BRAVE NEW WORLD. NINETEEN EIGHTY-FOUR.
A CLOCKWORK ORANGE. BLADE RUNNER ...

Visions of the future such as these reach out far beyond the boundaries of conventional science fiction. In doing so, they give the reader a genuinely engrossing and convincing experience of an all-too-possible tomorrow – engrossing because of their sheer narrative power, convincing because that tomorrow is clearly rooted in the reality of an all-too-recognizable today.

STAR BEAST and its 'prequel', the acclaimed SHADOW HUNTER (also a New English Library paperback), offer just such a stimulating experience of future shock in their compellingly detailed depiction of a world only a few generations from now. A world in which, after centuries of abuse and exploitation culminating in an apocalyptic war, the natural world is at last fighting back with some bizarre and ingenious weapons of its own ...

'Exciting and inventive to the last, that kind of wholly engrossing novel that can make you shiver in scalding sunlight'
Washington Post (reviewing SHADOW HUNTER)

Also by Will Baker in New English Library paperback

Shadow Hunter

About the author

Will Baker lives in the rain shadow of California's North Coast Mountains where he raises almonds and teaches at the local university. He is the author of several acclaimed novels and works of non-fiction, as well as two collections of short stories. He is married and has three children.

Star Beast

Will Baker

NEW ENGLISH LIBRARY
Hodder and Stoughton

Copyright © 1996 by Will Baker

First published in 1996 by Hodder and Stoughton

First published in paperback in 1996
by Hodder and Stoughton
A division of Hodder Headline PLC

A New English Library paperback

10 9 8 7 6 5 4 3 2 1

British Library Cataloguing in Publication Data

Baker, Will, 1935–
    Star beast
    1. American fiction – 20th century
    I. Title
    813.5'4[F]

    ISBN 0 340 65774 X

Printed and bound in Great Britain by
Cox & Wyman Ltd, Reading, Berkshire

Hodder and Stoughton
A division of Hodder Headline PLC
338 Euston Road
London NW1 3BH

To Rella

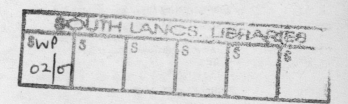

BOOK ONE

CHAPTER ONE

When the moon was full they ran along the dry streambeds. Now and then they lifted over a gully or slanted around an upthrust brow of stone, but dewfall settled the dust, so the herd could see and move freely. They were a swift river of shadows in the pale light; and, gathering and ranging and mending itself, this river always found a way over the land.

They had never been in these canyons before, had never run so far or so steadily into the wind, night after night. The new mothers and their young and the day-guards slept, rocking in their slings. The others occasionally called to one another or to the birds that skimmed overhead, debating their route. Sometimes a guard shifted to adjust one of the sacks on a flank, or to swing low and snatch a pebble or a handful of dry grass from the ground.

At a place where water trickled from the rock or had collected from a transient thundershower, they would finally halt. They would loosen the slings or remove them, take turns drinking, and then separate for a time, to eat and rest. The long-legged runners looked for the glow of certain blossoms on banks and low hills, lifted their wide nostrils for a scent of certain tough, small trees. Everything here sprouted thorns or appeared a shriveled skeleton, but they knew how to nibble away shreds of bark to reach hidden, tender layers, and how to paw the earth to expose bitter but nourishing roots.

The singers stayed together, usually under an overhanging wall or shelf of stone. From the sacks made of skin they scooped yellow curds, formed by the heat and constant motion, or handfuls of seeds or slivers of dried meat. As they ate, mothers nursed their young, the old rubbed their sore places, and everyone listened to the singing, for they needed to hear again and again the story they were making, the story the black bird had begun for them.

It was not a new story. It was the one they had always known and told, but now it was fearful and fascinating and different because it

3

had actually begun to be. They felt as if they were always running even when they were not; or as if a voice were singing to them even when they slept. They listened now to the young teacher who had been visited by the black bird, who moved her hands like wings to show them how the bird had broken the light and opened the world for her.

This was her teaching, her song: the one who had dreamed the world was about to be born again, and in the dream they were in, had always been in, there would be a crack, as a seed splits. Through this crack the great dreamer would come like a serpent, slipping into the dreamer's own dream because it had become disturbing and wrong, yet the dreamer did not want to wake, for then this world would vanish and the dreamer remembered how it was once good and beautiful and infinitely changing, like water and fire, and how it bore the dreamer through a sleep of ages, like a hawk riding the wind.

Because they lived in the sky, birds first saw the place where the dream would darken and fold and the newborn would wriggle out. (*It will squirm and squall and piss on itself,* their singer cried as if amazed, and all of the listeners laughed.) But the birds were in turn following the migrations of the great hives, which had learned everything from the earth since the beginning, and so knew before anyone that the birth was coming.

First they would be led into fearful places, the story went, and so the black bird signed them toward the land of square stones and blinding light. As they all knew, in this land lived creatures who had lost part of themselves, which made them eternally ravenous so they ate everything and multiplied, beyond counting, even as they were burning alive in their hunger. The long-legged singers had always defined the boundaries of this land simply by keeping as far as possible from the murk and smell and roar of the eating. So they remained a few small, dispersed herds, moving and hiding, and so the eaters of everything ignored them.

But now in the story that was taking shape they were running toward this land. They would be helped by the birds, and by others – creatures who were actually distant relatives of the eaters, but who now lived apart and worshipped the hives. But only they, the long-legged singers, could tell the story and carry the story and *be* the story, all at once. It was their purpose, the reason they were dreamed: to witness the birth and steal the dreamer away from the diminished creatures, the eaters, and then carry the little one everywhere so everything alive could see how the dream would change and become as it was before, beautiful as fire and water or a serpent with wings. Finally, so the story finished, even the eaters would see, would become whole and not be forever hungry, and would even run and sing with them.

It was quiet for a time after this story. Some were seeing inside themselves, seeing the old dream. They all knew that once the long-legged singers had gone everywhere except the sea, and there was deep green grass and pure cool water all around; but later they had become the eaters' slaves, had been cut in two, before they ran away and hid in the burned, cold, empty lands their masters had fought over and abandoned. For this reason the end of the story was still difficult to imagine. It made them uneasy, the idea of sitting down beside an eater.

The long-leggeds had drifted back to drink again; the young cooed and belched; a few of the old ones were dozing off. The mothers and guards talked a little, wondered if they were being watched by the bright, moving eyes the eaters put in the sky. Some said they were always watched, but at night the eyes could see only the runners. They wondered when they would meet the dark ones from underground, the followers of the hive, who would help them steal the dreamer. It would be soon, they decided. Soon the wind would bring a hint of the smell they had always avoided, the smell of something rotting and charred yet still alive, still digesting. Then they would concentrate on the song inside; they would hear the singing beneath silence, in their bones.

The moon was burning down directly overhead, through the scattered frost of stars. The long-legs were beginning to switch tails and pace. They blew noisily into the fresh night air, at the coyotes who had gathered on a low ridge to watch. They stamped and reared and their impatience made the singers laugh softly and move toward them.

The singers tied again their slings and sacks and mats. There was a creaking of dry, woven grass, a rustling, snorts of warning or agreement. A current of movement, an eddy . . . and then, as at the breaching of a dam, the river of shadows began once more to run, to shift and hang and lunge, running faster and faster, running now inside a cave of thunder, inside a story and a dream.

CHAPTER TWO

The grunts charged with the detail of clearing away the new flops had mutinied that morning. They couldn't stand the Gink stink any more, they said, and the crazy doctor was wasting everybody's time, holding up the flow of refugees, and filling the freezers with her tissue samples. The lieutenant had carried the men's grievances to Colonel Randolph White, who had come to see for himself.

Smell for himself, too, despite the nosehose and airpac the lieutenant had warned him he should wear. The colonel stood in what was left of a cotton field now serving as the yard for the field hospital tent, and surveyed the two long windrows of loosely stacked corpses. A layer of dust skimmed over the dry earth whenever the wind gusted, giving the illusion that the bodies made a reef in a flowing brown stream. The dust was stirred up by transport vehicles lumbering past, and by the great crowd gathered at the entrance to the hospital, the dark skeletons that had crawled over the border at dawn.

The lieutenant and a sergeant were explaining the situation to him, speaking in a low shout in order to be heard over the sing-song chanting of the Ginks who were still alive. It seemed the whole problem could be solved if the wagon drivers simply gathered the flops at the front entrance – almost half of those showing up expired before they got through the door – and hauled them to the landfill two kilometers away. Colonel White had nodded judiciously, even though they all knew they were going to run out of room there, too, within a few days. A portable furnace had been ordered, but other border stations were similarly overrun and the colonel didn't count on any relief very soon.

"Ever Gink or Pobler or whatever we sposed to call 'em that gets this far, we got to process 'em, sir, and the way she's doing it takes a good ten minutes, average. Some of the live ones she spends a *hour* on. But, hell, most of 'em comin' from the same area, same stock, couldn't she take just a stat sample?" The sergeant spat defensively in the direction of the twin reefs of decomposing flesh. "I mean, they're all swarming with the same ticks and lice and worms and Haysoos knows what, so what's the difference? Except my men have to spend an hour, minimum, scrubbing down. Sir."

"She's taking the same risks." The colonel gave the sergeant a hard, level look. He had made a career-long habit of dealing with complaints this way. Remind the bitchers that everyone suffered, everyone had a missile with his name on it.

"Yeah, well, sir . . . " The sergeant grimaced at the lieutenant, showed his palms in a gesture of helplessness. He did not have to complete his thought; they all understood. *But she's crazy.*

A wagon rattled around the perimeter of the tent, driven by a hulking young man wearing only khaki shorts, boots, and a set of earphones clamped over his head. He swayed in his seat, in time to the music. The wagon itself was merely a motorized platform, a rectangular metal bed and railing, on which was mounted a pair of pincers capable of taking a one-ton bite. The platform was heaped with bodies, propped up against each other, legs layered like jackstraws. Many of them, the colonel saw, were still moving. The young driver shifted into a higher gear and steered toward a dim track leading away over the field, before he saw Colonel White and the other two men. Then he did a remarkable portrayal of a man recollecting himself – slapping his forehead, downshifting, swerving back the way he had come.

Colonel White waited while the cloud of dust from the wagon blew around them, then flattened over the field. "I see you have already adopted more efficient procedures," he observed, with a very faint shade of amusement. The lieutenant and sergeant had apparently located something of interest on the horizon behind him. "Including dispensing with required safety dress."

"I reprimand 'em every day, sir," the lieutenant said. "They won't wear the suits now, demerits or not. They say they absorb the odor. And they insist on their own music. Say the Pobes' humming and howling gets to them."

Colonel White did not doubt it. The filters on his brand-new airpac were overwhelmed. He found himself pinching his nostrils around the intake tube, exhaling through his teeth. And the constant chanting was like the hacksawing of crickets. Abruptly he raised his flatttened hand to his brow and chopped down, as if cutting away an invisible cobweb.

"That's all, gentlemen. I understand your problem. Now *you* understand something. All along the border, for two thousand klicks, it's just like this. These . . . Pobla are putting tremendous strain on . . . on everything. A lot more of them than anyone foresaw. Too many. But you remember this: in this district, this station, the little fuckers are *your* responsibility. If orders are to process, you process. You stack them where you can, when you can. Inventory can't be too accurate, of course. Load here, load there. You understand me? But you dress this outfit in proper gear, Lieutenant. Do what you have to do, but do it *in uniform*."

Finally the lieutenant met his gaze, and the colonel could see the man's relief, almost joy. They would say no more, and continue to sneak loads around the field unit to the landfill. In the kind of shape most of these Ginks were in, they would be dead on arrival anyway. "Yes, sir," the lieutenant said and gave a very respectable version of a review salute. "Thank you, sir."

"You leave Doctor Fanny to me." The colonel favored the sergeant with a thin, tough smile.

"Yes, sir, thank you, sir. We'll take care of them Poblers." The sergeant saluted and the two wheeled and almost trotted back to their Jumper, parked beside the colonel's staff vehicle in the slice of shade from the tent.

Colonel White signaled his driver, who had opened a door and set one foot on the ground, to remain at ease, and began a rather slow march to the rear entrance. Every few moments, as they were talking, an orderly had pushed a cart out this entrance, bearing one or two, sometimes three flops, which were quickly dumped in one of the rows. Every third trip the cart was replaced by a small band of still-ambulant Ginks, who shuffled up a loading ramp, still singing, into the bed of a waiting wagon. This wagon was still less than half full, the colonel noted, and its driver was sound asleep in the cab.

So he could calculate, simply and graphically, how absurd the situation was. The Ginks were arriving at the rate of a hundred and fifty a day; dead or alive, each took ten minutes to process, plus another two or three minutes for transport, error, or special procedure. Even working twenty-four hours a day without meals or rest, no doctor could have done it; and especially not some dithery, owl-eyed frump with more than one hole in her bucket.

Doctor Tiffany Orr, known everywhere as Doctor Fanny in honor of her impressive beam, had been a disaster from the first. When she

9

came to his quarters to log in and present her work plan, she was wearing fatigues with no insignia and lugging a big wire cage with a bird in it – a ragged thing with a long tail, oversized horny hook of a beak, and tiny red orbs. Doctor Fanny's old-fashioned spectacles, on the other hand, made her own eyes huge and swampy.

Colonel White had been so stunned he couldn't begin to speak, so she informed him in her maddening, bubble-brained chatter that she knew he was surprised but he must understand she was one of a special team of scholars - not *doctors* plain and simple, but *scholars* – named by President Stockwell's new fact-finding Commission to conduct some basic research in the field. Her own specialty, Doctor Fanny noted with a giggle, was paleobiology, her subspecialty the semiotics of polynucleotides, but her actual real love was studying how all things in creation *sang* to each other, harmony and rhythm and variation being the key to all things – she was already trilling and warbling all this at him – wasn't it so, Colonel?

Even the fleeting memory of this scene gave the colonel indigestion, and the fact that the realities had soon jolted the giggle out of Lady Mountainbutt was no longer any consolation. The woman had become a fanatic, a headcase, an utter loony as far as he could tell. She spent sixteen hours a day in verbal testing and tissue sampling, to no purpose he could fathom. He had done his best to get her transferred, only to discover that she had superior juice, a line into the Commission, and the Commission was getting its own way in this grand new exercise in compassion, this Operation Life Line.

Just as he reached the entrance the door wagged again, another cart of flops pushing through. The orderly looked startled, gave a vague salute. The colonel glared and held the door open with an elaborate, savage irony. The stiffened hand of one of the corpses brushed his trousers as the cart passed, and the orderly gave him a fearful, inquisitive smile.

Operation Death Camp was more like the truth. Colonel White strode through the door, reaching finally a state of calm fury. For two months, in Operation New Broom, the order had been to hunt, zap, and count Ginks; he had dutifully sent his men into the sandstorms, flea infestations and bowel disorders of Wasteland duty. Now the policy was a neat, complete reversal: coddle and coo over the same creatures, the hordes of starving derelicts the government had themselves created.

But the armies were not designed for coddle and coo, so the colonel's job had become simply separating the dead from the nearly dead, and feeding the latter until they became the former. It was idiotic, maddening, lunatic. No wonder Doctor Fanny fit in, had her juice. He picked his way through more tagged bodies and gurneys and apologetic nurses to the space partitioned off as her laboratory, where she bent over the electron screen from her scope, surrounded by a clutter of printouts and strewn disks. A dried-up old Gink lay naked on the examination table, staring up at the ragged bird in its cage which hung from a tent strut.

The bird saw him, squawked loudly, and the Gink's eyes clicked shut.

Doctor Fanny heard Buster and just managed to quell her own urge to scream. She hit a key to save the image of the spectroburn of the section of chromo she was probing and looked up with a bland, toothy smile.

"Why, Colonel, my colonel, how nice of you to drop around. Hush now, Buster. You know the colonel, you know you do." She rolled away from the desk, still smiling, moving a stack of papers from a single, hard-backed chair. "Sit down, Colonel. Goodness, you make me ashamed of my own poor posture, hunched over this silly thing all the time, and you're so perfectly, perfectly *straight*. Maybe we should trade jobs."

"No, Doctor Orr, thank you. I will not sit down. I have no time to sit down. I— "

"Fanny." She wrinkled her nose at him, a schoolgirl conspirator, and with the very slightest shift of shoulders and hips gave her large, compactly upholstered body a subliminal wriggle, at once naive and obscene. It was her most powerful weapon against the colonel. He hated the gesture so much that he had to look away, and often lost the train of his thoughts.

But this time he managed to maintain his glare. "We can't continue with these examinations, on this scale. A hundred and seventy-four new ones today. We have almost a thousand now in the holding tank, and not more than a week's rations for them. It cannot, just cannot be done."

He looked at the papers on her desk, as if to accuse them, and she saw his expression change slightly. She had copies of old inscriptions, carvings, and tapestries mixed in with the columns of figures and branching equations, including some reproductions of mythological figures, marvels and monsters. "Cannot be done," he repeated, and glanced at her warily. She allowed her fingers to dance and dawdle

11

ver the papers, arranging them so he could see better. *Have a dragon, Colonel, or a unicorn, or this hairy penis with legs and one eye.*

"I know." She sighed deeply and reshaped her smile into a pout of sadness. "It's terrible, I know. And just as I'm getting such good results. Really, some marvelous things. But I know it's so hard on your men, they might break down and so forth, poor things, so I know I'll have to be content with a percent sample. Say fifty?"

Colonel White had opened his mouth to continue the argument, but now had to close it quickly, and blink. When he came in she had judged, by his pale, narrow-eyed countenance, that the old dick was finally wound up enough to take some nasty action. Of course she knew her research was the big bottleneck, knew they were already ferrying some of the incoming refugees around her and directly to the trenches. Probably they were burying many alive. She had determined to give in all at once (just like a woman), and propose a tearful compromise that would catch him off guard.

"Cannot be done," he repeated again, and the bird squalled as if to protest.

"Buster! That's impolite. Oh *Colonel*! Only half, *half* of what I was sampling." She looked as devastated as she could without making herself ill, and adjusted her spectacles, having trouble, apparently, believing that the world could maintain so cruel a guise.

"That's ridiculous. Fifty percent. Why, already—" He stopped himself just in time. She knew what he was going to say. She was missing about that many now. He waved, rather violently she thought, at the pictures she had arranged on the desk. "What is this *for*, anyway? What in hell are you after?" He looked briefly at the form stretched out on the examining table. He had asked the question before, more than once, but this time she saw he was serious. The whole insane, ghastly business had finally offended him professionally. The colonel could kill, or the colonel could try to coo, depending on his orders, but he was only human too, and wanted some reason for it all. In that sense, she realized suddenly, the colonel was not really a very good soldier. She regarded him for the first time with a tinge of honest curiosity.

"Well, I know of course how pompous it sounds, but actually the main point is the advancement of knowledge. I mean plain, pure science." Doctor Fanny got to her feet and approached the examining table. "We've never had so many of our little relatives to study, and we're finding out some pretty surprising things."

12

Buster began to chaff and shake his wings one at a time. The eyes of the old creature on the table clicked open again. Fanny stopped her advance and spoke in a lowered voice, rapidly, not looking at the colonel. "This, ah, subject possesses a gene that I've been tracking for a long time. It's very rare, and takes several probes to pin down. The bigger the pool you are sampling, the better your chance of finding something."

The colonel did not answer, though Fanny could sense him there, straight and stiff, waiting. She was trying to think of some plausible explanation for the direction of her "research" – a compilation of molecular oddments that correlated, at least in her imagination, with startling behavior, puzzling metabolic shifts, coincidences and intuitions. She could not, of course, render the final, speculative edge of her thinking. A practical military man was probably not prepared for a tone poem about dragons and stars.

"It's a very, very old gene," she said primly, a shade defensively. "Present before *lapsis* and *sapiens* were differentiated. Or *troglodytes*, for that matter."

The old Pobla's lips moved, made a tiny, sipping noise, and Buster hurled himself against the wire mesh of his cage, fastened there by beak and claws, horizontal, battering with his wings. Fanny reached up on tip-toe and sprang the door. The bird was immediately calmed and hopped in a leisurely way to balance on the threshold. *Tak!* Its call was not so strident, rather like a subdued cough. *Tak! Tak! Tagak!*

"Yes. Interesting, I'm sure." Colonel White's voice was tightly leashed. "But we have an emergency here. All along the border. This is not the place for" – he delivered the phrase with a fine spray of acid – "pure science."

"I didn't mean to suggest there mightn't be very practical benefits. There almost always are, eventually. The way this gene programs or decodes enzymatic interfacing could—" She glanced now at the colonel, saw she was losing him. "But what a silly I am, lecturing on like this, when you know, Colonel, so much is just chance, funny things that happen."

She had moved with alacrity, for her girth, to a console on her desk. "I can show you something . . . just a jiffy . . ." After a moment's fussing she twisted a knob and the room was full of throbbing sound, ancient music, the folk material known as rockenroll. The form on the examining table twitched slightly and emitted another faint sucking or kissing noise. Immediately Buster launched into a long swoop, alighting with three rapid wing-beats on the creature's sternum, between the wrinkled pouches of its breasts.

For several moments the bird turned in place, picking up and planting its claws as if to test the surface. The eyes, bright red beads, flicked here and there in the room, but always came back to the skin under its feet.'

"Doctor Orr." The colonel sounded weary. "Everyone knows their capability with other animals. I came here—"

"Watch now," Fanny said brightly, sweetly, peremptorily. "Watch."

Buster rocked abruptly, the long tail flashing into the air as he pecked at the creature's hide. The beak came up clacking, then speared down again. In another second or two the motion was constant, rapid, almost frenzied. Doctor Fanny beckoned to Colonel White stealthily, formed two words with her lips only. *Come closer*.

The colonel took a step, leaned forward with a frown. She knew, by the way he froze, that he could see the fleas now. They were hopping, zig-zagging, scurrying out of the old one's hair both above and below. They gathered at the bird's feet, a swarm so dense the tiny carapaces formed a single, glittering brooch. Buster bobbed up and down, gobbling furiously, but then in two long, springy hops he was on the Pobla's chin and slid his beak into the creature's mouth, apparently disgorging some of his meal.

"You can imagine," Doctor Fanny whispered, "what an advantage it would be if we could isolate the pheromones produced here, and perhaps selectively breed enough of this genetic type to supply them in commercial amounts?"

She had him. He cleared his throat aggressively, but failed to come up with a rejoinder. His troops had suffered terrible agonies from fleas during Operation New Broom. There was no question the number of pests had reached plague proportions during that assault, especially rodents and insects with a history of cohabitation with the Pobla. Most scientists assumed some direct biochemical connection, but so far no hard evidence had been collected.

Doctor Fanny had no such evidence either, but she had learned to spot certain external physical characteristics that seemed to correlate with the gene she was looking for. Brachiocephalic, partial epicanthic fold, small feet, hermaphroditism, tendency to epilepsy, a certain *attitude*, even – like someone used to waiting.

She felt close, closer than she had ever been, to breakthrough. This old one, for example, underneath the ruin of his mind – or her mind, as it sometimes was – might be the crucial case. Carried a version of the gene, anyway, and had struck up this peculiar rapport . . . but she knew she would lose the colonel for good if she got into the psychic stuff.

Colonel White had such a genius for barging in at the absolutely worst time. She heard whispers and wheels bumping in the corridor outside, and knew the gurneys were piling up, the Pobla gathering like shadows all around her. She could see, too, that the colonel was preparing to blather on in his flat, hard-ass voice about new orders, no other option, standard statistical samples . . .

"Let's be frank, Colonel White. Oh dear, how can I say this, because of course I respect you and your job, but nobody really knows, do they, what to do with these refugees? Where to put them even, let alone what should be done with them?"

"I know that," the colonel said between his teeth. He made a face at the corner of the room where the speaker was still throbbing. . . .*holaddashakingowinan*. . . .

"So what if we – you – could report some little useful thing, some *reason* to keep counting and burying or tending them? We all know they could supply organs for transplants but we also know how skittish people are about the idea – the old prejudices and so forth – but using Pobla subjects to generate bioproducts, like an insect attractant – now that might make us all feel better about . . ." she waved her arms to include everything around them – ". . . this."

There were little spasms in the muscles of the colonel's neck, a sign of some mental activity. "I think ten percent is a reasonable sample. A *generous* sample." He glanced again at the bird, still pecking avidly on its platform of withered flesh. "I appreciate that what you are studying may have, uh, some application, eventually. But we can't—"

"Oh Colonel," Doctor Fanny wailed. "Flea traps would just be the *beginning*. I really need to see at least, at the *very* least, a quarter of them."

Holadashakingowinan . . . oh baby . . . She saw the jaw set, and he met her big, bleary eyes with his commanding officer's line-of-duty, end-of-all-argument look, but just as he opened his mouth to refuse, the ancient Pobla on the table uttered a sound, a single, long, sighing exhalation. Buster lifted and spread his wings at the same time, and turned the tiny coals of his eyes on the colonel. Under the bird, the patch of fleas began to disintegrate, to disperse, and in a moment

15

ere were black specks popping over the paper cover of the table, onto the floor, in every direction.

Doctor Fanny moved instantly to the table, her plump, soft, white hand at the old Pobla's throat, palping for a pulse. Buster shrieked once and exploded into the air, where he circled the room in eccentric orbit, flapping mightily.

"Oh *oh*!" Doctor Fanny was biting her lip, stamping a foot. "We've lost her! The best subject I had! Oh *damn*! Buster, stop it, we've lost her . . . " She returned to her desk abruptly, snapped off the music, and sat down, her fisted hands in her lap. Just as abruptly Buster arrowed back into his cage and huddled on a perch. Neither the bird nor Doctor Fanny looked in the colonel's direction.

After a considerable pause, he said. "I'm sorry, Doctor." She did not reply. He cleared his throat and stepped backward. "All right, a quarter. Twenty-five percent. Absolutely the maximum." He turned and was just reaching for the door when she spoke.

"Thank you so much, Colonel. That is a quarter of *all* the subjects?"

When he looked over his shoulder she smiled at him brightly through her tears, and with two fingers of one hand imitated the action of someone trying to circumvent, stealthily, an imaginary sentry. "No more little unofficial trips to the landfill? Everything tagged and counted? Promise?"

There was nowhere for his fury to go, so he gave a single, savage nod and bolted out the door. The violence of the movement dislodged his nose hose, so he was both gagging and cursing when he went by the orderlies toward the entrance to the yard. A quarter of the whole was the same as a half of the half he had assumed they were talking about. Four times the number he had decided privately would be his ultimatum. He wanted to strangle her, slowly, but even as he entertained this immensely gratifying fantasy, he grew uneasy. At the edge of his vision the darkness swarmed, a pulsating border of black flecks, a sound like fine sand blowing, a hiss out of heaven.

Doctor Fanny did not call in her next examination right away. She was allowing the tears to come in big, fast drops. The optimism that exasperated even her friends had not vanished, but was now held in abeyance by an honest grief, mingled with awe. The old one's sudden death had not shocked her; she had seen these creatures – people – expire at will before, use their departure to sharpen her apprehension. They were, she guessed, trying to train her for further revelations.

She began to hum the poem she had composed, a chant designed to gather and focus her own intuitions. It was not finished yet; it would never be finished, nor would her investigations. Her own body, like the still form of the old Pobla, was made of stardust; every element in her being, every pattern, was as old as time itself; she and Buster had memories of the same dragons, their common ancestors spun from the same fiery hole, the salt of their blood the same too, another memory of the Flood. And in ordinary history, as she moved further and further into its images, the rotting stones and mouldering graves, she found the beasts, great and small, always allied with her own kind.

The old friars marveled at the savages of the New World, who remembered not only the mammoth and the saber-tooth but even the feathered serpent – archeopteryx – and their mating with flowers – the angiosperms' sweet invasion of tongue, flank and hide.

What Doctor Fanny marveled at was the ignorance of those prideful clerics, and the Men of Reason who came ridiculing after, neither wise enough to glimpse even a scrap, a bit of edgework in the great and powerful design that linked all life, spoke in and through every cell, to every other cell; and finally of her own thick-headedness, she who – until these shadow brothers and sisters had signed to her – had also known nothing, really, nothing at all.

> *Star beast, star beast,*
> *Ravening in the night!*
> *Swallow my heart,*
> *Hosannah of light!*

She suspended her chant then, long enough to add silently, *And swallow Colonel White's, too.*

17

CHAPTER THREE

Two people were trying to escape on a catwalk above a fiery inferno. She was guiding, step by step, because an acid-slinging terrorist had blinded him earlier. As the pennons of flame darted higher, he balked, shouting over the roar.

"Go on, Casey! Go on! Somebody has to stop them before—"

The woman turned and seized the blind man's head between her hands. The catwalk swayed and a section of the handrail gave way. "No!" she cried, "Don't you *see*, Mark, you crazy wonderful fool! I *love* you . . ."

She began to kiss him voraciously. There was a squeal of rending metal and behind a veil of sparks the two bodies began to entwine. The sound of zippers mingled with the crackle of flame.

The symphony launched into a thundering, ominous chord, but PJ silenced it and tossed the remote aside. He belched, picked up his gin and tonic, and looked away from the bright little figures miming inside the box. He had already seen four versions of the ending, including this limited adult extra, which would feature Casey and Mark fornicating on the steel lattice. They would come, just as the fire reached them.

In the last six months he had watched so much holo, done so many interactives, that he could establish the whole range of plots in the first minute. He was running out of ways to numb his brain. A steady force, like gravity, kept pulling him into the past, cajoling him to go back to the manuscript, which he didn't want to do because then he would be depressed again. Or more depressed, rather.

He couldn't do any more gin, or the blue tablets that contained big velvet sledgehammers, because he was staying up to watch his performance on a yakshow at eleven. An interview, less than a minute long, which would very likely determine his future. Also, he had a lecture tomorrow morning. To whom, he no longer remembered.

The designed cheerfulness of the little room was ghastly: the plum-colored drapes, the yellow and orange coffeemaker, the gleaming shower. He had spent a hundred nights in rooms like this one as he junketed around the country. Lately, however, the quality of his accommodations had been deteriorating. He was aware he was no longer a top draw, and for the upcoming month his agent had managed only three confirmed bookings.

On a local channel earlier he had scrolled an E-poster for himself, with sidebar windows of lurid footage from his most famous exploit.

Friday! Former Insec Superagent Phillip ("PJ") Feiffer! Meet the professional hunter-killer from the Border Zone who brought back little Ronnie Drager – alive! A man of a thousand adventures – he lived, fought, and loved, with the Pobla in their own land, and dealt a deadly justice to the most notorious of darkside assassins – the Snuffer! A story soon to be released as a major holo . . .

It was unbearable, and he switched himself off. Oh yes, he brought little Ronnie back. Back to a private nutbin, where he remained. Superagent Feiffer was, actually, himself hauled back by a fifteen-year-old Gink bitch code named Duskyrose, who fucked him over in every sense of the term. And the Snuffer had in fact snuffed himself, in a stupid, freak accident. And the major holo was mainly a blast of hot gas confected by his agent. There was not even a script yet, only this found notebook around which they had artfully spun a lot of rumors.

He glanced once more at the antic figures in the holobox. Casey and Mark (no longer blind) were resurrected, speeding across the City of Angels in a limovan. Their faces were smudged, their bodies fetchingly arrayed in charred rags. The Immortals. They could re-live these exploits, with variations, endlessly. Which was why holo was better than life, and why he, the Superagent, was contemplating the rape of a dead man.

His best friend, in fact. A man who truly had lived and fought and suffered among the Ginks. Who had even been in love with them, stinking cannibals that they were. But maybe he was distorting the issue. Was your best friend still your best friend if he was dead? And wasn't rape too strong a term for a little creative editing, touching up a manuscript never intended for development?

He allowed himself another glance at the tattered notebook with a filthy cover which he had hours ago removed from its plastic case and left on the stand beside the bed. Remarkable, that Tickles had

20

kept this diary for so long, writing by firelight with a sharpened reed dipped in plant resin and soot. Amazing, that some trooper had found it in the boneyard around that underground temple. Incredible, that it had then come to PJ, with no strings.

Charlie Fat, just before resigning as Director of Border Operations, had sent him the notebook, still in the lab's plastic bag, with a single, handwritten comment. *Inherit these bones, or burn them.* PJ had no idea what that meant, but apparently the old Pacrim never logged the notebook into an official file before clearing out his office and going off to his meditation retreat. PJ's agent had understood immediately the cash potential of this inheritance. It was the only personal manuscript to emerge from the Drager affair; and it was also the authentic journal of the first military agent to survive among the most peculiar and most fascinating species on the planet. Lieutenant Ted ("Tickles") Kelough, ace hunter of live specimens, had one day gone on solo patrol, parked his vehicle in a blind canyon, stripped off his uniform, stacked his weapons, and vanished for almost ten years.

A flipout, presumed dead. But PJ guessed immediately where his buddy had gone. The hunter had fallen under the spell of his prey. The Pobla. *Homo lapsis.* Or the Ginks, in vulgate. Humanity's bastard cousin, the most degenerate of the primates. Naked and alone, Tickles had entered this underworld; and however mad, he not only survived but became a trusted counselor to the ancient queen who was head of their weird termite cult.

So when the Ginks and their trained bear snatched little Ronnie from a Hunting Preserve, Tickles was appointed his guide and teacher. Teacher succeeded, all right. By the time PJ located the kid, they had smeared and slashed and anointed him the new prince of bugs, and mated him to a teenaged witch, the very same Duskyrose who – but his mind shied away from the memory of that humiliation. The whole thing was a creepy tabloid miracle: precocious upperclass lad transformed into depraved maniac by bloody rites, orgies, and hypnosis. And Tickles's journal was the only extant record of the whole process.

Fantastic positioning, PJ's agent gloated. But the notebook posed a little problem. It was mostly what the agent called mystical crap. Worse, it contained no oral sex and very little of the other sensational stuff – cannibalism, fetishism, sacrifice and mutilation – the average person now expected to hear about the Ginks. And it would be tough, the agent pointed out, to sell a script by somebody named Tickles.

21

On the plus side, their author was conveniently dead. They could doctor the thing extensively, do a based-on presenting PJ as colleague and closest friend, introduce juicier material. PJ had, after all, himself spent a few weeks as a captive of the cannibal fiends. The cyberscum nets had already offered modest deals for a swifty docudrama or home interactive, but they wanted to go for a class market, something longer term.

They would have to work fast, because the refugee crisis at the border was stirring up the whole Gink thing anew. Major people would be making moves. Very early, as part of a divorce settlement, the Dragers had sold rights to their son's story, and even the two-hour swifty that resulted, *A Kid In The Cannibal Kingdom*, made almost six bill. Thing was, feeding frenzies didn't last. Couple of months, max, to pull the script into shape and get it to producers. Otherwise – the agent had shrugged, glanced pointedly at the floor, as into a pit.

At this critical juncture, they had gotten what might be their biggest break. A rep from the Beaufort Winger show had called, offering a fifty-second face-to-face. Big Beau was doing a retro on the whole story – the deals, the indictments, the careers launched and ruined – and he needed bites. PJ would get primetime exposure, a chance to goose their emerging project. Winger's yakshow was the hottest in the country. The marshal of malice had a huge and devoted following, and he was moving now into mainstream politics. With an election approaching, Winger was attacking the Conservative incumbent Stockwell, focusing on his handling of the Drager incident. For one thing the doctors were still dawdling over Little Ronnie's diagnosis, almost a year after his ordeal. A whole lot hinged, politically, on whether he emerged an abused disturbo or the victor in a heroic personal struggle.

So they had to plan the Winger gig carefully. For fifty seconds hundreds of millions of people would be watching PJ's every twitch, hearing his every word. He was the man who brought the young hero – or pathetic monster – back into the civilized world, the only man with authentic, firsthand knowledge. A tremendous window, but very, very narrow.

"It's simple," his agent had told him in their first strategy session, at a classy midtown restaurant. "Your experience is worth a fortune because it's unique and it's finite. Great stuff. But it has a half-life, it's perishable. That's why we have to get the script idea out and bowtied in the first fifteen seconds, before any maggots crawl out. Then what we do is, we shift the emphasis to you. We begin to create—" he took a crab fork, twirled it, and speared a hunk of pink flesh which he held up to steam a moment between them "—the Legend."

At that precise moment PJ had felt an odd queasiness under his ribs. It was as if he had seen his fate in that skewered bit of meat, which came, he knew, from an arctic seafood farm. This crab had been born in prison. So had its ancestors. Freedom, for luxury edibles, was out of the question.

Finite. Finished. Of course he understood that to be a holo personality he had to abandon intelligence work. No more skimming the border in the fastest hovercraft; no more patrols into the Wastelands – those radioactive desert canyons for which he had developed a certain perverse affection. No more risky darkside ops, knowing the best and worst ahead of everybody else.

At the time he thought he was glad. The prospect of being rich and famous and safe was tremendously appealing. He had been through actual hell, the agent reminded him, which was exactly why people loved his story and why he should accept big rewards for telling it. "Listen, Bucko," the agent said, "nobody ever gets tired of hearing about dirty and down. If this were made-up, we'd have to rate it late-night adult and compete small-time with the interactives, but this is *real.* You *did* it, man! You've done the laps. Eaten them. Fucked them. Killed them. Like nobody ever before."

There was passion in the agent's voice, hints of both greed and revulsion. His blouse was open for three buttons, and the silver fork flashed again and again into the splintered carcass between them. "Bucko, you have to see yourself as the guy we'd all like to be. A hero, a type the world doesn't produce any more. Oooo, tasty bit, that one. All you got to do is learn the part, the moves, the style. We got coaches, got models, got writers. But *you*, baby, *you* got to step into it and *be* that hero. Have some, man, this wine sauce is so good it's porno. So the meaning is here: Winger will showcase you to 250 million viewers, minimum, and for fifty seconds, baby, you will be at the center of the fucking *universe*."

He saw by the chrono on the night table that the show would not be on for another ten minutes. He slugged down the rest of his gin, picked up Tickles's journal and sat back on the bed. It was an old-fashioned waterproof notebook, much thumbed, limp and ragged as a dead bird. Tickles had covered every page, back and front, margin to margin, with a sprawling, spidery script.

He did as he had done before; he let the book flop open arbitrarily and then began to read blindly, knowing he would stumble into a memory he couldn't erase, a memory of being sick and starved and exhausted and at the same time mysteriously grounded in himself and alive and terrified and happy and free . . .

Today they (Tsitsi and Kapu) asked me if it was true piksis, especially females, cut off parts of their bodies, noses and hips especially, and if they saved these bits to eat. I said yes and no. They were trying to teach me how to listen to beetles. Big, black hardshells, perfectly harmless. These fellows eat damp and rotting plant matter, and sing constantly about the depth and quantity and freshness of water in the earth. Tsitsi claims all water, below or above ground, is connected and carries messages. They are impatient because I hear nothing, so far. I believe it is April, or early May.

He believes it is April. He is listening to big black beetles. The waters are all connected. Christ. This was the guy who was at the head of his class in fractal extrap, polypsych, and judo, who brought back more live specimens than any rookie in the history of border operations. This was the best and brightest, his pal and rival. Christ. PJ laughed. He flipped over an indeterminate number of pages.

Third winter. Keep warm with rabbit and squirrel skins mostly. Thought is corrupt, I think. Ha. Can't stop though, as this demonstrates. At least I know the evil. Piksi thinking is just take apart and reconstruct, so you can control. Brain as tool kit. Pobla think by listening, smelling, tasting, watching for what they call harmonies. Adza says I belong with lemons and ashes.

PJ went on a page or two, stopped at the rare entry with a date.

3/21/27
Solstice. Calendars in the head, based on the four hinges of the year. It's been twenty-six, tho who cares. Pobla believe every day is a different length. For some insects, one day a lifetime. Bergson. Was wrong about Pobla philosophy. Original sin is for them loss of shadow – what happened to us piksis. The word shadow, or ghost, is too weak. Cannot grasp or express so many dimensions of this concept. But essentially . . .

* * *

Essentially, PJ thought bleakly, this would be stupendously boring to the ordinary holo-goer. No producer, not the freakiest, most far-gone drug blowout in the biz, would ever dream of trying to turn this stuff into a script. Even reading it hurt his mind, through the gin and fatigue. It made him remember his madness in the underground burrows, the hallucinations, the waking dreams.

A poor sick bastard he was then – thirty pounds down, covered with scabs, a ratty beard. When he brought back Ronnie and Duskyrose – though by then he was using their Pobla names, Pahane and Tima – they thought he was delirious and kept him in a headward for a week. He remembered that week with a wince of disgust. They wanted every detail. What Tickles said. How many times he had eaten Gink. And Tima – especially Tima. That was what they really wanted to hear, how it was with the horny little lap prodigy.

He went to the last entry. Tickles had written it at the beginning of the end, when the troops of New Broom had invaded the tunnels and Adza, the old medicine woman, was hurrying to the last ceremony at the great termite hives, when their whole world was collapsing and they were losing the connection to the Big Shadow, their god.

Yano! Yano! Death everywhere. The Shadow of Shadows is fleeing, Kapu shouts at me. The patrols are coming. Tomorrow the great Going In. My God, what have we done? No matter, must go. Purification time. I fear tomorrow at the hives, so many of us exposed.

Tickles had reason to fear, since twenty-four hours later the Snuffer lasered his brain out. Maybe he would shoot himself now, if he had survived, because he would see the species he loved becoming a herd of walking dead. Fighting among themselves, too. The refugees were stunned at that. *Pobla kill Pobla*, some of them said over and over, their eyes completely empty with the shock of it.

Must be, PJ thought, *the traces of chimp blood in them*, some primal cement of a band of gatherers against outsiders. They could bear heat, cold, disease, starvation, even genocide, with an equanimity that struck him as lunatic. But the idea of killing your own, deliberately, was unthinkable. As unthinkable as the final horror, which was, for a Gink, letting the piksis suck out your shadow.

PJ got up from the bed, tossing the manuscript onto the night stand. It was time for the Winger show and he needed a few seconds to relax, to stop thinking. Tickles had the right advice there. He moved to his open travel bag and rummaged for a tray of light spacers. He might be a little fuzzy for the next day's talk, but better fuzzy than haggard. If the bite was good, and things went his way, he might be surfing again on the mightiest, most treacherous comber of them all: daily holonews, the racing edge of the nation's attention span.

He picked up the remote and switched on the visual only. Credits were rolling over a scene from the border refugee camps, a horde of thin, dark creatures behind a chainlink fence. Yes, welcome to the new world. He put down the remote and picked up the plastic pitcher to pour out a half-glass of water. Brave, too. Brave enough to wipe out all the creatures who don't see things the way we do. Conquer and control. Build a statue, a monument, over the bones of our victims. Compose the anthem, write the history, watch the holo. Triumph.

Long fingers, like worms, wriggled and thrust through the links of the fence. He shook out three tabs and palmed them into his mouth, then drank two swallows from the glass.

The next shot was an aerial one of great blocks of darkness on the sandy plain. The refugee pens. Then a close up, a diamond of heavy wire around a single eye, black and bright as a flake of wet stone. The last wave of would-be immigrants. He gestured with the glass in a grand semicircle, as if welcoming them. He imagined there would be loudspeakers. *Welcome*, they would say, *welcome to humanity. You must learn a new language here, with many new and unfamiliar words. Your first new word is: holocaust.*

The credits were over. The border scenes were replaced by another closeup, this one of a face. It was a broad, grinning face with tight, full cheeks, as if some radiant force had been pumped under the skin. The lips were already writhing around words that seemed to be coming fast. PJ took the remote, fell back on the bed, and flicked on the sound.

CHAPTER FOUR

"Howdy-ho-ho-ho, Holodicts and Dick-tettes! It's datime again, and dabig fat guy's cominatya, got a few gems this Pee Em, some words of wise-dumb . . .

"Yassuh, folks, the Beaufort Winger Yakshow! So cuddle up to the box and prepare for audjo an' vizjwul violashun, because today, kiddies, we got a real full plate! Gotta old slimeball scandal that just won't go away. Gonna show you *bald* and *straight* just what the Stockwell regime been hidin' from the poor downgestomped taxpoopers."

To a driving surge of music, Beaufort spins in his huge console-chair, a gimbeled and geared and gyroscoped contraption built especially for his hundred-and-forty kilo frame. The armrests curl into a control panel whose buttons and joysticks co-ordinate the manipulation of backdrop, lighting, sound, and a bank of feeder channels, cueing a final mix accomplished by engineers poised in a control room. Beaufort touches a pair of these buttons and his body in its chair appears – to the millions watching his evening show – to rocket through the ceiling and soar far above a tremendous map of the continent, where he hovers and tilts, peering down.

"Now, we're not gonna do the whole tour, tour of the sewer – daily doo-doo of the admaxistration of Prezdunt Stockwell Swelltalk – only gonna take a nanobite: one quick peek at what's happenin' in this grand land. Better than the beeg peekchur sometimes, that one bitty clue. Nittygritty Humpos lookin' for a broken twiggie . . . but as we go . . ."

The satellite map begins to stream by swiftly, and a wind machine straightens Winger's tie and hair into fluttering pennants. He grins at viewers over his shoulder like a gargantuan schoolboy on a carnival ride, and plucks from a recessed well in the chair a plastic soft drink container. He pops the container open and shows off its red, white and blue logo before he guzzles the contents.

27

"Ah-h-h! Hits the A spot and B spot and the C and right on through the alphabetty, folks! Beau Winger Show, courtesy of the Big One – Big drink, number One. Hey, just remember, ain't nutrition and ain't medication, ain't stim and ain't tranque – it's pure, one hunnert and ten percent toe-squirmin' *pleasure*!"

Winger sighs and tosses the plastic shell, and a trashbin with swept wings arrows up beside his chair in time to catch and ingest the refuse, then zips away. The Big Fat Guy winks. "Robot Recycle. Remember, people: Big One. The Unique Giant. The taste at the top and you deserve it, so treat thyself. Now where are we – ah yes, our intro, a little hook, sneak in on the edge, go small first – vwah-lah! Weeniest Mini-Preserve in all NorthAm!"

Big Beau is operating a control, banking his chair in a tight circle over the continent, above sworls of cloud partly veiling great checkboard blocks of black earth or green or yellow crop, above mighty cities reduced to circuitboards, wired into nets of Thruways and pipelines and canals, above the resource basins – vast irregular tracts flayed by strip mines, contoured by lumber plantations and dotted with reservoirs and bright chips of solar collecting units. Here and there are the Preserves, small islands of irregular green broken by eruptions of dark stone with white tips, like pimples.

"Gonna look first at the comic side of the conspiracy, loyal fans! I mean straight bureauboozling, sheer propagoofy and disinfo, designed to convince the average yoyo that the Cons are lookin' out for the resource base, in harmony with ol' Mama *Nature* – you 'member the Big Mama Myth, the Dowager of DNA, Queen of the Green Machine? – gonna take care of every li'l thang?

"Well, folks, we're gonna show you how it actually works, the Big Mama Nature scam. Lookahere . . ." Beau points, straightarm, finger like a gunbarrel, at one of the wrinkled humps making up a minor range of mountains. In a zoom of dizzying speed the holo eye seems to rush down hundreds of miles to bring into clear view a single tree.

It is a ragged thing, barely alive; whitened stubs of dead limbs protrude from the crooked trunk, and in several places slabs of bark have fallen away to reveal a honeycomb of rot. A rusting fence, some panels sagging, is strung over the rocky slope around the tree, and a concrete pillar with a bronze plaque stands beside it. Just outside the fence is a small group of people, unkempt and shivering in motley coats and old blankets. They appear to be singing, and hold up a banner warped and tattered by the wind. The message on the banner is SAVE THEM ALL.

"Take a good gander, goosies – you're payin' for this particular pile of kindling. This ravishing subject is two acres of rock in the middle of which grows some kinda *ponderosa*, supposedly a true blue wild thang – that's Conspeak for old and worthless – which means the only pure specimen left, no sign of tinkerin' with the original genes. These weedgie-heads claim it's alive, see, and they're demonstrating to keep funding the Preserve Bio Research, which is a hundred mill for *measuring* and *sampling* this old wreck.

"Why? *why*? You ask that. You do. You sourheads, you numb nutooskis, you scheissfaxers! What kinda pregunta izzat? What are you, a hasslemacher, a buttrocker? Some kinda *Progressive*, tryin' to inject *reason* into the situation? You never quit, doya? *Why*? Simple. They gotta celebrate failure. They love sacrifice. They *unravel* at the idea of age and rot and ka-ka and death. Whatever's ancient and not making it, they love it.

"Now, you good people are thinking so what, so few of these spookyjooks, who cares, let 'em blather, just for laffs. What you got to recall is that these goofies split off the old Ecomini party, which has plenty influence with the inner Con circles. They got enough juice to maintain several of these weenie, raggedy-butt Preserves, keep some of the last creepy species on a very expensive life-support system. You know, the Adobe Lilly, the Hairy Vetch, the Bulbous Spikenard . . .

"Thing is, that's not gonna satisfy these Ecomini moles. This ain't about the Hairy Vetch or the Pink Ginko, students. It's about shapin' reality forever. They gonna tell you it's all for the children, posterity, the unborn bozos of an endless future, so humanity will never forget the beauties of yatatayatata. Ha! Forget, I guess, what failure looks like.

"No, folks, we got ourselves a *cult* now. True fanaticos. They ain't gonna stop with a few mall bushes. They take a secret vow to restore – now focus here, folks, absorb this one – the *old giants*. The original gods, they call 'em. I am not kidding, seetwayens. These people think God is a *tree*, and they want to bring Her back! Just a little matter of two thousand years, people. They want *more* preserves. For the Sequoia! The biggest dump of inefficient cellulose ever evolved!

"Well, lemme tell ya about the Sequoia, good people. Listen to a little Sequoia paranoia – these were the original watersuckers and land-wasters, folks; the primo fire hazard and soil-poisoner of the last century, not redwood but deadwood mostly, all rot except for the last ring and needles to make a mess the size of a football field. Our ancestors – bless 'em – had the good sense to phase out these stacks of junk. Of course they kept the faster-maturing hybrids, but unfortunately they also held onto a stock of the old cones. God's dandruff, huh? And this new cult – it's a religion, these are eco-fundies – they want that seed *grown to maturity*! Two *thousand* years, people! And then – get this – *they're not gonna harvest*!"

Reclining again in his chair, Beau has drawn a window in the sky with one finger, a mini-holo, in which a series of scenes has unspooled to illustrate his commentary. Ancient film and video footage, ghostly in holo, shows men with primitive gas-powered hand saws falling the immense trees, other men and women marching with upraised signs in front of standing specimens. Then come shots of a modern plantation: several mower-chippers eating a broad, neat swath through rows of perfect cone-shaped saplings; scientists in lab coats overseeing an apparently endless block of seedlings; and finally a factory bounded by a yard stretching almost to the horizon and stacked with slabs and cubes and girders of an identical pale yellow material.

"Naw, nothin' useful like you see here, good people. The fundies wanna *worship* the old lunkers, or rather they want their grand grand grand etcetera kids to lay around and grovel in the sacred groves. But even that's not the whole bill, Jack and Jill, o-o-oh no! There's a whole 'nother agenda, my frienda. Hold on to the old chapeau, Bro, 'cause we're just gettin' started. We're gonna dig down, Charlie Brown, to the *roots* of this whole deal.

"Which brings us to . . . the *Bleeps*! Know what I mean? The *bleeping Bleeps*! Ha!" Beau whirls in his chair to face the viewers, his great bulk shivering as if with fever. "It's unbelievable. We can't say it, taxpoopers! Those li'l cannibal critturs certain beanheads call our relatives . . . we can say shrink, we can say dink, we can say stink, but we can't say . . . eeeee! No, on public stations now we gotta say *Pobla*! Po-bah-la. Oh yas, yas, Percival. Indeed, indeed, Prudence. Pobla. Short for Ghoul Indigie Noxious Kaka, ha ha! Well, let's not get into that just yet, kids. I can tell you we – I mean Fatguy Foundation – is fighting this one in court. Gonna win, too, neighbors. Free speech, right? We're a yak show. This is our life, our country, our language – you and me and bobbymagee – and we gotta right to stand up and call a *bleep* a *bleep*!"

Winger is, in fact, inspired to stand up and walk out into the empty air, his arms lifted as if to bless the continent below. There is a rare moment of quiet, only a sound of wind or perhaps a humming choir. Then he snaps his fingers and a new sequence begins in the mini-holo window, accompanied by a chamber orchestra. It is a tall man in a suit strolling through what appears to be a museum.

"Anyway, we gotta get down to the real disease, Louise, and we start with an update on the barefact background . . . courtesy of Professor Roland Ashbert . . . hiya, Professor."

The tall man looks up, smiles. "Hi, Beau. Your viewers are interested, I understand, in new developments with the Pobla. Well, we've got a wonderful new display on that topic."

He hesitates before a tableau, a static scene on what appears to be a desert highland, rock breaking out of earth seared by some conflagration. On the horizon are towering clouds of black smoke. There are two groups of figures, staring at each other, frozen in attitudes of alarm. One is a gang of men, mostly dark men, though several are extraordinarily pale. Some wear a few rags, others are naked; they have long hair and carry sticks or metal rods, the ends beaten flat and shaped to a point. The other group is composed of seven apes, all chimpanzees except for one gorilla who cradles a small dog in her arms and stands apart from the rest.

"On our way, we might reflect for a moment on this very famous and primary event. These are, of course, the male *Homo sapiens* escaped from the underground concrete vaults of that maximum security prison during the last convulsions of the Great Southern War; and the apes who were abandoned by the panic-stricken staff of a primate center in the same remote area—"

"Fascinatin', Perfessor, but whaddaya say we hasten to the goods . . ." Beau has regained his chair, parked and tilted for viewing comfort before the window, in which Professor Ashbert wheels as if surprised, and chuckles.

"Pardon me, Beau. Digression is the curse of my profession. Anyway we all know the story of how these two populations interbred and the hybrid offspring miraculously survived to mate with other scattered bands of human derelicts. Thus *Homo lapsis* – a remarkable chapter in evolutionary history."

Ashbert has strolled on past a series of other displays: a cutaway model of a maze of caves and tunnels with air and light shafts, the ruin of a subterranean stone temple, Pobla figures (apparently stuffed) bent over fires or chipping rock, a case of artefacts – bone clips and whistles, sacks of woven grass, wooden spears. He stops before a strange, box-like vehicle made of sticks plastered with mud, on stone wheels, surrounded by the naked Pobla in a threatening dance.

"An amazing, primitive culture, though until very recently our science had no inkling of its inner character. Few of the creatures were ever captured alive; even the young died within minutes of encountering humans or their machines. Also they lived in an environment so toxic that life-expectancy remained under thirty. It was unimaginable that intelligence, as we know it, could grace lives so filthy, brutal, and brief.

"But now we know more." Professor Ashbert lays a hand lightly on the contraption of wattles and stone wheels. "They were capable of ritual sacrifice. Consider this novel structure, called a *mudlati*, a Pobla term apparently meaning any mechanical device. The Pobla, frenzied by narcotics and dancing, destroyed these iconic structures in an elaborate ceremony designed to ward off evil.

"For years anthropologists were baffled. Only recently they determined the word is actually a borrowing, a corruption of the old NorthAm expression for the first mass-produced internal-combustion personal vehicle – the 'Model T' that caused a profound cultural revolution two centuries ago. How the Pobla could have acquired the word – let alone a crude image – is still a mystery.

"That mystery may soon be unraveled, for the old arrangement between Pobla and human is changing rapidly. Our fearful, secretive, vicious 'cousins' no longer hide beneath the earth. Now they are crawling to our borders, creating a far more serious crisis. Even as we learn more about them—"

"Thanks, Perfessor. Been a help but we gotta run." Beau has brushed a button, and Ashbert vanishes. "On to the Drager Affair, extravaganza bonanza, 'cause that's where the Pob-ah-la question really gets hot, and we got ongoin' scandal, kiddies."

Another rapid montage of scenes fills the window. Homeholo footage of a man and boy in camou jumpsuits, loading gear into an all-terrain sport vehicle; then a medivac jetcopter descending swiftly onto a rocky slope, where the sport vehicle has become an overturned wreck. What looks like a ragged old rug, but in close view is a dead, eviscerated bear. A man with a horribly scarred face beside a tall, athletic woman with a gaze like a blue torch.

"So y'all recall, Frank Drager took his son a-huntin' and an old she-bear and a hill of ants caught 'em out of their vehicle. Ants ate out daddy's eye, while the bear swiped the kid and – everybody thought – snacked on him later. Stockwell's stooges spun it as a fatal, one-in-a-million accident, but the Insec gators *knew* all along the laps were involved. Oh, the Cons were nervous about that, good people, I mean petrified petoonias, and we all know why! Their whole futzathon about diversity and keeping the Wastelands as toxic dump and habitat and hunting as controlled agression therapy and blah blah blah – it was all on the line, if Ghoul Indigie raiders had, like, actually kidnapped and maybe tortured and barbecued this winsome lad.

"The Progs were drooly, of course, at that very same notion. So they hired Danielle Konrad – Ho! Piece o' work, fans, was she not? Mama Media! – to write the script, and what a ride she gave us! First ultimo all-out completely real national holosoap! Made Little Ronnie the biggest horrorshow headline on the planet, and stole papa Frank away from his wife! Bitchadonna and Scarface! Cauldron of passion, intrigue, etcetera, and as you know the rumor was, at her trial, that Konrad found out the kid was alive and winked a snuff to make sure he didn't stay that way."

Beau stretches out in his console-chair, hands laced behind his head. His look is wistful, far-seeing. "Ah me, I fondly dream. Whatatime and whatashow it was, kiddies, all that deep and devious darkside dealin'. Adultery and murder and resurrection of the innocent – how could a guy miss? But – hey! It ain't over until it's a sequel, which is our job here . . ."

Beau sits up, works his shoulder, cracks his knuckles. "Gonna dive deep into the Con messorama, wh-e-e-w! Gonna concentrate on one very special little Ghoulie Ka-Ka, no doubt you know of whom we speak. Lookahere."

Beau snaps his fingers and a new image appears in the window: a still hologram, apparently from a medical or police file, for a string of ID digits runs across the bottom. The figure is naked: a dark, slender and intricately muscled body. The eyes are huge, lemur-like, the hair a river of night above, a dense crow's nest below. Her features are quite human, the nose perfectly shaped by surgery.

Then come animated scenes: dressed in blue fatigues, she operates a terminal, hangs in harness on a rock face, takes apart a lasergun, runs through an obstacle course with extraordinary agility. The sequence ends on a repeat of the first hologram, the stark, nude figure. But in all these poses her eyes attract the viewer's attention; they are holes into some infinite darkness.

"H-e-e-e-re's that Duskyrose! Charlie Fat's little dirty secret, the notorious experiment! Only Noxious Kinky of our era to survive in captivity and be actually *trainable*. Idiot-genius type crittur, able at the age of fifteen – that's an adult animal – to memorize and follow procedure. Tima the Noble Sewage and Cybernymph! Her job, under the supervision of Insec's two top agents, to track down Little Ronnie – and guess what? She ditched the so-called Superagents and ran back to the nekkidness and filth of her early childhood, found the boy and taught him some tricks, oh yeah! Never explained, how she managed this maneuver – until now!

"We logged a headbanger with the only surviving principal, former agent 'PJ' Feiffer, handpicked by Chuck Fat. You've seen this guy maybe, since his new career is sucking the tabshows to pump himself in this affair. He's been cruising the burbs, personal apps, trolling for a docudrama or maxiseries. Watch close, people, and you can get a glimpse of the wiring behind this mini-mystery and segway to the beeg peekchur, the general Con debacle of *species preservation* – ha!"

Beau has drawn a second window beside the first, from which the naked Tima still gazes out. In the new scene two men are talking from comfortable, ordinary chairs on a studio set. Beau is one of the men, and he simpers and gestures coyly as he speaks.

" . . . so you were deep darkside, you devil, on search and rescue in the heart of desolation . . . you and Jack Skiho with the best recon craft in the NorthAm arsenal, right?"

"Right." The other man leans forward, smiles. He is of athletic build, but his face is a touch gaunt and overdue for a tuck at the eyes. "We flew south—"

"South into a nest of Pobla tunnels, the undiscovered city of Sopan! Whata mission! Just two against a whole colony! Wait, *three* it was, no? You had a tracker, at this point?"

The Superagent's smile broadens, but with an ironic curb. "We had a trainee with us. Yes. Rather special. A—"

'*Female* trainee, hey, PJ? A dark 'n slinky unortho-doxy! Now we know we're into classified stuff here, but come on, Agent Feiffer, everybody has heard about Duskyrose now, the amazing little Pobla assigned to you personally on this mission . . ." Beau has rolled nearer his prey, lays a huge plump hand on the man's sleeve. "We know what the quarters are like on those ships, what the normal policy is on

34

personnel interaction, but men are men and looking at a picture of this musky little Dusky, Captain I *have* to speculate you *noticed* at least, I mean blame it on diet or the cosmetic job they did but . . . Woooo! Makes a guy curious, you know what I mean . . ."

Beau has moved his big hand to the man's lapel, and his voice has gone thicker, smoother, and hot with implication. Feiffer's expression alters. His eyes slide to one side and something happens to his smile; and at precisely that instant his image freezes, pulsing. The Beau in the window is also static for a moment, but then animates to leer at the agent, mug at the audience, and finally tiptoe out of the frame, as the bigger Beau who has been watching turns to address the viewers.

"*Does* he know what I mean! You see that look, kids? What shall we call it? Lust is too weak a word. This is dirt and drool. It's all right there, people. The eye don't lie."

Feiffer's eyes indeed appear to be crawling over the naked form in the adjoining window. The merest tip of pink tongue has slipped between his smiling lips. He seems to radiate self-satisfaction, a not-quite-hidden lewdness, the manner of a triumphant violator.

"No need to allege anything, no need to advertise this hustler any more. One look is all it takes, you see the capitols of Conservatism, Slimeopolous and Scumstadt. Animal lovers, oh yeah!"

Beau zips shut both windows and when he turns back to his viewers his face is in close-up, a complex map of tiny squint-lines of amusement, a knotted brow and hooked mouth signaling disgust, eyes slanted up in mock prayer. "Who can explain? Mysterio profundo. Trained intelligence officer twisted by a little Ghoul Indigie bitch. Sign of how the Econinnys are eating up the Con system from the inside out. But at least we know the starting point. With Danny Konrad's supersoap, the little Ronnie Drager saga. And that's where we'll pick up the story tomorrow. Da Fat Guy never lets up, dear public. Never compromises. Never—"

All light is sucked out of the box. But the man on the bed, who has caused this extinction, continues to stare. In the dark, blank interior he sees his future. The air in the room is dead, but circulated by a ventilator. The current is just enough to curl a page of an open notebook on the nightstand and then turn it, with a sigh.

CHAPTER FIVE

"The circuitry of genius is always devious," Mr Foster observed, holding the image in front of them while he roamed the conference lounge. "That's quite different from the old saw about many paths to the temple of wisdom."

"Wisdom is not genius," Batboy said in a whispery falsetto. "Is it?"

"Of course not." Mr Foster favored Batboy with an abstracted smile and pressed his remote. The holo of the cuneiform tablet was replaced by another, this one of a tremendous, tetrahedral structure of stone blocks.

The thrill of recognition came too swiftly for Ronald to intercept it, but he disconnected his stronger emotions immediately and managed to restore the current of ordinary curiosity, mild and generalized excitement. There were six monitors in the room and all the patients were spiked for classes; but only in Ronald's case were the psych stats logged into an open file, always online.

This particular squiggle in his profile wouldn't surprise them. Any image of an ancient temple or grave could cause it. They were only probing routinely, hoping Snaketongue would be weak or careless. Snaketongue was the deepest and most powerful being alive in the cave of his skull. In Pobla the name was *Pahane*, which translated roughly as "alert-sleeper-who-tastes-everything." Pahane had already struck, had swallowed and dissolved the image of the blood-stained altar, had flashed back into the darkness. Teotihuacan would nourish a secret memory of another temple where Snaketongue had been born and tutored and sanctified, a temple now ruined and buried with the bones of so many of his kind.

But the patient Ronald Drager said nothing. Slender, of medium height, hair and eyes a plain dark brown, he was not particularly remarkable in this group. They were all between fourteen and sixteen years old, very bright, from good backgrounds. They all suffered from

Multiple Personality Disorder, and they all possessed at least one animal identity. They were a set, in fact. A very narrow set, determined by him. Therefore a set of which he was supposed to feel himself a comfortable member. Just another adolescent psychotic on the mend.

An observer might have recorded two small differences in Ronnie Drager. From a few inches away, faint lines were visible on his cheeks: cosmetic surgery could not entirely hide the scars from diagonal slashes of a dull blade. And now and then, behind his mask of solemn attentiveness, there was a sudden vacuum. The eyes went strangely opaque, and his breathing suspended, though only for a second or two. The spike revealed simply the onset of a theta pattern, hardly distinguishable from drowsiness.

Anyway, Ronald could not speak because it was not his turn. Foster was winding up for a lecture, so they would have to set up a pattern to derail him. Ronald cleared his throat, and on the rug behind Batboy's chair he saw a gray flake of movement. Simultaneously Touchy, sitting alone as always on the big sofa, stretched out her legs.

"We could cite this example of barbaric splendor – Teotihuacan, of course – characteristic of ancient so-called civilizations – and we might add the Mesopotamian and Egyptian here—"

"Ye-e-e-chh! More *mummies* . . .?"

Touchy sounded on the verge of losing her breakfast, and the others also groaned. They foresaw another graphic representation of prepared corpses. A light pulsed on Foster's remote, indicating a dangerous metabolic surge in the room. He punched again hastily, and Teotihuacan was gone.

"People, *people*!" Mr Foster sighed deeply, and pressed the remote to his forehead like a cold compress. They all laughed, spontaneously and affectionately.

Of all their therapist-tutors, Foster was the only one they genuinely liked. Tall, cadaverous, with thinning hair and an immense blade of a nose, he had been hired for his solid reputation in reaching otherwise terminal young headcases. His chief technique was a revival of old-fashioned pedagogy – the lecture and Socratic seminar – in which he played (almost parodically) the role of gadfly and devil's advocate.

"I *know* what you are doing, young lady." Foster stood over Touchy, one fist on one hip, using the remote as a baton to mark the beat of his words.

38

"Long is the way,
And hard, that out of Hell leads up to light;
Our prison strong, this huge convex of fire . . ."

Petite and prim, Touchy regarded him, her exquisite features perfectly still. The baton would come no closer, for no one risked physical contact with Touchy. Her bimonthly check-ups were robotic or self-administered. Everywhere except in her own room she wore a pair of clear plastic gloves. Once, soon after her arrival, an orderly accidentally brushed against her and none of them – doctors or staff or other patients – wanted to see a revival of that murderous she-wolf.

"Yeah. Uh-huh." Touchy's voice was cool, breathy, dismissive. "I myself am Hell. And so are other people."

"Yes. That is quite true, if trivial. One could spend a whole life wallowing in these old poets and their pompous blather. As I practically have. Trying to warn sprouts like you . . ."

Mr Foster looked around at them, exasperated. He understood that they were covering for Ronald, exaggerating reactions so as to overload the wire, and he knew that Touchy was designated speaker and would remain so until he turned deliberately away. He didn't, however, know why this pattern existed. It fascinated him and drove him to distraction. None of the computer analyses of class dynamics had adequately explained it, nor had hours of direct surveillance. With a very audible huff of disgust, he undertook to examine the ceiling, arms crossed.

Chairs creaked, someone coughed affectedly, the atmo unit hummed. Finally Feely spoke in his quavering, childish voice, "Well, of course it was a wonderful *structure*, in its way. They were great engineers. But the awful . . . I mean the terrible *sacrifices* . . ."

Batboy and Squirrels made slurping and panting noises, which made Touchy whimper again with revulsion. Ronald allowed himself a brief bubble of laughter. He had seen Foster look instantly down, hoping to catch some signal among them, and then grimace again at the tiny monitor on the remote. The whole group had no doubt generated another surge to protect him. They knew which ideas were triggers. *Sacrifice, mummy, anthropophagy, ghost, immolation.*

The others had guessed they were part of the experiment of Ronald's therapy. He was the reason they got to see exotic programs and ancient texts, however fantastic and ghastly. He was the reason they got the most radical treatment, the most advanced medication. When he came

39

to the Institute he was the most notorious nut in NorthAm society, the one the doctors most wanted to crack.

He was Little Ronnie, the former cabinet minister's son who at the tender age of fourteen had gone feral, had learned from animals, from the Ginks, how to mutilate himself, eat the flesh of his own kind, and have bestial sex. Little Ronnie, who became Snaketongue, and who – this was the ongoing controversy – had been unwilling to abandon his nightmare personality, even after a mass-release holo docudrama on his adventures had secured him world-wide fame and fortune.

"There are those," Foster said acidly, "who would be in the very front row. Or so they flatter themselves." He glared at Squirrels and Batboy. "One should remember that even in the darkest, most barbaric periods of early human society – the Celts or Pythians, for example – ritual victims were not simply *spectacle*. Even in Greek tragedy—"

Foster was pacing again, looking over their heads as if watching for little thought-balloons of the sort found in ancient books for children. Now they would be able to shift speakers again, create a stack, and their trained investigators would be mystified again by the unpredictable pattern. They established this random order by means of a very simple device: they relied on a stranger.

Snaketongue had first found this new friend, and Squirrels, who had a terrible accent in French, named her Emmy Gray. She was their secret link, at once messenger and mistress, a group facilitator. In exchange for a few scraps of cheese or apple, she made a reality of their dream to pass through, literally, the very walls. The Institute was an antique structure, never modernized to include an electronic pest control system, so for Emmy transit along its plumbing and wiring was relatively easy.

In any case, Emmy Gray could have fitted into a large thimble. She was small even for *mus musculus*, which had always adapted to persecution by shrinking dramatically. She was also very quick and understood perfectly the need to keep out of sight of all staff. So it was she, by regal whim, who gave them license to speak. She usually arrived in someone's pocket or in a cuff or collar, and circulated by darting behind chairs and sofas to wriggle up pantlegs. Whoever had her, or was nearest, could speak, and nobody else.

"Please, darling geniuses," Foster was now saying, in his long-suffering manner, "let's forsake your little game of who's-the-speaker and get back to work. I raise the issue of sacrifice for a *reason*. The concept is, at the most *profound* level, an evasion of responsibility. May I please retrieve the Aztec monument, and demonstrate the point?"

"Touchy might throw up," Feely said anxiously. His sallow features had a permanent expression of eager concern.

"Maybe on you, lucky boy." Emmy was with Squirrels now, behind his shoe. He hurried on. "Anyway, I don't think it's so irresponsible. I mean, what about fierce tribesmen like the Huns, thirteenth century, or the Conquistadors themselves? Killing for loot? You put Tehooie in there to bring in cannibalism, so you could work on Snake, which is mainly what is going on here, right? Our famous pee-er, our holo star who had the whole world *waiting* for his big bourgeois self to crawl back?" Squirrels shot a mocking look at Ronald.

"That's beside the point, William. And mean-spirited as well." Foster was stern without a trace of humor, the beak of his nose trained on Squirrels. "And you are distorting our lesson. The Aztec preoccupation with ritual murder, on such a scale, was one reason they were so easily–"

"Wasn't that," Squirrels retorted. "Couldn't be that simple. I mean the odds were a thousand to one in favor of the natives. What it was was the *horses*. The indigies thought they were one creature, a monster, the guy in armor and his . . . "

When Squirrels got to the word *thousand*, Ronald's eyes had gone empty, and he exhaled slowly, steadily. He had guessed the direction of the sentence, the impending collision with the dreams Snaketongue had been having. Those dreams had been magnetizing conversations around him for weeks. He could not avoid the shock of his response so he tried to precipitate it early, so the monitors would pair it with *ritual murder*, and not the image of a swift running thing, a beast with four long legs and the head of a man.

" . . .anyway the Aztecs had another god, right? Quetzalcoatl. Linked to Cortès and then to Jesus Christ, 1519, and what's Communion but just a little quiet personal cannibalism to prepare for resource extraction and—"

Mr Foster had closed his eyes and covered his head with both hands, while others in the room groaned or looked pointedly out the window. Squirrels treated facts as nuts: store them everywhere, for you can never have too many. Emmy took the opportunity to run back to Batboy, who merely yawned and hissed, to give them all a moment's rest.

"William, please." Mr Foster sighed in relief. "If you are to prevent the ultimate triumph of the Second Law, you must *prioritize*. I am trying to make the same point for *all* of you, not just Ronald. You are all, my darlings, victims of the myth of sacrifice, just like the Aztec. You are sacrificing *yourselves* to various defunct and dangerous myths, various, uh, cultural, uh . . . "

"Fruitcake ideas," Batboy finished in a loud whisper, and spread his thin arms and showed his teeth.

Foster ignored the laughter. " . . . obsessions. As *you*, Felix, dedicate yourself to *chiroptera*, which is, we may all agree, a fascinating group, very interesting, vampires and so forth, *but* – to return to the point – you can study them without suppressing your own human nature—"

"I'm *not* human," Batboy said. "Mostly."

"Mostly?" Foster said, with arch astonishment. "Mostly? Here is a change, people. Change for the better I take it, Felix? What part of you, may I ask, has been reclaimed for our species?"

Batboy looked slyly, wickedly at Touchy. "Don't ask."

There were whoops and unkind cackles, as Touchy's pale cheeks took on color. Then Feely burst into tears, and the raillery ceased. They looked down or away in embarrassment. Feely always felt everything, the pain even of raindrops crashing into the tile roof. He could be as effective as Touchy in bending the rest of them into a careful avoidance of emotional intimacy. Foster moved quickly to the boy's side, smoothed Feely's flat brown hair with one hand and patted his tear-bright cheeks – rather briskly – before glancing at his watch.

"Walter, Walter, you know Felix meant no harm. You and Melissa are both very *sensitive*, and sometimes the rest of us are a little *thoughtless*." He levelled a glare at Batboy, then stalked to the door. "You've all been a *tremendous* bother, as usual, but I suppose you're worth it, little geniuses that you are, if we can only convince you *not* to sacrifice this high promise, bliss is it in this dawn, et cetera. So unplug yourselves and begone with you. An extra half-hour break. Garden areas."

Feely broke into renewed sobs, but this time of glee, and the others cheered and scrambled from their chairs. They removed the tiny somatic-monitor buttons from behind their ears and tossed them in a foam-lined basket on Foster's desk in their jostling rush to the exit.

How they can empty *a room*, Foster was thinking, as Touchy, always the last to leave, wafted through the door with a fleeting smile over her shoulder. He walked from chair to sofa to cushion, looking for some clue to the dynamic of this group – a thread, some scuff marks in the fabric of carpet. . . .

Ah, *la belle fantôme! Le petit ange de bavarder*! Once they had told him, as a spoof, that a little French elf determined their protocol. An agile, adventurous faery whose cavaliers they were. He had come almost to believe in her, though he was aware of the danger to therapists of falling under the spell of a patient's gorgeous fantasies. He caught himself expecting to find a tiny scarf or garter, a slipper no larger than a bean. He laughed silently, sardonically, recalling that he had never found anything but, once, a little dark comma – a mouse turd.

CHAPTER SIX

It was not really her job to save Doctor Marvin Petrasky's foolish ass. What he did with that little tramp of a graduate student was his business – a sordid enough business, no doubt – but his inattention and sloppiness were endangering the whole project. Which included her position as Chief Administrative Assistant, the highest rank and salary Robin Florence had ever received.

So in that sense it was, exactly, her job to save her job – to avert imminent catastrophe, represented at that moment by a person who identified himself as Harold Fitzgibbon and who convinced her he had the authority to wait in the inner office until Doctor Petrasky was available to answer a few questions. After he showed her his badge, Robin had given him the first quarter's report and background files, harmless stuff, and made up an excuse for her boss's tardiness. An early morning meeting in the city. A guest panel and breakfast. She was certain Fitzgibbon didn't buy it. He was a fleshy torpedo of a man who winked at her and made her shiver. Petrasky wouldn't make three bites for him.

Her desk was at the big window overlooking the driveway, parking lot, and Institute grounds – a lovely park, really, full of rare big trees and flower beds and flagstone paths. A few patients drifted along the paths, but she didn't see their prize, the Drager boy. Nor the Gink bitch, Tima, who could give you chills even at a distance.

Something was going on with those four. Little Ronnie and Tima his cannibal playmate; Doctor Petrasky and Cynthia the tramp. She didn't even want to know what it was. The whole project was goofy, as far as she could see. They were supposed to unscramble Ronnie's schizoid personality, developed in his year with the Ginks. Pardon, the *Pobla*. Robin emitted a sibilant noise of disgust. The new Conservative korrektspeak. The Administration now required contract employees to call the filthy little buggers by their own name for themselves.

Then she saw Petrasky's sportcraft flashing through the trees lining the driveway. Almost an hour late. Simultaneously, on a stretch of path through a clearing bounded by spreading oaks, she saw little Ronnie – not so little, any more – walking with Scratch, the old groundskeeper. They were laughing. Jesus. If she could see them, Fitzgibbon could too. The primary subject, dawdling along after class with a *groundskeeper*. No supervision whatsoever. Sweet Jesus.

Snatching up a printout on the budget, Robin left her desk and set off through the building to intercept Marvin and give him an earful. She flapped through Accounting and Personnel, her own province, without a glance aside. Soaring down the hall, she couldn't resist one look through an archway opening into a ward, where she saw hypnosis tanks and feedback fantasy screens in use. She took another, more searching scan of the next big room, filled with aquariums and cages and glass apparatus. The room was empty, so she frowned and hurried on. She had half-hoped to glimpse the tawny outrage of Cynthia Higgins's hair.

Absolutely a violation of the rules, that hair: longer than prescribed and not contained. How did she get it to flare like that at the shoulders? Impudent little thing. Petrasky thought she was such a genius. Cunning was what she was. And only in a crude way, seeing that the first brazen hussy to blow in his ear could have him and so set herself up very smartly indeed.

Robin was so offended she slowed her pace, clacking down the mezzanine stairs. She felt like letting Petrasky walk right into the meatgrinder of Fitzgibbon's investigation. Stew in his own juice. But she remembered her job, having her own private office and access to what was really going on, and recovered her velocity. She was no fluffhead. She didn't need to diddle the boss to advance herself. She had only to tell him what nobody else would: what was what.

Springing up the broad staircase three steps at a time, brow furrowed and briefcase clamped under one arm, Marvin felt himself apprehended, even seized, rather than merely intercepted. Robin was misnamed, he had thought more than once. She descended like a great, squawking scavenger, hungry for his liver. At first he tried to secure with his free hand the paper she was waving, before he understood that it had nothing to do with her problem.

"Robin," he said finally, with an edge of asperity. "Robin, *please*."

She fluttered back, adjusted an earring. "Oh yes, sir," she said with a terrible smile. "But you *are* late, sir. Very, *very* late. And

I don't think we have very much time. I would appreciate it if you would just please listen a few moments to my opinion, and forgive me for being very very frank."

"Yes, hmmm, of course." Marvin had begun to mount the stairs again, but this time in single steps, head bent as if in thought. She matched his pace, one lift ahead.

"He's an investigator, this man. For a Grand Jury."

They had reached the mezzanine, which was the security office on one side and the employee lounge on the other. A uniformed man behind a counter looked up, inquiringly, from something he was reading. Two lab people in white coats, on coffee break, also glanced toward them, and immediately lowered their voices without interrupting conversation.

Petrasky stopped, and the first faint current of alarm went through him. Robin took his sleeve between thumb and forefinger and tugged. "Not here," she hissed, and drew him on to the next short flight of stairs.

"The whole staff knows, Doctor, and people gossip. You haven't been, if you'll pardon me, a model of discretion. But that's neither here nor there, now. We have much bigger problems. Our files." Now they were moving quite slowly, as if, Marvin thought suddenly, this were the way to a guillotine.

"What about our files?" In his own ears his voice was reedy and insincere, and Robin uttered a quiet but intense whine of frustration.

"He wants to see them. I told you."

"Who does?"

"Harold Fitzgibbon, the investigator. Please listen to me Marvin. He's in your office right now. And he wants to see *everything*. He is not a very nice-looking person."

Marvin switched his briefcase from one arm to the other. His shoes flexed and turned, like big, blunt compass needles, aligning him toward the entrance to the lab, toward Cynthia. He longed for her; he was, this very moment, growing longer for her.

His mind, meanwhile, seemed paralyzed. The files. The record of his examination of Ronald Drager. And Tima, the Pobla female with hypnotic and possibly telepathic powers. The invoices for exotic fauna and rare medicinal plants. His unauthorized experiments involving same. The encrypted holos. Overdue physicals. The files.

Robin had folded her arms and positioned herself to block his access to the lab. "I've given him the early stuff, just the clinicals

47

and diagnostics. But the next thing he'll want is the research plan. For your principals. And he'll see–" She looked over Marvin's head to the spot where the great, shining blade would be hanging, and took a slow, deep breath.

He'll see, Marvin thought, *what must not be seen.* That the new Director of the Institute had, apparently deliberately and repeatedly, violated the cardinal rules of psychometric research. Not on some routine control experiment, but with the most sensitive and sensational case he had ever undertaken. That he had selected as his partner in these infractions a young and inexperienced but ravishingly beautiful female graduate student. That unusual pharmaceuticals had been ordered in quantity. That very odd animals were kept in the lab. That the records for this radical approach had been very imperfectly kept. That, from a hard science perspective, the Doctor was arguably as deranged as his patients.

"Marvin."

Without thinking he had been edging around her in a desperate, constipated parody of a stroll. Again, of course, in the direction of the lab. He had to see Cynthia, talk to her, hold her. They would figure it out, in each other's arms.

"That won't help!" Robin was now clearly blocking his path, the heaving front of her blouse only inches away. She went on in a hoarse, intense whisper. "He's waiting, Marvin, right *now*. Get hold of yourself. *Please*. For all our sakes."

He stopped moving. He looked at her, then away, and cleared his throat. He knew Robin was right. Harried, unprepared, guilty, sweaty, too pale – no matter; he would have to go in anyway. Talk, explain, smile, make words, pretend puzzlement, invent, conceal. And he would have to go in alone. He had known, somewhere beneath his reckless ecstasy, even as he was making time vanish in a golden net and seizing day after day for almost six months, that this moment would come.

He took a deep breath, and plunged. "We'll start with the Drager file. Everything medical, every scrap. Blood pressure, stool, reaction time, whatever." As he spoke, Robin released her own long breath and gave him a first, wan smile. "I'll take all the time I can with that, try to spin things out until lunch. In the meantime go through and find the first diagnostic that mentions the gender switching. Look under the stuff for Pahane. Oh yes, and start that overdue physical on Tima. Put Cynthia in charge of it. That will tie up the file temporarily."

The Administrative Assistant was nodding now, almost beaming, encouraging him to leadership. They swung into their office complex in a semblance of good order, chatting about a remodelling project. He felt weak in his bones, but cooler, beyond despair. A saying from an old professor came back to him: If you have a plan, you have a chance. Tying up the file was an excellent delaying tactic, and a plan – or at least the wisp of an idea – had come to him.

Harold Fitzgibbon, coat off and shirtsleeves rolled up, was sitting with his feet propped on Marvin's desk. He was leafing through a folder removed from Marvin's heirloom cabinet, whose lock had been forced, apparently with the small steel bar glittering on the desktop. The man glanced up and smiled at Marvin with a sympathetic, leisurely amusement.

"Petrasky," he said. "Nice place. Very nice. I see why you like it." He went back to reading.

Marvin, arrested in mid-stride, saw with horror that the folder in Fitzgibbon's large hairy-backed hand was his private correspondence, including all the letters and notes Cynthia had slipped under his door. "Put that down!" he blurted and, galvanized at last, rushed to his desk.

Fitzgibbon lifted his feet and dropped them casually to the floor, then held up one finger, perfectly steady, as if sighting at Marvin's nose. "Petrasky, Petrasky. This is no time to get tight. Sit down. You and me, we're going to be talking a lot for the next couple days. We should get to know each other."

Marvin lunged for the folder and found his own hand neatly and snugly contained inside Fitzgibbon's, which was soft but exerted an uncomfortable pressure. In spite of himself, he uttered a subdued yelp. Somehow, bending naturally to the compression on his fingers, he found himself on his knees before the other man, who still seemed to regard him benignly.

"No, no, Petrasky. This is not your specialty. You're a scientist, an excellent scientist they tell me. You listen to reason, right?" Fitzgibbon leaned nearer, and Marvin saw with unprecedented clarity the creases in the man's thick neck, the misalignment of his nose, and the sheen of his dark, neatly parted hair. The pressure on his hand increased.

"Yes," Marvin said quickly. "I am a scientist."

Fitzgibbon released him with an easy laugh, and turned back to the papers before him. He closed the folder and, with a bureaucrat's practiced skill, snapped a rubber band around it.

"Get up. Listen, Petrasky, we're not really interested in the girl. A little insurance, so you take this thing seriously. The Grand Jury is concerned mostly about Ronnie Drager, as I'm sure you know already."

Petrasky had gotten to his feet, and as gracefully as he could, retired to the visitor's chair with his briefcase in his lap. He saw now the small pad and stamp, and on several folders an official seal and the word *Exhibit* in red ink.

"Though I did get a look at Higgins, and must commend your, ah, taste. Terrific, I can imagine. But so what, right? Sort of thing happens all the time. Also, you got a good secretary there, Doctor. Real good act. Only she shouldn't have put me in here by myself. Must be hard of hearing. Damned file cabinet of yours squealed to wake the dead. Anyway, where were we? Might as well get started—"

Fitzgibbon had opened another folder, but now shook his head in a slow, almost sheepish way. "Christ, I forgot. You *do* know you're being investigated, indictment coming down, and so forth? Misappropriation of funds, breach of contract, professional misconduct, falsifying government records – shit, Doc, it's quite a list—" He grimaced humorously, teeth bared as if at some too-raucous sound. "I'm *supposed* to read it, serve a subpoena, etcetera, but why? If we understand each other already, right?" Marvin was sitting very straight in the chair, away from its plush back. "That is my desk," he said. "My file cabinet. You have no right to break in here."

Fitzgibbon sighed and smiled again, but this time with a touch of weariness. "No, Petrasky. No. Not right. The desk and the file and everything else in here belongs to the Institute, which is currently funded by the NorthAm government, which I am sworn to support and which is empowered to impound records, preliminary to proceedings against you. And so forth. But let's not play it that way. Don't try to be tough. Don't be an asshole. Just listen, talk to me, okay?" Fitzgibbon eased out of the chair, leaned on one arm over the desk, and with his other hand patted Marvin first on one cheek, then the other. A good-humored, buddy-style slap, pause, slap. "Okay?"

Marvin said nothing, but after a long moment he swallowed audibly and Fitzgibbon sat down again. For a large man, carrying extra weight, the investigator moved gracefully. He seemed confident and obliging, as if Marvin had come by to apply for a small loan.

"I'm a spontaneous type of guy, Marvin. And I liked you right away, muff-diving off a cliff the way you did, so let's you and me be real open, off the record, just talking. Okay?" He smiled and Marvin nodded, just perceptibly, thinking *He's got a transmitter, of course. He's looking for a confession.*

"Sure, why should you believe me? You think I'm wired. Natural. So just let *me* talk for a while, give you the situation. You don't have to even nod."

The situation, as Fitzgibbon sketched it in colorful, sometimes vulgar idiom, was that Marvin's worst fears were about to become national news. They knew all about his allowing little Ronnie and Tima to interact, unobserved. They knew about the experiments with – Fitzgibbon hooted loud laughter – birds and bees. They knew the gist of his work in inter- and intracellular communication. Most of all they knew that, from their perspective, he was no longer even pursuing the goal he had been assigned – the whole reason for his being appointed Director – the traditional, ethical goal of restoring a damaged person to health.

So they were ready, in Fitzgibbon's unlovely phrase, to pull the plug. Which meant hand down an indictment, go public, ruin Doctor Marvin Petrasky professionally and personally. Absolutely no malice involved, however. The whole thing was strictly and purely political. Marvin must have raised his eyebrows, unconsciously, for Fitzgibbon went into detail.

"Everything these days, Petrasky, is political. You must know that. Election coming up, less than a year. Now, when Dannielle Konrad hired you – before she fell on her ass – she wanted to find Ronnie so she could have him wiped. Right?" Fitzgibbon cocked and uncocked his head in swift, rhetorical inquiry. "For her own very good reasons."

"I was not responsible for her motives."

"Sure you were. We always are. You knew the Progs were funding her show. You were willing to work for her, just like you're working for the Cons now. You scientists." Fitzgibbon brayed briefly. "Innocent whores. Ever done anything darkside that you *know* about, Petrasky?"

Marvin shook his head, repulsed. He was only half listening, stunned by the realization that someone on the Institute staff had betrayed him, had no doubt documented every transgression. He was also beginning to dread what would happen to Cynthia – how that sunny radiance around her, that faith and joy in what they were doing, would wither. The whole thing, in a certain way, was her idea.

She had brought things – astonishing things – to his attention . . .

"Ah. Too bad. You'd see then. Any number of degrees of allegiance and betrayal. Anything possible. You gotta be more flexible, Petrasky. Think."

Marvin stared at him blankly. What was there to think about? The Cons had expected him to make Ronald Drager normal again, dispel the rumor that the Pobla had tortured the boy, prepared him for sacrifice, driven him mad. If there was a psychosis, it had to be corrected – by drugs, conditioning, therapy, whatever it took. They needed at least the facsimile of a normal NorthAm adolescent, for in the public eye Ronnie had become the test case for certain policies: in particular, keeping the Pobla alive for sport or study, and allowing unmanaged genetic diversity in the Wastelands.

Marvin had thought he could do honest research anyway, could probe a fascinating, unique case and come up with a theory that would persuade everyone. He had assumed that once explained and illuminated, the boy's psychosis – his invented persona of a Pobla warrior – would probably vanish, or at least yield to a program of intensive treatment.

Instead, Marvin had awakened a sleeping demon inside his famous young patient. Pahane. Snaketongue. A stealthy, scaled intruder with dangerous powers. The biblical dimension to the whole affair had been a joke between him and Cynthia; now it appeared that retribution for their sin was at hand. Marvin allowed himself a small, bitter smile, which Fitzgibbon – cast as the avenging angel – quite misinterpreted.

"Good. You see. You are wondering, okay, why don't we just go on with the process, get you out of here and into Jury chambers – unless we want something else. Very good, Petrasky. You see I haven't got a wire or I wouldn't talk this way. And you haven't either; I know, 'cause I combed this joint. We *need* you, Petrasky. Dumping you would be embarrassing, since we've let you fuddle along for months already, and also you might, at this point, make yourself useful."

Marvin's upright posture, the stance of a man before a firing squad, gave way visibly. He blinked. He was not going to be immediately charged, exposed? His mind was released all at once from its paralysis, like an arrow. The Grand Jury wanted to make a deal? But he had nothing to offer them, and anyway the facts were plain. Ronnie was, from an orthodox clinical standpoint, deeply schizoid, probably incurable, and nobody believed any more in divine possession or demonic messengers, not even in mystical identities.

"One thing, Petrasky, is really bothering me. I'm not an investigator here, not part of this scene professionally, no axe to grind. Just a regular, curious guy. Okay? Buddy to buddy. I can't quite figure how you veered off your track so far. Into this radical bullshit." Fitzgibbon waited, his chin cradled on interlaced fingers, elbows planted on the desktop.

Marvin exhaled and closed his eyes. In the first dizzy month after Cynthia had seduced him in a hidden glade on the Institute grounds, he had wondered the same thing himself. She took over not only his metabolism, but the direction of his research. Though "direction" was hardly useful to describe the methods Cynthia invoked.

Bird-watching, eating strange plants, dreams, hypnosis, transcendences – trances and dances, Cynthia sang – with his *subjects*! Doctor Petrasky's heart had become heavy and cold as an iron wedge whenever he imagined what other members of the scientific community would say, if they knew. But of course Doctor Petrasky had been less and less present over these last months. Marvelous Marvin had replaced him. Or just plain Marvelous, in Cynthia's phrase. And Marvelous was not good at foreseeing dire consequences.

"So." Fitzgibbon looked indulgent, and a shade disappointed. "Just the usual. Sweet little poke, anybody could see that, but also a smart one, right, Doc? Knows how to get her way? Some of her old professors wound up as pelts on her wall, too, you know. You didn't know? Ah."

"That's a lie. You are trying to provoke me." Marvin gripped his briefcase to stop the trembling of his hands. "You wouldn't believe the truth if I told you."

"Maybe not. That's one of the hazards, you know, of this job. You have to assume nobody ever tells the truth. But I'm surprised, man, that it never occurred to you. The young lady has connections to some pretty strange groups. I mean *radical* radical. Free love, who cares, but these creepos do the occasional bomb also. You never thought she might have an agenda? Might be, uh, taking advantage?"

Marvin was very pale. He hated Fitzgibbon with a cold ferocity he had never seen in himself before. An image of himself lunging over the desk and bludgeoning the other man played swiftly in his mind. But instead he said, slowly and definitely, "You are a despicable person. You deal in vileness and treachery and cruelty, everything

I detest. But I understand what you have the power to do. And I will co-operate, fully. On two conditions."

Fitzgibbon hunched forward, his chin now resting on one hand fisted into the other. "I like this, Petrasky. And I like you, you got style. You're going to say leave the girl alone, that's number one, and the other – maybe save your employees?" He watched Marvin's face for a moment, then nodded. "We can deal. Go ahead. Your version."

"I want Cynthia absolutely out of this. No investigation, no mention of . . . of us."

"You got it." Fitzgibbon held up one finger.

"And I want the Institute to go on. Not with me as Director, of course. But—"

"Why not?" Fitzgibbon shook the finger reprovingly. "You are an innocent babe, Petrasky. You got to learn how to really deal. I told you we needed you. *All* of you."

Marvin did not move, except to blink. Fitzgibbon found his expression comical, and laughed. "You still don't get it. Listen close, Petrasky. We'll set it up so *nothing* has to change."

Marvin went rigid again, and repeated, as in a foreign language lesson, "Nothing has to change." He understood, in a flash, what going insane was actually like.

"Right. You're still the Director, and you and sweet stuff can keep whatever you've got going. Only play it careful around the office. You know, the other help – like your Robin out there – get jealous. Somebody will eventually feed the story to the newsvultures.

"You only have to do a couple of pretty simple things, Petrasky. Don't see how you can refuse anything so easy. One, you prepare a final case report on little Ronnie Drager, all the tests and procedures and dates and so forth, which will show that his schizophrenia predated his abduction by the Ginks. His school and health records, as you know, give us a little hint in that direction, and we can make some additions. Then you release the kid to his father's care."

"His *father!*"

"What I said. I know everybody thinks old Scarface has become a hermit, out of the action, but I can tell you Frank Drager has been rehabilitated and is about to enter politics again. He can testify to those early tendencies in his son. He was there when that agent brought him and the Gink bitch in. And he *is* the kid's father."

"But—"

"The mother? She's through. Trust me." Fitzgibbon beamed in professional pride. "She and Charlie Fat went into some bizarro cult. We know all about 'em – shaved heads and vows of silence, fasting, the works. Court wouldn't award her custody of a family dog."

In his most desperate moments, Marvin had always reverted to what seemed the fundamental pattern of his consciousness: the inductive and speculative mode of pure science, a painstaking review of fact in order to hazard new hypotheses. He was such a serious student just now, biting the inside of his cheek, his brow knotted intently.

"You want the boy," he whispered.

"Right." Fitzgibbon nodded encouragingly.

"Given to the father, who is going back into politics." Marvin pressed the fingers of one hand to a temple. "A Progressive extremist – the Exterminator, I believe he was once called – a mental case himself some believe . . ."

Fitzgibbon was grinning from ear to ear, making a boosting motion with both hands. "Petrasky, you are amazing."

"You want me to invent a new case history for Ronnie. Falsify the record."

"Hey, doc, come *on*. Don't exaggerate. Like I said, even his kindergarten teacher described him as one weird kid. His grades were going to hell, just before the bear and the Ginks took him. Moody, dreamy, no center. All you got to do is *restructure* some facts."

A light began blinking on the desktop, and Fitzgibbon pressed a button on the small, recessed panel there.

"Doctor Petrasky?" Robin's voice was charged with careful cheer.

Fitzgibbon nodded at Marvin, who spoke finally, his voice gone reedy again. "Yes?"

"The files on Ronald Drager are ready, sir. But Tima has gone for her physical, so Cynthia Higgins has her current folder I'm afraid."

"Thank you, Robin."

"Shall I bring in the files, sir? And will you be going out for lunch?"

Fitzgibbon shook his head.

"Uh, no, Robin, not yet. And cafeteria, uh, will be fine."

Fitzgibbon flicked the switch again and turned back to Marvin, rubbing his hands in anticipation of some delicacy. "Excellent, Petrasky. You were going to bury me in blood pressure and urine, hey? No need, you catch on so quick."

Marvin continued to frown with concentration. "What is the other simple thing?"

"You hire a couple of new nurses. Perfectly qualified. They get assigned to the Gink bitch. Absolutely simple and safe."

"Nurses." He thought hard a moment longer. "You occupy my office. You break into my personal files. You tamper with evidence. You want me to fabricate a medical history." Abruptly, he stood up. "You are trying to blackmail me. You aren't from any Grand Jury." Still clutching his briefcase in both hands, he began to back away from Fitzgibbon.

The large man oozed out from behind the desk. Marvin hurled the briefcase at him, turned and ran. He got his fingers around the doorknob before Fitzgibbon's big hand closed over the whole top of his head and hauled him back by the hair. Marvin was not aware of his feet touching the floor, but he was somehow returned to his seat.

Fitzgibbon leaned over him, his smile now mournful. "Petrasky, you hurt me this way. And you could hurt yourself. I never said I was working *only* for the Grand Jury. The fucking FedJud is small stuff, my friend, compared to the people I represent on the side. We can play it official, of course, if you want. I got a warrant–" He reached inside the coat hanging on the back of the desk chair, took out a thick envelope in official gray, and spun it into Marvin's lap. "I wasn't shitting you, the indictment *is* being prepared, this *is* an investigation. Sure you can claim you were offered a bribe and so on, but after these so-called files of yours come to light . . . who'd believe you? Be wise, Petrasky. Be thoughtful."

Again Fitzgibbon took Marvin's hand into both his own. Marvin felt a forefinger being separated, positioned. There was a muffled crack and a bolt of pure, white pain drove all his breath out in a small, gagging scream.

"Just one finger, Petrasky, to keep your mind from straying. You got the chance to hold on to everything. Or we can bury you in shit so deep you will never, buddy, ever see the light of glorious day again. We'll get the kid sooner or later, anyway; but you could make it quicker, save us some time. So easy, so simple."

The door opened then and Marvin saw Robin's face, white and stark under her make-up.

"What is it? Sir . . . Marvin . . .?" She took a faltering step across the threshhold.

"No problem, ma'am." Fitzgibbon laughed genially, draped a hand over Marvin's shoulder, massaging lightly. "Little muscle cramp. Right Marvin?"

Marvin cradled his exploded finger in his lap, with the gray envelope. He breathed jerkily, shuddering, making a querulous humming sound. He managed to nod.

"You don't . . . need me?"

He shook his head. Then he laughed just once – a sharp, high bark.

Robin stared at them, her mouth open and working long before the words came out. "Higgins wants to see you. Something about the physical?"

"Sure. Doctor Petrasky and I are almost done. Just give us another minute. Thanks, Robin." Fitzgibbon showed her the palm of a hand in benevolent but brisk farewell. Slowly the door closed, eclipsing the pale moon of the secretary's face.

"So, Petrasky, I leave it all to you." Fitzgibbon hooked his coat from the chair back and picked up the stack of folders. He took the steel bar from the desktop and slid it into an inside pocket. He was once more polite and businesslike. "I'll be back day after tomorrow at nine sharp. Pop a couple of painkillers and get that finger splinted; then think it over, discuss with your girl if you want – but remember what I said about that – and let me know what you decide. Okay, buddy?"

From some macabre distance, beyond even the steady current of agony running up his arm, Marvin heard himself groan an acknowledgment. He watched the big man roll out of the room, heard Fitzgibbon's amiable chuckle as he addressed some pleasantry to Robin just before the door closed gently. Then Doctor Petrasky was alone, at last, in his office. As his final act on this unusual morning, the Director of the New Life Institute – barely thirty years old and on the threshhold of a brilliant career – staggered into his private executive bathroom and vomited into the sink.

57

CHAPTER SEVEN

"Night mare, night mare," Scratch said, with a sidelong leer at Ronald. "My horsies in your dreams, big scare."

Ronald frowned and ignored Scratch's soft snort of laughter. The groundskeeper always talked in riddles and rhyme, which sometimes had an uncanny relevance. He supposed the old man meant people could become each other's nightmares. As humans projected their own worst features onto the Ginks, and the Pobla, in turn, perceived piksis as robot ghouls. *Piksi* was the Pobla word for the NorthAm populace. It meant "eater of shadows" – one who sucks out souls, like the marrow from bones.

The spooky part was that Scratch seemed to *know* what none of the doctors even suspected. His dreams were in fact intense these days, and haunted by horses of fire. They were lingering at a fork of the path leading to the old arboretum. Scratch was on his way to the plant nursery, where he kept a few tools, but the monitor on Ronald's leg had already emitted a warning ping. He had only another twenty meters of range in that direction. At the base of an old oak – one of only three native trees on the property, Scratch had told him – they stopped and faced each other.

"Late date today, hey?" Scratch's singsong conveyed mischief and glee. "Somethin' shakin' and breakin'?"

Ronald watched the old man place his hands on the bark of the tree. Scratch was poised, his eyes bright and quick under the brim of his frayed straw hat. They had seen the Doctor's car pull up an hour late, and the Doctor was supposed to clear Tima for their session.

"Mad boy bad boy," Scratch went on, beginning to grin. "Don't hafta be a sad boy!" He bounced on the balls of his feet, embracing the great trunk.

Ronald could not help smiling. The groundskeeper reminded him of Adza, the ancient matriarch who summoned Snaketongue and ordained him *tagak*. Adza had also mingled the silly and obscene and magical.

She had no doubt been, from one angle, senile and unbalanced, but the Pobla believed the Great Shadow, *wonakubi*, only spoke through these simple, perfectly open minds. Ronald's smile broadened. An underground tunnel straight to the Temple of Wisdom.

"Grow up to be an old boy, bold boy, like you," he answered, and reached up with both hands to touch the rough hide of the oak. He felt instantly the force driving up out of the earth, the humming life interconnecting and conversing through the great frame. It was like embracing the leg of the giant who held up the sky.

"Ya, good wood," the old man said. "Today's the day. Doc on the block, girl in a whirl." He unhinged his arms from the trunk and stepped back. "All up to you, Baby Blue."

He gave a sharp, sudden whistle, and a big bluejay alighted just above them. The jay delivered a loud, abrasive jeer, then cocked its head expectantly. Scratch answered with a churr and squawk, and the bird jumped to the next highest branch. The old man laughed and moved off, a hand on his hip to imitate a hobble, but in fact quick-footed and spry.

"Git there anyhow," he called back to Ronald, before turning into a broken puzzle of light and shadow, disappearing down the leafy path. "Keep flappin'! Gotta try, gotta fly!"

On his way through the arboretum, he found himself following Scratch's clue, searching the branches overhead for a migrant, a plover or swift or flicker coming in after a day's flight. But there were only the local birds, quarelsome and discontent. The gaudy flowers on the path also struck him as melancholy, like lonely girls dancing by themselves. Everywhere there were signs of bewilderment and loss, and these signs only confirmed the heaviness in his own heart.

This world they had once imagined they would cleanse and bind up was now beginning to shiver in its fever, its delirium. And the tremors had reached them, begun to sunder them. In recent days Tima had been strangely distant, or inattentive. Even in their free sessions, wrapped in each other, alone except for the robot holomonitors, she could sometimes be blank, her shadow turned away from him completely. If he reacted with impatience, she only smiled a remote smile, or pretended to awaken with an odd, silly laugh. When he rolled off her she would ask if it was lunchtime.

She was not like the *tohanaku* who had run away with him in the Wasteland, to buck and nip and play and then talk away the night beside a fire in a cave by the sea. For the first time he had almost doubted. For the first time the chain of miracles seemed to have broken.

After old Adza had gone into the Great Hive to embrace her sister-queen, the other *tagakin* had seen serpents come to encircle an egg of light exactly where he and Tima stood. That was a sign they were to be together always, were to unite the Pobla and the piksi. They would be the first *tak tagak* in two bodies. They would be twin gods.

But what god went around with an electronic shackle on his leg? Or had a mate in a cage? He grimaced. He was like Atlas, Prometheus, Osiris, Orpheus – all the pathetic ones. Each night he lay awake staring at faint stars through the shatterproof plastic bubble of a skylight, sealed by an electromagnetic field that tripped an alarm and snapped a steel shield into place at any sign of an approaching object. God might have two bodies (and three personalities), but for the last six months all of them had been teenagers in captivity. He allowed himself a small, bitter grin. Gods were under a lot of strain in this age.

He was now at the edge of a small outdoor court and garden, across from the door to Cynthia's office, which was open so he could see her framed in wisteria, bent intently toward a screenful of text with one finger poised on a key. An open mailer and heap of cartridges on her desk indicated that she was going through a collection from some old, offnet archive. He lightened his step and glided nearer on the entrance walkway. She did not look up, and he watched her file something, sigh, and shift her position in the chair.

He stepped over the threshhold, and the location monitor on his calf clicked. When she looked up he caught the expression on her face just before her smile. It was a reflection of his own state – the worry and uncertainty and even desperation of a creature in a corner – but with something new as well. Something at once reckless and secretive, which he recognized instantly. He had already seen it in Tima's eyes.

"Panny! Come in. How'd it go with Foster?"

"We kept him occupied."

Cynthia had a quick laugh, a kind of loud hiccup of joy. "I bet. Was he obvious again?"

"Completely. Today was sacrifice. Teotihuacan and so on. We multiple disturbos are unnecessary martyrs to false myths."

They gave each other the same wry smile.

"You must get tired of caverns and temples and serpents and termites."

"No, not the stories. I – we – just get tired of being fished in." He made a nasty noise around his protruded tongue.

She flushed a little and looked away. "I can imagine. Dimly, at least. I'm sorry, Panny. We do the absolute minimum. Which may be getting us into big trouble, by the way."

He waited, and saw again, fleetingly, the strange, reckless expression. Then she was cheerful again, with a determined forcefulness.

"In trouble – hey, it's our natural condition. And widespread, these days. Some mean viral mutations popping up, the Fed is giving us shit for lagging behind the Pacrims again, another story on the nonumbs–"

"Where's Tima?" He interrupted curtly, even meanly, because he already sensed the special session was in doubt. The Doctor must not have cleared it. Ronald had gained the rudiments of Pobla skill in apprehending meanings beneath a voice. In Cynthia's he heard the breath of evasion, the shadow of apology.

She was gazing back at him now, blushing. "Okay. All right. No use trying to fool you guys. I should have told you. Marv has been tied up in some unscheduled appointment. He had Robin call me to start Tima's physical, and didn't say a word about the free session, which is right on his calendar. And he's not taking inhouse calls. I'm really worried. And Tima's not feeling so good anyway. What's been happening on the border . . ."

It was his turn to look away. That was part of the trouble. Not widespread trouble, but narrow and very deep. The Pobla killing their own kind, the refugees, the forms with no shadows – everything since the New Broom invasion was a horror so great they could witness it only at intervals, when they were especially strong. That was because they were themselves, in a way, partly responsible for the horror . . .

When he could speak, he asked in a neutral voice, "So what's happening on the border?"

"The count is still going up. Another sanitation battalion mobilized. And it's still a hot campaign issue. Some mediaheads think it will be the crusher. Whether they can adapt to captivity and make themselves useful." She paused, and Ronald waited without expression. "Your name is coming up again. And so is your father's." She hesitated, then spoke softly and carefully. "I could show you a clip."

"I don't want to see him."

Ronald had turned away to stare out the open door, through the wisteria, at a green-throated hummingbird stitching along a row of roses. A hole had been seared in his mind, in the place where his memories of his father should be. The smouldering aftermath of explosion and fire. His father's nickname was the Exterminator; the twisted ruin of his father's face had become the symbol of a final, simple policy for all dangerous species.

The notion of death, of course, did not upset the Pobla. They often rejoiced in death, took refuge in it. They thought of death as a dark, swift river that bore all beings into a great sea of shadow, where a serpent of light and another of darkness spun out all things, all events, in a joyous geyser of being (like these hummingbirds feasting on red hearts). It was the loss of one's shadow, one's connection to his kind, and of his kind to this sea of creation, that terrified and shattered. That was what had happened to the piksis. What had almost happened to him.

"Now, they don't even know they are in captivity," he said finally. He was thinking not just of the Pobla, but of all creatures that adapted to cages and moats, and this simple statement struck him as bleak beyond anything he had ever said before. He shook himself slightly and took another breath. At least he still *knew* he was a prisoner. He re-membered – Snaketongue remembered – what running free was like.

Cynthia understood him, and was respectfully silent for a few moments. He turned back then and managed a thin smile. "So no session today," he said neutrally.

Cynthia mused for a moment, bit her lower lip first on one side and then the other. She frowned at her desk chrono. "Fuck it," she said then, her tone soft as the stroke of a moth's wing. "I'll tell them Marvin is on his way and to log Tima down here for the physical. You stand behind the door."

Fascinated, he watched her talking into the intercom, chatty and bright. This was a rule they had not broken before, and Security would know because of his leg monitor. Protocol was definitely unraveling. His heart was all at once quick and light as the hummingbird.

"Okay. Absolutely. My responso all the way. Thanks, Joyce, see you in ten." Cynthia flipped off the intercom and twirled in her chair, letting out a long breath. "If it's all going to collapse anyway . . . why not blow it up? We haven't done what we're *supposed* to be doing all morning. Marvelous is not supposed to be late. I'm not supposed to be

giving you the headlines. Or allowing you and Scratch to goof off together. Or discussing your case with you – uncredentialed as I am."

Ronald glanced at the screen where the ancient type still shimmered.
"What are you digging up these days? Still on werewolves and
lamias?"

Cynthia gave her little hiccup of laughter. "No! No time for
metaphors. Real thing now. Ferals and hairys. Heralds and fairies."

"Beg pardon?"

"The borderline human. Or subhuman, as it used to be called. Our
usual charming arrogance about which direction the universe points.
There's actually quite a literature, though very biased." Cynthia moved
a knob and began to scroll through the text.

"Look at this, from an old print journal way before the Fed, when
we were part of the United States."

Ronald stepped nearer to read. After a moment he laughed softly.

. . . not hairy men in the ordinary acceptance of the term, but more
resemble some of the monkey tribe (the Diana monkey, cuxio,
etc.); while their edentulous condition carries them yet lower in
the animal scale. The eldest is a man aged over 55, Andrian by
name, said to be the son of a Russian soldier from the district
of Kostroma. He was born during the period of service of his
reputed father, and has no resemblance to him, to his mother, or to
a brother and sister whom he possesses. To escape the unkindness
of his fellow villagers, Andrian fled to the woods, where he lived
in a cave, and was much given to drunkenness . . .

"I bet he was," Ronald said. "If that was the state of science in
those days. This was a reputable—"

"*Scientific American* was the name. Supposedly authoritative, for
1895. But other doctors were dismissing such hairiness as just the
persistence of infantile lanugo, or sometimes, as in the case of the
Ainu people, a genetic aberration in a whole subpopulation . . ."
Cynthia punched up another text in the same old-fashioned type.

. . . of a girl, six years of age, covered from head to foot with
soft, silky hair. Upon first sight little Kra-o, as the child is named,
would appear to be the "missing link" between the ape and man,
but a closer examination of this peculiar being will prove that
this diagnosis is faulty in all respects. Kra-o, who is being

exhibited in London at present, is quite an intelligent child, and had acquired enough knowledge of the English language within a few months to be able to make herself understood; and this is an ample proof that, although her outward appearance is that of an animal, she has a bright mind . . .

"Whew! *Although* animal in appearance, she has a bright mind." Ronald laughed again, then suddenly sobered. "Exhibited. I suppose that's what I'm supposed to be, eventually."

Cynthia frowned at him affectionately. "Let's not cross any quagmires before we come to them. It's at least a little more subtle now. That century was really one of the worst ever. Even the doctors and scientists, who should have known better . . . they were terrified of their animal origins. You know that expression 'sherlocking a solution'?"

Ronald nodded. "Yeah. Some old story about a detective? Always had the rational approach?"

"Whole series of stories, terrifically popular for more than a century." Cynthia rolled her eyes comically. "Quaint stuff. Written, actually, by a doctor, and one of the characters is a retired physician. Anyway, several of the stories involve apes or dogs or snakes, or a primitive pigmy, as killers. In one a doctor worried about his virility injects himself with orang-utan hormones, and winds up swinging in the trees, howling and beating his chest."

"So they shoot him."

"You guessed. There were more sympathetic portrayals – guys named Mowgli and Tarzan and King Kong – but in all of them the human has to triumph in the end. We—"

She stopped at Ronald's raised hand. The look they exchanged took the place of a long, fruitless conversation. It was a recognition that there was no further use in talking about these things, these movements and pressures, this feeling that great tectonic plates of history were about to slip.

There was a soft harmonic chime from the door. He moved quickly to take up a position against the wall where he would not be seen, and Cynthia rose from her desk and smoothed the front of her smock. Then she stepped to the door and opened it, without releasing the handle.

"Oh hi, that was fast! Yeah, I better just take her right here. Come in, Tima. I'm just *buried* today, Joyce, haven't got a minute, sorry . . . Let me initial that . . ."

Ronald did not hear any more. Tima had of course detected him in the room before she stepped over the threshhold and did not look at him when she entered. She wore a faded blue paper jumpsuit without zippers or buttons or laces, and paper slippers. It was the garb prescribed for potentially violent patients, though she had of course no status as a patient. On the record she was a lab animal, like the rats and tropical fish. Then the door was closed again, and they were moving toward each other. He took her hand and lifted it to his face. She did the same, so he felt her warm breath on his palm, and they inhaled together. She would take in all his anxiety and pain and doubt, know the inexpressible richness of his yearning for her, and their shadows would mingle . . .

Snaketongue had reared in him with the suddenness of light, fierce and alert. He smelled the apprehension and grief, the burnt residue of suffering, but these only floated on a deep weariness, and she also stank of sleep, a heavy and dull and drowsy inwardness. He would have thought some illness, but she seemed, in spite of fatigue, perfectly solid and healthy.

"*Tohanaku*," she said, with just a suggestion of a growl. He looked deep into her, into those eyes of moonless, starless night. She blinked and then her mouth curved around white, strong teeth and in a moment she would laugh.

He stepped back. "*Na, tohanaku*. You are tired. You turn away and now you laugh. Why?"

"Because you are such a sulky *dako*. Your *delo ogan* arrives first, as usual." She glanced down below his belt, and now she did laugh. Not a full Pobla whoop, for that would have carried through the walls, but a laugh that went over him like a clout of wind, and took with it all his desire.

He saw Tima and Cynthia exchange a look, a look so swift and stealthy that his surprise gave way in an instant to anger and humiliation. Ronald slammed back in, speaking NorthAm, his voice choked almost to a whisper. "What is this? What is this shit? What is the matter with you?"

Cynthia was blushing furiously. "Ronnie . . . we . . . look, it's an *awful* day – an awful time all around, and we all know it – but this may be the last session we can do for a while. We . . . we'll explain why after it's over. Please, let's just start the exercise, because—"

Tima interrupted, speaking still in Pobla. As usual she used few words, but they were thoughtful and emphatic. They could not forget they were mirrors, were *tak tagak* and their *kubin* together was a creature far greater than they were, a twin shadow with the burden of binding all the Pobla now scattered and empty and desperate, bringing them back to Kapu's band. They had to put aside the old games. There was no time left.

She turned and walked to an open area, covered only by an old rug. There she sat down and closed her eyes, waiting. He stared at her. The weariness was gone. She was poised and erect as an antelope, even sitting in her paper clothes. No matter how many times he saw this strength and resilience, this ability to move calmly and surely into the moment, it still amazed and humbled him. He had to labor to put aside what he had just seen, this collusion and deception. He had to ignore his own ignorance. He had to—

Tima spoke once more, eyes still closed. "We cannot do it without you."

He knew what she meant by "we". Their shadows, impatient with the bodies they were tethered to. The *tak tagak* that gave them visions. He took one more long breath and moved then to the other side of the rug and sat down to face her. He could hear Cynthia's quick steps behind him, the opening of a cabinet and a click of switches.

They began the breathing pattern, the flowing back and forth, until they were perfectly together. Through lowering eyelids he saw Cynthia bend to lay the little drum in Tima's lap. It was only a child's toy, a thin shell of wood with a skin drawn tight over one end and laced at the back.

An image flashed up in him, as if illuminated by a single stroke of lightning, and was gone again. Horses running, foam spattering their reaching necks, and among the whipping manes here and there was a face . . .

With her breath only Tima gave his *kubi* its female name; he gave hers its male one. Pahane and Tima were disappearing, dispersing, transforming. Feathers were sprouting, scales wrapping in an iridescent sheath, hair shimmering out in waves of electric silk. The drum tapped, and the first syllable came.

She sat very still, except for two fingers of one hand which tapped on the drumhead. The resulting sound had the faint, penetrating resonance of drops of water falling into a deep well. She had strength only to breathe, to lift these two fingers. All of her being was concentrated in the effort of sending her shadow away, to make a path for her *tahanaku's* shadow. They would be seeking the place where the last *tagakin* were singing the songs of death. She could only gather the image-making fire of her nature and open the path for him. Then he would have to meet the vision, witness it, and return.

For her *kubi* was, like this drum, male – a sun, a spear, a masked dancer, a brilliant fan of feathers, a cunning fire-shaper. And Pahane's was female – the force that created all these, boundless and agile and powerful as the sea, the force that wove all shadow into being and all being into shadow – and then *saw* what it wove. Her male ghost could go anywhere, his female would see what was there.

Ya tohanaku kishta tohanaku, her ghost recited, matching his chant to the slow tap of the drum. *My words shall be your wings, my mind is the wind. Hawk ghost, you must see for us all.*

The chant ran on, and the language began to seethe, to gather under them like a racing wave. She – his ghost – would be circling soon, hunting the hole into the world of shadows. He must be there for her, with all his power. His words had to vanish into sound, into song, crying like the great birds in flight. She had to open her eyes on the lost world. There was no more time. After this he would be thrown back into a female body, could voyage no more because of what grew inside that body. And Pahane – with his woman's shadow – would have to bear the drum.

CHAPTER EIGHT

His *kubi* was rushing into a fissure, tunneling further and further until she was swimming in a darkness so dense it undulated with current and pressure. There were others beside and behind her in the black flow, driving further, blind and reckless, until ahead now they sensed light and swam faster, lunged and leaped, became finned, flashing lances breaking the surface. The fish of fire!

The power lifted her, twisting and hurling a diamond, rainbow spray against the sun, and in this shimmering fan of light and air she entered the sky again. She was nothing, only awareness. The waves rose long and slow beneath her, gathered to plunge into the shore and sprawl full length, running fingers of foam over the smooth bed of sand.

On a high dune, where grew the last dwarf shrubs, flattened by the wind, she could see the ring of dark figures seated around a single prone form. She could hear their singing, the voices emerging from the last hisses and whispers of the racing foam. It was one of the old rockenroll chants that Adza had often asked Pahane to sing for her, in between her fragmented prophesies at the temple of Sopan.

> *Rollan-rollan*
> *Rollanonda reeba,*
> *Rollan-rollan*
> *Rollanonda reeba!*

When the voices died away, Kapu waited to let the surf reassert its rhythm. The breeze from offshore was steady and chill, occasionally lifting a veil of fine sand to sting their faces. Except for himself and one other old one from the original group of Elders at Sopan, the Pobla in the circle were all young, *tchat* warriors with a couple of raids to their credit.

Tsitsi looked much the same to them, two days after his death. He was propped up in the center of the ring, facing the sea: a rack of bones over which a wrinkled hide had been stretched. To them, as children, he had always been a joke – mumbling, winking, tottering along with his staff and pack of fat rats. He was just the old rat-herder, the timekeeper and gatekeeper, whose chief accomplishment seemed to be a miraculously long life.

But Kapu could remember Tsitsi as a *tagak* of middle-age, skinny and active as a grasshopper, full of jokes himself. Silly, made-up words and songs, games with numbers, burlesques of old stories. He had, even then, the mind of a rat. Once through a complicated chant or history, he never forgot it, never made a mistake repeating it. It was obvious to everyone that he would be the chronicler and record-keeper for the *tak tagakin*, for as long as he lived.

One of the young raiders shifted his buttocks in the sand, and others were beginning to look here and there, waiting. Kapu sighed, and picked up the drum. It would be no use to recall the younger Tsitsi, enumerate his exploits. There were no flowers, either, and there would be only a short, symbolic feast. Nothing was as it had been the year before – before the piksi soldiers had descended, like a whirlwind, into the most sacred of all the Pobla ceremonies.

"Vasan kubi tak mahanaku, tak zelag," he crooned, and struck the drum lightly. He saw them looking, listening. They cared about the drum, mostly, wondering what he would do with it. Their barely concealed curiosity irritated him, made him close his eyes and concentrate on the song.

> *This ghost of a great teacher goes a great distance,*
> *Goes to the shadow of shadows.*
> *Ya! This meat goes a small way,*
> *It has no shadow. It is his gift.*
> *Yano! Yano! Yanaku yano!*

Greeting death with this last, loud cry, Kapu struck the drum in rhythmic beat, a multiple of the slow march of the waves. Others around the circle began to sway, their eyes now closed. Kapu watched covertly, warily, until he felt them all breathing together, then sang quickly and smoothly.

> *Sky in his bones, sky in his bones,*

> *He flies round and round!*
> *This meat we give away,*
> *We give it to the sea,*
> *Great keeper of time.*

A couple of the young *tchatsinakun* blinked, gaped at him. He softened his stroke on the drum, let it fade into the sound of the waves, then stopped. There were uneasy movements now all around the circle. He stood up slowly and wrapped the tattered dog-skin robe around him more tightly. It occurred to him that perhaps he was himself only a few years from appearing to the young as a harmless, lunatic skeleton.

"Take only the heart, then throw our old brother into the sea," he said. He spoke deliberately, very clearly, but as he expected they only stared at him. The death of an Elder was always, had always been, followed by a curing of his flesh for future ritual feasting.

Then Yata and Apiso got up, looking troubled and embarrassed. "Why?" Yata asked in a quavering voice, though already he had taken hold of Tsitsi's stick-wrists.

"He was our great marker of time. Now he shall count the waves forever, for *wonakubi*."

After a long moment, Apiso nodded too, and seized the ankles.

They watched as the two strong young *tchatsinakun* took the body as far as the tideline, where they stretched it out again. Apiso stood with a foot on each thin arm, and with a stone knife from his shoulder-bag Yata swiftly opened up the chest cavity. The heart was dark, the blood already too clotted to run. Yata wrapped it in an old woven grass mat. He sluiced the knife clean and laid it on the sand beside the covered heart; then the two of them heaved Tsitsi's hollow corpse into the surf.

"*Kish*," Kapu said. He did not wait for the tide to carry Tsitsi away, but held the drum under his arm and marched back into the dunes. He knew the others would follow, or most of them, anyway. He could not predict, any more, when one of their company would vanish, drop away. Some, he knew, returned to what was left of Sopan to beg Sayat's mercy and take vows to him. Others wanted only to wander or die alone in the Wastelands.

Of course some of Sayat's people ran away and came to them, too. These refugees were often sick or mad, useless as scouts and

71

a burden on the other travellers, but Kapu always took them in anyway. It was not their fault. They had lost their shadows, so there was in them no depth or resonance or perspective, no dark, comforting space between being and suffering. In the old days they would have been abandoned as already dead, but Kapu had learned that in time some overcame their listlessness and terror, and revived.

It was the other kind of madness and death he could not understand: the kind Sayat had been consumed by and now spread among his followers. The fanatic will to create and then slay a monster, to purify the world of every enemy. And all who did not worship Sayat, of course, were the enemy. This was the piksi way, brother shedding the blood of brother. It was the sign of those who ate shadows.

"Kapu, *mahanaku*, go slow."

It was Tasimo, the other Elder from Adza's old council. He smiled one-sidedly at Kapu, a little out of breath from propelling his heavy, short body up the sandy slope. Tasimo was an early deserter from Sayat's group, a careful and apprehensive advisor whose views Kapu respected – though his deferential manner and skittishness were irritating.

"It was good, I think, sending old Tsitsi into the sea. Things are so changed, so must we change. Where . . . that is, how did you think of it?"

"The singing," Kapu said shortly. "One of Pahane's songs. About the proud one who burns in water."

"You . . . you saw Pahane?"

He had not actually envisioned the piksi boy until just now, but knew as soon as he said it that the notion was true. That presence had been there, had urged a simple but dramatic innovation. Pahane had always been unorthodox, if not shocking.

'He was near."

"And, uh, the . . .?"

"Witch?" Kapu smiled sourly. "No. You are safe. She was not near."

"And the drum, too. I knew you would save it. I mean I *hoped*."

"Yes." Kapu trudged straight ahead, concealing his surprise. He must have made some slight movement when they pitched Tsitsi into the water. He *had* considered throwing the drum in after the old one. Just to clear up one more muddle, and simplify their lives a little.

72

And then, just as if they had been there beside him, he knew Pahane and Tima would keep the drum, would approve.

"So glad you did. The young ones, you know, they want to hear it. They all do. And of course I know Sayat uses it, in the wrong way. I saw some of those . . . those awful nights. All night and the next day sometimes. The stones slippery with blood and the ones who had never been mothers–"

"I don't want to hear." Kapu felt the drum under his arm grow suddenly light, as if it had come alive. It was the simplest kind of instrument: a hoop of thin wood rubbed smooth, with a deer-skin stretched over one side and cross-tied across the back. For most of Kapu's life it had been sealed up in a cave with certain other objects associated with dangers and evils of the past. But, as Tasimo said, things were changing.

"The drum is to allow us to recover the Holy Time. For the ceremonies of the *tak tagak*." Kapu said this in a way that meant the subject was finished, but Tasimo did not take the hint.

"Yes, yes. *Takish*. But you know, we have no *tak tagak*. Here now, with us, I mean."

Kapu scowled down at the short, thick man, who had looked away to avoid just this glare. Like many among his followers, Tasimo was tactful in mentioning the absence of a great teacher to take the place of Adza, who had gone away to the Hive Dwellers in their last journey, at the time of the terrible piksi assault. No one spoke of these things openly, but they were always there.

Only a *tak tagak*, chosen formally by the Hive Being, could interpret the signs from *wonakubi*, the great shadow. Only a *tak tagak* could make them whole again, alive again. They all knew that Kapu, able and shrewd and courageous as he was, could never be such a leader; he offered only a strange vision, glimpsed even as the terrible piksi machines bore down on them, of the piksi boy and the witch, joined by a dark serpent writhing around a pearl of light.

"At the same time . . . well, these young *tchatsin* . . . you know, we were their age once. They mean only to have a good time. They have – we have – seen so many terrible things. And if singing the rockenroll brings Pahane to their minds . . ."

Out of habit, Kapu had diverged on a path parallel to the sea, now out of sight behind the first row of dunes, though they could still hear the surf. He was bent forward at the waist, the dogskin robe

73

pulled over his head, leading them in an imitation of a wandering herd of antelope or deer or wild ponies. The sky-eyes were watching, as always. Yet for several moons, ever since the Pobla began gathering at the border, no attack vehicles had struck deep into their land. The piksis were apparently content to wait for them, and bury them.

"This is true, *takishta mahanaku*." It was Yata, who had drawn near, without being asked. He lifted up the packet of woven grass containing Tsitsi's heart. "This old one is rejoicing, *na*? He would say to us celebrate, eat my heart and make it dance. Adza too. And Pahane, if it is as you say."

Shocked, Kapu came to a halt. The others gathered around them now, listening attentively. He clutched the drum, looking from face to face, and found that except for Tasimo and the youngest, no one looked down. He felt suddenly weary, and old and weak. They had no respect for him, for his vision. They were pups, greedy pups yapping for a treat, ignorant even after his efforts to teach them and protect them. And Tasimo – Tasimo had no doubt been talking to them behind his back, seeking to undermine—

He shook himself, alarmed at the sudden upsurge of rage, the impulse to fling the drum at them and stalk away. He recognized the danger, the madness that had lurked among them ever since they were driven from Sopan. It was their blood bond with the piksis, among whom to lead was always to be tempted by this ghastly hunger for respect, this suspicion and rage. Yet he was also afraid – even more afraid – of *not* leading, of leaving his band to Sayat and that madness.

"Those who have lost their shadow dance to the drum," he said. "They slaughter and torture and dance. Tasimo can tell you."

"We have not lost our shadows. We have not followed Sayat. For this we thank you, Kapu." Yata spoke and the others nodded. "You are a great raider and guide, as Tsitsi was a great marker of time. But you cannot do everything." He smiled tentatively. "Quite."

"You do not see how tired you are, *mahanaku*," Tasimo added. "*Yano* bears us well, we need not paddle faster."

It was an old and commonplace proverb. Do not try to hasten the river of death. Kapu smiled a little, in spite of himself. He could sense the affection in Tasimo's voice. He saw also the shewdness of linking the drum to the rockenroll chants, which were in turn linked to Pahane, who sang them over and over to Adza in her last days.

"And since we have no Tsitsi now," Tasimo went on, "no one who knows so many chants and rhythms and stories, then how shall we find a new timekeeper, except by trial? Perhaps one of these young ones—" He gestured at the others.

"*Na!*" There were grunts of approval from every side, quick and eager smiles.

Kapu waited, thinking hard, and in the silence the sea boomed, a big wave coming in. He had envisioned returning to the main group, only a short way off, and conducting the last ceremony for Tsitsi as another occasion to invoke their vision – seeking Pahane and Tima as the new *tak tagakin*, reconciling the piksi and Pobla. He would, he imagined, tell them again of the hardships ahead, the need for vigilance and purity in observing what old rituals they could manage in their new, fugitive existence.

Abruptly he shoved the drum into Tasimo's arms. "*Na.* Let it be so. You are the keeper of the drum for now. You shall send our offering after Tsitsi." Again the sudden silence. Tasimo stared at him, wide-eyed, stricken. Then the whole group broke into exclamations and laughter; two or three even fell over on their backs, legs kicking wildly in the air, and gave the Pobla whoop of sheer hilarity. Kapu felt hands on his forearms and shoulders, gripping and patting him happily.

He was once more astounded. What he had thought was lack of respect was in fact too much of it, a fear that he would be harsh and closed into himself. The wave of relief swept over him too, and his small smile widened quickly into a grin. Tasimo was right – he had overworked himself, consumed too much of himself. He had lost touch with the currents of feeling in the group, especially their yearning for joy, for release. Surely Pahane had been with him this morning, had moved him to take the drum along, not to throw it into the sea but to give it to the young Pobla. Seeing Tasimo sober-faced, holding the drum gingerly, Kapu burst into laughter. His friend would have a turn now at bearing the heavy load of prophesy.

He also saw that this was the way to advance his vision, to capture the imagination of his desperate, scattered tribe. A leader had to bring some promise, some delight even into the heart of suffering. How could he have forgotten so simple a thing? After all the hours he had spent observing Adza, nearly blind and with a mind mostly gone, swaying to the distant music coming through her battered little radio? A leader had to *sing*, or at least let her people sing.

"Ya takishta!" He gave a lusty whoop of his own. *"Vasan tchatsin, leeman shima rockenroll!"*

They laughed with him, no longer timid. They set off at renewed speed for the canyon where the rest of the group awaited them. They did not bother to imitate deer, but walked and trotted and flung themselves along in their own way. Their movement had attracted a flock of gulls, which veered and hooked behind them, hoping for scraps. *Sky in our bones!* the young *tchatsin* began to chant joyously, *Sky in our bones, we go round and round!*

This time they were not thinking of death, but of dancing. This night they would dance by firelight, and taste the heart of a great maker of rhythm, and the young would slip away into the shadows and make *naku*, and they would – for this night, anyway – be together in their vision. The new *tak tagak*, the twin shadow, would be with them, would bring them this gift!

She fell away from them, twisting and diving again, arrowing down into that place of pressure and darkness. She retreated into him, gradually yet swiftly, as the shadow of night races over mountains and seas after the setting sun. A moment of stillness, of calm. A spotless pool, reflecting the sky.

When he was aware again, he was Ronald, hearing Cynthia's voice. Her tone was matter-of-fact, crisp, with a trace of humor. " . . . what he thinks. Anyway, now that we're sure, we've got to move, got to tell him."

"Thinking," Tima said, with a burst of laughter that was like a bird shaking and fluffing out its feathers. "Thinking has nothing to do with it. But yes, we do."

In their voices he detected, more surely than ever, that secret, sly, knowingness, that evasion and pretense and smugness which infuriated him. Move? How move? With stone walls and electrical fields and security guards monitoring their every step? He supposed he was himself the "he" they were talking about. He had been absorbed more deeply than usual, giving himself wholly to the work of seeing. While they laughed and chattered as if . . .

"That song was so graphic. It's like they were trying to draw you in with a magnet. As if they *knew* this would be your last session . . ."

He started then, opened his eyes to find Tima already staring at him, reading the surge of bewildered anger in him. His hand brushed an object in his lap. The drum.

76

"Panny?" Cynthia was kneeling beside them, collecting her spikes and microphones. Her voice was brittle with cheer. "Ronnie? You okay?"

He blinked, made an effort to concentrate. For the first time ever he felt Ronald and Snaketongue align perfectly. They were together, a unified field of concentrated suspicion and frustration.

"No." he said. "Not okay. *Ya geenta pakish sa.* Tell me what? That you hide from me? Leave me out? I *know* that. You giggle and wink and . . ." On impulse he threw the toy drum onto the rug between them. "Play games."

Tima made no move to accept, and he could not read her expression. She was still opposite him, but squatting on her heels, the long stroke of her black hair reaching to the rug.

"Listen, Panny," Cynthia said with the same artificial brightness, "it's not like you think." She was back at her desk, rewinding and filing, moving in haste. "We didn't know for sure until just this morning."

"Know *what*?" He made no further effort to conceal the fire that leaped in him.

Tima grinned, a white slash of teeth in her dark face. The grin barely contained some fierce, opaque joy.

"Panny, we've fudged the rules here already. Haven't got a lot of time." Cynthia rose from her clicking, whirring desk and came toward them. Her brightness had begun to vibrate dangerously. "I can't reach Marvin. He doesn't know either and we've got to make sure you are stable before—"

"*Know what*, goddamn it! *Chonpatsi osta tak belik*! I know who I am." He gathered himself, ready to spring to his feet. "I am *tagak*. And I am tired of this. *Sa geenta ya pakish*."

Tima's grin widened. "But now you are more than you were." Her tone was mischievous, taunting.

"I don't know if we should." Cynthia hovered over them, distraught, like someone gathering up her possessions in a burning building.

"He knows," Tima said, and relaxed into a pensive smile. She seemed all at once weary, cool, and affectionate.

Another maddening pulse of rage went through him, and he opened his mouth to speak his bitterness. Then she told him, without uttering a word, simply by lifting one corner of the smile and reaching out to tap the drum playfully.

77

He could not breathe. He could not think. He was dizzy from the impact of seeing everything in an instant: the distance between them, the evasions and anxiety and secret glee, the naps and early lunches. He was conscious of smiling himself, idiotically. At the unimaginable thing he now was.

"*Pomogan!*" he whispered.

Father!

CHAPTER NINE

Though the Institute had nurses on duty, Marvin drove himself to a municipal hospital thirty kilometers away to have his finger repaired. He wanted to avoid the embarrassment and risk of fabricating lies for his own staff – a staff which included, he was now certain, some traitorous gossips.

The pain was still pouring up his arm and into his skull, but the white capsules from the hospital moored him just out of that fiery stream. He sat quietly and carefully at a table in a café at a gleaming, downtown mall. He was waiting for Cynthia, pretending to read a few papers drawn at random from his briefcase. She was late, and his thoughts had taken a turn that hurt him more, much more than his fractured finger.

Though he had only been able to manage a ten-second, furtive conversation on the intercom, he was sure he had communicated to her the extreme gravity of the situation. She knew the way, since they used this café often as a rendezvous. Traffic was normal. She had no pressing duties for the afternoon. That he knew of, anyway, and he should know. He was the Director, her superior. And he was also – or had been – her Marvelous Marvin.

Marvelous Marvin allowed himself a very low moan. The tables nearby were unoccupied: flat plastic disks, supporting napkin holders and white porcelain vases, in each a single paper rose. So many times in the past he had sat here with her, talking intently, completely oblivious to the synthetic music, the shoppers whizzing by in their electric carts, the sandwich in front of him. Now he saw the whole place as sinister, a fraudulent veneer of cleanliness and efficiency over some reeking secret. A reflection of his own life. He jerked his head once, sharply. Projecting. He must stop projecting.

He tried once more to concentrate on the article he had copied only the week before – a time that now seemed as remote as a vanished geological era. It was one of a series of publications by another

79

research institute, a medical foundation investigating new and mysterious disorders. It was material that – only a day ago – had fascinated Marvin utterly. The sort of thing he had loved showing to Cynthia.

She was always aware of what she called the political dimension of facts, how a bit of research confirmed or undermined some grand social myth. It had always amazed him that this wild-haired, reckless elf of a woman, willing anytime to experiment with ancient hallucinogens or trance techniques, could also be a profane pragmatist. *The real shit*, she said to him often, *happens before and after the truth.* He knew now, too well, what she meant.

In desperation he forced himself into the article. It mustered evidence for a new, devious assault by mutant viruses – especially the arbos carried by the ticks, lice, fleas, biting gnats and flies that prey on rodents, deer, domestic animals and humans. In the first notable case, a team of scientists had successfully spliced a modified rat gene into the human endocrine system. Antibodies the animal had evolved against strains of bacteria were thus added to the human repertoire. Unfortunately, it appeared that the gene also piggy-backed, from the fleas that passed the bacteria to rodents, a hidden template for the production, under certain conditions, of a new virus. This virus was harmless except for one embarrassing symptom – a slight swelling and irritation of the sinus, giving one a disposition to a rattish nose-twitch. The twitch, however, distracted a sufferer from fleas at work elsewhere, allowing a somewhat higher tolerance for their bites.

It was Cynthia who pointed out to him that this virus was a corrupt cop, an antibody gone wrong. Further research had revealed a whole complex of such venal enforcement personnel, most uniformed to look like legitimate molecules of the immune system. What excited Doctor Petrasky was the article's suggestion – guarded and tentative – that there might be a direction and purpose to the proliferation of these false police agents. They might actually be gathering and transmitting, flu to fever to pox, information useful in circumventing human biological defense systems; and might even be – Marvin exclaimed aloud at this daring confirmation of his own private speculation – securing databanks which allowed them to manipulate the behavior programs of host organisms.

A pox could thus enlighten the duck, or a flu instruct the swine, supplying them with new strategies to approach and infect humans (a coy quacking over crumbs, a docile snurfle). And since viruses mutate and hybridize directly, almost instantaneously, without any cumbersome reproductive cycle, these strategies could be coded and refined and traded and pooled rapidly in blood or saliva or excrement; they could be – Marvin was in a cold sweat now, both from excitement and fear – *organized*, like an army . . .

Here was a sort of connection to their own work with Ronald Drager. The intricacies of genetic coding and intracellular communication might be crucial to human affairs, but they bored ordinary citizens to death. No such thing as the tragic molecule, the heroic enzyme. But the case of a human being, a young boy, who had been mentally "infected" by the one animal capable of deliberate malice – that was news, that was high holosoap, that was supremely political.

The issues of biodiversity and responsible genetic engineering and resource management and so forth were all engaged, implicitly, in this emotional, this human drama. And with an election coming, Marvin thought he saw another key question beginning to take shape: If ducks and pigs had shown the way, was it possible that *Homo lapsis*, a hybrid primate, could establish – even *deliberately* – a pernicious symbiosis with some of these clever viruses? That the largest and smallest of creatures hostile to man might form an alliance?

It was well known that *lapsis* could communicate with an astonishing range of creatures, including insects. Old tales hinted that primitive man possessed a similar knack, developed in his domestication of the dog, cat, and horse. He had himself observed Tima summoning birds, squirrels, and bees with the simplest of gestures.

But what if a superior, hidden influence ran the other way? Their interlab scanner had picked up a rumor that the distinguished Doctor Goldbarth was conducting experiments on suggestive patterns of infection and immunity linking various species, including *lapsis*. Marvin was tremendously excited by the possibility that so-called higher organisms were in fact innocent pawns of a kind of viral intelligence network.

To test such a hypothesis of course required that the Pobla and their habitat be preserved, as invaluable research material. As subjects who had been exposed for months to that environment, Ronald and Tima were also unique informants. In the Conservative view – which was Dr Petrasky's view – scientists would, given time, supply a perfectly sound explanation for these emerging patterns, without relying on superstitious notions of an evil conspiracy. But there were other powerful interests with very different ideas, insisting that civilization was at risk and there was no time for experiments.

That was why Marvin dreaded Fitzgibbon's proposition even more than the ruin of an indictment. To protect Cynthia he would have to join a simple, brutal plot to discredit everything she believed in. A plot to eliminate one of their subjects and label the other a freak and lunatic. He recognized the ideology, knew its power. The fanatic Progressive stance: outlawing unmanaged adaptation, or any interaction of controlled and wild genetic material – and especially between Pobla and human.

If only, he thought abruptly and unscientifically, they weren't so dirty and unfriendly. If only their ancestors were not the worst criminal dregs of humanity, crawling out of radioactive rubble to mate obscenely with a lower species. If only – but then he saw Cynthia striding through the cavernous, bright mall toward the café, toward him.

The train of his thoughts – finally for a few precious minutes wrenched away from his despair – crashed immediately into a smoking ruin. His mind was again empty of everything but pain, the particular agony of watching her long, swinging gait, the luxurious, unkempt hank of golden hair. He swallowed quickly half the glass of mineral water he had ordered and left untouched for nearly an hour.

She wore workingman's pants with tool loops and multiple pockets, canvas shoes, and a loose, plain turquoise blouse. Her only ornaments were a pair of earrings, small fire opals in silver. He could see her capacious, woven bag was as usual stuffed with infodisks, old books and printouts. Her expression was abstracted and intent, until she caught sight of him, and then she smiled in a way that was quite new to Marvin. It was a brave, determined smile, but with a core of pity and a shell of impatience.

She slung the bag beside a chair opposite him, leaned over to kiss him swiftly between the eyes, and then put her cool fingers on his wrist just above the new bandages. "Poor Marvelous," she said. "They hurt you." Her face underwent a slight, rapid spasm. "And I've got to hurt you some more. My God, what an absolutely insane day this is." She released his hand and sat down hard enough to make the paper rose shudder in its vase. "I'm so sorry."

"Your professors," he blurted, "how many of your professors were you—" He gasped, stunned to realize he had no inkling of what he intended to say. "Why?" he went on miserably. "Why did you go with me? D-d-do those things . . .?"

She looked at him carefully, closed her eyes and exhaled, then opened them wide again. "Marvin, what is this? We don't have

82

much time. What things are you talking about, and who did this to you?"

"Fitzgibbon. An investigator from FedJud, planning a Grand Jury indictment. He had another scheme, too, a darkside business of some kind, offered me a bribe. But I don't care. They won't come near you, I made them promise. They will *not* drag us into their slime . . . that is, what we had . . ."

"Jesus. Jesus and the Twelve Apostles." She was sitting back in the chair now, very still. "That creep, the one who came to-day?"

Marvin nodded, unable to speak. He realized tears were dripping from his cheeks.

"So he told you all about me, I gather. My lurid past. Marvin, Marvin. You—" She bit her lips, looked into her lap for a moment, and then gazed at him again with her odd, new smile. "Well?"

"Your professors," he said again. This word now fully occupied his mind – the same mind that could juggle complex equations, devise intricate experiments, build whole hypothetical systems. There was room now only for penumbral images of snuffling, porcine beings, bald heads damp with sweat, hairy backs heaving. He felt, for the first time in his life, completely and hopelessly out of control, mired in a misery far deeper than his known universe.

"Oh, Marvelous." She reached across the table and brushed his wet cheek with the tips of her fingers. "This has never happened to you before, has it? Tima warned me, you know. She is going through something similar with Ronnie. She says—"

"Answer me." He leaned away from her. There was something horrible to him in her sympathetic, conversational manner. He could not keep his hands and mouth from twitching.

She flushed, and after a moment puffed out her cheeks to expel her breath in a small, audible detonation. "Okay. Okay Marvin. You are hurting and you think knowing will help. I doubt it, but – you asked, so here it is. Okay. Yes, I fucked two of my professors. Way before I even knew you. One when I was very young, second year at PolyTech. Very stupid and very vulnerable. He dumped me after a month, and I felt sort of like you do now. The other was a year ago and a little more serious. He was young too and didn't know himself very well and I didn't see that in time."

She looked at him, then at the stream of shopper-driven carts hissing by on rubber tires. A little boy on yellow skates waved at her. When Marvin did not answer she went on, and he saw that a tear had made a crooked, wet track down her cheek also, and into the corner of her mouth. "And then – I know this is the hard one, and I should have told you – I had a boyfriend when we first got together. I liked him, quite a bit. He's not like us, which was part of it. He's – well, it doesn't matter because he's also nuts. I mean he's a great person, and we belong to some groups together, but he's nuts. Not in a dangerous way, except to himself, but I could never—"

Her voice was squeezed upward into a little catch and sob. She put a hand over her face, and Marvin wanted, more than anything, to touch her, but her words had petrified him. She spoke then through spread fingers, her voice small and unsteady but rapid. "We can't do this, Marvelous, we haven't any time. I'm not seeing him any more and that's because of you. I have a thing for smart guys, boy geniuses I guess, but you are also the sweetest man I ever met, so serious and good you're hilarious too–" She laughed and the laugh turned into a sob that she managed to throttle.

"Listen, we're in real trouble, Marvin. Our experiments, everything from viral organizers to telepathy, the deep stuff we're getting from Tima – Pahane beginning to emerge – it's over. I mean *over*. For as far as I can see, anyway. We've got to bail out."

"Fitzgibbon told me it could all stay the same," Marvin said dully. "The Institute, you, me, everything. All they want is Ronnie." He made a vague, hopeless gesture of release.

She cocked her head, lifting her chin. When she was absorbing what she termed the real shit, her gray eyes were formidably steady. "Really. Interesting." She laughed again, quietly sardonic. "They don't even know, yet, how much they want him. Anyway, we've go to run. All of us. You, me, Ronnie, Tima. Tomorrow, or the day after. No later."

He stared at her, jerked out of his suffering by a new and startling possibility. She had lost control, too. The pressure of the situation had unbalanced her. "Run? What are you talking about? I'm the Director—"

"Were. Think were, Marvelous. It's *over*. I couldn't tell you on the phone. I had just finished Tima's physical, so I had verification, but I wanted you to be stable before I told you."

"Told me what?" He frowned pettishly. "About your . . . your history—"

"Oh Christ, Marvin. Forget that. Forget yourself for a second. About Tima. She's pregnant."

He opened his mouth and then could not close it. The whole vast floor of the mall tilted and he gripped the table with both hands, then yelped at the stab of pain from his bandaged finger.

A table nearby had been taken by a woman with two children, and all three now turned to regard them.

"Easy." Cynthia smiled and nodded at the woman and children. When she turned again to Marvin, he could see a flush in her cheeks, the glitter of more tears.

Yet her expression startled him. She seemed nervous, furtive, fidgety . . . and something else. Something she was struggling to hold back. She was stimulated, *aroused* somehow. She was – it struck him all at once, like a blow to his back – she was *happy*!

"Oh my God," he whispered. Tima was carrying a child. Ronnie's. Therefore a mixed. The most unwanted and shunned of all possible children. Half *sapiens*, half *lapsis*. A saplap. A freak and a felony. "How?" he whispered. "We monitored—"

"We should have known. Tima can pretty much screw with her hormones and metabolism whenever she wants. So our BC monitor was useless. She doesn't even apologize. She says this one *had* to be. It's a girl, and she's . . . well, like *special*." Cynthia uttered a soft, wild giggle and glanced upward.

The enormity of this new problem overwhelmed the Director, paralyzed his mind again. There was no covering up, now. Falsifying the record was irrelevant. Fitzgibbon's bribe was moot, canceled, a ghastly joke. Monstrous, monstrous scandal was now inevitable. Unless – he tried to keep the thought from forming, sensing its horror, but could not – unless Tima and the unnatural embryo were . . .

What jarred him out of his paralysis was Cynthia's laughter. He knew his face was red, and the family at the next table was again looking their way.

"I'm sorry, Marvin, really am, but—" She had to look away to master herself. "You should see yourself. This gives new meaning to the concept of wo-wo-*woe* . . ." The word escaped into a whoop, and Cynthia was curled over as with a severe abdominal cramp. She could not get her breath, she was sobbing with laughter, the tears coming steadily now.

After several seconds of furious silence, to his own amazement, Marvin emitted a small *humph* of amusement, then a sort of modest, melancholy bray. He saw the absurdity of tragedy: one's whole world – love, work, future, everything dear – smashed to smithereens, and yet everything appeared to go on as before. A man sitting with a pretty girl in a well-lit and comfortable place, sipping mineral water and laughing.

In a moment she was up from her chair, around the table, and in his lap, her wet face against his. She kissed him hard. He made a sound and she pulled back far enough to see his eyes shift, a signal that others were in the room, probably watching. "Fuck 'em," she said softly, and kissed him again, with more care. In spite of the horror and the ruin – Fitzgibbon and the swollen finger and the professors and the pregnancy – he felt himself rising to the occasion. His blood was heating and gathering with new, frantic urgency, as if pumped with a thrilling stimulant. Despair, it seemed, could be a powerful aphrodisiac.

Without thinking he put his good hand on her thigh and earned an immediate breathy, deep hum. Dimly he was aware of an exclamation, chairs skidding, departing footsteps. Their tongues were playing roughly, mimicking both courtship and consummation. It was mammalian and predatory, this time. Large, hungry, swift and careless creatures. Usually they would be able to guess, at least the genus, well before climax, but this time there was an experimental or mythological dimension . . .

The distraught shift manager had to speak to them three times, though he was only a step away. They unwound slowly, tugging dazedly at their clothes like people emerging from wreckage. They got up, smiling stupidly at the man and laughing with a perfectly false note of light-hearted apology. Marvin dropped a token on the table, not even remarking its denomination. Then they picked up the briefcase and bag and moved away, glancing back and giggling like children.

In the middle of the mall causeway Marvin stopped short and looked at Cynthia, blinking rapidly like a man trying to stay awake. "Where are we going?"

"My friends," she said. "They are going to help us. We've got to go underground. We're on the run, Marvin, already, but we need one more action to set us free."

"Free." He nodded slowly. "Us."

"That's right, Marvin. Us, from now on. And just us." She smiled at him with her old, ebullient radiance, and shifted her bag on her shoulder.

"You know," he said in his normal, measured, Director's voice, "this is the worst day of my life. And yet I . . . I feel—"

"I know." She wrinkled her nose ruefully and tugged his sleeve until they were moving toward the exit, in stride with each other. "Kind of fun, isn't it?"

CHAPTER TEN

It was the sort of off-campus housing Marvin had always been careful to avoid during his own university career. The weedy yard was full of big-wheeled solarcycles, elaborately painted in shades of puce, fuchsia, and tangerine. Graffiti decorated the fence and front door, the letters so stylized he could decipher nothing but the word *Stop*. From a staff on the roof fluttered a number of ragged flags, imprinted with faded hieroglyphs.

They went quickly through the gate, without looking back at the taxi. Marvin was balancing a large, flat carton emblazoned with the logo *Power Pizza*. Cynthia shouldered six beers in her book bag. The door opened for them, making a rectangle of deep shadow, and then they were inside. He could see only a spangled darkness, and before his eyes could adjust someone had him firmly by the arms and someone else ran light, probing hands over his body, between his legs. Startled, he tried to step back.

"Trigbee," he heard Cynthia say.

"Trigbee. How are you Ribs?" The voice was a tenor, amused and faintly sardonic. "And how—"

"Fine so far. Both of us. Marvin, these are my good friends."

He could now make out the figure directly in front of him, a hefty young woman with extremely short red hair. Behind her, stepping away from Cynthia – they had apparently just kissed – was a tall, wide shape.

"Sorry," said the young woman. "Didn't mean to goose. Pleased to meet you, I'm Red Wolf and he's Sharpshin." She jerked a thumb at the man who had held his arms, but was now smiling at his side and lifting the pizza box out of his hands.

"Very pleased," Marvin said, and took a step to meet the tall man. "Sandhill."

They shook hands with a swift, hard grip. Sandhill, Marvin saw, wore his black hair in a single long braid. He would have been

89

handsome, but for a flattened nose and cheekbones. These could indicate a Pacrim ancestor, but they were also – depending on precise measurements – sometimes a sign of *lapsis* blood.

"Trigbee," Sandhill said, grinning suddenly. "And welcome to our humble revolutionary cell. Everything permitted except anchovies."

Marvin felt foolish and disoriented. He was not even sure which of the city's campuses he was nearest, for he had been too preoccupied talking with Cynthia to look for a street sign during the taxi ride. She had told him briefly about these people, an offshoot of the old Ecomini party, but he had no clear idea what they actually taught or plotted or did. He understood Cynthia was sympathetic to their cause, but he had never guessed the depth of her involvement. Ribs?

"Trigbee?" he wondered aloud.

"Big tree, scrambled," Cynthia put in quickly. "Password. Can we sit down somewhere? And get started?"

"You bet." Sandhill put his palms together and bowed low. "Would Her Majesty like to join us for a sweat in the underground lodge? We'll stick the saucer of doom in the warmer and the suds in the cooler, and you and the Doctor can loosen up and get pure while we work the situation out." He gave Marvin a slight smile and a wink.

Cynthia swung her bag onto the table, with a muffled clank from the cans inside. "Typical," she said. "Disrobe now, talk later. Listen, Sandy, this is real shit we're in. We have to figure it out *now*. So whatever, but let's stick to the business."

"Don't worry, Ribs. He's under control these days." The big red-haired woman hooked the bag of beer and books from the table. "Sharps and I will get this together, so you guys go on down." She winked and followed her partner, who was already bearing the pizza through an archway to the kitchen.

With a finger crooked over his shoulder, Sandhill led them to the rear of the apartment, where a narrow section of the floor had been cut out to make a trapdoor. Beside this opening, under a row of coathooks on the wall, was a bench heaped with towels.

"So," the man went on conversationally, unbuttoning his shirt, "what about this Grand Jury stuff, this guy they sent around?"

Cynthia sat on the bench and bent to unlace her shoes. "He waved a subpoena at Marvin. Then offered him a bribe. They'd drop the whole thing if we fake the data to justify discharging Ronnie Drager to his nutty father, and hire a couple of designated snuffers as nurses so they can get rid of Tima."

Marvin was glad for the poor illumination in the room, for he knew his face was aflame with embarrassment. He removed his watch, trying not to look at Cynthia as she wriggled out of her workman's pants.

"And you said?" Sandhill threw his shirt on a hook without even looking, and raised his eyebrows at Marvin.

"I . . . of course I said no. I tried to . . . " He raised his bandaged hand.

"They broke his finger," Cynthia said tightly. "Their version of a reasonable approach. Assholes."

Marvin was fumbling now to get out of his clothes, for he perceived the others would simply stand there chatting, completely naked, waiting for him. He saw also that Sandhill bore tattoos: a sword on his left arm and a flower on one buttock.

"Ouch. Not nice. Sounds like the old Network to me, or whatever they call themselves now. I know what you mean, man." Sandhill turned to show Marvin his broad back and narrow buttocks, drawing a fingernail along an irregular series of pale spots, whorls in the skin. "I've been interviewed by these gentlefolk, too." He laughed, apparently in genuine amusement. "Good at what they do. Persuasive."

Setting his jaw, Marvin turned to the wall, unfastened his shorts, and let them drop. "I disliked this fellow Fitzgibbon," he said, " very, very much."

Cynthia and Sandhill laughed, so spontaneously and heartily it startled him. Cynthia snatched up two towels, tossing one to Marvin and draping the other over her shoulder. "Don't jump to conclusions, Marvin." She smiled at him, impish yet affectionate, then slid off the bench to lower herself quickly through the trapdoor.

Sandhill gave him another droll wink. "After you, my friend. Ribs is right, you are hilarious."

Stiffly, determined not to groan again, Marvin eased down the ladder into a chamber dug from the raw earth and lit by a single low-intensity bulb. At one end was a rectangular steel box full of bare white stones, and benches lined the two long sides. A great, mottled, dark mass loomed from the fourth wall, and a thick, spongy slab hung beside it. The air was dank and fetid.

He realized the box was radiating heat, even as he watched Cynthia lift up a large metal pitcher and slosh a stream of water over the stones. Instantly, in a roaring hiss, they were enveloped in hot, suffocating clouds of steam. Marvin could barely breathe or see, but Cynthia found his good hand and brought him to sit beside her on the bench.

Sandhill, a shadow in the hot fog, sat on the bench opposite them. They heard him blowing, taking a deep breath, blowing again. "Trigbee," he said softly. "*Sequoia gigantea. Pseudotsuga. Thuja plicata. Pinus ponderosa.*"

He heard Cynthia sigh and mutter a few words. He thought he heard *om mani padme hum*. Then they fell silent, and the steam dissipated a little so he could see their faces. Cynthia and Sandhill were breathing in measure, eyes closed. Marvin stared at the mass bulging from the odd wall. Not mass, he saw then, but moss – or rather mosses, and lichen and spiderweb and mushrooms also. A dense colony of various growths, bright green to black, rust and mustard, ochre and saffron, with here and there a flicker of movement, some insect darting out of or into a niche.

The object fastened to the wall, he decided, appeared to be wood, a section of log with fragments of bark, very old. It was being consumed by the growths around it, was, in a manner of speaking, alive. The moss shrouded it in rich color, and even as he watched he saw a very small, pale worm twist inside one of the holes pocking the surface.

"Piece of a section from one of the old Park Trees." Sandhill had pulled up his legs, chin on knees and great horny, toenails hooked over the edge of the bench. He was unbraiding the dark rope of his hair, and watching Marvin with the same bemused, sardonic smile.

"Really." Marvin tried to sound politely interested. As a schoolboy he had of course seen preserved sections of these huge trees, and holoized old filmstrips of their harvesting. He recalled dimly that controversy over the parks had launched the first underground predecessors of the Ecomini party, though the old forests were doomed in any case by airborne acids. But this sample was barely wood at all: a lump of decay; moss-root and worm-fodder; a bacterial jelly. He suspected a joke.

"This our god. A rotten mess."

"Sandy," Cynthia said with a long, angry look, "that's enough bullshit."

Sandhill laughed. His teeth looked very large to Marvin in the dim light. He had never seen a man with hair so long, or anyone naked with tattoos. "You told me Doctor Petrasky was an expert on the psychology of primitive belief, the Pobla termite cult, if that's the right language."

"No," Marvin said. "Cult is not a useful concept. Belief system, or cultural matrix, would be better. Though I have also done work on alleged communication with insects."

Sandhill laughed again, a loud and genuine hilarity. "Bug blather. Fly philosophy. Tick talk. Good, Doctor. Very good."

"That's enough." Cynthia had drawn the towel around her shoulders and clutched it into her face, so her voice was muffled, but Marvin could tell she was in a temper. "Let's not fuck around. We have to have some *help*, Sandhill. I called you because you've run actions before, and you once said to me—"

Sandhill lifted one open hand in a pacific gesture. "The man needs to know who he's dealing with. A sketch, no more." He smiled, waited, and when Cynthia grimaced he went on. "Worship may be an exaggeration. But consider, Doctor. The ancient trees – largest living organisms in our planet's history. Each one a planet itself, in fact. A canopy a hundred meters into the air, cooling and humidifying and sheltering. A net of roots that covered a half-acre and stabilized several hundred tons of soil. A structure to utilize and circulate energy, convert waste into nourishment, and support fungi, bacteria, slime molds, lichens, arthropods, spiders, salamanders and snakes and squirrels and mice and weasels and owls and hawks and on and on.

"We know many creatures can palaver, Doctor Marvin, thanks to research like your own. A wondrous thing and worthy of study. But they don't speak in a sterile place, a dead room, a cage. They *sing*, in and through a living, green universe. They can drum on its body, claw marks into or whisper messages under its skin, swallow and spread its seed. Each one of those old titans, Doctor, was an entire, complex, intelligent system – a model of a perfect world."

Marvin hummed and swiveled his eyes covertly toward Cynthia. A demented lecture seemed to be underway. He had heard this kind of fulsome rant before, this rhetoric of idealized nostalgia. How could a brilliant student like Cynthia tolerate such romantic delusions? Fall in with these zealots?

"Look at the common oak, the way ancient Celts invoked it—"

Cynthia emitted a muffled groan through her towel. Sandhill unfolded swiftly from the bench, reaching for her knee; and awkwardly, too quickly, Marvin tried to place his arm around her shoulders. She twisted and kicked to fend them off, then took the wadded towel from

93

her face and glared at them. "Just leave me alone, okay? And listen, we haven't got time for you guys to sniff each other all over. We've got *thirty-six* hours to put this thing together."

"Right, sorry." Sandhill controlled and then erased his grin. He glanced at Marvin and lifted one shoulder. "So, this enforcer is coming back day after tomorrow for your answer? Hmmm. Well, could stall for a few days, but any moment some attendant might spy out the pregnancy. That would send up the whole thing. Woo! They wouldn't indict you then, man, they'd *dismember* you. I mean, Insec and the President's darksiders and the Con party's and Moses knows what free agents – they'd be all over you."

Marvin shifted uncomfortably, and his sweaty buttocks made a small, unpleasant sound pulling away from the bench. *Thuck!* He was all too aware of the enormity of his transgression. He would be responsible for probably the worst scandal in the history of Conservative government. He knew what the media carnivores would say. Far from delivering a healthy, sane, rehabilitated adolescent boy, Director Petrasky had – under the aegis of a Presidential Commission – apparently encouraged his patient, a minor already suffering from a multiple personality disorder, to commit sodomy, copulate with a creature still legally classified as an animal . . .

"So did the radical Progs buy off Fitzgibbon? That's one question. But a deeper one is, how would they react to the arrival of this wee saplap? Sure, they'd be happy to see the whole Drager thing blow up in Stockwell's face, but it wouldn't exactly support their argument that the kid was driven mad by depraved brutes. I mean, you guys made some holodisks, right? And everything was healthy and creative and . . . enthusiastic?"

Marvin's face burned, and he could not even clear his throat. Cynthia had already revealed their most intimate research! To a stranger and outsider who—

"Oops." Sandhill grimaced and laughed softly. "Sorry, Ribs. Don't mean to ruffle any feathers, but it makes my case. They can't blame this one on the Pobla."

"I don't think that's their real agenda any more." Cynthia's voice was taut and quiet, but she picked up the pitcher and savagely sluiced another dollop of water on the stones, as if to underline her statement with a loud, angry hiss of steam. "Look at the Prog party's reaction to the Pobla refugees from the Wastelands. You'd think they would be screaming for a final strike, the big hit. But they've actually accepted the recovery camps, the testing and experimentation. Bipartisan study, science ahead of politics, all that bullshit."

"The wipeout position went down with Konrad's and Papa Drager's ship," Sandhill remonstrated. "Otherwise they'd be out there slaughtering away."

"Maybe not. I think there's a new vision."

Marvin felt her settle back on the bench. This second roiling cloud of steam was dense, omnipresent, searing; but he welcomed the discomfort and low visibility. His mind was still spinning with shock. His Cynthia was revealing a dimension he had never seen before, a cunning and combative intelligence that was capable of − well, if not deception at least calculated omission.

"Vision?" Sandhill gave the word ironic emphasis.

They waited, but Cynthia did not go on. She seemed to expect them to guess. She raised one slender leg and was examining the spread of her toes. The towel had already slipped from her lap.

"Slavery," Marvin blurted then. He had no idea why the word came to him. He had actually been thinking of Cynthia's full, firm breasts, the curve of her bare haunch. The heavy, kneading heat had not only invaded and unstrung the muscles in his back and shoulders, it had apparently fogged over his reason, so that only these odd and random thoughts could slip in.

"Exactly. Marvelous, you always come through. Though they won't call it that, because you have to be human to be a slave."

"Ah," Sandhill said. "Daring. Too daring, I think. That's a raving one eighty, after all. The Prog right wing always stood for the total wipe."

"But Progs also stand for efficiency, hardline economics. They'll argue these new derelicts are cheaper to work to death than exterminate. And now − first time ever − there's a tiny band of militant Pobla lurking in the canyons, so they can promise the hotshot hunters even more exciting prey. But we're off our subject again. What are we going to *do*?"

"Getting to that." Sandhill gazed levelly at Marvin for a moment. "I'm thinking Mr Fitzgibbon might be very interested in your private research. He's only heard, you say, about the disks, the . . . informal sessions with Tima and Ronnie?"

Marvin nodded. The steam had effaced his embarrassment, so he spoke almost casually. "He hasn't *seen* anything."

Sandhill clapped his hands once. "Thank Trigbee. An opportunity there. He's bound to be curious. The juiciest material, and he may be tempted to market some of it himself. The tabs would pay a fortune. Now if you have other stuff with more straightforward scientific value . . . "

"Well, actually . . . " Marvin glanced at Cynthia. Amazing was by no means too strong a word for some of their results.

Sandhill laughed. "Great. I thought so. What we need then is something that would appeal to Mr Fitzgibbon's official employers, so he can see the possibility of a safe double deal. Offer everything, suck up like you were anxious to secure the bargain. Promise telepathy and kinesis as well as hot disks. If you can get him hooked into a terminal . . . "

Marvin sat straighter. "I haven't done much acting. As a student, just carrying a spear—"

"No, Marvin." Cynthia shook her head violently. "No, don't. Just tell him what you've got, and that you'll make him a major player. That's true enough, in its way. This is just a diversion to occupy the man, right?"

"Right. Then we have to occupy everybody else. I'm figuring we could provide a demo at the main gate. There must be a service entrance somewhere. And you've mentioned one of the maintenance personnel is friendly?"

"Sweet, tough old rooster. He would sneak us out in a utility truck. Or whatever it took."

Cynthia was thinking of Scratch. Marvin now felt loose, easy, intuitive. He had forgotten entirely his throbbing finger, the impending collapse of his whole world. These nuances of politics and strategy were fascinating. Possibilities seemed to be appearing, one by one, like stones under his feet as he felt his way into an unknown swamp. They would be doing things unforeseen, unplanned, unimaginable. *Fugitives*! The word was like a beating of wings in his skull.

"But how do we get around Security? As soon as your demo gets going they will call a lock-down. That's the first thing they do." Cynthia's voice was low and fretful. "All doors and windows and entrances, including the gate to the service drive."

Sandhill was humming to himself, a stirring victory anthem of some kind. He ended with a dramatic flourish and an outbreak of laughter. "Fire," he said cheerfully.

Marvin sat up, alarmed. "No, please, this is not—"

"Fake fire, my friend. Small fires. Papers in a file, in a stairwell, couple of ounces of smoke-a-go-go in the odd office. No real threat. Cyn, you could do that job. Surely the fire control program would open the gates, override security?"

Marvin looked doubtful. "That's true. We do the drill once every thirty days. The main and utility gates would be open. But we cannot risk—"

"We won't. Idea is to spring you from the main building, get you into the utility truck and *away*, fast, because as soon as they turn off the sprinklers and see it was a fake, they'll begin to put it together . . . "

"And what happens to Fitzgibbon while this is going on?" Cynthia said. "He might catch on and muck up the whole thing."

Sandhill began his humming again, in a deeper tone. "Depends on what he wants to grab first – you or the disks. It's a gamble."

There was silence for several moments. "Well, I'm now glad," Marvin said finally, "that we have interesting material on those disks."

The others laughed, and laughed louder when they saw his surprise. Cynthia took his hand and squeezed it. "Marvelous, you have a genuine gift."

"All right." Sandhill's smile had concentrated, gone speculative. "Assume you can get yourselves off the Institute grounds and to the nearest Feederway. We'll have another vehicle waiting, a big van where you can change clothes, get your hair cut and dyed. Then to a safe house . . . a relative term. I'm afraid, Doctor Petrasky, you will find the accommodations very modest."

Marvin did not respond, was at the moment involved with a new problem. He saw that Cynthia kept up a brave face, but he could guess all too well what she felt. Cut that glorious, golden tumult of hair? Dye it some nondescript shade? As if she were a prisoner, a disgraced person? He sensed the distant footfall of a great sadness. Fugitives, he understood then, did not really *escape*. They had to creep in darkness and live a lie, like slaves.

"Well." Sandhill stretched his arms, rolled his shoulders, and clamped his hands on his knees. "That will have to be it, more or less. Lots to do between now and nine-thirty tomorrow morning. Never tried to put an action together this fast, but then what we have here is no ordinary deal, is it folks? You guys take it slow, come on upstairs when you get hungry." He stood up, rangy and relaxed

97

as a big cat, his hair a loose mane over his shoulders, and smiled down at them a little pensively. "You got things to talk about, no doubt."

Cynthia reached out, took his hand and squeezed it. "Thanks, Sandy. I – oh, you know. Just thanks."

'Yeah." He bent slightly, kissed her knuckles before letting go her hand, and went swiftly, lightly up the ladder and through the trapdoor.

The steam was now only a faint, luminous halo around the bare light. He could see her clearly, all of her. The lovely, trim body, an apricot color; her delicate, deer ankles and wing-like collar bones. And that cascade of hair – honey and brass and gold with a hint of fire. His breath caught, tears began to blur the vision of her. All at once he was tilting into a profound sadness, a pity for them all in the face of new trials and threats.

"Your friend," he said, and swallowed. "It's very k-kind of him to help. I'm sorry about . . . about . . . "

"Don't be." Cynthia lifted one shoulder and looked down at her feet. "Careful with Sandy. We need him, he's great at this, but you have to be careful."

He waited for her to go on; but the next moment she lifted one hand, turned his chin so she could kiss him almost roughly, and said all in one rush, "Because I want to live through this and be together and work together and make tremendous discoveries that save the world and have a house and roses and a wine cellar and babies, all those stupid old middle-class things, and people like Sandy – maybe you noticed, they all took the names of extinct species? – they don't have any hope, they don't want any hope, they don't *like* hope. Hope is too human for them."

"I see," he said, though he didn't really. He was only aware of the yearning and bitterness behind her words, and the sudden bump of his heart at the word *babies*. He wanted immensely to let the tears come and put his arms around her, but he sensed that it was not the time. They were fugitives first, together now in fear and isolation as much as love. They would need food and rest, and also their apartness – as pillars sustain an arch, or magnetic poles a world, which would otherwise collapse.

Marvin did not know these things clearly, as he knew the isotopic variants of certain amino acids, but he was discovering that this maelstrom of unfamiliar emotions could impel him sometimes, as if by magic, to say the right thing. First he returned Cynthia's kiss as a business-like token, and then went on with a brave, if unsteady heartiness, "I am hopelessly, hopelessly in love with you, Cynthia. But maybe you'll have dinner with me anyway. Pizza and beer?"

CHAPTER ELEVEN

"A Conservative Prez must think
We all love the scum and the stink.
For he hints what we need,
To spice up our seed,
Is a roll in the mud with a . . ."

Beau Winger clamps both hands over his mouth, muffling the final rhyme, and his considerable bulk writhes with throttled force. When the fit passes he gasps, throws himself in his console chair, which is cocked for launching, and addresses the tiny eye through which a quarter of a billion people are watching him.

"A-a-a-rgh! Still, *still* not allowed to use our native tongue, Seetwayens! We can say pink or zinc or mink or tinkle, but can't say da liddle G-word, kiddies, that we all know, not on nashnul holobelt broadcast! Still they dodge and slither and delay us in the courts! Even as we present the hard facts, expose the ongoing slime of Stockwell's poopy *Po-ba-lah* policies! Policies to gag a duck with diarrhea!"

Beau wrings his fingers as if to rid them of some viscous horror. Then he settles into his chair and, with a flourish, pushes a button. A jet of blue fire blossoms under him, and the chair appears to blow through the wall of the studio and begin a steep climb into open sky.

"Back on the track, faithful fans! Who-o-e-e-e! Now while we're in flight, recall where we pushed pause yesterday. We traced the ongoing Drager drama through the Duskyrose episode, Little Ronnie's recapture by the so-called Superagent, the media megastrike, and right up to the kid's incarceration in a fancy psychotel."

Again tilted over a scrolling continent, his tie and lapels fluttering in the gale of his progress, Beau lifts a forefinger and crooks it in a beckoning gesture. The map below expands suddenly, rushing nearer. Canals, Thruways, grids of housing units define themselves. Beau uses a thumbnail to cut out what appears to be a suburb, which he stands upright. He pushes another button; he and his chair shrink abruptly to a mere dot which flies into the upright square. The holoeye telescopes after, bringing the viewers again to Beau, now perched over what appears to be a park and estate: ponds, groves, and a cluster of buildings.

"What kept you, kiddies? Don't dawdle, this is Alice in Blunderland. You will recollect the hot dispute over what actually *happened* to the little fella during his sojourn with the Sewages? Did the Ghoul Indigies torment him completely bananas, or did they just convert him to a weird spirituality? Centralissimo question, pupils. Now pay close 'ttention."

The magic chair swoops lower and hovers over the main building, a structure of old stone shaded by rare large trees. A mower is crawling slowly over the lawn. The figure riding the mower removes and waves its hat, revealing a tiny patch of white hair.

"This is where the Cons sent our li'l victim to have this question answered. Supposed to be the best Docs, highest tech, newest theories – the fabulous Institute for New Life Studies! They got other subjects, as cover, but the bigtickee contract is to *analyze* little Ronnie, figure out, see, whether he's boy or rootabega, sane or badoobadooba."

Rapidly, with one hand, Beau appears to reach down and pry up the roof of the building. After a peek inside he jerks his head to invite his millions of onlookers, and the holo unit glides into the crack to oblige. First visible is a young man at a lectern, apparently conducting a press conference. Then come a series of labs and storerooms, in one of which a slender blonde woman carrying a clipboard seems to be observing a tankful of tropical fish.

"Now you may ask, hasslemachers, who's in charge of this operation, funded by two bill of the taxpoopers' browsweat? You're lookin' at 'em. That's Herr Doktor Director Marvin Petrasky, wonderboy in exotic brain bends. Geewhiz hair and dorkshoes aside, good people, can you *imagine* putting a major research facility in the care of this little puppy? He's barely out of diapers, but don't be deceived. Oh he's done some very, *very* creative experimenting, has Herr Doktor Petrasky! None of it made public – after eight months of supposedly intensive research – for reasons we will explore.

"And who do you suppose is his very special little helper? See her right there. Cynthia Sue Higgins, age twenty-six, doctoral candidate in Psychobio. Honor student. Year at Oxford. Covergirl for campus humour magazine. Hire her myself if I just listen to the hormones mumble – a teamster's damp dawn dream – but check this background, good people: Econinny radical, arrested three times for demos or destruction of property, known affiliate of the Thorgs – you know, the Terran Holistic Organic Revolutionary Guard – can they be serious, folks? How about the Teeny-brained Hideous Oafs with Regressive Genes?

"And these are the people, ladeez and gennulmen, *these* are the people Stockwell Fullstocking put in charge of Little Ronnie's case! And what is their approach – I know you wanna know, gotta ask – what's been happenin' with that child for eight months? What *is* the Consuhvatiff plahn? Ai-i-e-e-e-ya!"

Beau drops his corner of the roof with a resounding crunch and rockets his chair higher again, as if to escape a bad odor. "It's a scrofuloso cesspit, my Dames and Dandies! So reeky I can't plunge further without a bath and shampoo and some refreshment! So before we get to the real slimeorama, time for a quick 'n glossy uptone. So prepare, lovely ladies, you're about to glimpse one of the gods' great deeds, the big guy bare, and I'm talkin' all dimensions, girls, I mean FAT RULES!"

Beaufort seems to blast away from his chair, fall free in space. Items of clothing – coat, shoes, shirt, trousers – peel from him, the last shreds fluttering off even as he splashes down in a blue pool surrounded by jungle. Rising from the water is a marble dais, upon which recline two young, slender, beautiful women, a blonde and a redhead, clad only in ingeniously positioned triangular ribbons of watercress. They are holding large bottles of shampoo and rinse, and when Beaufort surfaces, a white whale beaching itself on the dais, they begin a stylized ballet of ministrations to his large, round head. His voice carries over the scene.

"Big Cool is right for all cabezas, cavaliers – and don't forget Cool Coquette for the ladies too – body and texture and gloss that say you're there, you're a factor, you can power up! Big Cool is right for me, the big fat guy always cominatya, and right for you, too. Not to say you can *be* me, dreamers. *I'm* me, already, and nobody else gets the job. I lu-uv my job, kids. You warthogs blame me? Huh? Ha! Hey, FAT is good, FAT is me, FAT is where it's at! Send for my holo, Frontal Attack Therapy, autographed, four fifty-nine ninety-five. Build esteem for your own big bod, be a wide bride, a groom who looms . . . Oops, there goes the plug—"

The women are planting a kiss from each side on Beaufort's round, grinning face, while they hold up the Big Cool bottles. But there is the sound of a great onrushing wave or cataract, and as his eyebrows go up in mock alarm, Beaufort is sucked down into a sudden whirlpool, and his voice is transformed into a bubbly boom.

"—just when the fantasy is getting inarresting, they *always* do this to me – but we do have this responsibility, do we not, to *expose* these houndawgs—"

The pool has become an ocean; its surface bulges in the center of the holo and like a launched missile Beaufort erupts, again reclining in his chair fully clad, his coiffure gleaming and perfect. He soars over the city, kamikaze-dives directly at a great shaft of concrete and glass, bullets through a sliding window and decelerates swiftly until he rocks to a stop in his studio again. There he expels a long breath and drinks from the can of Big One that has appeared in his hand.

"Ah-h-h-h! The one and only, the Biggie, the slaker and shaker. Need it today, fans, that little sip of ecstasy to boost us over the steamin' swamp of corruption we got ourselves into here." He drinks again, eyes closed and great throat convulsing, then palms the empty while he once more gazes speculatively at his viewers.

"Thing we must remember, fair folk, is that Stockwell's facing an election. He's gotta figure out what to *do* with these refugees, these Po-ba-la ghouls, and fast. They are stinking up the whole border area – just ask any grunt who's been there. New Broom was such a gigantissimo costly bungle people are afraid of extermination – the *obvious* solution – so we begin to hear rumors. Talk of actually *assimilating* these sick boogies and their black hole culture.

"Oh, I know, you just can't believe this. You think old Beau has ninetied straight up and out. No, friends, I fear it's a facto exacto: there are people, there are groups out there talking about giving these li'l critturs *rights*, a new *status*, a place side-by-side with *humanity*! Proof, you say, where's the proof? Assimilation, whaddaya mean by assimilation? Well, you remember yesterday's show? You saw this huckshyster Feiffer, a former Insec superagent, slobbering over Duskyrose. Everybody can guess how she assimilated him, and Little Ronnie too, it turns out.

"Here it is, hasslemachers, bombshell uno. The fact is she's living at the New Life Institute, now! She's part of Petrasky's so-called *therapy*. Not a patient, not listed on the staff roll, no ID file – completely dark, baby. We got it from the inside, but for six months nobuddy sees, nobuddy knows, what this "therapy" involves. But we know the situation: we got two horny teenagers – one serious

104

disturbo and one mutant nympho – and a Director with connections to the creepo Conservative right. Gettin' the picture, seetwayens?

"Oh, but there's more, fans, much much more! You are still wondering, lookin' for some harder evidence? Well, we're gonna give it to ya, kids, gonna wrap it all up for ya – right here on the Beau Winger yakshow – tomorrow!"

Beaufort actually *means* "we"; he has stomped a button with his empty can and now two images of him in identical chairs regard each other. After a moment of mugging, one image salaams elaborately to the other.

"Oh yes, noble master! Director and Producer and Performer of the world's biggest yakshow, oh Big Fat Guy with all the answers! I do your bidding . . . tomorrow!"

"Tomorrow! I can't stand it! I'm drooly already for the inside take on the Institute's wacko experiments, for—"

"Oh wait 'till you hear what they eat, and what funny games they play! These mushrooms, and drums, and hankypank with spooks . . ."

"Indictment? Do I smell indictment?"

"Now, now . . . *tomorrow!*"

One Beaufort lifts up a Big One; the other hoists a bottle of Big Cool. As they move in unison, their images slide together; one bulk beaming magnanimously around at a distant multitude. The holoeye withdraws enough to reveal the studio around the office set, other recorders and engineers at their terminals.

"Yeah, tomorrow, class. Tomorrow we begin a three-day series of blastorama exposés. We reveal the, and I mean THE, major conspiracy of our time. Mean it, kids. Don't miss this one, 'cause we're gonna name the names, and the old world ain't gonna be the same ever again. Guarantee. And the whole shooterama, like always, brought to you by Big Cool and the Big Number One beverage. So waddle on, waddle on with the Big Fat Guy, always cominatya!"

Beaufort's image begins to swell and spin and glow at the same time, as the surrounding studio fades to black. Theme music modulates into celestial chimes, a reverberating cosmic hum, a deep electronic shimmer suggesting solar wind. The effect is that of a star birthing, taking its place in the firmament.

CHAPTER TWELVE

When Robin looked up from her desk, like a small animal caught in the highbeams of an onrushing vehicle, Marvin knew that events were once again out of control. He had guessed as much ten minutes earlier, driving up to the gate. Already there was a cluster of media vans, and lights were pulsing on patrol vehicles. The demonstration was larger than he expected; and as soon as his car came into view, booms telescoped out of vans and swooped alongside, cameras tracking him. Nor could he make sense out of the garbled questions reporters shouted at him before the security officer checked him through. His "reaction"? To what?

"Oh Doctor!" Robin wailed. "Doctor, Doctor!" She stabbed a finger at his office door, ominously ajar. "*He*'s here already."

Marvin stopped short, briefcase dangling from one hand, the other curled over his heart, protecting the tiny, swaddled infant of his broken finger. It was eight-twenty, and the appointment with Fitzgibbon was made for nine. He had been up since four o'clock, going over the plan with Sandhill and his team. Cynthia was supposed to be in the lab already, infernal devices in her purse. Timing was everything now.

'What—" he began.

"He looks . . . upset." Robin was pale beneath her make-up, and her expression was reproachful. "I suppose he wants to know what happened. With the Winger show."

"The what?" Marvin heard in his voice the irritable falsetto of desperation.

"Oh my god." Robin was suddenly hushed. "You don't *know*. You actually . . . Beaufort Winger? The yakshow?"

"I do not—" Marvin began, but then Fitzgibbon pushed the office door open and beckoned him.

The man's face was pale pink, his hair not quite as neat as before, and the gesture he was making – a single finger crooking in front of a squint-eyed smile – had an extraordinary, sinister cuteness. Marvin detected the radiation of fury and potential violence, but he marched toward the door anyway. With the help of the white capsules he had already achieved a numb momentum which got him through a parting with Cynthia, an hour ago. Locked in a long kiss, they had thrown themselves over this precipice, and were now in a sheer, simple vector of gravity, of fate.

Over his shoulder he spoke to Robin. "Tell Higgins to get Drager and Dusky, and line up the telekinesis stuff." He strode past Fitzgibbon, who had moved back in surprise. Slinging the briefcase onto his desk, he waited for the big man to shut the door and then said, "I have decided to accept your offer."

"What offer?" Fitzgibbon moved in his lumbering glide, teeth bared in a horrible parody of geniality. "You miserable little fuck, Petrasky. Maybe I should break your neck, this time. You had a sweet proposition – we went out of our way to keep your dead ass in here – and now what? A leak from somebody in this nutbin to that fat prick Winger."

The big soft hands were reaching again for him, but this time Marvin did not retreat. He crossed his arms over his chest and looked Fitzgibbon in the eye – not a difficult feat, since the wide, pink face was only inches away now.

"I do not have the faintest idea what you are talking about. Or whom. I don't know anybody named Winger."

There was a moment of stillness. An odor of cologne and gunmetal came from the big man who rocked slightly back and forth, studying Marvin intently.

"And I would appreciate an explanation." Marvin put his good hand against the lapel of Fitzgibbon's coat and pushed. "At a distance."

The charged silence lasted another moment, and then Fitzgibbon laughed. It was a brief, gravelly sound. "So," he said, "the pup found his balls. Probably the truth. Somebody like you, with his asshole between his ears, wouldn't watch anything that vulgar. Too bad. You could have used the morning to commit suicide." He stepped back and gestured at the file cabinets behind Marvin's desk. "Instead of cataloguing your shit and turning in your keys."

"Please," Marvin said as steadily as he could. "What are you talking about? I came prepared—"

"It's nice you found your balls. But you're a couple of days too late. You just got famous, Petrasky. Or infamous, rather. You and your poke both. So there is no deal. And then you screwed it up worse, going to that little gang of misfits and setting up that demo outside. What the *fuck* were you thinking, Petrasky?"

Fitzgibbon rolled to the window overlooking the grounds, stared briefly out. They heard a scatter of shouts, a siren in the distance. Marvin could not trust himself to speak. A holo-program, one of those popular yakshows, must have mentioned him or the Institute unfavorably. And he and Cynthia had of course been followed to Sandhill's apartment. So Fitzgibbon's private employers had cancelled their offer, were instead going to allow the prosecution to go forward immediately, he supposed. The whole escape plan was a ruin.

"You are a baby after all, Petrasky, and you cost us. We could have had Drager out of here in two, three days, and now, with this publicity shitstorm, it'll be weeks. Prosecutor's paperwork will be done in a couple of hours, and a team will be here to seal these files and take you in for arraignment. But my employers want another look first, so let's get busy." Fitzgibbon left the window with a sigh and positioned himself before the files.

"But I have some remarkable experiments under way." Marvin tried to purge his voice of supplication, of panic, of despair. "Your employers would be interested, and I have planned to show you—"

Fitzgibbon stepped near again. With a thumb and forefinger he flicked away a bit of lint from Marvin's lapel and then, like a solicitous wife, straightened the Doctor's tie. "You dumb little fuck," he said, almost affectionately. "You're dead. Now let's get the files on Ronnie and little Duskyrose, see what we want in and what out. Okay? Or you want to go for another finger in splints?"

Marvin closed his eyes, took a breath, then shook his head. Fitzgibbon smiled, nodded, held out his hand. In the instant before he moved toward the drawer where he kept the key cards, Marvin had an idea. It was the most daring idea he had ever entertained. Simultaneously he opened his mouth and drew in his breath sharply. "I . . . I'll have to get the right card from Cynthia. She keeps it in her lab, in the safe."

Fitzgibbon pursed his lips, amused. "Clever, Petrasky. You want me to wait here while you run for the parking lot? Forget it. I told you, Doctor Peterhead, you're just meat now, waiting for processing. Come on—"

"No, for heaven's sake! It's just a precaution. Cynthia is . . . she has control of many aspects of . . . But fine, good. Break the locks. You've done it before." Marvin was genuinely angry, and again this seemed to please Fitzgibbon.

"Sure. I just told you these files are going under seal. Would look great if the deputy finds 'em crowbarred open. So you're saying your punch holds the whole deck? Whipped you into line?"

Marvin compressed his lips and looked at the floor.

"You disappoint me again, Petrasky. Tell you what. I give you ten minutes." He looked at his watch. "Starting now. You don't want me to come after you. Believe me."

"Fine." Marvin set his jaw and walked with dignity to the door, while Fitzgibbon picked up his briefcase, opened it and dumped the contents on the desk.

He shook his head at Robin, who was pantomiming questions at him, and hurried on. When he came into her lab Cynthia was standing by the window, looking pale and anxious. Tima sat cross-legged on a chair, her eyes closed.

"Oh Christ, what is it? You look awful. Is he—"

"The arrangement is off. Some commentator or yakshow person named Winger has leaked the story, and they've decided to indict, arrest – I need a . . . that wrench you had for the acetylene bottle, where is it?"

"Marvin, Marvin—"

"Where is it?"

She pointed at one of the lab counters. He approached, saw the wrench hanging from a hook under the sink, and removed it. When he turned, Cynthia regarded him with a peculiar, almost comic mournfulness. Tima was watching him too, now, and smiled slightly.

"Now give me your office and file keys, and go ahead and set up our, uh, release materials. Where is Ronald?"

"Next door. Pretending an exercise." She took a ring of narrow plastic cards from her lab coat and handed it to him. "But this is twenty minutes too early, we—"

"We can't distract Fitzgibbon now, and we can't wait. So in about five minutes – if there is a miracle – I will be back and we're going anyway. If I'm not, then . . . then I'm sorry and I hope . . . I hope . . . " He swallowed and shook his head. Awkwardly, because of the bandaged finger, he put the keys in a coat pocket and the wrench in his trouser pocket. The handle protruded, so he had to hold his arm in such a manner as to conceal it, which gave him a certain stiffness of bearing, like one who compensates for an old wound.

When he reached the door, Tima spoke.

"Don't try to hide it, you call attention to it. Hold out the keys right away. Try for the temple."

He hesitated, then moved to loosen his shoulder and arm. "Thank you," he said, and left them.

Coming through his office door he had the key cards extended, jangling, but Fitzgibbon barely looked up, and then glanced at his watch, before putting aside the stack of papers from Marvin's briefcase. "Lucky you," he said, and got to his feet.

"If you don't mind, it's hard for me to go through these . . . my finger . . . " Marvin jangled the key ring again, almost under Fitzgibbon's nose.

The big man hooked the ring with one hand and began to flick through the cards, which were color coded. "What are we looking for?"

"Uh, the green one. For the first cabinet."

Fitzgibbon found a green border and turned to the files. He inserted the card in a slot at the top of the cabinet. Marvin removed the wrench from his pants pocket and held it still and heavy, parallel to his leg. Fitzgibbon pulled out the card, turned it over and reinserted it. He jiggled the handle of the cabinet and frowned over his shoulder at Marvin.

Marvin sidled a step nearer, pretending to peer at the ring of cards. "I meant that – is that turquoise?"

"Another fucking PhD," Fitzgibbon said, with a huffing sigh. He flicked through more cards, separated a blue one. "This one?"

Marvin moved another half-step. "Right."

"You know, Petrasky, this whole experience might turn out to be good for you." The big man pointed a corner of the card at him, before sliding it into the slot. "You don't see real life in–" He released another explosive sigh. "Shit." He reversed the blue card and jammed it into the cabinet, which now began to emit a pinging sound. He had clamped his mouth tight in irritation and was turning back toward Marvin when the wrench caught him on his exposed right temple with a muffled smack.

Momentum kept him turning, turning and falling at once, a full one hundred-and-eighty degrees, his eyes swinging past Marvin as if he were on a departing, sinking platform. One arm hit the desk, scattering a few papers, and the thick body struck the floor with an astonishing crash.

There was, to Marvin, utter silence after this tremendous sound. Two or three sheets of paper were still banking and sliding obliquely through the air. Before they completed their fall, a great strawberry patch appeared over Fitzgibbon's temple, and Marvin became aware that the cabinet was still pinging. He stepped over the body and pulled out the card, stopping the signal immediately.

He stood for a few moments longer, the wrench still hanging in his fist, and took deep breaths. The sequence of events had, impossibly, occurred exactly as he had imagined it, as if his nerves and muscles had been replaced by some inexorable robotic apparatus. A terrible thought came to him, but even as it did, Fitzgibbon lifted a forearm from the floor and uttered a long, soft, bubbly sigh. The arm flapped back and then there were two quick taps at the door, and before he could respond it opened wide enough to admit Robin's head and one shoulder.

He saw her eyes register the body at his feet, then swivel to meet his own. She was blinking rapidly, as if to restore her vision after a flash of too-bright light.

"He's taking a nap," Marvin said. "Don't disturb him." Now she was staring at the wrench, so he put it carefully on the desk before he came toward her.

She stood aside as he exited the office, closing the door firmly behind him. Her extreme pallor made her make-up seem garish and theatrical, but her voice was barely audible, a kind of controlled gasp. "Doctor Petrasky," she said. "I believe I am going to submit my resignation."

"Yes, good. Good idea." Marvin gave her shoulder a quick, friendly squeeze. "Anyone asks, I've just stepped out for a moment. Lab prep. Right back. Talk to you later . . . "

He was already hurrying away, and when he reached the hallway and found no one there he ran. When he burst into the lab, they were all three waiting at the side entrance. At the sight of him Cynthia swayed, her eyes tightly shut. Ronald looked startled and pleased, with also an alertness or anticipation, almost a hunger, in his manner. He was holding, on one knee, a small drum. Tima looked at him exactly as she had a few minutes before, only her smile was a little wider.

"In the lavatory wastebin and in our custodian's closet. I set them to blow eight minutes from now." Cynthia had recovered herself and managed a grin. "I just assumed you would . . . somehow. And you did." She opened the side door carefully and looked both ways in the corridor. "Let's go."

It was their usual route to the arboretum and gardens. A few technicians and research personnel greeted them through open office doors, and they passed through a ward rec room and spoke to a pair of orderlies there. Cynthia had thought to bring a notebook and small holorecorder in a shoulder case, so it would appear that they were working.

To Marvin she seemed her sunny and congenial ordinary self, while his own smiles and waves felt like horrible spasms of nervousness. One of the researchers, he was sure, had stared after them suspiciously. They had until now been careful about appearing together; usually he and an orderly accompanied Ronnie to the gardens, and Cynthia and Tima came only later. It was utterly unbelievable to him that they could simply stroll through the building in this perfectly normal way, while a government investigator lay bludgeoned insensible in his office and fire bombs ticked away their final seconds.

When they came out of the freight elevator on the ground floor, he saw that his disbelief was justified. The security station there was crowded with men in uniform, both his own staff and city police. They surrounded a group of young men and women seated in a huddle on the floor. He saw that these were captives. Their hands were clipped behind their backs, one woman had a nosebleed, and there were several torn sleeves and collars. A moment later, with a considerable shock, he saw that the boy called Sharpshin, who had searched him at Sandhill's, was one of these captives.

"Doctor Petrasky, sir!" It was Dwayne Simpson, Captain of Security for the Institute, bearing down on them. Simpson was, like many career officers in law enforcement, very swarthy and notably taller and heavier than average. Just now his features were even darker with exertion, and shiny with perspiration.

"I don't think you should be out on the grounds right now, Doctor. This whole situation is getting touchy. They charged the gate, and you see a few of them got through." He shook his head and expelled his breath in a decisive blast. "We really should seal the whole perimeter."

"Oh, now," Marvin said, and tried to laugh. "Surely . . . "

"They're screaming about the *Bastille* and liberating all creatures and that kind of crazy stuff." Simpson glanced in obvious disgust at the huddled figures on the floor, who had in fact begun a chant.

Free them all!
Fish, flesh, or fowl!
Come on, saps.
Learn to howl!

"Oh Christ," Marvin heard one of the police say, and a guard kicked one of the singers tentatively.

"So if you don't mind, Doctor—" Simpson was interrupted by a tremendous clanging from a speaker recessed into the ceiling. Everyone was silenced, even the singers, and looked upward. Then the captives began a series of whoops, yips, and yowls – an imitation, Marvin recognized, of the cries of several extinct species of *Canis*.

"Shit. Fuck." Simpson had lifted his spread hands as if to receive some large object from heaven, but now dropped them and looked swiftly at Cynthia. "Excuse me, I'm sorry Ms Higgins, you'll have to leave the building now, all of you—"

"Fire? Did the bastards get in somewhere—?" A short, thick man in a dark suit had broken away from the ring of uniformed men and charged toward Simpson, who was making grand, sweeping gestures toward the wide glass doors leading to the sunlit grounds.

"Out! Get 'em out of here! Yes, shit, yes, fire! Perkins, get to the main station and clear all exits, put your people on the floor and start moving patients, soon as we got this thing located . . . Doctor, please, let's get outside?"

Marvin nodded dumbly, even as his feet accelerated under him. He had gripped Ronald by the shoulder, and Cynthia and Tima were hand and hand as they left the building, which was disgorging a few people now from every exit, some of them running. Others had gathered in groups on the lawn or garden paths, pointing. They could see two windows on the second floor that had shattered and now emitted a steady, boiling column of gray smoke. The clanging seemed to come from everywhere now, and a siren had started up too – a skull-ringing electronic lament.

Behind them the officers were dragging and shoving the captive demonstrators, who continued their caterwauling, through the glass doors. This spectacle, and the general confusion, allowed their small group to move unnoticed to the maintenance shed. Its wide, sliding door was open, and in the shadow of the interior Scratch stood – or rather danced in place – beside his old utility vehicle, its engine idling.

He cawed at them, and jerked a thumb at the open cargo area in the back. "Hey, lookin' fine, Clementine, and you ain't starvin', Marvin! Right under that big pile of shavin's and leaves, behind them barrels, put on the masks and let's go, Joe!"

The truck was half full with a heap of leaves, lawn cuttings and mulch chips, in which four depressions had already been scooped. A dust mask lay in each trough. The other half was a row of barrels stamped with red letters: *Danger, Flammable, Toxic.*

"This is . . . all?" Marvin's heart once more contracted in a chill of apprehension. He had not imagined anything so crude.

Scratch made an absurd, inquisitive whistle – *wat? wit? poweet?* Ronald handed the drum he had been carrying to the old man, then vaulted onto the truck bed and gave his hand to haul up Tima, then Cynthia. Red-faced, Marvin scrambled up beside him and, following the example of the others, he donned a mask, then covered his head with both arms and lay on his side in one of the shallow depressions.

Cackling, whistling, muttering, Scratch took a rake propped against a rear wheel and jumped up onto the bed. A storm of debris covered them, dimming the light and filling their nostrils with a dank, moldy odor despite the masks. It occurred to Marvin that the old man was demented, believed himself actually to be some kind of prophetic bird, burying them like a cache of nuts or bits of colored glass. Perhaps their whole scheme was demented, a madness so elementary it might succeed.

He could feel the weight now of the loose organic material above him, and they lay in utter darkness. Small shocks in the frame of the vehicle told him Scratch had jumped down again and climbed into the cab. When the engine raced and the gears engaged he heard Cynthia's voice, muffled and remote, but he registered only the word *possum*. It was an old game, part of their play of love, to imagine themselves to be a certain animal, to nuzzle and spar and evade accordingly.

He began to concentrate with all his strength on remaining motionless, insensible, a mere lump of dead matter. That is what Fitzgibbon had told him. Dead. The deceased Doctor. He gave in completely to the jostle and sway of the cargo bed, the settling of his weight. He felt the change in their velocity, heard another change in the sound of the wheels on the roadway. They lurched slightly, coming to a stop.

Distantly he heard footsteps, then indistinct voices and the sound of the cab door opening. A moment after that the voices were louder, moving toward the tailgate.

"Reg'lations." It was Scratch's voice, only drawling and without its customary energy. "Flammable and dang'rous m'terials. 'Count of the fire."

"I don't know. They said only medical, injury or something." This voice was young, doubtful.

"Hell, you git a spark in that orange barrel there, you gonna have *plenty* of injury." Scratch laughed, a long salvo of wry hilarity. "You want to answer up for that, fine with me. I can park 'er here and walk back. You can mind this stuff, sonny, but I ain't gonna get within a half-mile of it. For love nor money."

There was a pause, and then the young voice said, "I guess that's medical, sort of."

"Will be if the sumbitch goes off."

"Yeah. Right. Well, get it out of here then."

Marvin heard the cables squeal to retract the service gate even before Scratch slammed the cab door, and then they were moving again, swinging into a turn. Soon there were more turns, too many for Marvin to co-ordinate in a mental map. Once the truck seemed to pull off into a lot, reverse, and retrace its way. Finally they stopped again, and he could hear the steady rushing whine of a major Feederway nearby. The cab door opened, and seconds later the tailgate banged down.

"On yer feet, Pete!"

There was a rustling above him, then a foot nudging his leg. He began to squirm and thrash with one arm through the layer of chips and leaves and grass, emerging finally into the glaring morning sun. Shrouded in debris, their masks like hoary snouts, the others looked to Marvin like creatures from a horror holo. Scratch stood over them, grinning and baying his laughter. Behind him, at the tailgate, stood Sandhill and another man in white jumpsuits, a uniform of some sort.

"Come on, compost heads," Sandhill said. His smile was a quick reflex, his eyes full of urgency. "Let's fly."

They ripped off the masks and brushed their faces clear before jumping down, one by one, to the pavement. Scratch gave each of them a quick, hard handshake, and presented Ronald with the drum again. The truck was parked next to a large delivery van, white with bright red trim and lettering, its rear doors open. A thick, pungent odor struck his nostrils just as Marvin registered the logo on the van: *POWER PIZZA*, again. He also had time to see that they were at the rear of a card-operated fueling station, one without attendants, before Sandhill hustled them into the hold, and pulled the twin doors shut behind him.

Marvin heard Scratch's truck rev, then pull away, before their new vehicle began to slip forward also. It was a smoother, quieter progress, and a whole section of tray holders had been removed, creating a compartment with benches where they took seats. He felt exhausted, dazed, empty-headed. Cynthia had her eyes closed, taking in long, deep breaths. Tima, he noted in dumb astonishment, was yawning. Ronald was perfectly still, but it was the stillness of something coiled.

"*Yanaku.*" Sandhill said quietly, and extended one hand, palm down. Tima hesitated, then took his hand in her own, carried it to her face, and inhaled.

"*Yana.*" She released him. "My pleasure. Trigbee . . . right?"

Sandhill gave again his rapid, urgent smile, and then looked at the boy. "*Pahane,*" he said, even more softly. There was a long pause before the answer, a single syllable that seemed to come from the boy's chest, for his lips did not move and his eyes did not change. "*Na.*"

Marvin's brain reeled into painful, unsteady motion. They should be careful with an MP disorder. Ronald's fantasy *persona* was volatile and should not be exposed to trauma, outside a supportive lab situation. He was about to speak when he remembered that his lab might be, at the moment, in flames – a thought which aroused a terror he had managed to suppress.

"The Institute," he bleated, and looked wildly in what he thought was the right direction.

"It's okay, Doc. We caught a newsbreak just before you showed up. Contained, probable arson but nothing firm, demo leaders being questioned, some injuries . . . no mention yet of any missing persons. You guys did a terrific job. Ahead of schedule, too."

"Sorry." Cynthia took another deep breath, released it, and then laughed unevenly, ending with a gasp. "Plans had to change. Marvin clubbed the goony inspector with a pipe wrench."

"No shit." Sandhill clapped his hands together. "You didn't! With that bum finger?"

Marvin flushed and looked at Tima. "It wasn't . . . that hard. You were right, he just never even saw it."

"Whe-e-ew, Doctor Marvelous! I'm beginning to see why Ribs is nuts about you. A dangerous felon, not unlike myself." He clapped a large hand over Marvin's knee and hoisted an eyebrow in wry conspiracy. "And you're about to collect the usual reward."

"Where?"

Sandhill looked at Cynthia and shook his head. "This guy wastes no time. He already knows *where* implies *what*. Okay. First you get new clothes and haircuts and tints, and then you guys get sentenced to what a hundred million kids would give – think they would, anyway – their eyeteeth to be doing." He paused, exaggerating the drama, looking somberly from face to face.

"Come on, Sandy." Cynthia's smile had faded. She too had been hiding from a fear, Marvin realized. The fear of losing her golden hair.

"You will have the privilege, for three whole days, of living . . . right here! Your new home." He threw out his arms to indicate the racks of trays, the warming chambers with their rows of indicator lights. "A little cramped, but all you have to do, you lucky contestants, is drive around all day and eat pizza!"

They heard the electronic sensors lock into the Feederway traffic monitoring system, and they immediately began to accelerate, the force of inertia pressing them together on the bench.

"Sandy, that's *crazy*! We've got to get away from—"

"You will, Ribs, you will, but they're going to expect you to run for the border. So we'll pick our time later. We will have opportunities, probably soon. Meanwhile . . . " he grinned at them, "we just take care of mama and baby. Got a couple pretty safe holes to hide in. And you and Marvelous will maybe find a new field for research – a little glimpse beneath the surface of NorthAm society." He laughed to himself. " Meet some others in the pipe wrench gang."

BOOK TWO

CHAPTER THIRTEEN

At midnight Professor Joseph Goldbarth, the world's leading authority on intracellular communications, stormed out of his laboratory and down the hall toward Image Repro, where he could hear laughter. He had been fuming for several minutes, waiting at the light table for Hendricks to come back with the plates.

It had been an eighteen-hour day of relentlessly tagging isomers, sectioning tissue, and mapping with laser diffraction. They were all blear-eyed with fatigue and had eaten nothing since the snack lunch wolfed down in midafternoon. Beyond that, Professor Goldbarth was seventy-six, and stricken with rheumatoid arthritis; he depended on Hendricks – a brilliant boy, his protégé – for help with dealing with the avalanche of Doctor Orr's samples.

So Hendricks had set off with their last selection of slides, knowing his senior professor was anxious to have a look before they went home – and had promptly drifted away again, as if indulging in morning coffee break on a slow day. And this wasn't the first time such a thing had happened. Hendricks had developed a disturbing habit of smiling without cause, whistling under his breath, even dozing on his feet. This odd behavior was especially remarkable because a colleague over in Biophysics, Professor Marjorie Tadlock, had noticed a quite similar trend in one of her own prize students.

Just before he swung around the open doorway to the IR lab, Joseph had begun to frown, signaling the revival of an old anxiety: that the most promising young scientists, in this particular age, might be predisposed to mental disorders. But when he saw Hendricks, lounging on a sagging, threadbare sofa and guffawing, soft drink in hand, he was stung again into rage. A pretty PacRim girl whose name he had forgotten – she was here on some kind of exchange program – was laughing with him. They were watching a tiny portable holobox, on which he saw, in the briefest of glances, nothing humorous, only a fat man in a chair flying over a building with smoke belching from its windows. The girl was leaning against the counter, her shoes were off, and just as Joseph came in she lifted one slender foot and prodded Hendricks's knee with her toes. On the counter he could see the plates, processed and invoiced and ready.

For a moment he was so stunned and furious he could not speak, but Hendricks smiled broadly and lifted the plastic soft drink bottle in a toast. "Hey, Goldie," he called, "Come in and sit down, Ruby's taped some funny news."

"Hi, Doctor Goldbarth." Ruby straightened up with a nervous smile, waved to the stack of plates, then glided beyond them to switch off the holo. "Hen was just coming."

Goldie. *Goldie*? Professor Goldbarth was now so flabbergasted he forgot even to be angry. *It's the work. He's having a breakdown. My God* . . . Of course he knew students used nicknames among themselves, but only his oldest colleagues and his wife would risk calling him "Goldie" to his face. He had won both the Gandhi and the Watson for his contributions to science, and students from all over the world dreamed of working with him. Those who did have that privilege generally addressed him as sir, with downcast eyes.

"The plates, Hendricks," he managed to get out.

Ruby was already recovering them from the counter, beaming ingratiatingly at Joseph and shooting warning glances at Hendricks.

"Full plates, kiddies," Hendricks said and laughed immoderately. He finished off the soft drink and stood up to stretch. "Big scandals, Goldie, over at New Life. So happy I'm here with you."

Hendricks was a skinny young man with large hands and ears, straight hair that wouldn't stay put, and brown eyes that were both large and close-set, giving him – normally – a lemur-like alertness. Now, suddenly, he grinned idiotically, threw wide his arms and, moving toward Goldbarth, said, "I love you."

Joseph stepped backward smartly, alarmed. He glared at both of them, then at the empty bottle left on the sofa. Spiked. That had to be it – alcohol or drugs. He might have to dismiss them both . . .

Ruby was shaking her head and moving to intercept Hendricks. She shoved the stack of plates into his abdomen, so he ended by embracing cold metal. "Back to work now, Hen. He's coming, Professor Goldbarth." She steered Hendricks toward the door, looking a little frightened herself.

Joseph strode ahead of his assistant on the way to the lab, and did not look back. His irritation had gone out like a candle in a gust of wind, displaced again by anxiety. The young man's behavior was, he realized, symptomatic of other mysterious changes on a much grander scale.

In the last year, debates over the ethics and economics of various biopolicies had grown intense and acrimonious. Scientific management of living systems – the ideal of his own generation – involved many unforeseen contradictions and dilemmas, the source of political turmoil. Now these public controversies had come to be haunted by rumor, scandal, and darkside maneuvering.

As a young man, Joseph had heard his grandparents describe the horrors of the *laissez-faire* approach: the deadly nuclear and biological wars, the near exhaustion of vital resources, the spoliation of continents and the creation of the Wastelands. His own career had matched the rise of the Federation, joining the Three Worlds, and he had dedicated himself to the Federation's elemental goal: total utilization of, and maximum production from, every molecule in the universe, for the benefit of humankind.

But nowadays a proposal to make the most minor alteration of a gene, or to boost an indicator stock by a fraction of a point, at the expense of a tiny tilt toward toxicity – these could embroil one in very nasty business. Investigations, Grand Juries, media scams and smears, even blackmail and assassination. The ancient greed for power still distended and warped the concepts of "utilization" and "production" to serve private ends. Then there were the zealots who challenged all precepts of civilization, and even the notion of "humankind" – the tree worshipers who argued that *Homo sapiens* was a dangerous genetic freak. To say nothing of the appearance of peculiar new psychoses in the public at large, like the dementia of those who began to behave like lower life-forms, even insects – the notorious "bugheads."

He wondered if Hendricks had developed some such delusion, which had then become exacerbated by overwork. It was imperative to persuade the young man to undergo a thorough examination. But when Joseph had ceremoniously shut the door and turned to confront him, Hendricks collapsed into a chair, the plates in a heap on his lap. He was pale, unsteady, and looking at Joseph with an expression that came close to blank terror.

"I did it again," he said, and then went on in a rapid, unpunctuated monotone, "I did it again and I watched myself doing it and couldn't stop didn't want to stop because I couldn't see any reason to . . . to . . . "
He hesitated, took a quick, uneven breath, and rubbed his right temple

with the fingers of his left hand. " I'm sorry, Doctor Goldbarth. I don't know what it is. I just – I *knew* you were waiting for those plates but when I walked in there Ruby wanted to play me just a little of this show – the Winger show – talking about this bizarre thing at New Life – and it's like all at once I feel so *good*, really relaxed and at ease and like I've *never* felt before—"

"Good?" Joseph stared at him. "You feel *good*?"

"I mean – it's so comfortable all of a sudden, and I feel warm toward Ruby and . . . and you, Doctor Goldbarth, and I lose track of . . ."

"Of the fact that we are engaged in some potentially vital, not to say *revolutionary* research." Joseph intended a steely sarcasm, but was himself surprised at a deeper, melancholy note in his voice. He tottered to the light table, lowered himself stiffly into the swivel chair, and signaled for one of the plates, noticing as he did so how much his hand resembled a claw. "Call me Joseph, please. You forget what we are doing tonight?"

Hendricks reddened, blinked at him, and then began to talk again, pell-mell, even as he fumbled the first plate out of its case and handed it to Joseph. "No! No, I haven't. I know exactly: I mean if we do establish that there is a feedback link between calcium ion action in gap-junction signaling, and the penetration of what you, uh, Joseph, have so eloquently called a smart bullet virus, to which Fan – Doctor Orr's – new gene carries a vulnerability, then . . .' Hendricks stopped because Joseph had raised a claw in a cautionary gesture, before switching on the imager and booting up the plate.

"It is not quite time for 'if, then'. Everything depends on isolating the virus, which is at the moment a shadow – a shadow of a shadow – at best." Joseph began to adjust knobs, setting the beam to do a preliminary moving scan of the whole plate. He was surprised, and secretly pleased, that when the boy concentrated he seemed able to locate himself in his work. The abruptness of these shifts was nevertheless puzzling, and unsettling. "You say you . . . lose track?"

Hendricks had moved the other plates to a rack on the table and now stood just behind Joseph, both of them watching the shifting image, the gobs and coils and spidery latticework of a cell's interior. For a moment they heard nothing but their own breathing and the hum of the machine. The cell was from the pineal gland of one of Orr's Pobla subjects, which she called her Omegas. The tissue had arrived only that morning, along with a scribbled note urging them to process as quickly as possible.

"It's not like forgetting," Hendricks said finally. "It's like losing your will-power, your *ambition*. A sort of wave of pleasure without any thoughts or desires, a . . . a totally *dumb* pleasure. As if I had taken a huge tab of some euphor along with a very heavy tranq – but of course I haven't. It's just, bang! Right there."

Doctor Goldbarth hunched his shoulders, as if at a chill. Now the young man sounded like any common cotton-headed adolescent. Perhaps he was an extremely late developer sexually. The Pacrim girl had flirted with him outrageously and Hendricks had been confused, disoriented. But he hadn't looked like a blushing bumpkin. *Goldie*, he had trumpeted with coarse self-assurance. Happy as a clam.

Joseph started slightly. That was an old expression, and an odd one, too. Anyway, the lad had blurted out a declaration of love at *him*, senior professor and prize winner, and come lumbering after him ready to administer a bear hug. That was quite another pathology. Another odd one, too. Ambiguous, surely, to be embraced by a huge hairy carnivore. He squeezed shut his eyes and then opened them wide, several times, and stared intently at the screen. Concentration, concentration.

There were a few ruptured membranes, a little cytoplasmic aberration here and there, but no sign of massive invasion. Why did Tiffany think the virus – if it existed – would manifest itself in the pineal? Because, he answered himself, she believes – on the basis of no discernible evidence – the mystical nonsense about the third eye.

"Ah," he said, and Hendricks grunted assent a moment later. They had entered a region of more significant distortion, so Joseph switched to manual control and began to dial them here and there in a random pattern, looking for an ideal view. The cells were outsized, heavy-walled, a touch granular, but he hesitated to use the word *damage*. There were signs that Secondary messenger molecules had been active, certainly; and there was a certain clotting and stringing that suggested lipophilic transduction. But the abnormal patch was limited in range, and not sharply delineated from the surrounding tissue.

"Hmmm. Subtle." Hendricks spoke almost in Joseph's ear, leaning over him to peer into the monitor. "Don't see any reason, though, to think virus at all. Has Doctor Orr, uh, really . . . "

"No. Beyond the fact that they are cannibals, and some of their rites involve blood-letting." Joseph did not elaborate further, for his own opinions on Tiffany Orr were troubled and complex. She had been perhaps his best student ever, but as in Hendricks's case, her

125

brilliance was clouded by aberrations of character. Tiffany was, in the old-fashioned vulgar idiom, a flake. She insisted on synthesis, long before evidence warranted, and forged outlandish analogies and speculative models, citing various quaint poets, alleged seers, and ancient prophecies as justification.

"Though they are getting tricky. Hardly ever see a filovirus nowadays."

Hendricks sounded regretful. Joseph turned away from the monitor long enough to deliver a stern look. "We may be thankful. We do not wish a return to the directness of Ebola. Ever."

"No, no, of course. I mean . . ."

Hendricks's voice failed him at this mention of holocaust. Both men were studiously silent for a time, steering the craft of consciousness carefully around the whirlpool of that memory, the looming images from lectures they had attended – and later given themselves – in introductory virology: snarls of thread-like molecules with their deadly program to assemble crystalline bricks in the body's cells, sunder and scatter until whole populations, mostly in the southern continents, swelled and bubbled with a fatal pestilence. When the cities were emptied, power stations, factories and mines abandoned, then whole economies collapsed; hunger and civil war galloped after the plague.

The hundreds of millions who perished were not, however, the final horror to the survivors. What Joseph and Hendricks avoided was not any discussion of symptoms or the uglier stages of the Marburg strain, but a more shameful knowledge. A secret speculation, never openly stated: that only this sudden diminishing of starving, fanatically warring populations had allowed the northern tier of nations to survive and prosper, given them the breathing space to develop vaccines, then to organize and enforce their world order, the Federation.

"We are most likely merely eliminating an outside possibility," Joseph said in his professorial manner, easing them out of these deep waters. He returned the scanner to remote. "Tiffany's inductive leaps are often rather like shots in the dark. And, you know, it is rather dangerous work. Things seem to be very chaotic there, and she is under great strain."

"Sure. Right. But also, what an opportunity. I kind of envy her. I mean, so much new material!"

Joseph could hear the yearning behind the young man's exclamation. He had never thought of Hendricks as an adventurer, and certainly counted him less eccentric than Tiffany Orr. But probably any young scientist with a passion for discovery would dream of an assignment like hers. Danger was a precondition for heroic triumph, risk the only route to great gain; and all these were in the very wind blowing from the dying hordes of Pobla at the border.

The beam had now picked up another patch of the thick-walled cells, and this time Joseph noted that the membranes along a capillary corridor, in certain transections, were also uneven, but in a roughly regular way. Like . . . waffles. Possibly receptor sites. For what hormone? He went back to manual and scanned in a spiral. Again, the abnormal cells formed a loose patch that dispersed, at its edges, into ever smaller clumps and tendrils.

"Hmmmm. Ha." Hendricks was intrigued, amused. "Like a topo of a city, with burbs and Thruways and so forth. It could go either way, of course. With Fanny's subjects, I mean."

Joseph grunted. The point was obvious. Some had always wanted to exterminate *Homo lapsis*, given their genetic link to *Troglodytes*. Others at another extreme clamored for special efforts to protect them, establish "relations" with them, as had been done with the smaller cetaceans in marine parks. The sensible majority – Joseph among them – argued vigorously for the maintenance of the species for research. Especially now, with thousands of live subjects appearing at the border, almost as if *offering* themselves; whereas before the collapse of their primitive culture, *lapsis* would not tolerate captivity.

"She describes the camp as a ghetto, and a stockyard," Joseph said. "Unprecedented numbers, most of them merely ambulant corpses. Not a 'suburb.' A benign strain, certainly, is all the more unlikely."

"I meant these cell colonies, these jumbo waffle-walls. They look like a city. So what else did she say?"

Joseph did not answer immediately. Though Hendricks had a point. The patches of variant cells were perhaps arranged along the capillaries and ducts of the gland like villages strung on a Transcon Thruway. Waffle burbs. He winced. Metaphors. His students were perhaps infecting *him*. Why had he suddenly suggested that this gangly youth – whom he had been on the verge of chastising severely – call him by his first name?

Hendricks cleared his throat, and Joseph remembered the question. "For Tiffany, only a short note. She continues to . . . speculate. She believes certain of her subjects – androgynes of a dark hue, with Mongoloid skulls – carry the gene. She endorses our suggestion that we look for a hypothalmic connection."

127

"Right." Hendricks laughed, and Joseph felt a twinge of guilt at the weight of irony in the word "endorses." He recalled her communiqué – filed, doubtless, before dawn of the day just past.

Yes! Yes! Find it! I know it is there. They read our feelings as easily as you and I read posters. You know yourself the endocrine system is an intricate, endless symphony, horns and strings and percussives composing and blending even as it creates 'monuments to its own magnificence'! Why? To charm disease and disorder, to enthrall death, to maintain the whole being like a mighty chord against chaos! Mythopoesis and Autopoesis are the same! And how else could they overwhelm their own autonomic nervous systems, die at will, expiring as casually as you or I would fart or belch? The hormonal must precede both word and dream, must determine them. Find it!

Joseph sighed, and his shoulders drooped a little. He was too old for eighteen – now nineteen – hour days. Too tired to combat Tiffany's frantic enthusiasms, Hendricks's feckless delayed adolescence. Like other endocrinologists, neurobiologists and biochemists, he was in headlong pursuit of clues to the structure of the complex, dynamic equilibria of the hormonal system; already there was evidence pointing to astonishing sophistication in this apparatus. But to believe that it was supreme determinant, arbiter, monitor, *soul* – that quote Tiffany had thrown at him, "God is a good mood" – was absurd.

He changed the subject. "What was it you said about the New Life Institute? Has Petrasky been fired?"

"Not exactly. More creative than that."

This time Joseph's frown was perfunctory, indicating only a touch of impatience at the undercurrent of excitement and pleasure in Hendricks's voice. Every psychobiologist in the country knew of the gossip surrounding New Life, the rumors of the Director's affair and unorthodox research methods, the failure to publish on the unique Drager case. Petrasky was in fact a chief exhibit in any theory concerning the tendency to derangement in young scientists of promise. Joseph was not, however, one to revel in the juicy details of a rival's precipitous decline. He toyed with a dial, pretending to forsake his curiosity.

"He's disappeared. And his chief subjects with him. Perhaps taken as hostages."

Joseph reared away from the monitor, turned to confront his young associate, who was beaming at him in triumph. He had been more out of touch than he realized. "His subjects? You mean—"

128

"The Drager kid and the Pobla known as Tima – the one Insec trained, you remember? And the Doctor's girlfriend too. She may actually be behind the whole plot."

"Plot? What plot?"

"Got the Thorgs to stage a demonstration and fire-bomb the Institute. That's what Winger claims."

"Good God! What do these people *want*?" Joseph glared at Hendricks, who nevertheless broke into a short laugh.

"Well, influence, I guess. Notoriety. And Petrasky was already looking at dismissal, maybe an indictment. So he was persuadable." Hendricks looked sly and winked at Joseph.

For the second time this night, Joseph found himself momentarily speechless. He collected himself enough to stop the remote scan, in the midst of another patch of the waffle-cells, and got painfully to his feet. He started toward his desk, then reversed himself to stand before Hendricks. "When I came to get the plates," he said, laboring to force the words out, "you were laughing. Laughing at this event."

Hendricks's face was a study in contrary forces, deforming now in a smirk, now in puzzled dismay. Another laugh gathered in the young man's chest, even as his eyes registered panic. "I did . . . yes . . . ha! My head off! Sir . . . Goldie . . . ha! They . . . they went on a sort of . . . double date! Hokery-pokery . . . old in-and-out! Hee-hee!"

Joseph made an enormous effort to speak clearly, matter-of-factly. "You believe there has been miscegenation, then? That the Drager boy has been with . . . intimate with . . . the Pobla girl? Under Petrasky?"

"Under?" As if struggling against a cramp, Hendricks bent slowly at the waist. "Well . . . huh huh . . . don't know about . . . huh huh . . . *that*, Joe!"

Joseph colored to the roots of his gray hair. "With his consent. You believe him to be a pander."

Hendricks had staggered to the light table, unable to suck air into lungs empty with silent hysteria. " . . . huh huh . . . a . . . pander bare!"

Joseph swayed on his feet. An astonishing medley of feelings had coursed through him in the last few seconds. He had been appalled, enraged, frightened, dumbfounded, desolated. Most of all, try as he might, he could not seem to fend off an infinitely remote, and tiny, but unmistakable urge . . . to smile! A colleague, a fortunate and reputable young genius, had ruined himself, scandalized his profession, committed a crime; and these acts had in turn seemingly ignited a similar derangement in others. And these tragedies – condensed into a terrible pun – were tugging at the corners of his mouth!

It took every milligram of his strength to speak, though his voice was barely a whisper. "You must go home and rest. Now. You are not yourself."

Hendricks lurched away from the table, holding both arms crossed over his middle. His face was still writhing. "I know, Goldie sir, I know, god I know . . . It's just . . . Ruby and I, we . . . we wanted to make it a *triple* date and . . . ah god! I've *got* something, haven't I?"

Joseph took a step, watched his own crooked, ancient hand lift and grasp Hendricks by the shoulder. He had the sensation of discharging static electricity. He moved his lips, moistening them. The name came to him finally and he used it for the first time.

"William," he said. "Bill, is it? We – I don't know. But go home, now, Bill. Go home, rest. We . . . we may all have something."

Hendricks nodded and, moving in a kind of dignified stagger, made his way out of the room, leaving the door ajar behind him. For a long minute, Professor Goldbarth did not trust his frail limbs to support him. He remained frozen like the image on the humming light table. Another line in Doctor Orr's hasty letter had come back to him, a bit of mere chat that now suddenly acquired a sinister dimension. *The grunts who shovel and haul,* she had written, *have taken to jawing like insolent scavenger birds – won't wear their masks and gloves – discipline gone utterly to pot.*

Clams. Bears. Crows. His own hands turning to claws . . . The death-mask of Ebola victims, their hostility and personality change . . . Joseph propelled himself, with utmost care, like a tiny shell boat over a puddle, to his desk. In a kind of staged collapse, he sat down. Doctor Orr's letter was there, and he fingered it like a charm, not reading. The infinitesimal urge grew suddenly stronger, by several orders of magnitude, and jerked his mouth into a rictus-smile.

To hell with it, then. He would speculate along with her, be silly for once. He was only an old, dry stick, his work almost over, and he was worn out and it was nearly dawn. He could think about whatever he damn pleased. Like the oldest living thing, the ultimate myth, the first intelligence – as Tiffany insisted. A virus. A code. Matter with spirit. A system with no principle but adaptive change.

130

A system invading and utilizing – yes, here was "utilization"! – every subsequent form of life. The prokaryotes, information warehouses, soon absorbed into eukaryotes, mobile hunters that learned to multiply and combine into armies, armies whose conquests were consolidated as unique nations – great complex organisms with diplomatic as well as martial strategies, whose administration was invariably subverted by two agents: chance and . . . virus again, always.

Joseph grimaced at these metaphors, but found them unshakeable. A virus was, Tiffany argued, loose genetic refuse, dandruff of the gods, a kind of star-dust from unimaginable early detonations, patterned into syllables so numerous and flexible that Shakespeare – Shakespeare backwards, even – was inevitable. So why not an innovation that altered the body's internal communication network, tuned the mysterious harmony of hormones to new melodies? Melodies in counterpoint with those of other species, the whole a grand symphony – a tremendous overture begun in thermonuclear cymbal-crash and winding, soaring, building, echoing and varying in endless composition . . .

He was startled to notice his knees were flexing rhythmically. The smile that had taken him unawares was responding to a rhythm. He remembered all at once a news story, something about the remarkable time-keeping of the Pobla – sidereal precision, by means of song. Soothing the savage. Music of the stars. More odd old ideas – summed up by means of Tiffany's definition of their own species: *dancing star beasts.*

Joseph swayed a little in his chair, eyes closed. A symptom of this shadow-virus might be a sense of rhythm, along with a euphoric mood. The Pobla shamans might be defined by a genetic vulnerability to this virus – lovers of music and play, it was said – and the virus in turn might, through an intricate endocrine chain-reaction, alter the gene. Converse with itself, so to speak; give itself new and infectious ideas. Jawing like a gang of crows.

He was giddy with terror and excitement. Hendricks had something, and Professor Goldbarth was now beginning to believe he might have it too. A molecule that compelled hymns to itself. Forced the soul into self-consciousness. Made him, the Gandhi prize-winner, into a monument to its own magnificence. And it was being spread through their tissue samples, was perhaps already an epidemic. The Pobla, even as they seemed to be expiring, were grafting a mysterious legacy into a new host.

131

He gave a groan which, nevertheless, he recognized as vaguely musical. One old habit would stay with him. He would insist on confirmation. There either were, or there were not, waffle cells in his own pineal gland. He knew only one way to find out, which would require a most unusual gift to his brilliant former student. No one would perform exploratory on so thin a hypothesis. Only an autopsy would do. Yet another old phrase came to him, making his heart lift. The dance of death.

CHAPTER FOURTEEN

Kapu had chosen a spot under an overhanging cliff, where the sun struck only late in the day. Here it was cooler and protected from the wind, so he did not mind sitting near his small fire. He took a handful of leaves from the pouch beside him and strewed them over the coals. When the pungent white smoke swirled up, he inhaled deeply and stared out at the horizon.

The land he overlooked was murky with dust, and deeply fissured by erosion from rare, slashing rains. In one direction was a distant haze – the sea – and in another, a low range of mountains. Sayat's raiders had cut them off from the coast, but Kapu did not concern himself with this problem now. He was concentrating on the astonishing portents he had received just three suns ago, and on the meeting he would have with the strange ghost who had come to them out of those mountains. A ghost of the tribe of the Little Horses.

A bird they had never seen before, fiery red with a huge yellow beak, had appeared first, after a long night of *tchatsi* drumming and dancing. it had signed, unmistakably, the coming of strangers, six-legged beings. Then his own messengers, returning against the heavy current of *yano*, had brought knowledge of a change, at last, at the border. It was none too soon. The drums – they had made new ones, of shape and sound different from the old original – were making him uneasy again. Under their influence the young grew restive and impudent. Many still disliked and mistrusted the mission he had set for them – to move the dying Pobla toward the piksi border stations.

One of the last elders to go, however, had managed to return. She was one of the *tagakin*, and revived to claw her way out of the earth the piksis had pushed over her and a hundred others. She crawled back to a burrow, met a small band of raiders, and gave them her message, before she let herself be taken by the long river into night. She had found one piksi with a shadow: a fat *pomasu* who looked inside mouths and sucked up tiny vials of blood or shreds of flesh, yet who had listened and seen and even spoken a few words of Pobla. Also, this big piksi lived with a very old *chintsa*, one of those with a white tail who could mock the Pobla with their own words.

Kapu had known, immediately, that before this moon was round he would have to go himself to the piksi camp and try to speak with this female blood-taker. It might be the last good chance to contact that rare one among their persecutors with a sense, however faint, of the shadow within. Everything depended on such a contact, on finding a *mahanaku*, a shadow-mirror. Someone like Teeklo – who had taught him a little of the piksi language and quite a lot about their peculiar ways.

The smoke had drifted through him now, clearing away anxiety and uncertainty. He felt his *kubi* poised and light, able to range at will. A cloud of gnats, attracted by this power, hovered nearby. He sang to them for a while, let his thoughts imitate them. A scattered, loose weave of image and reflection, moving over the surface of the tremendous, dark river of *yano*. It was carrying them away, more and more of them, sun after sun.

For a time now he had felt the heavy, swift current lifting his own bones, like a cage of sticks. There was a sour ball in his gut, growing slowly, and he sometimes retched a little blood. The smallest scratch from a thorn or sharp rock was likely to fester. He knew this was because they were living more often above ground, in the deadly invisible breath from the craters of ancient war and the mountains of piksi excrement.

Just now he heard the stone at his back creak ever so slightly, expanding in the last light of day. For a moment the wind died and the ribbed and canyoned plain before him seemed tranquil, each thing perfectly itself. Then he detected movement, someone coming up the path. Through the smoke he saw the ghost of the Little Horses.

He felt prepared now for such an encounter. His *kubi* rode like a watchful hawk above him. The two-legged one, leading the four-legged, was a powerful *tagak*, perhaps *tak tagak*. They would find some way to speak to each other. Kapu would be alert for hints of what these strangers knew of the piksis, of ways to reach them, show them their own shadows.

"*Yanaku*," the two-legs said, and stopped several strides from the firesite. The shaggy horse flared its nostrils, neck arched.

"*Na*." Kapu replied and made a slow, quiet gesture of invitation. He had never seen a live horse so near, and this one made him apprehensive. It was not, by Pobla measure, a little horse at all, but long-legged and thick-bodied, the mottled gray and black hide sheathing great knots of muscle,

The strange ghost, on the other hand, was slender as a *tchat* boy. Her teats were small and high, though she was surely eighteen winters, or more. Perhaps their *tak tagakin* were also childless, Kapu thought.

This one glanced at the swirl of tiny insects, which was dancing away now. Swiftly she held her two forefingers side by side, then hooked them together.

Kapu smiled and moved his chin to one side. No, they were not his *mahanakun*. Or only for these few minutes. Again he indicated a place before him by the fire, now down to a few winking red eyes, the smoke almost gone.

She said something to the horse and ran one hand along its long, matted mane. "*Klat,*" she said to Kapu, tapping herself on the nose, and "*Yeklat,*" tugging on the mane. He nodded at the introduction. The horse sidled a step or two away and lowered its head, the dark opals of its eyes intent on Kapu even as it smelled the earth.

"*Ya . . . ya chosa Pobla delo. Delo pakish chosa.* Spik piksi?"

"Liddle," Kapu frowned. "Onally liddle."

"*Ya me. We tohanakun.*" She matched and hooked her forefingers again.

Kapu laughed and she sat down quickly then, her back straight and head level. They looked at each other, frankly and completely. Kapu signed the sky and then his mouth, and she understood; they began to measure their breath to the wind. The Little Horses were a different color, close to that of the rocks made of sand, and their eyes were set wide. In the old stories he had heard about them – he had never seen one before himself – *wonakubi* made three beings of clay and put the Little Horses beside the fire of his creation, baking it like a brick. The Pobla he thrust into the coals, which blackened the first of their race. The piksi he forgot, and left in the snow.

He wondered if the Little Horses knew the story, and on impulse he scooped up a handful of earth. "Pobla," he said, and tossed a little clod onto the coals. The second clod he dropped half an arm's length from the fire. "*Delo sabool.* Liddle huss." Then he held the remaining earth in his outstretched hand, cocking his head at Klat. "Piksi?"

She grinned at him and made a motion of throwing something useless or befouled over her shoulder. Both of them burst out laughing. Kapu had not laughed in this way for a long time, with such a deep, easy release. This slender *pomasu* was not like a stranger; her *kubi* was not hidden. He threw the clods behind him, and after a pause that seemed expertly timed, both of them cringed, holding their arms over their heads, as if a great rain of stones had come back at them.

This final accord in their beliefs sent them into an even longer burst of hilarity. Kapu fell on his back, kicking his feet into the air, whooping. Klat hugged her knees, shoulders shaking with wild laughter. Yeklat snorted and stamped, lashed out with his hind hooves at an invisible attacker. That was always the problem with the piksis: you could not throw one away without a hundred springing up in his place.

So they began to talk, intensely, finding words in three languages and signing often. Meaning leaped like lightning from mere fragments, a syllable or slight gesture, because their two shadows were running together, impelled by a common urgency. Klat knew more of the Pobla than Kapu did about the Little Horses, who were all nomads, great travelers, and stealthy as fog. For some time now, Klat informed him, they had followed and observed the Pobla. They knew of the great temple at Sopan and of other holy places, other tribes, even some far across the water. But it was not their way to interfere, or in any way to call attention to themselves.

Klat's people were inseparable from their horses, moved only in their company, and could escape detection by hanging on the side or underneath their mounts. Every birth, Klat told him, was dual; each member of her tribe began life with a twin; or – as they looked at it – each was a being of six legs. They suckled on both mothers, slept and played as one. Kapu was amazed, if a bit troubled, to think that often when he had seen a herd galloping away over a hill or up a canyon, creatures much like himself had been hidden behind the hooves and flanks and tossing manes.

He learned other startling things from this slender, alert *pomasu*. She told him of the old tales of the Little Horses, which included stories about the Pobla. *Nacuatli*, the Little Horses called themselves. The word meant "swift singers." Both tribes, in Klat's telling, had been slaves of the piksis long ago, but the invention of so many *mudlati* robots had rendered them of no use, so they were exterminated or kept in pens until disease and hunger reduced their numbers. But the piksis had also bred with them, taking the childless young *pomasun* for their pleasure, and some of the mixed offspring survived.

Nacuatli and Pobla had also intermingled, thrown together as refugees or prisoners. The two of them might even be – Klat grinned at Kapu – related. Even some piksis, she claimed, had joined this population: especially the undesirables, those too deranged or criminal to prosper in the great cities. Just as in Kapu's own tales of the beginning of things, these stories always linked the fate of the tribes to the animals who sustained and instructed them. The Hive Beings for the Pobla, and the raven, the night-in-day jokester, for the Little Horses. And also like the Pobla legends, these stories tended toward a tragic, frightening conclusion.

Klat paused after her account of the coming of the piksis, and how her tribe had recognized and liberated their horses. In the silence they both felt the sun go out, and the rock at their backs clucked its tongue at them.

"Then bad," she said softly. "So bad."

"Bery bery bad," Kapu agreed.

In the desolate southern lands, where the piksis were last to arrive, their ancestors had made a terrible, terrible mistake – the source of suffering for generation after generation. It was only necessary for Kapu to strike his breast and make the sign for eating, and Klat hid her face in grief. Again they understood each other perfectly. The piksis had eaten out the insides of their captives, made them into docile *mudlatin*, so that whips and cages were no longer necessary. In fact the Pobla and Little Horses had become soldiers, skilled fighters in the wars the piksis started with each other.

Yet, Klat said, there were some lands across the sea, ruined by these wars, where the remnants of tribes somehow survived and learned again what they had forgotten. Like the Pobla and *Nacuatli* these peoples could hide and run. They threw away all the weapons the piksis had given them, and studied the strategies of their more ancient allies and teachers. Birds, fish, snakes, wild dogs, salamanders, bears and crickets – many, many creatures had once more agreed to speak to the holy ones, to travel with them, to feed them.

These wise ones, usually grandmothers of great clans, began to remember the old ways, the old chants, the old ceremonies. The graves of their important sons were rediscovered. The ghosts reclaimed their bodies. Evasion and camouflage even allowed them to strike indirectly against the piksis and their machines, without being blamed. They numbered very few, were as nothing to the vast piksi race, and for that reason, they survived.

137

And then just a few years ago, from their desolate haunts, the Little Horses noticed that the world of the pale masters had begun to darken ever so slightly, to labor and lurch unevenly. Certain slopes, certain streams and marginal strips, were being patrolled less often. A few blades of grass were springing up between the steel ribs of abandoned diggers and cutters.

Kapu was uneasy during this narrative. Everything Klat said confirmed his own life, but this auspicious movement no longer meant very much, because the Pobla were in a tragic, a terrible and sudden decline. He was about to interrupt, to warn this youngster that the Hive Beings, much more ancient than any other creatures, had been—

"Me too, bery bad! *Tak pakish!*" Klat said quickly, her face taut and cold. "Boot . . . *ya chintsa!*" She showed how the bird came to give sign. Then she pointed north, tapped Kapu on the knee. "*Chintsa* coom way Pobla. Show beeg got." She pointed skyward, earthward, threw out her arms to the horizons, then signed a swollen belly. "Bery bery beeg got! Snek got! Beby Pobla!"

Kapu himself cried out, his heart kicking at his ribs. His vision! "*Na! Na!*" He nodded violently, but held up one forefinger. "*Delo* Pobla!" Then he held up the forefinger on the other hand. "*Delo* piksi." He hooked the two fingers and pulled tight. Swiftly Klat was on her feet, staring at him, and Yeklat was beside her, stamping, nostrils wide.

"*Pakish.* Bad!" Her arm went around the horse's arching neck; she was uncertain and alarmed, he saw. She could not believe such a thing, that a holy birth could stem from union with a piksi.

Kapu remained motionless, closed his eyes, spoke into the darkness. "Liddle one, come piksi. Den piksi goway, come Pobla. Pahane. Snek." He made a wiggling gesture with one hand, then held two fingers forked at his mouth. "Oder Pobla *pomasu* . . . weetch wuman . . . goway, come piksi. Fly holycaptor. *Chintsa* wuman, birt wuman. Snek birt. *Tak tagak, kishtak kishtagak.* Beeg beeg beeg sun." He described a wide circle in the air, then pointed a finger between his still closed eyes. "I see. Liddle liddle one, snek birt, piksi Pobla."

There was silence except for Yeklat's blowing, the hooves grating on rock. He could feel Klat's *kubi* circling his own, watching. When he opened his eyes she had sat down again, but her face was empty, her look that of one who can go no further and must rest. It was dusk now, and the wind was rising a little, sending a few sparks skittering away from the remains of Kapu's fire. He waited, and finally she spoke in a low monotone.

"*Na*. Liddle huss spikstory. Bery owd, owd spikstory, snek birt beeg beeg *tak tagak*. Nem *Ketzicat-lee*. Beeg beeg bad, den come *Ketzicat-lee* one more tam. *Ya!*"

Kapu swayed back and forth, his heart already out of him and blowing like one of the sparks, into the sky. It was true, then, everywhere. The Little Horses knew the vision already, from an ancient story, and there would be others – the tribes Klat spoke of, far over the sea – who had seen or heard it, at least a fragment. As the great river of dark light was bearing him, ever swifter, to *wonakubi*, he would know that young *tagakin* like Klat were preparing for the birth, taking care for the holy one. "*Ya!*"

"Beeg bad here," Klat went on, again springing to her feet. "I come for *Ketzicat-lee*, snek birt. Tek him away. *Tak zelag*, bery farway."

Kapu held himself still then, barely breathing. That was the disturbing new element in Klat's story. The birth would be heralded by some terrible evil, and surely that was what had befallen the Pobla. Perhaps they were surviving only to guide the Little Horses, who would carry away Pahane and Tima and the *tak tagak* they yearned for. Were they all to sacrifice themselves, then? Had the Hive Beings forsaken them?

He broke into a ragged cough, a wet sound. When he spat into the ashes he tasted blood. There was something . . . he knew in some mysterious way that the Hive Beings, when they took Adza, had also given the Pobla a message to bear north. He could not read that message. In his mind it existed only as feverish fragments – urges, scraps of dreams, a pattern of leaves or pebbles or migrating birds – but his bones moved as if to a drum whose music set all things spinning into one intricate dance. He had assumed that in this way he would draw ever nearer the holy one, would finally touch her. But perhaps that was not what he was doing, not what the Hive Beings wanted. He could only follow his bones, and see.

"Find snek birt, den spik," he said. Painfully he got to his feet and came to stand before Klat. "*Yakish mahanaku*. Goot. *Yanaku*." He took her hand, brought it to his face and sniffed deeply. She was alert, excited, warm. No fear, and nothing hidden.

Awkwardly, she returned his gesture, and Yeklat, too, smelled his forearm. They laughed, and then the Little Horse ghost moved, all six legs together. She was swinging up, throwing a length of grass rope over the muscular neck, even as the hooves dug into the earth and the great body bunched. There was a loop in the end of the rope, where Klat hooked one foot, while she wrapped the other end around her hips and took it between her teeth, so that as the horse stretched out into a gallop she clung almost under and along the neck, moving in rhythm, hardly distinguishable after only a few paces.

Kapu watched, gaped after this thing that hurled over the land like a thrown spear, the flashing hooves seeming not even to touch the earth. He knew a certain desolation and envy, for he could imagine – not without a thrill of terror – the excitement of such speed, of suddenly expanding one's range to mountains and canyons never visited, beyond the edge of the world. It made him uneasy to think that his people had remained ignorant of these places and the beings who dwelt there, that perhaps the Pobla had hidden too well, had allowed the piksis to obsess and thus restrain them.

Yet the Little Horses, too, had relied on camouflage and stealth. Like the Pobla, they could maintain themselves only in those Wastelands the piksis had poisoned and then abandoned. And Klat had been deeply shaken by his vision of Pobla and piksi joined in a sacred birth, perhaps a return of the great god of the Little Horses, who was both serpent and bird. Kapu realized, yet again, that at the heart of his vision was – by the traditions of both people – a monstrous and unnatural idea: that the piksis could be kindred shadows, quite like the bear or cat or coyote.

The whole world was disturbed and reeling out of its known paths, Kapu thought, as he made his way down the trail toward their encampment. He could see a few smudges of red light on the canyon walls and hear the pulsing of the drums, indicating the young *tchatsin* were beginning yet another night of revel and speechmaking. He had tried, and failed, to convince them these sessions were dangerous, since Sayat's raiders could so easily locate and track them. And now he would have to leave others in charge, while he traveled to the border station and found the fat piksi woman, the blood-taker.

The pain in his bowels bent him and slowed his pace, and his joints were too stiff to allow more than a half-sun's travel at a time. He would have to start soon, and allow at least three suns for the journey. Since Tsitsi's death, he had become more conscious of time and its counting, realizing that his *kubi* was gathering itself for the last strokes, the final step into *yano*, the river that ran always and without end, outside of time.

He would not, he understood all at once, see the holy birth. He might not even reach Pahane and Tima, or have the comfort of hearing the heart through the wall of her womb. He probably would never return from this border station. They would push him into one of the trenches with a *mudlati*: but first he would find out where the holy one was. The piksi woman would help him.

So it was good that the Little Horses would care for the holy one. His work was only to live long enough to scout for this rescue. The work of a new *tchatsin*, a green boy. This irony pleased him, and he was ashamed now of his envy of the Little Horses. The new *tak tagakin* would have a horse-sister, perhaps, and would go like the wind itself. She would belong to all peoples living in the shadows, all those who had hidden and survived, and also – in some way he could not grasp yet – she would give the piksis back their ghosts, bring them again to *wonakubi*. Besides, he thought with a little smile to himself, who would want four more legs to go stiff and lame?

CHAPTER FIFTEEN

"Guy is big, I'm telling you," the agent had said. "Really, *really* fucking big. And he wants *you*, baby, nobody else but."

Even through the phone PJ had detected the adrenalin simmering in the agent's system, the aroused greed. The restaurant picked for the meeting was also impressive: a rural mansion three stories high and three centuries old, in a countryside that was practically a museum (restored farmhouses, ponies behind white fences, weathervanes).

At the door the maitre d' met PJ with an obsequious flourish and led him upstairs to a private dining room, plain stucco and dark beams and a fireplace, where there was a table set for four. A waiter materialized, bearing a single glass on a tray, and then disappeared.

"Your host has been delayed just a *few* minutes," the maitre d' said. "Do make yourself comfortable. Hors d'oeuvres on the sideboard. I recommend the hot banana pesto on flatbread." He made a slight, swift bow and was gone.

PJ picked up the drink and sniffed, then set it down. Whoever his hosts were, they knew his habits. PJ wanted the gin very, very much. He had overindulged several appetites the evening before, after an appearance at a run-down urban campus, and now felt like a ruined building, every window out and a cold wind blowing through. He still had, however, the instincts of an intelligence officer; and these instincts told him that there was no wealthy eccentric dying to toss a couple of billion at their non-existent script. That the story was bogus, except for the element of wealth.

Since the agent's call yesterday, he had reviewed other reasons why someone powerful but anonymous would want to see him, and the results were not comforting. He had personally sunk the fortunes of the Progressive party, at least temporarily, by fishing Ronnie Drager out of Ginkland. And before that he had spoiled a big firm's scam to pump from a Wasteland aquifer. And then there was the poaching case involving a three-star general. And then . . .

But why would anybody treat him to a two-thousand-dollar meal before they maimed or killed him? Also, unless the guy was so really, really fucking big he could buy off the whole restaurant staff, there would be a number of witnesses to this meeting. Maybe, he thought, looking longingly at the fizzing drink, he actually had a rich fan somewhere. Someone who wanted his services. But he had no darkside vantage now. He had recently been famous, and an active operative cannot be famous.

It was true that his visible fans had become odder as their number shrank. He saw a lot of retired military men, eager to reminisce about hunting Ginks in the early days on the border. Then there were the child-abuse types, who thought he had, because of his rescue of a feral disturbo, some expertise in that area.

Even a few young ecorads were showing up, imagining that after his stint with cannibal spear-carriers he would be ready for conversion to raw veggies and straw shoes. He had even pretended to entertain such ideas last night, in order to encourage the attentions of a young woman who lingered to ask questions, then for a beer, then for a walk back to his room, where she demonstrated convincingly that a believer in the simple and natural could be guilty of quite sophisticated invention when it came to certain elemental acts.

They came in then, his hosts. The woman looked vaguely familiar. She was not striking, but not exactly nondescript either. Slender, fit, in a straight business suit with just the necessary touches of jewelry and cosmetic color. A spokespersona, a diplocrat, a femex. Neutral eyes, pro smile, just enough heat to indicate the equipment was all there.

He recognized the man. A big one, because he did the work of the very biggest. Skin of a golden oak hue, long lashes and luxuriant brown hair with hints of sun, enough lines to indicate experience and concern. The suit was conservative, the color of dark smoke, but cut so perfectly the effect was almost flamboyant, like the burgundy silk tie. He came at PJ with white teeth, a big hand open, as if they were already good friends.

"Phillip James Feiffer," he said, "an honor and a pleasure to meet you. I'm Josh. You know Dorothy Smith?"

"Ah." PJ bowed, smiled, and shook once the cool, muscular hand she offered. "Of course. I saw the hearings. Magnificent performance."

"Thank you, sir. My first acting job."

They all laughed, briefly. It was the inexorable record-keeping of personal secretary Smith that exposed Danielle Konrad's possible connection to a darkside assassin. Soft-spoken and infallible, she had grounded a number of Grand Jury indictments in the Drager case. PJ had seen her on newsholos several times, and was now surprised at his inability to recognize her right away. It was true, he reflected, that certain actors made a virtue of their generic faces and bodies, could transform themselves into a great range of types.

"How is your former boss?" PJ spoke as the waiter reappeared with an ice bucket and three glasses on his tray, and when the tray stopped in front of him he lifted off a glass with a slow exhalation of gratitude. A rude question, he was aware, but Dorothy laughed and wrinkled her nose at him while the champagne was poured.

"You teaser. Minimum security, of course. Plays implacable tennis, I hear, and is working on a holo script. Has her first shot at parole in thirty days."

"She'll get it," Josh said. "Tough competitor. Looks like practically everyone in that affair has landed on his or her feet, no?" He extended his glass, watching PJ with easy, comradely attention.

PJ hesitated deliberately before meeting the toast, and held it to the faintest tinging of rim to rim. They would know perfectly well that, after his little hour of fame, he had landed flat on his back. They would know the current state of his career, especially after the trashing on the Winger show. They would have sniffed the rumors of a major holo, and found them only empty hype.

Josh Tremain was lawyer, lobbyist, and political consultant, an inside player with clients from both major parties and the international corporate community. He did deals for governments, into the trillions, as well as for the richest people on the planet. Such a person would be aware, to the dime, of just how badly former agent Feiffer needed a break. Question was, of course, why would Tremain be interested in a burned-out intelligence agent who drank too much, took too many pills, and had no cover anyway?

Josh laughed in an affectionate, sympathetic baritone. "It's relative, PJ," he said. "Look at *your* former boss. They say he doesn't talk any more. Has no worldly possessions. Sits in an unlocked cell and stares at the walls for days. But his fellow monks say Charlie Fat is the happiest of men." He shrugged. "And maybe he is. Who's ahead, really?"

You are, PJ thought, *you phoney asshole*. He smiled. "Whoever's closest to the exit," he said.

"Right." Josh's eyes had narrowed into a companionable squint, as if they were all braving the same cosmic wind. "The scale is individual, we run against our own shadows."

"Right," PJ said, and drank. He did not think he could stand very much more. It might be best to drink a great deal rapidly and then say or do something too obscene to excuse, something that would end this relationship, whatever the fuck it was, before it went any further.

"Hope your agent isn't too furious that we didn't ask him to come along. Fact is – you probably guessed – we take an unconventional sort of approach to scripts. Politics as art, art as life."

"I'm so glad." PJ aped as well as he could the other man's affable cheer. "So sick of empty show."

"Would you gentlemen mind, terribly, if we had lunch while you continued this fascinating philosophical discussion?" Holding her drink in both hands, Dorothy made a cute, lateral, little-girl movement toward the table, at which three waiters were now unloading a cartful of steaming delicacies. In the quick glance she gave him, PJ saw amusement, warning, and something he could not name – something speculative, cunning and avid.

"My navigator," Josh said and made a humorous gesture with the flat of his hand, half approving pat and half spanking. "Never had anyone like her. Dorothy absolutely *never* forgets what the business at hand is. A tigress of agendas."

"Silly me." Dorothy said as she slid into the chair held by one of the waiters. "I care." She smiled at PJ, in such a sunny and open way he had to laugh.

He sat down opposite Josh, Dorothy between them, leaving one empty chair.

"An associate may drop in later for coffee," Josh said. "And Navigator Smith is quite correct, we do have things to discuss with you before that. Let's just pick and sip along here, while we do a quick sketch of our situation."

"Sure." PJ took up a pair of silver tongs and ladled a half-dozen tiny clams onto his plate, then laid in a side of the greens and goat cheese, and a couple of strips of a rich, dark meat that had been broiled with capers and peppercorns.

"That's antelope loin," Josh observed. "The real stuff from the veldt parks. Very good choice."

PJ did not bother to nod. "I've lived on it," he said, "a time or two."

Any dish from the few large game ranches was a rare delicacy. Wild meats had to be licensed and inspected and auctioned, and the fees and taxes were exorbitant. But as a rookie PJ had hunted poachers at the fringe of one such ranch, and whenever they caught someone with a kill, they were allowed a steak or two from the carcass, as field rations. He nibbled at one of the strips, and the flavor matched what he remembered – the hot, dripping chunks from an open fire, dusted only with salt.

"We know," Josh said easily, but with a certain off-hand authority. "You've got a remarkable background, remarkable resources, and a reputation that is, simply, the best. I don't mind telling you we've run a very deep check, PJ. At least for a private consortium." He smiled at Dorothy. "And Dot can get deeper, I would guess, than a lot of probes inside the Administration or the Fed."

"I believe that." PJ met the Navigator's eyes, and found them amused, still calculating, and interested.

"But I think we both dislike a lot of circling and feinting, before the plot is even visible or the players known. So let me be frank." Josh paused to fork in a shrimp dripping with lemon and butter, lifting one shoulder casually to show that frankness was an everyday quality in his life. "We think you could be of great benefit to us, if you would consider going darkside again, probably for a month or two. We have in mind an assignment with some risk of legal problems. The reward, of course, would be commensurate with that kind of risk. This script of yours, for example, would be eminently doable. *If* you were an active outlaw, a sort of darkside hero."

"Darkside. Really." PJ kept chewing the antelope around and between the two words, so as to emphasize their vitriolic irony.

"Of course, you're thinking this is a line of crap. You left all that behind. How could you go darkside after being splashed all over national holo? What we mean, actually, is a *fugitive* into the darkside."

PJ belched. "You want me to commit a crime."

Josh smiled. Dorothy smiled. One of the waiters hurried across the room with a freshly opened bottle of wine.

"Leave it," Josh said. "And leave us, for now."

As soon as the waiters had withdrawn, Josh filled PJ's glass, shaking his head indulgently. "You are a tease, as Dot said. You know of course we would never, under any circumstances, hire you to commit a crime, Mr Feiffer."

"Of course not." PJ struck the knuckles of one hand lightly on his skull. "You want me to commit a great and noble act, for a very large sum of money."

"Precisely. You quite live up to your reputation for cleverness. And, further, it is a great and noble act that only you can . . . perform."

"Actually," Dorothy said thoughtfully, "let's say you already have done it, in a sense. Only you would have to take *credit* for it."

"Well, I'm a self-effacing guy. Don't even realize, sometimes, what I've done. But if there's a check coming I'm glad to hear it."

Josh finished scooping out a helping of smoking couscous, saffron-tinted and speckled with aromatic herbs, before sliding a hand inside his coat lapel and producing an envelope. He propped it casually on a salt shaker before PJ. "Certainly. Thanks for reminding me. Consider it an instalment, in the neighbourhood of, shall we say, a fourth."

PJ had lifted his wine glass to the light, appeared to examine it for a fleck of cork or some aberration of color. He was thinking of a passage in Keelough's journal, one of the few that twisted into obsessive fulmination, like a tirade by a loony Old Testament prophet.

Money has teeth. A rabid golden dog. Whosoever is bitten becomes its slave. Soon there are no free men, and all are howling and tearing at one another, consuming one another, and God is revealed as a set of fangs.

He drank, savored the wine. A more than passable pinot. "Not enough," he said. "Not enough for my brave and noble act."

Dorothy clapped a hand over her mouth, but could not block the laughter. She laughed with a pure, artless joy, the sound of cold water on stone. "I like this man," she said to Josh. "A match for anybody in my files. We're going to have fun." She turned to PJ, happy and a touch wistful. "Too bad we didn't meet years ago, before you committed completely to Insec, but regret is *such* a useless emotion, don't you think? And you're right, it isn't enough, up front. But look at our investment in building a new image. One you could exploit for years. However, the deal is strictly one way, PJ. No exit."

Josh's smile was lacklustre, a little weary. "I'm sure PJ knows that, Dorothy. I'm not sure he meant the *money* was insufficient. No doubt he appreciates the gesture, modest as it may be. He would just like us to provide some kind of *context* before he makes a decision, am I right PJ?"

PJ nodded judiciously. "Right. Like who the fuck are you, for example?"

The two hosts laughed again. He was clearly a comedian this afternoon. "Good question," Josh said, and rolled his eyes. "Wish I could answer it. Seriously."

He put down his fork and looked directly at PJ. "Seriously. I know you won't believe it, but I swear it's the truth. I don't know every facet of my client's affairs, in the usual way. I hate pretension, hate to sound this way, but . . . how else to say it . . . we're talking *spiritual grandeur* here. Something almost off the human scale. In the practical everyday mode, what I can tell you is this: it's a foundation to support the Creative Arts. Absolutely nonpartisan, and – of course you won't buy this one – ultimately nonprofit. At least in any ordinary sense. I could give you some names, sponsors from development finance and information markets, but you won't find anything registered with the Fed or on the Exchange." Josh glanced at Dorothy and lifted his eyebrows in silent inquiry.

"Correct." Dorothy held her fork with a charming insouciance, as if she might spear a morsel of meaning out of the thin air over the table at any moment. "There are a few small visible units – foundations, thinktanks, study centers – but these are just contact points, to maintain public perception. Actually, at the very top we're an extension of an old tradition. A kind of private club. Like-minded people gathered around a great leader in order to . . . make things happen, get a show together. Like an amateur troupe. Just a much, much more ambitious version."

PJ had abandoned the meal to concentrate on the wine, which had real presence now in his bloodstream. He felt warm, free, careless. "My question was," he said with an affected tolerance, "does the ambitious version have a fucking name?"

"You *are* an investigator, aren't you?" Dorothy bit her lower lip tentatively. There was something at once kittenish and mocking about her, and PJ found himself in an odd crosscurrent of revulsion and desire.

"You may be thinking of the Network, and it's true some of the people here were associated with that group, but the name doesn't fit now. Myself, I call us Wavershaft." She put on a swift, droll *moue* to defuse any pretension. "Because your next question, Phillip James, is certainly going to be, what the fuck do they *do*. And they don't *do*. They shape. They interpret. They create the plot."

"Excellently put." Josh shook his head and smiled at PJ. "She is a genius."

"*Please*." Dorothy made a pretty grimace. "Time is short. We haven't given Phillip James *any* idea of the brave and noble deed we want him to perform."

"Oh yes," PJ said. "You have."

Josh and Dorothy waited, pleased. He was a good student, as well as a comedian. He drained his glass and set it down with precision and care. "We all know this has something to do with the Drager case. That's what blew me out of the dark, and Skiho and Tickles are dead and Konrad and Fat might as well be, so I'm the only active survivor of that caper, which also brought the Network to the surface for the first time."

PJ picked up the bottle and swirled the little wine left before pouring it into his glass. "Summon the waiter. Anyway, I merely have to recall the lead story of this past week: ecocrazies have busted our little hero and his notorious Ginklette out of the bin, and the horny young doctor and his beautiful assistant as well. So we have a big story, big scandal. Of course various people want them *back* for various reasons. And of course I did that very job, only a year ago. But I'm not an operative anymore, boys and girls. No access, no clearance, no *nothing*. I'm the last guy in the universe you would want for that assignment. Anyway, the perpetrators are a gang of amateurs. Even the local police ought to be able to apprehend them, fairly soon. So no, I still don't have the context. And if this is really a one-way no exit, then you probably won't answer my last question – namely what the fuck do you want from *me* – unless I sign on first. And you know I've run out of options. This is the only game I can play. So summon the waiter, let's pledge the deal with a drink." He took the empty bottle by the neck, smiling encouragingly at Josh.

"Look, PJ," Josh said, "if you feel uncomfortable . . . "

Without getting up, PJ swung his arm in a grand circle, endowing the bottle with enough centrifugal force, when he released it, to loft across the dining room, bound off the wooden door, and shatter on the tile floor. In the interval that followed they could hear one of the larger, curved fragments as it rocked briefly, a slight, grating ring into silence.

"Good eye," Dorothy said. "I believe Mr Feiffer is accepting our offer. I'm just surprised he hasn't guessed his assignment yet."

"You mean what I've already done. What I take credit for."

She responded with only a sigh and pout. He had disappointed her. And then it hit him. So obvious he laughed for the first time with sincere gusto. "Decoy," he said, and laughed some more, then quacked like a duck. "Fucking *decoy*."

The door opened and the waiter came in one step before seeing the broken glass, but he reversed instantly, smoothly, saying "Yes sir, just a moment sir." He came back seconds later with a broom and pan, followed by a second waiter pushing the wine cart.

"*Very* good." Dorothy clapped her hands. "Both the guess and the duck call. But that's only part of it, you know."

PJ unloaded a single bottle from the cart, one with a wax seal and dust on its shoulders. Swiftly, wordlessly, the waiter dealt out three snifters and wheeled away, the sweeper in his wake now, bearing a panful of glass out of the room.

"Why would this wooden duck want to nap away a couple head cases? Must have a motive." PJ peeled off the seal and blew the dust from the label on the bottle. "Mmmm. My god, pre-Federation. This must be an occasion."

"Things have not been going so well for the duck. He apparently doesn't care for being legendary." Dorothy bit her lip again. "And he feels unappreciated. After all, he *found* this waif, restored him to his mama's bosom. But the reward has been, let's say . . . disappointing. And now he can't go back to the life he really loves – roaming the Wastelands, undercover and da. gerous – and too young to retire . . ."

"Ronnie Drager is also a very *rich* disturbed kid. A trust fund from the holo." Josh had recovered his easy charm. "His rescuer might feel this good fortune should be shared."

"The duck also drinks too much," PJ said helpfully. He wrenched out the cork, then tinkled a thin stream of rich, amber liquor from the bottle into each of the glass bubbles before him. "Which might help explain why he would attempt anything so lousily imputterible." He squinted at Dorothy. "What say, navigator?"

"We thought of that," Dorothy said. She gave him a slight smile, a shrug. "But we *do* need a wooden duck, PJ. Not a loose cannon. We understand you have been under pressure. Your buddy Keelough, the journal, and what that agent of yours wants to do with it, an understandable temptation, of course . . ."

151

PJ had been inhaling the fumes from the ancient brandy, eyes closed. Now he opened his eyes and set down the glass, quickly and precisely. "Careful," he said.

"No doubt the man was extraordinary," Josh said, leaning forward to set his elbows on the table, the snifter cupped in both hands. "If not exactly balanced. Anyone who ate——"

"Just shut the fuck up." PJ also leaned forward, hands resting lightly on the table cloth, his gaze steady and unblinking.

"You don't like me, do you PJ?" Josh lifted one corner of his mouth in ironic wistfulness.

"No. Definitely."

"No problem. It's mutual. You're a lout, and an asshole, as well as a lush. But we offered a job – happens to be the one job you can still do – and you accepted the terms. In your own loutish fashion. You're now an employee under contract, so listen closely, my friend, to what you're going to do, or – let us put this clearly – you'll be a sack of fishfeed by tomorrow, sundown." Josh grinned. "My word on it."

"No! You wouldn't." PJ covered his mouth with three fingers, eyes round with horror. Then he was reaching across the table, but Josh had rocked back in his chair, and Dorothy intercepted and captured PJ's yearning hands.

"Whoa, *whoa*, gentlemen, please!" She pushed firmly, and PJ turned his palms out in a pat-a-cake of yielding. He was entertained, intrigued by this small contest.

"Let's not strut, let's not get off the track now, please. We were doing *so* well, and now we're just wasting time. Let's be comfortable, let's be easy." She had a hand up to caution each of them now. "Josh, you *must* realize top agents are never tractable people. They are independent and creative and a little wild, and that's exactly why we hire them."

She smiled encouragingly at PJ, and spoke to him in a confidential, concerned tone, like a camp counselor. "And *you*, PJ, you are in no position to blow this opportunity. You are a professional and should realize a client does have legitimate demands, and an investment. And this client, make no mistake, will fulfil contracts. Josh was too blunt, of course, but he *is* giving you the facts. Now let's all allow each other some room to play."

PJ picked up his brandy again and winked at her. "Okay, you're right, Boss. I forgive this blunt instrument."

"How kind." Josh turned to Dorothy with a thin, brief smile. "We do have more important business, and there's still somebody outside for him to meet. So let's do it." Josh tilted his snifter, and yawned at PJ, or rather at the wall behind him.

"Thank you, gentlemen." Dorothy took a small notefile from her suit pocket, tapped a few keys, and considered the tiny display screen briefly. "Just to answer a few questions in advance for you . . . Yes, there are safe houses, and a regular contact. Wavershaft has extensive assets in the intelligence and judicial communities, so you should be a step ahead of any investigation. Itinerary . . . a bit complex. You'll be doing some actions and we have a narrow escape already scripted. We've composed your statements for you, and a secret interview with an alternative media source. As you could guess, we are loaded in that department, and we should be able to make you, rather quickly, into a romantic outlaw – cowboy, robin hood, guerilla commandante, that type. Really just an amplification of what you—"

"Hold it, hold it." PJ was shaking his head, grinning. "Who's going to believe I'm in league with these jerks? The *Thorgs*? Feiffer the master ecoterrorist? When have I hung around—"

"You fucked one last night." Josh saluted with his snifter.

"Ah." PJ looked at them in turn. "I see. Not a coincidence."

Dorothy delivered a quiet, lilting laugh. "She's very good, no?"

"And I guess Tickles is a kind of cult hero in those circles. And I have put myself forth as his spokesman. Jesus Christ. I see." He looked at Dorothy now in frank admiration. "I suppose you've organized the past three days for me."

She reached out and picked up the envelope, which had slid from the salt shaker to lay flat. A corner was wine-stained. "Indeed. Including this. It's an account statement and access card, established according to your demands. This meeting was the first negotiation in the contract process for your holo series rights. You chose Josh because of his financial and political reputation, me for my, what shall we say, credibility with dates and names and sums? But you *do* have to take the money, PJ."

"Suppose I do, at that." PJ took the envelope, opened it and removed the statement slip and code card. He glanced at the statement. "I see why your boss doesn't turn a profit." He slipped the paper and plastic into his coat pocket. "But there is one other little problem I see. This elaborate masquerade will last exactly as long as it takes to find Little Ronnie. What good am I when that happens? Like I said, any dumb cop might—"

"Oh, PJ." Dorothy laughed her pure delight again, the rapid, cold brook over rocks. "We know where he is."

Josh had gotten to his feet and moved toward the door, but PJ heard him laugh too, in satisfaction and triumph. PJ made no further effort to pretend detachment. He wished he had not drunk so much, could frame a better question.

"So what's the point?"

The veiled mockery was more intense, and kittenish, he now saw, was the wrong adjective. An adult feline, and quite large. She cuffed him with one paw. "Suspense."

PJ thought hard, found the idea bizarre, opaque.

She batted him again."Drama."

He managed a smile, though barely. "So I just read the lines."

"With feeling. On cue." She was rising now too, and PJ saw that Josh had let in a newcomer, a big, broad man in a blue suit, wearing a hat.

"One thing. How come your client is so hung up on this kid?" He spoke swiftly, watching the big man approach. The man's small eyes were active, appraising PJ's girth at waist and armpit, a weapons check.

"Remember Caliban." Dorothy's voice was soft and insistent, a schoolteacher's tone. "Shakespeare didn't like savages. Or anybody who fooled with the order of things. Genius always tries to tame chaos. Yes, nice to see you . . . " She nodded at the newcomer, already on her way to the door.

"Harry Fitzgibbon. Harry, PJ Feiffer."

PJ could see why Harry wore his hat indoors. It covered a bandage over one temple, and the eye on that side was still puffy, half-shut. The hand that gripped his was a very powerful instrument.

"You gentlemen will have to get acquainted on your own, for obvious reasons. We can't stay." Josh was smiling genially again, a charmer in his smooth slalom to the nearest exit. "You do have common ground. Harry is also a disgruntled former investigator. We got him fired yesterday. You now provide him with an opportunity to redeem himself, and even perhaps advance his fortunes." He clapped Harry lightly on the shoulder. "All our fortunes. Harry's a bodyguard – within, of course, the guidelines we set for him. And our former Secret Agent here, pride of the Border Patrol—"

Josh seemed to be appreciating PJ's prospects, reviewing his promising record, comtemplating promotion. He smiled affably and winked.

"The SuperAgent will be known as Joe One. Joe One will follow the orders he receives. Or his bodyguard will kill him, promptly. Gentlemen." He moved away, joined Dorothy at the door, which the two of them left open behind them.

PJ was the first to break the silence, which had lasted down two flights of stairs, past the maitre d' who did not seem to recollect their faces, then out the front door and as far as the gate to the parking lot, where they stopped, apparently to meditate on the pastoral landscape.

"I won't lie," he said. "It's not a pleasure to meet you."

"Mutual." Harry seemed to scan a far horizon, where he was not finding something he very much needed. "Can we leave this fucking picture book? Your car. I'm dumping a rental. They gave me the itinerary for the next week."

"All it needs," PJ said, using one finger like an eraser, "is to get rid of the white fences and a few lawns. Gouge out a gully or two, couple sand dunes – what happened to your head, by the way?"

Harry did not answer. His bulk rocked very slightly back and forth, and PJ sensed the man was radiating a single emotion, hot and deep. "That's private."

"Sure. I've had those embarrassing things happen, myself. You must have been the dick on duty when the little ones stole away. They terminate one for so *little* these days . . . "

"Don't." Harry had turned, finally, to look at him directly. Even with one eye half-shut it was a very meaningful stare. "Don't, please, be a wiseguy. Don't tell jokes. We do our jobs, professionals, by the book, and that's the whole burrito. Period. After this week you'll be running the basic op, and that's fine with me, but I know where the lines are, Feiffer, and it is my fucking call, when to enforce."

"I do not doubt." PJ gave Harry a quick, jaunty salute. "No jokes."

"And just one other thing." Harry's face had warmed slightly. "One thing I want."

"Name it," PJ said. "It's yours."

"You give me Petrasky. Whatever else is going down, I want Petrasky."

"You have him. Absolutely." PJ smiled. "Your party."

CHAPTER SIXTEEN

After two days in the delivery van, Ronald was so nauseated by hot salami and tomato paste that he was grateful for the odors of their new home: acid and metal in the subway, detergent and excrement in the sewer. Their passage into these underground tunnels was swift. Only for a few minutes had they enjoyed the open air.

Sandhill had driven the van to a narrow alley in an industrial sector of the city, a slot between two immense warehouses. They were far away from the impromptu wedding to which they and their cargo had supposedly been despatched an hour ago. Perfect way, Red Wolf laughed, to leave this crappy job. Power Pizza would make a charitable contribution to the lower orders – once the Great Unwashed, now the Great Uncounted – the Nonumbs.

A small crowd assembled quickly, some with hand trucks and shopping carts, and the van was eviscerated in a matter of seconds. Then the dark figures, lumpish from cartons of food stuffed into coats and waistbands, began to disperse into doorways and side alleys. Sandhill and Red Wolf seemed to know the scavengers, who were not, Pahane could see closehand, ordinary laborers. They were young and old, men and women, dressed in an odd motley of clothing. One gnomish old woman, in galoshes and headscarf, pushed into their midst and, laughing soundlessly, began to hurl shirts, shoes, trousers and coats from the heap in her cart.

"Knobs's exclusive line," Sandhill said, grinning as he unzipped his white coveralls. "Obtainable through a simple, tax-deductible contribution of the shirt off your back."

Knobs collected all their clothes, cackling triumphantly over Doctor Petrasky's white nylon shirt and expensive suit. But she frowned at the institutional blue jumpsuits from Ronald and Tima. "What's this pigeonshit?" she demanded, and peered warily at them. "Who these motherfuckers?" Her stare came to rest on Tima.

Sandhill shifted his shoulders, adjusting them to his new jacket, a frayed and wrinkled affair with a skull in flames emblazoned on the back. "She cool, Knobs. They all cool. Swear my pride on it. Goin' under for a while, now, baby, you know how it is." He threw an arm around her and squeezed, before she could push him away.

"Motherfucker. Kahonies where you brains s'posed to be, foolin' with these chi'ren." Knobs uttered a sharp, hoarse laugh. *Better* go under, what I hear. But take this motherfucker outa our street." She jerked her scarfed head at the van, and then, from an old, cracked plastic purse, removed a notepad and stub of pencil.

Sandhill nodded to Red Wolf. "She's right. Grab a couple armloads of these originals, and let's hop. Power's gonna put a tracer on the vehicle any minute, and we still got to shear our little lambs. Your job, Wolfie." He waited while Knobs scratched a few marks on the pad, tore away the sheet, and handed it to him. He nodded and shoved the paper into a pocket. "You can have the blues, free."

Half-dressed, they took the rest of their costume wardrobe back into the van. Red Wolf set up a bench and from a locker produced shears, clippers, comb, and tablecloth. The van's tiny sink supplied basins of water, which slopped and shuddered as Sandhill wove them into a cruise lane. Her broad, maternal face set in a smile of perverse joy, Wolfie lifted the chattering metal jaws. "Line up."

So they were cut, and Ronald most of all. Red Wolf shaved his head into a dome of dull ivory to match his tight pants, spike bracelets, and a shirt of cheap, imitation chain mail. Then, from a little suitcase, she gave him a wisp of moustache, so he might look eighteen. He was supposed to be a mall roach, one of the welfare youths who haunted parlors offering simusex and freefall virtuals.

Cynthia also lost most of her hair, wiping away tears as the sheaves of brightness slid away to scatter on the floor. The small mop she had left was dyed brunette, and with lurid make-up and jangling earrings she looked barely older than Ronald – a slovenly schoolgirl runaway, perhaps, or an unemployed sales clerk. Doctor Petrasky received a simple dark tint and, unable to shave for three days, had already acquired a blue stubble. But even in baggy, castoff clothing, his shoes taped at the seams, he was not convincing.

"Marvelous," Cynthia observed, "you can't hide the professor, no matter what. Don't even *try*."

That approach, in fact, seemed to improve matters greatly. When he reverted to his usual habits, squinting and frowning and moving his lips as he debated some hypothesis with himself, the doctor became a credible version of a deranged derelict. "Mumble aloud," Red Wolf advised. "Throw in a Jesus or Eternal Fire now and then."

They had all thought Tima would be the most difficult. They had neither the chemical preparations nor the time to lighten her color, and even with most of the heavy black flag of her hair shorn away, she looked too exotic. Even her slight, sinewy body, at once agile and undulant, marked her as Pobla. Seeing the anxiety in their faces, she smiled and bent to rummage through what garments were left.

She found a battered hat, a long shabby coat, a pair of boots three sizes too large. When she turned to them again, and clumped a few steps in the van's narrow aisle, between the rattling trays, a miracle occurred. Red Wolf gave a low howl of astonishment, and Cynthia clapped her hands.

As Pahane Ronald had of course seen this transformation before. Usually the air around Tima warped ever so slightly, as in a thermal current, and her form itself blurred, as if another, slightly different shape was emerging through it, a kind of superimposition of images. It was her *kubi*, her shadow, flickering in polymorphous play through the envelope of her flesh. This time a diminutive, ancient man was revealed, a cage of brittle bones, a chin permanently wrinkled, a mouth in withered pout. His skin seemed dried and darkened with age and the elements – many years, perhaps, on a tree plantation or border patrol.

"Oh my girl," Red Wolf whispered in awe. "And *pregnant* girl, too. I don't believe this."

"You see why we wanted to keep experimenting." Cynthia looked both proud and wistful. "She can do this all day."

Ronald and Tima had exchanged a glance then. He alone guessed what effort these guises and transformations cost her, how painful it was to concentrate her vital energies in this way, when her whole body was organizing itself around the new life inside her. But his sympathy was not untroubled, not quite pure.

It was true the misunderstanding between them, his bewilderment and irritability, had been swept away by the revelation. At first he had been giddy with excitement, relief, wonder; but soon enough he began to sense the tremendous, subtle influence of this little knot of multiplying cells. It radiated like a tiny, invisible sun into every corner of his being and alternately warmed and quickened, seared and paralyzed.

159

Yet, oddly enough, the fragile integration of his identities seemed strengthened by this new turbulence. It was as if Pahane the Pobla mischief-raider and Ronnie the piksi dreamer now had something in common; they could commiserate with each other, and – would it not be natural? – thrill to the idea of a final bond, symbolized in this worm of plasm, feeding and growing in Tima's darkness.

So he had crept and trotted and slogged beside her, at once proud to be a protector and inexplicably glum at what felt like constraint. They were only three – or four, depending on how one looked at it – just now, he and Tima with Sandhill, making their way through a subterranean complex of tunnels. After ditching the van they had split up, intending to rendezvous within a few hours and begin making long-range plans.

They had traveled first in a sewer main, an old concrete-lined section whose iron grates and ladders had nearly rusted away, and then for hours in subway utility corridors, deafened by the shriek and rumble of trains, skirting showers of electric sparks. At each juncture of trunk and branch lines, they encountered people like those who had emptied the van, and each time Sandhill talked with one, he showed the bit of paper given him by Knobs. Then there were others, sidling beside them or peering from the shadows, whose appearance and demeanor startled him even more.

Everyone, even the child of a well-connected energy official, had at least glimpsed the Nonumbs, and knew that they were a permanent, if indeterminate, population in cities. They had survived for at least two centuries by making themselves unobtrusive, almost invisible. They shared a few false identities and stolen or forged cards, took handouts from embarrassed relatives, moved in and out of the margins of legitimate society. Abandoned buildings, terminals, and barges provided shelter. In exchange for squatters' rights, they acted as living fire and burglar alarms, and even did a certain amount of maintenance work. No taxes were paid by or for them, no claims filed in their name. In fact they had no names, officially, nor had their ancestors, sometimes, for several generations.

It was rumored that Nonumbs were capable of living quite well. The shrewdest of these survivors had a hundred ways to trick the older credit machines and ticket dispensers. There was also trade in contraband, primarily drugs or exotic folk nostrums, and some prostitution, despite the universal availability of simusex parlors. Even the wealthiest Nonumbs paid no rent, and Ronald had heard his father talk of the wholesale pilfering of power and water from remote substations.

But in these reeking, dripping corridors he saw many who clearly had not walked the face of the earth for a long time. With their unkempt hair and huge eyes, garbed in filthy rags, they reminded him instantly of Pobla. Especially the young, who scampered barefoot only inches from a steel rail carrying fifty thousand volts. Tima, too, was amazed at the resemblance. She turned to him with a wild, gleeful grin. "*Tchatsinakun*! *Yita piksi tchatsinakun*!"

And, as if they had understood her, some of these children whooped and waved, making strange gestures with their hands. Pahane thought he recognized the quick turn and point of a rat, then the rapid squirm of a heavy body – a snake. Two young men swung down then from a catwalk that served a bank of transformers; as they approached, Ronald saw a pigeon, its breast a spatter of black, white and gray, with a head and cape of iridescent violet and green, perched on the shoulder of one.

The man bearing the bird wore the grease-stained coveralls of a Transit Force mechanic, his companion a cheap suit but with no tie. They could have been recent dropouts from a rehab or recon program, still eligible for food credits or a night's sleep at a shelter. Apparently they had been waiting for Sandhill, and knew the identity of the dwarfish old man and the shaven-headed mallroach who accompanied him, for they gave a quick thumb-jab in the air to signify triumph. The man in coveralls spoke first.

"You got the back?"

Sandhill nodded and patted the breast pocket of the flaming skull jacket.

"O-h-h-h, man. Gonna taste *so* good." The man wet his lips and laughed. He had the look of a mixed. The surgery on his nose and eyelids had been poorly done; and although his complexion was light, his hair was thick and glossy and coarse as any Pobla's. "Come on, man."

"Her Majesty got us a zone?" Sandhill touched the pocket again, but waited, his look penetrating.

"Definitely. Good for the time bein'." The man lifted the first two fingers of one hand, twiddled them rapidly. "Okay?"

Sandhill took out a small box, flipped up its top, and extended it to the pair. Their hands were swift as sparrows, pecking out the thin white sticks and flying up to their mouths. The man in the suit had already produced a teardrop of flame from a little tube, and in an instant they had sucked bright coals at the tip of the sticks and were exhaling soft jets of smoke.

"Oh, Jesus, man. M-m-m-m!" The man in coveralls had closed his eyes, letting the smoke crawl from his nostrils, then inhaling it back again. The pigeon turned its head and uttered a kind of purring growl.

Sandhill laughed and winked swiftly at them. Ronald was shocked and intrigued. Cigarettes had been outlawed for nearly a century, along with pipes and cigars and chewing preparations. Ronald had seen them, and the cases and holders and other paraphernalia of their use, only in the crime museum. Though he had never witnessed anyone actually smoking, he had been exposed to the instructional holos that detailed the horrors of lung disease in a previous age, and the massive public health campaign that had criminalized tobacco and converted most of the population of advanced nations to modern, safe, synthetic stimulants.

Nonumbs were indifferent to that historical lesson, and everyone knew they peddled a certain amount of illegal tobacco to old people and workers in mines and tree farms. But Sandhill too took a cigarette, inserted it between his lips, and leaned to light it from the tip of one of the others – a jousting kiss of fire. The smoke drifted all around them, and Pahane and Tima breathed it in, tentatively but of necessity, and found the aroma fascinating.

"The others?"

"Yeah, they coming. Dizzy here just give us the word." The man in coveralls turned toward the pigeon. He worked his tongue between tight lips to free a fleck or two of tobacco, then opened his mouth slightly and the bird's beak darted in, delicately, to nip up the offering.

"Picked up another skippy, too. Slick boy."

Sandhill was suddenly alert, poised. "Another? From where?"

"Same do. That hospital. He get out on his own."

"How?"

"That all we know, man. Not followin' the number close, you dig? Got our own thing, here, you know that. Makin' shit for the man, makin' shit for the people. We—"

"Wastin' time, Tyrone," the man in the suit said in a soft tenor. "Talkin' that talk." He was handsome, a pure NorthAm of the desired golden shade, with shaggy, coppery hair and a faint band of freckles over the bridge of a button nose. "Sandyboy want all his chicken in the bucket, man. His people notorious. *He* notorious. See his ugly face on the box every day. Some people already askin' down here, man." He looked meaningfully at Sandhill. "Serious people."

"Deah, how re-mahkable." Sandhill sighed, and the other men laughed spontaneously. "But you right, Humper. We got to go under all together. Way under. Queen give us a righteous zone?"

Tyrone nodded and laughed. The pigeon growled again and retracted its head between its shoulders, causing a shimmer of rainbow color, darkening to purple. "Oh it under. Oh yas. It one bad, bad mother-fucker of a zone."

It was, indeed. It smelled terrible, the lighting was poor – either gray gloom or the high glare of utility light – and there was a constant, strong draught – a cold dank wind that carried grime and soot. The cavernous place they came to, their zone, was an abandoned section of the subway maintenance system, an empty shop, crew station, and emergency car barn where malfunctioning engines were once shunted until they could be hauled off for salvaging.

The zone was part of a whole underground network – the water, power, drain, and sewer conduits of the previous two centuries. Many of these caved in or were sealed off as the city migrated, or were replaced by newer and larger units, but the scavengers had re-excavated certain sections, extended others and connected them by cross-tunnels. The whole was now serviced by a complex of parasitic syphons, pirate pipes, and stealth wires.

So it was also good. Exquisitely, deliriously good – a restoration and nostalgic release long before they expected it. For this was very like Sopan, the Pobla's great city beneath the Wastelands, only in concrete and rusted steel. In her excitement, Tima forgot her role as little old man. She went light-footed beside Ronald, her head high, the old hat stuffed in a pocket and the coat unbelted. Their radiance was so pronounced that people stepped now and then from the shadows to peer at them and call out good-humored appreciation and lewd encouragement.

But Ronald remained stunned and more than a little apprehensive. The scope of this labyrinth and the number and variety of its in-habitants overwhelmed him. He had difficulty believing some of the things Sandhill and Tyrone and Humper had told them on the way, in a tone of casual amusement.

The Nonumbs had been forming their lifestyle for a hundred and forty years, the men claimed. Lifestyle, subculture, ghetto, hood, tribe – all archaic notions that had their little flare of notoriety. Actually, the Nonumbs had another name for themselves, which Ronald heard as "O'Malleys." Whatever you called it, the situation was the same. Sandhill's grin was demonic, provocative. *Some can eat shit, some can't.* Tima had laughed at that, and a knowing look flashed between them.

Every society in the north, Sandhill went on, the Pacrims and Euroslavs too, undergoes this division. Every nation has another non-nation hidden within, a faceless horde, imperfectly counted, existing outside the fluctuating graphs of production and consumption, the flow and eddy of wealth and power. The existence of this non-nation is acknowledged, to be sure. Everything, Sandhill reminded them with a wide, savage grin, is now acknowledged. You number it, you numb it. The news stories, the statistical reports, the Presidential Commissions – all part of the apparatus of ignorance.

"What he sayin'," Tyrone interrupted at this point, "is they can fo'get anythin' by advertisin' it enough."

"Talk theyseffs dumb," Humper added. He gave Sandhill a slight, crooked smile. "Like he doin' just now."

Sandhill took a breath, then hesitated. He was, Pahane saw, discomfited, and for the first time at a loss for words.

Ronald seized the opportunity, asked the question that had been on his lips for several minutes. "O'Malley's? A . . . a family?"

Humper and Tyrone stared at him, then laughed. "You got a O," Humper said, snapping his fingers in a beat, "to go."

"You got a M," Tyrone joined in, and slapped his thigh, "to get a fem."

"Got a A, to stay."

"Got a L, to yell."

"Got a Y, and why?"

"Cause ever cool fool got a mama to shake it and ever li'l muthuth git old and cold, say diss me jack we take you back and lay out the sound, survey the ground, lemme free lemme see, 'cause we goin' wild like a child, goin' down you clown, gonna quit this jive *alive!*"

The two men punctuated their chant with an elaborate series of handgrips and slaps, mock blows, body jerks, peculiar gliding or shuffling steps. Sandhill seemed to know the ritual too, for he recovered his grin and joined the others in their last few motions. Tyrone and Humper erupted into hoots of laughter, watching Pahane's face.

He recognized this ancient, forbidden "music". Rap – the last form of rockenroll, marking the terminal stage of decadence in a culture of violence, which ushered in the final, catastrophic wars before the Federation. Such material was prohibited except in the classroom, preceded by a proper introduction and holos of the horrors of that age. Rap was a code, as his teacher had explained to them, for rip and rape – primitive regression to a state of dangerous emotionalism. To absorb a small sample, they were given buttons linked on a circuit, so they could signal when the bad images began to arise, and he heard only a few notes before a chorus of buzzers drowned out the sound.

"They say it stands for *Old Muthas And Lazy Youngboys*," Sandhill said.

"That was the folks went under," Humper said, still carrying a rhythm. "Mamas with no papas and so many mouths to feed . . ."

"No jobs, no pay, a boy don't try, just get high," Tyrone cut in. He looked away, somber. "Say it stands for homeless, too. What they called it a long time ago. And that story. What that story, Sandy?"

"Ones that walk away. Some old tale about this utopia, kep' an idiot girl in a closet." Sandhill shrugged. "All that stuff, crazy stuff, they locked up with rockenroll. I've also heard homely anomalies, and gnomely homilies, and some others, worse."

"Anyway," Tyrone threw out one arm casually, "we the Omalys and this *our* home now."

They had lingered at the entrance to the old car barn for this discussion, except for the pigeon. Dizzy had departed with a burble of discontent when the impromptu chant and dance had begun. But now he returned, riding on the shoulder of a majestic figure, an extremely tall, narrow woman. Her posture, her regal smile, and her measured stride removed all trace of incongruity from her dress – an evening gown, soiled and often mended, but once, long ago, stylish and very expensive.

She picked her way over a runnel of black water wandering across the sagging concrete floor, and extended the long, thin fingers of one hand.

"Sandy, how perfectly daring and irresponsible and wonderful of you to bring us these celebrities." While Sandhill took her hand and bowed, she looked at Ronald and Tima, swiftly but carefully. Her voice was a rapid whisper. "You've quite outdone yourself. What ghastly disguises for such lovely young things. Dizzy was beside himself. That's your doing, I dare say."

She was looking at Tima intently. Eight decades had faded the blue of her eyes to a steely tone.

"Ours," Tima said.

"Oh, of course, I forgot. You are two, at the moment. Anyway, Dizzy likes you both. Do you mind?"

"Not at all." Tima smiled, and the pigeon erupted from the woman's shoulder, a brief, loud clap of wings, and alighted on Tima's. The bird chuckled softly, and ran its beak swiftly along Tima's cheek.

"Or rather three. Tima, isn't it? And . . . Ronald?"

In turn they held the thin fingers, which were stiff and dry as paper. "Pahane," he said with a wry smile. "I am a multiple person."

"I've heard." She laughed. "And I'm jealous. A single identity can be insufferable. I fear I am only plain old Eva. Who is pleased, however, to welcome you to her humble lodging."

They were strolling inside the barn now, and as if on cue someone hailed them from above. Smiling faces leaned over an iron railing, beckoning and clapping. This gaiety echoed strangely in the huge, gloomy corridor, spanned with girders and hung with tangled vines of electric cord, bearing occasional blooms of yellow light. The dank wind swayed these bulbs, so the shadows under their feet twisted and gyrated.

"Your friends are here before you," Eva said, and led them to an ancient lift, a steel cage once used to carry men and their tools to the second level of the barn. Humper and Tyrone put their shoulders to the sliding door and moved it aside with a squeal and rumble. They entered and Eva pulled at a bit of cord hanging inside, jingling a bell. They heard a series of heavy thumps overhead, and with a little shudder and sway the lift began to rise.

"Counterweights," Eva said with an indulgent little laugh. "My impossibly Victorian taste."

When the lift was half way, they saw that it was indeed propelled by nothing more than a cable leading over a pulley to another platform, where seven smiling men stood and waved as they passed, sinking to the floor below. Arriving with a clang on the second level, the steel mesh door shoved aside, they found themselves in an even more arresting scene. There were sofas and lamps with lace shades, a towering grandfather clock, several ornate dressers, a whole row of refrigerators. Many of these furnishings looked used or repaired, but some were nearly new. There was barely time to register this impression – much like a huge second-hand warehouse – before they saw the column of smoke, the group rising from a circle of chairs and lounges. It took an extra second to recognize the couple beside Red Wolf, for Dr Petrasky was so pale and Cynthia, without her golden hair and flashing smile, was truly a different person. And a second after that Tima opened her mouth wide, her throat contracting, yet Ronald heard only the hiss of breath.

Then he saw who it was. The smallest of this group was almost hidden in a rain poncho, mouth wide like Tima's, showing teeth. Batboy. Ronald grinned in delight, gave his best imitation of a squeak and chitter.

"Ah so! The new skippy." Sandhill glanced at them. "You know him, I guess?"

They did not bother to reply, but gathered around their friend, hugged him and laughed and spoke disconnected phrases of delight and amazement. Cynthia, too, embraced them as if it had been days rather than hours since their parting, while Dr Petrasky shook hands, even clapped Ronald awkwardly on the shoulder. They were almost like a family, celebrating the safe arrival of new emigrants. He was aware that everyone touched Tima with a special, reverential enthusiasm.

"Quite a young man," Eva said from behind them. "Quite a story of hanging for hours from a heating conduit, and getting some help from his winged fellows. And of course you all have a marvelous tale to tell. But I wonder if you wouldn't like to see your quarters first, have a bite, and perhaps take a good long nap? I assure you my friends and I will be all too happy to squeeze out every tidbit of narrative, before we let you go."

They noticed then the others, some of whom had regained chairs arranged around the little spears of fire and waves of smoke issuing from a topless fuel drum. A thin man with a white goatee, who lifted a hand in greeting or blessing, a short, plump woman wearing an absurd hat, her features obscured behind a veil of black gauze, a middle-aged man, bald and smiling affably. Like Eva, they were dressed in what was once elegant, even formal attire.

The newcomers had only to glance at one another to know she was right. Ronald was exhausted. He supposed he looked like the others – bright, feverish, fragile, dazed. They had come to rest, at last, like the shipwrecked on a strange island; and as soon as they found food and a quiet cave, they would fall into each other's arms and sleep like stones.

"Humper, won't you be a dear and show these distinguished guests to their rooms? Tyrone, you might set out snacks and fire up the teapot, and so forth?" Eva turned to Sandhill and beckoned him with the slightest of gestures.

He came to her, taking from his pocket the slip of paper from Knobs. A curl of flame from the barrel threw an uneven light on his high cheekbones, the long hair again in a braid. With his tattoo partly exposed in a wide notch of unbuttoned shirt, and the death's-head jacket, he reminded Ronald of pictures of famous outlaws and deviants from the previous two centuries, or illustrations of the still earlier indigenous races, in their feathers and hides and ornaments of bone.

But this vision vanished in a blink, with the mocking, debonair smile, the deep bow Sandhill made as he presented the paper. "Always a pleasure, my lady. Arrangements for five, I think, and adjoining if possible?"

"Oh Sandy, you're going to rush off, aren't you? Cavalier, I believe, is the right word. Positively ingrate, some might say." Eva folded the paper without looking at it and slid it into a tiny, embroidered belt purse. "I'm sure this will do, two nights, three, whatever. But we *will* see you for breakfast? We must tell you there has been some pressure down here, since your little, uh, vacation. You have some interesting friends you may not even know, and I wouldn't be surprised if you get some very promising inquiries quite soon. Actually I'm not convinced it was a terribly good idea to come so far so fast."

"Our choices were limited," Sandhill said with another bow. "And this is of course the finest establishment available." He had, unobtrusively, taken out the cigarette box and now pressed it into Eva's hand. "A small token of our gratitude."

"Oh Sandy! You are a shameless and outrageous seducer, which is the most lovable kind."

Eva held the box for a moment against her cheek, then inserted it swiftly into the purse, where it created an oblong bulge. "You make a miscreant of me. But unfortunately for you, I am too old for flattery, and you'll have to account for yourself tomorrow all the same. Eight sharp." She gave him an ironic wave of imperious dismissal, then lifted her arms, the sleeves hanging from the long bones like spread wings. "Welcome and good night, my dear guests. We honor your achievement, and we will help you as we can."

She blew them kisses before turning smartly to join her group around the fire. The flames reached higher now, since the old man with the goatee had thrown in what appeared to be the leg of a chair and slats from its back. A conversation resumed, the plump woman laughed behind her veil, and after Humper led them again to the lift, they saw the chiaroscuro tableau of Eva and her salon appear to ascend, a little shakily, toward the great pipes and girders of heaven.

Getting out on the ground floor, Dr Petrasky broke the silence. "But then, this is . . . this is a . . . "

"Hotel." Sandhill was amused. "And a hotel of dignified lineage. You never heard of the Morphopolous chain?"

"Holy shit." Cynthia puckered and blew a long, audible jet of breath. "Of course. His first wife. She must be—"

"Nobody knows. Almost a hundred."

"Don't," Humper said softly, "ever let her hear you speculate on that subject."

Dr Petrasky had taken on his look of an anxious metaphysician. "A fortune. Trillions, I believe . . . but she had a breakdown in *Africa*. An operation, wasn't there? Experimental? A rejuvenation . . . " He stopped, his mouth still open.

"And her husband was the big hunter. Homer, right?" Cynthia turned to Sandhill. "Barrelhead. Bought up most of what was left of the old Hong Kong?"

"Bought up a lot of things. Cosmetics. Transport. Junkfood – including Power Pizza and Big One. Pulp and fiber. Gold. Oil. Entertainment. Especially entertainment." Sandhill smiled. "Or entertainers. Like Eva – one of the last of the screen stars, you know, to make the shift to holo."

"Say one more time," Humper sighed. "Leave it."

They had stopped before the shell of an ancient subway car, crumpled in a wreck and then beaten out crudely. It was divided into four sections. "This is your private zone," Humper said. "Towels, soap, all that inside. Tyrone be along quick with some snack." He turned to Sandhill and Red Wolf. "You comin'?"

"We hang around, say good night, be along right away."

Humper nodded. His handsome NorthAm profile was thoughtful, even somber. There was a distant, muffled rumbling, a train passing near enough to make the concrete underfoot tremble ever so slightly. The pigeon, still on Tima's shoulder, purred softly.

"Need anything, press the button say *Call*. But don't go walkin' 'round here. Don't do that." Humper looked at each of them in turn. "Please." He glanced at Sandhill as he turned to go. "He tell you."

They listened to Humper's footsteps, fading swiftly into a background of distant clangs or thumps, rustlings, perhaps voices, their origin uncertain in this echoing cavern. Ronald heard the squeal of a rat, and saw Tima turn her head to listen, raise a hand to calm Dizzy.

"Well?" Cynthia said finally.

Sandhill laughed briefly, softly. "It's raw capitalism down here, friends. A no deficit, no credit, free trade zone. The pizza got us this far and made arrangements for maybe three nights, here only. Step outside Eva's, and you owe, right now. You pay, right now." He stretched, yawned, smiled at Cynthia. "With whatever you got. Ring, chrono, shoes. Your hair, maybe. Or a nice tooth. Or all your teeth."

"I thought . . . I thought these were friends, and we were . . . " Marvin was blinking rapidly with bewilderment and indignation.

"Free?" Red Wolf gave her raucous whoop. "Oh you *free*, Doctor. You free long as you got somethin' to sell. After that, you free for anybody *catch* you."

"How can I put it?" Sandhill touched his temples in playful cogitation. "Ah. The simplest of definitions. You know how the Omalys distinguish gender, Marvelous?" He gestured toward the shadowy corners of their concrete and steel cave.

Marvin bit his lips, waiting.

Sandhill said, "You a two."

"Or a three." Red Wolf laughed, her arms akimbo in triumph.

"Two or three?" Marvin was staring now at the floor.

"Holes. And if you got nothin' else, to supply the plumbing in between, that's what you sell."

"Oh freedom!" Red Wolf crowed. "Freedom just another word, Doctor, the way Omalys think. Now a *hole*, that get you a cup o' coffee!"

CHAPTER SEVENTEEN

As soon as they saw the black flecks in the colorless sky, the old one began to sing to himself. They were vultures, Tiffany supposed, and she heard the sorrow in his voice and was immediately anxious. It was a kind of miracle that Kapu was alive at all, given the tumor in his bowels and the fact that he ate no solid food now. If some disaster had visited his community, the shock would likely finish him. He might, like that mythic leader she had been reading about, vanish in a puff of smoke.

"*Uh, pakish . . . pakish geenta*?" Immediately she felt foolish, and touched Kapu on his bare, brown arm. A bad thing – of course it would be a bad thing if hooked beaks were dragging out the entrails of those you loved. If your mate, your children, your home, your friends – everything, absolutely everything, was gone. But the old one did not seem to notice her touch. His eyes had turned inward and the rhythmic song went on, as she increased the speed of their Bantam another five klicks. She couldn't do more because the arroyo they were running down was strewn with boulders and the occasional rusted vehicle frame, and warped by fans of alluvial debris from side channels. She was also avoiding bursts of speed that might indicate to Colonel White's Comm staff – who were certainly tracking her by now – a problem of some kind.

A problem beyond the tremendous mess he already had on his hands. Tiffany felt genuinely sorry to have abandoned poor Colonel White, even though her hospital had its routines down and she had left quite specific instructions on her office computer. Then there was her lame excuse for this expedition. She said she wanted to explore the possibility of an experimental substation in the Wastelands, and hence procured – some might say purloined – this vehicle, which was really just a runabout and not armed for scout or research duty. And he would be upset – well, apoplectic, possibly – when he found out she had taken a Pobla subject as passenger and driven right out the gate with a cheery wave at the dumbfounded grunt guard.

Tiffany was, actually, a little appalled at herself, when she stopped to think about it. But this venture was not about *thinking*, in the commonplace sense. Intuition was her primary tool of investigation. Intuition had made her famous. And (it was only fair to admit) intuition also got her into a deal of trouble. Which she was most certainly in just now. A glance at the onboard's 3-R gram told her the option of going back to the base, without a refuel, would soon no longer be available. If Kapu did die on her . . .

None of that mattered, of course, in the face of what was happening to these people. To Kapu. She grimaced, as the Bantam whacked its underside on a sandbar and careened around a curve in the arroyo. He was not dying on her, he was living for her. He cared nothing, she knew, about his own death. In fact he was impatient to enter what he called the dark river. He had stayed alive, he told her first thing, only for the purpose of bringing her here.

He had been at the head of the line yesterday; the others had obviously yielded to him, were gathered around him, listening. He looked up and shocked Tiffany with a smile, a true smile of gratitude and affection. Then she nearly fainted, for he said, almost cheerfully, "Gat mirnin. I hef come."

None of these pathetic zombies had smiled at her, let alone addressed her in recognizable English. The possibility of ordinary, direct conversation had never even occurred to her. When she got him into the laboratory she was shaking with anticipation, still half-believing she was hallucinating. She had a million tests to run and questions to ask.

Only a few days before, looking in old chronicles for analogs to the magical gene (as she termed it to herself), Tiffany had stumbled on the case of Tupaq Amaru. He had appeared in the SouthAm jungle, a full century after the royal line had been extinguished, and claimed to be the last Inca king. A clever, opportunistic shaman, the historians ruled – and yet they were impressed with his influence on the aborigines, both from the selva and the highlands.

He spoke to all of them, including the Spaniards, in their own languages, and began a remarkably sophisticated military campaign against the colonial government. The lone dependable drawing of the period, crude and faded, showed him in elaborate feathered crown, pistol in hand, a monkey on his shoulder. When the conqueror's cannon and flintlocks finally prevailed, Tupaq called together what remained of his forces, exhorted them to eternal resistance, and then, according to legend, vanished in a cloud of smoke. It was a story like the others: a hero or king or lama appears from nowhere, is recognized by certain signs, performs miracles, then vanishes – walks out of his grave, or ascends on a beam of starlight, or whoofs away in wind or cloud.

Tiffany had collected hundreds of versions of this archetype, from Krishna to Wovoka, looking for details that would correlate with the profile she was sketching from her research on the Pobla. She had managed only the most basic tests on Kapu, just enough to suspect that he did not, in fact match that profile. A keen disappointment – she had to turn away, her face hot and her eyes brimming with tears – but soon assuaged by startling revelations in a new dimension. The old man–

Kapu lifted his hand in a simple, formal gesture, without breaking the rhythm of his chant. On the monitor's telephoto, the vultures were near enough that she could see their naked heads swiveling, watching the approach of the Bantam. She switched on the topo and saw that they would have to leave the arroyo and find a route overland in the direction Kapu had indicated. She slowed and fussed for a moment over the control panel, deciding finally to convert to cleated tracks. The terrain looked uneven and braided with steep gullies.

The old man. She hesitated over this slip. Was it a slip? In scientific literature the Pobla were identified as male or female *lapsis*. Man and woman belonged only to human. She clucked at herself impatiently. Kapu was right. Such identification was a waste of effort. Before she could continue her tests, he had pushed her hand away. "No tam," he said, with authority. "I spik now."

And spik they had, non-stop, in a hasty, *ad hoc* idiom of words and signs and images. She called up a special graphic program for aphasics and, sketching with a mouse, Kapu had gotten across to her that he came because a piksi *ogan*, which meant a human man, and a Pobla *pomasu*, a lap female, had run away together. They were going to have a baby, which was for his followers a tremendous event.

Tiffany had hardly been able to believe those simple, unmistakable drawings. Easing over the top of the arroyo bank and into a broken, empty landscape, she still experienced a surge of elation at the memory. Less than a month ago the scandal at the New Life Institute had erupted. A day later little Ronnie Drager escaped the Institute and disappeared, along with the Pobla female prodigy used in his therapy. And just a few *hours* before Kapu appeared on her doorstep, the sensational media – the tabs and yakshows – had begun to circulate the rumors of a cross-species pregnancy.

How could this old, dying Pobla, crawling in from the Wastelands, have known about these things? He knew them exactly. She had recovered a segment of an old newsholo, a shot of the Drager boy entering the Institute, and Kapu at once cried out and pointed: *Pahane*! This was, he indicated, the piksi *ogan* who had lived with them, become one of them, and was now on his way here again. This boy was the father.

Tiffany remembered the name. She had seen it in the one cursory article emanating from Petrasky's lab. *Snaketongue*. The name for the other half of Ronnie's multiple personality. There were only two possibilities here. Kapu was clairvoyant, or he watched a lot of holo.

Retracting the Bantam's radiation shields, going direct visual, Tiffany ruled out the latter alternative immediately. Except for the wheeling, dark birds, there was nothing alive anywhere, as far as she could see. The surface of the land was gray or dun, but its cleavages showed streaks of rust and mineral green and a sulfurous yellow. It was gouged and riven periodically by the rare, violent rains; meanwhile blowing dust and sand filled in some cracks, beveled and stripped others. Nothing electronic or mechanical could long survive here, without an elaborate support and resupply system. A branch research facility in this environment would be, in the kindest view, difficult.

She was following a zig-zag path, crossing the shallower gulches, threading between the steeper ones, trying to get nearer the slow, spiraling column. She heard a hitch, a breath out of rhythm, in Kapu's song, before she saw the sudden burst of black wings climbing away into the sky, then the body they left behind. There was no way for her to go around, and when she glanced apprehensively at Kapu he only lifted his hand again, straight ahead, so she slowed to a crawl. The cleats made a soft, regular thud and stirred up a thin veil of dust which failed to hide a horror she could not stop herself seeing.

The body looked like a child's, so thin were its limbs, but she could not tell for sure because the head was detached, lying only a step away, the skull beaten in and then hollowed out. The chest, too, gaped open, and the vultures had strung its contents over the stones. She thought she was going to be sick, wanted to be sick, but Kapu's singing had grown softer and its steadiness, on the border of silence, kept her from crying out or retching.

She had been seeing Pobla corpses for weeks, thousands of them. She thought, after the horror of her first few days at the field hospital, that nothing would ever shake her that badly again. Dissecting, analyzing, laboring furiously to understand, she could look at the procession of skeletons without flinching. But this was different, immediately. She was looking at a murder, at the grotesque mark of some colossal, mindless malignancy.

They came to the tip of the spine of rock they had been following, found themselves on the brink of a deep, serpentine canyon. There were a few pools of water near the opposite wall, and around these were clusters of the vultures, bowing and strutting over their feast. Tiffany could see that their leathery heads were slick, see how they waddled in satiety. There were many bodies strewn on the banks of the water holes, and others here and there along the canyon floor in both directions, as if the victims had tried to run away.

Kapu was barely whispering now, but there was no variation in the beat of his chant. Tiffany was afraid to look at him. She was concentrating herself wholly on simple, physical acts, on the mechanical recording of data. Take a reading on the slope. Set anchor spike. Prepare to belay down the wall. Open a voice-activated file. She was blinking rapidly, did not take time to wipe away the tears.

Two hundred and eighteen feet down they came to the canyon floor. She stopped the winch, unhooked them from the line and staked it. The shadows of the big birds were shuttling over them, crossing and recrossing. Tiffany hesitated only a moment, then switched the locks off and retracted the side doors. Regulations called for rad suits and sidearms, after notifying a standby backup, but she had no intention of observing these rules now, She stepped into the heat of the day, the fine scrim of dust blowing around them, taking only a remote microphone for her audio log. Kapu swung out on the other side of the Bantam and tottered toward the pools, which shuddered in the wind.

The old man had altered his chanting to a higher, more resonant pitch, something like the drone of insect. Tiffany kept a respectful distance behind him, mumbling into her microphone. The corpses were all like the one they had seen on the way in. Decapitated, the rib cages sprung open. The carnage was methodical, maniacal. She logged the number around the pools: twenty-seven corpses. Male and – she bit her lips and corrected herself. Men, women, and children. A massacre.

Kapu spent a few moments beside each body, singing to it, and then sat down abruptly, and was silent. Tiffany had gone on a little longer, whispering her estimate that the killing had been done less than forty-eight hours ago, before her voice faltered too. There was only the sighing of the wind, a hiss of wings and an occasional croak overhead. This world felt utterly empty, an emptiness somehow as terrifying as the ghastly scene before them.

She had asked, almost the first thing, why his people were drifting in hordes, mindless, dying without a sound. Were they not cannibals, could they not hide and survive as they had before? They had lost themselves, he had answered. But there at the hospital, the stacked corpses outside and hundreds dying in holding pens, he had seemed less affected than he was by the sight of this slaughter and dismemberment. What was the difference?

Kapu spoke abruptly, as if he had heard her. "No it hem. Kill far kill." He made the motion of stuffing something into his mouth. "No it hert. It shidow. Lak piksi."

He meant, Tiffany guessed, that certain Pobla were now spiritual cannibals. They consumed another's shadow to enhance the power of their own. What piksis do. She had colored at that, had taken a moment to dismiss her irritation. And in another moment she was hot with shame, even self-loathing. Her obsessive sampling, avid research, grandiose theorizing in search of her magical gene – what were they, but a feeding upon lost souls? She had told herself it was all for knowledge, for science, to blaze a path into the heart of the most ancient mysteries – those surrounding the human psyche – yet what was she, after all, but another ghoul, advancing her career and her species? Locating "subjects" and sucking out of them every nanoseme of information?

It struck her all at once that she wanted to do more than identify the magical gene: she wanted to subjugate it, control it, make it into a *resource*. She almost gagged. It was not mere death that was so fearful. One could bear even the horror of these gutted and rotting forms scattered around them; but to see your faith annihilated, your self, your *kind*, the very ground of all being devoured by an alien thing that grows fat—

Kapu had tilted up his face and was singing now into the sky. His hands were weaving and floating about, and after a few seconds she realized the vultures were settling again, some walking stiffly with wings extended, as if mimicking his gestures. The whacking of wings as they alighted, the rustling of feathers, went on until almost all the birds were down, prancing slowly and stiffly, or hunched around Kapu. Only a half-dozen remained aloft, very high, moving on invisible spokes.

Kapu's insect-song was nearly inaudible, interrupted now by an occasional, grunting cluck. Tiffany had the impression the old one was offering some tribute, like a choice bit of offal, and the vultures were appraising it. They lurched and peered in a fashion she might have thought comical, in other circumstances. Kapu watched intently, and then, in one breath, stopped singing and dropped his hands.

Several of the birds opened their beaks in a chorus of hisses, and made short, symbolic jabs in Kapu's direction. A moment later they began to lumber and flap into the air again, some rising into the spiral pattern and others veering away to the south. Three of the largest banked down to perch on a ledge midway up the canyon wall behind them. Kapu turned toward her and beckoned. She clutched the useless microphone and plodded toward him, her face still wet from the tears.

"Sayat goway," he said, pointing after the broken line of birds moving south. "Op dere more." His finger swung to indicate the three black hulks on the ledge.

Tiffany could see now the cracks along the ledge, some large enough to qualify as narrow caves. Could there be more bodies hidden there? Painfully, using a staff he had picked up from among the corpses, Kapu got to his feet and moved toward the steep, stone wall. She did not see how one so decrepit could climb to the shelf, a good twenty meters above them.

Yet the moment he put a hand on the bare rock, the old one was surer of his footing, more agile than she was. Her bulk made it difficult to balance on the tiny ledges and crevices that seemed to appear spontaneously in Kapu's path; and she soon found herself too afraid to look down. Kapu was humming to her, something reassuring and encouraging. *You can do it*, she imagined him saying, *if I can*. She heard him laugh softly.

An incongruous sound in this valley of death, and even more so because he appeared to be simply gazing into the rock. But when she reached the same place, she saw there was a small lizard the color of slate cleaving to the vertical surface, its throat inflated. Kapu was nodding and beaming down at her. "*Apati*, he hissed. "He show. Mek sem."

Tiffany nodded back, a careful tilt and return of her chin. Make same. Good advice, no doubt, but she certainly did not have the best shape for such imitation. Still, pressing herself flat to the warm stone, her fingers spread wide and digging for purchase, she wormed and wriggled her way to the shelf, which was just wide enough to sit on, if she let her feet protrude over the edge. She leaned back against the stone to catch her breath, and heard the sound.

A throb so faint she thought at first it was her own heart, but the beat was too slow. It came from the left, and her eyes began to pry quickly along the ledge. The three vultures were gathered before the largest of the narrow caves, and she guessed the sound came from there, from within. Kapu signed her to stay a few steps behind him, and began to move sidewise along the ledge. Holding her breath, she followed, clinging spread-eagled to the rock face.

At the mouth of the opening, Kapu called out, and there was an answering cry from within. The throbbing went on, recognizable now as the hollow percussion of a drum. They entered, and before her eyes could adjust, Tiffany saw only dim shapes amid fiery tracers and whorls, after-images of the sun-glare outside. She heard, however, grunts of astonishment and alarm, then a squeal she could not identify, though she was certain it came from no human throat.

Kapu was speaking rapidly, explaining and placating. Several times she heard the words *piksi* and *tagak*, in connection with her name (*Fannhee*, as the old man pronounced it). There was a sharp clatter, another squeal, and even as she recognized the sound she saw that the largest of the shapes in the gloom was a horse. A very small person hung at its neck, while on the cave floor sat two men, one with the drum between his legs; and beside them crouched another animal, a desert cat whose black lips were peeled back in a snarl too soft for her to hear.

The cave was actually a narrow, miniature canyon whose walls had collapsed to make a gothic arch over the entrance. This crack in the stone receded into a very dim glow, which Tiffany guessed would lead to a maze of similar cracks, perhaps with connecting passages. She was familiar with the sophistication of the Pobla underground settlements, which had been fully disclosed only in the notorious New Broom operation in the preceding year.

She knew as well – everyone knew – about the unusual symbiotic alliances among species in the Wasteland, with the Pobla often at the center of the network. She had seen for herself the instant bond between Buster and the ancient, hermaphroditic Pobla who, Kapu claimed, he had sent. But unlike snakes or owls or dungbeetles, the horse had been, for more than a century, a textbook *negative* example. It was one of the few domesticated animals (the pig was another) that had reverted to a feral state, had become a useless, ill-tempered scavenger whose survival depended on a vigilant avoidance of all things human.

This animal, for example, was trembling all over, its head thrown back and nostrils wide, breathing like a bellows as it stared at her with white-ringed eyes. But then the slender girl beside the horse, fingers knotted in its mane, also looked frightened out of her wits. The man without the drum was also uneasy, crouched on his heels and looking ready to bolt. Tiffany had remained still, two strides behind Kapu, smiling tentatively, but this stance did not seem to reassure anyone.

Piksi pomasu tagak. That meant something like important doctor-woman. Or witch, perhaps. What was she supposed to do, then? She had only her microphone, mindlessly recording and transmitting, and a little beltpack of common medicines . . . The cat was coiled on its haunches now, its growl high-pitched and sounding to Tiffany melancholy and desperate. Kapu had sidled back towards her, still talking, and he touched her lightly on the arm.

"Da clos," he whispered. "Tek off."

She kept smiling, whispered, "*What*?"

"Tek off clos, plis." He plucked at her sleeve.

It was true everyone else was naked or nearly so. A first principle of anthropology. Of good manners. Gently, in spaced increments, wincing because they all reacted to the sound, she unzipped. They stared, fascinated, as her generous bulk began to emerge from the straps and panels that contained it. Her areolae were dark and rich, prominently and generously mounted; her hips and buttocks were firm, despite their mass. She was a very big woman, undeniably and irrevocably, and long ago had resigned herself to the fact. She had even taken a perverse delight in her dance exercises, giving her heft a surprising resilience and momentum, an imperial cetacean grace.

So Tiffany braved their rapt and fearful stares, feeling as if she were metamorphosing on the spot into a pink diplodocus. Then, just before she let down her panties, she heard Kapu exclaim again, and felt simultaneously a tickling up her backbone. She froze. There was a soft chorus of admiration from her little gallery of spectators.

"Apati!"

She swiveled her head, trying to look over her shoulder and down her back. There, indeed, was a tiny, wrinkled knob with a slit of mouth above leathery jowls, peering at her from eyes like chips of dark, glittering glass. The reptile must have come aboard as she inched up the sheer face of the canyon, clung to her fatigues with its little claws even as she tried to imitate it. The creature darted now as far as her shoulder. The prickly scales of underbelly and tail were a dry, light caress, giving her goosebumps.

Kapu said something and laughed. When she looked again he was seated opposite the man with the drum. The young woman and the horse remained alert and poised, but the whole group seemed to have relaxed a few degrees. There was curiosity now in their staring, even a measure of something like respect. The lizard, clearly, had influenced their estimation of Tiffany. She moved very carefully, back straight, and lowered herself to sit beside Kapu. She was conscious of the reptile, like a small, calloused hand, resting at the base of her neck.

The young man tapping at the drum was also chanting under his breath. It was a sound like the murmuring of bees, incessant, with complex overtones and harmonic resonances. Tiffany guessed, from the concentration of Kapu's expression, that the singer was recounting the massacre. She noticed he was as emaciated as the refugees, but full of a subtle, electric energy focused within. He alone seemed to take no notice of her. He was caught up in his story, seeing something else beyond the group before him. Perhaps seeing with the third eye. She wondered if his pineal gland showed the enlarged cells, if he had the genetic predisposition to the ecstatic "infection" – as her old professor Goldbarth had suggested in his strange, last letter.

Kapu began then a hesitant translation of this *spikstory*. A few broken words, many gestures, and a certain look, eyes glowing like moons behind the clouds of his cataracts. It was indeed an account of horror, and Tiffany had the peculiar sense that she was being made witness to it. Despite Kapu's crude vocabulary, only fragments of a narrative, the scene grew so vivid she found her heart battering inside her ribcage. The old one's hands were shaping for her the whole settlement: the women among their baskets, preparing food, children playing, the men twisting grass rope or singing over the drum . . .

Then the invaders came. The man beside the drummer took over now. He was young and, she could see, sleek and well built. His hair was oddly cropped, and there were many scars patterning his arms and ribs. His expression was vacant, exhausted, trance-like. *Sayat*, she heard again and again, *Sayat*. A company of warriors, faces streaked with blood, wielding spears and clubs. *Pakishta Pobla*, the drummer hissed. "Bed Pobla," Kapu echoed softly. "Bery bery bed Pobla." She was aware that they were all – even she – confronting now the most unspeakable horror. There were no words. Hands mimed clubs on the heads of children, stroked as knives across the throats of women – split and ripped and dashed—

Tiffany thought she could bear no more, that she had yielded to a panic that would carry her into insanity. The young man chanted on, his voice choked. This Sayat and his followers were howling with glee, dancing with joy, as they went about their butchery. They held up the heads and spoke to them, made faces at them, rolled them and booted them for sport. Tiffany then understood, that this young man with vacant eyes had been one of that company, one of Sayat's band. Of course! Of course! That was the final unbearable illumination!

Sayat and his followers knew their victims, had once sat at the fire with them, laughed and played together. They were . . . the drummer, Kapu was signing to her, the drummer here writhing and moaning . . . the drummer and Sayat . . . the drummer and Sayat were – brothers!

Tiffany saw herself momentarily from outside, at a great distance, like the miniature image in a reversed telescope. The naked pink diplodocus, sobbing over a handful of hollow corpses, soon to be bones under the drifting sand. The remains of savage creatures held by her scientific peers to be a nasty, degenerate species declining into extinction. Colonel White and Professor Goldbarth would probably agree on that much. And as for her . . .

Had she been stretching herself further and further to bridge an unbridgeable contradiction? Her respect for old texts, her imaginative reconnection of myth and science – the pathology of vision, the genetics of mystery – this whole fabrication of her intelligence, meant to dignify and redeem (she had believed!) these beings – had it all been an elaborate mask to keep her from a final transfiguration, the annihilation of her own selfhood? She thought then of the avatar, the Dracula legend. For disease and starvation were nothing, compared to this terror of discovering that one's brother or sister – or father, mother, lover, child – had become a grinning ghoul. A thing without a shadow. And a terror beyond that – that one's own shadow was devoured, and one's self become the devourer . . .

In her bewildered heart, Tiffany could find nothing to say. She could no longer follow the agonizing story, no longer bear her own imaginings. She caught her breath to moan aloud, but before she

181

could utter a sound they numbed her again, made the whole world shift treacherously around her. They began to laugh. *To laugh!*

The young man was pounding his breast, triumphant. He had awakened! His shadow had come back! He was Ap, he was Pobla, the old Pobla, before Sayat! So, he gestured, he had run and hid, found a crack that led finally to this cave, where he found the drummer . . . asleep! It was his pantomime of this discovery that provoked demented laughter, his portrayal of astonishment followed by a mournful dilemma: how to gently rouse an innocent to the presence of disaster?

The drummer resumed the story again, and Tiffany gathered he had withdrawn to this spot to practice drum chants and had fallen asleep and begun to dream. His dream had been good, very good, and an important dream. Again Tiffany heard *Pahane*, the name for the Drager boy, and *naku*, a term Kapu had trouble rendering, but which she thought meant tribal identity, *Volksgeist*, or the like. The dream was good, the dream was true, but it faded. He had been shaken awake to a nightmare. So he kept drumming, as he drummed now, to restore the first dream. And thus it had happened! The great birds had signaled, as they used to do, and brought Kapu and this stranger, who surely could return Pahane to them, the mother and the child, as it was promised.

He ceased drumming and the silence was like a final hammer-blow on the great gong of the world. He raised his eyes, still luminous with hope, to stare at Tiffany. They were all staring at her. She felt open and defenseless and ripe as a new continent before a conquering horde. Her own soul – or shadow if that's what it was – fluttered in alarm, flew everywhere and nowhere.

"Hep," Kapu said, so softly she barely caught it. "Nid hep."

It seemed to Tiffany that her flesh burned away under his look, this plea for help. The heavy pink body was gone, and in the space it had occupied something else shimmered. Kapu, too, was only a husk, a bit of gauze before a dark radiance that flowed and shifted, a plasm between them that conveyed everything perfectly. He would stay here with the others who would drum and sing while they waited. She would begin organizing the research station nearby. The preposterous had become all at once a certainty in her mind. She would bring Pahane and Tima and the child to them, somehow.

"Yes," she whispered. "Yes. Na."

All at once the cat yawned and groaned, got to its feet and slunk around her on its way out of the cave. She felt the lizard scramble from her shoulder along her arm, then spring from her wrist to the ground. Kapu took a long sliver of stone from beside the fire, drew it over the heel of one hand. Then he reached to take Tiffany's hand, and she watched the blade glide along the base of her thumb, felt the hot wire of the cut.

He raised her hand, covered the bright wound with his mouth; and when he lifted his own dripping palm she met it with her lips, found and swallowed blood. The raw, cloying taste brought her back into her body with a shock. She was part of something quite new for her – a conspiracy. She saw it as inevitable. The lab she would build, her "research", her *life* would be dedicated to this cult of an approaching messiah. Her mind brushed the Dracula story again, and Doctor Goldbarth's letter. Curse or infection or illumination; whatever, she had it.

CHAPTER EIGHTEEN

The dumpsters were half in shadow, because one of the overhead floodlights had gone out. The organic unit was the smallest size (four to a rigload), because the Trencherman was a hole-in-the-wall café, and not very prosperous. Only twice had they seen a cart whiz out of the kitchen with a cargo of refuse. They were observing from a BulletBus stop on the main avenue, and hadn't been able to tell whether the attendant was resetting the alarm.

"Ah shit," Humper breathed. "D'sizjun time." He looked mournfully at Tyrone. The two of them occupied a bench, while their students loitered behind. It was late and the others waiting in nearby alleys or hunched under a loose drain grate would be restless.

"We wrong, Sandy fry us," Tyrone said, "but these slicks got to learn." He turned his head a fraction of an inch, to indicate Ronnie and Tima and Batboy. "Let's poke it."

Humper sighed and lifted one hand. The three acolytes drew nearer, hovered at his shoulder. "Clean up, now, and get on the muthufuckn channel. You gonna watch close, learn the move. Takin' a d'sizjun, evah pro and evah slick know what goin' down."

Ronnie was Pahane now, whenever he wished, so he listened mostly to what ran beneath Humper's words. He could hear the anxiety, the doubt about this whole mission. And he could smell the amusement and mischief in Tima, whose shoulder touched his.

Humper and Tyrone had a conflicting, dual duty: they were supposed to score the dumpster and at the same time teach a trade, with minimum risk to their pupils. It had already been impressed upon the newcomers that without a scam they would have no identity here, would stand out as starkly as egrets in a flock of ravens.

Almost everyone, in the Omaly world, had to have a scam. A Nonumb, by definition, was raw and exposed, possessed no codes, no complex digital identity, no deck of plastic slices that gave access to the goods. In any foray aboveground, one needed camou, a stolen wallet or a garb and manner that looked genuine. Below, one was defined by one's skill in such trickery, by one's reputation as a supplier, entertainer, or predator. A great mistress of fakery, like Eva, held a very high position: and as new recruits in her band they were expected to earn their keep.

So they were out to establish new selves again, and there was always risk in that. Batboy, light as air on his feet and alert to the night, was the lookout and would be scanning the darkness for any approach. Pahane and Tima, as notorious political fugitives, were only supposed to observe. "You just shadows," Tyrone had said sternly – at which the two of them exchanged a swift grin.

"Could be hot," Humper went on, as if talking to himself. "Dangerous. Place look jus' right. Kind the Man love. Setup. You recall?"

They all made a low noise of assent. Humper had already explained how restaurants had to send organic waste to Compost Centers, which tested randomly for quality and decay time, as well as the common toxics and bacteria. Whenever a manager was buying substandard produce or doctoring overripe meat, he had an alternative – to leave the dumpster disarmed and let the Nonumbs empty it overnight. The problem was, there would be no overt signal. An eatery could be heavily fined or lose its franchise for deliberately inviting scavengers. On the other hand, a business already charged with such a crime might earn clemency by agreeing to bait a trap.

So the custom was for an attendant to leave the lock imperfectly secured, the alarm disengaged. If you had your people ready with carts and bag coats, the dumpster could be emptied in a few minutes. Problem was, the smack team couldn't tell for sure until they broke the lid free. Sometimes searchlights speared the raiders and a squad of StreetSweeper cops erupted from the dumpster or the back of the restaurant. Then everybody had to scat.

"Nevah know," Tyrone said. "But people hungry, man. Got to smack sometime." He shrugged.

"True." Humper set his hands on his knees, preparing to rise. "Nobody know. And dey hungry, like you say. So let's do it. You slicks pay mind, we check it out."

"I can find out for you," Tima said then, as the two men stood up. She was diminutive, shrunken in her greatcoat and boots, her voice soft as the brush of a wing; yet the men stopped. Pahane smiled to himself, for he had seen this reaction before.

Humper turned, slowly and carefully. "Say what? How you gone do that, girl? You what, sixteen years old?"

"Bring me there, I will show you."

There was a pause. Pahane could see her *kubi*, like a blowing flame, shape the space around her into a funnel so that the others could see nothing else, wanted to see nothing else. They were held, transfixed, by mere darkness hunched in a coat, a glitter beneath the brim of an old hat. A vehicle went by. Far away a siren could be heard briefly. A couple came out of the restaurant and moved down the street, the woman laughing.

"You'll see," he said then, grinning. "Let's go. Walk on over there."

All four of them moved together. Humper was still waking up, his mouth working a little. Tyrone looked frightened, his glance skating over Tima as if she were a bright light too near. "Juju, girl got juju," he whispered, "now what we doin'?"

"Watch," Pahane said.

It was easy working with these teachers, and Tyrone especially. The man had many piksi habits, like all Omalys, but Pahane was sure the corrected ears and nose indicated mixed blood; Tyrone seemed to sense, and yearn to recover, his departed shadow.

They moved into the alley and approached the dumpster, the two men shaking their heads and blinking like roused somnambulists. Humper lingered near the avenue, as they had originally scripted, because of his more or less presentable suit. Pahane and Tima pretended to be an unrelated pair, regular trashies cruising the shadows for overlooked scraps. The siren seemed to be drawing nearer. Tyrone licked his lips and peered at Batboy, still at the bus stop, but there was no signal. "What she doin' now?" he hissed. "What—"

Tima had tottered all at once directly to the dumpster. With one hand she braced herself against the steel wall, while with the other she clawed under her coat at her crotch. An old man, perhaps drunk, was urinating unsteadily, mumbling and crooning to himself. Pahane was concentrating with her, knowing what it took to bend the world even this minute degree, to squeeze one's shadow into a single new form, among its infinite possibilities.

He alone understood her whining song; he alone saw something more than an old man pissing, saw two flakes of dull light skitter along the extended, braced arm. The flakes stopped just short of the mumbling lips, then flexed, rocked, and flattened again. The antennae he could not make out, but they would be stroking, tapping, vibrating. As the old one finished and reached for his zipper, the roaches skittered back and were gone behind a flange of the dumpster's lid.

Lurching away from the wall, Tima reeled one step in their direction and then the world unwarped again. It was like the sudden angle of light out of water into air. The old man was gone with a shrug, and she was among them, talking.

"Just food," she said with a wrinkled nose. "The alarm's down. Chicken's pretty ripe and they want to boost out some old bread made with hot milk. No cops."

Humper and Tyrone did not seem to hear. They were staring at the glistening, steaming pool by the dumpster, a finger of it wandering even now toward a drain in the middle of the alley. Pahane laughed and jigged to one side, so that the light chains around his neck rang.

"Just a matter of practice," Tima said. "It's all in the lips." She smiled disarmingly. "Not much distance, of course."

"Well," Tyrone said finally, with quiet reverence, "I say you one juju muthufuckuh, an' I goin' along, any talk you talk."

"Fine." Tima's smile widened and took on a certain cool glee. "So you go'n' poke, or you go'n' talk all night?"

Tyrone grinned, tentative at first and then in a wide, white slash. In three strides he was at the dumpster, and Batboy had given his impossibly high, thin shriek. They heard the shuffle and slap of many feet on concrete, and before the dumpster lid had grated against its backrest the tied plastic sacks were blooming out of the steel maw and tumbling into wheeled carts or vanishing again under long, loose coats, while they, the smackers, stepped away smartly, pretending surprise and apprehension at this outrage, until they were well along the avenue, then down a cross-street where they could exchange surreptitious hand-slaps and even do a little version of what the Omalys termed an old boogie.

"Jus' fine," Humper pronounced, and then, like a bird, turned his head but not his eyes slightly away from them. "But who teachin' and who studyin', 'round here?"

As a mark of his new respect, Tyrone left them with a special cigarette. It was not back, but a cheap relaxant which had long ago gone through the medicinal-forbidden cycle and then been forgotten, supplanted by more modern pharmaceuticals. They smoked it later that evening, in the larger apartment Eva had assigned them. At the first whiff, they recognized *bitsa*, the "handleaf" which was burned by the basketful at many Pobla ceremonies.

"One good piksi idea," Tima said, hollowing her cheeks and half-closing her eyes as she drew on the cigarette. "Putting just a little bit in a tube like this."

Ronald only hummed idly. He was Ronald because he was watching the end of the news, just before the Winger show. The holo had been hung from the waterpipes crossing the ceiling, so he lay flat on the bed looking up. Tima sat on one of Eva's old fur coats spread directly on the concrete floor.

Most of the news was about the refugee crisis and the election, but again these events were tied into their own story, which had developed an exciting new twist only a week ago. Out of nowhere, ex-superagent Feiffer had claimed credit for the breakout and announced a guerilla assault on the bio and eco policies of the NorthAm government. So an all-out effort to find the fugitives was supposedly under way: teams of investigators combing the streets, every rumor tracked, and every known ecoradical group under surveillance.

"Ratshit," Ronald said. "Not even convincing ratshit."

He accepted the cigarette from Tima, inhaled from it. Since their flight, no station had mentioned the abandoned delivery van, or even hinted at a connection between the Thorgs and Omalytown. A deliberate evasion of evidence, they assumed, and now they had confirmation.

"Is this what piksis do when they are married?"

Ronald blew out sharply. His eyes still feeding on the box, he extended the smouldering stub into the air between them. "Stockwell doesn't want the embarrassing stuff to come out, okay, so it's a pretend dragnet. But they would *never* hire PJ to run a decoy covop, especially one with an Ecomini connection. And now we have this mysterious offer. Whose scam is that? What do they want?" When she did not answer, he glanced quickly at her. She was sitting perfectly still, her hair undone and falling in a thick, black bolt to the floor. "What?"

She laughed, raucously. "You answered," she said. "You could answer your own question, too. It's always the same answer." She pinched away what remained of the cigarette and rubbed it out on the concrete.

"Control, you say. What all piksis want. But they didn't offer Eva big money. Didn't ask anything except were you actually pregnant and could she get a message to us. And the message was 'How can we help you?' What kind of control is that?"

She cocked her head sardonically at him.

"What? You are *always* doing that." He made a madman's grin, and reached as if to throttle her, but remained flat on his back. "I wish I had been able to see the guy."

"Smell."

"Yeah, okay. Better. Anyway, Eva says he came on very polite, but very sure of himself, like a diplomatic envoy. So they already think we're down here, whoever they are."

"Everybody knows we're down here." Tima yawned and got up.

"In a general way, maybe so. But the Administration wouldn't want us back, we know that."

"O-o-oh no. Bery bad."

They laughed together, at her accent and at the thought of what ruin their stories – especially the holos – would wreak on Stockwell's chances in the election.

"They could just hire some darkside team to wipe us. And if it was the Progs, they would simply buy us alive and feed us to the tab shows, right?"

She shrugged, and took his drum from its nail on the wall.

"So who is it? And why did they get PJ into it?"

She twiddled her fingers on the taut head, a light parody of a portentous roll. "The riddle, the secret, the mystery . . . "

He sat up and looked at her, frowning a little. "Well?"

She laughed again and rapped a beat with her knuckles. "You piksis are funny. Everything is a knot to be untied. I don't know who these people are, but they don't want any mystery either." She tossed the drum at him. "That's why they got PJ. So they can make up our story for us. That's why Cynthia and her friends are so upset. The Thorgies thought *they* were telling it. Now you answer me a question, and then do me some rockenroll." She yawned and began unbuttoning her baggy old-man's shirt. "Who sent those horses you dream about?"

He had forgotten the holo overhead. He was floating in the handleaf, yet concentrated wholly on Tima. By themselves, his fingers and the heel of his hand began a soft, urgent rhythm on the rim of the drum. The dreams had become clearer, and they always assumed the horses were running toward them, but he realized they had never spoken the obvious.

He grinned suddenly. "She sent them, our little witch, big as a mouse now." He went through a swift run, a complicated but free-ranging weave of resonances, his speculations and ponderings of a few moments ago scattering like leaves before a gale. Of course it was so: all of them – the Cons and Progs and Ecos and darksiders and the Pobla and the dream horses – they had all been summoned, by *wonakubi* in the end, but for this time and this place by the little knot of cells they had made, an egg of light mighty as a star, their witch-mouse . . .

And Tima – how happy he was that she was laughing again! This night they had only stolen a bin of half-rotted food, a little *tchat* raid, and breathed the smoke of Pobla ceremony, but it was enough to make them forget the bad time at the border. The Pobla had that strength, to go beyond suffering, in one clean stride . . .

She was smiling back at him, stepping now out of her trousers and flicking them with her toes to a far corner of the room. He always liked watching her come out of her clothes, because she left behind every trace of her piksi pose; she emerged all at once, with perfect grace, as a slight movement will break a fully formed lynx or deer out of a pattern of shadow and light.

Her head was thrown back and she crouched a little, swaying to the pulse of the drum. She was imitating, playfully, the dances they had seen the Nonumbs doing around their fire-barrels. That was, he realized, also the source of the song he was reshaping into a richer, but softer and more sinuous form. He knew these melodies and rhythms were themselves reworkings of more ancient songs, chants from the old continent from whence both his and Tima's ancestors had come. To rock or to roll, one of the old books revealed, simply meant to fuck.

Tima moved as he drummed, and around her a light was gathering, tinged with violet, for her *kubi* was concentrating in her bones. Her breasts swayed, full and tight, the nipples ringed by darkness. The lithe body had now a softer outline, and she moved with a careless new power, undulant and luxurious.

He was fascinated, his hands flying as she shook and curved and pumped; he had the startling sensation that the drum had become her body, the two fused into a pure energy that was stroke and sound and a breathtaking excitement, running like a tongue of fire up his spine. She was beside the bed now, her hair around her shoulder to run between her breasts and fan out over the writhing fork of her body.

191

"Tonpah tohanaku . . . vasa ya vasa ni . . . " she was crooning to him, her voice charged and thick with a nectar new to him, and he answered with the insistent, fervent syllables in his hands. His hands were on her, in her, and she was around him, over him, rippling and convulsing, though they were joined only at the eyes, a ray between them that burned away the whole world.

His body had turned incandescent, pouring through his hands into her, and the drum was no longer speaking in percussion alone but as a seamless surge and drive that took him into her, bent her to him. Her hips, at the level of his eyes, began working in a sweet, parallel complexity: first the long, regular, hooking strokes of the oldest rhythm, then with her back in a taut arch, a series of rapid circular pumps, and then a final thrust, swift and voracious, that gave way to a bucking shudder, which in turn worked through a syncopated counterpoint to settle again into the old rhythm, but at a heightened intensity.

He could hear himself moaning under her honeyed coo and knew a fleeting, fiendish joy. They could make *naku* this way, with the power of the drum alone. Something had happened to him, since Pahane's shadow moved in. He was not only Pobla, not only *tagak*, but had also the divine disorder of the chanters and counters. For him play and music and love were becoming one force, a fever joining him to Tima and both to their people, spinning everything into dance.

But just this sliver of reflection caused a divergence from their momentum, troubled the perfect harmony. He tried to find the beat again and could not. A moment later he groaned and smacked the drum impatiently and tossed it aside, but before he could roll to his feet she was straddling him, laughing. She uttered a sympathetic, humorous whimper of inquiry, and picked at his belt buckle. Her hips still rocked a slow rhythm, and she let the black column of her hair swing over his face, tickling him and making him sneeze.

"Wait, goddam it . . . " he began, and tried to blow aside the skein of hair. She threw her head back and laughed, and then so did he, a laugh as free and loud as her own. He relaxed, breathing slower and more deeply, and let her quick fingers open his pants and strip them off. Then she was settling on him, but tentative and delicate as a hummingbird or butterfly, and he quieted his urge to take her buttocks and reassert the pace of the drum.

She enfolded him gently, yet with a supple strength, so that even wet and slick she could hold him firm, worry him, even lift him slightly. She had found a slower, more deliberate rhythm, and moved so softly he felt it as the very pulse of his blood; and her motion was even more complex – slight tremors and twists and contractions that shaped his breathing, and hers, into a pattern of sobs and grunts and sighs . . .

They had never before been so quiet and ecstatic, so able to float and flutter inside each other. So many times they had been at each other like big cats, but this was the long, slow, intricate dance of certain insects or snails. He was aware – and knew she was too – that this change was because of the new life between them, the little twist of flesh where infinite darkness had whirled into itself, had swallowed itself and become a seed of light. And they were the bridge that sheltered and nourished that seed; they were celebrating it; they were together and they were one and everything was one and the light was breaking now all around them in these slow, soft, infinite waves . . .

In four extended, powerful contractions she emptied him. Their tears ran together and they breathed as one, so deeply they shuddered. They had burned into nothing, a lovely nothing, and lay heavy and still as earth, and went on breathing until they were in the even, hypnotic harmony of utter exhaustion. He was just tipping into sleep, a black shimmer like her hair, when a shift of light on the wall roused him. He glanced up, at the holo, which was still running though he had apparently flicked off the sound.

Elongated in his angle of view, the image loomed over them. It was the famous yakshow host, his expression one of demonic exhilaration. The lips were clipping and spitting inaudible words, and in Ronald's last flare of consciousness he was able, without effort, to divine their meaning, which made his own mouth twitch in a smile.

"Oh we know," the Fat Man was saying, *"we know what they're up to, we know what they're doin'* . . . *"*

CHAPTER NINETEEN

"There you are, sir. Enjoy your stay."

The captain grazed his temple with cupped hand, and the launch pulled away, moving with a barely audible whisper over the glassy sea. Old timbers creaked, a gull flapped aloft with an irritable squawk, and Josh could smell tar and a hint of rotten fish as he made his way along the dock toward the beach.

Except for the great white yacht standing a half-mile offshore and the little dunejumper waiting for him on the beach, the place was a perfect version of a tropic port abandoned a century ago. The sheds on the dock were boarded up, a few derelict sailing craft, caked with barnacles, bumped the pilings in the swells, and a pair of tall, ragged palms made a dramatic statement at the crown of the highest dune.

He supposed there were surveillance lenses buried in some of the sheds, or lurking behind the black portholes of the derelicts, but you would never see them. Just as you never saw the metal detectors or alarm switches, never thought of the polite launch captain or the groundskeepers or valets as security personnel. Everything on Barrelhead's island was rustic, informal, and unobtrusive. Everything was also artifice.

The Great Artificer. Josh smiled, supressed the impulse to wave cheerily. Homer Morphopolous preferred that guests be charmed and taken in. It was not considered good taste to remark how the Island moved, sometimes overnight, to a new location. He slid into the dunejumper, where music was already playing softly and the air was cool and fragrant.

The drive was also part of the beautiful illusion, for the main lodge was actually within walking distance, had there been a direct route. But a road wound cleverly along the coast, skirted tiny, secluded coves and twisted up and then down a couple of cliffs. One got several views of the lodge before one arrived, and passed through several microclimates.

Josh drove rather faster than he meant to, but then this was his fourth trip, and a working conference. He hoped Dorothy had already arrived. The old man liked her a lot and seemed to be willing, in her company, to forego some of the affectations of his paradise. His studio. Josh pursed his lips in a quiet spasm of hilarity. A humble garret. Four hundred and eighty floating acres that ran on the budget of a small nation.

He was breaking away from the water, making the final approach through the desert. The great, clear plastic shields were retracted in this season, when rain was not frequent. Some work was under way, new ravines cut beneath an escarpment, and patches of dense, high grass transplanted among the rocks. An empty insulated cage sat on the edge of a pit ringed by freshly turned earth. Some new specimen, he guessed, was arriving to supplement the Island's remarkable population.

On every visit Josh saw species he had supposed were extinct, including some rather intimidating creatures: a Komodo dragon nearly as big as the jumper, and an anaconda that liked to hang in the low branches of a caoba tree by the swimming pool. These residents were Barrelhead's hobby, but no more exotic than some of the human specimens one might encounter on the Island. The thought made Josh take a couple of deep, measured breaths and focus, for a few seconds, on the Big Zip. Years ago he had done some puja therapy and yoga practice on a lux tour of Pacrim shrines, and he still used certain techniques in stressful situations.

He pulled up in front of the lodge, which on this approach was a rambling portico of adobe brick and handhewn timbers, overgrown with bougainvillaea and trumpetvine. A young man materialized from these trees, ready to whisk the dunejumper away to the underground garage. By the time Josh emerged into the balmy, late-morning air, his valet – the same one he had been assigned before, he noted – was waiting on the steps with a broad, welcoming smile and a bath kit in hand.

A refreshing shower and touch-up shave, a change to jeans, safari shirt, and antelope boots, a glance at the beepscreen on his notebook before he slipped it into a shirt pocket, and Josh was ready for drinks in the courtyard. He would be working, of course, immediately. Morphopolous had a saying: all work and no play makes Homer a very successful sonofabitch. The old man had a lot of sayings. Proverbs that could strike you as imbecilic or profound, depending on the mood. Play is serious business. Creative mind is god. There is no time but showtime. The future is only a first draft. This last was the homily they currently bore, Josh reflected, graven on their asses.

Coming into the sun-dappled courtyard, Josh noted with satisfaction that Dorothy had predicted exactly the seven who would be there. Robert Adamson, the Progressive candidate for President, sat on one side of her, and next to him was another woman, a big, lithe woman with close-cropped hair and blowtorch eyes. Danielle Konrad had accepted their invitation, delivered the day she was released from a minimum-security correctional facility. She now sat calmly only a step away from Dorothy, her former secretary, the woman who had betrayed her and ruined her and was now offering to save her.

He barely remarked the others. Yamaguchi was expected, a drop-by, and of course Tasha was there, curled beside Morphopolous with her notepads and colored pencils strewn before her. In swift and formal sequence, like the preening and dancing of certain flocking, migratory fowl, they went through greetings and small pleasantries, quick handclasps and nods, even as Josh warned them to stay comfortable and took the remaining empty chair. As last arrival, he had an excuse for his demeanor of modest, quiet receptivity. Meanwhile, he worked to figure the import of the constellation at the table.

"Sam was just chatting with us about the situation at the border, Josh. Incredible stuff. So thematic it breaks my heart." Tasha turned so as to regard Barrelhead and at the same time strike Josh with her Nephertitic, ex-supermodel profile. Josh could see on the tablet under her hand a big black loop with red, blue, and yellow lines starring out from it. On the red line was scribbled *prim agress*.

"Let the man relax, let the man listen." Morphopolous smiled at Josh.

It was a slight, ironic, comradely smile, and Josh mirrored it carefully. He was meeting a personal challenge. His employer stirred him at some primal level, for Morphopolous was at once his commanding officer and a father figure. Of course Homer had once been, not unlike Josh himself, a very shrewd young buccaneer, and even now he was an impressive ruin: an oversized head with waves of dark silver hair, the body still athletic and tanned – flesh and skin trimmed and smoothed or replaced until nearly three decades were sloughed away.

What a piece of work, indeed, was this man. A cortex fortified with foetal tissue, a third heart, a baboon liver, and a complex of hormone supplements from several branches of the primate tree. Yet Barrelhead was still the patriarch and master, capable of the startling, perverse maneuver. It made Josh wonder if the old man was proof of the final authority of random change, of divine whim. The arbitrary exercise of great power, even in the service of the most foolish idea, might be a kind of ultimate glory.

"This man is here to do both," he said easily, and cocked his head at Yamaguchi. "Please go on."

The Director of Intelligence and Security for Border Operations in the NorthAm Division of the United Federation of Nations was the only one among them who currently held a permanent position in government. Samuel Yamaguchi was therefore constrained to "chat" as a personal guest, dropping by for a drink and a swim after a visit to his Pacrim homeland.

It was doubtful, Josh thought, that the universe contained anyone less gifted at casual banter than Sam Yam. The Director followed a profession, after all, in which words served mostly to conceal or mislead, but almost never to entertain. Yamaguchi was also unbribable, yet they had turned up in this most secretive of bureaucrats, a yearning to participate in their enterprise. He had become a kind of informal consultant, for the simple pleasure of manipulation; he seemed to enjoy lending authenticity to the most daring of the thrillers being concocted and consumed every day on the planet.

After a nod and his version of a smile, Yamaguchi continued his presentation. "I summarize. The holding camps are overcrowded; arrivals are increasing, disposal falling behind. This is of course popular knowledge, because the camps are too large to hide from satscans. The research people are also very anxious. It seems there is an outbreak of some mild disorder of the nervous system, brought by the last few waves to come in. The doctor more or less in charge is unfortunately a bit of a troublemaker. She wants a new post, over the line into the Wastelands." He paused.

"So?" Josh shrugged. "If it's just another flu, then why go to the expense?"

"This," Tasha said in her throaty, dramatic whisper, "is not an ordinary disorder."

Yamaguchi's small smile was quick and efficient, like decapitation. "We encounter an odd side effect. Most visible in the morale of troops assigned to the camps. Exceptional rate of disobedience and malingering, also odd behavior – short attention span, euphoria, even hallucinations."

"As a candidate, I've had a briefing on this," Adamson said with a frown of concern. "Pretty bizarre." He broke into a rueful laugh. "The one about the impromptu naked concert? Dancing some old step called the *jitterbug*?" He puckered his mouth and blew, rolling his eyes, to indicate outrageousness. "We used to get crazy when I was a young recruit. Guys on patrol needed some way to cut loose. But nothing this weird, even coming off a combat situation." He patted a thickening midriff and uttered a cluck of nostalgia, though for what was not entirely clear.

"This assignment is a sanitation assignment," Yamaguchi said, his tone colorless. "There should be no casualties except by accident, and no particular stress. So although there's no appreciable physical impairment – sometimes a rash and mild headache – the psychological impact is significant. We would not be deeply concerned, except for another development, which might require deploying combat-ready units in this very same area."

"We're going to craft new policies for tactical medical response, Sam, and those policies will prevent this kind of epidemic in the future. And provide a boost to the economy at the same time."

Adamson had shifted gears, seeming to take on color and stature as he spoke. Light bronze skin, fair hair, tall and solid, he was a publicist's dream of the bold young reform candidate. His gestures were informal, yet incisive, styled for the holocamera shooting from below, in quarter-profile.

"Let me guess – save Sam a summary – the second development," Josh interrupted, cued by a glance from Morphopolous. They knew all about the new defense package, since Dorothy's team had put most of it together, and no one wanted to hear the speech, however short, that the candidate was about to give. "I heard another rumor, about more conflict among the Pobla. Rather ugly massacres, almost a little war. Flop counts in the thousands, ritual mutilation?"

Josh was pleased to see a flicker of what he took to be respect in Yamaguchi's glance. Dorothy's true identity was master thief: she was at the center of a legendary web of electronic parasites that fed on info from every power center, official and darkside, in the known world. The Secretary from Hell, he thought privately. She had pilfered and shown him holo and 2D images of the atrocities, lifted from Insec's own files.

"I cannot divulge that. Confirm or deny." Yamaguchi waited a long moment, staring at Dorothy, who only raised her eyebrows in innocent curiosity. "But there are important developments. Also, one other matter of discussion with us. Former agent Feiffer has drawn us far too much attention. We are being asked to investigate ourselves, get rid of such opportunists."

Yamaguchi directed a blinkless, lizard-like stare at Josh. "The sum you paid for his holo rights was leaked. Very unfortunate. Mr Feiffer has become popular among certain fringe elements, is perhaps receiving help from high people. These people should be very careful. Mr Feiffer is an unstable and violent person. So. That is all the story available, for now." Very precisely and ceremoniously Yamaguchi lifted his glass, which contained a clear, effervescent liquid and two ice cubes, and sipped from it.

"Sam, that was fascinating and we appreciate it no end. I know there's a lot you can't tell us, and we shouldn't ask, but just the atmosphere you provide is invaluable. I mean it. And if we do something, it will have a documentary edge because of you, and Insec will come off looking *very* good. But listen, you're on a day off, for the love of God!" Morphopolous slapped the table lightly, decisively. "And Bob – I know it's tricky, as an official candidate – but you guys might talk *around* the idea of self-insulating investigations. Especially without the rest of us amateur scribblers to muddle the protocols. So why don't you guys take a walk before lunch – one of those coves on the lee side – and have a heart-to-heart? Rest of us will gossip on with Josh here, until he catches up with the party."

Yamaguchi was already on his feet, and Adamson, though he could not entirely hide his dismay, was not far behind. The candidate understood the virtue of swift, graceful exit, whenever his cash value was to be discussed. The others waved, pretended envy, promised to follow soon. Josh crossed glances with Dorothy for the merest fraction of an instant. Konrad remained, which meant she already belonged in the studio. Dorothy must have arranged it, without asking him. His partner's audacity left him, as usual, both fuming and respectful.

"Well," Morphopolous announced with an exaggerated, humorous sigh, "that was a hint as broad as a bulldozer."

They all laughed.

"I'm flattered," Dorothy said. "We are high people."

"Careful high people," Josh amended. "Sam's right there. Feiffer is working our way now, but he's got to be watched."

"I'm more intrigued by the heating up of this ugly little war," Morphopolous mused. "Thinking back to our first treatment."

Josh appeared thoughtful, as if examining the idea from two or three sides. "The difference is they're attacking their own kind, not us. The public would never go for even light probes over the border, without real provocation. It would take a threat of major atrocity to generate an action. And atrocities are tricky." He looked at Danielle Konrad. "Am I right, Danny?"

"You are right." She did not blink, and gave him a slow, easy smile. She was shameless. Everybody at the table knew Danny Konrad had done her time for plotting atrocity at a new order of magnitude. The actual charges – lying to a Grand Jury, misusing classified info – fooled no one. She had been at the center of the juiciest scandal of the decade, perhaps the century.

It was widely believed that after hyping the Drager story into a defining national myth, she had tried to arrange a darkside wipe of Little Ronnie, even while she was sleeping with his father. And she almost pulled it off, almost capsized the Con government. She worked at that time for a small, highly influential group of info dealers and system developers. She had made one mistake. She had trusted Dorothy Smith, the woman now sitting an arm's length away, smiling sisterly encouragement.

"And even a major atrocity, acceptably lurid, wouldn't displace the refugee problem." Danielle made a wry face. "That's the issue with real specific gravity, especially with this new whiff of possible epidemic."

"Christ, those refugees." Barrelhead exhaled between his teeth. "For a hundred years they hid underground, shocked themselves out at the mere *sight* of a human. And now they crawl for miles to stink up a holding pen or die in a lab."

"Not," Josh commiserated, "great material."

"The Holocaust overtone would be a possible angle," Morphopolous mused, as if he hadn't heard. "Except that they are degenerates."

"Major guilt," Dorothy said cheerfully. They all looked at her. "The dominator feels debased. A superior warrior needs a noble adversary, not a skeleton begging for euthanasia."

"Of course," Tasha said, "that's obvious." She picked up a yellow pencil, stroked it irritably over her tablet. "Guilt is always part of the tragic mix. Wavershaft knows that, it's figuring in, it's a factor, but—"

"Now, now," Morphopolous said with a little burble of laughter. "Ladies. I just got carried away, thinking back to when we had a simpler thing going, our old Western movie as Dorothy once called it." He seemed wistful for a moment.

"Was a great script," Josh sighed. "Absolutely made for Bob Adamson. Young leader standing tall, hurling back the savage hordes, making a desert bloom. But now the wily natives just lie down and die. Or massacre each other. And stink. So I see no way to wayne it now."

"But what a shame to waste a war!" Danielle interrupted. "I'm sorry, Josh, I haven't had exposure to such stimulating talk for six months, so I can't contain myself. But is there anything like armed conflict, when it comes to zesty roles for a NorthAm leader? For *generations* we've had only border actions, recon probes, surgical punitive strikes. Even New Broom was just a big search op. Nothing like even a *tiny* war. I mean, what an opportunity!"

Josh grinned at her, teeth clenched. "Yes?"

"And now the refugees no longer fear armored vehicles? And an organized lot of them have started exterminating their own kind?" Danielle frowned prettily.

Dorothy joined in then, wrinkling her brow too. "It almost sounds as if you were saying . . ."

Josh could hear his molars grinding, but he saw the target now. "Of course before the Federation, the developed countries often supplied weapons to . . . "

"Wait. Wait a minute." Morphopolous had planted both fists upon the table, his forearms cording with tension. "Do you see?"

Tasha played her part perfectly, pleading with the intensity of unfeigned ignorance. "See what, milord?"

Homer gazed around the table, a slow sweep of judicious majesty. "The threat is there. A real possibility of deadly conflict. In fact, it is probably inevitable. We just haven't seen it until now."

They joined in a ritual display: they pressed temples with massaging fingertips, appeared to question each other with urgent looks. "You mean . . . " Dorothy began, her voice hushed.

"Arms." Morphopolous sat back in his chair, his hands relaxed, and drummed his fingers on the table top. He favored them with a quiet smile. "Light stuff to begin with. Portable, lo-pro, easy to smuggle.

You might say no one could sink so low. But some evil party will try it, if the little buggers have actually reached the point where they could learn to squeeze a trigger. Then we would *have to* intervene."

"My God, that would be awful." Dorothy had her hands over her face, pressing in. She was, Josh guessed, hiding the upward twist of her mouth.

"Pobla panzers," Josh said. "Genocide. Horrible." He raised his glass to Morphopolous. "And I think you're right, inevitable. Visionary." *Brilliant bitches*, he was thinking, *I'll bet the stuff is already on order*. Beads of moisture were beginning to form at his hairline. This session was turning up too many surprises.

Morphopolous inclined his head in acknowledgment. "Well, my boy," he said expansively, "the future is our first draft, remember. Flexible rewrite is our creative ideal. Barding off the flux and turbulence of every day, inspiration and risk and so forth . . . we need a sketch of this new wrinkle as soon as you can get it out. Also, the more I think about it, opening that Wasteland research station is a good idea. Could be a dramatic location for this kind of thing. Remote outpost and so forth."

He dispatched Josh with a forefinger that mimed the barrel of a handweapon, and then turned to Danielle, genial and avuncular. "I think this young lady would most like to hear about our major plot element, since it was inspired by her own magnificent work." Danielle smiled in self-deprecation. Her lips were moist and slightly parted, her eyes lowered modestly. It was all Josh could do to keep himself from gagging.

"Of course, as you know, we didn't plan that stupid escape – and we intended to go with Stockwell for another term of office. We *certainly* didn't count on a little cross-species bastard, which we are now almost sure of." Homer wiped his brow in mock dismay. "But Josh and Dorothy here have turned the whole thing around, made it actually the *strongest* feature of a whole new scenario. So, guy, why don't you fill Danielle in on what's happening with our little runaways? I'd like to have her input."

Josh was still trying to fathom what Dorothy and Danielle had going. The speed with which they had sketched this arms deal was unnerving. Also, he did not like the way Dorothy had worked one of her sandals out to swing on her toes insouciantly as she listened. He flipped open his notebook, pursed his lips as casually as he could, and punched up a screenful of data.

"As Morph said, we have built on Danielle's idea of managing political reality as a holosoap keyed to one family. Of course all political parties are thinking that way now, offering their version of the Big Show. What brought *us* together" – he rotated one finger in a swift circle around the table – "was Morph's incredibly simple, incredibly selfless—"

"Oh please, Josh.' Morphopolous made a coy move to repel some invisible, onrushing force.

"—incredibly brilliant insight. That an *independent* genius could absorb all these productions, script their positions and play them against each other as pure drama. And the key was – also a Danielle Konrad discovery – to find the characters and events that were going to be most potent thematically – the vital, mainstream juice – and develop them, shape them, direct them. And then, after they've lived out the story . . . " Josh shook his head, still unable quite to believe in genius of such magnitude. "We do the holos. We *mythologize* them. We make them permanent cultural icons. Ideally, the survivors will play themselves, and then go on as *both* media stars and candidates for the highest offices . . . "

Morphopolous, he noted, had taken to closing his eyes and pinching in his nostrils slightly, as if to refine and concentrate some odor. A pose of meditation, a gathering of forces, a trance.

"So when the New Life thing blew, Stockwell's regime already shaken by the refugee crisis, and on top of that a rumor of sodomy and species miscegenation – well, we certainly had our creative stew bubbling. The prob was, nobody could figure out exactly how to handle this new warp – the possibility of a saplap embryo. As expected, the Cons denied everything and are trying darkside to neuter their own rescue effort, while the ELFs and extreme Progs scream for apprehension and termination, which sends the fundies into orbit. Meanwhile some of the rad groups are treating it as a divine visitation. And underneath all that, the old sneaky doubts about one's ancestors, one's neighbors. Bad genes, the Omaly issue, and so on."

Josh hit a key on the notebook, then read from the new screen. "'Deep cutaways, broad dredges, and simusurveys all show the same confusion. This issue has extraordinary penetration and durability, but cannot be readily vectored to allow for consistent prediction.' That's from a new SOA firm called Pollstergeist. They're willing to say, off the record, that it is the most powerful emotional maelstrom they've ever dealt with."

"I know the people," Danielle said. "They don't exaggerate. You must be . . . excited." She looked from him to Dorothy, maintaining her novitiate's pout. "To be involved in creation, at such a level! But how did you manage to monitor the situation, track the principals?"

"Can tell you in two words." Josh bowed and pressed his palms together in the Pacrim gesture of honoring. "One is Dorothy and the other is Homer. Dorothy has incredible street contacts, and one of these led us right into the heart of the Thorgs, the group that raided the Institute. Ironically, these scruffbags had already infiltrated one of our junkfood subsidiaries, so it was easy to track them. We pretty quickly located the fugitives in Omalytown, where, as you may know, we have an excellent network of informants."

Danielle tactfully said nothing, and Tasha ran reassuring fingers along Barrelhead's wrist. Everyone knew the duty of these informants and private agents was to monitor and keep out of public view Morphopolous's mad first wife. Josh allowed himself a moment to appreciate privately the beauty of this arrangement. Ecorads and Eva Morphopolous together represented everything the old man detested; no one would believe he had personally managed their collaboration in a conspiracy.

"Ah yes," Danielle said then and laughed, almost girlish. "So Feiffer was a decoy. He releases statements, makes robinhood raids, takes the headlines. The authorities will be looking for *him*."

"It's been free-flow," Morphopolous said, "improvisational. I knew you would like that, my dear. But this gives us some time to decide on our slant, our approach . . . "

"He sees everything," Tasha announced possessively, and made her profile available to all of them.

"Stunning, absolutely." Danielle regarded the younger woman with deferential admiration, beneath which Josh detected a strong radiation of contempt. "So what are your little darlings doing?"

"Tell," Dorothy said with gleeful anticipation.

Josh grinned. "The unvarnished truth is, they've become a pack of petty thieves. They're working the malls and tubes almost daily, and doing quite well, thank you." Josh bowed to acknowledge the chuckles around the table.

"Except for the good Doctor, who hasn't been able to fit in except as . . . you will appreciate the irony . . . a street headcase. He prophesies to commuters on the approaching apocalypse, which he sees as some kind of bacterial invasion."

Josh paused to allow more laughter, handclaps and exclamations, before shifting to a more serious tone. "Actually, his mental health is a matter of some concern. We don't want him picked up, obviously, but risks are increasing. Also, his assistant and lover, the Higgins girl, is hooked on nicotine, so the romance may be unraveling."

"Oh, that's just *marvelous*! How *rich*!" Tasha uttered a laugh designedly silken and wicked. "We could go a *scad* of ways with that."

Morphopolous smiled, Josh noted, but his eyes remained closed, the nostrils pinched. A breath control technique, or was he dreaming of his new wild specimen? Or asleep?

"Our other up story, already mentioned, is Feiffer. Our people have done a terrific job there. He's firmly soldered to the whole Ecomini agenda now, with extortion as motive one and revenge a close second." Josh glanced again at his notebook. "About twenty-three percent of the public now list themselves as 'sympathetic' to the whole big-tree-free-river dream, even though they also recognize it's completely impossible and most believe it's only a shrewd scam – build-up for an eventual cheap holo. But they enjoy the show, the last outlaw hero angle, so we have a number of daring raids scripted for Feiffer. We can safely say the ecorads are commandeered, neutralized. *We* can vector whatever they do. Our edit. Period."

He stopped, gazed at Danielle, his manner frank and open. He wondered if she would savor all the ironies in that collective pronoun.

"Incredibly well done," Danielle said. "My compliments."

"That's high praise, my boy." Morphopolous was grinning, almost salaciously. "You know, my dear, you *did* inspire our own efforts. We've only really refined the Konrad technique, made it a higher art form . . . "

"You have indeed." Danielle's glance was aflame again. "It's just breathtaking. After so many centuries of greed and ego, to think of shaping the world to the mold of sheer, magnificent *drama* . . . " She closed her eyes and seemed to undergo a spasm of ecstasy. Then her lids flew open and she gave Morphopolous a full, hot gaze of worship. "No wonder they compare you to Shakespeare."

Morphopolous smiled in Olympian modesty. "A little joke of Tasha's. Of course we all strut but a brief hour upon the battlements, and so forth . . . But we hope, Danny, you will consider joining our informal workshop? Give us your input?"

"Of course, of course, *of course*!" Danielle had tactfully closed her blowtorch eyes to take this sacred vow. Out of prison and on to the pinnacle of power, in partnership with her former nemesis. She had to be, Josh assumed, coming all over herself.

"It's a fantastic positioning," Danielle went on, "and all I can do, as the newcomer, is applaud you all. I did think, while you were laying it out, that a lot seems to ride on the wee one." She looked tactful, concerned. "And I thought I heard an *almost* next to that subject, a shadow of a doubt . . . "

"We can't do an exam, obviously," Josh said in his frank, low-keyed manner. "But we know they were sexually active – some disks were made – and Doctor Petrasky's girlfriend did do an exam on Duskyrose just three days before the breakout – and destroyed the results. It's the most obvious way to explain the panic at New Life, and our contacts in Omalytown tell us that it's common gossip there." He lifted a shoulder with a smile. "I don't have any doubt, and of course the tabs and yakkers and anchors are already speculating."

"Yes," Danielle breathed back a smile of her own, "but we don't want to confuse echoes with confirmation."

Dorothy laughed, and Josh felt the warmth in his face before he could control himself. But before he could respond, they heard voices from the outside courtyard. Sam and Bob were returning from their stroll.

"Ah, lunchtime already!" Morphopolous beamed at them all, and rapped the table sharply with his knuckles. "Good session. Lots to work on. An immensely talented new member of the workshop, and Sam's report and this Holocaust factor – gruesome prospect – genocide, Pobla panzers as Josh said – looking very possible . . . wow!"

The old man was getting up, they were all getting up. The gruesome prospect was already a done deed, in Josh's mind. Dorothy would have made all the arrangements, as she had whisked Danielle Konrad in here ahead of him. As she had decided already, no doubt, whom she would sit next to at lunch, and feed on.

But Morphopolous was turning to him, eyes crinkling in a fatherly appraisal, as Yamaguchi and Candidate Adamson came into view. "Josh, we've got to get clear of these Amazons this afternoon. And you're looking a little pale and overworked, if you don't mind my saying so. Now this afternoon why don't we take these guys . . . " He turned to the other two men, arriving now, and gripped Adamson's shoulder in manly solidarity. "Who don't get enough of the outdoors either, and make a little shooting party to the jungle? Some thinning to do – very critical, keeping the balance here – and we use antiques, the old cartridge-type, so it's a sporting proposition. Sound good, after all this palaver?"

Josh and the other men traded looks of a mature heartiness. Barrelhead was inviting them to his own favorite diversion. There would be bearers for each man, and others for the drinks and holorecording. They would make no mention of the coming election, or the state of the economy. They would talk only the animal, the approach, the shot. Josh hoped he could run on automatic playback, appear fully engaged, because he already knew his mind would be occupied chiefly with quite another sporting proposition. *Who would be in whose room, tonight?*

BOOK THREE

BOOK THREE

CHAPTER TWENTY

Tak tagak – Most High, One Among All, Greatest of the Great – Sayat peered over the last stone ledge above the floor of the narrow canyon and watched, intently, as his three emissaries approached the piksi man. The man was stark naked, curling his toes and lifting his feet alternately, for the sand and cinders were already hot in the mid-morning sun. A few steps behind him were the three oblong crates, their lids standing open.

Sayat's messengers moved very carefully. Yema was advancing by count, tapping his spear on the ground, and might have appeared dignified except for his trembling. The two young, alert *tchatsinakun* were fanning out to flank the naked man and watch for any sign of movement at the piksi camp, which was four or five hundred running strides away, against the canyon wall. The piksis, of course, had their metal eyes and could no doubt see well enough. Could even see Sayat, behind this rock.

The thought caused him to frown and rearrange the necklaces hanging on his breast, one of miniature jawbones and the other of twisted bits of burnt metal, debris from various piksi *mudlatin*. They would see that he feared no ghost-eater, for he had eaten himself, and that he would not lose his shadow to any machine.

But a moment later he forgot his appearance, fascinated by what he had never seen before, a piksi utterly bare, and at close range.

A pitiful creature. Pale as a toad's belly and sheathed everywhere in a thumb's thickness of fat. Dwarfish ears and a bent back. Almost hairless, with the merest stub of a *delo tchatsi* between the legs. They were nothing without their *mudlatin*, especially their long-strikers – what was in those open cases. And now, it seemed, they had come to offer the Pobla – to give *him*, the *tak tagak* – their secret power.

It seemed. You could never trust the piksis. But so far they had agreed to all his conditions: the open-cabbed cargo vehicle without escort, the crew of only three, the unspecified waiting period (now

211

in the fourth day), even the humiliation of exposing their leader, his baby's feet scorched while Sayat observed at his leisure. Sayat was beginning to entertain the suspicion, amazing as it was, that the piksis – or at least some enlightened few of them – had learned of his greatness, his vision, and had realized their own inferiority.

Yema was now only a dozen strides away from the piksi, and his courage was failing him. He tottered to a halt, the lance still lifting and dropping rhythmically. The piksi's face contracted in what Sayat supposed was a smile, and he dropped to one knee. Both the *tchatsin* tensed immediately, drawing back their spears, but the piksi did nothing more. It was a gesture of submission.

Yema managed to get out two verses of the most formal and wary of welcoming songs, before resting on his lance. Then, voice wobbling, he asked for a name and a purpose, and beckoned to the piksi. Sayat leaned a little further over the rock ledge, ignoring the worried rustling behind him, where fifty of his best *tchatsinakun* crouched with their clubs and spears in a tight grip. This was the crucial moment. They would know now if it was an ambush or a true trading.

The piksi pointed to his fat middle and said *Joe*. The rest of his response was garbled, barely intelligible. They were poor mimics, these creatures, and had managed only the most rudimentary vocabulary; but that was not important here. Yema and his guards were listening only for the timbre and resonance of intent. In the very first encounters, the Pobla had been astounded to discover that their old adversaries could not hear or understand the most essential components of speech. Piksis missed or misread motive and feeling all the time, even in the simplest greeting.

Apparently what Yema heard was satisfactory. The man got to his feet then and came forward slowly to extend one hand. The old advisor took it and smelled the fingers, knuckles, and hair of the forearm. The piksi uttered a short, foolish laugh. When Yema offered his own hand the man shook his head. They were crippled in this way, too; they could apprehend nothing directly through their noses or tongues, and very little by ear.

Sayat remembered how he had once watched from the mouth of a burrow when a team of piksis arrived to poke about the wreckage of another *mudlati*, which a *tchat* band had enticed into a prepared avalanche. They gathered their samples with tongs and pumps, wore thick garments that sealed them off completely from the earth, put everything into bags. They had felt nothing, smelled nothing, sensed nothing.

Now the piksi had beckoned Yema to the cases of long-strikers. Yema swayed on his feet, looking at whatever was inside. This Joe was urging, gesticulating, laughing his foolish laugh again. Yema motioned him to step away, and after a long pause, ten deep breaths at least, reached out finally to touch the frame of the box. He jerked his hand back as if burned.

Sayat uttered a sharp hiss of impatience. Even his closest followers were still like children, gullible and fearful despite the new teachings. He heard more uneasy movement behind him, and lifted a hand irritably to quiet his raiders. Only he understood the momentousness of this meeting; only he grasped what the future might be, once the strikers were theirs. He would have to show them, as usual. Correct them, and demonstrate the consequences of their fear, the necessity of serving the true and inexorable vision of their *tak tagak*.

He could see no sign of movement at the distant camp. Although the piksis had metal fleas who could transmit messages for them, the naked man would have to speak aloud and Yema would have heard the treachery under the words. Anyway, there were only three of them, and no one had spotted any weapons outside these crates. He arranged the necklaces again, and spoke one phrase, calling for his drummer and the six guards, two for the sun-shade and the other four bearing sharpened lances, the hafts dark with old bloodstains.

He stood up and waited for his company to form, then strode along the ledge, which slanted down gradually to the canyon floor. Yema wheeled about, saw them, and lurched again toward the nearest open crate. This time he managed to keep his hand on its edge, but he was shaking so badly he lost his grip on his lance, which fell against the crate with a rattle. The sound unnerved Yema completely, and he sank to his knees. By the time Sayat halted, four strides from the piksi, his former chief emissary was vomiting on the sand.

The piksi carefully avoided looking at Sayat. He kept his head bowed and both hands raised, palm up. Something something Sayat, he said in his own language. There was respect in the voice, also a sliver of fear, but nothing dangerously concealed. *"Tak tagak Sayat,"* the man said then. *"Kishta kishta Sayat. Kishta kishta Pobla."*

"Kish Pobla," Sayat corrected. *"Ya kish piksi."* He loaded the words with obvious duplicity and malice, an open insult even a deaf dog would have detected, but the piksi of course heard nothing. On

213

impulse, he added a short speech, now affecting a benevolent tone but stating plainly that this Joe stank so badly not even a maggot would condescend to eat him. He heard one of the sun-shade bearers swallow audibly in the ensuing silence.

Sayat himself knew a deep thrill of mingled excitement and apprehension. No Pobla had ever spoken so to the ghost-eaters, or approached them so near without falling sick immediately. He felt a little weak, and his heart pumped faster than usual, but there was no sense of the great river of *yano* rising, the dark silver current that swept one into the shadow-world. It was simply not true that, in the presence of piksis, death was the only alternative to being devoured, to losing one's *kubi*.

He, Sayat, had proved the old teachings wrong, and now everything was changed. They would learn about the *mudlatin*, how to use the long-strikers. They would be powerful, in the way of the piksi, but they would have also their own secret knowledge. A tremor of discontent followed this reflection, for the Hive-Beings had been withdrawn and even hostile since the catastrophes of the previous year. Sayat explained over and over that until Kapu's heresies were cleansed, they could expect no revelations from the Shadow of Shadows, and many of their former allies would avoid them. Still, he knew his followers were nervous because they had no queen, who could speak for them to the ants, wasps, bees, and termites who wove the world.

He dismissed these bothersome thoughts and signaled for the drum to begin its solemn beat. He strode to the open crate and gazed down at the packed weapons, straight and solid and giving off a dark sheen.

The piksi man spoke, and Sayat heard his excitement and anticipation. Without looking he knew the man's little *tchatsi* was enlarging slightly. He sucked in a full breath, seized one of the long-strikers, and dragged it from the box. From the ledge above them he heard low, throttled moans and the scrape of a spearpoint against stone. The drum faltered, then recovered at a faster beat.

The thing was heavier than he would have believed and had an attractive force. He was reminded of the great black stone, the jumping stone, discovered long ago by his people and serviced by its own tunnel. Metal bits would leap to the surface of this stone and cling there, as this striker clung to his hands. He felt the *yano* coiled inside, the bright tongue. Experimentally he pointed the mouth here and there, at ground and sky.

Very slowly, palms still upraised, the piksi edged nearer. He was speaking continuously, soothingly. Sayat turned the striker suddenly on him, and grinned to see how he froze and how his voice was momentarily striped by terror. But then Joe was smiling again, speaking confidently and signing that he wished to approach even nearer. Sayat nodded. He understood that the instrument would not bite arbitrarily.

Gently the piksi reached out to the striker, turned a round knob, then brushed a switch. He pointed at a lever on the underside and said *"Delo yat,"* before stepping back and indicating an imaginary path out and away over the canyon floor, a corridor between their two camps. A small danger. Sayat could feel that the striker was awake now, humming. He lifted it, groped for the lever, found it.

The striker's tongue was like a perfectly straight thread of lightning, gone even as it appeared, leaving a dark line burned across one's field of vision. Sayat frowned, tipped the weapon downward and moved the lever again. This time the lightning thread sent up a smoking geyser of sand twenty strides away. The third time he struck a small rock and saw it fly into fragments.

The piksi raised his hands again, cautioning, and moved in to advance the knob to a new setting. *"Tak Yat,"* he said.

Sayat touched the lever and this time a thicker cord of brilliance unzipped a tunnel of darkness. The jet of sand was higher than his head and the heat from it was like a slap from the sun. Again and again the cord lashed out, exploding rocks into a cascade of powder, furrowing the earth, slicing at the sky. The drum was pounding and Sayat could hear his *tchatsinakun* moaning like doves.

He became aware of Yema, still huddled on his knees over his own mess. "This one!" Sayat said loudly. "Afraid! *Yapa ya mahanaku!* He is meat already!" He worked the lever and the bright streak ate through Yema's arm, left it dangling by a charred flap of skin. Yema's eyes remained blank, staring up at Sayat, who worked the lever twice, irritably. The spitting and sizzling were startlingly loud at close range. Most of the middle of Yema exploded into rags, and the remains folded into a smoking, oozing, nodding heap.

"Ya! Ya! Takish!" Sayat cried, and lifted the striker high. It felt as if it had grown into his hand, as a tree root grows into and around a stone. He wheeled and faced his guards, the raiders peering down at him from the ledge. He looked deep and long, and saw everything he needed to see in those faces. *"Tak tagak Sayat!"* someone shouted. Then another, and another, following the drum. *"Tak tagak Sayat! Tak tagak Sayat!"*

Sayat laughed, as he had not laughed in many suns, and turned back to the piksi. The man had maintained the foolish grin, but the smell of fear was rank around him. Then his lips moved, though Sayat could hear nothing, and his look was riveted on the necklace of little jawbones. Sayat held the weapon aloft in one hand, cutting off the drum and chant, and then lifted the string and jangled it in front of the man's nose.

"*Pakish dako Pobla*," he said, leering. He pointed at his skull and snapped his teeth together several times, to demonstrate how they had eaten the brains of the young in Kapu's band.

The piksi man nodded, simpered, and made a slow, tentative gesture of switching off the weapon. Sayat uttered a contemptuous grunt, but moved the switch and felt the tongue of light retract and go quiet again. The man let out his breath in a rush, swallowed, and his lips moved again. No more than a whisper, but Sayat understood and laughed in derision.

The piksi was uncomfortable. His baby feet were frying, the sun was making his belly uneasy. He wished to talk somewhere in the shade, away from the smouldering heap of flesh that had been peeled away from Yema's shadow. He wanted a little ceremony, a little respect, in exchange for the strikers.

Sayat shrugged and made a foul noise between his lips. He pointed at the crates, and watched keenly as his guards approached them. Two hesitated before grasping the metal handles, glancing at their leader with white-ringed eyes. Sayat lifted the weapon in his hands, set a finger on the switch, and stared at them, waiting. The guards seized the crates then, hoisted them and set off at a staggering run toward their fellows behind the ledge.

He would have to free the shadow of one of those two, Sayat decided. The big one with the shine of perspiration on his brow and muscles convulsing in his back. And there would surely be others – those hiding some weakness, still corrupted by Kapu and the teachings of that old crone Adza, who had led the Pobla into disaster. But the strikers would provide an admirable test, and he could now afford to purge the weak and fearful, since a single dependable *tchatsinaku* bearing one of these tongues of light was worth a hundred armed with lances.

Sayat allowed the naked piksi to follow, mincing over the hot sand, while he strolled to a place where the canyon wall leaned outward and made a band of shade. There a drip of water fell from a crevice into a tiny pool worn in a plate of rock fallen long ago from the wall. A few stones had been dragged into a circle about this pool. Sayat sat on the largest, the striker across his knees, and only one guard on either side of him.

The absurd naked piksi used his few words of praise over and over. Sayat the High, the Good, the Big, the Strong. Sayat had begun to frown and yawn, drifting off to fret about his raiders, whom he imagined hunkered around the crates, still moaning like disturbed doves. They might start tapping the drum again, and Sayat's preoccupation for some time had been with this penchant among the *tchatsinakun* for miming – rather than actually performing – the story of their adventures. They needed a major raid, larger than ever before, a scattering of shadows by the thousands. They needed discipline, not more dancing.

Finally the piksi spoke new words, words that excited him, almost brought him to his feet. Not only Kapu, but *Pahane* and *Tima*, and then *delo dako paya*. The little runt-snake, the offspring of the hated union that had almost destroyed the Pobla! Where were these demons? Tell! He glared at the piksi man, gripping the striker until his fists were mottled white. In the silence following his demand, he did hear the drum, only a soft pulse at this distance. Sayat felt rage leap in him like a grass-fire. He could do to any of them what he had done to Yema. To all of them.

Joe was whispering hoarsely, rapidly, and making marks in the sand with a finger. Kapu was invading, in the company of a piksi woman. They were making a new camp not far away, as Sayat The Most High surely knew. A camp to capture more of the Pobla and eat their ghosts, fill them with Kapu's false visions, turn them into slaves of the piksis, and then take back the desert, the canyons, all the way to the sea. It was a secret plan, kept even from the piksi leaders, hatched by a group of traitors.

The camp part was true, Sayat knew, for his spies had already reported the cargo vehicles, the new buildings. And it was true that Kapu had been taken in by some piksi woman, one of their *tagakin* who lived on drops of blood. Runaways from the old faker's group had reported it so, and quite possibly this unholy pair would come to the new camp.

But what about the *dako pa*, the runt-snake? How near was the *mudlati* witch to giving birth to this demon? He watched the piksi, who was nodding violently, excited now. If the toad lied this time Sayat would twist the knob and turn him to ashes.

217

Joe held his forefingers and thumbs together in a big circle, then showed five fingers, one bent at the knuckle. Almost six moons. Then he pointed to the mark in the sand that represented the new camp. All Kapu's people would be going there. To wait for the birth, for they thought this bastard-thing was the true *tak tagak*.

Sayat uttered a sound between a growl and a groan. It was the truth. The evil Pobla were offering this runt-snake as his rival. He shook the long-striker, and his two guards took a step away from him. Joe was going on, his voice low and insistent. Here would be the place, here the chance to take vengeance on those who did not believe in Sayat The Most High. The bad Pobla would be gathering there, all the old and sick and confused that followed Kapu's false vision. With the long-strikers, Sayat's raiders could turn all the traitors into ashes, and they – Joe and the other piksis who had learned of Sayat and admired him – would help by persuading the soldiers to look another way.

"*Ye!*" Sayat grimaced. He had been thinking of a great raid, but only against Kapu's scattered clan, the encampments in the canyons. The idea of attacking a piksi post was startling, unsettling. But the man was saying they could possibly obtain much more powerful weapons, and in a moon's span the *tchatsin* would be trained well enough for such an assault.

There was, however, another reason for Sayat's unease. The piksis seemed quite unaware that they had built their new blood-taking camp in a place sacred to the Hive Beings, a place where offerings had been made and celebrations conducted for generations. Those from Adza's old colony in Sopan had been the most frequent visitors, and had dug an elaborate system of tunnels connecting to this small valley. Sayat knew the place well, but so did Kapu.

On the other hand, the mention of bigger long-strikers was enticing. And the Most High need not be concerned about the soldiers, Joe was now saying. He made a circle with one hand. The *tchatsin* would only surround and wait. Their piksi friends would give them a signal when it was safe. They would only have to begin the attack and then withdraw a little, for the soldiers would open the pens and drive Kapu's followers away and Sayat could hunt them down at leisure.

Sayat reviewed the naked piksi closely, from head to toe. He could see no advantage for the piksis in this plan. They were giving up some of their weapons, and might even lose a few soldiers in such an attack. The man began to smell of fear again, and something else that puzzled Sayat and made him stare a simple

218

implicit question. *Why?* Why did these piksis want him to do their killing for them?

Gesturing, smiling his sickly, foolish smile, the piksi conveyed that they were together, companions, *mahanakun*, in their thoughts. They both believed Pobla and piksi were separate, and should always remain separate. Most piksis believed this. Only a few were mad and dangerous, like Kapu among the Pobla. But these few lunatics had tricked their way into a position of control. They actually wanted to mate with the Pobla, breed a population of slaves. And the hybrid demon-child was their symbol, just as it was to the corrupt Pobla. Joe mimed the expression of disgust he saw on Sayat's own face.

Sayat frowned and looked away. The whispering was peculiar, confusing. Under the voice and gestures there was truth, but a crooked truth. Sayat could not see its final direction. But the wish to remain separate was clear and strong. The piksi was full of terror and revulsion at the idea of mingling with a Pobla. On this point, at least, they were together.

Sayat signed abruptly that this meeting was ended, that he would consider everything that had been said. The piksis would have to wait, coming no further into the sun's belly, and he would send a *tchatsinaku* to summon them. They should prepare to bring more long-strikers and also perhaps – he uttered this new thought on impulse, and watched the man closely – a *pam-pam*. One of the huge, swift spears that could fly many suns' journeys in the space of five breaths. That would prove the piksis meant what they said.

Joe seemed pleased, even excited, rather than shocked. Sayat identified at last the nature of that other, obscure feeling he had detected in the man, right beside his fear. It was the odor of simple, directionless lust, like the itch in the hands of a young *tchatsi* to play with himself. Sayat laughed aloud, startled at such a bizarre connection. The man gave off this stink around the long-strikers, and when they were speaking of the possible raid. Play with weapons apparently aroused piksis, made them want to mate indiscriminately.

Sayat made the foul noise with his lips again, and waved at his guards to follow. But before he could turn to go, the piksi gestured in urgent supplication. Joe displayed his shoulders, the backs of his arms, which had grown gradually pinker, and hopped back and forth on his bare feet. He was begging to be allowed, next time, to wear a garment and shoes. Sayat grinned unpleasantly and shook his head, then extended a hand palm up and curled it closed.

Joe nodded ferociously. *"Na, na!"* He made the motions of carrying and distributing. There would be gifts for all. He appeared to look into his own open palm. He pretended to drape new necklaces on Sayat. He upended invisible handfuls into his mouth. Mirrors and ornaments and things to eat.

"Candy!" The piksi man beamed at Sayat, an expression of avid certainty. *"Chocolate! Kish! Kish! Kish!"*

Sayat wrinkled his nose and shrugged. They were all mouth and eyes, the piksis. See and eat. Still, the man's face was for the first time truly radiant, as if a sacred ritual had been completed. Perhaps this was their holy pattern. Killing with the long-strikers, then copulation with whatever, then candy. Obscene and repulsive, but certainly curious. He shrugged, and signed the man to wear what he liked at the next meeting. For the Greatest of the Great, the novelty of staring at a humpbacked hairless toad was already exhausted.

CHAPTER TWENTY-ONE

Derrick threaded the tippet through the eye of the Black Gnat, size sixteen, and secured it with a behind-the-bight slip knot. Then he snugged the knot, clipped the loose end with a silver tool dangling from his vest, and released the fly, which seemed to float free before him, the leader invisible. With a flick of the ultra-light rod, he made the lure vanish, sent it hissing back and forth overhead as he stripped line from the magnesium spindle of the reel. Fifteen meters. Twenty. Twenty-five.

He smiled to himself, aware that his breathing was synchronizing with the casts: a great, arcing belly of line behind, then the snap and a long, snaking reach out over the spanking bright water. The rhythm was coming to him, and as that happened the tangle of his thoughts began to unravel. Soon he would enter that exquisite, mindless state of alertness known only to the advanced practitioner of this art. Every nerve would be connected to the tiny dark dot of the gnat, which at any moment could disappear, sucked under by one of the hybrid lunkers that had been released that morning into the lake.

You needed that total absorption on a day like this one. Hectic, from the first peep of the alarm at 5:15 a.m.: the Pacrim market in an unexpected roil and Josh Tremaine on the line in the middle of breakfast. Then Michelle dawdling over her choice of a dress for tonight, and a whining call from his eldest son at Geo Tech, wanting an advance. His cellphone was even now in his creel, in case there was an unforeseen move in a couple of major ongoing merge negos.

But he was beginning to relax. Friday fun time. Michelle was parked at the club lounge behind him, might even be able to see him on this little landspit finishing the cast – almost thirty meters now, the line straightening a meter above the water, the leader with just enough momentum to hook and let the fly waft down and kiss the surface first. There was a holocorder tastefully recessed in the branches of a small tree nearby, and later they would review his tape and he would explain the perfection of this cast.

His smile broadened, and he squared his posture a little, imagining the beautiful ex-model, twenty-two years his junior, watching him do yet another thing with mature skill. It pleased him to remember the envious glances from other club members, when he touched her back lightly and left for the locker room. Donning his waders and vest, fitting up the rod, he had taken a ribbing from Woody Packhurst and Amad Benara. "You *must* like to fish," Packhurst had observed. Benara, CEO of PetroPlex and famous for his impassive Bedouin mien, had actually winked.

A heavy swirl appeared under his Gnat, capsizing it, and Derrick reacted too slowly, popping the fly back with a wet smack. Damn it, damn it! A big Brownbow, two kilo range. Woolgathering, plain and simple. Presentation was perfect, but then he had lost concentration. Ah well. Spooling in the loose line, he let out a deep breath and relaxed another notch. Today he wasn't going for score, hadn't wagered with Pack or Benara. Recreation, pure recreation, today.

It was remarkable how the little lake had been contoured and landscaped to screen out the city. A lane of impressive artificial conifers had been erected to mask all but the tallest skyscrapers, and the growing shrubs and smaller trees hid the Trunkways and burbs completely. The treatment plant from which the lake drew its water deliberately pumped into an elevated settling pond, so that a long cascade over concrete boulders could produce a deep, natural rushing that obscured, by melding with, the sound of traffic.

It was worth every penny of the eight hundred thousand a year Derrick paid for membership. He kept his gear in a club locker, so he could drop in for an hour or two any time. Starting from his midtown executive suite, in just minutes he could be in a natural setting, the sun flashing on the water, casting for the big fellas. They were always big fellas, tough and canny, and this club catered to real sportsmen who used only light tackle.

Derrick uttered, to himself, a small, hearty grunt of anticipation. He was feeling keen, zestful, steady; that Brownbow was worthy, perhaps a champion, you could count on it. The fish would have begun the day in a quiet holding tank, undergoing sonogram and x-ray to verify health. He would have had no food for at least twelve hours, except for a few artificial insect placebos employed to provoke a feeding pattern, just before his release into the lake.

222

One feisty, ravenous chunk of a trout, with Derrick's name on it. Who could put a price on things like that?

It was a marvel, what the staff biologists had accomplished by selecting and improving the strains of *salmonidae* drawn from hatcheries worldwide. Forty years ago the common domesticates had all but lost the impulse to strike at surface or near surface food – insects, larvae, tadpoles – and rose only to the roar of trucks, a dump of hard protein pellets made from slaughterhouse waste. But by isolating a sample from the stock of remote, primitive farms in late-developing countries, and identifying a gene complex that fostered both muscular development and surface feeding, scientists had brought back several solid game fish.

These breeds were enhanced still more when a rare species had been discovered in an underground stream in the Wasteland. A big red fish had adapted to the extreme cold and utter darkness of subterranean caverns. Blind, with an armored snout and huge, feathery fins, it nevertheless had kept the instinct for taking flies and – even more desirable – had welded that instinct to a brute, aggressive vigor. The red hybrids, with the blindness and unattractive jaw eliminated, were the valuable foundation of every lunker prepared in the club's lake.

Derrick knew their value, because he traded the stock of the small but prosperous company that had patented the gene complex. Such stocks and such companies were a significant share of his business, Sporting Chances. Derrick's love and his work were thus one. These afternoons at the club crowned his career and made sense of his life; he was demonstrating, personally, that recreation was industry, and vice versa.

As his second cast arrowed out over the water, the wind kicked up suddenly and caught the fly, doubled it back into the leader. He let the mess drop, and eased himself down the bank to enter the shallows. He would move a few steps to avoid casting directly into the wind, and wade nearer the big Brownbow. Another beautiful thing about angling: it was a perfect analog of life, of business. You had to adjust constantly to the unexpected.

He pursed his lips and almost frowned, gathering in the tangle of line and leader and beginning to sort it out. He was reminded of Tremaine's call. He was flattered, of course, because Tremaine was a very big player, a major dealmaker with connections to both parties, and a serious factor in the entertainment industry.

But the call seemed only routine, Josh making a contribution from an anonymous client to a charity Derrick had founded. Then they chatted about the market and the economy generally. Josh wondered about the impact of these ecocrazies, their kidnapping and extortion, on the outdoor leisure business. Were sport stocks wobbling because of this sort of violent wilderness fundamentalism?

Derrick knew, of course, that Tremaine had done the deal for holo rights to that outlaw agent's story, in effect making the first ransom payment for the Drager boy. The more outrageous that story turned out to be, the better. There had been a daring raid or two already: junk food for the Nonumbs and a thermite job on a pair of artificial oaks providing canopy in a downtown park. So he could guess Josh's views, or thought he could, and had tried to be diplomatic. The truth, in any case, made it easy to do so.

"Fundamentalism everywhere," he said. "Nuts galore. The thing is, people *like* to see it. From a distance. So we may actually go up a half-point, maybe three-quarters. These ecofundies have a certain *cachet* right now. But it won't last. They'll catch 'em. Surprised they haven't already. I'm more worried about the Ginkpool on the border."

"Bugs again," Josh had replied. "Germs. That sort of thing?"

"Sure. The old negative association. Tends to spread beyond the laps and their lice to all undomesticated or marginal creatures, and the sports industries *depend* on a careful connection to certain of those creatures, even extinct or in zooparks. You know, the mythics – Bison Boots and Eagle Irons and assault vehicles like the Choctaw and Leopard and so on. Lots of money there. You remember two years ago, when that Drager hunting accident—"

"Right, almost ended the National Preserves. Shook the sport vehicle people badly."

"You bet. Shook *everybody*, eventually. Bugs, bears, Ginkies – wanted to exterminate them all. New Broom, that whole mess – whew! Anyway, what we have now is more benign. I hear the polls even show a sneaking sympathy for the big tree scam. Absurd, of course, to wait a thousand years for some so-called sacred slow-grower, but myself I'm an old-fashioned Conservative and I do support managed and monitored diversity. On marginal land, of course. I'm more concerned now about the opposite fringe. Beau Winger and the loonies behind him."

"Indeed," Josh said, after a pause. "Dangerous."

It wasn't clear to Derrick just what danger was implied, so he changed the subject, thanked Josh again for the generous contribution.

They should have a drink together soon. Not today, Josh replied, Friday a fishing day, right? Derrick was surprised at the man's sharpness and passion for detail. He wondered what else about his life was laid out on Tremaine's screen. Then came the remark that still puzzled him.

"You sportsmen are notoriously kind-hearted. So don't be surprised if somebody goes trolling for you," Josh had said. "You're a pretty visible corporation."

He had been about to ask what he had done to be visible, but Tremaine was already winding out of the conversation, so Derrick could only guess the charity work had touched some important people. Business was also good, he had to admit. Maybe one of the holoshows planned to feature his success with sports-related investment, how a share always went to introducing city kids to the outdoor experience. Which of course – beautiful congruence – made them potential customers some day.

The line was loose and clear now, coiled in one hand, so he began a new cast, glancing at his chrono as he did so. Twenty minutes before the NorthAm market close. He usually made a last call to the office, checking final performance, but if that big fella hit now there wouldn't be time. Forget it. Exuberant, confident, just a shade reckless, he put everything into the whip of the rod, and saw the Black Gnat soar, slide, hang, and then settle, soft as a snowflake's shadow, thirty-three meters out on the blank lake.

A wavering column of deformed silver bubbles rose from the rubber-clad quadruped hanging motionless before PJ. The bubbles curled around a long, thin shaft that led to a clump of lilypads on the surface. Beside him, Fitzgibbon was clawing and reeling, still unable to manage his bulk in its new, buoyant condition. PJ wanted to laugh, to hoot like a mad loon. He felt utterly, monstrously silly.

"He's into it," Bottlenose said. The voice was grainy, metallic, with a slight echo, coming through the receiver built into their hoods. Bottlenose could see and hear the target via the fiberoptic cord running through the stalk to the lilies. He was a deepdark marine demo man, their op field support and guide. "Fucker's really into it. Guys better move in to about eight feet."

"Fucking freezing," Fitzgibbon croaked. His arm, gyrating in slow motion, bumped PJ in the chest.

225

"Unhand me, you abominable groper." PJ wheezed out the gale of his mirth, sobbed, wheezed again.

"Careful. Come *on* guys, move it!" Bottlenose turned his rubber head, jerked it up and down. "He could get one any time."

PJ's eyes were filling with tears, so the terraced and scalloped bottom grew indistinct. Here and there a dim, torpedo shape glided in or out of an overhang or between the rough, algae-covered concrete boulders and imitation stumps strewn about. He was imagining headlines, and suffocating from hilarity. *Daring agent hooked on job. Finny tribe offers phoney bribe. Whale of a scam.*

Fitzgibbon had hold of his arm now, tugging him clumsily toward their goal. PJ worked his flippers, coasted laterally a few feet until the bottom began to slant upward. The cold helped, all right, to combat the absurdity of the situation. At first they had work to keep themselves warm and distracted: they went in hand-over-hand on a line shot through the outflow culvert, Bottlenose cutting the grates and screens with his acetylene backpack. Before that they had coveralls and tools, posed as a utility crew servicing the exit pipe. But they had been in the lake twenty minutes now, mostly waiting. The chill was into his bones, and he felt ready for action, however ridiculous.

Near the shimmering surface a heavy dart of pink shadow shot past him, and a second or two later he heard the splash, saw an expanding bloom of concentric wavelets.

"Yeah! Got one, got one on! Get in now, close . . . be ready to slip out, like I showed you . . . " Bottlenose modulated his excitement into a professional's intense, contrived calm. "Going to be slick, guys, slick and quick . . . check the weapons, check your footing, want to sort of ooze out . . . let him work this baby almost to the net, I'll give you a green . . . "

PJ unfastened the holster flap and slid out the handweapon. He would only pretend, as usual, to be the hot dick. The little phaser was actually harmless, a fake, able to deliver a charge barely sufficient to stun a subject for a few seconds. Fitzgibbon and Bottlenose, on the other hand, packed entire tiny arsenals for darkside wipes. All designed not for their target, the angling executive, but for PJ, in case he grew so demented or unwise as to deviate from the script.

"Don't get creative," Fitzgibbon rasped through the headphone. "And no fucking jokes. Just do the job."

They had to flatten themselves now, and PJ could pull himself along from boulder to boulder with one hand. They were side by side, spread-eagled over their own shadows, which floated in an intricate mosaic of squiggling light and pulsing shadow. To his right PJ could see the man's legs in waders, breaking at the plane of the water into a warped and blurred figure holding aloft a curved, throbbing wand. The heavy pink dart was convulsing, bucking, thrashing a few feet away.

"OK . . . he's unfurling the net . . . nope, Jesus! Another run . . . don't bust off, baby . . . OK, OK, he's turned . . . coming back . . . coming home, baby . . . fold in the flippers, guys . . . net down, net down . . . OK! Slick and quick now, guys, GO!"

PJ lifted his head and simultaneously raked back his mask, pulling the rubber hood and earphone completely free. A sunny, solid world with startlingly loud birds, a roar of wind and traffic. Fitzgibbon, lumbering aloft also, sounded like a walrus, but the man on the finger of land was wholly absorbed in landing his fish and remained unaware. The trout was flopping and shuddering on the surface of the water, while the man strained to guide it into the cocked net. PJ had time to orient himself toward the holocorder, so his image would be clear and identifiable. Most important, his employers had stressed.

"Move on this asshole," Fitzgibbon hissed, his own mask banging free as he blinked furiously through rivulets of water. His face was poached a pale blue, and he looked simultaneously enraged and miserable.

"Oh, Asshole," PJ called to the man holding the jigging rod. He moved closer in a kind of mincing shuffle, holding the phaser like a small bouquet.

Fitzgibbon was acquiring color now in his cheeks, fumbling at the pack on his belt. "One of these days I'll kill you, Feiffer, just do—"

"Asshole can't hear me," PJ said cheerfully. "Preoccupied." He walked to a position not two strides from the man, looking, in effect, over his shoulder. Fitzgibbon, hissing a steady stream of curses, edged up behind him. "Quite a nice one you have there," PJ said conversationally.

"Oh, you *beauty*! You magnificent, magnificent . . . Oh, easy now fella . . . " The man was muttering, cooing to himself, but sensed the presence, finally, of the figures now only an arm's length away. "Oh hi hi," he said with a quick glance over his shoulder. "Yes, yes! He's a slugger, isn't he? A real champ . . . ah, little stuff left, careful . . . "

PJ grimaced humorously at Fitzgibbon, lifted the phaser and shook his head. The man either didn't see it, or didn't appreciate its significance. *Let's wait*, he mouthed, and grinned into Fitzgibbon's broad face, now bright pink. "I think he's tired," he said to the man, who nodded but did not look aside. Then, with a smooth hooking motion, the man slid the net under the trout and lifted it free in a cascade of flashing water. The thick body bent; the dark, liver-colored gills flared open.

The man hoisted his prize high, and gazed at the two others in rubber suits with a great, boyish grin. "Look at that!" he yelped. "Ye-e-ow! Two, two and a half at least!" His eyes swiveled in the direction of the clubhouse. He hoped, obviously, someone was looking and would admire his good fortune and skill.

"Beautiful." PJ nodded appreciatively, then sighed. "Fine fish. But look at this." He held up the phaser, waited until the other had focused on it, then extended it gently, almost tenderly, to within three inches of the man's nose. "Derrick Gifford?"

"What?" Derrick's smile lost force, and the net sagged under its twitching weight. "What is this?"

"Deadly weapon." With his thumb PJ moved a small lever on the side of the phaser, which emitted a tiny beep and then a very faint, steady hum. "Better put the pole and the fish down, Derrick. It's all right, he won't get away. Then take the phone out of your bag, please."

"What . . . " The smile lingered without purpose, a ghastly thing. "What do you . . . " Derrick's eyes strayed to Fitzgibbon, looming now beside him and removing the net and the pole from his paralyzed hands.

"Don't ask any more questions," Fitzgibbon breathed into the side of the man's head. "You fuck, you just do what he tells you, you won't get hurt."

"Pardon my associate's rude ways," PJ said, and retracted the humming weapon a handspan. "But we do need your co-operation, and we only have a few minutes. The phone?"

Derrick was galvanized, at last. He jerked open the flap of the creel, plunged in one hand.

"Easy." PJ kept the phaser trained steadily on the man's nose. "Hand it to my associate. He's going to call your office. When they come on, you tell them to jack you in at the top, private channel. You're going to make some moves before closing."

Derrick produced the cellphone, a slender bar of dark silver, which Fitzgibbon picked off like a banana and prodded with his stubby fingers. PJ saw his bodyguard's lips moving in methodic recall of memorized digits. He sighed. *The sums of money involved here, one might have expected a higher grade of employee.*

"You're a conscientious businessman," he said to Derrick. "You care. You've had a change of heart."

"What?" Derrick's voice was barely a whisper, he was staring at PJ in embryonic comprehension. "You . . . you're . . . "

"Yes I am. PJ Feiffer. Swashbuckling ecorad. Don't forget, you have me on holo too, for confirmation." He tilted his head cheerily toward the camera in the tree. "Anyway, you're about to contribute heavily to a daring new project to bring back the great trees, giants of the earth—"

"Got 'em," Fitzgibbon interrupted. He held out the phone to Derrick. "Careful what you say."

Derrick took the cellphone, cleared his throat and spoke into it. He stopped, listened, and began again.

"No, no . . . touch of a cold, but I'm fine. Yes, yes . . . a good fish . . . uh, Frank, I want a line, full service all options. Secure, yes, secure. I know it closes in a few minutes. Yes, I *know* it's the weekend." Fitzgibbon slid one big hand to Derrick's shoulder, to the back of his neck. "Frank, just give me the goddamned *line*."

"Good." PJ had opened his beltpak, removed a small roll of waterproof printout. "We'll give you numbered accounts and the sums for each. Rest of your selloff is on the open market."

Derrick worked his jaw, glanced down where his fish was convulsing, still in the net. "Selloff? No, right now—"

"Oh yes." PJ smiled encouragingly. "Large selloff. Two or three of your prime stocks, in the outdoor line. Afraid those shares will depreciate pretty steeply, come Monday."

"No!" Derrick bleated. "They're growth, they're—"

"Now, now." PJ frowned and Fitzgibbon's hand clamped tighter, bringing the man erect, back arched. "Trust us. Only temporary. We're nailing down some options for you, a buyback on the right date. We'll split the margin and you'll do quite well. Line open?" Derrick gaped at the display slot on the phone, nodded dumbly. "Then here's the first transfer. Keep the display so my friend can see it. I'm going to read fast, so pay attention."

In a few minutes their work was done. A long chain of numbers and letters had shifted radically the investment pattern of several companies. Derrick Gifford had gambled his whole career on a lightning, brutal dumping of stock and a criminal agreement for secretly recouping on the surge that would follow the publicity from this hold-up. PJ had explained the deal rapidly and clearly, as he restored the printout to his beltpak and holstered the phaser.

"There'll be a sympathy buy, from the public," he observed with an engaging grin. "Also, as you would yourself admit, the outdoors *is* fashionable and these stocks *are* sound. But you don't want us to be caught, Derrick. Those options would never come through. The fad for eco-action would end. Depends on the wild and free, and that's me. Remember, trigbee, not pigmy. Be on the side of the giants." He took the cellphone from Derrick's hand and pitched it, underhand and smoothly, into the lake.

"How," Derrick said plaintively, "how could—"

"How *could* we have known you were fishing today, how could we know your inner office number? How indeed. Think about it. Your lucky day." PJ leered at him. "Say, occurs to me it would look good if you tried to fight back, tried to restrain us until help could arrive."

"Shut the fuck *up*, will you?" Fitzgibbon spoke in a throttled roar. He jerked the rubber hood over his head. "Let's get out of here, Feiffer." He clapped the facemask into place.

But PJ had stepped nearer to Derrick, his grin constant and re-assuring. "Go ahead, take a swing. Try." The man did not move. He looked dejected, utterly. PJ extended three fingers and pushed him lightly in the chest. "Like that. Little shove. Go ahead." Derrick made a vague gesture, batted at PJ's chest. PJ turned him firmly and carefully around, seized a handful of trouser seat and knotted a fist into the man's collar. "You *do* swim, Derrick?"

"Ah – ah – yes! I mean no . . . " On tiptoe, waders flapping, Derrick was propelled along the spit of land and into the lake, windmilling frantically. PJ released him, slipped on his own hood and mask, and dove into the water. He nudged Derrick a stroke or two further out, gave him a friendly tickle under one arm, and after extending his flippers again, flutter-kicked hard after Fitz and Bottlenose, toward the outlet pipe.

Derrick gasped and blew, thrashed with all his might toward the shore. Finally one foot struck a boulder and he managed to stagger into the shallows. Streaming small rivers from his vest and the collapsing waders, he stood motionless, blinking through the blur of water and hair in his eyes. He had lost his hat. Perhaps he had lost everything. And only minutes ago he had been happy, ecstatic, exactly where he wanted to be.

He could.see the clubhouse now, its windows dark and blank. No movement, no activity. Perhaps no one saw. He could say he fell in, landing the fish. He would say nothing! He would foil their stupid outrageous publicity stunt! He took two joyous steps and stopped. It occured to him that then he would be personally responsible for those erratic – no, insane – purchases, would have to explain his funding of a whole battery of mad Ecomini schemes. He was caught. The fisherman was caught.

Think about it, Feiffer had said. He did not have to think long. The call from Tremaine. The talk of fishing, of the unexpected activity in his specialty stocks, of the ecoraiders. Josh Tremaine, who had the rights to Feiffer's story. And knew his office number, his habit of calling in late sometimes. It had all been thought out. *You sportsmen are notoriously kind-hearted.*

Squishing, he walked to the dead trout in his net. Or perhaps not. He thought he saw a faint shudder along the glistening side. He picked up the net, reached in and unstuck the Black Gnat from the fish's jaw, then carried his prey to the edge of the water. When he spread the knotted cords carefully with his fingers and slid the frame out from under the fish, it floated still as a log, bobbed a little in the slight wave action. Then the gills flared again, contracted, opened partially. The tail waved, feebly. The fish tilted on its side.

He waited. The gills worked, stopped, worked. All at once the whole body squirted forward a few inches, tilted still further so the dark back was visible. The fish hung in the water, the gills pumping twice more, and then it was gone. Derrick got to his feet, cast aside the net. He was, he understood now, only a player in some complicated plot not yet revealed. Tremaine had involved him in something deep, and he would have to go with it. There was no alternative he could see. He had taken the lure. He began to jog heavily toward the clubhouse, stumbling and waving his arms. "Help," he called feebly, practicing. "*Help.*"

CHAPTER TWENTY-TWO

Marvelous Marvin was examining his shoes, or rather his footgear. First three layers of paper, then a sort of bootie of light plastic, and finally the shell of heavier vinyl fabric. The whole was held intact by various bits of twine, staples, and industrial tape, but Marvin kept the surface clean and applied a dab of polish every day, so that with his baggy trousers worn low, he presented twin respectable toes to the world.

He was thinking of layers and surfaces, of how many great sages had gone barefoot, worn only a simple shift, or made a point of sitting on the ground to teach. They seemed to want very little between themselves and the raw weather. On street no one ever went barefoot, of course. It was illegal, to begin with, and even here in Omalytown one needed protection from glass and concrete, and the corrosive fluids that leached down from above.

In his former life Marvin had never thought to question shoes. He had never thought to question many things, except within the confines of his discipline, where he had been considered rather a maverick. But since becoming a fugitive and passing through what he now thought of as a dark night of the soul, he had discovered a new and daring curiosity in himself. Without his disk library, without his daily updates from the research scanner that policed every infoband relevant to his work, without the weekly brainstorming sessions and monthly conferences, he had begun to see new questions, more and more of them, including some so monstrous – and at the same time so idiotically simple – that he had terrified himself.

Why one was the creature one was, for example. A craven nocturnal shrew weighing a few ounces did not *imply* an eventual Michelangelo. There was no particular *reason* a coelacanth should bumble along, unchanged, in the black depths of an oceanic trench for twenty million years. What imperatives and opportunities made one a man, or a mastodon, or an amoeba?

Finally, painfully, he reversed the classic formula: what you became was a function of who you were to start with, which was something (he discovered with a nasty shock) he did not actually know. He *did* know that he wasn't what he thought he was. Doctor Petrasky had thought – had simply assumed – that he was one of the most successful adaptations of the most successful species on earth: a well-off, extremely talented young professional scholar. (His shoes had then been hard and bright as mirrors.)

Yet here he was, a penniless, ignorant wretch, waiting to solicit permission to beg in the streets; and his patroness, who could grant such licence, was the queen of fugitives and addicts and wretches and lunatics. So yes, he was now one of the poor in body and spirit, and yes, he knew practically nothing about the most fundamental matters, but – and this was the final and greatest miracle, which had given his unshaven, sallow features a permanent, ethereal smile – he was *happy*.

His suffering had brought him joy, sometimes ecstasy. A preposterous idea! An idea he would have dismissed, before, as psychotic nonsense. Now the truth of it was as irrefutable as his own heartbeat. He had been miserable beyond the reach of his imagination – his career ruined, estranged from his beloved, exiled to this sinister and brutal shadow-world. He had *envied* the amoeba, in its place far beneath possible humiliation. And then, looking up from his stupifying agony . . . he had seen a stroke of sunlight through a grate, falling onto a stained and pitted concrete wall, and there was the delicate, shimmering billow of a spiderweb, whose threads of light had become . . .

The problems came when he tried to communicate his visions. Words were not things. You could not explain how a gossamer net the breadth of your hand revealed the moon and clouds and horses running in the snow. He could not even make clear how he had come to see his great body of knowledge as exactly that – a writhing body, lacking a head; or how knowing so much *about* living things and their interrelations had kept him from instanding them.

He smiled to himself over this new word, which Tima had one day coined to illustrate the difference between her people and his. To instand another was nothing like understanding them. It was to live and feel along with, or even simply to become another, losing track of oneself, as the Pobla in trances could be ants and flowers and even stones. Was it, he had asked, the "secret" of their ability to "communicate with animals?"

Tima had whooped in mirth. She pointed out to him that he *was* an animal, and that he had a host of other creatures living on him, and in him. He might begin a conversation, she suggested, with those nearest at hand. It was a startling idea, to imagine signaling to the benevolent bacteria in his digestive system, or the tiny arthropods on his scalp. But very soon he underwent a familiar jolt in the frontal lobes, the sign of discovery. Such a conversation, he realized, would be only the beginning of deeper discourse, at the level of the molecule.

The old fellow who acted as Eva's butler appeared on the catwalk above him and beckoned. Marvelous nodded and rose from his bench, then made his way to the dim stairwell that wormed up through the bowels of the repair barn. Eva maintained her office at the very top level, where a ventilation shaft led to the street and admitted a faint gray light and a whisper of traffic noise. She was a superstitious ancient, who claimed she could read the mood of the city from this sound alone.

She reclined in her salon chair, before a low table on which rested a small silver samovar and a tray full of cups. She was wearing a purple cocktail dress trimmed in black, set off by an orange sash and opal earings. Ranged against the far wall were her three desks, littered with printouts and infodisks. Each desk also had a keyboard and screen, and two displayed an open file. Along the joining wall were two refrigerators and a holo running without sound.

The Doctor was a touch more presentable, she noted, but had not altered his irritating expression, which reminded her of the unfocused satisfaction of an infant shitting its pants. Eva had composed her own amiable smile, and now lifted one of her long scarlet nails to point at the upholstered chair nearest her own.

"Doctor, I've been heartless and rude to keep you waiting. Please make yourself comfy and have some tea. It's been such a – forgive me – colossal bitch of a day, but I *do* want to discuss this plan of yours and get things decided. Sugar?"

He shook his head to decline, trying to co-ordinate the cup and the samovar handle to dispense his tea. *A congenital klutz*, she reflected. *How had he ever made his way in a laboratory? Above all, how had he felled a trained operative with a pipe wrench?* Her profound pity for the man carried a border of exasperation, and another of curiosity.

"The market," she went on with her apology, "had a touch of indigestion this morning. That wild man's raid on recreation stocks

235

and the news at the border and the election, et cetera. Of course you are interested in much more vital things."

"Oh, vital . . . I don't know, I think everything is . . . bears on . . . the living system." Doctor Petrasky had settled tentatively into the chair and now took a polite sip of the hot tea.

He looked so earnest, so vulnerable. Of course he was very bright, too. Eva took Cynthia's word on that. But he had absolutely no trace of the abilities esteemed in her world: camouflage, subterfuge, mimicry, the ploy and the bluff.

All the others had fit in quickly. Tima had become an invaluable consultant, skilled in every sort of ambush and trickery. Ronnie had revealed a knack with his drum, and anyone with musical talent had some respect, could travel in the hoods and free zones without hassle. Cynthia and Batboy picked up the lingo and postures of young smackers, and were perhaps ready to solo.

Petrasky had seemed actually to regress, to lose even the veneer of confidence. His pose of a street headcase was not in fact a pose at all. He went on mumbling about the origins of matter and life and thought whether or not anyone listened. But now, in what appeared to be the early stages of a major delusion, he had acquired – Eva wanted to laugh and wince at the same time – a kind of *following*, a niche, a possible career.

"I want to hear all about this new proposal," she chatted, "and your thoughts. Astonishing, from what I hear. Humper told me they already know you as 'Preach' all around Bankers' Park."

"Yes." The Doctor's cheeks were pink with modesty. "I was very surprised myself. Just people passing by at first, but they began to come back with friends. I . . . I didn't know *what* to say at first. I suppose they were sermons, but . . . " He looked again at his shoes. "Without my research, I've been able to think more *deeply*, actually. More generally and . . . creatively."

"I'm sure you have. Very exciting. And now you've got a congregation! You're a . . . Pastor! Imagine."

"Well, only in a manner of speaking. We wouldn't be registered, of course; there wouldn't be any church – no edifice, I mean – and the . . . uh . . . contributions would not be in any traceable currency or credit."

Petrasky was looking very earnest. And he was not entirely out of touch with things, if he had thought of these arguments himself. Eva's main worry was that the Doctor would call attention to himself, cause a disturbance or complaint that would draw the police.

"What sort of people are they, your congregation? I gather you deliver God in terms of germs and genes and so forth?"

"Ah, no. Not exactly . . . a kind of *translator*, rather . . . science is only a metaphor I am trying to explain."

"Hmmm. Yes, how intriguing." Eva smiled, lifting her cup in a gesture meant to convey both accord and dismissal. But the Doctor was growing animated.

"The great forces driving our universe apart and binding it together are actually engaged in this wonderful dialogue, which takes the form of a sort of story or song. Every bit of germ plasm is telling its part of the story, and also listening to the others—"

"Absolutely fascinating!" Eva's smile brightened and sharpened. "No wonder they flock to you. But I do worry that any sort of crowd, any notoriety . . . "

"They are mostly elderly," Petrasky said quickly. "Some mothers and children, a very few Nonumbs and those just the old park people. I think sixteen is the most I've ever talked to at once." He looked at her in frank supplication. "They just want to listen. And I feel – selfishly – fulfilled and safe and . . . *validated* somehow. And I would at least not be so . . . so dependent on the rest of you." Hurriedly he drank from his cup again, an excuse to lower his eyes.

On Cynthia, he means, Eva mused. She had noticed how the lovers had grown awkward and glum around each other. They seldom talked any more about their former life, the promise of their research. Cynthia had let drop a half-joking remark that she and her old professor had switched roles; she was now the hardhead, he the fringie. It would certainly do Petrasky good to have, as one said, a life.

It was also possible that a lone nut ranting on the street was more ostentatious than a handful of rag-tag dissenters. A tiny cult had a sort of legitimacy, implied duration and regularity. The police would not be as likely to jerk someone around if there were respectable citizens present.

"Your friends think you are perfectly valid as you are," Eva lied, "but of course we would be happy if you felt better." She laid one hand on a carved wooden box at her side. "You would have to promise me not to perform any miracles or become a great teacher. We do have to protect our little one."

Doctor Petrasky looked nonplussed for a moment, then blushed and laughed. "Oh no! I mean, there are enough miracles every day, all around us . . . in us . . . and most people are rather afraid of miracles, I think, so I am not going to be . . . *popular*." The word seemed to astonish him slightly, like a burst bubble. "So, it . . . it would be all right?"

Eva again lifted one long, red nail. "It would. Just be careful, and keep us informed of your daily schedule, any new additions to your flock. Okay?" She put the finger swiftly to her lips, before the Doctor could get out the profuse thanks she could see him preparing. "Good luck. I think you will make a darling prophet. Now I've a scad of calls to make and some more people to see. So off you go, and we'll talk soon."

"Thank you. You are a very kind lady." He said it with a touching gallantry, and bowed before he turned to go. As soon as the Doctor was out Eva flipped open the lid of the box and took out her ivory and jade holder and a cigarette. She wanted to giggle, and at the same time knew a pang of anxiety. Petrasky's innocent delusion was itself a kind of miracle, one bright strand in a dense weave of intrigue and deception and danger.

She lit the cigarette and inhaled the rough, aromatic blend of black Balkan leaf. A dot of green light appeared on a monitor deck across the room. That would be the Plenipotentiary. She had given him that title ironically, but had come to recognize its etymological accuracy. He called himself, with his own twist of irony, Joe Seven.

Let him wait, she thought. Of all those who had sent out feelers or made blind propositions, the organization behind Joe Seven was the most mysterious, and the most powerful. They seemed to know, with certainty, the identity of her famous guests. They also knew her own schedule, her habits. They had sent the black Balkan as a gift. They were, therefore, almost certainly an instrument of her ex-husband. And she would, therefore, have to control her revulsion and think carefully in any further negotiations.

Meanwhile her charges had ensnared themselves in their own net of risk, trouble and pain. Tima would soon be too pregnant to do her old-man act, but Ronnie needed to keep working, to learn every bend in the labyrinth he now lived in. Against her better judgment Eva had granted them a few more outings together, evenings in a free zone. Cynthia was spending too much time in political meetings, arguing and plotting with Sandhill. Eva did not consider this an auspicious development, especially with Petrasky out from underfoot. She intended to pair Cynthia with Ronnie, perhaps Batboy too, and let them run easy scams in the transit tubes, where they could dodge and disappear if any hitches occured.

All these solutions were temporary and uneasy. Eva felt a little overwhelmed. She had known the rumor of the pregnancy would reach the world and create a great stir. She had expected bribes and threats from many quarters, as in any delicate political situation. She never ruled out an offer before hearing it, and trusted her ability to balance and betray in such a way as to protect her world and its inhabitants.

But this odd teenage couple and their developing embryo had boosted things to a new order of magnitude. They had become a symbol charged with immense, ambiguous significance. Some were calling them tragic lovers, and others prayed for their extermination. The whole NorthAm continent was dividing over whether to forgive or persecute them, and as the rumor of the hybrid foetus spread, the polls showed an unprecedented intensity and volatility in public opinion. The only constant was a growing voracity for more sensational detail, more conflict, an eventual trial and judgment.

Eva sighed, blew a jet of smoke at the green light, pulsing now. From the ventilator shaft she heard a faint but insistent droning. Another lockup of feeder lines, or general traffic system overload. She had her own theory about the burgeoning hysteria above. The NorthAm populace was afraid to admit what Omalys took for granted: that there might be a lot of Gink blood loose in the gene pool. Bestiality was not something you bragged about, and yet . . .

She shook off the reflection. There were hard facts to deal with. From the start she had received disturbingly large offers for information on the whereabouts of Ronnie and Tima. They could have come from Stockwell's intelligence apparatus, from the Progressive opposition, or from freelance darksiders interested in a bidding war. But Joe Seven had said, the very first thing, that his employers would match any offer. Yet they didn't ask her to turn the kids over, or to reveal a location – they already knew it, apparently – but simply to keep everyone safe.

Safe for what? That was the question that troubled her. *Our future*, Joe had said with his maddening, deferential confidence. *We want to see potential realized.* That sounded like her ex-husband, indeed. Though it was uncharacteristic of him to dabble directly in such a political issue. Homer had always bought whatever he needed from whatever President or party reigned at the moment. The sonofabitch had no ideology she knew of, unless insatiable vanity and boundless greed could be called ideas. Perhaps his floating island and collection of rare carnivores had grown tedious, and he was under a new influence. A new influence, she would hazard, with big tits.

She made a decision, ground out the cigarette, and got up to approach the monitor with the blinking green light. She took the portable board and keyed in their usual trapdoor channel, blind on his side, before returning to her chair. As usual he was in an office, behind a generic desk, a neutral wall behind. His tie was loosened and his sleeves were rolled up. He wore the same cool, easy smile, and spoke as soon as his image steadied.

"Good morning, Eva. Very glad you were there and ready to link. How are you?"

"Ninety-three years old, and curious."

He did not laugh, of course. He made a point of not laughing, but she worked at him anyway. A remnant of her old pride as an actress, a prima donna bitch.

"Beautiful at any age, and always famous for your wit. As for the curiosity . . . let me mention some new developments with us, which might answer some of your questions." He waited, holding the smile, his bald head gleaming in the desk lamp.

She watched his eyes for any nuance, any shift of concentration, but he did not flinch. A perfect messenger-man, an antiseptic, electronic diplomat. She regretted now insisting on only a voice line for herself. He might have betrayed more if he had to stare at the wreck of a great beauty.

"The flim-flam at the trout pool? Are you disavowing or taking credit?"

To her great surprise, Joe Seven did utter a laugh, so swift and slight she almost missed it.

"Doesn't really matter, does it, Eva? But Agent Pfeiffer has – you must concede – deflected the search away from your own territory."

"He's an absolute phoney. You *must* be taking credit."

"I suppose your friends the Thorgies were thoroughly outraged. One would think revolutionaries were above jealousy."

"Have you ever been a revolutionary, Joe?"

She got a slight thinning of his smile, but he went on as if he had not heard.

"We're a little concerned that speculation on the pregnancy has hardened and some wipe offers are going out. People down there are going to snoop, and find traces. You know the situation in your districts, and you know that everything under the street has a price." Joe shrugged his understanding and forgiveness. "So—"

"So I have mine. Which you know, but I'll name it again. You want my co-operation, you tell me what you want to do with my kids."

Joe beamed. "That's simple, Eva. As I've told you from the start, we want them to achieve their destiny."

She hissed between her teeth and almost reached out to kill his image, this conversation. Her ex-husband must have given this asshole particular instructions to drive her into a rage. But he had hurried on, aware of treading a dangerous border.

"I know you think we're hiding something. You think we have a blueprint for that destiny. But we don't Eva. We just don't. And that's the amazing, the entirely new approach we're taking – we *have* to take – because this thing is bigger, has more momentum, than any of our blueprints. It's a unique and tremendously powerful convergence. This is *history* being made, Eva. We don't control history." Joe's smile warmed and widened. "Though with luck we just might be able to shape it so the beauty and truth of things are clearer."

"Ah. Beauty and truth. By my troth." Eva had adopted a throaty whisper full of sweet venom. "Every man's bullshit sweet to his own sense doth smell. Spare me, Joe. You tell me how your employer – that dried up old prick – sees this 'destiny'. Tell me right now. Or I cease returning your calls." She put her finger on a key.

For several seconds Joe said nothing. His smile now conveyed careful concern. His eyes were clear, unblinking. When he spoke his voice was soft and deliberate.

"All right, Eva. You want some cards on the table, and we understand that. I think you will have to admit that the situation is unstable and deteriorating, that your . . . kids . . . need a more secure haven. You've worked wonders these last two months, given them a home and something to do, but – let's be honest – your resources are limited. Some very big players are interested in these assets, and you would eventually – painful to say this, and don't take it wrongly – have to sell them to save them. You need our help, and believe me, we have exactly the same priority. We want, first of all, to keep this family together and

241

guarantee this child safe delivery. That's absolutely bottom line."

"Noble words."

"We will back them up. Let me point out we've made two generous payments already, merely for confirming information we already possessed. Let me also mention that so far we have never intervened, though we've known your program for some time – the dumpster diving, the back deals, Ronald's drumming in free zones, Cynthia's involvement with the Thorgs – all of it. If we had wanted to nab anyone, we could have done it weeks ago. We do have resources."

Eva did not reply. It was not an idle boast. Joe Seven had first appeared without warning in the midst of a deeply encrypted, tripwired file, and none of their subsequent transactions left any trace on her logs. That casual reference to dumpsters told her that her wards had been under surveillance since their training began. She suspected also that these people had bribed one or more of her close subordinates for off-line information. How else did they know what she liked to smoke?

"We do understand your hesitation. We don't expect you to compromise your position, unless we can guarantee you a better one. We are working up a proposal, but in the meantime, with the situation so unstable, we want to provide you with an emergency exit option, with secure transit and a safe destination."

"Why? Have you scheduled an emergency?" Eva gave the question a deadly, companionable lilt.

Joe Seven looked patient. "Hardly necessary, Eva. They are arriving on their own. It's four weeks to the election of the century, and everything rides on what happens to these star-crossed youngsters. Certain parties, I'm sure you know, would take desperate measures to ensure their recapture. And others are just as anxious to make sure they disappear for good."

Again Eva did not reply. What Joe said was true. So was what he did not say: that his employers might be among these certain parties.

"We have trusted you, obviously; and soon you may have to decide whether to trust us. All we can do now is make the opportunity available. If you will give me a free-standing dead-end vault, with a one-way, one-time release, I will log in a single entry, an address. You need only get your kids to that address – any hour day or night – and we will move them out of the city and to a secure place. A place where they will feel at home."

As he was speaking, a display code ran under his image. She exited the file on her second deck, then pulled up her deep tomb and split off a new insulated space. When her system read the code and turned up no virus or fuse, she signalled open access. She would take any information from this source, true or false.

"Thank you, Eva. You won't be sorry." He pressed a key at his station and she heard her deck swallow the entry. "If anything should happen and you can't retrieve this vault, we have a backup contract who can lead your friends to the right place. You have an assistant, you see. Quite near."

"Thought so. How comforting. What did he or she cost you?"

He paused, maintaining the frequency of his smile for a perfectly timed interval. "Good bye, Eva. Always a pleasure."

The light that had composed Joe Seven was sucked away through a point in the mathematical center of the screen. She stared for a moment at the file that had resurfaced, then turned to the second deck. She dropped the tomb back through layers of guard system, sealed it, and killed power on both decks.

It galled her to admit that the Plenipotentiary made sense. Omalytown was really no place to have a baby. She probably wasn't the right godmother, either. And the dying refugees, the whispers of an epidemic, and the impending election were creating terrific pressure for some quick, symbolic solution – like a sacrifice.

From the beginning, of course, they had talked about making it to the border and crossing into the Wastelands. In their trances Ronnie and Tima claimed to communicate with the few Pobla still holding to the old way, and it was clear they yearned to rejoin Tima's tribe. There was simply no credible plan for such a journey. Nonumbs survived under the street because they *couldn't* go anywhere else, and the Thorgs would hardly drive through a sensitive military zone in a pizza truck.

A place where they will feel at home. Eva knew a dreadful, deep spitefulness. *We have exactly the same priority.* She closed her eyes and released a long, uneven sigh. She was an old woman. She should be too tired to hate this much. After almost fifty years of spurning him and everything he stood for, here she was, set up again in helpless dependency, once more a thing to be calculated and played like a token in his endless egotistical game. But fact was fact, however intolerable. Barrelhead had the power to get her kids home.

Her eye was caught by the holo on the side wall. The Fat Man in his flying chair. The unstoppable mouth. Another media sensation feeding on the Drager saga or scandal or whatever it was to be. Eva had seen many of these sensations bloom and fizzle in her long career. Beau Winger had bottom. He seemed to be enduring. They said he might even make a difference.

The idea unsettled Eva. She had other appointments, a list of calls scheduled. She could hear Dustin's ostentatious tread behind her door, reminding her. That big toad was appalling. He was a monster of tinsel light, a gale of foul gas. He was also – her hand was already foraging in the carved box, releasing the strong, rich smell – addictive.

". . . the fat man's shnozz is infallible, pre-shunt, the shnozz of doom, ain't I told you a thousand times? Beginning to get da beeg peekchur, taxpoopers? Beginning to get a whiff?"

Beau's chair has swooped down and shrunk to the apparent size of a dragonfly, whisked through an open window into his central studio, where it inflates again to normal size. But now the chair is an office variety of elegant leather and dark wood, and the only other furnishings on the set are a NorthAm flag and a tremendous map of the continent. The lighting has modulated into a somber chiaroscuro. Beaufort is calm, his clasped hands resting on one knee of his crossed legs.

"We think, good people, that the whole soap is a Con con job from the get-go. This so-called kidnap was a fully funded, professionally arranged political picnic. Okay, obvious, so next question. We're getting to that, the ultimate slimoscam, and with the help of yerstrooly's investigative piranhas we'll expose the really Big Issue. Because who do you come to for the final take, the total wrap? Dabig fat guy, right? So here it is, dear publick, in a nutshell: the Con party, ladies and gents, has been completely infiltrated, maybe overgetaken completely, by the rads, the closet Thorgies like Cynthia Higgins, with all their terrorist leanings.

"And what's their agenda, folks? Well, what bombs won't get you bamboozle will. They start with Biodiversity and Ecobalance and all that old flapdoodle – Save the Sharks, Hug a Cobra today, no poison on Pissants, et cetera – and *especially* protect the Po-ba-la, the ghouls, because *eventually* – enough propagoofy and duplicitistics down the line – they're gonna push for some kind of *equality*, for admitting these critturs into *human society!*

"And you know what that means, you guessed, dincha? *Mixing*. Interbreeding. Your daughters, folks. Your lovely sweet precious daughters. These nutcakes would mate them with beasts. Dafat guy doesn't mince his metaphors, kiddies. Beasts, capital B. The lap goes on two legs, he has a language of sorts, he can sing a simple song, but he *ain't* human. Ever. Period. Laps barbecue their own parents in ritual feast, they sniff crap, they howl at the moon, they nibble each other's lice – must I go on, I got lunch ahead of me – they are a degenerate species. Freaks. Muties. The worst ever evolutionary error. And that, class, is that. End of lesson.

"So you can't believe it, huh, Seen Yours and Seen Your Eatahs? Too way out, beyond flash, absurdorama preposteroso – how would they ever *do* it? Well, I'm gonna tell ya, kiddies, tell ya exactly – after this Public Infodrama Spot Message!"

Beaufort licks his finger and reaches out with it as if to touch the lens of the camera dollying in. The whorls and ridges of skin on the fingerpad expand to fill the field of view and then dissolve into another topography, a low, hilly terrain contour-planted in dense, conical green bushes. A machine moves along the slope, gobbling up the small bushes and extruding a moist coil of matter into a wide, deep bin rolling behind. In a rapid montage, this fiber pulp is followed through heat-vats, injection chambers, chemical baths and a shining, whirling array of cutters, rollers, and stampers, from which emerges a dizzying variety of panels, fabrics, structural beams, cabinets, vehicle fenders and doors, rugs, lampshades, pillows, paints, unguents, lotions, preservatives and cosmetics – all of which assemble themselves into and around a scene – a happy, handsome family in front of a trim, landscaped home. While their two children cavort, the husband and wife are setting out tasty snacks and iced drinks on a patio table. A female voice, crisp yet cheerful, provides commentary over a track of carefree holiday music.

"The new Euroslav trade agreement, providing access to the fresh quick-grow plantations of the taiga, recently boosted the output of consumer goods, especially this low-priced house-'n-car complex. The agreement was hammered out between Federation's Secretary of Trade, NorthAm President Stockwell's Econ team, and Euroslav ministry delegates.

"The new 'Holistic Lifestyle' approach uses every ounce of raw resource – from root to leaf – for maximum biomass release. And as this family – Al and Sally Wilson from the WashYork corridor – can testify, it makes a real difference. Their home and vehicle are an integrated biosystem, part of their green commitment to 'use it all and use it right.' Sally?"

The woman looks up from the fruit bowl she has been arranging, a little flustered and embarrassed but smiling with sunny good humor. "Well, Al and I – gosh, we were going to remodel and refurnish our old home, you know, but when we compared prices, this Cellufab Omniplex unit was so—"

"And they mean *omni*." Al has popped up beside his wife, grinning boyishly, holding a golf club which he now flexes, as if lining up a chipshot. "Would you believe this seven iron used to be a hunk of *bark*?"

"Al, the *price* was what turned us around. That's the important—"

"But honey, there's so much in the Omni." Al pinches the lapel of his natty sportshirt. "Even the shirt off my back – it's spruce needles – and—"

Sally has put a shoulder in front of her husband and cupped a hand around her mouth to insist, in a loud confidential whisper, "*Under* five, girls. An absolute *steal*. It's not only made entirely from the green and growing, it will keep your household budget the same way!"

The female voice-over laughs affectionately and continues while Al and Sally mug a mock spat. "We'll have to let the Wilsons work out priorities for their purchase, but any way you slice it, the Trade Agreement is a big plus for NorthAm buyers. Conservative and Progressive spokespeople both take credit for this economic coup, but this is a pubinfo break, so we go back now to—"

"—the Beaufort Winger show, sponsored by Big One and Big Cool, from Greenpro! The most humongissimo, the most monsterama yakshow on the globe, Job! Dabig fat guy is cominatya!"

Riding his chair, Beaufort appears to glide above the Wilsons' patio and park in the air at a comfortable, conversational distance.

"Time for People's Plaza, where you pose the preguntas, seetwayens. You ask the expert – that's me – and you can come back on the answer, as long as you stay under forty-five seconds and you do not just babble propadrivel from some madrad goofinsky perspecto, okay class? We got the comlink terminals open, folks, ready for your holocalls, so ring up and get in the yak stack. But let's start with Al and Sally. Listen up for our special focus today. We were suggesting that the Conservative Party has caved in to extremists who secretly want to – I shudder, I gulp, I hate to spoil this happy hour for a coupla beautiful kids like you guys, but hey, the truth takes a strong stomach – legalize copulation with animals. With *Homo lapsis* in particular. Lemme get just a quick reaction on that from Sally – Mrs Parent-of-the-Year . . . "

Sally has lost her smile. In fact her eyes glisten with tears and her chin has acquired dimples, a dermal contraction induced by powerful revulsion.

"I really don't have words for . . . for anything . . . so *awful*. When I think of my own children . . . I . . . I just don't understand how any *sane* person—"

"*Sane*? Oh, Sally, these people can't have minds, as we know them, intelligence as we understand it. These people worship lizards and talk to rootabegas. They need professional assistance."

"They need a professional kick in the old watooski," Al says stoutly.

Beaufort laughs with gusto. "Big Al, you tiger man, I think you got it right. I think the average taxpooper would agree. But we are, uh, nonviolent, of course. Only encourage the creative, haha, incentive for behavior change, right, kiddies? My question is a fine-tuner, a nuts-and-bolts. If, let's just say *if*, there was a conspiracy not only to accommodate this sudden wave of Po-ba-la, but actually to give them *rights*, legal status, then how are they going to bring it off? What's their strategy? What should we watch for?"

Al and Sally look at each other, scratch heads, then look again, pleadingly, at Beaufort's floating image.

"Well, Beau," Al says with a sheepish grin, "I enjoy your show so much – it's so full of so much info and good sense – I guess I'd just tune in to find out!"

"Great taste you got, Al, and thank you, guys for that little testimonial. But you're already *on* the show, you pudinskis. We need some ideas here, folks. Creative thinkers, serious hasslemachers. Come on, now! Ah! Here's somebody. Morning, sir, you are . . . ?"

"Luke Landsman. Love your show, Beau."

The Wilsons have vanished, are replaced by a lanky man in work clothes, who is standing, rather ill-at-ease, in one of the comlink portable studios.

"Thank you, discriminating viewer. Now, right to it, Luke. What do you think these beanheads and bentbrains are up to? What's coming at us?"

"Well, Beau, they could do a lotta things. These people. They're nutcakes, like you said."

248

"I know what I said, Luke. Appreciate your support, but have you got something? Otherwise . . . "

Beaufort touches a dial and the image of Luke begins to fade. Alarmed, it speaks rapidly, gestures with great animation, and as a result waxes vivid again.

"Well, I think they'll try to get the mixeds in first. Yeah, you bet! Change the rules for that, the sterilizations and all. There's a lot more of them than—"

"Whoa, whoa there, Luke. Do I hear – is there static in the beam, sunspots, gremlins? Are you saying we have a prob with our mixed pop?"

"Well, Beau, I'm in the service department of a public utility so I get around doing new hookups and I see a lot of kids, lot of bandages on noses and ears. In lo-cost, sure, but also in some pretty fancy places. I mean doctors and businesspeople and even—"

"Now Luke, be careful here, be very careful. Are you saying that the mixeds are on the increase? In spite of the duplicitistics our gummint feeds us? That these throwback cases are *not* being reported, not being sterilized?"

Luke appears nonplussed and confused, a little bit frightened. "No, I mean . . . shoot, Beau, I don't know. But if like you say they wanted to bring the *bleeps* in on us as equals, wouldn't they have to stop cuttin' the mixeds?"

Luke is fading during this speech, dialed down by Beaufort, who modulates his own voice with a deep, prophetic echo.

"'Course you don't know, Luke, and they ain't gonna tell you, either, or anybody like you. They're gonna keep you scared and dumb, because in your own wonderful simple-guy populoso way you figured out the *obvious*."

Beaufort's chair has whizzed back into broadcast headquarters, and he is being recorded now from an angle that shows the stage and its flat walls, the crossbeams of the holo projectors on feed, the engineers' booth and technicians working the lights and effects. Beau leaves his seat for the first time, lumbers to the center of the stage, again speaking directly to his viewers and striking now a pugnacious attitude.

"Sure, everybody knows somebody who had to have a bleach or cut, and everybody knows those ops are supposed to go with a sterijob, privacy protected by law. Fact is, the laps did have human ancestors. Fact is, it's nobody's fault some of the first generation took their unholy offspring and slipped back over the border. Fact is, a hundred seventy years ago, before the Fed, we didn't have the tech tools to geneprint accurately. It was only fair to treat the occasional throwbacks as unfortunate quirks. Idea was to correct, sterilize, and keep confidential. Problem would just gradually fade away in a couple of generations.

"Wrong. Not. Monumentoso a-roar. The beanbrains forgot something. Uno, you make a judgment call on a baby's ears, you can miss and one slips through. Duo, mom and dad maybe got the juice to bribe a surgeon for an illegal bleach and tuckeroonie, so the genes are loose, goose, and fertile, child, and at large, Marge. Next thing we have folks high on the pole, *very* high, who may never know until one of their kids – number four, maybe? – has a troglo nose or a lot of hair. You flash? Coming clear?

"All that buzz manure about diversity and compassion for the starving hordes, our cousins? Hey, gets you taxpoopers in the mood for the idea that we 'owe' the ghoul kakas a refuge, at least. Gets you used to them. Pretty soon your daughter wants one for a pet. Factor in now, good seetwayens, the dark and devious radwing of the Con party. Thorgies like this Cynthia and Commandante Sandhill and their agenda of liberating and protecting every weird and dangerous molecule in the universe.

"That's why the Drager kid and his little kaka prodigy poke – trained by the Con Insec machine – they're the perfect enterin' wedge! The monster to be born! It's the Frankengeek story, the new guidin' myth! Everybody's talkin' it, walkin' it. You see it now, doncha? Only here, kids, only here with the big fat guy cominatya are you gonna get the truth. We got ourselves more than just a lickyslurpy story now, more than a handle on a scandal, we maybe got ourselves a conspiracy – a conspiracy not to suck up a little cash or muck up an opposing candidate, but – are you ready? – a *conspiracy to corrupt the human race*!

"Holy baloney! Did I say that? Really? You bet your kiester, meister, I said it! You wanna get the true doo-doo, you tune in tomorrow, class. We got some serious fragos for Prezdunt Stockwell Swelltalk. Like, why don't we make public all records from the New Life institute? Where are those porno tapes we hear about? We're not gonna ask for proof of insemination. If the bitch wasn't pregged before the breakout, you can bet all your bonbons she is *now*. Count on it!

"So we ain't gonna wait. Besides our campaign to restore *bleep* to the vocab, we want a retesting of every dubious woggle in the geneprint files from every agency that logs 'em. We want a requirement for a card or even a tattoo in every borderline case. Also, just how many illegal cosmetics are there, and how many public officials have had one? We got some names, people, and we got some numbers. Not factoids, not infoscams. Just like we always end up here, in the studio, where you see everything out in the open. Genuine value – like Big Cool and Big One, our revered sponsors – so remember, tune in tomorrow, class, and meantime waddle on, waddle on – fat rules! Together, we'll crush 'em all!"

A feeder channel cuts in logo and theme music, and Beaufort stretches his face in a great squinty-eyed silent yowl and does a shuffling dance step to the edge of the stage. Production personnel, sexcretaries and techies are gathering there, applauding and cheering.

"Hot? Was I a hot mutherfucker? Woo!" He shivers and gasps. The studio lights reveal that Beaufort is sweating under his make-up. A young woman hands him one cool, wet towel from the stack draped over her arm, and before he buries his face in it he puckers momentarily in her direction, an air-kiss.

"Jesus, Beau, you have *done* it! I mean that was dynafuckingmite! Outrageous! Max impact!" The producer, himself flushed and perspiring, grips Beaufort's meaty shoulder and is thus dragged along toward a row of desks at the rear of the studio. There, several people are talking excitedly into intercoms or holophones. The whole retinue swirls and eddies in the wake of Beau's progress.

"Living history," one of the production staff says to another beside him.

"Unstoppable," she replies, with a headshake at the sheer miracle of it.

"Terrific, terrific, Beau." A gaunt, middle-aged woman at a battery of monitors looks up, her face transfixed. "Eighty-seven point six faves, sixty-two of those very strong. Estimated three hundred mill on line."

"What's the down?" Beaufort tosses the towel over one shoulder, and behind him someone catches it. He flaps his elbows against his huge torso and grins at the woman. "I can take it, sweetheart."

The woman scans the monitor; her mouth twists with supressed excitement. "*Too* powerful." She giggles. "Too good to be true."

There is laughter, more cheers. "The Mixed angle, *tattoos*, that was the killer." The producer seems on the verge of tears of ecstasy. "We have really . . . *really* . . . "

"Beau! Beau!" A young man with his loosened tie askew is gazing into the holophone chamber on a desk. He slaps a hand down on top of his head, as if to keep it from blowing off. "Alex Waters just said on NHC – holy shit! – he said you were—" The young man's brain volcanoed his hand straight up into the air. *"The greatest menace to public order in the nation!"*

There is a mighty cacophony of hoots and whoops and whistles. People are embracing, doing impromptu dances. Beaufort Winger blows kisses and does an elephantine curtsey, then raises his joined hands in the victor's gesture. The hubub diminishes then, to allow him to speak.

"You ain't pernouncin' it right." He puts on a mock scowl. "It's pernounced *mean-ass*. I'm the greatest mean-ass in the land, kids. And you're gonna find that out, Waters – you and the other so-called pundits. Get the dicks on the job, people, open the files, we're gonna put some of these buttholes on the griddle. And—" He sighs, wistfully, and is suddenly calm, businesslike, looking from face to face around the room as he continues.

"—we got to start with ourselves. Everybody in the entire team – all staff, including gofers and doorpeople and caterers – gets an up-to-date geneprint on file. No exceptions. Hey, you got a cousin once removed, some in-law, who is a possible streak – we just wanna know. Doesn't mean your job, necessarily – unless you try to hide it. But let's all come clean, okay? Absolutely clean, Eugene."

It is quiet now in the room, except for intent murmurs and soft exclamations of approval. "Absolutely," someone whispers, and others chime in: "Right . . . full disclosure . . . with you, Beau, all the way . . . "

Beaufort grins and ambles toward a door leading to his inner office and studio. Only the towel girl and the manager follow this time. Hand on the doorknob, he glances coquettishly over his shoulder and deliberately sways his great behind. "You all workin' for the biggest mean-ass in the universe, kids. Better love it."

They recover, break into grins and cheers again, send him out of the room with affectionate yells.

"Love ya, Beau!"

"Dabig fat guy!"

"Love ya, Mr Mean-ass!"

252

CHAPTER TWENTY-FOUR

They were in trouble because of the drum and a sewer dog. The drum because they had cajoled Eva into letting them have a last night in a free zone, where he was getting a reputation for his mojo, even as the rumors spread of a new hunt for them under the street. Then the dog, because Tima had looked at him when they came in and when he ran whining to her she touched him before she thought and made him instantly her *mahanaku*, and even if the dog gang hadn't been specifically sent after them, the leader couldn't overlook such an insult.

They had a few minutes to think, because in a free zone the doggieboys were powerless until the drumming stopped and the crowd dispersed. But that would happen soon, and he could see the hate and anticipation in the twist of the headboy's mouth, and the signs he gave to his companions, to watch every passageway out.

They were on the first level of a ruined parking station, where sections of the broken concrete had been turned into makeshift benches. The drummers were ranged around fire barrels, and behind them in the shadows some couples were dancing the ancient forbidden dances. Old people, lifelong Omalys with their fantastic patchwork clothing, huddled even closer to the barrels and occasionally sang or hummed a melody that seemed to fit.

There were only three drums still working when Pahane finished a sequence and got up to move with Tima a little way from the others. She had whispered to the dog (a snow dog, rangy and black with some silver on his face and chest) and the animal remained by the fire, watching her for any sign. Tima lit a cigaret and passed it to him so he could drag while she talked.

"I didn't see in time, I'm sorry. *Ye tohu pakishta*." She inclined her head very slightly toward the huddle of dogboys glaring at them. "These *dakos* are trouble. We will have to run them, string them out, and then spook them."

"We haven't run much for a long time." Pahane glanced uneasily into the huge, shadowy chamber, connected by old shafts to the subway and an abandoned jitney tunnel. "And you . . . "

"I'll be fine." Tima smiled a little. "She likes to run."

He grimaced. A good part of their child's life so far had been on the run. The new freedom they had thought to find here, the chance to talk and dream together, a place of their own – these had resolved into yet another labyrinth, another minefield.

"You got to them again. I heard some of the old ones talking. They remember when a half-a-million people danced in the streets." Tima took back the cigaret, played with it for a moment, holding it like a candle. "They were flying."

"*Kish.* It happens a lot these days," Pahane said. "*Wonakubi* is speaking, not me."

He was refreshed at some deep, physical level by the drumming, and the travel it induced, though he was sobered by what he saw. Usually he drummed along with Kapu's band, so he knew about the horses, and the people who went with them. They had, he understood now, broken into his dreams months ago.

He followed other remnants of Adza's clan, those without shadows who were drifting toward the border on some slow, implacable tide. There was now a mysterious quickening of this current, as if the horde of skeletons bore some new gift of spirit, subtle and unfathomable. And now there were Omalys who followed his drumming, or rather were absorbed into the power emanating from the migrating Pobla. He was not a dazzling performer, not even very practiced, but something turned his hands into wild birds at these times. A whole people spoke through them. The other drummers and dancers, without being aware of it, adopted this new tongue, and found themselves soaring into a landscape they did not know, amid great-winged birds they did not recognize, into the company of ghosts whose intensity disturbed them. Before they knew what was happening some glimpsed their own lost shadows and believed they had gone mad.

"Anyway," Tima drew on the cigaret and exhaled the smoke through her nostrils all at once, dragon-like. "I think you even reached the headboy over there. He still wants to slit me, but maybe he imagines you could be his bonus."

She smiled again and they were silent. Pahane understood her. The headboy would be wondering, *Why pop them both?* This odd little slick with his hot drum, he could have all the back and progirls he wants, and instead the fool stays with some pregnant bitch with a flat nose who looks like a little old panhandler. Maybe – the headboy might think further – somebody should wipe the three-hole and hump the kid for a while, use his talents, because he definitely had a touch.

"Wolfie warned us," Pahane said then. "She said the doggies are very territorial, very hierarchical."

Tima laughed. "Here, that means something."

The drum sessions brought people from the whole intricate mosaic of clans and gangs under the street. In free zones like this one even bitter enemies could bargain and trade or witness an entertainment together. These zones were a necessary element in the Omaly economy, which was as ruthless and complicated as the one above ground.

Securing a place was everything, in the under-economy. In the beginning their clothes and the vanful of pizza had bought them scrip from old Knobs, good for their first nights. Eva guaranteed basic services through payoffs to city officials in transport, water, and energy, which protected them from closures or inspections. Thus every tunnel had a toll, every dumpster and culvert a rental, every Omaly a price. The only stability was the precarious one of incessant struggle – a fine, calculated quadrille of alliance and betrayal, self-interest and common good, designed to occupy and defend a space in which to *be*.

Once again, a mirror of the bright overworld. Competition. Combat. The highest and most honored of traditions. Since the Federation and its strict control of weaponry, conflict under the street was resolved by ancient methods – the bludgeon and cold steel. The principle was everywhere – even in the drumming and dancing.

When Red Wolf had taken them to their first session, they were startled at the lashing feet and hands like blades, the convulsions, the sweating and eye-rolling intensity. Pahane had been almost overwhelmed by the visions that came. For the first time he had glimpsed what he assumed were Sayat's *tchatsinakun*, the raiders whose shadows had turned inside out and become devourers. His own effort became one of resisting this influence, of weaving in subtle syncopation, of laying off the beat, riding for something more intense, something final and whole.

"I doubt I can win him over. He knows we're the mark." Pahane looked toward the fire barrels. "What about the dog?"

"He won't cross into the rats' tunnels. I'll send him back. But he might be able to help a little, confuse them." Tima sighed. "I shouldn't have touched him. But his ancestors and mine, and his life here . . . " She flicked away the cigaret butt, a tiny fiery parabola into the dark.

Is just like ours, Pahane completed the thought in silence. Some gangs hunted the dogs with flashlights and nets. They ate the weak and slow, and trained the better breeds – the long-limbed former trackers with night-vision – to hunt with them or stand guard. In Eva's district, the rats performed similar functions. Just as he had once studied living things as "resources" and Tima had been an Insec "experiment" learning to catch her own people. Just as they were both training now to survive in Omalytown, ever alert to borders and margins and allegiances.

"Prisoners," he said, and they looked at each other for a long moment. They felt the pressure of this underworld, bending them as the dark imperative of gravity bends light; they yearned into each other, desperate for reconnection to their vision – the play of wild freedom and perfect harmony, the song of things.

Simultaneously they reached out. His hand on her womb, hers on his heart. A small bright fish in a cave. Was between them. Was them. Was.

"*Sehapsi*," she whispered. "*Tohu.*"

"*Tohu.*"

When they were breathing together, they stepped apart. Tima grinned. "*Ya*. That's better. Now – can you go again?"

"Hold them? I think so. A few minutes." He flexed his hands, the one still tingling from the current that flowed through their three hearts.

"*Kish*. I will send him his dog. Then we run. We'll take the small tunnel for buses."

She was already concentrating herself. He could feel her effort, see the odd indistinctness of her figure in the red light from the barrels. She was the projector, he the receiver. He walked back toward the light, funneling his mind through the maelstrom of phantoms the other drummers had spun from desire and the thrill of striking. The gang headboy was watching him and Pahane opened to this desire, the curious testing and provoking, like a cat teasing a mouse with sheathed claws. *Now we will see*, he thought to himself, *which is which*.

He picked up the drum and did a one-handed riff. It was a simple center-to-rim pattern with a rap on the hoop to separate phrases, a deceptively simplified imitation of what the lead drum was doing. He delayed the rhythm by a just detectable margin, a kind of query, which he answered by laying off for six whole beats, then coming in by an equally slight margin ahead, thus tripping the others imperceptibly, so that he could catch them up, the one hand hot suddenly, a drive so swift they could not pause or react, could only follow, and they were no longer swinging or kicking but running, bounding, then flying . . .

He saw the dog slink along the edge of the circle, its ears laid back with dislike for such hard duty. The headboy's attention divided. The blur of Pahane's hand could no longer hold him, and he looked down at the dog, now wriggling slowly nearer, almost on its belly. The headboy's lips peeled into a snarl and he reached for the back of the animal's neck.

Pahane had moved a few steps away from the circle, even as he drummed again his simple opening statement, lost now in the complex drive of the others, and then he was hurrying into the gloom toward the entrance to the jitney tunnel. He stumbled once over a broken block of concrete, but as his eyes adjusted he moved more surely, avoiding the collapsed pillars and potholes, until he arrived at the black mouth of the tunnel.

Even as Tima hissed at him from inside this mouth, he heard the rapid footfalls behind them. He had stuffed the drum into the front of his shirt so he could reach out with both hands, palping the darkness. She was emitting sharp clicks of the tongue to guide him, and in a moment his hand fumbled into hers and they were moving faster. They loped in the Pobla's long-footed glide, Tima ahead. Behind them he could glimpse the beam of a light probing and glancing along the tunnel walls.

"He'll go with the light," Tima whispered. "When we find a place I can give him something to see."

They kept a steady lope, but the light was getting nearer. They heard a yell then, a sign they had been glimpsed. Soon they could hear a new sound, a softer, more rapid pattering, a hoarser breathing . . . Pahane heard Tima laugh under her breath. It was the dog. In a few moments the animal was running beside them, whimpering in joy, matching them stride for stride. The tunnel had inclined upward slightly, but they did not slacken the pace. Pahane could feel the pull of the ground, the distension of the bellows of his lungs, and began to work toward the empty serenity in which, the Pobla taught, one could run forever.

When the tunnel leveled again they found the spot they needed: an indentation in the wall, wide enough for three workmen abreast, with a callbox and tiny toolshed with no door. Tima drew him into this space, flattening against the ledge nearest the pursuers. She held the dog with a word, until the bobbing light was a little more than a hundred meters away, then released him onward again at a dead run and yipping. They heard another shout and a string of curses. The light advanced, gyrating wildly, glancing from the wet walls; they could hear the thud of feet and heavy breathing.

In the faint reflected glow, he saw that Tima had found something of interest in the tool shed. It was very old, for the thin walls were of wooden slats. She peeled away one of the slats and snapped it in two, and took a bit of string from one of the pockets of her shabby coat. When she huddled again beside him, he could feel her concentrating, coiling into herself, as she did something with the slat and string in her hands.

He quelled a sudden, mad pang of jealousy – it was always she who knew how to strike in these situations, her man's *kubi* with its power to evoke brilliant nightmares – and forced himself to add what he could of his own strength. Mainly he could scan for the headboy, who would be radiating murderous lust; for his shadow's gift was to apprehend, to see even in darkness.

When he felt the ugly knot of the headboy, to the right and a half-dozen strides behind the light-bearer, he laid his hand like a pointer across her shoulder.

"Good. When I stop them, you take the light." She breathed rapidly. "Easy. Don't jerk. Then turn it off and wait. They will be afraid and huddle together."

His hand was cold now, so cold he could not feel her shoulder any more. Though he knew what was coming he could not wall out the images Tima was calling from the darkness, the swirl of shadows growing luminous. The light was glaring off the tunnel walls now, the yells echoing like thunder.

"Got the muthufuckuhs! Got to be—"

She was gone from under his numb arm in an instant, and the hard white light from the hand lantern seemed at once to explode and expire around her moving shadow. What she did with the loose old coat he did not know, but the effect was of a huge, swooping creature with a mouth impossibly distended, a tongue writhing forth with the swiftness of a snake. He knew the image came from within

258

himself, that Tima had only drawn it forth and made it live, but he trembled and staggered anyway, moving after the light, which skidded crazily along the ceiling of the tunnel.

The boy holding the lantern had apparently fallen down and others of the gang tripped over him or wheeled about in fright, so the light fragmented into silhouettes and great lunging shadows. There were shrieks, startled bellows, and he was only one of the struggling bodies until he thought to go down on all fours. Someone was screaming, "*Get him! Get him!*" The beam swung around and down the tunnel again and . . . nothing! An empty, curving shaft with glistening black walls.

The sound from behind them was a deep, lewd gargle. Pahane had reached the lantern-bearer, now on one knee, and could see an outline of the boy's gape of fear. As the beam reversed once more he closed his hand over the lantern, partly blocking the light and tinting it the red-yellow of flesh. He was careful not to look up, but he heard the boy fighting to get enough breath to scream, and the lantern came into his hand as easily as a picked fruit.

Just as he switched it off he felt the pressure, the darkness collapsing in on itself. It was a kind of slithering advance, at once heavy and thick. He froze, pressed himself into the cold concrete floor. The boys made noises like motors unable to start, or soft yelps, or humming grunts, as they scrambled and stumbled away, colliding with each other and the walls.

"Fuckin' light! Where's da muthufuckin' light!"

"Ah shit! Shit! You see it? You see it? Fuckin' god, man, you *see* dat thing, dat lizard or what—"

"Gimme ya hand, Tony! Shut up, Kicks! Quiet!"

"Ah shit, Shag! Dat Pancake *toll* us not to mess wid dese people until—"

"Shut up, I said!" There was a muffled impact, another yelp and then only the sound of hard, irregular breathing, a sniffling.

Then whispers. "Whaddaya mean, ya *dropped* it? Find da muthu-fuckuh!"

Pahane had not moved, though he guessed he was less than ten steps away from these voices. In the utter blackness he could see the shapes beginning to swarm again, and before the gang made a move to feel for the lost lantern he heard the low, deep hum. It was a sound that made his whole frame vibrate, and it seemed to come from everywhere, from the whole darkness, and pass completely through him.

Panic lifted him for one instant, and then he almost laughed in exultation. A *vum-vum*! A toy for Pobla children. Also an instrument in some of the *tagakin* night ceremonies. It always terrified the very young, until they saw that it was only a blade of wood on a string, swung around and around overhead. Tima had made it from the shed slat and her bit of string, and the doggie boys had never heard its like before . . .

They were already babbling, breaking into hysteria.

"Whazzat? Whadafuckizzat? Ah shit! Shag, whaddawe do? Let's go, man, let's fuckin' *go*!"

He slipped the drum from his shirt and began a rapid tapping on the rim, with an occasional bump from the heel of his hand. Tima swung the *vum-vum* until it had the throbbing resonance of a great motor revving. In the distance the dog began to snarl, then yelp in terror, coming nearer . . .

"*Ambush*, man! Fuckin' ambush!" And in a stumbling, headlong rush they began to run back through the tunnel. Pahane heard a thud and a shriek of pain – someone colliding with the wall or floor – then bellows of sheer terror. They were beginning to see in the darkness the shapes Tima had summoned for them. He heard her moving after them, still swinging the *vum-vum*, so he came too, hammering a steady tempo on the drum. They would not, it appeared, have to run any more this night.

After following the jitney line to the old terminal, they found a sewer shaft up to the street and decided to pick a circuitous way back to Eva's. They were exhausted and talked only intermittently, once the euphoria of their escape had dissipated. They had, oddly, experienced the combat with the doggieboys as a kind of freedom. For a few moments, whose duration was intensified luxuriously, they had been wholly themselves and wholly together. Their future – again a matter of moments – depended completely on their agility, their insight. It had been a pure risk, a coincidence, a variation from the invisible pattern that held them fast.

"So you see where we are now," Tima remarked with a slight gesture of her hand. "Our horizon."

They were in a back street, where big ventilators sent steamy breath over their heads and a few delivery vans were already unloading onto the condo service lifts. But Pahane understood she meant much more than this scene: she meant this pattern which linked them to a two-faced society, made them notorious fugitives in a world-wide political scandal and simultaneously shrank their field of action to a goblin-game with idle boys.

"Better than the Institute," he said. "As prisons go. At least they are trying here. They believe in the trees—"

She made a small sound of disgust and he did not go on. In the pizza van they had listened to Sandhill and Red Wolf give sermons on the great trees, the vanished giants. Privately, Tima had pointed out to him how even here the piksi mentality prevailed. "They want the *idea* of the thing," she had argued wearily, "always. They want *their* kind of garden. They don't see that trees are not important. Bears and whales and hawks are not important either. Nor mountains and oceans. *Nothing* is 'important.' Including – especially – them and their ideas."

He had been shocked at the time, but he had come to see her point: she was thinking of the same old piksi compulsion to be boss of the universe, to assert dominion over every living thing. And he supposed it was even true, to some extent, of their new allies. They were constantly plotting and performing actions to "shape perception" or "create momentum." It was a battle, Sandhill had said, for the public's attention, for "narrative control."

"But they must believe in us . . . in Sehapsi . . . in some way," he said finally. "In what we . . . " He stopped, seeing her wry pout.

"Oh yeah. We can *represent*. Hey, that's what we *do* these days. We're instant myth."

He laughed, looking sheepish. "Okay. But I don't think they'd trade us in for a tree memorial. And they wouldn't separate us."

"Only as long as they think we can save *them*." She uttered a soft hoot. They were now skirting a minirig drawn up before a loading dock. The driver had just swung down from the cab, his powerplant burbling, and was staring at them with hostile contempt.

"Pancake," Tima said then.

"What?" They had eased by the driver and were hurrying now. It was near dawn, a dirty gray light behind the blocks of buildings. They would have to go under soon.

"One of the dogboys said they should have listened to the pancake."

"Oh yes. I heard that. Not to mess with us, until . . . " He frowned.

"Yes. Until. So what's a pancake?" She glanced at him, amused. "In your curious tongue?"

261

"Never heard it before. Omaly slang, I guess. But I would guess it is someone who" – he described a series of ascending loops with one hand – "turns around and around. And then comes back where he started, only reversed."

They walked on for a time in silence. Then they looked at each other, a common surprise.

"This pancake in the air," Tima said, "must be one of us."

CHAPTER TWENTY-FIVE

The dark egg of Josh's jetcopter dropped swiftly onto the shoreline pad, where the driver and valet were waiting for him with a limovan. Normally the old man allowed only boats, mostly old-fashioned launches, so this was a sign that another creative crisis had developed. Engineered, no doubt, by the all-devouring sisters.

Josh didn't bother to hide his irritation when the valet replied that indeed Ms Smith and Ms Konrad had arrived last night. They were supposed to be partners, but he was doing all the gruntwork. He was authorizing and then reviewing polls, co-ordinating market and campaign strategies, doing all the shmoozing and lobbying and fixing necessary to direct the grand drama they had conceived. Of course this was his gift, he was right for the job, but still it bothered him that his associates were getting cozier, and winding themselves further into Barrelhead's soul.

The valet had brought a shaver, hot scented towels, and a fresh shirt for him, so he felt much better when he stepped out of the limo and made his way to the inner courtyard. They had conferenced on holophone that morning, so he only traded nods and quick smiles as he took his seat. Only five now: the three of them and Tasha and Homer. On the phone the talk was in code, about the weapons delivery, the massacres, the rumors of a pregnancy; but here the discussion had clearly already moved on to more basic issues.

Danielle was talking, while Dorothy sat with chin propped in her hand, legs crossed, one sandal swinging idly. These small informalities suggested a new order of belonging, a family scene.

"I hesitate, the situation is so complex and fluid, and I'm the newcomer here . . . " Danielle shrugged. "But I wonder why we haven't been talking more about some of the psychosexual aspects."

There was a stillness, during which Josh heard for the first time the trill and cluck of birds in the greenery around and over them. Tasha was staring accusingly at Danielle, pencil arrested in mid-stroke.

The quiet extended itself, the birds louder still. When Danielle went on, her voice was soft and reserved. "The idea of a mixed, a saplap if you will, excites a lot of contradictory emotions. No one wants – consciously – such a connection to her own blood, but everybody wants to dream about it in some highly placed family. Dark secrets of the highborn. But you know all this, of course. I'm only underlining." Danielle folded her hands and looked at them, calm and retiring, a nun.

Oh, she was good, Josh had to admit, no question. The witch had seemingly been reformed, tamed, devoted now to a higher purpose. Close-shorn, eyes downcast, simple jade earrings. The bold media sorceress was nowhere in evidence. The intelligence emerging now was prehensile, insinuating, stealthy in its predation. She was shuffling and sighing her way into the heart of their little troupe.

"I only wanted to emphasize – and again I'm sorry for being so obvious – we're dealing with the miracle of new life, and with a *family*, however weird. The fundies and orthos can cry monster, freak, beastie – and the public seems to agree. But I'll make a guess that a cutaway would show, underneath this expressed revulsion, a curiosity, even a little excitement. A *frisson*."

Dorothy smiled encouragingly. *Her favorite*, Josh thought. *The chill thrill.*

"Ambivalent." Josh interjected crisply. "Plus we're dealing with a very young couple, and Duskyrose is almost attractive, in a certain pornofunky way, and of course she has a freak IQ. They're also outlaw lovers, which is always holopositive."

"Romeo, with Juliet as a kind of elegant female Caliban." Tasha had turned on him, offended. "Certainly not 'pornofunky.' Please."

"There you have it." Danielle seemed both saddened and satisfied. "We're demonstrating the ambivalence right here. A paradox, like the refugee thing, which makes both situations highly unstable. And we have a new pressure, an unexpected bump. In minimum security, you know, we sucked a lot of holo." She smiled demurely to defuse her prison slang.

In the ensuing silence Dorothy laughed. "Sir Beau," she said. "The monster mouth."

Homer cleared his throat. "That man." He frowned, and all of them shifted in their chairs.

Winger was a touchy subject. Weeks ago Dorothy warned that the man was dangerous and ought to be removed. They hadn't listened and now it was too late. Winger was too popular, a daily narcotic for the half-billion worldwide who tuned in expecting him to pump and blow them into frenzy. And his current appeal was based squarely on his manipulation of the very material they were trying to master – the New Life scandal, the issue of genetic purity, the refugee mess.

Normally Morphopolous would need only to say "that man," in the tone of voice he had just used, and within a few days Dorothy would see to it that the individual in question suffered an unfortunate accident, financial or physical. That was one of her specialties. The old man, though he might express chagrin at the unfortunate coincidence, would never allow any insinuation of any connection between his staff and such a tragic turn of events.

But the Winger case was more complicated. Morphopolous companies – Big One, Power Pizza, and Eyeful – were his sponsors, and the Fat Man had boosted sales impressively indeed. Nor was it clear yet what impact his yakshow was having on the campaign, though Adamson would probably benefit from the attacks on Stockwell. Also, at a certain order of megastardom, an entertainer was protected by his fame: discreet arrangements to interfere with such a career were no longer possible.

"He is a force," Dorothy said pensively, "a terrific actor. I wish . . . " She stopped and bit her lip. Josh watched her work the swinging sandal out to the end of her toes.

"He's like the evil fairy godfather for a cursed child," Danielle said. "Together they're developing a real tension. If we don't shape it, figure it in . . . " She heaved an apologetic sigh, reflected for a moment. "We might find ourselves not in control."

"Isn't it funny," Dorothy said then, chattily, and held up one cupped hand. "Just two or three ounces of tissue over here, a speechless brainstem and a couple of flippers. And over here" – she swung the other arm to encompass a great bulk – "a human hippo with a bellow that goes around the globe. The extremes, and yet because of high exposure, we're already past the, uh, radical solutions."

"Yes! If we were *really* operators!" Danielle laughed girlishly, and then the two of them teamed to spoof this droll contrast further. Danielle pretended to struggle with the elephantine shape, tip it finally over the edge of some chasm; Dorothy squeezed shut her cupped palm and twisted off a tiny head, like a bottle cap, and pitched it after the plummeting hulk. There was a moment of shock before she wrung both hands in front of her face. "Out, out, damned spot!" Her voice was comically wretched, and they all laughed, even Tasha.

"Yes, good!" Morphopolous had looked uncertain for a moment, but this reference to a favored text restored his high humor. There was a touch of rose under his tan. "Nor all the Arabian perfume, nor multifarious oceans of grenadine . . . and so forth and so on, eh?" He nodded archly at them all and they nodded back, respectful and admiring. "But we're living in a subtler age, where a few points on the market, a soupçon of scandal, a crazy yakshow – they're as potent as . . . as . . . " Morphopolous was gazing at something far off now, on a metaphorical horizon. "As drowning the little princes in a sackbutt of ale."

"Marvelous," Tasha breathed.

Josh watched her scurrying marker pencil: *indv & mass – Aris – pit – fear – cath – boff –*. She was clearly well along the path to a private climax, her whole body writhing as she scribbled. Josh wondered briefly if she brushed her teeth and took a crap in the same center-stage manner.

Josh had been around long enough to catch the hint of impatience, the desire for reassurance, in the old man's voice when he continued. "Now what do we *do* with this connection? The refugees and this yakshow fool and our own rough little beastie swaggering toward Babylon? Bottom line?" The old man paused to allow Tasha's knowing giggle, but kept his gaze unswervingly on Josh.

Here was pressure. Morph was still counting on him for the real production and accounting savvy. Eldest son and so forth. But he would have to have crossfire for this one; he would need the Brilliant Bitches. Easy now.

"I'm only picking up on some of your insights," Josh said, matter-of-fact. "If we assume with Danny that the public is *enamored* of this scandal. With Winger juicing it, I think we've got a major, make-or-break opportunity. Terrific pressure building, people wanting release, wanting *something to happen*."

"Beyond the election," Dorothy said. "Which is already choreographed beautifully. Josh has done a really professional job there."

"Brilliant." Danielle patted her hands softly together. "The staunch old Ginkophile versus the tough young slavemaster. A terrific toss-up. But yes, something *transcending* politics."

"Nothing—" Josh began.

"Have you noticed," Dorothy said impetuously, "that we hardly mentioned Ronnie Drager today? Certainly not *little* Ronnie Drager?" She blinked at them, the innocent smartypants in the front row.

"Interesting." Morphopolous administered a small, mock, self-sock to the jaw, meant as a sign of shrewd cogitation. "Meaning?"

"I just wonder if our outlaw lovers aren't becoming a bit dull – and maybe therefore . . . irrelevant?"

They all heard Tasha's sharp intake of breath. The young illicit lovers were her favorite. But she was too dumbfounded to protest and Dorothy pressed on.

"The baby has the mojo, the real juice. As Beau understands so well."

"The foetus fascinates," Danielle breathed, captured by an internal vision. "Keeps people guessing and keeps them pumped. World waits on wee saplap embryo."

"But Winger is already styling the crib," Josh said. What they had to do had been obvious for some time, but again he was nettled, seeing how the two subtle serpents had taken the initiative, tilting the discussion toward the very major proposal he was planning to deliver in his own style. "He's establishing a perception. I think we should at least make contact with him."

Homer was alert, his eyes narrowed but unblinking. "He's a clown. An entertainer – rather a fool, even. Really, Josh—"

"A fool!" Tasha had awakened. "You know we don't have a fool, actually, in the piece?" She nodded, agreeing vigorously with this insight. "A wise fool. We really should."

"I'm suggesting we feel him out," Josh said. "We give nothing away. Strictly chat, to establish if there's some way we might work. We have – assuming a normal cycle – another couple of months before the new messiah shows up . . . "

"My God." Dorothy uttered a short, desolate laugh. "I just thought, I mean, at this point a miscarriage . . . " She shuddered and felt blindly with her foot for the loose sandal.

Josh felt a bolt of pure horror pass through him. He had never considered this possibility. The multitudes behind Winger, slavering over the idea of miscegenation, rooting out the taint in their midst – they wanted to *see* the freak offspring, the nightmare incarnate. The Ecominis and Thorgs wanted their living messiah. Everybody yearned for this cursed child. So they had to deliver. Without this unholy birth their whole script would collapse.

"Miscarriage?" Barrelhead was animated now, looking hard at each of them in turn. "There can be no miscarriage."

"Of course. No." Josh felt panic beneath his assured manner, as if the whole three-hundred-and-twenty-acre raft under him had been lifted by a monstrous, maverick wave. "Of course we don't have a hospital—" He felt the depths yawning below, realized how far, how very far, he could sink.

"—in the ordinary sense." Dorothy, offhand and mildly amused, threw him a slender lifeline. "But there are alternatives."

"Yes?" Morphopolous peered at him, frowning.

"An alternative that would solve several problems at once." Josh was surfing now on his panic, working for control and rhythm that would give their proposal an irresistible momentum, the smooth, powerful glide that always captured Homer. "We've mentioned before the risk that one of our principals will be picked up in a routine police sweep and the media will get wind of it before we can arrange a case of mistaken identity or accidental release and, although we have great penetration of law enforcement, it's not perfect and one obstinate dimwit with a badge could cause great damage. And meantime one of our Joes reports that various darkside players have been combing Omalytown. Big offers are floating."

"That would not be good." Morphopolous's frown deepened. "In terms of our story. So what do we plan?"

"A move." Josh made his smile quiet but intense. "A *sensational* move."

"How do we accomplish that? And *where*?"

Josh shook his head, pretending disbelief at such astuteness. He was improvising at the speed of sound. "Exactly. That's the thing. How and where." He smiled confidently, stretched his arms and flexed them. *Help me. Help me, you fucking cobra cunts.* "We're most afraid of Petrasky's being picked up, as we said last time. So we . . . " He made a snatching gesture.

"Pick him up ourselves." Dorothy wrinkled her nose in fun. "Pretend to be police. Our man PJ."

Josh manufactured an easy chuckle. "Nab Petrasky. Then the rest of them will have to run, too. They will expect the authorities to squeeze names and addresses out of the poor deranged captive. So we arranged a place with medical care and tight security. A place no media team would think of."

"PJ was a border agent," Danielle hinted sweetly.

The path they were tracing led to a brink. Josh expelled a long breath, smiled, and leapt into the abyss. "Right. Once we started kicking the idea around, things fell right into our hands. That overborder research post Sam wanted to scrap, remember? Remote, well-equipped, top pri classified, limited personnel? A controllable environment."

"But . . . " Morphopolous was, for the first time, manifestly irritated. "You must be joking! Yamaguchi would not allow——"

"He made only one condition, very simple." Josh shrugged. "After the show we let him have Feiffer. To cleanse Insec's image. Sam let this crazy doctor set up her post – they're a disease control unit – but insisted that the base has to be available for Insec operations. The agency can send in gear and agents. Supplies come in via transit units with black clearance, including live cargo under quarantine. Feiffer used to be a top Insec operative. It's credible he could get access."

Josh was talking too rapidly, he knew, but exhilaration propelled him. "So he smuggles in mama – Ronnie too, why not? – and stashes them in an off-limits ward. The whole place is effectively sealed, because of the epidemic. Also, an untried, just-promoted brigadier general is in charge of the post, someone easy to get around. And finally, this doctor is quite the space cookie, and we have good reason to believe she will actually *collaborate*. Then she and Feiffer are perfectly positioned to take the heat, whatever happens."

Morphopolous shook his head in pained wonder. "This is serious? This woman, this prizewinner, she would do such a thing?"

"Probably," Dorothy offered gently. She gave Josh a quick smile of approval. "I'm a screen person, and I review a lot of material, including this lady's research on the refugees. Tiffany Orr is a protégée of Joseph Goldbarth, the Gandhi winner who died under rather bizarre circumstances a while back? There are hints that our cannibal cousins are infecting their keepers – a disorder causing spasmodic movement and also euphoria – and Doctor Orr has been curiously eccentric since her arrival at this new post. She's also very headstrong, *and* with ties to the old Ecominis."

"Oh yes indeed," Josh said, and laughed. He felt full to bursting. "It's daring. It's juicy. It's creative. And we're protected. All we have to do is *get* them there. The situation will shape itself then."

"But why," Morphopolous broke in, almost shouting, "goddamn it! Why do we *want* them there? It's a dangerous situation, you said it yourself. This plague or brain fever or whatever it is, these new bloodthirsty Ginks in the area . . . " His flush was pronounced now, and they all went quiet. They had forgotten a first principle: genius had no rivals, and Homer was genius.

Then Dorothy spoke, her tone one of injured innocence. "But *you* gave us the reason!" She looked around the table. "Didn't he? Arms, Pobla panzers, the creature war . . . "

"Right." Josh grinned carefully at Morphopolous. "You're a sly one, Socrates as well as Homer! I see what you are driving at. You want us to appreciate the drama of creative risk-taking!" He winked broadly at Tasha. "You guided us all the way, and what a story! How about an unborn baby kidnapped by a bunch of ecorad terrorists, who want to crown it prince of apes, so they flee into the desert and are besieged by another bloodthirsty faction, *animals* armed for the first time—"

Morphopolous still had his mouth open, his eyes flicking around the table. They smiled at him, tentatively at first, then beaming.

"—and a remote post like that – of course the creatures would attack, with their new weapons, once they knew the demon-child was there."

"That's brilliant." Danielle sighed, a novitiate in orgasm. "Really brilliant. Of course Sam will have the mother of all covert ops in place to handle them. We synch with the election, and Adamson can wayne into it, finish the Ecominis and wipe the bad mutants, save the dark messiah . . . "

"But," Dorothy held up a hand in gentle caution, "no genocide. His compassionate spectrum in play here – he would protect the last of the refugees, argue for their domestication as an economic resource. Blow Winger away." She turned to Morphopolous, radiant. "All the things you have been hinting, and us so slow . . . "

Gradually, but unmistakably, Barrelhead's gape had become a loose, smug little grin. Tasha had slipped a hand through his arm and composed a real expression of her own. "Incredible," she said in her tinkling and intimate social voice. "The lovers could re-unite—"

"I hope," Dorothy turned to her, immediately solicitous. "Though there is some danger. War is war. But the embryo – we must save the embryo, absolutely."

"Oh God." Danielle laid her fingers lightly on Dorothy's shoulder, as if suddenly dizzy. "Think of having an *orphan*."

Dorothy closed her eyes and went pale. "A foundling," she whispered. "A cursed dynasty. A whole new—" Her eyes went wide again, as if she had been startled awake. "What are you saying?"

Danielle also seemed startled, flustered. "I – I guess I'm thinking of dramatic genius again . . . of tragic depths." She released the other woman's shoulder and appeared to collect herself. "Possibilities."

"We do have to be ready," Dorothy agreed, "for anything. However terrible. And magnificent."

There was another interval of silence. When Danielle had touched Dorothy, Josh experienced an odd, hot throb of some obscure feeling. He was at once exhausted and aroused, and just a touch uneasy about this last, unexpected twist of plot. The two cobras had braided themselves together before his very eyes, had surely begun their dance before this meeting. The final vision of them, brooding over a cradle, had shaken him.

He made a supreme, invisible effort and turned to the last maneuver he had to execute. An apparent detail, but one which required delicate engineering. "Getting the wee thing there," he said, as if musing aloud. "Safe transit. Completely dark." He grimaced. "Not an easy thing, even for Dorothy. But you gave me an idea, Homer – as you almost always do."

"Did I? Well, ideas *do* come to me, now and then." Morphopolous looked with fond good humor at Tasha, who gazed back with tremendously arch reproach at so outlandish an understatement.

"We needed a vehicle of some kind, large and designed for carrying a live cargo, discreetly. So right away I thought of that little company you employ for shipping your own specimens." An interval. Josh felt a faint sweat congealing on his brow. He nodded amiably. "You've often said that trading for those rare creatures is as close as you get, personally, to the darkside. Given the silly laws we have about rare game populations. So I took the liberty . . . "

To his immense relief, Morphopolous adopted an expression of shrewd amusement. "Of course. The notion occurred to me just as you were talking a while back. I picked up that firm years ago, for just such contingencies."

Josh looked full of admiration. "Don't they regularly handle exotic cargo, gene material for transport or disposal? Exempt from all inspection, except at destination?"

"Of course."

"That's so perfect!" Dorothy clapped her hands once. "We can list them as a rare infection, contagious tissue. Returned shipment. I can spin out the data for that, easily."

"Well, then." Morphopolous looked around, an expansive patriarch. "Poor players. You have your book in hand, and must ready the performance." He patted Tasha's hand. "The author and his muse are most satisfied with this new act, no?"

Josh watched the three women exchange their silent, bright snarls of submission. He folded up the screen of his notebook and slid it into his shirt pocket. His bones were already loosening, anticipating the great wide bed in his room, a nap before dinner – but it was not to be.

"Josh, speaking of those silly laws, I've got a couple of buffalo to thin out, and we could use a bit of sport after all this brainwork, eh?" Morphopolous had slipped from the clutch of his muse and was getting to his feet. "We'll leave the ladies to relax. Get you a heavier boot and a shooting coat and we'll be on our way."

Josh managed a grin, a small grunt of anticipation. It was father-son time. He understood the special favor. These mini-safaris were reserved for Homer's intimate chums, for the men who – as he put it – made up the world brand-new every day. There would be no discussion of current prospects, no citing of figures, no gossip. This was recreation, with now and then some talk of Life, and what it Meant. In a rare moment, one could share a personal philosophy; between shots, a conversation might touch on the dearest, deepest-down things.

No one would accompany them, except the small staff of bearers and trainers. Even so, Josh's heart sank. He wanted a darkened room and a soft pillow upon which to lay a head already overloaded. Instead, he was probably going to get a close view of a big, dead beast, along with a sunburn and burrs on his pantlegs.

CHAPTER TWENTY-SIX

Dying, Kapu had managed to amaze himself. Old taboos were blown away as dust. For one thing, he permitted the piksi attendants to perform some of their strange purification rites. Smiling and fluttering, they arrived with their sprays and swabs and filter masks. He remained cheerful and curious, and even (on good days) offered them a few words from his small stock. Fahnee had strictly forbidden them to touch his person, so the various ticks, fleas, and lice who acted as his confidants were safe. The attendants did not seem to mind. In fact, they begged him often to summon a gang of fleas and cajole them to dance.

Fahnee herself came twice a day, and they talked through the picture *mudlati* until he was exhausted. Mostly, he gave her old stories or the common lore of Pobla life. If he was particularly alert, they might trundle him into a vehicle and go on a short field trip to some nearby canyon where he could show her how birds signed or where an ant colony had marked a prophesy.

His own prophesy had been explained many times, but Kapu was not bored. The story of Pahane and Tiina, the vision of the serpent entwining an egg of light, the arrival of the horse-people – this story revealed more of itself to him each time he related it. He understood for the first time, as his life was ending, that *wonakubi*, the Great Shadow, was manifest not only in the wisdom of the Hive Beings, but also in the speed and alertness and power of other creatures. The horse people had contacted *wonakubi* in their way, through the nightblack bird; and Klat had told him still another legend of two-legged ones who lived in sea-caves and whose sacred knowledge came from the blowfish. Now he believed there might be still other tribes hiding in the Wastelands or on islands or on the continents of ice Fahnee had told him about, each with its own way of touching the Great Shadow.

The next three suns would be a revelation. He had known, actually, last night when the crickets started and the Pobla at the gate joined in, drumming with their feet. Then the piksi soldiers sent to quiet them had argued among themselves. Some had laughed and made noises, but a few joined the chant, at first in ridicule but at the end in delight. By morning Kapu could sense the excitement in the whole camp. The heels of orderlies in the hallways were rapping out anticipation, the animals in the lab were engaged in frenetic, cacophonous gossip, and the light beyond his window was shimmering with wings.

Though he had not had his shot yet, Kapu was already shaking free of his body. His *kubi* would soon leave this small, bloated planet of pain. A little death, like sleep, only he would remain present and aware, able to talk to Fahnee, even as he floated in the great river running toward the land of all shadows. The new energy around him came from this shadow-land, from the *kubin* of all the *tagakin* who had become and then gone and then become again.

The young piksi female who arrived to adjust his tubes and give him medicine was happy and humming. She smiled and stroked his hand once before placing the gleaming nozzle against his withered arm. "Hey you, chief," she said, and pulled the trigger. He felt the small, sudden spot of coldness, but did not change expression. His eyes were open, unblinking, dry. "You big. Big bad boy." The girl set down the silver gun and held up three fingers, passing them slowly back and forth in front of his face. "How many, Kap?"

She was a slender girl the color of the bark on his favorite desert tree, the one called sun-skin. She had told him by elaborate gestures that her people were piksis from another, far-away place. Pock-reems.

"How many?" She waited, a bubble of laughter on her lips. "You gone? Gone to *yano*?" She flapped her arms like a bird, then pinched her fingers together to make a beak, which she used to peck him lightly on the forehead.

He waited until he sensed the first trace of uncertainty in her, just before she glanced at the glowing screen. He had learned to control the bumps of light on this screen, slow them down to an interval just before the buzzer went off.

"One," he breathed, not moving his lips, but she heard – or thought she did – and leaned to stare hard into his empty black eyes.

"*One*? You bad! Always one." She pecked him again and laughed. "Big night last night, Kap. You hear the singing? Soldiers too. And dancing, we hear. And all you care about is big black birds!"

"It," he said, in his normal, wheezy voice. "It me. It bren." He allowed his eyes to move quickly over her face.

"You naughty thing. You bet I will. No birds necessary, Kap. I'll it you first. It your amazing bren." She pushed him ever so lightly on the shoulder and his face, so wrinkled it seemed to contain every possible expression, bent at last into a smile.

Joke. He liked the piksi word. It had a ho-ho of deep laughter bounded by the slap of brisk consonants. Their joke was his long breath, how he lived on and on, festooned with tubes, far beyond any expectations. The birds were a reference both to Klat's ravens, hanging around outside his window, and to scenes they had shown him of a tribe of piksis long ago, living among great mountains draped in white. These piksis were shown chopping up their dead and feeding them to scavenger birds. Kapu had cried with delight at this parallel with his own beliefs, and sang over and over the saying of the Pobla: *Sky in our bones, sky in our bones, we go round and round!*

This young female, Roo-bee, and her *ogan*, a gangling youth with ears so large Kapu suspected Pobla blood, appeared to understand. The boy, who called himself Hen, once seemed to sign obliquely that he, too, had taken the brain of a *tagak*. Kapu was so startled he gave a Pobla whoop, registering amazed joy. Hen immediately pretended a misunderstanding, but Kapu saw the sly and satisfied look that passed between the lovers.

Roo-bee finished recording her readings from his bottles and the *mudlati* screen, smiling at him now and then over her shoulder. "Wonderful day, Kap. You old geez, you're wonderful too. You okay? Good? Good one?"

"Goot." He sank back a little in the bed, to show he felt comfortable. It was much more pleasant, this new camp. They were in Pobla country here, so they were not so crowded. Through his messengers, Kapu could now keep in touch with his followers, and influence the flow of refugees. Consequently, fewer soldiers were needed, and the laboratories, hospital, and library were calm and orderly, carrying out Fahnee's plans. Fahnee and he were the only *tagakin* here, and in her group there was now high humor, compassion and, of course, making *naku*. Kapu could smell, even now, a night's *ogan* stuff on Roo-bee. And some of the soldiers were doing it too, in the equipment yards at dark.

"You look great." She imitated his steady, blank stare for a moment and then grinned. "Look dead already. Ready for the boss. Feel anybody coming?"

He moved his chin imperceptibly. "*Tak tagak* come," he said. "Fast. Tree day."

She cocked her head at him, widening her eyes. Her mirth was partly suspended by curiosity. "You don't say. Maybe that's why everybody's so juiced. Our wee *tak tak*, eh?"

"*Delo tchatsi* gurl. Yas. *Tak tak tagak.*" His wrinkles organized again into a smile. "Beby."

She smiled back, and he caught the shade of melancholy in her. "Well, maybe that will balance your bad news. About the bad Pobla. Hope you were wrong about them."

"Yas." Kapu made a slight gesture toward the window beside his bed. "Know awready." He had heard his people singing, seen the raven's sign. Sayat possessed *mudlatin* now, the long-strikers. Some piksis had given him many of them, and he had been slaughtering ever since, and was coming nearer.

Kapu did not, however, consider this massacre an omen of the future. The *mudlatin* had arrived too late. *Wonakubi* was woven into the womb of a young holy witch, who was coming – was almost here! The new *tak tagak* of his people would turn the long-strikers back on all who gripped them in fear and desire. It would happen here in this very place, which was, he had explained to Fahnee, a very holy place. Then the baby would go with the horse-people; her snake-bird spirit would bring together all the tribes who belonged to *wonakubi*, and they would go forth to show the piksis their own darkness and give them back their ghosts. So he smiled again and wheezed, "No worry."

"The old geezosopher knows everything, huh? Your wigglies told you, no doubt. Quite a spy network you got, Kap." Roo-bee surveyed the pillows she had just plumped, the small bunch of aromatic leaves stuffed in a beaker, and the screen with its pulsing green line of light. "Well, maybe the tiny *tak tak* is on her way. Hope so. 'Cause if this Sayat you talk about has firepower . . . sho-o-o! We're hanging out here without—"

She stopped, interrupted by a howl of jetcopters, coming in very fast and low. She went to the window and watched the first two fan out overhead to cover the third, which plummeted to a landing behind the roofline.

"Ah-ha. The brigadier is a-comin'," she said. "Oh boy." She

waggled her fingers at Kapu and flew out the door. But his eyes were already closed. The piksi dream medicine had turned his pain into a chameleon shimmer of brilliant colors. But he did not stay for the show. His *kubi* was soaring free, skimming the desert like a hawk's shadow, hunting those angry ghosts Sayat had liberated.

CHAPTER TWENTY-SEVEN

He and Batboy and Cynthia were teamed for this smack, their first solo pocketpolo and a complex routine for apprentices. Cynthia loitered on a bench nearest the credit machines, and finally gave them the target signal. A big red-faced man in a badly fitting suit, who seemed in a hurry.

"Okay, Pahane, your guy ready?" Batboy's narrow features had taken on a luminous energy.

He eased one hand into his pants pocket, ran a finger along Pepper's flank, noted the bristling whiskers. Behind them a whisper grew rapidly into a racket of wind, then a tremendous hiss as the train decelerated out of the tube and into the station. "Ready."

"Salty too. So here we go . . . we *swoop*."

Wearing the fluorescent orange jumpsuit of a market runner, Batboy moved at a bouncy, slouchy walk toward the same machine the big man was approaching. Pahane came two steps behind, dressed in his black mallroach jacket and chains. He felt alert and clear, light on his feet, happier than he had been all day.

A *tchat* raid, with an element of the hunt as well. More freedom than he had expected, after their imprisonment in the pizza van. The fleeting memory of that time – the odor of asphalt and tomato sauce – made his stomach clutch, so he emptied his mind of everything but the trick in front of them.

The man stopped in front of the machine, took out his case of credit slices, and selected one. From his fumbling, Pahane guessed the man had spent a little too long in the bar after his business hours, and was late for dinner. He would be wanting quickie clearance, for sure. A cold dinner and an irate wife awaited him somewhere, no doubt. The whisper started again, became a whirlwind, which faded abruptly as the train shot away and left the station full of desultory, hollow echoes.

Batboy was whistling noisily and impatiently. He craned around for a peek as the man punched in his code, still holding the gaping wallet in one hand. Pahane had looked down, as if bored, and now saw the sharp, black nose protrude from Batboy's trouser cuff. Then the whole body poured out, lithe and gray, almost the same color as the scuffed concrete floor of the station.

The man squinted at the screen, muttered something, glanced over his shoulder with a frown. Pahane smiled to himself, reached in to tweak Pepper's tail, and felt the rat twist out the hole in his pocket and climb down the seam along his leg. When the little claws reached his instep, Pahane lifted a big toe to signal a halt. Then Batboy sent Salty Lady streaking across a meter of bare floor to the mark, who rocked on his heels a bit, exhaling in anticipation as he reached for the deck of transit passes that had popped into a tray in the machine.

The timing was close. They overestimated the effect of alcohol in the man's blood, and his fingers actually brushed the passes before jerking back as if he had been burned. The rat was up his pantleg almost to his crotch by then, so his tiptoe jitterbug across the floor also involved a rapid unzipping and digging with both frantic hands. The curses he was bellowing brought startled glances from other commuters, but none of them saw the second rat scoot out from Pahane's pantleg and snatch the wallet from the rubber mat in front of the credit machine.

Pepper lumbered along the splashplate, behind softdrink and nutribar machines, until he reached a bundle of pipes and conduits running vertically up the wall. In the meantime the man had succeeded in getting his pants half-off and Salty had spilled onto the floor and bolted back toward the credit station. Pahane ran to the man, whose face was now a deep, solid rose color around his writhing lips.

"Hey! He's gettin' away!" he shouted. "Look!" He pointed at the wall, where Pepper had almost reached a junction box, connected by a section of conduit to a ventilator. The rat paused, the slab of leather dangling from its mouth, watching Pahane's gestures.

The drunk's eyes were unfocused, rolling from side to side. "You seen that thing? That sonabitch! Right in my pants?"

"*Sir*! Your wallet! *Look*!" Pahane gripped the man's sleeve and tugged hard. "It's got your money, we got to stop it!"

Finally the man saw the rodent, recognized what was in its mouth, and uttered a hoarse bleat. Clutching his sagging trousers, he waddled toward the wall, Pahane hurrying beside him. Pepper scurried along the conduit to the lip of the ventilator. Behind him, Pahane heard exclamations from those who had veered their way, curious.

By now Batboy would have punched the Accept button on the machine, removed the transit deck and lifted Salty swiftly to the slot so she could nip out the credit card. In a moment both rats would be into the utility corridors in the ceiling and walls, racing for the grates leading to the main tunnels.

He lifted one hand and Pepper darted between the slats of the ventilator. The drunk groaned out a curse. Pahane recoiled and turned to the spectators gathering behind them, some looking concerned and others grinning knowingly. "I'm goin' for Security!" he shouted, and broke into a run.

It was an unwelcome shock when, just after vaulting the turnstile, he in fact encountered one of the blue-uniformed guards arriving from the main lobby. The guard had already unholstered his stunner, but tilted it away from Pahane and moved in for a bare-handed grab.

"Just where you think—"

Pahane looked up with relief, and put a wobble in his voice. "Ga, man, I was *lookin'* for you! Man had me *down!*"

"What you runnin' from? You hook somethin', you little roach? Turn your pockets out."

He screwed up his face and uttered a sob, before fumbling in the jacket pockets, jerking them inside out. "Some ol' squeezgeez put a clutch on me . . . an' you guys—"

"Wha's 'at?" The guard frowned, a single, long crease in his thick brow.

"A perv, man. Ol' perv down there still got his *pants* down! Drunk and seein' rats and spiders and—" He sobbed again, even managed a tear.

"Yeah? You never—"

Pahane shook his head violently, fiercely. "Come *on* man, he's gonna get away—"

"You okay? Ga, that sleazo!" It was Cynthia, who had hurried up to cover, and was gazing urgently at the security man, giving him a close view of her rapid breathing. "Guy down there was all *over* this poor kid, I mean, max ex-*posure.*"

"All right all right." The guard released Pahane with a slight shove. "Getoutahere." He nodded at Cynthia with a fierce, deferential resolve. "I'll deal with this." His stunner aimed at the ceiling, he departed at a lumbering trot.

They traded a swift grin, and Pahane wiped away his tears on a .

sleeve, before they moved on toward the escalators leading to the park outside.

It all went beautifully, a perfect *tchat* by a team of naturals. At the fountain he picked up a wig from Cynthia's bag, and after tossing his jacket and the chains into a refuse compactor, the two of them waited ten minutes and went back down to the tubes. Batboy had slipped off his orange runnerboy jumpsuit in the restroom, and sauntered forth a studious lad with corrective spectacles and braces on his teeth.

They met on a platform one level down from the credit machines, drifted to the edge of the tunnel, and in the bustle of an unloading train, Pahane bent to check a shoe-snap and Batboy pretended to drop a transfer token. Salty and Pepper darted out of the shadows with their booty, traded it for bacon rinds, and scampered back into the tunnel. Somewhere above, they assumed, the red-faced drunk was trying to explain himself, his unzipped fly, his lack of identification, the outrages committed on him.

If the guard's superior officer was willing, the drunk would be allowed to call his furious wife, who might or might not agree to vouchsafe for his authenticity. The victim might also voice suspicion of those two adolescents standing nearby when he was attacked. (Easy to spot, the man would protest – one had a shaved head and wore sadogarb, the other was in a bright orange suit.) It was most likely that after an hour or two of wrangling, nobody would file any charges of any kind, and only then would somebody remember to call in cancellations.

Meanwhile they had a live card and would undertake a buying binge: new clothes, food for the week, transit and service decks and whatever else they could cram in before the first circuit shrieked alarm. In fact, within minutes they found Samuel Brady to be a rich lode indeed. Three more slices opened up, because good Sam carried an operator license and Fedsoc ID in his wallet, and like many unimaginative marks, simply borrowed the first digits from these for his PIN codes.

"Ga, what a smack!" Cynthia said, when they emerged from a tube station into the open plaza of a minimall on the edge of downtown. She dropped her armload of packages on a bench and affected coy wonder, batting eyelashes which she had cantilevered far out over cheeks of a fashionable, consumptive pallor.

Batboy giggled and nodded his appreciation. Part of the thrill of these expeditions was in practicing the street idioms, both word and gesture, so necessary to convincing deception. With his extraordinarily acute hearing, Batboy was brilliant at this mimicry, and schooled the others in nuancing their performances.

"Hunkysmack, what I say," Pahane ventured, with a cocky roll of his shoulders and a fair facsimile of a sneer. "But we gotta slide, feebs. Oughta rent us another locker and stash this, before we score the back."

"Good!" Cynthia clapped her hands and laughed aloud. "Very mallroach, very drooly. I would have absolutely *ground* my teeth, a couple months ago, at that sort of talk."

"Well, 'hunkysmack' not, I'm afraid. That's more a femthing." Batboy mused for a moment. "I mean, you could swish it, make it ironic, I guess."

Pahane shrugged and grimaced. "Anyway, we need the locker." He glanced around, checking to see if they were attracting any undue attention. Their heap of shoeboxes and garmentbags and thermopaks was, it seemed to him, overly conspicuous. This was not a prosperous district; the minimall had several closed shops and trash was overflowing the receptacles in the courtyard. They had to fit in, or the backpeople wouldn't land. But except for the stares of a few children, the other shoppers seemed to ignore them.

He found himself in the odd role of guide and supervisor on these sojourns, a counterweight to the impulsiveness of his companions. Once over the loss of her hair, Cynthia was, like Batboy, discovering an enthusiasm, even delight, in the risk and challenge of their new life. The costumes and make-up, the precisely timed performance for high stakes, excited both of them, made them reckless.

His multiple personality disorder, Pahane thought wryly, and perhaps the habit of camouflage learned from the Pobla, rendered these experiences less novel to him. Also he was now a father-to-be, and had begun to recognize in himself a certain grumpy pragmatism, streaked with envy. Unlike the others, he would not be able to relax until he had brought the food and clothes all the way home. Responsibilities. A long and heavy word, he was learning.

"Point," Batboy said, with a slight grimace in Pahane's direction. "Old Sam was a real cornucopia." He reached inside one of the packages, removed a candy. "You guys truck, and I'll be lookout, case a backman cruises." He plucked away the wrapper, winked at them, and tossed the sweet into his grin.

283

"A sugarbat," Pahane said, and bent to begin sorting the packages. "A sparetire vampire."

"Now, boys." Cynthia included them both in her maternal frown. "I mean ga, feebs, we gotta great trick running. Let's not rot."

All of them had to smile at that. They had laid in a good two weeks' worth of staples, including barter for rent, and it was barely a month since they began training for this kind of trick. Even a masterscammer would have been proud. There might even be a sort of celebration, tonight, in their honor. If they were lucky now and hit some good back they would save a little to smoke themselves.

Cynthia carded out a medium-sized cart from the lot and they loaded it swiftly and rode on into the main lobby. From there they trundled to the storage area, where a few shoppers were stacking purchases into open lockers. They picked a bin next to a salefreak, who they figured would ignore them, so busy was she heaving out box after box of what appeared to be disposable slippers decorated with a dinosaur motif.

"You cruising by Marvelous, on the way home?"

Pahane did not look at her as he spoke, pretending to deliberate on the positioning of a case of dehydrated soup. He was aware of the contrivance of his offhand manner, and knew Cynthia was too. One disadvantage of their newfound talent for camouflage. The fugitives could no longer conceal themselves from one another.

"I suppose." She shook out a jacket, an old-fashioned leather dyed a stormcloud gray, with black piping. "You'd look star in this, Panny. But I think it's not glit enough for your act."

He heard the tremor in her tone, beneath the cheerfulness, and took the jacket from her as an excuse to clasp her wrist for a moment, reassuring. "He . . . he's really *trying*."

The way she turned from him, a jerk of her whole body which she tried, too late, to restrain, told him it was the wrong thing to say. At the same moment, holding up the jacket by the shoulders, he saw it was far too large. Too large for Marvin, also. Maybe Tyrone. Or Sandhill. "I guess that's the whole trouble," he said then.

"Right." Still turned from him, Cynthia picked up a package and slung it into the locker. "Right. Smacko."

As abruptly as if he had been that package, only thrown from a window a hundred stories up, Pahane plummeted into misery. Their common misery. He and Tima, Cyn and Marvelous, Sandy and Red Wolf, Batboy too. They loved each other, they depended on each other, they protected each other, and they were gnawing each other to rags. Soar and crash, that was the street expression. But the proportion of crash to soar seemed worse for the newest lovers, and for Marvelous in particular.

"Why are there no brilliant men?" Cynthia faced him suddenly, and he almost stepped back from the flame in her eyes. "Why are they always brilliant fucking stupid little *boys*?"

He flushed and looked away, lifting one hand a few inches, palm out. The salefreak was smiling at them, interested. She raised her hand tentatively too, but clenched in a small fist. "Yeah, sister," she called out. "*Good* question."

Cynthia gave her a bitter, fleeting smile, but lowered her voice. "Forget it, Panny. I'm sorry. I'm sorry all the time."

She was biting her lips, fumbling with the last of the packages. She was going to explode if he said the wrong thing again. Of course she felt sorry. And guilty, and angry. Because Marvin did try – and try mightily, with a glum, bewildered doggedness that made them all wince – but the results were not encouraging.

Though they all avoided discussing it, the brutal fact was the Doctor was a liability. He was too absent-minded and easily distracted even to serve as lookout; and two weeks ago he had appeared so glazed, so utterly lost, they had begun to fear breakdown. It seemed a lesser risk, overall, to give him some simple practice.

Marvelous seemed minimally able to perform only two roles. Holy crank and authentic feeb. Unshaven and unwashed, dressed in a grubby suit and grease-spotted tie, he stood in parks and on streetcorners at the edge of the market district, beside a folding table bearing a sign, some leaflets, and a basket. Four days a week the sign said *Help the Disadvantaged: Private Foundation accepts food or trans tokens.* On the three other days, *Save Creation! Support the Teaching! Give generously!*

Meanwhile, Cynthia worked further into her own new identity. She was spending a lot of time with Sandhill, whenever he was not on a dark run somewhere. There were meetings and intensive workshops, liaisons with other groups, strategy and meditation sessions. Commitment was total and irrevocable, and they lived always in the shadow of the memory of the vanished giants, the great trees.

At the moment they were scheming hard to figure out and combat the force that was trying to take over and manipulate their cause. So far they had determined only that this force was very powerful, and totally dark. The ruse of the extortion plot, involving the former

Insec agent, was very effectively undercutting the message of political idealism the Thorgs had intended; and with uncanny timing, Feiffer's statements and movements upstaged their own.

Sandhill was getting thinner, his eyes too bright and his laugh too sharp and sudden. The daring, dramatic action at New Life had given way to the petty, daily business of stealing or dealing back. All of them, Pahane thought, were smoking too much, the hours stretching out in an interminable idleness between tricks.

He noticed, even as he thought this, that Cynthia was licking her lips, glancing at him impatiently. The fit was on her, the inadvertent flexing of the first two fingers of her right hand, nostrils contracting in anticipation. A good investigator might notice something like that, might recall a report filed by someone they had smacked. He should warn Cynthia. It occurred to him then that Marvelous, at least, wouldn't betray himself that way: he couldn't bear the merest whiff of nicotine. Another source of tension between the two of them.

He closed the locker and sliced it to pay for twenty-four hours, which would give the retrieve team plenty of time. When they had climbed back into the empty cart, he spoke once more, as if thinking aloud. "Money is the piksi prison, Tima says. I guess only losers are free."

Cynthia didn't answer. She was fidgeting, looking straight ahead, and probably regretting the whole conversation. He wondered if she, too, secretly missed the Institute sometimes. The quiet, orderly laboratory, the brooding old trees full of birds, the exciting discussions and plans – and of course a handsome, confident *Director* Marvin Petrasky.

He could see the sadness and inevitability of what was happening to them. They were, in a way, merely adapting to a new habitat, as the rats and roaches and pigeons had. And this adaptation was supposed to be a sacrifice to the memory of the big trees, bright water, and throngs of colorful creatures – and of course for themselves, their great cause, the voyage backward in time toward a green and wild planet, where all sentient beings were respected, where diversity and balance and hoo-ha . . .

He was sneering, he realized, and felt even worse, felt something very close to terror. He blew through the automatic door into the plaza a little faster than he should have, and barely avoided a couple with a baby in a sidecar coming the other way. He rolled into the lot with hands clamped on the wheel to keep them from trembling. You couldn't afford such mistakes. Humper and Tyrone had warned them, again and again, to smack the trick and slide, fast; not to relax and start jerking off.

He switched off the cart and glanced at Cynthia. She was staring at something, and Pahane did not like the look on her face. He tracked her line of sight and saw Batboy still sitting on the bench. But now he was doing something very foolish. He was talking to strangers. A young girl sat on one side of him, a teenpro in a very scant skirt, with a heavy pendant of cheap crystal to divide her perky breasts. Her bossboy sat on the other side, a muscular young man holding a shopping bag in his lap, but tilted so that Batboy could see within.

"Oh shit shit," Cynthia breathed, and neither of them moved from the cart.

"Don't take it," Pahane whispered intently, as if Batboy could hear him.

There was back in the bag, he could tell this much from Batboy's flushed face. A lot of it, apparently. Two, perhaps three cartons. Batboy was giggling, looking now at the girl, who had her thigh plastered against him and was running a pink tongue deliciously over her lipstick. Batboy removed one of Sammy's slices from a coat pocket and the young man plucked it from his hand, examined it as if in admiration.

Pahane groaned, as the man shifted the bag over into Batboy's lap, then said something and got to his feet, keeping the card. The girl laughed and leaned to whisper in Batboy's ear.

"Oh Bats, Bats, Bats. Don't."

"Maybe he hasn't told them he's waiting." Pahane was scanning the plaza, looking for loiterers or shoppers who might be stakeouts. The crowd seemed to be thinning, no one paying particular attention to the threesome at the bench.

The man was walking briskly away now, angling toward a row of dispensers at the main entrance to the street. Maybe he was only going to test the card, slice a Big One or a Sugar Smear. Maybe he was just a reckless backdealer and this was a jit deal; it could be the final flourish of a great day. Pahane started to exhale, slowly.

Cynthia had been pretending to look through her bag, while he pretended to wait impatiently, an excuse to remain crouched in the cart. "Shit, double shit," Cynthia hissed then. "That couple, the baby. Don't turn around. They're still there, just inside the glass door. It isn't a baby. It's a fucking *camera*."

287

Pahane did not need confirmation. He was watching the young man, who was standing in front of the Big One dispenser talking rapidly into his other hand, cupped in front of his face. "The trains. You up and me downtown. Don't move too fast." He stepped off the cart, turning away from the automatic door, which hissed at him as it retracted to release the salefreak, who had apparently finished caching her dinosaur slippers.

"Oh hi!" she said brightly to Cynthia, who had also turned toward the escalators leading down to the subway terminal. "You know, what you said about *men* and *boys* . . . "

But her voice had drawn a glance from Batboy, who of course then noticed Pahane and Cynthia, and, intoxicated by the girl's perfume and mouth and thigh-pressure, fatally raised his hand in an unmistakable gesture of joyful beckoning, and called out as well. Pahane did not register the words, at first because he was staring into the eyes of the young man, who had finished confiding into his cupped hand and was lowering it when he discovered this new reason to lift it swiftly for an important addition; and then because he was running, and running hard, bumping past startled or blank faces, shoving past people on the escalator as he leaped down three and four steps at a time.

CHAPTER TWENTY-EIGHT

"And who hath wrought this fearful symmetry?" Marvin intoned, as he shoved a leaflet at the stream of passengers plunging into the tube station. One man gave him a sickly, sidelong grin, and at the last moment snatched the paper, before he stepped on the escalator and accelerated downward into an echoing gloom.

"Praise you, may you multiply," one of the old women called, and there was a low chorus of amens from the small band who had begun, in the last weeks, to assemble daily around Marvin's table.

"The El'mental Patter." It was a boy perhaps seven years old, earnest and excited. He was obviously the grandson of the well-dressed elderly lady holding his hand.

"Pattern," the grandmother corrected, with an apologetic smile at Marvin.

"Yea, and from the mouths of babes ye shall hear truth." Marvin looked fondly, if solemnly, at the boy. "For we do but patter, we but chatter, of a mystery far beyond these poor words. A mystery as old as time and deep as the universe."

"Hallelujah, brother!" It was the Omaly. He was a ragged coat draped over a frame of sticks, with the shriveled, yellow face of a lifetime back addict. "Ain't sayin' nothin', 'less we singin', and ain't no singin' but yo own seff high!"

"Amen," said a very thin, very old woman with sharp gray eyes and a huge handbag. "Who knows the singer from the song?"

"Yea, and the twin serpent rose, writhing 'round, and spake with the tongues of angels, in the alphabet of life." Marvin lifted up his forearms and twined them from elbow to wrist.

"Day-o," chanted one.

"Ribe-o," chimed in another.

"Nucle-o," sang the whole group, with a rhythmic clap at the end.

"And so there was life, and it was good, and it was *everywhere* and in *everything*, without end. And everything that moved upon the face of the earth or swam in the sea was one song, one symphony, and its echo is eternal."

"Tha's right, he sayin' it," the Omaly crooned. "Ev'body changin' jus' de same, gettin' de same bug, and 'at bug gotta bug and *it* gotta bug an' so on an' so on to de *las'* mama bug and she ain't nothin' but a song an' dance like we gone do right here one fine day – whoooeee!" The man twirled completely around, with surprising grace, the tails of his old coat flapping. With relish he lifted forked fingers to his puckered mouth. "Gonna *smoke*, folk!"

Marvin frowned and lifted an admonitory finger. "Give thyself to riotous song, but forsake not the melody. You know how bad tobacco was, Johnson. We have children among us, and you know better." He looked beyond his little flock to the hordes of passengers flowing in currents and cross-currents, rushing or eddying to the rhythm of electric signboards that flashed times and destinations. "We are as vibrating lutes, struck by an unknown hand. We are a divine hum, and holy intelligence sings in every atom. Oh chromosome! Chromosome, light and dark – binary chant in the mirror of creation!"

"Oh chromosome! Oh chromoso-o-o-me!" The gathered faithful swayed, eyes closed, listening to the last syllable resonate through them.

"And genome! World within world enfolding, compression most dire, self of self itself!"

"Got hisseff by de tail!" Johnson twirled again, grinning wide.

"Yea, a mighty round." Marvin shot a forgiving and appreciative glance at the old Omaly. "And every cell sings in harmony with every other, and every being with its kind, and every species with species, even unto the smallest; and every molecule is star-born and star-bound, coming and going without end, as all are born and sing and die to be born again."

"Hallelujah! Born again!" There were radiant faces now in the circle around Marvin. They even won a few smiles from passers-by, or those lingering at nearby tables. He nodded to acknowledge the attention of several gathered to sign a petition against cosmetic surgery on pets.

"Born as beast or tree or tiny spore, one poor instrument in this great and endless symphony – until, one day, the breath of God stirs us into higher life, that life for which we strive – creative life!"

"Yea! Hallelujah! Song of songs!"

"Breath of God blows! Elemental breath, playing through the reed of matter, roaring in the smithy of our souls, trumpeting a melody eternally new! Oh holy matrix, ever-weaving, ever-unraveling one! Oh smallest, swiftest intelligence! Oh changer of change! Thou who livest only for and in others, who dost create and destroy! Oh parasite without peer, parasite most high! Oh Virus!"

"Oh Virus! Hallelujah! Oh Virus!"

Some were shuffling now in a slow dance, the infirm merely leaning from side to side on their canes. A tremulous voice began, others joined in, and Marvin swung his arms to mark the beat as they sang.

> Oh Thou art one with me-e-e,
> The serpent and the tree-e-e;
> Daily bonding with thy ho-ost,
> Thou joinest all,
> Into the holy gho-ost . . .

When the song ended and eyes were open and shining again, Marvin delivered a short prayer to the Elemental Pattern. Then his followers came forward to shake his hand, and at the same time unobtrusively place on the table their offerings. In the small shopping bags and plain wrappers, he knew, would be jellies and cookies, neckties, underwear, transport tickets, and sometimes a pawnable ring or brooch. He gave them in turn his own slightly dazed smile, his murmured thanks.

"That was so moving, Mr Holzkopf, as usual." It was the very thin old woman. She set her loaf of nut bread on his table and peered closely at him. "But you look peaked, Mr Holzkopf. Things on your mind and I am certainly not going to ask but you *must* take good care of yourself, for your own sake too as well as all of us in Holistic Covenant. We depend on you."

"Thank you, Margaret." Marvin bowed. She was among the first to become a regular at his talks, to insist that he give a name to himself and his doctrine. He had conjured up both, in the beginning, to be ironic; but his listeners had accepted him so earnestly and solemnly he was touched, and found himself engaged in perfectly serious speculation and prophesy.

"Caesar and his legions may mock and the mighty may revile, but we happy few must endure and prevail, and that means nutritious food and a good night's sleep."

"To endure together is to prevail, Margaret. In wholeness is all."

"Yes, I know." Margaret did not abandon her sharp scrutiny of him. "But for every weaving is a riving. And you do look riven, Mr Holzkopf. Though it's none of my business, and I know you have friends to comfort you in your tribulation, like that young person who comes by here sometimes in such flimsy dress, and whatever the weather. As you say yourself, the Great Pattern always contains the germ of evil, yea, which is given us that we may consume it and so be nourished, for all is phagery." She looked away from him now, and waved a gnarled, small fist at the street, the crowds, the towering buildings.

"Yea," Marvin said, and lifted his head, his expression almost fierce. "We are the Lord's lymphocytes."

"Ho-o-o, Baby!" The grinning old Omaly man dipped and swayed next to Margaret. "Big biters! 'As what we are, Baby! Soopah-powah snackin'! They some *bad* muthuhs gotta be re-e-cycled!"

"So it is, Johnson." Marvin smiled. Margaret also favored the Omaly with a benign if prim glance. Johnson and Margaret were his most intent and thoughtful audience, always lingering to help him pack his folding table, leaflets and gifts into the shopping cart. It pleased Marvin that he had brought together these two old people from opposite ends of the social spectrum. He even thought it possible they were beginning a kind of platonic, twilight affair, founded on their mutual love of learning.

He had been amazed and made humble in the course of his career as a sidewalk teacher of holy mysteries. The translation of abstruse scientific problems into the quaint idiom of religion was begun as an exercise simply to alleviate the misery of being deprived of his lab, his work, his position, and the humiliation of being an incompetent fugitive and criminal. But he found that many of the most fundamental concepts of his profession were expressed admirably in old metaphors and mysteries, anticipated by ancient thinkers and prophets – some of them illiterate. *In the beginning was the word.* And the word spelled itself. And the word was nucleotide. *And the spirit of God moved on the face of the waters.* Wind and lightning over the protobiont soup of the sea. Genesis. Gene.

People like Johnson and Margaret were an even greater surprise: they knew the parables and stories, the cadences and flourishes of the old texts better than he; and they were quick to apprehend his analogies, the connections and patterns he wanted to suggest. He had been startled sometimes at how Johnson could distil an intricate

292

point into a compact and colorful – if occasionally rude – phrase; at Margaret's shrewd appreciation of the nuances of promise and terror that linked such elemental ideas as chaos and free will.

The ultimate and most shocking discovery was that he had never, until he began preaching and singing with this group of derelicts and children and elderly, understood how an idea could send its roots into one's heart, into the blood and nerves, and then blossom from one's tongue in ecstasy and carry seed into other minds and hearts, until they all joined in a mighty hosannah that multiplied their happiness, their understanding, their power, a thousandfold.

He recognized now, as Margaret and Johnson helped him pick up the last crumpled and shredded leaflets from the concrete, that religion had always depended on a community of souls, brought into literal harmony. A community made luminous and whole in ceremony, in dance and song. He grasped, finally, what Tima and Pahane had tried to show him about the world: that all living things had a soul like his own, and all souls became one, as shadows become the night, or notes become a chord.

He even understood the Thorgies' fanatic worship of the *memory* of the ancient groves of big trees – a notion he had formerly ridiculed as psychotic delusion. But such forests had, indeed, once been whole worlds unto themselves, with their own climate and population and history. They had survived from the Age of Dinosaurs, marking every season, every drought and hurricane; they shaded, protected, nourished, and supported a tremendous proliferation of fungal, microbial, insectile, avian, reptilian, and mammalian life. They had been the oldest and largest cities on earth. If one imagined them devoutly, in deep meditation, one could hear again the sacred song of creation.

He sighed, recollected himself and his lot, and caught another shrewd look from Margaret. She had seen through him. After the exhilaration of these sessions, almost a trance sometimes, he invariably slid back into the same melancholy. All very well to celebrate the union of souls; but he was not in touch with the mortal shell of one in particular, and it was no good pretending he was above caring.

He tried to keep from thinking about Cynthia, as he gathered up his stack of good leaflets and squared it on the table top with a sharp rap. "I can get everything else," he said to Margaret, rather more brusquely than he meant to. "I'm—"

He saw the four men and marveled at their purposefulness a moment before he understood it. The men had pinned him with their eyes, fanning out even as he watched, the leaflets clutched to his breast.

"What is it?" Margaret blinked at him, alarmed, then swung her huge handbag around as if to keep the intruders away.

Marvin recognized Fitzgibbon, who was smiling and flushed with a murderous anticipation, but none of the others. They had to be plainclothes officers of some kind. He could run for a few steps, at most, before they caught him, and no one would interfere with the arrest of another street headcase. So he moved only to put himself in front of Margaret, noticing that Johnson had already faded into the crowd.

"Join me, sister," he whispered, and began to sing.

"Twine thy love in every strand,
One life in sky and sea and land—"

Fitzgibbon's cuffing hand sent the leaflets into a fluttering storm, but his grip was thrown off because Marvin did not shrink or flee. He met Fitzgibbon solidly, surprisingly, in an embrace.

"Petrasky, you miserable . . . "

But Fitzgibbon was drowned out by the voice in his ear, strong and hearty, booming on about the holy code. He found himself struggling to peel Petrasky's arms from about his neck. A moment later a heavy object struck him in the back, and he glanced over his shoulder to see an old lady winding up for another swing of her purse.

"Philistine! Don't you dare profane—" She was interrupted when two of the men took her elbows and lifted her from the ground in order to move her swiftly aside.

The third man worked a hand between Marvin and Fitzgibbon, who was now stuttering in rage and alarm, and managed to pry them apart. He kept the hand lightly wrapped in Marvin's lapel, and waited courteously for the stanza break in the song.

"Good afternoon, Marvin," he said then, with an engaging smile. "My name is PJ Feiffer, and I'll be your abductor today. You know my associate of course. He's been very anxious to renew a conversation with you, but this is not quite the place for it. Shall we?"

The man tugged playfully and Marvin came along, so they began to walk together, away from the tube station. Fitzgibbon fell in on the other side, breathing through his clenched teeth. Marvin ignored his hissed curses and glanced back once. The two other men were coming behind now, expressionless and watchful. Beyond them, beside his forlorn table, he could see Margaret, transfixed amid the scattered leaflets. But she was not gazing after him. She was looking at another figure beside her, a figure bent intently to listen. This newcomer was staring after him and his escorts. It was young Ronald Drager, in a wig.

"You're not under arrest," PJ Feiffer said cheerfully. "Put thy mind at ease. I'm only your host for a little trip."

"We are all hosts for the Elemental Pattern. A colony for Its holy messengers." Marvin murmured, speaking by rote to cover his shock. He slowed his pace a little. "I would like a few minutes to meditate, before—"

"No, no, Doctor." PJ shook his head and laughed indulgently. "Nothing like that. Relax."

"Let me have him a few minutes. *Medication* is what he'll need." Fitzgibbon lurched to one side, jostled against Marvin. He was still flushed, but now his broad face bore a worried frown.

"Bless the avenger." Marvin stopped and took one of Fitzgibbon's hands in his own and squeezed.

"What the fuck!" Fitzgibbon shook free, backed away. "Goddamn it, what is this?" He glared at PJ, wringing the hand Marvin had touched, as if burned.

Marvin stole another glance down the street, saw Ronald hurrying now after them, darting between and around other pedestrians. He bit his lips to keep from crying out a warning. What was the boy doing? He should be running the other way! And where was Cynthia? Marvin smiled idiotically at Fitzgibbon, allowed PJ to tug him again into a brisk walk.

"You better relax, too, Fitz. You're in the presence of divine inspiration." PJ winked at Marvin.

"Fucking nutcase. I'll goddamn *normalize* him. You wait, I'll . . ." Fitzgibbon bunched one hand into a fist, but his voice had lost power. He blinked as if his vision were blurring. Marvin realized, in amazement, that the big man was feeling wretched, was on the verge of tears.

They had reached the middle of the block, where a parking ramp led into the bowels of a tall building. Beside the ramp was a sidewalk deli, presenting a counter of fat sandwiches and cups of salad, pickles and sodas and popcorn. PJ steered them to this counter. "Going to be a slow trip in rush hour," he said conversationally. "You want something before we board?"

Marvin shook his head dumbly. He was afraid to look around again, afraid that Ronald was almost on them.

"Fitz, get me a coffee and a three-star special. Sorry we had to leave all your cakes and cookies back there, Marvin. Can't beat the home-made stuff."

Scowling, Fitzgibbon moved to the counter and began loading a tray. Then, with a cold surge of fear, Marvin saw the Drager boy appear beside the big man, not six feet away. He was afraid even to breathe. He knew of course that Feiffer had hunted this boy down in the Wasteland tunnels two years ago, had brought him back to his former life. Ronald was older now, wearing the wig, and stood with his back to them, but still . . .

Fitzgibbon had filled his tray and ran a slice through the slot at the end of the counter. His eyes flicked once over the boy, a look of perfunctory disgust. PJ seemed to be watching the ramp into the parking garage, whistling just audibly. Marvin saw Ronald nip up two bags of popcorn. Then a dark blue economy limo rolled up the ramp and stopped.

"Ah hah. Perfect timing." PJ lifted his coffee from the tray and beamed at Marvin. They strolled toward the limo, where the two men in suits had materialized to wag the doors open. Marvin found himself shoehorned into the vehicle swiftly and smoothly, between PJ and Fitzgibbon. The driver was only a shape on the other side of a tinted glass shield.

"Sorry about these cheap rentals," PJ said, and raised the paper cup to sip his coffee. Then, just as the two guards began to swing shut the doors, there was a startled cry and a commotion at the rear of the vehicle. Marvin felt a slight shock through the frame. Through the side window he saw a cascade of white flakes, like a sudden tiny snow squall.

"Shit! Goddamn!" Fitzgibbon slammed the flat of one hand against the tinted glass shield. "Go!"

Marvin twisted around, and as the limo jerked ahead, nosing aggressively into the stream of traffic, he saw one of the guards run a few steps and make an obscene, dismissive gesture. He guessed that a disturbance further off, a few faces turning, was a sign of someone dodging through the crowd. Ronald, he had to assume, but he could see nothing more because a dark, beating cloud had descended. He heard a scrape and rattle on the roof of the limo.

"Pigeons!" He heard Fitzgibbon bellow, in a voice brimming with revulsion. "Fucking flyin' *rats*!"

CHAPTER TWENTY-NINE

"You are an absolute Sybil, my dear."

Eva had finished logging her purchases, and now folded up her portable and nested it carefully in the coarse grass of the bank where they were sitting. Before them stretched three huge, shimmering plates of water, linked by low waterfalls and descending, stepping-stone fashion, from a squat, plain building where pumps hummed.

"Of course, the poets might rather grimace at the notion of spelling out destiny in sewer algae. Our poets, I mean." She sent Tima a swift glance embroidered with apology.

For a moment longer Tima watched the tiny fry of a mosquito fish as it nosed a fleck of larval husk. The green-gold scum to which Eva had referred was already dense, caking the reeds in shallows and incubating an early hatch. "The association with the bond market wouldn't bother them?" she said finally.

Eva giggled, so infectiously that Tima smiled broadly too. They had come here every two or three days, since their first stroll, to enjoy an hour or two of sunlight and ease, and to allow Tima to make her selections. It had delighted Eva immensely to discover that this treatment plant, processing releases from the city's business quarter, was rank with information on investor confidence, currency supply, and interest rates.

Of course everyone knew about garbage archeologists, but Eva was amazed and fascinated at the power of instant prescience in her new friend's nose. From a faint aroma of certain solvents, Tima could infer that mainframes were rotating into downtime – a sign that the big players did not contemplate major strategy shifts in the next few days. When an orgy of deal-making was about to begin, a particular reek arose from the jakes of expensive restaurants, and the alcohol content of their refuse inhibited yeast action in the settling pond. Or a drop in the population of fungus-gnats might signal an increase in graywater, an obsessive showering that surely heralded some investigation, indictment, or sting.

Relying on Tina's ability to read this affluent effluent, and her own long experience as a coupon-clipper, Eva was earning a steady, modest fortune from the one trading fund she still controlled. The only time, she announced with a cackle and hoot, she had profited from her conviction that the rich were full of shit.

Tima accepted a commission only large enough to cover rent and extras, but the real advantage, for both women, was the occasion to lounge by these pools and explore their odd but deepening friendship. Despite a difference of almost eighty years in their ages, and the fact that they were, in the view of orthodox science, of different species, they had discovered a certain common ground. They were both outcasts: self-exiled, eccentric freaks. Both survived in the shadows and lived on the dream of apocalypse – with a healthy dash of bitter wit – and both saw very deeply into the souls of those around them.

"Our poets would shock you," Tima observed. "They sing about eating their mothers or drinking each other's blood."

"Well, actually, ours do, too. The ones respectably dead for a few centuries. Only I believe it was the mothers who served up their children. For good reason, as I recall. Anyway, this is no chatter for a woman in your condition." Eva held up a long, thin hand against the sun and squinted at the dim shadow of her finger bones. "Or mine."

Tima shrugged. They had noted before the irony of another bond between them: one soon to give birth, the other nearing the grave, they mitigated anxiety in small talk about their diets or discomforts or the stress of waiting. Now these subjects were taken for granted, and in the last month they had begun to speak at a deeper level, confessing doubts and speculations they shared with no one else.

At the moment they were both worried about the trouble between Cynthia and Marvelous. Sandhill, they agreed, was only a symptom, not the cause. "A criminal life," Eva had observed drily, "is hard on a couple." She knew from experience. Her own career, as holo goddess and wife of one of the richest men in the world, had involved years of lawyers, trials, and appeals, terminating in heavy illegal addiction, commitment to an institution, and bribery to facilitate release.

In turn, Tima related some of her own history with Pahane. How she had to be (at seventeen) a mother to him, sometimes a sister too, as well as his sex instructress and teacher in Pobla ways. He was such an odd mix: Pobla and piksi, child and adult, fool and seer. And of course he was a she, inside. The exact reverse of

Tima's own makeup, a male mind concealed in a female body. This idea, which she had thought might appear bizarre to the older woman, was understood immediately.

"Oh girl," Eva said after a long burst of laughter. "It happens all the time. I saw it immediately, that *he* wanted to carry the baby, was going to go through every contraction, whereas you would much rather be running with the hustlers. I was the same way – Lord, how I hated kitchens! Anyway, that makes you two a rather good match. No wonder you are going to give birth to a goddess."

Of course they talked about the baby a lot. Eva had also known at one glance that it would be a girl, though she had never had children of her own. She also believed that the birth would inaugurate a cycle of great upheaval, radical change. It was clear already, she explained, from what one saw on holo. The whole nation was getting the jitters, trying to interpret this illicit union: they couldn't decide whether they detested or desired a mixing of blood, wanted to kill or control the creatures arriving on the border; so the Progs and Cons were jockeying furiously to maneuver the situation to their advantage – if they could only divine where such advantage lay.

And besides these obvious macro-indicators, one saw little anomalies in the everyday life on the street. Eva had her own sources of divination. She read the subway flow, the power surges, the shifts in Omaly population, much as Tina deciphered the financial import of sewer fumes. Last week, for example, after Tima had pointed out a strange influx of pipers, gulls and herons, two workers from the plant below had sauntered out at lunch break. The men spotted them, but had not – as they expected – turned back to phone for security. Instead the workers had broken into a jigging dance, definitely obscene, and beckoned to the women.

"Never, never see that any more," Eva had said, in a tone of real awe. "They could be fired for an impromptu boogie like that. That's at least as weird as your herons."

Tima expressed surprise. She pointed out that the Sanitation Bureau had authorized shade trees here, a pair of benches and a dedicatory plaque. They must have once expected a few idlers, a public that could relax in view of its own excrement, perhaps toss a ball or romp on the grass?

"My dear, you've spent your whole life among us either in institutions or on the run, so you assume it's different for the ordinary citizen. But we're *all* prisoners here. Idlers are definitely discouraged everywhere. So is public mirth." Eva gazed with a certain melancholy yearning at the naked concrete block of the treatment plant. "Freedom under democracy, eh? Fud. Freedom to kiss the ass of whatever bunch of bandits currently owns the franchise. Or else, if you start kicking, they lock you up. Those two sanitary engineers act like they've got a whiff of real freedom. They could be in trouble. Did I tell you my first serious affair was with a sanitation engineer?"

Tima had laughed, delighted. "So. That's why we come here. Sentimental reasons."

"No, not sentimental. I knew very well I wanted to smear myself – the part of me that had been auctioned off to Homer – in the gutter. I wanted the bottom. Mental health required it. I was just shocked at how much fun I had. This randy, funny roughneck, who had come with a backhoe to our exclusive estate . . . "

Eva had told her that story, and others involving mechanics, magrig drivers, and unemployed drifters, a series which led quite naturally to the hotel in Omalytown. Of course her establishment was no ordinary one, for she had discovered in this underworld a surprising number of others of good education and some means, eccentrics who gravitated naturally to her circle and formed a salon. Most of them backheads, Eva was quick to admit, but nonetheless a good-tempered, peaceful, and interesting lot. They dabbled in psychic research, undertook the occasional mild, septuagenarian affair, and discussed holosoaps and the news with considerable vigor and astuteness.

This select company (Eva called them the upper crust of the lower depths) had quite agreed that by every portent and augur they were approaching a time of marvels and prodigies. The obscene boogie of sewer-men, the flocks of shorebirds, the torment of lovers surely foreshadowed some strange destiny; and the psychic contingent, at least, harbored no doubt that Tima's baby would figure in that destiny, both as cause and effect. Madame Ondine, a matron who was leader of this faction and always wore a hat with veil and a single flower on her bosom, had declared the embryo an angel, probably of the avenging kind.

Tima had smiled at that announcement, and wondered privately what the occult group would make of the hairy being growing inside her. She had already seen her child – who would develop early, she already knew. The vision was as bright as any dream: a black pelt, rich and smooth as velvet, curled around a perfect body; eyes of gray-blue, like arctic ice; already strong enough to grip and lift herself, or roll over. This vision of power and beauty held her, sometimes, mute and still and radiant as a stone in the sun. She had shared it with no one, not even Pahane. So Tima was prepared for the oblique question in Eva's next remark, framed between the swift, furtive actions of notching a cigarette in her withered mouth, and lighting it with a tiny plug. "I suppose if the notion of children had ever appealed to me, I would have picked the seed out of that pack of brawlers and outlaws I ran with on my way to Omalytown. Hoping, I suppose, to birth some rebel saint from the gutter."

"Fun," Tima noted slyly, "was mentioned as a motive."

"Oh yes, they were healthy animals, many a fine and furious fuck. But I was quite mad with idealism in those days, my dear. I wanted my rebellion to *mean* something. Now I suspect my own previous lives were all hellions who abandoned their progeny, if they had any, and worked for noble but conveniently abstract causes. Maud Gonnes and George Sands and the like. But if I could have been guaranteed Sun-Yat-Sen or Ataturk or *Joan of Arc* . . . " Eva blew smoke casually at Tima's midsection. "Or even a mystery woman of rare extraction . . . "

Tima laughed and waved a hand into the smoke. "But this is a completely new shadow. No one knows. She is . . . herself. Unique, like all of us."

Eva looked at Tima sardonically around the white thread unspooling from the tip of the cigarette. "Surely there are no accidental ghosts, on such an occasion."

Tima looked away, laying one hand across the swell of her belly. "No, no accidents. We do not believe in chance, as you define it."

"Oh, forgive me, child! I'm a nosy old bat sometimes, but I am so thoroughly enthralled by this whole world you've introduced us to. Brave and new, indeed, and rather shivery at times. But if you don't want—"

"No, it's all right." Tima touched the old woman lightly on the shoulder. "It is only that words do not help us much, here. This little ghost does not speak to us. She emerged in Pahane first, as a sensation of warmth and dark, growing inside a shell of brightness and cold. He could tell she was fearful, as he had been when his *kubi* awoke. She was in flight from something, yet also toward something."

Tima sighed, seeing that Eva was disappointed. "You must understand 'she' is only a scattering of memories at this point, so incandescent they burn through thousands of years, but puzzling and discontinuous, like pieces of a dream. For Pahane these memories began to glow when I became pregnant, to make patterns like filings near a magnet.

"Our first name for her was Sehapsi, which is Pobla for 'runner', because that was Pahane's sense – something moving like the wind. He dreamed of horses the night she was conceived. On the run from the start. The way we have always dodged your copters."

Tima tried to smile, but it was too late. The weight of these last weeks had slammed down on her, without warning, and left her barely strong enough to lift the corners of her mouth. Her people had always feared these prowlers on land and in the sky, had always preferred to dive into the great, silver-dark river of *yano* rather than be taken into that shrieking, blinding death brought by men. For centuries they had cowered before these *mudlatin* predators, hissing overhead, infrared eyes eternally awake, poised to peel flesh from bone with fire.

"Oh love!" With one skinny, beringed hand Eva had forked her cigaret from her mouth. "You simply have too much on you. It's absurd! Seventeen, pregnant, on the run – the last thing you need is some dithery old puss to remind you of hiding in caves from gangs of mechanized killers—"

Tima shook herself, lifted her hands. "I'm all right, Eva. Really." She managed to widen her smile. "And the company in this particular cave is most charming. You've been very kind. It's just, you know, the waiting . . . "

"Of course. Of course! And kind of you, my dear, to say all that, but we're not actually very charming, even at our Sunday best. It's true – don't shush me, child – we are only as good as the next scam or lucky smack or back deal allows. Pays your money, takes your choice, we say, and that's the law of our Omaly universe. No money, no choice. We're all consumers, love, and all consumed."

Eva looked, for the blink of an eye, as if her skeleton were emerging from its sheath of papery skin, a luminous rack of bone grinning at some mad, sinister joke. Tima thought of the chain of hellions her friend had imagined: a flickering of thin, ravening shadows receding from this bright skeleton. The piksis. Ghost eaters. They *were* different.

"You know, don't you, my dear?" Eva asked suddenly. She had looked away as if distracted, toward the tall shafts of office buildings beyond the trees that ringed this desolate small park. They could hear the steady, heavy noise of traffic, like a waterfall, with an overlay of click and chatter, the sensor switches opening and closing like the mandibles of billions of metal insects.

Tima did not answer, and Eva went on. "I'm sure you do. You must. You worked in border security with Charlie Fat. They are not fools, at least when it comes to finding people."

Again, Tima felt as if the force of gravity had doubled, or tripled. Apparently some perverse spirit could spin a dial, and her flesh would begin to sag, pull from the bone, like a shroud of lead. Even the baby, with all her power of promise, like light compacted, became merely a dumb, downward pressure. She gathered herself, lifted her chin imperceptibly. "Yes," she said tactfully. "We are all prisoners, as you say."

"Undertown is full of people they are careful *not* to find, for the time being, anyway. But my ex-husband always knows who is near me, what I am doing." Eva kicked at the computer case nested in the grass. "His people monitored every transaction we made this morning. If I tried—" Eva looked away again, her head swiveling as if she had received a firm, invisible slap. "I hate that sonofabitch. I'd kill him, I'd kill him if—"

"Please," Tima said, "let it go. You have done everything you could."

"No, I haven't." Eva's voice was pettish and sniffly. She had ground out her cigaret and was dabbing at her face with her long fingers. She abhorred, Tima knew, any deterioration of her make-up. "I *should* have killed him years ago. That time he stood in front of the car at the beach and dared me—"

"Eva, Eva! We are at least better off here than at the Institute. For now we are holding on. We can watch too, you know, and something may come along. Only we mustn't let the others know, Cynthia and Marvin especially. For them freedom, even just the illusion of freedom, is all that—"

She stopped, for Dizzy had fluttered down to the grass at their feet, cooing and chucking furiously, strutting back and forth. Tima's shadow rolled and rose within her, staggering at first, but then shouldering aside the heaviness. She was up on the balls of her feet, scanning the perimeter of the park. Beside her Eva had recovered the case and was checking its snaps. "What was it?" the old woman hissed. "Should we leave? My dear, I can't *gallop*, you know . . . "

Tima saw the figure, moving through the trees at a kind of sprinting walk, a poor imitation of someone hurrying to a subway or bulletbus stop. The Omalys had taught them this gait, to be used only in emergencies. For the sight of a bizarre or shabbily dressed person running, or even skipping, was an immediate alert to any security apparatus.

"Who is that?" Eva allowed herself to be helped to her feet, clutching the case under one arm.

"Cynthia. We'll stroll . . . easy now . . . to the street exit." Tima set off in her old-man's hobble, her hat tugged down over her eyes, toward the fringe of trees. The sight of three Omalys scurrying together would also attract attention, so she angled to intercept Cynthia obliquely, casually, as by accident.

"Why is she . . . oh dear, someone has blundered. Shut up, Dizzy." Eva moved like a rickety swan, covering ground with deceptive, if perilous, speed. The pigeon swirled around them, batting its wings now and then at Tima's hat. Cynthia, they could see, was stiff and awkward with inner tension. She careened over the grass, her skimpy clothes and handbag incongruous in this setting, her face a dim, pale flash, like a worn coin spotted on a sidewalk.

Tima did not have to wait for the words. She read agony in Cynthia's motion, her blank face, the eyes that would not close for a long time. This agony was for herself, Tima could see, some deep and final guilt. So she was not surprised when her friend cried out hoarsely, still twenty strides away.

"Marvelous!" The word was not so much spoken as pulled forth, like a knife from a wound.

Tima made a gesture, half greeting and half caution, or perhaps supplication. She appeared to crouch a little and set a controlling hand on Eva's elbow. "Hey, girl," she croaked. "Easy now. We good folks, here."

Cynthia came on, a jerky somnambulist, fumbling now in her handbag. "Marvelous," she cried again. "They picked up Marvelous. Batboy too. They'll break him. They'll—"

"Easy now." Tima moved sidewise like a crab, holding out a begging hand. "They maybe watching, girl. Holdona yuhseff." She had concentrated her *kubi* into her role, as her people did when they threw a hide over their backs and moved like deer or antelope, to fool the satellites.

"Oh my God, my God." Eva's voice wobbled with anxiety. "That's terrible. Did they make a mistake?"

"Bats." Cynthia compressed her lips to a white line. "He fell for a sex and back hook. Panny and I saw it coming and blew. And we had it. We *had* it! Smacked a whole deck of big slices and we were on our way home . . . " Her face seemed to collapse, writhe, then reconstitute itself in a terrible smile. "*Home?*"

"Easy, easy, easy." Tima had edged them under one of the scant trees. She gripped Cynthia by the wrist and drew her near enough to whisper. "How long ago?"

"Hour and a half, maybe two." Cynthia had found the cigaret pack in her handbag, but it was empty and with two savage strokes she crumpled it and threw it on the ground. "Panny and I split up. We were supposed to do a couple of transfers and then double back to meet at the park Marvin likes. His table was there, the flyers out, so I thought he'd just stepped away—" She quelled a sob, reduced it to a muffled whimper. "Oh Christ. Jesus fucking Christ. I did it. I nagged him to keep going there. It's me—"

"It is not." Eva looked down on both of them, imperious. "It is *not* your fault. He did need something to do. We all thought so. You are under tremendous stress, sweet, and it won't help to blame yourself. It's not—"

"How do you know he was picked up?" Tima interrupted. She kept an eye on the traffic flickering through the trees, the occasional pedestrian glancing their way with distaste.

"A woman who was leafleting right beside him. She saw them bust him, four men in an unmarked van, but she is sure they were cops, Insec or Fedjud. Then she said a young roach showed up looking for the Preach, so Panny was ahead of me. I didn't want to wait, didn't know how long we had, whether to warn the hotel first. Sandy's gone . . . " The sob tried to erupt again, and became this time a hiccup.

Eva and Tima exchanged one quick glance. Eva had fingered two cigarets from her own pocket and hung them in her mouth. With her glow plug she lit both, then picked away one to set between Cynthia's first two fingers, already extended and trembling. "You did the right thing. Sandy can care for himself. Always does." Eva's eyes slid sideways. "But we mustn't tarry. Tima and I have been here two hours already, and this is highly illegal."

"Fuck it," Cynthia said in a low, passionate tone. "Everything is highly illegal." She sucked on the cigaret, its tip rousing instantly to a bright, hot lacework. "But I thought I could handle it. With Marvelous, I mean. But I was just avoiding, taking for granted. And I was, I don't know . . . "

"Bored," Eva said. "He is wonderfully sweet, a real dumpling despite the loose rivets, and when this is over you should take him, but when one is under for a while, smacking and backing, soar and crash, one acquires a rather high threshold for excitement."

"Oh God." Cynthia dragged again on the cigaret, hard, and then talked out the smoke, smiling wanly. "Guess I didn't fool anybody but myself, did I? I was tired and nervous and I don't know . . . crazy I suppose. It's always been crazy around Sandy. Yet how could I—"

"Forget it." Tima had flipped up the brim of her hat and leaned wearily against the tree, just below Dizzy who was parading nervously along a branch. "All of it. We have to contact the others, and we'll have to move, that's clear. If it was a squad operating officially, they may turn him loose and then follow him, to locate the rest of us. We'll assume Panny also shook loose and is hanging somewhere, probably not far from" – she gave Cynthia a quick, ironic smile – "home."

Tima knew, in fact, how to find her mate if he was still on the street. Peppercorn and Dizzy could show her. But she did not tell her friends as much. She cared for them, but they were distraught and they were piksis to begin with, and thus not trustworthy in these situations. "We ought to split up too," she said matter-of-factly to Eva. "You could return to the hotel and gather some information, find a safe envoy to meet us at a rendezvous. You know a place?"

Eva, too, had been sucking smoke with furtive industry, her brow corrugated with concern, but now she looked dismayed. "Ah no! Separate? Oh child! You and our precious little . . . But yes. Yes, you're right of course." She dropped the cigaret and rolled her heel over it. "We should. Hard as it is. And I do know of a place. I hope it's secure. A dark sanctuary, I was assured." She showed her teeth. "Better be."

She squatted abruptly, unsnapped the case and set the portable on the grass. "Anyway, it's all we've got." She was running her spidery hands over the keys, her mouth still a tight, straight line. "It's a one-time release, so when I uncrypt you've only got ten seconds . . . "

"I'll memorize it. Cyn's got enough to bear just now." Tima pushed away from the tree and leaned over Eva, watching the screen. Cynthia's glum expression showed that she understood this precaution. If she were caught, the investigators would go to work on her with drugs and psych probes. Harsher techniques than those allowed at the Institute. She would end by betraying everything, weeping and laughing.

The portable murmured and clicked. Tima read the half-dozen words, the string of numbers: a name in capitals and an address. Then the message swallowed itself.

"Anybody else got a copy?"

Tima made the question simple and gentle. But Eva looked away, and when she answered made no effort to hide her weary disgust. "Our benefactors have a backup, they tell me. Someone among us."

Tima shrugged. *Our pancake*, she thought. She felt lighter, as if the demon had turned his gravity dial in reverse. Her *kubi* floated too, alert and agile. She was certain Pahane was still free, and would know she was free as well. Or as free as this twisted piksi system would allow. She would find him and together they would scout this dark sanctuary.

"Well, then," she said. "You'd better go. I'll wait here a few minutes, give you time to get to the tube." She flipped her hatbrim down again and her body shrank and twisted. One hand hooked out irritably at the others. "Got no stim, no back fo' decent money! Git on, git on!"

Eva laughed in spite of herself, a hoarse cackle. "Amazing," she said. "You know, you could have utterly *conquered* the stage. Break a leg, as they say. I do love you. And you, too, my sad young friend." The old woman touched Cynthia's cheek, as if it had been fine china. "I was much like you, a long, long time ago. I know what you think of yourself right now. But you're wrong. Believe me, this is also wonderful. Wonderful and awful. I'd give anything to go through it again. Anyway, come along."

Computer case shut once more and tucked under an arm, Eva set her course toward the street. In her wide-sleeved coat, very expensive in its time but now much patched, her upswept hair, and trailing violet scarf, she glided like a rakish old craft under full, if makeshift, sail.

Cynthia managed a brave, rueful smile. "Who *you* call a muthuh? And I love you too." She turned abruptly and strode after Eva, not sprint-walking now but rolling, swaying a little like the brash, provocative runaway she had taught herself to be. Tima did not watch for long. Before the others were out of sight, Dizzy was on her shoulder. She put out her chin to accept the stroking beak, listened to the anxious, urgent churring. She was becoming one with her shadow, and her shadow would move with the bird, and together they would begin a swift, sure scavenging after her mate, her twin.

307

BOOK FOUR

CHAPTER THIRTY

The hard running was over, so they gathered now like rain pools in the narrow, crooked canyons, or scattered in bands too small to attract attention from the sky-eyes. Their movements would, they hoped, appear random; their numbers only the result of seasonal grass along the border of the Eater's land. Sometimes they were sure the black bird spread its wings and hid them from the eyes of all creatures.

The long-leggeds had begun to lose their thick coats, as they went lower and the wind brought them the rank smell of the devourers and their refuse heaps. From the ridge they were on they could see distant strings of lights crossing a plateau of the Eater country. They were closer than they had ever been, and this chain of sparkling, sinister jewels was both frightening and fascinating. The singers and the runners kept close, the little ones hemmed in and watched so there could be no accidents.

The Nacuatli had never lived in such fear and anticipation, had never spent so much effort in intricate, careful wandering, snatching mouthfuls of food as they moved and watching keenly every tilt and flap of the wings of their sentinels overhead. They knew many of the hive-worshippers had left their burrows and gone toward the Eaters' land, anticipating the birth of the Great One, whom they called Sehapsi. These Pobla were diverting the Eaters, making a shield for the six-leggeds. This was an act so brave and mad the Nacuatli were full of awed respect.

Klat told them the story of the coming snake-bird child every night now, so they would not yield to the fear or lose the scent of their own purpose. She told them also of how the dark bird had rolled a bit of clay into the First Beings, those who had found the long-legged runners and mated with them in a country that was all grass, between the fingers of the white god's hand; and how the original six-leggeds ran everywhere, even over a frozen ocean into other vast lands where it was always summer, and there the first snake-bird god was born and taught all creatures how to live together.

They listened, under the stars, and felt that their running was part of a migration that went back to the beginning. The runners of the light and those of the dark were racing, and the earth beneath them had become unstable, because the Eaters could not control their ravening hunger. They understood that the birth was happening because the Great Dreamer was having a nightmare and might wake up, and then everything would vanish as smoke from a swift, hot fire. So they had to gather, unobtrusively, here near the little valley only three ridges away from where the old Pobla man told them the birth would happen.

There would be a great battle, and much fire and smoke, like a volcano, and they would ride into its mouth and take the snake-bird child and then run away again, like a thousand small rivers. Some of you will be lost, Klat told them. The Eaters have terrible snakes of light that can reach across a canyon and strike us down. But they too want the child, want to make it into a hungry corpse like themselves, so they will be careful at first. We must confuse them, and then they will go back to their eating for a while. But eventually they will learn about the snake-bird child, some of them see already that she is the Spirit of the Dreamer. They will come for her, and she will give herself to them and save them and the Dreamer will dream the beautiful world for us again.

Klat was thinner now, and her eyes were bigger. When she laughed they saw through her, as if she were air, and on the other side there was sunlight and cool wind and the young ones were playing happily. Sometimes her hands did something and they thought she was the black bird, shaking its wings and fixing them with an eye like a hole into the dream world. We are all the same now, she admonished them, we are all in the mother of Sehapsi, and we will all be born together. And so we will run together, not six-legs but a thousand thousand legs, until we run like the fastest river, no legs at all, only running . . .

And so they would be up again, moving without thinking, easing their way in a long and winding and doubling path toward the valley. And on the next ridge over they saw other bands, six-leggeds and four-leggeds and even twos, all of them gathering or waiting to move. From the wheeling great birds they knew there were beings approaching from all sides, from very far away, and so the story was going on, just as Klat sang it every night.

All stories had of course a place where the things that have been

312

foretold happen, and then the story sings itself. They were almost at this place, for they no longer were certain some nights whether Klat was speaking aloud or not. They did not so much hear the story as see it and feel it and move in it. The sun came up and they were moving and inside it was exactly as if they were being sung. The sun went down and they slept on the river-race of that same song.

No one spoke of time, but if they had it would not have been measured in moons. Two hands and six legs were more than enough to count the suns that would rise before the song would speak the holy name. Already they could hear its echo in the marrow of their bones. *Sehapsi! Sehapsi! Sehapsi!* She was turned in her dark chamber, readying herself for the first wave of light.

CHAPTER THIRTY-ONE

Skirting what was left of the great desert at sundown, Hank Freeman liked to retreat to the observation port above the sleeping cabin and go direct visual for a few quiet minutes. Out here you still caught a bit of primitive skyline, crags and black stumps of mesas, before a red-hot sun rolled over the edge of the world.

Hank also liked how the Feederways radiated out into the darkening land, bearing vehicles like tracers of light, with here and there a constellation burning – a pumping station or power plant or com tower. It was the only place along the Orleans-Paso-Angeles corridor where you could overlook the whole grid, no interference, a hundred miles in every direction. In daytime you saw the great irregular swatches of claywork and concrete, catchbasins for an annual four or five inches of rain, the potable supply funneled into the pumping stations and then underground to the cities. You could see the banks of tilted mirrors and solar panels, ringing the power stations like petals of some geometrically perfect flower. Sometimes you even caught a work crew in their huge beetle-like machines, pincers and jaws dredging a canal or slicing away the top of a mountain to use as aggregate or fill in a new Trunkway.

It satisfied Hank, deeply, to cruise by these scenes, these glittering strings and spokes of light. The power ran the pumps and belts to push the water and ore out of the ground into the cities, which in turn circulated an endless current of goods. A living, pulsing organism, and he was one of its hurrying corpuscles. As Hank saw it, everything connected and came to life through the magrigs rolling on these arterials, eighteen lanes now, nearly half a million kilometers of them spread over the continent.

His old rig was pooping along pretty smartly right now. Two hundred and twenty klicks an hour, and nearly five klicks a gallon efficiency. They had a tail wind, and for this season traffic was light. There was time to catch a little holo after this sunset, before popping a sledge and switching into a sleeper lane. He appreciated the chance to ease up, dream a little, consider this weird haul and what he thought about it.

From the cabin below he heard the phone beep, but he decided not to take the call. He knew it was his wife, her usual after-dinner check when he was on the road. After she came on to leave a message, his baby girl burbling in the background, he only half-listened. He was staring out through the glass port at a hot pink sky.

"Sweetheart? Are you hiding back in the bay? Can't *imagine* what you've got, all this hush-hush! Anyway, sweets, if you have time, give us a jingle before Jennifer goes beddy-bye? Oh, and if you jitney back tomorrow . . . "

There was a slight increase in the flutter of the sensor bands underneath the mag's big wheels. This stretch was the last one where the NorthAm Trans computer would still allow mags to cruise over two hundred. At this speed the landscape seemed to be in constant motion, rotating slowly around a series of dark lumps on the red-streaked horizon, a range of mountains bordering the Wastelands.

Somewhere over there those Gink hordes were pouring in. The big story on nightly newsholo for weeks. Another crisis for the Con government; another opportunity for expert heads to yak away, chew over their new concepts.

Or they would all do their folksy chuckling, the panel and the visitor, just another small joke in front of a quarter-billion viewers. "Maureen may be right. This may be the first virus with *style*. Moving now to the political front . . . " The moderator would break away then from the intimate circle, head-on serious, yet with that lurking we-all-know-what-it's-really-about smile. "Candidate Adamson has nixed Total Wipe as a strategy and is listening to the Balbuds among his advisers. Adamson is thought to favor the border Factocamps idea . . . "

It wasn't even news, this Gink thing, to the drivers. Months ago they had begun reporting more roadkills. You had to be looking – no noticeable impact – and sightings had always before been rare. Just lone strays spattered and within minutes pounded down to a mere stain on the concrete. (After all, a series of hundred-and-twenty-ton projectiles travelling at high speed, three seconds apart, could disperse an elephant in a few minutes, let alone a fifty-kilo bonebag.) But now those stains were multiplying; Ginks got smeared every day. It had even happened to Hank.

Two at once, in fact. The funny thing was that the female and the young one had just appeared there, on the inside sleeper lane. They weren't running, didn't even seem aware of the phalanx of hurtling mags. He had just awakened, poured himself a cup of coffee, and flipped on the monitor. He was only doing a hundred and ten, so he got a good look, even the faces. Hard to tell with the dirt and hair, but he would have called the female's expression blank. Took some kind of self-executed lobotomy to go anywhere near the maglanes on a Transcon Trunkway. Validated ELF, too. Eco Legal Fund, or so registered, but everybody read it as Exterminate the Little Fuckers.

Hank laughed briefly, silently, then dropped again into his melancholy musing. He hadn't even noticed when his wife hung up. The problem with being a rigdriver was too much time to wander around in your own mind. The guidance systems took care of everything but deliveries, delays and accidents. Most of the time you could watch holo, use the exercise chair, or sleep. With this current cargo, a one-shot hipri special, he had nothing to do but keep himself amused between log points.

A little later he would catch Winger, his favorite show. Massive Man had a whole campaign going on this refugee thing, and the kidnapping of that Drager boy from a fancy high-security nutbin. He had cojones, you had to give the Big Guy that: he had even filed suit to challenge the official renaming of Ginks as Pobla. He claimed it was part of a conspiracy to legitimize mixing species. Fuginking, in the people's NorthAm. The BFG was hinting very big players, major money, a new political machine. Well, Big Beau himself worked for The Big One, which included not only the softdrink and shampoo empire, but Sportsorama and VitaVirtuals as well. All of them in a conglomerate headed by Barrelhead Morphopolous, reputedly the richest individual on the planet. Hank was interested in this fact for a personal reason. He was pretty sure he and Beau Winger were, at the moment, employed by the same boss.

Mama's Mini-Zoos was part of the Morphop empire, if he believed the underground broadcast he just happened to catch a couple of weeks ago. *This mummified imperialist toad*, the commentator foamed, in his whiny, vitriolic soprano, *has acquired bioindustries from Alpha-Gro to Mama's Mini-Zoos . . .*

The line stuck with him, maybe because he laughed at the idea of a giant toad wearing a crown, buying his own cage. About the crown, however, there was no question. A Lebanese Greek, the young Morphopolous had inherited a dying dynasty – a family trade

317

in pulp, fiber and fertilizers. Borrowing and buying recklessly, he plunged into the most risky and exciting new industries – especially the packaging and distribution of information and fantasy. Within a decade, he had taken over his former creditors and was chairing the Fed Central Board of Econovisers.

Anyway, when Hank checked in at the dock and saw the printout listing Mama's as the shipper, and the Apollo Terminal in Diego as destination, he was fairly certain, and pretty excited. Apollo MultiTrans also belonged to Morphopolous, and it was fairly well known the old guy owned a private artificial Pacrim island which was supplied out of Diego. Hank guessed his rig would be hauling something unusual, something very special to this particular multitrillionaire. Then it turned out he was not deadheading on the return. Another cargo from Mama's was booked on a completely dark run. He wouldn't even know the destination himself. He'd be on standby until a pilot came aboard.

Yet there was no mystery at all on this first leg. He already knew – through a lucky accident – what cargo he had back there in its climate-controlled, intensive-care suite. Nothing to justify the precautions the shippers took. He couldn't figure the secrecy. His company specialized in live cargoes, fragile biostuffs, and of course security was sometimes elaborate because gene patents were involved or the strains were not sufficiently tested for release. But usually the guys in the office could tell him, at least, whether he would have a hundred tons of hexagonal tomatoes, or black cotton, or wingless chickens strapped to his ass. This time, not a peep.

At the dock when he arrived was a medical, young and efficient but with a cold eye. She was there to supervise the loading of the big container, equipped with its own heat control, filters and a lockable keyboard. He had already guessed, by sneaking a look at certain gauges, that it was an animal, and probably large, when a monitor alarm began to oogah. The woman started swearing, with surprising crudity, and went for the main doors.

She ordered the foreman and lift operator back into the warehouse and they went without a word. Hank had retreated to the cab of the rig, which was idling. Since he was out of sight, she forgot him and he simply flipped on the rear video, and observed. The outer doors opened to reveal an inner compartment, a minilab adjoining a big cage, serviced by a blower, water tank and food dispenser. Straw littered the cage, and at first he thought the tawny lump at the rear was only a bale of the same.

318

Then the head came up, framed in a great black cowl of hair, and the yellow eyes, huge and unblinking. It was a lion, an old male apparently, and a large one. Nothing unusual in that. At the theme parks they were a common exhibit, sometimes allowed to wander. Defanged and declawed, the gentlest would tolerate the older kids on their backs for a home holo. This one looked drugged, and not in the best of health, its dusty, ragged hide draped over sharp hip and shoulder bones. The flanks heaved and collapsed slowly with each breath.

But it had teeth, the tips of long, yellow incisors showing now as it raised up on its front paws. He saw then they had a tube in it, taped to a haunch. The medical had shut off the alarm and was bent over a control panel, fiddling with dials, adjusting dosage, he supposed. Sure enough, in another few seconds the front legs splayed out and the big head flopped back onto the deck. The woman remembered then to close the main doors, so he switched off the video.

Her procedures, whatever they were, took another twenty minutes. Then they loaded the container swiftly and Hank was cleared to depart. The woman waved, smiled with her icy cheer and told him a bald-faced lie. "Your cargo is all bacteria cultures, sealed and coded, so it'll be a nice, quiet trip. And remember, we'll have another load from here going back." And that was all. A one-shot hipri express, costing probably half his annual salary, plus whatever they paid the medical. For one moldy old lion. He could make no sense of it at all, unless the lion was just cover for some darkside deal, and the return cargo was something really special.

The chrono beeped him a reminder. Winger was coming on.

He wondered what The Most Fat One would think of this matter, this screwball haul. He'd connect it to the refugees, no doubt, since he was completely wound up on the subject. Especially after he broke the totally weird story about the alleged hijacking of the alleged hybrid bastard embryo, and started hinting the whole thing was a setup, the Ecominis and Cons collaborating to advance a secret agenda – which was to develop a whole generation of mixeds that would seize power and drag civilization back into the slime.

Hank couldn't tell if the Big Guy was serious. It was true a lot of families hid the rumor of odd blood somewhere. Grand-parents who had a nose and bleach job or a dubious miscarriage. The joke was, a King was just a dyslexic Gink. And it was true the notion of mixed blood seemed to shake up a lot of people

319

nowadays. Both Thorgies and Elfies, representing the extremes, had expanded their membership. Nervous people throwing money around, hoping to save their asses. And Winger, of course, thrived on it all.

It struck Hank all at once that NorthAm society might be undergoing a giant cell-division, like the Ginks were going through, each side accusing the other of being cancerous. He couldn't, himself, make up his mind, and had ceased to take the whole thing seriously; it seemed to him a lot like a splashy but disorganized holosoap. Mostly he had to laugh, but it was irritating, too, and sometimes a little bit scary. The idea of gene clearance, a card to show you didn't have any Gink, for example. Or how much, if you were unlucky.

The Fat One was dangerous there, made people *really* uneasy. Gink in the woodpile. Skeleton in the closet. If you actually *found* one, of course, you made him a Pobla, immediately. That hypocrisy, as much as anything, irritated Hank. He had done his military training on the border, shot a few, told his share of jokes. Now all at once, by government decree, the common words were unacceptably crude. No more laps. No more bucks and bitches. Male and female "subjects," a possible "resource."

Well, fuck that. They couldn't stop him from thinking to himself anything he wanted. What difference did it make what you called them, anyway? He had no particular animosity, one way or the other. If they had given up their noxious habits, like eating each other and inciting other animals to sabotage, and if it was cheaper to use them than wipe them, then organ banks or border factories would be fine with him.

Hank had now waited long enough for the ads and infomercials to be over, so he punched up the program. He was curious to know how Winger's challenge had fared in court. The Big Guy would be funny either way. He had such a way with words, so it made sense he was taking this issue to the wall, and if he lost the decision he'd only leer at the camera with a wink, a wink that said go ahead and *think* Gink. Which was exactly what Hank was doing as the great yakker's image flared up, blasting in on the rocketchair until the broad face filled the whole box, eyes shut in a trance and mouth already stretched wide around a yowl of wicked ecstasy.

CHAPTER THIRTY-TWO

"Ginkoblast! Fanginkotastic megagink! Ginkocrat reginks the ginka-tonic funginkus! Ginkophobes of the ginkosphere, agink! We got nogink to ginkup but our chaingink ginkofences! Hey, bubaginks! Guess who-o-o-o! Da Beeg Fat Wan cominatya widda bran' new roolin' from dee high court, a smokin' decree, a habeus ginkus and stay of exeginktion, the proseginkor foiled! Ha ha!"

Beau Winger looms, a sheaf of papers crumpled in his big hand, words exploding out of his mouth in a fog of spittle. He has just wheeled out of a jetcopter onto an outdoor stage, positioned in a playing field at the center of a huge colosseum. Despite amplification through a two-story bank of speakers, he is barely audible over the mighty, sustained roar from the crowd, the hundred and forty-six thousand fans who have paid dearly to celebrate his victory, live and in person. His pudgy arms straight above his head, ramming the papers and a fist at the sky, he lets the avalanche of sound roll over him. He moves to the left, then the right, in a kind of mincing waddle; he makes faces of astonishment, wonder, puzzlement, idiotic awe, both at the crowd and into the holocameras on booms over the stage.

"Izzis for *me*? Little ol' Beaugink? Oh, peeple, *stop* it now!" The sound grows even more thunderous, a sustained detonation. Winger allows it, makes a motion of gathering in, a copious embrace. Finally the tone changes, a soft rush of laughter invading the howls of triumph. Winger has fists on hips, now, and surveys the crowd with a familiar leer.

"Yas, yas, I'm wonderful. This I know, my dear subjects. And there's so much *of* me, too, you lucky hogs, but let's not waste any more time being modest, we need this little victory toot, and then we got a whole new convoy of ginkoids, Draculaps, Frankenginks, and lapasstrophes to bring you."

Beau holds the papers now at top and bottom, like a proclamation, and swaggers back and forth on the stage. "Hear ye! Hear ye! In the matter of Winger Productions and Maxmondo Holos – tha's us, seetwayens – you hasslemachers, you holohogs – versus the Unified North American States of the Federation of Nations – which is bustagut bloatarama, the flubocracy, the immensoid bucksucker, your own troo gummint, the *Conservative administration* of Presigink Stuckwall, our chief Execugink—" The applause drowns out Winger once more, and he bows in acknowledgment, then quiets the crowd with a tolerant frown and goes on.

"—the Federation High Court rules as follows – sorry 'bout this, loyal pubalick, but we got to hold the shnozz and go in deep cheekies here – rules as follows: the prohibition against 'usage'" – he takes a deep breath and begins to accelerate his reading – "'ofagivenword-inofficialdocumentsexceptingdocumentspertainingtocourtproceedings orjudicialreviewshallbeheldtoapplyexclusivelytosaidwordinitscon-ventionalspellingand/orpronunciationwithoutmodification . . .'" He glances up, grinning, and reverts to stately declamation. "'Such . . . prohibition . . . shall not extend – *shall not extend*,' oh noble folk, oh loyal wallowers in blubberblabber – 'to satiric coinages or analogs incorporating the said word or its elements, or to the word qualified by suffixes, prefixes or other modifiers incorporated structurally, whether or not such modifications are grammatical' – Oh fugink it, fans! We git it, hey? They can't stop us, can't exterminate the basic rat, hey? With me? Rat to assemble, rat to jabber – jabber long, jabber free! – rat to bitch, sweetheart, right here on the cosmoscale yakshow! We cominatya *live* today, ginkophobes, gonna give it to ya *good*. But—"

Winger raises one finger and the crowd hushes, breathes as one organism.

"We make no cheap charges, no jealous jeers, my friends. We got the stuff, gonna lay it out for you. Let us review the case now, loyal swallowers. Primero: we reported already last month how the whole so-called kidnap served the Conservaginks' interests, a move to get the show offstage, and how their former Insec tool, agent Feiffer, shows up in the smack middle of the mess, trying to look like an Ecomini terrorist.

"Segundoroso: the Conswervos set up a whole network of so-called scientists – including a Gandhi winner – to build up a case for keeping and feeding these Pob-ah-la-te-das. They wanna *analyze* 'em, they claim, for sigh-ants, of course – but right away rumors of a mystery infection, a goofus bug that's makin' our fighting men into marshmellows – and meanwhile another band of Ginkies mutates into murderers, and some idiot genius smuggles *weapons* to them! All at thy expense, unfortunatos! Oh yeah, sigh-ants! They gonna find, you bet your buttons, how splendissimo excellentay it is to have just a hintita of a ginkomite in the old bod, just an itty whisperinkle of a ginkule. You wanna bet? Hey? How do I know this? How *can* I know this?

"Seenyours and Seenyoureatahs, I am the Vigilante Corpulante! The Fat One sees all! Prepare thyselves now for his revelations, two in numbuh . . . Yeeow!"

With remarkable agility, Winger cocks up one knee and spins at the same time on the toe of the other foot, leveling one arm at the giant holoscreen behind him. A tremendous image blossoms there: a foetus in rich color, the empurpled and blue-netted membranes of its nest glistening. The domed, chinless skull with great slitted eyes jerks randomly, the tiny gnarled fists flail. The thing curls and transforms swiftly, sprouts a dark sheath of hair; the lips thicken and widen, the ears unfold like sails.

"Oh, how better to begin the New Order, ladies and gents! How 'bout a wee one, a saplap succubaby, darkness and light, ape and angel! New messiah, hey? Oh messy, ah messy, ah messy-yi-yi indeed! Cominatya now, seetwayens! This ain't no rumor, this ain't no hype, this is a real live hairball, people, and the ecorad terror-folk wanna make it *yours*!"

Winger has squared off like a boxer, his pudgy arms hooking at an imaginary opponent. The crowd produces now a steady thunder, deep and passionate. They are standing, staring at the creature on the screen, many weeping openly.

"So we need your help, loyal seetwayens! To arms! We got a major menace in our midst, and time is runnin' out on the human race! The forces of disorder and destruction, of *adulteration* and *bestiality* are advancing, on every front. Everything we hold dear and sacred – you think the Big Guy has no ideals, Pharaoh of Fat is all ridicule and no heart, just another cynijerk and misanthrowup? – well, you wrong, babeez – everything we believe in as *human*, good ol' sapiens sapiens, I'm talkin' *Civilization*, if any dumbbell doubts at this point – it's all on the line!

"What we gonna do? Where we gonna turn? We got an election comin' down in a few *days*, and the biggest bugaboo boondoggle in our history is ongoin' as we speak – the stinking Gink horde now carryin' infection as well as deadly weapons, supported by a crazy cult of tree-humpers and loony scientists in Prezdunt Swelltalk's shadow gummint – a whole conspiracy organized around this little kaka mutant freak! Gotta have *help*, people! *Big* help. That's my cue; the Big Fat Guy is about to introduce you to the *solution!*"

There is a roar of anticipation, but for once Beau does not roll like a porpoise in this wave. He seems transfixed, and does not speak again until the sound has ebbed to a vast, but hushed murmur.

"One of the great professors of ginkosophy, maydumbs and maysewers, one who has witnessed the ultimato in the sinisters of this age, who has been to the bottom of the basement of the dismal abysmal and the last spasm of the chasm."

Beau bows his head. On the speakers the first synthetic sounds are introduced, the first earthquake-like chords of a mighty dirge. Some in the audience cry out, recognizing the soundtrack of the popular holo, *A Kid in the Cannibal Kingdom* – the based-on of Ronnie Drager's months with the Pobla.

"Not the least ashamed to be known as Scarface or the Great Exterminator, recognized everywhere for his uncompromising courage, formerly Secretary of Energy for Fiber Production – welcome, people, the father-figure agonisto, the hero-count-the-zeros of this modern tragedy – FRANK DRAGER!"

The crowd has already, instantly and eerily, fallen silent – so silent the microphones pick up the rustle of the flags, the footfalls of the man approaching now from the rear of the stage. He is in no hurry, for he knows his effect on them and is prolonging it. On the holoscreen behind is a giant version of himself in close-up. The head is thrust forward and he is, they believe, grinning, though it is difficult to be sure. That is partly because, on the scale of the screen, his features are like ridges and canyons and valleys, but also one side of the face is sheared away. The eye socket is a puckered slit and the cheek has sunk into a livid scar, the shriveled tissue retracted permanently to expose the teeth on that side.

His breathing, a rhythmic hissing, is now audible, as an engineer somewhere brings up the body microphone. He waits a few moments longer, enjoying himself – they are certain now – and staring down these thousands, who, as his cyclopean gaze sweeps over them individually, must look away, but then must look again . . . And even Beau Winger – an extraordinary thing – is wordless now, arms at his sides and head still bowed as if at a great ceremony.

"Good afternoon." The voice is soft, yet with a slight rasp, and the laugh that follows is almost soundless. Three rows back from the front of the stage, a woman topples over in a dead faint. Those nearby prop her up again, speak in urgent low tones, whip out handkerchiefs. Drager ignores this disturbance, and goes on speaking.

"I am here as an example. A testimonial. A symbol and a sign. Or, as one of my friends puts it, an unrestored national monument."

Frank Drager bows slightly, ironically, and there is the barest ripple of tentative, polite laughter. Winger lifts his head, brightens and begins to swing his arms slowly, like great sausages.

"That he is, good folk. A NorthAm treasure, a mighty river of resolve, a towerin' peak of performance, and a grand canyon of courage. We are so lucky he can give us a few minutes – and, by the way, he has a major announcement – a behemoth of a bombshell, people – and all of us poor bewilderosos and taxpoopers are mighty, mighty grateful for this opportunity. Understand you haven't spoken publicly, Frank, for almost two years. Can you tell us what's brought you forth now, one week before the election?"

"I wanted my fellow citizens never to forget." Frank Drager sweeps the audience again with the laserbeam of his one eye. "What those creatures of darkness, those beings that crawl beneath the earth, can do."

"Ah hey people, is that guts? Is that a leader among men? Not to forget the lovely ladies too." Winger also turns to the multitude, now become as somber and still as a church congregation. "Far be it from us to stir up that whole hyperghoulie horror, Frank, but tell us in general terms what you think we're in for, where you think we oughta go . . . "

Drager's voice becomes momentarily remote, cold, lunar. "I can tell you very specifically. Sacrifice. A great sacrifice. A sacrifice of blood, to avert the unleashing of the deadliest and most destructive forces in our universe."

These words hiss out over the crowd like an unfurling lash. Again there is utter silence, except for a laugh, begun and immediately cut short, from the backstage utility sheds. Frank Drager's face contracts, stretches, and those watching in fascination cannot say if it is a smile or a beginning scream. "For myself, it is the sacrifice of my son."

"Hey, hey, hey . . . " Beau Winger has rocked and shuffled at Drager's side, as if dodging the invisible, coiling whip of the soft voice. "This is what the show is all about, people, these moments, this kind of excrucifyin' deepdredger honesty, this flash cutaway filet of the freaky unique inside – that's yakkin' 'n' trackin', that's the Fat Man, what he stands for! Now Frank has got something more to say, fans, something that's gonna blow the whole holorama wide, and show ya, halleluja dooya, right here on the biggest yakshow in the known universe, just what a great man is, no slingo the lingo here, good people, just plain greatness, wide open and deep down . . . his only son . . . his flesh 'n' blood . . . "

"My son," Drager's hoarse whisper fills the stadium, like a rising wind, "my son was dear to me as life itself, and yet I knew long ago Ronnie was . . . tragic. Not like other boys – oh, he *appeared* gifted – but there was always an invisible spot, a faint shadow on that brilliance, and we would not accept what his counselors hinted, that his dreams, his fantasies and obsessions could be a . . . fundamental and terminal disorder.

"I hid these hints, these suspicions. I tried to raise the fine, pure, promising boy we thought we had. I took Ronnie on that hunting trip – our fatal *hubris*, the pundits said – in that spirit. And so they took him from us. The lovers of filth and darkness, who eat their own flesh. The brutes who trained the bear that sheared away half my face, and who summoned the ants that ate their fill of what was left. Our former brethren gone back to the beasts, who took my son for their plaything."

Winger is pacing beside the speaker, beckoning forth from the crowd a low murmur of sympathy and outrage. Drager's soft voice, coiling and uncoiling, has brought some to moan in anticipation. He is otherwise still as a statue, except for the ravaged head, which swivels back and forth.

"But it is time now for the truth, and nothing but the truth. We have watched our economy slide into stagnation, our productivity suffer from onslaughts of every sort – bacteria, fungus, malignant hybrids, genetic deviation. We also watched our leadership deteriorate into paralysis and evasion, victims of their own antiquated theories of *laissez-faire*.

"These things represent a dire and desperate crisis in our world, but we could conceivably meet such a challenge, if our own values remained strong and untainted. We have the technology and resources and research centers to combat every kind of virulence. We could eradicate *all* the remaining noxious, undomesticated species – every pest from the tiger bees and dump rats to the urethane fungii spreading in old landfills.

326

"But we now encounter a far more monstrous dimension of these evils, a threat unspeakable and unrecognized, except by a visionary few . . . " Drager's head swings further in its metronomic arc, so as to fix the single eye on Beau Winger for a respectful second or two. "You have heard Beau speak of a deadly, social mutation, a terrifying, swift cancer on the body of civilization. You have watched his exposure of a mad coalition, conscious or not, involving elements of our own population and that last, degenerate fork of the primate order, the inbred hybrid ape, the so-called Pobla, *Homo lapsis* – our own dark, nightmarish shadow!"

"Ah yes, yes, YES! This man, my man, *our* man, people! Can you *hear* 'im? This is magnifico, on-the-big-money head-on talk! Here it is, seetwayens, cominatya live, no escape, *right now*! Listen! Listen to the Exterminator!" Beau is swaying his great backside, clapping his hands rhythmically, eyes shut and mouth half-open. From the audience now come a few screams, hysterical and sobbing.

"We are about to face that shadow, that nightmare, which took my son's soul. We are about to face . . . " Frank Drager pauses, letting the chorus of cries and wails build; here and there is heard also an appalling laughter – a demented, non-stop, bellowing. " . . . *ourselves.*"

"Oh face the race, gimme some space, No Face got the ace . . . " Winger chants underneath the high sibilance of the swinging lash, and the audience has begun to take up his rhythmic clap.

"We all know, in our hearts, what is hidden. The operations and abortions, the sons and daughters shipped to distant cities, the names quietly dropped from membership in certain clubs. For generations now, we have ceased to count or track those who disappear and become human parasites, the invisible so-called Omalys or Nonumbs. Nocturnal, speaking dialects harder and harder to understand, they live by barter and theft and leave no trace in the record . . .

"What we do know is that a high proportion of them bear the stigma of Pobla blood. It is no wonder that the conspiracy Beau has outlined took root there, that this cursed and obscene experiment in 'new life' hid itself there, among the deformed and shiftless, the brutal and malicious dwellers in the subways and sewers of our own cities. We tried to seal off and ignore this foul basement; we fed it scraps to keep it quiet; we pretended it would die out of its own weakness.

"We did not see the Omaly beggar and thief and lunatic for what he was: our twin, our very self – only in the dark and distorted

327

mirror of failure! A degenerate god! Every ancient myth teaches us that nothing is more horrible than a rotting angel, a deity corrupt! And to see that is to admit we still need salvation, and thus sacrifice. What of this nightmare *in ourselves* – the ravening beast *within*?"

"O-o-oh! E-e-e-ow! The Hero speaks like thunder! You got the *truth*, you got the *word*, makes the follicles pollywoggle and the liver shiver! Listen to the man! Listen to the word!"

Beau is leading the crowd now, when he shakes his bulk they sigh like a gale approaching, when he claps they clap with him, mighty percussive strokes on the drumhead of the earth. Yet the other, the one-eyed man, threads his amplified whisper through these sounds, a violin solo riding like a small bird above the hurricane of a symphony.

"We know, we *know* this dark shadow-brother of ours! He creeps out of the pestilent Wasteland, he stalks the underworld in our cities, he lurks in our own skulls. He has reached the vulnerable and naïve among us and feels strong enough now to make his demand openly. Protect wilderness, encourage diversity, he used to whisper, but now he shouts to high heaven – accept the hordes of starving cannibal creatures, call them *Pobla*, feed them, care for them, embrace them, *mate with them*!"

"No! No! No! No!" Winger has united the handclaps and voices into single explosions, a cannon firing and recoiling, firing and recoiling in perfect rhythm. The Big Fat Man's whole body rocks and thrusts to enhance, to express that rhythm.

"That shadow came into my son, it consumed Ronnie, ate him from within. And now it may have reproduced itself, to serve as the model for a nightmare future. But it would not be enough to find the monstrous product of this mating, flush it from that creature's womb: Beau has shown us how powerful forces are moving to encourage, even to *honor* such debasement!

"We must purge this shadow from ourselves and from others, from our whole civilization! We must act, we must roll back the night. But we are like a surgeon operating on his own deep-rooted tumor: we must cut carefully, skilfully, to extirpate without too great a shock, for our malignancy and our vital substance are dangerously intertwined.

"I know I am asking you to undergo agony, and so I take the first step myself. You know my reputation, you will understand the import of what I propose. I must begin by renouncing my commitment to extermination, which I once thought unswerving and absolute. In my blindness I did not see how deep and widespread the infection ran, how variable its symptoms. I see the sacrifice must be, in a sense, even greater, that it forbids even the sweet balm of revenge and death. I tell you now that, if the thing that was once my son is captured, I will end the Drager name for all time. I will authorize his sterilization."

"*No! No! No! No!*" The multitude is on its feet, standing on chairs, screaming at the two figures on the stage, which are dwarfed by their own towering images, in close-up, on the screen behind.

"We must begin the cleansing, yet with an implacable compassion that honors our species above the individual! These are our children, our loved ones, our dear friends, who are cursed with the slime of that first evil union! Yet we cannot, absolutely cannot, be betrayed by the factions that are working to *ennoble* this degeneracy. I repeat, we must face ourselves, the shadows in our midst! Not tomorrow, not next week, but now!"

Beau Winger, amazingly, is on his knees, heavy thighs stretching his trousers to the bursting point, his body still pulsing with the rhythm of the crowd's clapping and chanting.

"Halleluja dooya comintoya! Man gives you his own story, his own life, his own *boy*, you hear? What he say? Gonna git his only one son unbegot, gonna take a supreme whackrifice, man has seen beyond the veil, the maya playa, this is the mysterioom tremendooom, this is spiritualissimo here now cominatya, right here, right now, the max, come on and do it, come on now say the truth, 'fess it up like this man done, his only son, y'all get down and testify, come on . . ."

The crowd roars with a new, frantic energy, for two, three, now six of its members have fought to the center aisle, one man in a wheelchair, and are coming toward the stage. Technicians have rolled into place a ramp, and when the first of these pilgrims reaches it one of the attendants clips a microphone to her lapel. A moment later she is on her knees beside Beau, her face wet with tears and drool. Her sobs are long, deep, primal. Beau passes his hand over her head, and the sound from the crowd is a sustained, rolling boom.

"She got the word, got the sign, logo in the hojo and a train in the brain, o-o-oh baby, you the first soul in the bowl gotta weigh it and say it, come on now baby you famous now honey now give us a name . . ."

"A . . . a . . . lu . . . lu . . . lice," the woman gags, "Wu . . . wu . . . wil . . . son. Oh, oh, oh . . ."

"Alice no malice you gotta be a talker, come on, Alice, you got

329

a shame to blame and a shade to trade, oh Alice, you the first not the worst, come on, Alice, sing it out for the man he give you his son his only one he the *man*, come on, on, Alice . . . "

"Ba . . . ba . . . ba . . . by." Alice has bowed her head, her hair hanging loose and hiding her face. She folds her hands over her abdomen. "Ba . . . ba . . . ba . . . "

"Wanna baby gotta have a baby . . . no *gotta* baby now and no room in the womb maybe two maybe three on the way and whadda we do for you, Alice, you gotta play gotta say now come on, come on . . . "

"A shadow," Frank Drager hisses, and leans nearer the woman. "You have let in the shadow."

Alice jerks her head up and down in a nod, coughs, retches weakly. "He . . . he . . . bu . . . bu . . . bu-leach, and ha . . . ha . . . "

"Hair oh hair beware, this daddy did a bleach, had a depil too, oh baby sure sign you gotta night-mite now, splinter of the deepdark growin', oh Alice no malice but whatcha gonna do don't wanna little zygink growin' don't wanna deny this hero count the zeros do you now baby do you . . . "

"No . . . no . . . *NO!*" Alice shakes her head violently, droplets of sweat and tears flying like tiny diamonds in the stage lights. She is convulsing, digging with her hands at her womb, and her voice is lost in the renewed chant from the crowd. "*No! No! No!*"

Two attendants rush to lift Alice to her feet, and Beau brushes her brow with his fingertips before they usher her to the back of the stage. Other attendants now restrain a man before the front ramp, a small man who is gripping his own ears as if to tear them from his head.

"Come on, babeez, come *on!* Gotta do it like the lady did it this Alice she a hero-ine genuine, take it out no shame start again with the trueblue men, oh all hail the female, mystery of history, but no shame you guys nowise, can't clean a dirty gene Eugene, see a spike just a spot, any nanogink still gotta think cut, think cut, can't wait to regenerate, and everybody cheer, here in the world's greatest yakshack, 'cause we got ahold of it now you wunderkinders givin' it all takin' it all, come on holohogs say it for Alice and these others linin' up, for the man our guest the best, nobody higher, cut his own son for you, babeez, for *us!* And now he's gonna give us *his own self!*"

There is a hole in the great cataract of sound, and again Drager's voice, almost a whisper, carries miraculously to every ear. "We are agreed," he enunciates, "to undertake the formation of a third party.

330

We shall support young Adamson in this election, to reverse the ghastly and sinister drift of Stockwell's administration, but thereafter, if enough of you join in this great sacrifice, *I* shall stand for the Presidency."

Beau is on his feet now, arms thrown wide to embrace Frank Drager, who rather stiffly returns the gesture and then steps back to stand immobile, his single, staring eye fixed on a distant horizon.

"Givin' us everything, givin' us his all! Gonna take it on home now, people! Got a hero, got a platform, one simple truth for a man to stand on! *Humanity! Humanity first, last, and always!* Frank Drager, good seetwayens, and the Humanitarian party! Now plenty personnel here gonna receive your pledges and those contributions we gonna need for this movement yas I say a tide gonna run now, a big wave a-comin', we all ridin' and slidin' on the big mamawave gonna wash the whole scene clean, oh yeah new day dawnin' and we the people – hey you all 'member that one? – we the people gonna get right!

"You look inside, way deep in the heartwell honey, you see the shadow in there, catch the whiff, you come on home here, don't be 'fraid my fans, gotta do it together, gotta purify this old planet and get 'er runnin' our way, hey hey, sapiens! Ma peeple! Come on home, now, get clean and flash some cash, you can always trust the Big Fat Guy cominatya, for the Big One and Big Cool!"

Beau's broad face is a plate, wet and shining and bare, tilted up to receive, and his arms are still spread and uplifted now to the audience. Behind him the rumpled and sweat-soaked giant of his own image could be embracing the whole of heaven. The multitude before him is still roaring, again in rhythmic chant, as the line of penitents writhes like a long snake in the aisle. But the great cannon now fires a slightly different syllable.

"Beau! Beau! Beau! Beau!"

CHAPTER THIRTY-THREE

She saw the flyers before Dizzy understood the pattern of the other pigeons. The leaflets were red, easy to spot against gray concrete or black iron. Tima wondered if the spoors and tracks and rumblings of the city had become her primary ground of perception, displacing the other sort of flyers – and crawlers and swimmers – she had always relied on. Dizzy, however, was visible over a greater distance, so the two of them were soon following scattered flocks of late scavengers as they rose and dipped through traffic.

Pepper, riding in her pocket, confirmed that it was Pahane who had laced the trail with popcorn. The scent ended twice at tube stations, where Pepper traced it to platforms and Tima boarded trains for a stop or two, realizing Pahane must have watched the bursts of pigeons from office buildings and guessed the direction taken by the vehicle carrying Marvelous. That direction seemed to be toward the ruburbs, where industrial parks and decaying housing units marked the zone between city and country.

What intrigued Tima was the fact that already they had passed two precinct stations, and the path so far led away from the main downtown police headquarters. It was also curious that, according to Pepper's nose, most of the leaflets had been dropped from a hand other than Pahane's. Finally, Tima had to assume that Pahane was following the vehicle for a good reason. If Marvelous had fallen into the hands of the police, tracking him would have been superfluous: the important thing would be to warn everyone else, as Cynthia had tried to do.

In her role as a diminutive, senile Omaly man, Tima could not hurry. It was tiring to maintain this crabbed stoop, to squint and sidle from doorway to doorway, and – especially – to generate the field of this image she was hiding within. She was afraid that the vehicle they were following would access a main Feederway and be lost in the high-speed flow. But oddly the pigeons traced a wandering route at first, as if the driver were uncertain of his destination. She was taking risk enough merely to appear in these districts, so she was relieved when the pattern changed, a definite direction was established, and office buildings began to give way to warehouses and yards full of spools of cable, girders, pipe, and cargo modules.

Walking so far, through so many neighborhoods, Tima saw further evidence of the changes she had been discussing with Eva. The tempo and tone of this great piksi hive was altering: the cacophony of traffic was detectably rhythmic, a hysterical syncopation was visible in the stride of pedestrians, and radios and holos on different channels could mesh in weird, surging waves. The smells were an equally rich record of urges and apprehensions, a complex palimpsest of desire and dread and indecisiveness.

Even the faces of passers-by had a certain murky radiance. They registered extreme reactions to the sight of her: though she made no gesture, some people thrust tokens or half-eaten sandwiches at her; and others scowled and spat, or even made a move to shove her aside. One or two women peered at her, looking puzzled. Tima assumed they were reacting to the new life assembling itself within her, a life already so powerful she could not, with all her skill, entirely conceal it.

She was not ideally suited to child-bearing. She had not the gift of giving in, of being a clear lens, a massive, maternal, mindless blob of cytoplasm. She took no pleasure in incubation – unless the seed was metaphoric, some clever plan entirely of her own devising. She delighted in postnatal visions: a furry, prehensile form at her breast, Pahane beside her, a roomy, safe cave overlooking the ocean.

Pahane, on the other hand, would have been perfect for pregnancy. They had joked about this anomaly often enough. He could be placid, utterly empty, at will; he did not project images, but he could receive them, or even entertain the actual substance of other shadows. Where Tima used energy to summon or manipulate the *kubin* of others, Pahane sometimes had not the resources to keep them at bay. He was a kind of open culture-dish for random ghosts.

Of course the fetus attracted every sort of powerful new shadow. Tima's baby was only a conduit, a minute configuration of the Great Shadow that would render the mystery of Itself present and visible; but already it was remarkable that a *kubi* from so long ago should appear. They had to surmise that the coming child had been a messiah before, a *tak tagak*.

Tima had lost herself in thought, and only when Pepper began squirming in her pocket did she realize how inattentive she had been. Looking up she saw the drive-through eatery, the Power Pizza sign, and Dizzy strutting amid the scatter of red and black leaflets across the sidewalk. She stopped short, stunned. They had come to the very spot. The end of the cross-city boulevard that started in Omalytown. The last ruburb access to the major Trunkways east and west. The transfer docks, magrig lots, fastfoodstops and rental garages. The very place Eva had named as a rendezvous.

Pahane was near, very near. Possibly Marvelous too, and also those who had taken him. For the first time, she felt a tiny foot thump on the wall of her womb. They were all here because of this little . . . fish, frog, salamander, lizard . . . on its way to eternity. The embryo within her, Tima realized, now enclosed her: she was at the center of the very design she had been meditating on.

It was no surprise, therefore, when one of the delivery vans paused before pulling into a loading ramp and disgorged Sandhill and Cynthia, tense and watchful, onto the pavement. She let Pepper, now frantic, escape from her trouser leg and begin snooping avidly along the heavy steel mesh bounding a warehouse and office complex. They were all converging, as infallibly as swallows or bats or cranes in annual migration.

She saw the big, pink-faced man leave his vehicle, noted his agitation. It was a limo, a rental, and as she watched, Dizzy fluttered down at the rear of it. The big man swung one arm wide in rage, and the bird erupted into the air again. Then he strode stiffly toward Sandhill and Cynthia, who stood a pace apart, apparently arguing. Tima felt, even at this distance, the distress in her friend. She hoped Cynthia would not shatter in the next few minutes, when she discovered how thoroughly and perfectly she had been betrayed.

Pepper had turned down the alley that formed the service road to the warehouse and offices, and Tima reverted to her shuffle and followed. She caught the startling scents before she registered the unobtrusive sign in the building. Large felines and snakes, fish and bats, many ungulates, and also the odors of molds and yeasts.

Mama's Mini-Zoos

EEE!

Everything from Elephants to Eukaryotes

All the windows on this side of the building were covered in the metal mesh, but several were open and she could hear a barking, snuffling, and caterwauling from inside. The inmates' excitement was obvious, and of course Dizzy and Pepper had picked it up. It was the analog to the complex beat on the street, the rhythm that made the sewermen bop and the traffic eddy and pulse. The rat skittered away from the fence, emitting his own squeal, and crossed the alley to a doorway on the other side; the entrance to what was once, according to the pale ghosts of letters now stripped away, a holovirtuals rental store.

Tima heard a muffled shriek from the doorway, and then Pahane's voice, low and reassuring. She sidled nearer warily, until she saw they were only two: Pahane kneeling to feed Pepper a few sunflower seeds, and the alarmed little old woman who had plastered herself against the dusty store window.

"Good gracious! You mean it's a *pet*?"

Pahane did not answer because he had spotted Tima and risen to take her in an embrace whose ferocity surprised her. She uttered an amused grunt and pushed him back a little, brushing his cheek with her nose in the Pobla fashion. She was for a second or two a ferret twining around him, her fur sparking with recognition and desire. He laughed in a wild, abrupt way, wanting more, but she shook her head reluctantly. They had to keep to the center.

Pahane groaned and placed a hand on her belly. "*Yanaku tak delo naku.*" He felt the difference, and in a moment the tiny foot bumped again. He murmured in surprise. "*Ya!* She's drumming already."

Tima laughed, a great spike of mingled mirth and melancholy going through her. "Just today," she said. "A few minutes ago. Because everything else is."

"I know who *you* are." The old woman was examining Tima with critical, maternal care. "But you don't of course know me. I'm Margaret. You should sit down and take a good rest, my dear. When they start thumping on you it's time to relax. And you see we *have* found Reverend Holzkopf – as I know him, and of course you may guess who I mean, but you can be very sure, my dear, nobody will hear it from me – and we can only wait now." She glanced meaningfully across the alley, toward the loading dock of the warehouse.

Tima saw the magrig, a waver of invisible fumes pouring from its exhaust stacks. It was entirely black but for the white ID plates and a small red triangle on the doors. She saw no sign of a driver or crew, though the back door of the rig was open. Judging by the coolers and ventilators on the cargo unit, the rig was designed for carrying live specimens.

"He's in there with an old friend of yours." Pahane gave Tima a pained grin. "And mine. PJ."

They looked at each other, and it took a tremendous effort for Tima to keep herself still. PJ reminded her of cunning, evasion, and revenge. Of her eight years as a piksi experiment, a toy and a slave. She wanted to keen, to wrap herself around Pahane, or flee. She wanted to reach that cave by the sea, to sit by a fire, the two of them once more mirrors to each other, their shadows deepening and doubling to infinity. Instead they were about to enter, once more, the whole sinister maelstrom of darkside dealing.

Pahane, she could see, felt the same way. The mad, bad *tchat* boy pacing in his cage. So she said, quietly and carefully, "Our new friends also just arrived. Cyn and Sandhill. It's a big trap."

"Maybe bigger than the trapper." He grinned without humor, like a coyote. "I guess we'll see."

"Well," Margaret said, with a small explosion of a sigh. "I think I've done what I can and it sounds like you have your own business to attend to, so I think I'll be toddling along." She gave Tima a quick smile and nod. "You will have a beautiful child, a special child, I can tell. And this young man of yours is quite the sharp fellow – you should have seen him stuff that bag of corn behind the bumper."

From her great, droopy handbag she produced a package and handed it to Pahane. "I thought to pinch this nut bread I brought for Reverend Holzkopf. You'll be on the road, most likely, and you know what atrocious meals they serve to travelers. Goodbye, young fellow, and our prayers will go with you all. Do watch out for Reverend Holzkopf, won't you?" She blinked earnestly up at him. "Whatever is in store?"

"Yes, we will. Absolutely."

"He *is* a marvelous man. His knowledge of scripture is a bit wobbly, but you know he really understands it all perfectly in his heart, which is where it counts, even though he doesn't know he knows it yet, quite."

Tima smiled at her. "Yes. Exactly."

On impulse Pahane kissed Margaret firmly on her forehead. "Goodbye, Margaret." He grinned and performed a swift, undulatory dance-step. "Hunkysmack, geez."

Margaret flushed and allowed herself a rather indecorous giggle. "Why, goodness me! Haven't seen that for – well, never mind! That's a boogie, we used to say." She recovered herself, waved once, like a small bird stretching its wing, then hurried from the doorway and in a moment was gone.

"She came after me, planting those leaflets," Pahane said, shaking his head affectionately. "Eighty-three years old. A born *tagak* and a *tchat* raider."

They were silent for a while, and then she spoke as if answering his direct question. "Batboy may have been an accident, a coincidence. A routine police sting."

He regarded her, thoughtful. They were both leaning against the abandoned storefront, worn out with the strain of projecting false identities and supporting the burden of true ones. They were also completely alone again. Alone in the gut of a mysterious, monstrous beast.

"They'll bin him again. Someplace a lot worse than New Life."

"Maybe not. He's tougher now. He has some acts." Tima looked rueful. "He's underage and it was a small buy. If they don't do a full screen on him he might be out this afternoon. Whereas in our case—" She glanced at the idling magrig. "We don't even know where we're going."

He tilted his head toward the ruburbs, the huge flat irrigated fields, the desert catchbasins, the border. "A long way. We saw them loading a couple of meals and a waste container. After all, we're escaping again, aren't we?"

She ignored his irony. "Or maybe the important question is why."

"PJ is doing it for money, for fun, I suppose. But this isn't just another darkside wipe. They want something from us."

Tima smiled. "They always do."

Pahane watched her speculatively. She detected a familiar ambiguity: admiration and reproach. "When did you know Sandy was rolling us?"

"*Know?*" her smile turned melancholy.

"Imagine."

She sighed. "After those three days in the pizza van. He was anxious, but it wasn't physical fear. Too much shame and doubt in it. And I had to wonder why the police couldn't trace the van, and why it was so easy for us to hide with the Omalys. Sandhill never seemed worried; and he had us out on the street right away, just to keep us *occupied*. He smelled sly to me. And finally . . . " She glanced at the warehouse across the alley, where the chorus of grunts and growls and whistles continued. " . . . I never saw Dizzy light on *his* shoulder."

"Then why didn't you—"

"But *know*? Not really, until a few minutes ago when I saw him bringing Cynthia here. This is the rendezvous he set up with Eva, in case of emergency."

"Where you were supposed to bring me, after you found me." Pahane appeared to be talking to himself. "Where a mag was already waiting. And PJ. And Marvelous."

"But PJ didn't know the address, right away." Tima made a wavy, irregular motion with one hand. "The first part of your trail looked like scouting. He was waiting for a call."

Pahane nodded, grimaced. "Yes. He did wander. Of course. Which means they don't trust him. Which means they are smart." He laughed. "Mama's MiniZoos. They're very big, and very fast, these people." Thoughtful again, he asked the question she dreaded to ask herself. "You think Eva knew, all along?"

"*Knew?*" Tima looked at the sidewalk. "Such a definite word. Eva maintains a certain distance between herself and her awareness of evil. She told me today that Barrelhead always knows where she is. Always. So she pretends to be free. That's her only possible defiance. Everybody, in this place, pretends that. Us too."

"I know and then I forget," Pahane said softly. He was staring at the faded imprint of the letters over the empty storefront. *Dream on.*

"Piksi." Tima lifted a hand and touched his arm, to soften the word. "Crazy to be in charge. They never see how the craziness controls *them.*"

Pahane looked away and bit his lips. She knew he was thinking of his father – Ronald's father. "One of the old rockenrolls has a line . . . Freedom's just another word for nothing left to lose."

She smiled, her teeth suddenly bright. "Yes, that's good. A piksi poem I actually understand. The Pobla say you can lose everything but your shadow, and still remain wild. *Kukulan* is our word, and 'wild' is closer than 'free.' "

"I can see that." Pahane gave her a sardonic leer. "Walking into this big trap is a wild thing to do."

"I don't see that we're free to do anything else," she countered. "And I don't think they have quite figured out how to handle the three of us. Or what to make of things generally. They sense the shadows gathering, beginning to dance, but they have no idea what it means."

"Do *we*?"

She laughed lightly, but he did not divert his steady gaze. Already, days ago, she had mentioned how the creatures at the treatment plant, the birds and frogs and scouting ants, had been patterning as if a Going In ceremony were drawing near. But the piksi *mudlatin* were also lurching to a new rhythm. Pahane had related in turn how his drum-travels showed the Pobla singing, chanting, counting relentlessly even as they entered the piksi death-camps. It frightened her a little to admit that she could not grasp the nature of this great turning and circling, yet she was utterly certain that the new being growing inside her was its center.

She was saved from having to answer by the sound of a vehicle entering the side street. It was not a magrig, but a smaller vehicle, moving swiftly. They retreated into the doorway, Pahane crouching behind her. The limo flashed past, then they heard it decelerate and stop at the security gate. Hinges squealed and, on the loading dock behind the black rig, three men appeared. One was in uniform with a holstered sidearm, the other two wore suits. Tima recognized PJ, his tie loose and askew, a carefree grin on his face. The others were visibly anxious and frowning.

The limo coasted into view and braked to a stop beside the magrig. The large man emerged first, his features a deeper shade of rose. He had a holocellphone in one hand and spoke into it. Then he shouted something to the men on the dock and jerked open the rear door of the limo. Cynthia got out first, her face blank and set, a somnambulist. Sandhill was next. He was talking intently and without pause.

Another of the men in suits came last. He stepped quickly beside Cynthia, ignoring Sandhill, and steered her toward the ramp leading to the dock. The big man was gesticulating with the cellphone. He seemed to want to throw it against the wall or strike PJ with it. By his puckered lips, PJ appeared to be whistling, and snapped his fingers. To Tima, the whole scene radiated an impressive tension.

When Sandhill threw up his hands in apparent disgust or frustration, Cynthia jerked away from the man at her elbow and sent two words over her shoulder, swift and definite as pistol shots: *Fucking bastards*. Then she marched up the ramp, walked to an overturned crate and sat down, facing the empty wall of the warehouse.

Inside, the hooting and grunting and chirping seemed to increase in volume and urgency.

Pahane looked at Tima and grinned, a *tchatsi* flash in his eyes. "I believe we're expected."

"Oh yes. Very much." She rested her hand on her abdomen again, and they smiled at each other, bravely and wearily. She was thinking of the intricacy of their weaving, sperm and egg and embryo, and how they were wound into the larger patterns of history and chance – the collisions and replications of molecules, cells, organisms, societies. A prison or a labyrinth? Perhaps the only difference was one of scale and complexity. She adjusted her hat and made her body crooked, sucked her face inward again. "Yeah. So we gonna slide, Clyde?"

They left the doorway and crossed the access road toward the security gate, which had squealed back into place. The tableau on the loading dock was unchanged, except that the big man was now shouting into PJ's smiling face. Cynthia was still staring at the wall, flanked by the man in a suit. There were now two armed men in uniform on either side of Sandhill who had ceased talking and stood with his arms folded, expressionless. As they approached the gate, one of the uniformed men said something and pointed toward them.

The guard at the gate was only a dark figure behind the glass of his cubicle. Dots of blue and orange light and a monitor screen glowed within. When they stopped at the gate his amplified voice came at them through a speaker port. "Move on, please. Private property."

Pahane hooked his fingers in the heavy mesh of the gate and tilted his shaven head insolently. "C'mon, feeb. We got *business*."

Tima leered from under her hat. "Yo, sweetpie! Gichoo a boy, gichoo some back?"

"*Step away from the gate, please.*"

They saw the dark figure rise. On the loading dock faces were now turned their way, and one of the men in suits was hurrying toward them. They heard the big man's swearing, the desperation and rage rising to a bellow.

"—fucking deadbeats *out* of here! That's the same kid . . . "

They heard PJ laugh, a cry like a loon's that rose over, and mysteriously quieted, the cacophony coming from inside the warehouse. Then he, too, was jogging toward them, his loosened tie blowing over one shoulder.

"Goddamn it, Feiffer! Stop! Jerry, throw those people—"

"Shut up, Fitz. These *are* the people. Hey, Ronnie boy, Tima the Creamathe. Oh captives, my captives!"

He was at the gate now, palm to palm with Pahane, grinning through the metal grid. Tima could see with one look into the white-ringed eyes that he was truly wild, *kukulan* even inside Mama's Zoo. When his eyes met hers, she found herself unaccountably disoriented. A man she had seduced and humiliated, a man whose career and reputation she had demolished, gazed at her with an overpowering mirthfulness.

"What's the matter, Duskyrose? Cat got your imagination?" He gripped the mesh and shook the whole gate in his exuberance. He was older, a bit thicker, and no longer exuded the cool, careful malevolence of an Insec operative. She inhaled deeply, but there was no odor of chemical modulation.

"Captain Feiffer," she said. "I see you have recovered."

"Never. I'm permanently damaged. Need constant care. Just the job for you and Tongue of the Snake." He winked at Pahane. "We were about to search desperately for you, and here you are! Ready to join our travelling Freak Show."

They stepped apart, because now the big man and two men in suits had arrived, and the gate was squealing open again. The newcomers quickly encircled them, and one pointed a handweapon vaguely at Tima.

"What the hell is this? Is this—?" The big man still carried the cellphone cocked near his face, and now spoke into it. "Yeah, I don't know. A street geez and a kid, a roach—"

"Fitz, let me introduce you. This is Ronald Drager and Tima. Tima the Terrific. We can go now. Everybody's here." There was a long pause before the big man spoke again into the phone, his voice now a falsetto whisper. "He says it's *them*. He's fucking nuts, like I been saying . . . Christ, I don't know. Yes. Okay, *okay*." He turned the phone around, held it toward Pahane and Tima like a talisman against demons, so the pinhole lens could transmit their grainy and indistinct images.

Tima took off her hat and shook out her bright black hair, grown now almost to shoulder length, and straightened up. The man with the weapon took a step back and said *Shit* so softly and suddenly it was like the sound of wind hissing over the wings of a bird swooping past. The twisted, driveling septuagenarian he had covered a moment ago was gone, utterly. He did not appear sure of what he now beheld.

The big man was listening to his phone again. They watched until

342

his color changed and his eyes riveted on Tima's midsection; then PJ, with a grand gesture, ushered them toward the loading dock. Cynthia was on her feet now, at the edge of the ramp, gazing at them in a kind of stupor. Sandhill was looking into the sky, his face a controlled blank. A homely man in overalls, wearing a duckbilled cap, had come onto the dock from the dark interior of the warehouse. He looked glum and bewildered, and carried a clipboard with a sheaf of papers attached.

When they started up the ramp Cynthia spoke. "This fucking bastard rolled us. Why didn't you run?"

Tima saw the tears streak all at once, on both cheeks, and she went to her friend and hugged her, let her begin the long, slow sobs, that hard taking-in of new breath, of birthing.

Only Pahane looked at Sandhill, curious, and in a moment the other spoke, his voice tight and quiet. "The trees," he said. "The trees will be. The rest of it couldn't be helped anyway." When no one answered, he went on. "They had us from the beginning, Ribs. Could have taken us anytime. So it was this deal or no deal." He glanced at the big man, now almost pale, who had clicked off his holophone.

"He's got that part right," the big man said. His voice was throttled back to an intent whine. "Listen, wrap it up. We gotta *move*."

"Oh fuck you, *fuck* you!" Cynthia wailed over Tima's shoulder, between sobs.

"Deal?" Pahane had not wavered in his long examination of Sandhill.

"They protected us from the authorities, man. Even with Eva and her Omaly connections, we wouldn't have made it through that first week. And all I had to do was watch out for you guys, stay down and cool and wait."

"For?"

"And in the meantime they set up the thousand-year project – what we always *dreamed* about, people!" Sandhill had taken a step nearer Pahane and stared at him with a searching intensity. "They *did* it! A piece of earth – a hundred and sixty *acres* I'm telling you – with all the wiff and hab coev to the Big Guys restored. Deep crypt deadbolt funding, supertrust Fed status guarantees, and—"

"Asshole." Cynthia punctuated this comment by blowing her nose on a tissue Tima had provided, but there was a shade less vitriol and revulsion in her tone.

"That's it. Enough fuckin' therapy. We're loading, Hank." The big man signaled the glum driver imperiously and then turned to Sandhill. "We didn't hire you to be a fuckin' historian, Mister. Don't say no more. Just find your way out. I get the impression that would be a real popular move."

"Ease off, Fitz." PJ had made a quick pointing gesture at one of the uniformed guards, who hesitated, frowned, and then walked into the open cargo bay of the truck. "Sandy has done a fine and delicate job. We are almost ready to become legends of our time. The narrative will go with *us*, my hearties – the famous outlaw and his band of rebel runaways." He shook Sandhill firmly by the hand, clapped him on the shoulder. "Good luck with the trees. Noble thing, really. Only wish I had a few hundred years more myself. But Fitz is right. Time for goodbyes."

"Wait a minute. Just a fucking minute. Who's—"

"I am, Fitz. In this situation." PJ laid a single finger gently on his pursed lips. "New chapter. The old procedures are too coarse for what we have here. These people came to *us*, don't forget. Distinguished guests. Great talent. Possibly divine." He beamed at Pahane and Tima. "They will be a great help, if things get difficult."

"Goodbye, Ribs," Sandhill said. He looked at Pahane, then Tima, and his mouth worked at something more.

"Goodbye, Sandy," Tima said. "It's all right. Just go."

"The trees," he whispered, and then turned on his heel and strode down the ramp.

"Right. Fucking nuts. And I don't like it," said one of the men in suits. He now carried his handweapon loosely at his side, pointing at the floor, and regarded the big man steadily.

"It'll be interesting," PJ said encouragingly. "Quite a new sort of country. Inspiring, though desolate. But Fitz *is* right, we should be going." He extended a hand invitingly toward the magrig.

"Please," the driver said. He threw an accusing look around the dock. "You people can argue inside. We got refreshments, climate control, holo, all that. I just wanna drive." He glanced unhappily at the sheaf of papers. "It's a haul."

Two men appeared at the entrance to the cargo bay then: the uniformed guard and Marvin, who stopped and blinked at them. His face, Tima saw, had been subtly transfigured beneath its blue stubble, and his posture was at once loose and poised inside the soiled, baggy suit. He did not seem surprised at the sight of them. His eyes were alight, glistening, wider than she remembered. *Kukulan.* She kept an arm around Cynthia, squeezing tight. No one spoke, and there was another surge in the chorus of yowling and snorting and trilling from Mama's MiniZoos.

Marvelous raised both arms high, fingers extended as if he were flying. He looked first at Pahane, then at Tima: a beautific, steady, passionate look.

"And in her was found the blood of prophets, and of saints, and all that were slain upon the earth! Yea, and this child with child – ye who cry Lilith, Jezebel, Whore of Babylon – I say unto you she is our mother! And the mother of all upon the face of this earth! For we are the stuff of stars, made each in dance various, molecule to molecule, the whole a harmony, breathing as one! Now rejoice and praise her who is come among us, and she shall bless us." Slowly he lowered his arms and looked at each of them, friend and foe, with the same radiant compassion. "We *are* the blessed. Now let us go *home.*"

CHAPTER THIRTY-FOUR

Tiffany and Henderson had retreated to the corner of her private lab where she composed her papers and poems. They had a number of disks decked into a portable light table, and the deepdark file on W-4 was open and running on the auxiliary desktop. They had just fed in a series of complete bioprofiles done on selected troops rotating out of the border battalion. Now they were integrating this data with the stuff from Goldbarth's lab, and matching the composite with the whole body of simulations and posited parameters in Tiffany's databank on shamans and messiahs. What they had seen so far had unleashed a major epidemic of speculation.

"So they would present the Reincarnated One – who was maybe eighteen months old – with a set of objects, right? Like an archetype recognition test, maybe." Henderson was shifting his weight, rocking from side to side, while he rolled his usual can of Big One between flattened hands.

"Possibly. We don't know, from the old texts, what the neutral objects were. Whether bright, jingly, or what." Tiffany was watching a series of slides the computer had selected for significant aberration. Three grunts had died in accidents over the last six months, and an autopsy of the most recent of these revealed clumps of the enlarged pineal cells with their grid-like membranes. "We just know what the holy ones *liked*."

"True. But it's not obvious that a *doortje*, for example, is a sacred power symbol. A more mature kid might say it's just an old dumb bell."

"Cultural contamination. That's surely one of the reasons they gave the test to infants." Tiffany looked away from the screen and glanced at her open notebook, full of scribbles and sketches. "Dumb bell. Hmmmm." She laughed.

A moment later Hen laughed with her. "Yeah. Sound of silence. One hand clapping."

347

"Simpleton. Favorite role of Holy Ones. Ringing soundless amid the babble of reason." Tiffany did her own little step, at once elephantine and sinuous. "Also the fool and the child, the 'poor monkeys' . . . "

They laughed at each other. Hen closed his can of drink in one fist and pounded it lightly on his chest as they shuffled a short, celebratory routine together.

Tiffany understood him. The reference was not only to the mating displays of great apes, but also to the thymus gland, the powerful memory-bank of antigen structures that lasted – in the Pobla and in certain far-off primate ancestors – well into puberty. It was currently the focus of their research – a hot, rich crevice in the chest that was displacing the old metaphorical heart as the dynamo of human destiny, just as the pineal had displaced the frontal lobes as chief instrument of human insight.

"Still hard for me to believe, sometimes," Tiffany said as she turned again toward the light table. "Let alone the public. My God, what would they say if we told them humanity was a sickness, and a rare viral symbiont from the hairy apes was the only cure?"

"Can imagine." Hen swigged from his can, then belched. "The fundies would have you drawn and quartered."

Tiffany batted her eyes at him in mock surprise. "You mean they wouldn't appreciate our ecumenicism? Linking Buddha and Jesus and Mohammed – the lot – to an odd scrap of protein shrugged off by *erectus* half a million years ago?"

"Forget that. Imagine what General White would do, if he knew he were sitting on the medstats for his troops. This fraternization, as he calls it, is making him ferocious."

"Yeah. He said to me last week it was like an epidemic." She giggled.

"From the mouths of old bulls." Hen winced and drank again. "Thing is, *we* don't know what other enzyme combos might show up eventually. Might be secondaries, side effects that involve more than attitude change."

Tiffany drew in a breath between her teeth. It was true, and kept her awake nights. They were fairly sure now that the waffle cells Hen had cultured from Goldbarth's pineal were the result of infection by a retrovirus picked up from her Pobla tissue samples. Just another retrovirus – except for one thing. Unlike the other fourteen retros known, it did not appear life-threatening. Its effects were almost entirely psychological.

Tiffany thought she understood the origins of this "ease". Living for generations in close proximity with various arboviruses and bacterial colonies nearly forgotten in the Northern Hemisphere, the Pobla had developed highly adaptive immune systems. Their resilient, long-enduring thymus gland sparred with a rich broth of viral nucleics and produced a mighty complex of hybrids and symbionts, including some exotic retrotransposons. One of these – still labelled merely shado W-4 – in turn transcripted new enzyme constellations that, so it seemed, radically altered consciousness.

This retro was common, among the Pobla, for three reasons. First, because it was constantly changing, absorbing new elements from other species (bird, rodent, insect). Just as influenza in the past century had been transformed by swine and transported by ducks out of Asia, W-4 renewed its virulence by experimenting in coyotes and fleas, or horses and midges. Second, it could be transmitted by direct ingestion, and of course the Pobla commonly ate their dead, especially the *tagakin*. Third, the Pobla normally produced an antibody that controlled some symptoms of the virus, especially visions and the impulse to sing.

But a very few – or so Tiffany theorized – carried an aberrant gene that curtailed production of this antibody. These few, she believed, were likely to become the *tak tagakin*, who were then compelled to transmit their "infection" in the form of prophesies, songs, divinations, games, drama. Invariably these expressions praised and formalized the link to the various other creatures that vectored the virus; thus the *tagakin* commonly maintained colonies of personal parasites, and at death offered themselves as food for their followers and wide-ranging carrion eaters. So the cycle was complete.

But among humans of the Northern Tier, it appeared, the virus might spread much more easily. NorthAm people had no controlling antibody. The three dead grunts were admittedly a miniscule sample; still, one of those three had the waffle cells. It was also hard to believe the man had contracted the virus in some weird cannibal rite. Tiffany and Hen had gotten the bug, they first assumed, as Goldbarth had – by handling samples carelessly. Now they weren't sure. Tiffany had begun to wonder if the endless chanting, by itself, could warp a gene or make it jump. More unsettling, as Hen had just hinted, they didn't know what new side effects their species might develop, over time.

"Nothing in the historical record," she said finally.

Hen did not bother to answer, because they both knew there

349

was, so far, no proof that various prophets and saviors over the centuries had all been carriers of W-4. Even the definition of "holy one" was uncertain. Gilgamesh, Quetzalcoatl, Dionysus were perhaps only legends, though it was remarkable that the stories of all three contained hints of cannibalism. Christ's peculiar invocation of wine and bread as his own flesh and blood was suggestive, and he was one of many great spiritual leaders who had been identified as criminal or demented during their lifetimes. St Joan, the Mahdi, Wovoka – one man's messiah was another man's mess.

"And nothing but that little rash and maybe a slight temperature for a day or two," she went on, but without notable confidence. "Nothing to generate a panic."

Hen looked at her with a wry hook in the corner of his mouth, and crumpled up his empty can with both hands. "Yeah? You watch the news last night? We already *got* panic. And what do we do if some bad sides turn up? Quarantine ourselves?"

They heard jetcopters pass very low, then hover, and Tiffany began to speak rapidly. "Hen, it's a risk, but you've already taken a much greater one. Nobody here knows about Goldie's work, or who you are, or what we've got. I mean, we *do* have something. Literally." She laughed in sudden, desperate mirth. "And so far the most *apparent* symptom is, uh, wanting to . . . to boogie, as the old people say."

"It's more than that." Henderson flushed and looked down. "There's increased . . . I mean . . . " He hunched his shoulders and laughed. "It makes you want to goof around. *Try* stuff. And . . . and not just with a partner. Speaking generally."

Tiffany gave him a droll squint. "You mean it makes you not only horny, but playful and creative. Yes! *Erectus* was well named. A wild one, I would imagine, when it came to fun and games. The champ of chimps."

Hen hooted. "Wound up as a chump."

She laughed through her nose, clicking her teeth rapidly at him. "So chomp 'im."

Together, like an old comedy team, they grimaced, and then Ruby appeared in the doorway, a forefinger aimed skyward. "He hath descended," she said. "The general. You want me to make some hemlock tea?"

"Iced," Hen said.

"Have you seen Hathaway?"

Ruby shook her head. Tiffany sat down and rested her chin on the heel of one hand while she tapped fingernails against her bared teeth. Hathaway was the Insec officer attached to the research center, supposedly to monitor military communications for efficiency and confidentiality. He had an office with advanced snoopgear and a hangar for a fast, light stealth craft. His real mission, Tiffany assumed, was to watch her and her crew.

"Find out if he's in camp. Make up something you want him to look into – say your lab auxcomp has a fudge virus, or—"

She stopped because they heard the boots thwacking down the hallway. The research center had been constructed swiftly, as a temporary installation, and the flooring now began vibrating alarmingly. "Never mind," she said. "Just get the tea."

Ruby slipped out, and a few seconds later General White was at the door, snapping off his field helmet and tucking it under his arm, saying over his shoulder, "She's here. Roberts, you high-tail it to the post command and start the FB report. Rest of you men wait for me outside. *Don't* wander around." He was in the room now, and glared briefly at Henderson.

"Doctor Orr. Speak to you privately, please."

"Good heavens yes, General White! This is my assistant George. Working very closely—"

"I know who he is. Excuse him, please." The general kept his head high, heels together, chest out. The impression he gave was that of a missile already fired and nearing ultimate velocity, spearing straight up, so steady in its flight that it seemed motionless.

"George, please, take a run down to the lab and have a look at that Rhesus with the runny nose? Thank you." Tiffany got up and gave her departing assistant a quick wave before she glided toward the general. "Since our last conversation – and I enjoyed that day *so* much, General – hearing about your promotion and taking a little tour of our humble station – I know you've been so busy—"

"Stop right there, Doctor Orr. I don't have the time for your performance today." General White directed his words at Tiffany's hairline. "We can't go on with this, what you're doing. When I approved the—"

"Oh, Doctor Orr, Doctor Orr – I know when you go back to that I'm in trouble." Tiffany reached out too quickly for the general to move and laid her hand on his chest for the length of a heartbeat. When she lifted her hand away she saw him, just perceptibly, sway. "I know we've been doing things a little out of the usual routine. And I know you have a tremendous responsibility—"

351

"You do? You know about responsibility, do you?" General White wheeled ninety degrees and took two long paces, wheeled and took two back. "You know about seeing the finest fighting units in the business go into a spin, unravel, *flip out*? Just as the first serious military threat of this operation comes at them? Just as some . . . some . . . *a little out of the ordinary* woman worms her way into the situation and *invites* that threat and then has the gall to pretend—"

"General White, if you please." Tiffany drew her considerable self into her own version of attention. "I have never disguised my gall. And I don't pretend, unless the advancement of science is at stake. I asked for a research station across the border and I got it, and my staff has worked very hard to make it produce. We knew there were risks, and we *appreciate* your protection, the tremendous strain of—"

"Strain? *Strain?*" The word peeled General White's lips away from his teeth, and darkened his face. "How about *insanity*, the goddamned outright fucking – I'm sorry, strike that from the record – goddamned insanity of this duty? For six months my men have been separating the living corpses from the dead ones, waiting for those fat-asses back home to figure out which group they wanted most, supplying you with your *samples*, trying to do a *job* and feel *right* about serving their country . . . "

"I know," Tiffany said. "Your poor boys."

"They are not goddamned *boys*," General White said in a kind of throttled bellow. "They are *men*."

"Just an expression, Randy. And we are grateful. Really. We're not inviting anything. It's just that we too are trying to do a job, a job as confusing – to us – as yours is to you. That's all I wanted to say. Okay?" She gave him a sunny smile.

General White made a rough, uncertain sound deep in his throat and frowned. "No, madam, I'm afraid it is *not* goddamned okay. I want some honesty here, first, and some straight information."

"Straight poop," Tiffany said helpfully.

"Precisely." White made the sound in his throat again. "This George of yours is some kind of ghoul, we've found out. His real name is William Hendricks and he's wanted for questioning in a little manner concerning the theft of tissue from an autopsy. I assume you know that, since it appears that someone on your staff supplied him with a false employment record. I suppose this must be an example of pretense in the name of advancing science." The general allowed himself a wintry

352

smile. "Hathaway has mentioned other infractions of code. The old fellow with the tumor – your witch doctor – has apparently been installed in a private intensive care room? And now, I find out, you have been broadcasting certain . . . *materials* to his followers?" General White delivered the emphasized word as if it had fouled his mouth.

Tiffany sighed and looked both reproachful and relieved. "Oh, Tibetan chants, some old popular songs, a Diné corn-dance – nothing of consequence. A little experiment." She watched his expression carefully. "That's the one that upsets you, isn't it?"

"For six months, this entire six months, these goddamned living corpses – skeletons – ice bags – have been . . . have been . . . "

"Singing?" Tiffany covertly signaled Ruby, now at the door with a tray of tea things, to enter swiftly and stealthily.

"Singing? Singing is just the start of it. Dancing, making a basically obscene movement, very suggestive, though they stumble and jig around so that . . . but the point is, the men can't take it. Some of them go *nuts*. I think there is actually some hypnotic thing going on. Some ultrasonic subliminal type of thing. Some men, been out here obviously far too long, are . . . " He stopped, swallowed, and shook his head violently, as if at an extremely bitter taste.

"Joining in? Dancing?"

Ruby had set the tray on the desk and slid away to the doorway again. Behind the general she exaggeratedly mouthed two words at Tiffany. *Kap. Dying.* Tiffany moved quickly to take the pot and pour, keeping her sympathetic regard fixed on the general.

White seemed finally to have reached escape velocity, or the apex of his trajectory. He was erect, his frown engraved now, his lungs expanded with air, but when he opened his mouth nothing came out. He discovered the helmet under his arm and set it down absently on the desk.

"Fraternizing," Tiffany said gently, a doctor piecing together a diagnosis. "Engaging—"

He stopped her with a look, and she only bit her lip, handing him a steaming cup and indicating with her other hand the chair behind her desk. She glanced out the window and saw some activity around the biosupply unit, where a large metal door was rolling aside.

"Anyway," Tiffany said softly, "we don't have to say more. I know what you mean. I see. Oh, Randy! This is *hard* for you." He sat down, slowly, balancing the cup, and she turned aside to drag nearer a folding metal chair. "And now this business with this Sayat character and the missile . . . "

The cup was almost at his lips for the first sip, but abruptly halted and lowered again. "How do you know about that?" He stared at her in alarm. "How in *hell* do you know about that?"

Tiffany *tsk*ed and winced in demure apology. "My witch doctor." The expression on his face made her hurry on. "It's the truth, Randy, though I absolutely can't explain or prove just how he does it. You saw that day when the old woman fed Buster her fleas, how they can communicate with other creatures. And their songs, the drumming with their feet, and smells . . . " She shook her head to indicate the strain on credibility.

"Two days ago. We picked up the first trace of this thing two days ago. Supposedly top pri darkside." General White inhaled, a loud, protracted sniff of contempt. "Last night the holohawks had it as a rumor, with no name or confirmation. Today you people act like it's old news. Maybe your witch doctor and Beau Winger have the same channels." He stared glumly into his cup. "You know what that gasbag is saying?"

Tiffany touched her forehead with two fingers. "I just don't keep up. Something about testing everyone? And mass confessions at some kind of rally?"

White guffawed sardonically. "That was *last* week. He's now accusing the government of a criminal conspiracy to adulterate pure NorthAm stock. He claims this whole business with the Drager kid and the experimental female lap was a plot to glorify miscegenation. Says the Ecominis have taken over the Conservative Party and want this symbolic love-child bastard-mutant – whatever it is – to rally around, so they can legalize mixing. And he's already hinting that, on the other side, the Prog extremists are smuggling weapons to the Ginks so they can massacre each other – and maybe a few of us too – and provide the rationale for another massive extermination campaign."

"Oh dear." Tiffany looked deeply concerned, but managed to glance again at the biosupply building. A crew was assembling to check and unload something. She spotted two people from epidemiology, but she could not recall any scheduled shipment of live tissue for the day. Something of Hathaway's, perhaps, coming in off the roster?

"'*Oh dear*?' Jesus Christ! And you and your new station – your ghouls and witch doctors – are way out here, the furthest outpost into the Wastelands. And I'm supposed to protect you. With troops who are completely losing discipline, falling into . . . "

He was, she could see, too miserable to go on. He drained the last of the tea, but did not rise to go. He seemed almost to have forgotten why he came. "Protect me?" she said very softly.

"I . . . the unit, I mean. The research facility." He looked at her and immediately away, as if he had come upon her half-dressed. "The . . . our morale . . . " He set his cup down smartly on the table, his ears now a radiant rose.

But before he could rise she had a hand on his knee, which froze him in place. "Thank you. I do feel protected. But it's you I am worried about."

"*Me*? No! Ha! That's ridiculous. I . . . I've gotten off the subject. I'm here to tell you we'll be bringing up two new companies, a transport and a light armored. Meanwhile I want you to begin wrapping things up again, ready for a move." He had his helmet now and made a brave effort to reach his feet, but the hand, surprisingly small for a woman of Tiffany's amplitude, kept him in the chair as effectively as an iron chain.

"But we have to do *our* job, Randy. We just have to. There isn't time for anything else. And I must tell you – please keep this in confidence – we are working now, directly, on just the problems that concern you. Data which will influence that whole question of genetic purity, of how to handle these . . . skeletons, as you call them, and . . . " She released his knee and took his hand in hers. "Tell me something."

She felt him sway again, and a sharp breath went in and then out of him, but he did not pull free.

"Why are you so upset by our playing music? By a few old songs?"

He remained motionless, a man of wood.

"Look at me."

He did, finally, and spoke at the same time in a whisper. "I . . . I find it . . . distracting." He swallowed. "I find myself . . . that is, something in me . . . has . . . has a response." He looked away out the window. A large transport rig had rolled into the yard near the biosupply unit, and one of the waiting crew was waving it casually into a berth.

"You mean a response not entirely . . . negative?" After a moment he managed a single, slight jerk of his head. Appreciating the tension in him, she waited for several seconds. In her main lab, far down the corridor, she heard Buster shriek three times. "That's what you meant by hypnotic, or subliminal, I guess. You find the chants are, uh, *attractive* in a certain way."

She smiled, but carefully. She was not yet sure what percentage of humans carried the gene making them vulnerable to infection from W-4; but it was already obvious that everyone in a community was influenced by its presence. The virus of happy spirituality, or spiritual happiness (she had expressed it to herself), attacked finally through the ear, as song. That it reached even General White was, to Tiffany, a miraculous confirmation.

"Attractive . . . no, I . . . more of a turbulence . . . " General White lifted his helmet, then lowered it again.

"Randy, can I ask you something else? Do you associate this turbulence with coming here? The singing was different last night, you know. More lively, more sustained, more . . . ecstatic. It made *me* want to dance." Actually, she *had* danced, with Henderson and Ruby and a few others. An informal party. "Do you associate the turbulence with . . . with me?"

They rose together, without any awareness of making a decision. Tiffany kept his hand firmly, and his eyes were inextricably involved with her own frank, warm regard. "Fanny," he whispered, "I don't know. All my life I've been a . . . a fighting man . . . "

"You're a very brave man, Randy, I know that. Now I wonder if you are ready to face the dragon."

He stared at her, and tried to smile. "Dragon?"

"The one inside you. You're not afraid of anything in front of you, anything you can *fight*. But inside, Randy, that's the big one! That's where you're afraid. Of these skeletons. Of your soldiers dancing and sneaking off in the dark with each other. Afraid of *me*. Afraid to dance with *me*, for example."

He let out a gasp, meant to be dismissive. "That's silly. That's preposterous!"

"Prove it." She released his hand and stepped back. She turned and switched on her desktop, punched three or four keys. From overhead came a soft hiss.

"For Christ's sake, Fanny!" General White looked away, again out the window. His voice was a cracked simulacrum of impatience and authority. "I have men waiting for me. There are armed renegades in this neighborhood. You have a shipment coming in. What is it, by the way?"

356

"No idea. It's a big black magrig full of dangerous tissue. The Arc of the Covenant, a Trojan Horse, ninety-nine cases of traditional Tibetan chants. Dreadful, no doubt."

The hiss ended abruptly in a crash and wail of primitive electric instruments, a driving, thudding beat, and a voice so raw and loud General White jumped slightly and went pale.

C'mon, c'mon, now touch me babe . . .

"I don't know, Randy, what or who's in the truck, and I don't *give* a fuck. I'm not afraid, and not afraid to ask you to dance, either. Have you ever seen these old styles, where you shake everything? Obscene movement, I think you said? You know how, fighting man?" Tiffany swayed, lifted her arms, and cocked one great hip. On the beat she gyrated, a slow but powerful undulation that compelled General White, in spite of everything he could do, to look.

She was now undulating and shivering simultaneously, and moving nearer with a sinuous lightness. She was concentrating on a memory, a boa constrictor she had seen in a zoo as a child. Its movements, the mazy curdling and flowing of its brilliantly patterned hide, the black lightning of its tongue, had hypnotized her, provoked a mad urge to climb into the cage. She wound her arms around the general's neck, let her fingers play with the cords at the back of his neck. She brought her face to within a hand's breadth of his own. "Prove it," she hissed.

She came up against him like the sea, or a rising sun: something big and rough and imperious. He had never known a woman like that, she could tell, and at first he set himself to resist. But she knew now what was under his alarm. She made him look at her, and when he tried to glare back, his ferocity turned into heat of another sort. The man of wood came alive, went green, and she felt him sway yet again.

"Yes," she breathed, "yes, General. Let's slay the dragon!"

CHAPTER THIRTY-FIVE

The Highest of the High, Most Powerful of the Exalted Ones, Giver of Life and Death's Master, Sayat found himself raging against the simplest, most obdurate of dilemmas. With all his power, he could not, it seemed, be in two places at once.

His raiders – those he had chosen and armed with the long-strikers – could of course swarm up through the tunnel into the place where his enemies were hidden. But then he would not have the immense pleasure of watching Snaketongue's eyes when he first prefigured his fate. Or, with careful instruction, someone – he was thinking of Ap, an important *tchatsi* he had won over from Kapu – could hurl this wonderful silver *mudlati* against the piksi soldiers' camp.

He was, however, loath to grant such a privilege to another. He had already a special affinity to this heavy, bright lance, the pam-pam. He was, in fact, straddling it at the moment, brooding aloft over his select company of guards, who had stacked their weapons in a rough pyramid, an imitation of one of the great hives, and then prostrated themselves in the dust.

It was pleasant to feel the hard metal skin of the *mudlati* grow warm between his legs, while he surveyed his legions and the terrain all around. The shaft was the thickness of a small tree, and he could sit comfortably there for a long time, legs dangling, the shining snout angling at the sky. It seemed to him the hidden fire inside the pam-pam inspired his thoughts, radiated a power into his bones.

His followers felt this exchange and had been moved to the prostration, to chanting prayers and hymns of praise, which were at once homage to his mastery of the pam-pam and a soothing support to his meditations. A happy phrase from one of these hymns called the pam-pam his *tak delo ogan*, his big little man. Sayat was pleased. Indeed, in this position of riding the great spear, he seemed to have a mighty silver seed-thrower, ever erect and ready for deadly ejaculation. It was an insight into the lust he had detected in the piksi Joe, when he brought the long-strikers.

But this tremendous new organ did not resolve the dilemma, or a number of difficulties that continued to trouble the Most High. The problem created by the drummers and tale-tellers, for example. Sayat knew he could not deprive his raiders of this diversion. Yet they were so enamored of singing about their exploits, and discharging the strikers merely for effect, that it was more and more difficult to get them to do any further actual killing. Then there was the matter of the lizards and sour lice. The Pobla had always lived intimately with both creatures. Lizards helped control flies, which, though respected beings, were sometimes too plentiful. When the lizards had eliminated most of the flies, a family would have to feed them on lice. If the number of lice decreased too much, the family would eat some lizards; and if times were so hard both species declined, a few elderly Pobla might allow *yano* to take them, so their corpses could furnish a hatch of flies and launch a new cycle of nourishment.

But now the lice were turning sour. Sayat's people made faces and spat. They were uneasy, for they could no longer exchange moods and feelings in the simple and direct way of sharing parasites. The lizards, meanwhile, had plenty of flies, and, also repelled by the lice, were drifting away from Sayat's settlements. Over and over he told his followers these ominous changes were the punishment for allowing piksis to live among them, and especially for harboring Teeklo and Pahane and Tima, but he could tell the Pobla sometimes doubted this simple truth. The humming and murmuring of his guards had altered subtly. Some were trying to stifle sneezes, brought on by inhaling the dust where they sprawled. One was approaching the pam-pam by inching along like a worm. It was Ap, who had introduced one of the subtle changes by hissing an apostrophe to his master, in a rhythm identical to that of the ongoing chant.

"Tak Tak Tagak Sayat is great in his wisdom, yet he is troubled, and we are too weak in understanding to aid him." Ap did not raise his eyes; he seemed to be confiding in the earth under his nose. "He has defeated the piksi sniffer-*mudlati*, he has eaten its brain, and now the pam-pam is his seed-thrower."

Sayat could repress a smile no longer. Ap was bold even in his crawling. From the moment he returned to their camp, a second-time defector from Kapu's band, the young *tchatsi* had shown a talent for reading the moods of his leader. He did not whimper for mercy, but confessed his treachery openly, and gave a plausible excuse. His friends, his mate and children, old Kapu – they had all conspired to delude him; also, Sayat's drummers had frightened him.

Ap had great prestige among the other *tchatsin*, because he knew the piksis so well. He and Sayat were the only survivors – excepting Kapu – of the raiding party with the old she-bear, which had first stolen the puling piksi *dako*. Ap had also been chosen to take the runt on his first raid into the Wastelands, after the naming ceremony when he became Pahane. For these very reasons, Sayat had absolved the traitor. Ap's devotion to annihilating Pahane's seed seemed to have become as implacable as his own, and carried the special venom of a faith renounced and now reviled. It was also useful to have one living example of the compassion of the Most High.

"You are not too weak to squirm," he said, just loud enough for Ap to hear. "And tricking their sniffer was no great work. Their *mudlatin* have no shadows."

He could see Ap convulse slightly in a spasm of mirth. "Only Tak Tak Tagak Sayat," he hissed, "could make eight children in a single sun."

It had indeed been comical. When the piksis came to deliver the pam-pam from a carrier-*mudlati*, Sayat apprehended their urgency, their nervousness, at once. Piksi Joe was dressed in a brand-new uniform and stank of chemicals. With great earnestness he insisted on a new condition for making a formal agreement. Sayat would have to allow the monitoring of a small sniffer-*mudlati*, a robot which could detect crooked speaking.

"Arm sniff, head sniff, no hurt!" Joe had exclaimed, simpering and bowing. He hooked himself up first, wires to his palms and temple, to show Sayat how the thing worked. It was only a wobbling line of green light on a tiny screen, a row of dials and switches. Piksi Joe positioned Sayat so only he and the other Pobla could see the screen. Then he said, "Talk. Sayat Most High talk question. Joe talk answer."

Sayat demanded to know if Joe had brought candy as he had promised, and Joe said yes. He asked about necklaces, and it was yes again. He asked if there were more long-strikers in the carrier. Yes again. How many cases? Joe held up one hand, fingers spread. The green line bumped and shuddered briefly. Sayat stared, frowning. Joe grinned and retracted two fingers. Three, then. The line remained flat.

So the sniffer machine was to tell the piksis when they lied to each other. Sayat laughed strenuously, in disbelief, and when he explained to his guards they laughed too, amazed at such pathetic measures. They had all noticed the deception in Joe when he first held up his hand, without even glancing at the screen. It was hugely entertaining then, when piksi Joe hooked Sayat to the sniffer and turned the screen away from them. They had only to look into piksi Joe's face to know what the line was doing. Immediately Sayat began to experiment, telling minor falsehoods, adjusting his manner in order to gratify the *mudlati*. Soon he could safely claim to be twenty-two winters, six more than his true age. He acquired two imaginary wives and the eight new children Ap had mentioned.

Of course he knew what piksi Joe really wanted to know. By the time the questions came, Sayat was able to shade his answers, pretend to be confused and furtive, make the green line wriggle and steady as he pleased, and thus deliver monstrous lies that his questioners swallowed whole.

He respected the piksis greatly (steady). Even loved them (wriggle). He had received signs from *Wonakubi* (steady). He was sorry he made piksi Joe stand naked in the hot sun (wriggle). He was eager to co-operate (steady). He only wanted to please his new friends (wriggle). The piksi plan was superior (steady). He would do as they advised: attack the refugee camps first with the pam-pam, then send a smaller force into the new station (steady). They would seize the runt and the pregnant witch, the false *tak tagakin* (steady). No, he would not torture or harm them (steady). He would trade them for pam-pams (steady). Only a few pam-pams (wriggle). No, he was not concealing a plan of his own (steady).

And that was the hilarious thing, for piksi Joe and his attendants, watching the line on the screen as a cat watches a rathole, believed it all. They closed their notebooks, relaxed, laughed, and praised the Most High in their execrable accents. The Pobla laughed in turn, with much greater gusto, and whooped their contempt, of which the piksis had no inkling. They practiced the piksi handshake, and were cheerful all during the unloading of the pam-pam and the painstaking instructions, involving diagrams and models, for its use.

Ap still lay in the dust at his feet, whispering more urgently now. "Tak Tak Tagak Sayat is always awake, always thinking of little No-Name Without A Shadow, thinking of how to use the pam-pam. How strange this tiny worm is powerful like the pam-pam – or worth many pam-pams . . . always Tak Tak Tagak Sayat is thinking . . . "

Sayat's frown was no longer indulgent. He glowered at the squirming one below. "Careful," he said, and resettled himself on the shaft of metal, looking swiftly out at the horizon, where nothing moved but a few low clouds of dust, a wheeling vulture or two.

"I am sorry ten thousand times, I live on my belly and stuff my mouth with earth if I offend. *Pakish leema dantakyat.*"

Sayat straightened, as if struck between the shoulder blades. He stared at the *tchatsi*, who was motionless now, face pressed flat to the ground. There was a long interval, while the others crooned and coughed, and the sun bore down.

"But Tak Tak Tagak Sayat is wise beyond all the children of *Wonakubi*, and I can only help by chance, in ignorance, as one hair of his head, or lash of his eye."

A pretty response, Sayat thought. He will pose as an insignificant, mindless helper. But he is the only one to hear as I did. He must have been the other who laughed. Perhaps that meant it would be better to kill Ap now, on the spot. But Sayat made no move toward the striker slung behind him on the pam-pam.

"They would not answer your questions, so wise and deep. They are restless as shrews, and cannot answer, and Tak Tak Tagak Sayat must seek in himself . . . but I am ten thousand times ten thousand times foolish to speak of what I know not. I would do nothing, because I know nothing. I do not understand what is so valuable about little No-Name."

"Doing nothing is doing something," Sayat snapped. He was breathing a little faster, staring at the back of Ap's skull as if he intended to burn a hole in it. "You know we must destroy the egg of evil."

"Oh yes, Tak Tak Tagak Sayat! You have taught us all this truth. We must. Always and always and always. But we begin with the hen and the cock, the outsiders. Then this tiny egg with no shadow, yet powerful as many pam-pams it seems, which only Tak Tak Tagak Sayat can match . . . and then . . . and then . . . " Ap stopped, as if confused or startled.

Sayat was now holding his breath, dizzy at this – so it seemed to him – invasion of his most secret mind. Ap had understood everything, had thought beside him pace for pace, spinning an appalling web of speculation.

It had begun during their sealing of the agreement with piksi Joe and his companions. He had pushed aside the sniffer and announced he had two or three more important questions, and needed no *mudlati* to assess the answers. He would try to follow the piksi plan, but what if there was a mishap and Pahane and Tima and the crazy lady and all the others were killed?

Joe's face went immediately translucent and still. Only the infant, he said. The others do not matter so much. But we must have the little one. Without the baby everything is lost. This was not a lie, Sayat saw.

"What do you want with it?"

With an ambiguous smile and shrug, piksi Joe signed he didn't know. There was quiet consternation among the Pobla. They detected again that strange blankness or crookedness in piksi speech. Joe's smooth, soft features seemed undisturbed by the admission of such ignorance, though it was nearly unimaginable that one negotiating such an important, risky raid would not be told its object.

"Why?" Sayat asked, actually curious. "Why do you not know?"

Piksi Joe had smiled wistfully, and delivered the very phrase Ap had quoted to him. *"Pakish. Pakish leema dantakyat."*

Bad to know too much? The Pobla had all stared, dumbfounded, before Sayat laughed again. Behind him someone else also laughed, and he knew now that was Ap. *Bad to know.* Of course. He understood, all at once. The piksis *did* realize they were poor liars, and weak besides. They kept their grand plans secret from the very ones who carried them out. Only a few – perhaps only one – would know how all the parts fit together. So Joe didn't know, *exactly*, even though he could no doubt guess with the slightest exertion. It appeared piksis could know and not know at the same time.

There was a kind of genius in it, this creative use of ignorance. Sayat had been intrigued, then excited. He grasped the advantage of the idea in an immediate, concrete way. From the moment he became *tak tagak*, he had harangued his followers on the need to destroy the evil embryo, and the parents who had brought it into being. But when Joe revealed how much the little one mattered to the piksis, a whole series of startling notions had flowered in his brain.

What if they did *not* exterminate the unborn, but cut it alive from the womb? There were female *tagakin* in his band who could do such a thing. One of his own pregnant concubines could nurse the creature. If these piksis wanted the child so much, what would they pay to get it? That was the meaning of Ap's sly hints about No-Name being powerful as many pam-pams. And what did they want it *for*? That question still vexed him and, turning it over in his mind, Sayat wondered for the first time if *he* had some advantage to gain from keeping the demon alive.

A moment later it came to him with the force of one of the long-striker bolts. The raids on Kapu's band, the hundreds of skulls split open and the brains scooped out, the endless drumming and chanting, the new weapons that made each of his chosen guards a thousand times more fearsome – all these followed from his dedication to destroying the demon infant. He, Sayat, had summoned this fierce energy, had stirred his people to life again and breathed fire under their ribs, but he saw in a flash that he had depended on the fear of an unborn horror to accomplish this resurrection. He had wondered only seldom and vaguely what would happen after his goal was reached.

That was the meaning of Ap's whispered "always, always, always", of his feigned stumbling over "and then . . . " How would he inspire his *mahanakun*, when there were no more corrupt Pobla to hunt down? When the demon-infant was only a memory, a story? What would the tribe blame for sour lice and fickle lizards?

He could foresee unwelcome changes. The singers would assert even more power. Everyone would want celebration, fires and feasting and new chants. The long-strikers might become mere props for display. Some of the young *tchatsin* would shirk training and drift away to make *naku*, perhaps start new settlements in the ruins of the old temples. Without a dire adversary, he, Highest of the High, might not be thought so necessary, might appear therefore less glorious, or even . . .

His heart went cold, then white hot. No one would ever dare to think him ridiculous. He could destroy them all, choke the river *yano* with a freight of shadows such as the world had never seen! He could – but that was the genius of this piksi way! There need not ever be a finish to the struggle. Suppose he decided – secretly, telling no one – to keep the demon-infant! The piksis could not attack, for fear of losing what they most cared about. He would demand to know the hidden power of this No-Name chit of a thing, so he could estimate its ransom value.

Meantime the raiding would go on and on. They could pursue the remnants of Kapu's band, allowing a few always to slip away. His warriors would never grow fat and careless; they would have to guard the evil sprout alertly, until the price was right, and afterward no one could be sure if the bastard mongrel creature lived or not.

He would need secret allies, and Ap had detected that need and offered himself. No doubt there would be others who would see, dimly at first, what he was doing. They would have to learn to know and not know at the same time. As long as they could live in this paradox and never speak it, they would be trusted *mahanakun*. But if they breathed a word of what they knew and didn't know, he would cut their throats before they heard the echo of their words.

Softly again, as if speaking idly or to himself, he said, "Every hair of my head, every lash of my eye is dear, but another will do as well. My big seed-thrower is different. There is only one. How can I leave it? And yet we must be first from the tunnel. And I alone must call out the little cock and kill him."

Ap sighed as if in pain. "Ah! Yes, Tak Tak Tagak Sayat, and slowly, too! The *dako* must know his fate, that he and all his seed are come to nothing, nothing at all, while you are restored and raised up, Highest of the High. Still, the seed-thrower is so beautiful. So long and straight and hard. We must take it everywhere, even in the tunnels."

At last Ap looked at him, his eyes rolled up and showing white beneath a contracted brow. Sayat was at once gratified and disturbed. Ap understood, he saw, that nothing was more vital to his leader than humiliating the piksi weakling who had become Pahane. Ap remembered how in the beginning Sayat had not been Most High, how others smirked and whispered *dako* behind his back, so that when Mata the old she-bear had dragged in a half-dead piksi pup, even Sayat could poke and jeer at someone. Yet this new runt, through the devious tricks of Teeklo and Kapu, had been elevated to a *tak tagak*! A perversion so great *Wonakubi* had brought down disaster on them all.

Yes, Ap understood, with uncanny swiftness, and had adopted immediately, audaciously, the *we* Sayat had thrown out. It was almost as if the young *tchatsi* in the dust were actually his shadow.

"But the pam-pam is coiled a certain way already. It will cast death on Kapu's brood from here, and hardly touch the piksi soldiers."

"We know its slant, and the slanting of its shadow, and how far away the soldier camp is. We can make it do our bidding."

Again, the quickness of the response was almost alarming. Ap had clearly thought of these problems beforehand. They had all grasped, during the piksi's complicated instructions, how procedures could be undone as easily as done, the shaft angled or swung to reach other targets. For many generations the Pobla had learned from their tunnel-guides, the rats, how to reverse and retrace the most intricate mazes; so the pam-pam appeared to them surprisingly simple in its assembly and operation.

"But they are watching us, surely, all the time," Sayat protested cagily. "They may strike at us if—" He stopped, seeing the tiny, incipient smile in Ap's face. Again, pace for pace, the other was with him. No need to waste time in voicing aloud what was obvious.

They had only to hurry the pam-pam into the nearest tunnel and move toward the station where their enemies hid. The idiots had put their dwellings directly atop a holy place, a great intersection of main corridors. In a few hours they would be so close the piksis could not risk an assault, for if the pam-pam went off it would blow up the demon-child along with everyone else. Then Sayat, the Most High, could release the great, bright lance at the refugees in the soldier camp and create a diversion indeed, even as he spirited away the cock, the hen, and the egg. He would do all the things he promised – only in a different place at a different time, for his own reasons.

"So," he said finally, and shifted his position in order to gaze again at the horizon, "it shall be as we have said. We shall move swiftly as those gliding black sailers. Then I will squirt death-seed over all Kapu's children. Ha!" Sayat slapped the gleaming bolt between his legs and rocked back and forth. "We will flush the little cock and cut off his own scrawny seed-thrower, and stuff it in his witch's mouth, and make him watch while we rip his pup out of her belly, *na*? Ha! *Kishta tchat!*" He rocked back and forth, grinning.

Ap had raised up on his spread hands, like a lizard, and his eyes still showed white in ecstatic adoration. "*Tak tak tagak Sayat*," he cooed. "*Most high! Most high!*"

"We will make the piksis pay! They will give us big pam-pams. They will fall down before us. They will be nothing. We are not afraid of the *mudlatin* any more. See!" His rocking was furious, convulsive. He felt his seed gathering, and for a moment thought the pam-pam might erupt under him. The murmurings of his guards had grown feverish, more insistent. The horizon around him seemed to blur and undulate.

"*Tak tak tagak Sayat! Tak tak tagak Sayat!*"

With a final, violent shudder he spilled himself, and the world rolled away around him, in awe of the *naku* of the Highest of the High. He felt himself soaring into night, like one of the stars that streaked down, and all creation was thrown back amazed. He understood the piksis now, why they had ridden pam-pams to the moon, hurled others around and around the earth, and he was not afraid. Now it was his turn, and there would never be an end to this release, this power to loft higher and higher . . .

Then he was aware again of the chanting of his followers, faint at first as if he were descending from a great height. There was more sneezing, and here and there someone gagged, giving the prayer a syncopated or uneven rhythm. Sayat felt a tickling in his own throat, and a compulsion to blink. There was dust or pollen blowing in, a faint halo around the sun. Frowning, he looked once more at the horizon and then at Ap again.

"The horses," Ap whispered and smothered a cough. "More came in the last two suns."

"Why? The grass is thin now. What do they seek?"

On the horizon the long plumes seemed to crawl back and forth, like great, slow, brown caterpillars.

"Perhaps . . . " Ap's voice was barely audible, as if only a trick of the light wind. " . . . they have come to be near the Most High . . . to worship what is greater than themselves."

Sayat inhaled, swelled his neck. That was it, of course. The horses had once travelled with the ancestors of the Pobla, and were returning to pay homage. All creatures would come to him, eventually. He would acknowledge them, as long as they behaved themselves and showed respect.

He swung down then from the pam-pam, and instantly the chanting was terminated, in a chorus of coughs and kachoos. Sayat sucked in a sudden breath, his eyes watering. These heavy-footed ones would have to learn to keep their distance on breezy days. He lost control then and emitted an alarming series of honks that caved in his chest and bobbed his head like a gourd floating over a rapid. He recovered and glared about, but every single one of his followers was preoccupied, head down, and had apparently failed even to notice this explosion of sneezes.

He stalked away toward the camp, and his six personal guards hastened to fall in behind. A chorus rose from the others. *Yanaku Tak Tak Tagak Sayat! Yanaku!* But beneath and intermingled with this obeisance and farewell were more honks and hawkings, sniffs and snorts, noises which almost suggested – at least for an irritating splinter of a moment in Sayat's consciousness – suppressed mirth.

CHAPTER THIRTY-SIX

Fanny and PJ understood each other immediately. They persuaded Fitzgibbon that the quickest way to get rid of the old Gink was to allow a ceremony in the pocket valley at the bottom of the canyon. They told him the truth, that the old one had waited on the threshold of death for weeks, and might continue to hang on, if they didn't give him his little song and dance. He wanted only to lay his hand on Tima's womb, see his people accept her, hear the last chants. Then he would go. And a Gink could go, everyone knew, whenever he wanted.

So they loaded Kapu into a field ambulance, climbed aboard Fanny's staff vehicles and, with a light armored escort, ran for the valley. The driver remarked in amazement that for the first time there were no refugees around the station or drifting through the landscape. When they crested the canyon wall over the trickle of water winding through the valley, they saw why. Hundreds of Kapu's followers squatted on the stones and dunes rising from the valley floor; and beside and around and over them were the birds.

The major in charge of the escort was immediately nervous and beeped Fanny from his command carrier. He wanted to halt the column and call General White for advice. "There could be hostiles," he argued. "With arms. We have a security problem here and I'm responsible for these boys."

Fanny overran his position with her sunny, implacable charm. "Don't you worry one *bit*, Major," she said. "They're starving but they won't eat *your* boys, I *promise*. Continue." Her driver shrugged and forged onward, accelerating downslope into the canyon. He had observed General White's conduct, retiring from Fanny's lab, and knew where the power lay now.

The major's urgent remonstrations turned into alarmed orders to catch up and throw a cordon around the staff vehicles and ambulance, from which Kapu was already rolling into the sunlight. A cry went up, and all at once the sky was full of wheeling, slicing wings.

When Pahane and Tima emerged, the cry came again, then sank to a whisper, and then vanished into silence. The major wanted to watch this pair more closely, also the new agents who emerged to picket themselves around Fanny's group, but he was distracted by the attendants hovering excitedly over the body on the gurney. Apparently the old Gink had expired en route.

Tima stood for only a moment, long enough to see the nest and walk to it. The colony was small and weak, yet the Hive Being was in it, they knew. The air all around became like clear water, magnifying, displacing, vectoring the light at a new angle. Some workers began to swarm, raising a pale, shimmering vortex. They both felt the surge of *naku*, that powerful magnetic force that held the Pobla together, as one.

In another moment Pahane and Tima were on their knees, foreheads against the crusted wall of the nest, listening. In the dark labyrinth they heard a minute and steady cataract, a faint, percussive sound which was the sum of thousands of heads striking the hardened floors of tunnels within. They let the cadence sink into their very bones, until their own bodies began to pulse and sway; then they rose to their feet, as the first drums picked up the beat and the ranks of Pobla began to stamp and clap.

As the couple glided, swayed, shuffled toward Kapu on his cart, the ambulance crew looked frantically toward Fanny. The young doctor was shaking his head and signing with a horizontal chop of his hand that the subject was effectively dead. Just before their arrival, they had given up on the respirator and gone to electro and then a syringe into the heart. Nothing. All the lines were flat. Fanny only motioned serenely for the crew to stand back.

Tima had begun a soft chant and, when she reached the gurney, she leaned over to breathe into Kapu's mouth. Then she stepped back and the corpse sat up and grinned. One of the medical attendants fainted, and then the hundreds of squatting figures began to breathe the chant along with Tima, barely audible at first but rising like a wind.

Kapu continued to grin, and one arm jerked in the rhythm of the chant. Pahane gazed into the dark face, every wrinkle and seam of it stretched tight to expose the yellowed stumps of teeth. He was seeing the old one not as he had known him, in an antic, unreeling present, but all at once, as a tableau through time. Crouched in a sun-dappled glade of high forest, beside the old she-bear, considering whether to kill or keep the piksi runt they had captured. Through a billow of smoke, a red line drawn by knife-point across his upper arm, peering into Ronald's blank eyes in search of a shadow. Erect with lance in hand, grim and hostile at the giddy runaways Pahane and Tima, rioting in their new *naku*.

His last glimpse of Kapu had been at the Going In ceremony, just as the deadly *mudlati* hurled into their midst, desecrating the joining of the queens and sundering the Pobla for the first time. The awe and terror of that moment were entirely absent now, even though hundreds of thousands of Kapu's people had lost their souls and forsaken their ruined temples. What he saw in the old one now was a shadow racing, expanding, leaping in joy; the body was only an empty room, a ringing echo after a mighty hosannah of ecstatic celebration.

He laughed, Tima laughed, the hundreds of Pobla around them laughed. Kapu turned toward Tima, and she took the withered knob of his skull in her hands and held it to her womb. They saw his lips moving, saw Tima bending to overhear. His message was not long, and then they saw him breathe again, just once, long and deep.

The air around them was still clearer and brighter, full of light except for the vortex of Hive Dwellers, which swayed in a column of darkening mist the height of a man. When Tima released the old head, this swirl of darkness rose and dispersed, vanished. The chant swelled to a hurricane, broken by wild whoops, as the Pobla began to dance. The earth beneath them vibrated, a great drum, and the wing-beats above were thunder.

The major watched in disbelief as Tima retired and four of the Ginks, young males, moved in to tumble Kapu from the gurney and bear him a little distance away. They stretched the body out on a flat boulder, and though he saw everything – the sliver of stone, the quick strokes, the cavern made by the frail ribs – when they lifted up the stark, red heart, it seemed a magical apparition. Then the birds were on the carcass in dark waves, and the chanting and dancing were everywhere, raising a veil of golden dust wherein figures whirled with their shadows.

Though he had his finger on the switch, the major never activated his hot line. After the heart, he had to labor next to understand what his eyes recorded, as he frantically reviewed his emplacements. He saw the crews on the personnel carriers grinning and nodding; he saw grunts in the security cordon, the ones nearest the gyrating dancers, sway and dip; he saw several men moving in time with other men, facing them. He heard an aide whisper behind him, *"Holy shit."*

The first lieutenant beside him was monitoring communications from the jetcopters, and now picked up his binoculars and scanned the canyon rim. "Sir," he said. "Up there. More company."

The major squinted through the dust, the golden light, which was making the horizon wobbly and insubstantial. "What? Goddamn it, hard to—" But he did see, then. There was a band of large, four-legged creatures on the rim, seeming to materialize out of the warp and waver of the atmosphere. Moving with remarkable speed, slowing, hooking back, then accelerating again in a spurt of dust. "What the hell is that? Let me see."

The lieutenant handed him the glasses, and in a moment he had them. They streamed in a torrent across the flat disk of his field of view – flashes of brown, russet, black, gray, white . . . Horses. More horses than he had ever seen.

CHAPTER THIRTY-SEVEN

It was like one of those desperate parties held on the fantail of a sinking vessel, or just before an execution, or in the last days of a siege. Technically, Fitzgibbon supposed, it was a wake of some kind, but the deceased was not present, was in fact most likely already picked to the bone by the million hungry crows that had shown up in the bleak canyon where they had laid him out.

More glum than defiant, he took another swallow of his rum and cola. He knew he shouldn't drink at all on this job, and the alcohol wasn't helping that much, but the weirdness of the whole situation required a stabilizer. Anybody would need a drink after watching those spooks eat a fresh heart from one of their own. Still, he didn't forget his job. He checked every few seconds to see that PJ was nearby, and four men covering the exits and windows.

What a zoo. Mama could put bars around this bunch and double the admission. The two teenagers, for example. The knocked-up Ginkette was cute, he had to admit, if you didn't look into her eyes or watch for too long. She could turn a certain way, bend herself somehow, and before you knew it you thought of something nauseating. A snake around your neck, or a crab with a claw on your—

He stopped himself, a spasm already in his gut. The boy was almost as creepy. He hung around his little mama like a guard dog. His eyes were at once too blank and too bright, and Fitzgibbon figured he was a serious headcase, like Petrasky. He turned to observe the doctor, deep in conversation with his beloved (transformed now into an ordinary street punch and backhead) and Madam Big Buns – this Fanny who was supposed to be the rank here, the famous scientist, and who was just as torqued as the rest.

Fitzgibbon winced and drank again. Petrasky – the main reason, besides the money, he had gotten wound up in this goofball kidnap. Petrasky was now pathetic, a joke, and Fitzgibbon found himself almost capable of a degree of sympathy for the poor bastard. He had lost his job, his girl, and finally his mind. Brain blown, he could greet tragedy with that radiant, idiotic smile. Maybe there were situations where common sense was a drawback, where being loony was an advantage. Doctor Dingaling seemed to be recovering his fair companion after all, whereas he, Fitz, had shit.

Things kept skidding around, reversing, vanishing. The original idea was to keep PJ under surveillance, make sure the ops went down right. Light stuff. No wipes. They wanted some kind of folk hero, was the original plan. Something they could turn into a major holo and a political cause. Also a way of winding up the Drager saga, or so Josh Tremain led him to believe. The pay was terrific, and it should have been easy duty.

But the deal was going on too long, and getting too weird. All at once here they were in the fucking *Wastelands*, without even a change of clothes. *Proceed with cargo*, the contact had said. *Cover in place.* There was no cover, and none needed, because this was the end of the universe, this was nowhere, this was *research*, with a bunch of crazies in charge and nobody, absolutely nobody else around but the singing skeletons. A new musical act. The stinking Ginkatonics.

For another thing, PJ was now uncontrollable. Far from trying to escape, he actually loved this adolescent wacko sabo stuff. He didn't seem to care about the money, or his reputation, or the future; he was reckless and unpredictable, endangering the whole scam. He was a type that irritated Fitzgibbon tremendously. The Jokers. The type that enjoys fucking with everybody all the time.

He had to keep an eye on Hathaway too, and of course Hathaway knew it. The agent approached him now, carrying his cup of black coffee and smiling. Fitzgibbon had noticed how all Insec people wore the same insinuating, ironic smile. A class exercise, no doubt. Establish dominance. Hathaway took up a position at his elbow, as if they were on sentry duty together. "Quite a party," Hathaway said. "Enjoying yourself?"

"Immensely." Fitz did not look at him. They had taken over Hathaway's office, his linkup and security files, very easily. They simply explained the situation, allowed the agent to glimpse a holstered weapon, merely as a talisman. PJ had made it a joke, of course: a mock dialogue between officers and gentlemen. The contact had already assured them that the grease was in, that the whole op would be a matter of gestures, of appearances. They were impersonating an Insec team of specials. Hathaway was impersonating a field agent fooled by their impersonation.

This made Fitz nervous. His job became a fake job, a part he was playing, but he didn't know where the action was going. Somebody high up at Insec had to know they were here, had to *want* them to be here. The impending election would probably bring a new configuration of power, and this op was surely an element in that shift, but he could not reason out the pattern. Adamson and the moderate Progs were talking tough now, tasting victory. They would do some showy business on the border, change the refugee policy, but . . .

"I like parties." Hathaway laughed, apparently musing aloud. "But one shouldn't stay too late."

"That so?" Fitzgibbon turned his head just enough to watch the agent sip his coffee. "Why shouldn't one?"

"One might miss the next party. Bigger party. Exclusive party. Very exclusive." Hathaway laughed again. "And these little scams that go on too long, they get sticky eventually. Call attention to themselves. You know, I'm sure. You can take care of yourself. Good talking to you." He moved away easily, his smile still ironic, but broader.

Fitzgibbon frowned, unsettled at how deftly his captive – if that's what Hathaway was – had expressed his own thoughts, and at the agent's carefree good humor. But he had no time to mull over these puzzles. Combe had sidled up, trying to look shrewd.

"I'm wondering if you're thinking what I'm thinking."

Combe was the youngest and dumbest of his men. He had a flat, wide, athlete's body and kept his blond mustache closely trimmed. He looked uncomfortable in the fatigues Fanny had requisitioned for the team, so they wouldn't look out of place. His job was the simple one of staying heavily armed and a step away from his boss. Combe was perfect for the work, which required a sincere love of enforcement and a complete lack of imagination. Fitzgibbon stared at him, unsmiling, waiting.

"I mean, why here, Fitz? This is . . . this is *way* out. And these people . . . you know who those kids are, nobody even tryin' to hide that pregnant freak . . . I mean this is *big* stuff, Fitz. And you remember that geez, the famous doc, the one whose brain—"

"Combe," Fitzgibbon said, and managed a weary smile. "Don't wonder any more. Don't think. We don't know these fucking people here. We're not supposed to know them. We just protect our target people. Okay?"

"Yeah, okay, Fitz. But why here? I mean, *Jesus*, this is weird. I feel set up out here. So do the other guys. Research, supposed to be, right? So we bury this old Ginko, and here come birds and horses, and those people dancing and *laughing* . . . I mean it's weird. Come on, Fitz." Combe's small, round, blue eyes were intent, unswerving.

Fitzgibbon sighed, sank into himself. "Okay. It's weird here. All right?" After a moment of inner contemplation, he raised his head again, looked around the room. "Now tell me something," he said. "Where isn't it?"

Across the room, Tima and Pahane had drifted apart from the others. This little gathering – a bizarre mixer for terrorist and hostage – was their first opportunity to talk after the ceremony. They were aware of how they shocked and intrigued their keepers when they crooned and gestured before the small termite nest, laughed uproariously and gyrated to the pulse of the drums, the stamping feet.

Since that letting-go, the effort of keeping their jubilation silent, interior, and private had tired them out. The baby had also been aroused by the dancing and had pummeled Tima unmercifully. She was sleeping now, but for the first time Tima felt her as a weight, a small ingot of force pulling down and away. This drag was distorting the mother's body, but Tima knew also that everything in her entire being, inside and out, was bending fundamentally and irrevocably.

Pahane, for his part, had been exhilarated by the miracle of seeing so many Pobla alive with *naku*, chanting and whooping their laughter; yet he was troubled by the speed with which the ceremony had been arranged, by the watchful presence of armed men who, despite their expressions of disgust, did not interfere. They had assumed that PJ was the leader of this group of agents, but very soon noticed that he, too, was kept under surveillance. Tima had noted this peculiarity, in their first brief conversation, and PJ had grinned in bitter glee.

"We're all prisoners together, mama. Including these fine gentlemen watching over us. You were in the agency. You should know. All we can do is sing in our chains."

"Who's the push?" Tima had asked matter-of-factly.

"Some old gang in a new bottle, I think. Only now they have a higher aim. Humanitarian."

Tima was amused. "What's the 'human' part? Deciding extermination wasn't cost-effective?"

376

"Oh, yes. Now it's ID tattoos, sterilization, and rehab camps. Your baby has a bright future, Duskyrose."

"So these are the new Progressives? A gentler Danny Konrad?"

"Ah, no." PJ was convulsed by a private joke. "They have, I believe, no affiliation. Only a higher allegiance. Above the mire. Beyond sluttish time."

Tima's laugh had a bitter edge. "Ah, yes. Art."

Then Fitzgibbon had lumbered up, puffing and frowning, and they had dropped the subject. It was merely confirmation of what they already accepted as the logical and obvious explanation of their "escape". They were moving through a script, as players. That had been true from the very beginning. Little Ronnie Drager's journey into the feral underworld, his re-emergence as a dirty, scarred pubescent with multiple personality disorder, his supposed rehabilitation – the whole had been transformed, even as it happened, into *story*. Within days of his rescue, the holo that made him rich was under way, while various political factions were working to portray him as hero or victim.

Now, Tima guessed, there was a single, simple change in this process. A change in scale. "They want to catch everybody – Cons, Progs, Ecominis, Thorgs, Fundies – everybody," she speculated. "Then they provoke a crisis, and conduct the conflict. Maybe not so much for profit, but for the sheer thrill of control. That's what NorthAms have always tended toward. Managed, dynamic spectacle. Continuous terror and delight. We're a juicy opportunity for them. We can represent everything dirty and depraved and fascinating."

"But not for profit?" He was Ronnie for a moment, playfully. "That's basic. The most basic, I thought."

"Well, the ultimate thrill is perhaps not just to own or coerce, but to have everything go as you wish, always, simply for your *entertainment*. Piksi gods – isn't that what they do?"

It was true in a way. In school he had learned about such primitive beliefs, and how scientific management had taken their place. But the purpose of such management – energy policy, land policy, economic strategy – was actually the same. Direction, arrangement, manipulation – all for gratification. "Well," he said finally. "That's an improvement, isn't it?"

"Might be a step in the right direction." Tima smiled wryly. "Though a backwardsass one."

"Backasswards," he corrected, grinning.

"Sorry. I always get that one . . . backasswards." She closed her eyes with a long sigh. "I'm tired. Tired of pretending and playing a part. Tired of this whole tale."

Watching her face, Pahane saw all at once that her features had thickened and tiny cracks had appeared at the corners of her eyes and in that neck once perfectly supple and smooth. The shock of this vision left him disoriented. He had always thought of her as a girl, with a girl's lithe resilience and agility; but he saw now she would wear into a woman, with a woman's heft and shape. He remembered that a Pobla's life expectancy was barely a third that of an average *sapiens* – a fact usually attributed to poor diet, disease, and toxic habitat. What if it was congenital? What if his love was already half-way to her grave!

He tried to say her name, but the sounds caught in his throat. He lifted his hand and when he touched her she opened her eyes instantly. A feeling he had not known before struck him like a great boulder in the chest and kept rolling, deeper and deeper.

"No, no," she said. "None of that, *tahanaku*." She took his hand, brought it to her face, and inhaled. "Remember."

"*Tahanaku*," he whispered. The word she had taught him when she brought him over her and into her and through her, that first time, when they ran away to the sea. When she explained to him that they were entirely alone: the first of a new dynasty of *tagakin*. He had to look away and rub the tears from his eyes, hastily and irritably. "Yes, I forgot. I'm sorry. So anyway, if they made everything up, this performance for their amusement, why did they bring us here? PJ doesn't seem to know. I mean, it's incredibly lucky for us, but—"

"PJ doesn't care any more. He's learned, finally, to ride the wind. Anyway, some reasons are obvious. We're easier to control here, media people can't snoop around, the refugees and Sayat's band supply a crisis backdrop. We provide the star for the big scene."

Tima spoke matter-of-factly, but Pahane heard the anxiety and anger beneath her voice. "Our star," he said. "Why are they so afraid of her? A little baby. A little saplap baby." He thought hard for a while and went on to answer himself. "Because she is beautiful and powerful, but she is not human, in their terms. She won't look human, will she?" Pahane did not even glance up to see Tima nod. "And she will tempt them, tempt them backward – as they conceive direction – toward their shadows—"

"We Pobla have always tempted you," Tima said. "And frightened

378

you. Like the dark, like shadows, like anything wild and beyond your control." She had gathered herself again, like a flame. "As if the only things in the universe were *human* wishes, *human* entertainment! As if the whole world came about just to suit you piksis." Tima huffed derisively. "No Pobla would ever assume such a thing. Kapu – you know what Kapu said to me? He wanted to know if the Hive Beings forgave him for being so happy for his own people! He wanted to be sure we sang for everything alive – the horse-people and the blow-fish people and the ice people – whether mythical or not – everything!"

"For Sayat too?" Pahane surprised himself with the question, which flicked out like his Pobla name, the tongue of a snake.

"Oh yes. And his tunnels."

"Tunnels?" He looked startled, then excited.

"Oh yes. Right under us, and well-known to *Tak Tagak* Sayat." Her mouth warped in disgust. "Who has weapons now, and wants our brains in his hand. Kapu told me he would come from below, from the earth. And told me to run with the horse-people."

Pahane looked uneasy. "Sayat would try that? An open attack on this place, on piksi troops? It would be mad!"

"Of course he's mad. But not stupid. I imagine they will try some *tchat* as diversion, then strike here, inside, and snatch us away before the carriers or copters can react. Once in the tunnels they'd split us up and fan out. No augurcraft here, so it would – normally – be a few hours before a full press pursuit can be launched."

"Would normally?" Pahane watched her closely for a moment. "Then you think . . . ah! This attack is also written into the story! A relief force will be poised to . . . to . . . " He laughed, so loudly he saw others in the room look their way. "Rescue us again." He stared at her in admiration. "How do you do it?"

"You forget half my childhood was spent as the ward of the Director of Border Operations for Insec. It's a fairly obvious setup. Sayat was given weapons precisely for this assault, to be a credible threat to the unborn mystery."

"Election coming up. The refugee issue. The turmoil over the mixeds and Omalys. Sure. You're right. A military operation right away, within days—"

"Hours, more likely. A quick delivery." She patted her womb lightly, again with the wry, melancholy smile. "And a great drama is not supposed to exceed one day."

Pahane was thoughtful. "I saw horses, just as in the dreams, but no people. And why are they so devoted to us?"

"Kapu said they have an old story of their own. To them we are a snake and a bird, and our baby is both. The highest possible *tagak*. And a throwback, according to our learned friends." She looked away toward the group where conversation was most animated: Cynthia, Marvelous, Fanny, Henderson, and Ruby; and now PJ was listening too, with Fitzgibbon hovering glumly beside him.

"Absolutely, absolutely." Fanny was agreeing with Marvelous so enthusiastically she had covered his knee with one soft hand. "Think of what *anthropomorphic* means. Giving human form to animals or things. *We* impose on *it*. Think of that tremendous body of myth dramatizing copulation with animals, hence centaurs and satyrs and draculas! Just metaphor, we say, just old tall tales, allegory and symbol. *Never* fact."

"And usually," Cynthia broke in, "divine males do the insemination – or rape, more often. In our versions the god transforms himself into an animal, but in the very oldest stories, the god *is* a bear or crane or snake, and only disguises himself as human in order to trick some innocent young thing. And from what I've seen of men—" She pouted as if at a very sour taste. "I'd take a snake, any time."

Doctor Petrasky turned to her, a study in puzzlement, concern, sadness. "He meant you no real harm, Cynthia. He believed in the trees—"

"I know, I know, Marvelous. And you're different. I didn't mean you."

Marvelous flushed, then beamed again. "We share our substance with many creatures," he went on. "They do, indeed, possess us, as your work has so convincingly shown." He covered Fanny's hand, still on his knee, with his own. "I wish in some ways I had been here when you were working this through. Spelling out that endogenous retrovirus, guessing how it hybridized with the strains from birds and fleas, how it came back after five million years . . . "

"And seeing the connection to the shadow gene, how it linked with shamans and prophets, their music and playfulness, and then tracking it to the waffle cells." Cynthia clapped her hands together softly. "That's a Gandhi winner, right there."

"If they don't indict you first." PJ leered at all of them as he shouldered into the conversation. "Do pardon the devil's advocate, but he has his duty. Some people, you know, will look at the whole thing very differently. They'll say you found this virus, this disorder, in a dying and demented population. A *nonhuman* population. Filthy cannibals, in fact, who once hid in the Wastelands but now are overrunning our borders."

"Joint discovery," Henderson interrupted, a touch officiously. "Doctor Goldbarth—"

"Ah yes. Thank you for reminding me. Your samples also infected a famous researcher, so you stole his brain right off the autopsy table. Then you set up a station to collect *more* samples." PJ raised his eyebrows high and grinned maniacally. "Because the directress of the program was busy composing an epic *poem*, celebrating famous martyrs and monsters and mental cases as beasts born from the stars. Not a scientific paper. Not an epidemiologist's certification. Not a simple memorandum to the authorities. Oh no. A *po-ehm*, to present the alleged greatest scientific discovery of the age."

There was a silence. Fitzgibbon's eyes had almost disappeared, were just detectable as a flicker from face to face.

"Song," Fanny said finally, soberly. "It's more of a song."

PJ laughed and did a little pirouette and bend. "Better. Still better. A boogie song, like the old rockenroll numbers. And this musical virus turns out to be a ribonucleic telegram from our primate past. A piece of pithicus gone astray and slumming with the chimps for a few million years, and from thence to the ginkoids of today, with a new wrinkle or two copped from insects and birds – if I follow this flapdoodle correctly – and thence, finally, to us."

His grin was fixed now, a carved demon's head. "Now one wonders. You've been out here a good while. So have some of these troops guarding the infected herds. I suppose you've been monitoring their health, no? I hear there's a problem with morale, short attention spans, disrespect, lot of impromptu parties and even some hanky-panky, eh? One wonders about autopsy records . . . " He cackled with delight, at what he saw in Henderson's face. "Oh boy. Withholding data, too. And on top of all that now comes our pair of fugitives and the fruit of their unholy union, our main symbol of the obscene and unnatural and perverse – not talking infection now, but deliberate fornication – mixing with a lower order, hurling *backward* into the bestial mire . . . whooo-eee!"

PJ was whipping back and forth now, lifting his feet as if from a too-hot floor. "Wow! That's what I *like*!"

"Feiffer, shut the fuck up." Fitzgibbon was red-faced, and his brow shone with a film of perspiration. "I need to talk to you."

Fanny had also risen to her feet, smiling. "Oh yeah, you got the beat, Pete. Fact is, you're now *responsible*, aren't you? You brought us this terrifying twosome – threesome – and posed as a team of government investigators; you've extorted money to support mad schemes; you've fooled with the forces of darkness – Feiffer the foul fiddler – and we're your helpless hostages!"

"Oh mama! Know what you mean, Darlene." PJ had bopped swiftly to one side, just in time to escape Fitzgibbon's wide, groping hand. "C'mon, you beasties and nuts!" He waved grandly at Tima and Pahane, then strode abruptly to the door, threw it open and shouted down the hallway. "C'mon hostages, shake them butts! Your host wants some *party*."

There was a murmur of voices, a hoot of laughter, and then a number of orderlies and lab assistants squeezed into the room. They were grinning widely, two young men were arm-in-arm, and some bore bottles clad in paper sacks. "Halleluja, do ya," one crooned. "Some funeral."

Hen had made his way to a small console against one wall and had already booted up the right disk, so the whang and thump that emerged on the audio system perfectly matched the undulations and pumps Fanny and PJ were directing at each other. This was old rockenroll, material forbidden to all but legitimate scholars, a moaning and panting of indulgence and excess. Bodies in the room began to move and twist, like trees taken suddenly by a long, driving wind from the sea.

Fitzgibbon's face was now a pinched and mottled lump, pink and white; one hand was thrust into his field jacket as he tried to glare into every corner of the room. Yet he somehow ignored Combe, who had come to his side looking wary and uncertain.

"Fitz," Combe whispered, as loud as he could in the din. "*Fitz*." But the big man's head kept swinging erratically, like a radar unit malfunctioning.

"What do we do, Fitz? Do we get in on this?" Combe's moustache twitched as he tried a one-sided grin.

Finally Fitzgibbon registered his bodyguard's presence. He glared at the other, his eyes opaque at first, then taking fire. "What?"

"This is kinda *strange*. But kinda *inneresting*."

Fitzgibbon reared, swayed back on his heels. "Don't stand so fuckin' *close* to me," he croaked. A guitar note bent, flexed, then knifed through the room at belt level. A long, happy sigh from the dancers followed, like a row of wheat mowed down. Fitzgibbon rocked back on the balls of his feet, his head tilting down until he stared at the floor. "And," he said, his voice rising to a bellow, "stop movin' your fuckin' *feet*!"

BOOK FIVE

CHAPTER THIRTY-EIGHT

They changed quickly, and the ancient Forager was waiting for them when they emerged from the gun room. The vehicle and the weapons were authentic history, as Barrelhead liked to say. The two-seater, open to the elements and without sound system or air conditioning, was noisy and rough-riding. To enjoy this experience fully, Homer took the long way around the island, passing Josh a leather-bound flask for a sip of warm cognac as they jounced along.

In the rack behind the back seat they had secured four weapons; two were old-fashioned cartridge-loaders of large caliber. He had a surprise, Homer confided, another situation that absolutely required this traditional gear. "Not an ordinary shoot," he yelled at Josh over the road noise. "One in a lifetime." He looked sly and utterly delighted. "Tell the grandchildren!"

The light rig pulling the supply trailer and the refrigerated unit bringing up the rear indicated that Homer wanted to preserve this specimen, whatever it was. That would mean an extra half-hour, at least. Josh maintained a smile and a wrinkled brow, to indicate both pleasure and curiosity, but he was actually fretting – stupidly, he realized – over Dorothy and Danielle. He imagined them in one room or another, lounging and playing, teasing each other. They were the kind who would interrupt their sighs and pants to murmur over strategy or giggle at their patron's pomposity. Or revel in their triumph, now almost complete.

That morning they had convinced Morphopolous to accept, as his own idea, their clever betrayal of the original script. The arming of the bloodthirsty faction of Ginks had set the stage for crisis; the principals were now gathered at the border research station; Beau Winger was already busy plunging hundreds of millions of citizens into a final convulsion of purgative xenophobia. They needed only a fillip, a last straw, a detonator.

That was to be PJ's role. The swashbuckler, the Robin Hood figure, the lovable outlaw they had carefully groomed was too dangerous. He had gained too much credibility for the ecorad position, had given the public an unhealthy taste for romantic adventure. They cheered when a newsholo showed him tossing an important executive into a pond by the seat of his pants, or when rumor hinted he was behind distributions of stolen pizza. A tolerant curiosity was developing toward both Thorgies and Omalys – the most dangerous trend of all.

So the new plan, what Josh privately called the python pussies' plan, was to flip PJ. Long John him. Strip away the romantic myth and reveal the monster beneath, the foul creep. With Winger's help, they were making him a mad cult leader, a psychopath and pervert who intended to offer up a pathetic freak in barbaric sacrifice.

Only that kind of reversal would justify and enhance the bold decisions they had designed for Adamson to take, in the first hours after his election sometime tomorrow afternoon. Generations ago the NorthAm constitution had been amended to transfer military authority immediately to a President-elect – two months before the inauguration. So as new Commander-in-Chief, Adamson could launch a top-secret rescue mission by a compact, élite force. Insec's finest strike team, supplemented by darkside freelancers and supported by Third Army armored units, was poised to assault the remote station, where – on cue – blood-crazed savages would besiege a band of suicidal ecofanatics. The firing of the obsolete short-range missile would supply immediate provocation. Nothing would emerge from the smoking rubble but the freak family, the sacred whelp delivered prematurely.

"Ever think of kids, Josh?" They had taken a fork in the road, away from the sea and toward the newly planted grassland. Josh looked startled, and Homer laughed and accelerated. "Whooo! Not yet, eh? Your age, I was the same, lad! So many lovely things, so little time . . . But now, when we're on the verge of making history, a guy begins to think—"

They were approaching a low knoll, and Josh recognized the site under construction on his last trip. A couple of skinny thorn trees had been planted on the knoll, and a thin cover of sawgrass was struggling for a foothold. One slope was sheared away, and here was a dark slot under the hill, a low cave. On the ground before the cave Josh saw a scatter of large bones white in the sun.

Barrelhead eased the Forager to a halt and switched off the engine, which gagged to death in the manner of the old internal combustion type. The other vehicles had pulled into a camouflaged parking port fifty meters behind them, and they heard the bearers get out, very quietly. A light breeze blew, making the grass tremble, and in the sky three vultures hung like broad, black blades on an empty blue wall.

"But now . . . ripeness is all." Homer winked at Josh and extended just the pale tip of his tongue. "Time comes for a man to think about passing on his heritage."

Josh nodded again. He was trying to control his breathing, do a very swift zazen routine to regain calm, purge his brain of the image of his two rivals writhing, whispering, devouring each other. And beneath this image was a deeper unease, the fallout from the first step in his own new plot. His private ten-minute conversation with Beau Winger. *A corpse and two cunts*? The Big Fat Man had laughed like a French Horn. *Come on, Sonny. Train's leavin'. Dump and jump.* "Time comes," Josh repeated lamely. What the hell was the old man driving at? Did he want Josh to make him a godfather?

"Tash and I," Homer prompted. He reached to the rack and removed one of the old rifles, gripped it in both hands and gave a slight, suggestive thrust.

"No!" Josh put a hand over his eyes, as if dazzled. "That's . . . that's great! That's *marvelous*!" He had almost said *incredible*. Homer had to be close to a hundred, could even be more.

Homer laughed gruffly. He did in fact look healthier, heftier than Josh remembered. No obvious seams, if there had been a recent tuck or pump.

"You wonder, you scamp! Couldn't be, you thought." Homer handed him the heavy rifle. "I'm like this old Kruger. Might grunt and make a lot of fire and smoke, but I get the job done."

Homer took down another rifle, this one with a curved clip and leather sling. From a metal box on the floorboard he removed two belts, one studded with bright, brass cartridges and the other bearing clips in sheaths. "Better get out before we load. These old guys have sensitive triggers."

Josh swung off the seat to the ground, still shaking his head and laughing. "Well, hell," he said finally. "So! Surprised me at first, but of course a moment's thought—"

"Not hard to figure, eh? You know your women. You see. That *resilience*, that *fire*. She's made me a young man again, Josh. A young *poet*, by Christ! She's elegance incarnated, mister, and at the same time . . . well, I won't go into it, but she knows every trick there is – intuitively – and she can give them all her own special twist. Here."

Josh accepted the cartridge belt and nodded when Homer lifted his eyebrows in an unspoken question. He recalled how to work the bolt, insert the bullets nose first in the breech, flip the mechanical steel safety. It was a marvel to him that men had once hunted and fought with these primitive, cumbersome instruments. "That's Tasha," he ventured.

"Yes indeed. We're like a couple of college kids. Horses of the night, holding off that old busy fool the sun, so on and so on . . . " Homer had detached, checked, and reinstalled the clip of his rifle, and now removed a cellphone from the pocket of his hunting coat. He switched it on. "Charles? Ready here." He listened for a half-minute, then frowned and clucked his tongue reprovingly. "Well, wake him up. Try sound, then the shock button if you have to." He set the phone on the fender and smiled ruefully at Josh. "Your old monarchs have their own chrono – I should know, hey? Anyway, not to mislead you, my boy, I of course had an implant charge from the cryo bank for the actual insemination. You never know, and I had a goodly store of prime, healthy gametes from, oh, years back, so why take chances? But everything else – her receptivity, the delivery, timing – bingo! Just perfect."

Barrelhead laughed expansively, with a kind of absolute heartiness, and Josh joined him. He was careful to look the old man in the eye, but respectfully. These were unusual confidences. Morph was in a rare mood. The result, Josh assumed, of nearing what would be the climax of their drama, a last act of bloody salvation, yet simultaneously the beginning of a new cycle, a fantastic birth which carried, in turn, a hidden curse from the past. They were going to give the world an exciting shape, a new narrative, for at least another generation. Their story would go on and on. Immortality, in short. Only the story wasn't going quite the way the old man thought.

The cellphone emitted a miniscule ping. "And now," Homer said, retrieving the phone, "we make an offering to my new son. We offer him the last of a noble, noble line." Abruptly somber, he looked significantly at the cave in the knoll and settled the rifle into the crook of his arm. "Yes, Charles?"

Get on with it, Josh was thinking, and in spite of himself he glimpsed again a few frames of the sneak holo in his brain. What the two women were doing disgusted him, yet he could not for a long moment turn off the switch. He looked away at the distant, blue water.

This area had been designed to make you forget you were on an island. He concentrated for a moment, trying to sense any slight movement beneath him. Nothing. The swells were not great today. Some time he would return to the lodge early, unexpectedly. Would surprise the girls. Teach them a thing or two. *Let me show you my little snake.*

"Was he fed yesterday? Phillips said he was responding, was on his feet . . . No, goddamn it, *today*. Prepare him an ampule. Wait two, three minutes, and then use the button. Get us two bearers up here." Homer snapped off the cellphone and grimaced in exasperation, before recovering his shrewd but tolerant expression. "Sorry. Bit of a delay. Old boy is taking his time. Well, he deserves it, I think."

When Josh smiled and shrugged uncertainly, Barrelhead laughed. "Come on. We'll stroll into position, and I'll tell you about Sun King." He nodded at the two men in camou jumpsuits and dark glasses, who were approaching at a soft, gliding trot. "Take those heavy strikers, fellas, and back us up. Stay on the flank, and stay ready."

The two men veered to the Forager and quickly lifted out the remaining weapons, which were phaser-compression jobs designed to stop personnel carriers. They came after the two hunters at a calculated distance, just out of range of any casual conversation.

"What would you say, Josh, if I told you there was one real lion left?"

They were walking at an angle to the knoll, so as to face the dark slot under it more directly. Josh considered a moment. "You can't mean a wild lion. The last were brought in, I believe, at the end of the last century. So, I suppose, speaking genetically—"

"I *do* mean a wild lion."

Josh frowned again and began dutifully, "But I thought . . . "

"An *Asian* lion. Little-known fact, Josh. A few were kept on a hunting preserve for some sheik or other, right up until the Last Wars." Homer stopped and turned to Josh, his face alight with anticipation. "Here is about right. Don't want to be nearer than forty meters. An adult male can cover that in a dozen bounds. Check your rifle."

Josh did some business with the bolt, peeked at the cartridge inside, and fingered his safety, but Homer shook his head. *Not yet.*

"The preserve was actually an oil field in what used to be called the Caucasus – where, you will remember, one of the last major actions took place, before the Fed. Neither side wanted to bomb that field, and during a long cease-fire and treaty negotiations it became a no man's land. A few of these lions hung on in there. Some local tribesmen knew, and would throw refuse over the fence now and then – sheep guts or the like – and take the occasional pelt;

but they were left alone until just a few years ago, when the field was opened up for waste injection, and the engineers sighted a lone male.

"The bio boys were sent in to tranq him. Old Sun King was unfit for any zoo, of course. Had his fangs and claws, and a temper to match, and couldn't get along with the domesticated. They studied him for a while, then got clearance to sell him to a wealthy collector, who liked to watch kills. The collector died and they were going to put him away when I found out—"

The cellphone again emitted a faint, muffled ping. Homer's mouth tightened and he rolled his eyes at Josh before jerking the phone once more from its pocket. He grunted a curt acknowledgment and then listened.

"All right. Whatever. But I want him *out here now*." Homer had turned a little, so Josh could no longer see all of his face. "I don't care. That's what I pay you for, isn't it? So do it, and don't call me again."

Even as the phone slid back into the coat, a utility runabout shot out of the parking port and ran swiftly to the mouth of the cave. Three men got out, dressed in padded jumpsuits, face masks and heavy gloves. They carried holdalls and a coil of light cable. Homer had turned back to Josh and taken his arm to resume their stroll, away from the sight of the men penetrating the cave.

"Stretch our legs just a bit more. Sorry about the damn delay. Our fella is well past his prime, and he doesn't travel well, but they're going to take care of it now. Beautiful day for a shoot."

"Yes. Nice breeze." Josh kept the pace carefully, held his gun with what he hoped would appear as natural confidence. He knew an intense urge to fidget, or guffaw, or deliver an oral imitation of a fart. The terror of riding this urge was exciting, somehow pleasant. He forced himself to think of a plausible question. "Will we have to figure that – the wind factor?"

Barrelhead laughed. "Oh no. Not at this distance. This is close-quarter work. You want to think only of a smooth swing, breathing out, putting the bead on his chest cavity, and a steady squeeze to get the shot off. Don't mind the smoke. Then just keep shooting, be methodical." The old man's grip tightened on Josh's arm. "You know, no one has had the chance to do this for maybe fifty years. With the old guns, in a setting like this."

Josh could hear the phlegm of powerful emotion in Homer's voice.

An experience almost too overwhelming for words. In a lightning glance, he saw that one of the men was operating the runabout's hydraulic winch, the cable running taut into the cave. "They would have given him the syringe, in a cage, and sliced him stem to stern for microanalysis." Homer spat to one side. "Without respect, without a sense of . . . of . . . " He looked intently at Josh.

"Denouement." Josh saw the word go in, drop out of sight. There was a ripple of recognition, but it did not expand into comprehension. Tasha and her fucking Intro to Drama. He wasn't absolutely sure himself. "Catharsis," he said, more emphatically.

"Ah. Exactly. *Exactly*." Homer stopped, drew back a fist, and administered a soft, old-comrade slug on Josh's shoulder. "You *see*."

Josh smiled, looked down, looked aside quickly and saw, in fact, the Sun King emerging, flat on his side, with an attendant fore and aft.

"So many don't, any more." Homer lifted his rifle, examined it with quiet admiration. "Respect for tradition. For the nobility of the great game animals, and those old timers who went for them with just a power-blast behind a lump of lead. On foot, just as we are now." He glanced swiftly over his shoulder, as if at a bright, oncoming light.

The three men working furiously, their holdalls agape. The head of the lion heaved up once and Josh heard a slight, hoarse cough. He saw a plastic bag and an immense, long needle glinted in the sun before sinking into the tawny hide. One man was assembling a frame of clear struts, from which swung a harness of some kind.

"The thing I can't stand," Homer said with a new, quiet virulence, "is this radical crap about *recovery* of the past – bringing back the big trees and creating habitat and – especially, of course, in terms of our project – breeding our own species down again to a more primitive form. You can't *relive* the past, you can't sacrifice the present to some ridiculous, fantastic dream. Crazy and dangerous as he may be, this man Winger is right about that. Ritual is all we've got. We'll never be *animals* again. Why, we–"

"*Sir*! Ready now!"

When they turned, the old lion had been slung in the harness, where he sagged to one side, the great head lolling back and forth, stringing drool. Whatever had gone through the needle made his flanks alternately hollow and inflate, producing a series of low, retching coughs. The attendants had withdrawn in the service runabout to one side, but they kept the motor running, their masks and gloves in hand.

"All right, Josh. We'll keep two or three steps apart. You're my guest, so the first shot—"

"Oh no, no, Homer! I don't have the experience. Please, you handle this one. I'll be first backup."

"Well, perhaps in this situation . . . But you take your bead at the same time. You can put your thumb on that safety now." Morphopolous called out without turning his head. "Ready, flankers?'

"Ready," the two behind them cried in unison.

"Very good. He sees us now. Now we move deliberately. This is a moment for us all, this is it, yes, yes . . . For you too, old fella. Look here now. Hey, King! Come on, old boy . . . "

Sun King had seemed to register their slow advance, but then lost interest. One back paw had scratched at the earth, skewed his body in the harness so that his glance rolled toward heaven. He heaved out another cough, this one deeper, and then all at once managed a mighty, groaning roar that made the air vibrate.

"Oh! All right!" Homer had jerked his rifle to his shoulder. He uttered a peculiar, soft, breathy laugh. At that instant Sun King's head drooped, his muzzle pointing almost straight down, and the big paws flexed once and then flopped loose. The lion's whole weight now settling into the harness, one of the rear struts collapsed and Sun King appeared to sit down abruptly, his hind legs splayed out like a child flat in a mud puddle.

"Sonofabitch. *Sonofabitch*!" Barrelhead jerked his rifle down again. The runabout was already skidding to a stop beside the lion, while two of the men were airborne out of it, bags in hand. Josh did not risk a direct look at Homer, but he muttered a supporting *Damn*!

They remained crouched, weapons gripped tightly at the ready, watching the men work to revive the lion and reinforce the strut. Josh managed to get in a look at the ocean around them, still calm and blue, and at the three vultures still hanging in the sky. Time seemed inoperative, meaningless. But then one of the men turned toward them, pulled away his helmet-mask, and shook his head.

Josh could not describe the sound Homer uttered, could not, for a long second, grasp the word that followed the sound, except to identify it as a question. When the bare-faced attendant groped a stethoscope from his bag, however, he understood.

"Pulse?"

The man snapped on the earpieces, rummaged with one hand beneath the shaggy mane. He listened, they all listened, and then the man cried out exultantly, nodded with all his vigor.

"*Back!*"

Homer was taking aim again. The men were scrambling, on all fours, to get behind the runabout or out of the line of fire. Sun King was still in his mud-puddle sprawl, his upper body held aloft by the harness. The head, however, had drooped so far Josh could not tell whether the eyes were open.

"*Shoot!*" Homer's voice sounded high and shrill as a bird cry. "*Shoot at will!*"

The explosions were not thunderous, a shock with an after-ring in the whole skull, as Josh expected. He was hardly conscious of them. He fired once, politely, then a second time with more attention. The lion was jiggling, flopping a little, but he could not tell if this was the impact of bullets or a muscular reflex. Homer fired bursts, then single shots, then more bursts, until there was only a clicking. He jettisoned the empty clip, inserted a fresh one from his belt, and went on firing.

Josh saw the puffs of dust from the animal's hide, then two red blossoms on its underbelly. The jaw was transformed, all at once, into a yawning mess laced with ivory splinters. He lowered his rifle, watching intently until Homer's weapon clicked again, and the second empty clip tumbled, smoking, to the earth.

The old man fumbled with another load, then hesitated. Josh realized he had been holding his breath. There seemed to be no sound. The seedheads of grass barely dipped in the breeze and one of the men had switched off the runabout's engine.

Homer slid the full clip into the breech, but did not raise the weapon to his shoulder. He uttered again his soft laugh, but it had shrunk now into something hidden and guarded. "Good. Good shooting. But stay alert, while we verify. Go ahead, boys."

They waited, while the two backup shooters approached the lion, probed it with their strikers and boots, and waved in the man with the stethoscope. Very quickly they got a thumb up, and three broad smiles. Homer had removed his flask from an inner pocket, and Josh noticed that the old man's hands were trembling slightly.

"A commemorative." Homer extended the flask. "Those who were there when the King went down." The voice was also a shade unsteady, and when he took the cognac Josh kept his eyes tactfully lowered.

"Long live the King," he said. In a corner of his field of vision he noted the refrigerated van had emerged from the camouflaged port and was now rocking sedately toward them. *King Beau. Beau-a-King-Stricter*. Hysteria throttled him and he pretended to gasp over the brandy.

"You see," Homer said, "I care about these things."

"Of course." Josh did his best to appear manly and cryptic, as if choked up himself. "Beautiful."

"If you consider the alternative."

"Yes. The alternative."

The refrigerated unit had arrived and its doors were open, releasing clouds of vapor. The attendants had disassembled the harness and stretched out the carcass, and were looking their way, waiting for some sign. Homer had the flask now and lifted it in salute. "End of an age," he said and drank in two quick swallows. When he lowered the flask he smacked his lips and blew. "Old as I am, this stuff."

"Excellent," Josh said. The sun on his neck was growing oppressive, and he shifted his feet.

"You want to look him over?" Homer capped the flask and stretched.

Josh thought a moment. "No. I'd rather . . . remember."

Barrelhead smiled and slipped the flask behind his coat lapel. "You're a gentleman, Josh. Old-fashioned. Just one reason I like you. And when these guys are finished . . . " He raised a hand and pointed one finger toward the open van, and the attendants sprang into action, rolling out the boom and hook. "The King will look just as he did today. Better, even."

"I believe it."

"And whenever you see him, this day will come back. And tomorrow we will have a new President. And a new Age. And a new World. Creation!"

"Creation," Josh agreed. *And how many serpents in the garden*?

"Well." Homer swung the rifle by its barrel across his shoulder. He had regained his jaunty, youthful manner; the color had come back to his cheeks, the glitter in his eyes. "What say? Back to visit the girls?" He twitched a wink at Josh.

"Back to the girls. Of course." Josh grinned through his clenched teeth. "Always."

CHAPTER THIRTY-NINE

> *All being birthed from a black hole,*
> *a rip of light and the dance begins!*
> *Twine, untwine, and twine again.*
> *Star. Surf. Thunder. Breath.*
> *A strike from the deep*
> *fashions our tongue,*
> *clapping shut the prison gate.*
> *Now must the dancer backward dream!*

Tiffany sighed and looked up from her notebook. The window sectioned out a strip of smudged silver on the eastern horizon. There had been no dewfall, and a low haze still hung over the station compound and the desert beyond. In his cage in a corner of the room, Buster emitted a gravelly whirr and fanned his wings; and from the interior of the building she could hear faint footsteps, the clang of a tray, the drone of a vacuum-sweeper. The orderlies were beginning morning rounds, Ruby would be along with tea in a few minutes, and her work on the new canto would have to end.

She clucked to herself in frustration and regret. It might be a while, perhaps a long while, before she could return to these lines, which she knew were not right. "Prison gate" was too obvious. She had wanted a subdued echo of Wordsworth and Blake, but her image yielded a clunk instead of the clang she was after. The slant rhymes were good, the association of lightning with speech was arresting, but the suggestion that words could blind and oppress was not subtle through.

It was an impossible task, writing a modern epic. No wonder so many of the Romantics unraveled. Sickness, Goethe had called it, and she was a literal proof. Yet she had never been happier than in these last days. Her malady was her ecstasy. She had glimpsed the outlines of creation, the twisting path of human destiny, and the omens of a remarkable fork in that path – omens that seemed to indicate that very soon she would see, right here, that serpent's tongue in time.

The details had fallen into a pattern so swiftly, so magically, that she had almost fainted with delight. At its grand level, the pattern was elegantly simple, established by the very first life-forms, bacteria and protists. She still liked the rude, reductive phrase she had scribbled soon after her epiphany: *a genome is only genius jerking off.*

Closing her notebook and slipping it into a drawer, she had to giggle. Perhaps investigators would find this distillation of her life's work and use it to diagnose her dementia. At best she could hope for incredulous laughter and frank dismay from a few of her more liberal colleagues. Such energy, they would say, wasted on so preposterous a theory. Yet she was telling them what seemed to her now only plain truths.

Most of the history of life on the planet consisted of a long dialogue between tiny packets of lively information, who learned from each other how to survive together. Not without cost, not without mistakes, but – considering the harsh conditions – very successfully. These bits of venturesome knowledge kept a coded record of their experiments and, even after combining into larger hierarchical units, they kept up their communication, exchanged tricks and solutions.

Onto recapping phylo was a sort of practice, a fast-forward of memory so one would never forget what one had been. The DNA of a living organism remembered every shuffle of itself back to the first, and as a kind of exercise ran through its own history *in utero*. It had also been known for generations that rare shifts in certain mistress genes – those that directed an embryo's development – could produce radical alterations in an individual – gifted monsters – and that these shifts could be the result of viral invasion.

Goldbarth had been first to grasp that one of these shifts was engendered by a remarkable retrovirus which affected the endocrine system by modifying cells of the pineal. Her own research led to the discovery of another shift, which altered the thalmus gland's coding of certain antibodies and left a carrier of the gene vulnerable to Goldbarth's retrovirus – now known as ShadoW-4, the waffle-cell bug, a flake of primate code as old as *Homo erectus*, harbored and transmitted by crow and flea as well. So they had between them identified this first primordial dis-ease of the rational mind: a predisposition to vision (hallucination, her critics would immediately charge) and sensitivity to rhythm, with occasional side-effects of hermaphroditism, unusual body hair, and a tendency to energetic play. But a list of symptoms conveyed very little of the range and power of this disorder.

Tiffany got up from her desk and moved to the window. The whole sky was now bright steel, and the haze that tarnished the horizon had thickened. The horses, she guessed. Or the six-leggeds, to be more precise. Klat and Yeklat and all their kin. A few months ago she would have thought such a tale a charming fantasy, a relic of mythology. It would have been impossible to believe that such beings had escaped scientific scrutiny.

But she had since learned a great deal about the shortcomings of scientific scrutiny. The two jetcopters she now descried on the horizon, no bigger than gnats, were probably cruising the canyon rims to verify this unusual concentration of ungulates. The bioteams would be puzzled and go over their data for the region to see what might explain the gathering. It would be unthinkable that the horses could have advance knowledge of an impending upheaval in human affairs. Silly to suggest that the last nomadic tribes of the steppes, the Turko-Mongolians who retreated with their herds into the most barren reaches of Asia, had not only survived but migrated to new continents, undetected. Preposterous to hint that these Khirgiz and Baktiari and Bashkir learned to decipher the signs of birds and insects, and to transmit through them prophecies from the blood of holy seers. Behind her she heard Ruby enter the room, and after a clink and rattle she smelled the sweet, rank steam from the pouring tea. She would need at least two cups, and a few minutes more to prepare. She *was* the Director, after all. She would have to comfort her staff when they saw Kapu's prophecies realized, when Evil burrowed out of the earth, and angels rode forth on a cloud, and the holy child vanished in fire.

"Burning the Muse at both ends," Ruby observed with a glance at her desk. "You ought to go to bed for a couple hours. How did it go?"

"Not so good." Tiffany took the cup Ruby handed her and returned to the window. "Did you make up the food caches?"

"Done. All dehydrated, plenty of bottled water, and med kits. How soon do you expect this siege to begin? Should we vote early?"

"Good God." Tiffany set her tea down hastily on the window sill. "Good God, it's today, isn't it?"

Ruby laughed, watched Tiffany's face, then laughed even harder. "Democracy in action. That's right, boss. It's Tuesday and by noon we'll probably have a new Prez. You look like you're not ready."

Tiffany blinked rapidly and shook her head. "I guess I'm not."

"Who is? Except our charges out there, the naked and starving." Ruby glanced toward the window. "They've got a nice counterpoint going today."

Tiffany listened for a moment or two. The Pobla singing had become so familiar she often failed to notice it consciously, but this morning there was a definite lift and drive to the chant. "Some newcomers?"

"A bunch. They seem to be real happy. Like they were expecting something." Ruby snapped her fingers along with the beat. "As we all are, right? Even our dear friend, the Big Fat Ass."

Tiffany had recovered her cup and taken a contemplative sip. She heard the unease lurking behind Ruby's brazen manner, and shared it. In the beginning they had laughed at the Winger yakshow two nights ago. They saw clips, heard the list of crimes. Drug traders, pornographers, child abusers, extortionists and ghouls. But their laughter soon grew outraged and then ceased. They saw the ludicrous distortions, the misleading images – but would the billions of Beau's viewers?

"What do the networks say?"

Ruby looked away, and Tiffany caught something like alarm in her expression. "You should see for yourself. We've been watching in the rec lounge. Some of the pundits are buying it, unbelievable as that seems. So there's an all-out, around-the-clock hunt for our little charges. You'd think Tima was going to give birth to the Prince of Darkness."

Tiffany did not reply right away. She drank more tea and watched a gathering of Pobla she could see through the window; the whole dark mass swayed a little like an anemone in the tide. She noted again the plumes of dust on the horizon and the jetcopters – six of them now – skimming the ridgetops. Election day. A day of choices, supposedly.

She moved to her desk and switched on the console for the station's intercom system. Two buttons patched in the large outdoor speakers that carried sound over the station compound and even

400

to the Pobla shelters on the surrounding plain. For a few moments longer she listened to the chant outside, then she punched up and cued her selections, opened the all-points line and began to speak.

"Yanaku, tchatsinakun! Vasan ito wonakubi. And Hi to you, too, friends and staff. This is Doctor Fanny. We've got a busy and probably stressful day before us, with some unusual precautions to take, so I'm not gonna chat along with you today, but dive right into business. First, we may have some unexpected visitors, so I want you all to be alert and ready, and don't stray too far from an intercom. Also, don't turn on any oxygen unless absolutely necessary, and keep doors shut unless they're in heavy use. Next, the weather's been wonderfully warm these last days, so I urge you to wear as little as possible. Shoes if you're around glass, and a little something for modesty's sake – for the modest among you – but nothing superfluous. Those of you in security who were issued those silly handweapons after General White's last visit, I suppose you have to strap them on, but please keep them securely locked and on safety, and don't activate for *any reason.* Finally, a number of you are already in the lounge, so just stay there and I'll be along. We'll have a short general meeting to run over a couple of options for the rest of the day. Meantime, I love you all. We'll just stay in the groove and do the job . . . "

Her last words were submerged in another of the old, forbidden songs she played for the refugees. She tried always to match the beat of their chants, and it pleased her that this selection (*Early Soul III*) seemed to fit perfectly. It was only 6a.m., but she set the volume at near maximum. That way, when Major Covington complained, she could reduce it a notch or two and appear reasonable.

"Visitors? And what's this, we're a nudist colony?" Ruby's look was now frankly forlorn. "Oh my."

Tiffany gave a deprecatory, reassuring wave before she picked up her private line, which now showed a stack of three calls, one an override that had to be from Randy. Ruby lifted away the tea set and moved to the door. On her way she whispered an ironic reminder to her boss: *vote early.* Just as she closed the door, she heard Buster chortle and flap his wings.

It was indeed Randy. He spoke in a tone Tiffany had never heard before, but recognized instantly as "combat readiness." He was telling her to make some of the very preparations she had just made, and a couple of interesting new ones. She was to gather "important personnel" and stay near the tissue locker, which was fire-proofed and had its own independent air and power supply. She was also to encrypt and seal all important files, according to instructions that were already cued and waiting in the second call on her stack.

She did not interrupt, but listened carefully to what she heard buried deep in this new tone. It was anguish, and uncertainty, and a heavy, dumb rage that grew – she felt intuitively – out of what could fairly be called love.

"It's an exercise. The highest pri, next to rehearsal. But I am not enlightened as to the scope of the operation. My units are deploying as back-up and containment on the eastern perimeter. We are supposed to be protecting you and your Poblers."

"Oh," Tiffany said. "From Sayat and the bad ones?"

There was a slight pause. "From whatever."

She thought she heard a tiny emphasis on *supposed*. For the first time she felt a thrill of alarm. If Randy, as a Base and Regional Commander, did not know the scope of the action, then it was no ordinary exercise – was probably not an exercise at all. "Some new friends helping you out?" she asked in what she hoped was an offhand way. "In the west, I mean?"

Again a pause. She guessed that Randy feared the call was monitored, and that would mean a higher level of intelligence was involved. Something beyond the military's self-surveillance arm. Probably Insec.

"We have a new unit in the field."

"That's good." She laughed, a cheery chirping that Buster punctuated with a squawk. "You hear? He wants breakfast. Big guys, are they?"

"Our force is sufficient." The general seemed defensive, yet his tone was singularly unemphatic. "Able-bodied. Prepared. As you have to be these days, Doctor Orr. For *anything*."

"So true! Goodness! What we've been hearing." She thought again, fleetingly, of Beau Winger's tirade. And now a special unit. A high-level, darkside maneuver whose purpose not even the general knew. He would of course suspect that she did know, but he could not ask. Not only because the line might be monitored, but because of his hurt pride. There was a deep ache in her heart, a powerful urge to blurt out the enormities she had kept from him.

She laughed, unsteadily. "Well, *I'm* ready for anything. And I . . . I can't thank you enough, General White. We'll certainly carry out the preparations. I know these exercises are not just for fun, though you don't actually shoot at anything?"

"There are some . . . " For the first time the general's voice wavered, almost broke, and became a cough. "Sorry. There are some simulated targets. Always a very slight risk. That's why these procedures are not *just* practice. Please observe them, to the letter. We will maintain an open, secure line; if we issue any further orders, please follow them also to the letter. I'll be here to the east . . . "

"It's my favorite direction, General. I happen to be looking out that way just now. I see the sun is popping up." She knew her own voice was bumpy, but she went on anyway, digging at her eyes with the heel of one hand, before she waggled it at the square of landscape before her, now gold and red with light. "I'm going to wave. I'm waving now. I'm waving at you, Randy!"

The bark he gave was meant to sound like a gruff laugh of dismissal, but she heard only the pain in it. No doubt he had requested permission to send a cover force to move her and the staff from the area, and been denied. He would realize she might be in great danger, and find himself quite ignorant of its origin and powerless to intercept it.

"Yes, yes, well . . . " The line was briefly empty except for the hiss of static. "Please be careful. I . . . I salute you." She compressed her lips to keep back a sob of laughter – there had been a joke – at their last meeting, their fabulous union – about his little salutes – and listened dumbly to the static until the line went dead. He might forgive her everything but her silence, for not at least hinting to him the reason for the trap closing swiftly now on all of them. Very soon there would be revelations scandalous enough to shake whatever faith he had in her. He would perhaps think she had seduced him, teased him into a tentative, painful commitment of the heart, in a calculated move to protect a gang of criminals. Or a sinister, fanatic cult. It appeared they were already acquiring a new identity.

Tiffany ignored the tiny, angry red eyes that signaled her remaining calls and used a corner of her lab coat to blot the tears from her cheeks. Then she removed the coat, jerking her arms violently through the sleeves. A curl had been dislodged to dangle on her brow, and she extended her lower lip and blew upward explosively to tumble it back into place. The next moment she took a deep breath, kicked off her low shoes, unsnapped the waistband of her slacks, and let them drop. With a couple of pulls to stretch it, her T-shirt reached just far enough to cover the shadowy triangle showing through her panties.

She giggled again, a frill of hysteria in the sound. Was she modest? She could not explain just why she had advised her staff to shed unnecessary clothing. Combat readiness, as she saw it. Uniforms and lab coats would only draw attention and impede action. What action? She did not know, exactly. Some movement, Kapu had predicted, from the very earth. And he had told her often that piksis were wrong to keep so much – clothes, vehicles, buildings – between themselves and the earth. She flexed, glided, undulated into the hallway. Things were reversing. Day broke and shadows advanced. The sun rose, and clothes were thrown off. She was dreaming backwards.

She smiled happily at the stunned orderlies who drew aside as she made her way toward the rec lounge. Some, she noticed, beamed back, and a few had even stripped as far as she had, to shorts or slips.

"Emergency?" one young man wondered, puzzled and intrigued, as she passed.

"Just emergence!" she called back to him.

The rec lounge was jammed with bodies, seated and standing, all engrossed in the newsholo which was going full volume to override the rockenroll blaring over the speakers. The few who glanced at her seemed dazed, did not even notice the mighty pillars of her bare legs. Ruby gave her a wan, desperate smile. No one was talking, and Tiffany had the odd impression they were breathing in unison, and shallowly.

In the box a topo shot from a satellite is tilting slowly, and a small, glowing comet moves deeper into the scene, on a path to intersect a cluster of specks on a ridge. A woman's voice is speaking rapidly, with a carefully modulated lilt of concern.

" . . . obsolete but operable warhead. The simu target in this excerpt represents an armored company, at a range of about five hundred kilometers, which authorities say is standard for the outlaw K-13 now in the hands of the Pobla warlord . . . "

The comet diminishes, falling more rapidly toward the specks, and all at once a bloom of brightness erupts, grows swiftly into a great flower filling almost the whole box, before it dissolves and another scene emerges, this one a scorched field where a few heaps of twisted metal are still smoking.

"The missile is dangerous, military experts say, because it is an old-fashioned 'stupid' bomb – indiscriminately destructive conventional explosives, guided by a simple, irreversible system. Now Mike Thomas is with us from NorthAm Border Command, where he has been talking to Insec's chief, Sam Yamaguchi, about this new danger. Mike?"

Tiffany hears a raucous hoot of laughter from PJ, across the room, as a middle-aged man wearing a slight frown replaces the smouldering wrecks. He speaks in a measured, yet rapid baritone. "Thanks, Donna. As you heard moments ago, investigators have now traced the group to an industrial ruburb. A freelance magrig leased by Mama's MiniZoos, a small firm supplying rare pets to wealthy collectors, was apparently hijacked there and used to transport Feiffer and his gang. It is believed Feiffer, a former agent under Director Yamaguchi's predecessor, Charlie Fat, used his knowledge of Insec codes and procedures to engineer the heist.

"Suspicion now centers on a remote and desolate area of the Wastelands, since the magrig entered and exited a checkpoint there, and was later found abandoned only two hundred kilometers further along the Pasodiego Trunkway. An intensive air search is under way, but the terrain is a rugged canyonland, offering plenty of cover, and Feiffer, of course, honed his survival skills as a hunter-killer Insec Special Agent. The search is also tremendously complicated by two factors, which we want to discuss with Director Yamaguchi. Sir, we understand this area is one of the regions frequently raided by the warlord Sayat?"

The holocorder has pulled back to reveal a Pacrim man in a dark suit. His narrow face is impassive, his smile only a carving. He lifts one hand to make a simple, horizontal gesture of underlining. "Yes. He is probably there now."

"Actually *there now*! And now much more heavily armed, right?" Mike's features contract with concern. "Do you think the K-13 is actually—"

"Yes. Probably near. That is our first complication. We cannot make any assault until we are sure we do not detonate. For this reason all regular forces in the area will stay in place or secure the perimeter only. General Randolph White has responsibility, and we work together."

"But there are already many Pobla in camps in General White's area, aren't there? And these are Sayat's sworn enemies, who believe the unborn hybrid allegedly fathered by Ronald Drager is some kind of messiah? So don't we have here, sir, actually, a kind of religious war?"

Yamaguchi's eyes glitter with an emotion – perhaps interest, perhaps contempt. "Precisely. That is the second very serious complication. If Sayat knows or learns the whereabouts of this messiah, so-called, he will attack, go on a killing spree. Very, very delicate situation."

"Indeed, indeed, sir. We see what you mean, and we certainly understand the intensive, all-out search for the fugitive gang. Or cult, as some now say. Do you have any reaction, sir, to the charges linking this group to a bizarre new sect – Church of the Holistic Covenant – which preaches the virtue of viruses and endorses sex with animals and deals in narcotics and pornography? Or to the accusation – we must play hardball here, sir – that high officials of the Stockwell Administration tolerated or even *orchestrated* the abduction of the disturbed Drager boy, and the pregnant Pobla female Duskyrose – trained as an Insec experiment, we remind you—"

"I am appointed by the Federation, Mr Thomas, and cannot comment on the NorthAm government's policies." Yamaguchi's stare is unblinking, lizard-like. "We all know this is a time of political sabotage and smear propaganda to influence an election. There are many charges pro and con. I have no role in this process, unless there is an investigation ongoing, and I do not comment on active investigations. I am surprised at this question."

"Well, Director, I had to *try*." Mike grins wide, chuckles in sly apology.

Without warning, another smile appears and then vanishes from Yamaguchi's face, swift as the flash of sunlight reflected from a speeding vehicle. "I am not saying there is an investigation. Or not an investigation."

"Let's take a different tack on this next rumor – the rumor that your élite Omega Force has been activated. *If* Sayat struck against a relocation camp or research facility – and we understand one such facility was established recently across the border – or *if* a band of fanatics tried to make a suicide stand, *would* you activate the Omega squad?"

This time Yamaguchi does not smile. His voice has a darker color of ambiguity. "I do not comment on hypothetical questions. I can say only that Omega is designed for crisis. Very swift intervention, decisive outcome, minimum casualties."

Tiffany has become aware of a new sound, a heavy vibration under the pulse of music outside. Jetcopters are coming in low and not very fast. People are also beginning to talk in low, urgent tones; many are looking her way, and have registered the fact that she wears very little. Still, she is sweating, for it has become uncomfortably warm and the air in the room is stale. A hint of dust is getting through the filters.

"I think we understand you, Director. And your candor is appreciated. We'll take that as a statement of the possible – and let it go. We'll hear more on these matters when we switch back to Donna, who is going to get reactions from both the Stockwell and Adamson campaign teams and also bring us up to date on the election results. We thank you, Director Yamaguchi, for being with us, and I must say you live up to your nickname, sir! Mike Thomas, folks, here with Insec chief . . . Sam Yam the Clam! Back to you, Donna."

"Thank you, Mike. The election is indeed complicating – and intensifying – what some are already calling a unique crisis in NorthAm history, the result of an amazing convergence of events. From the beginning this campaign has been waged over a single bitterly contested ideological issue: what some have called genetic insulation. But the candidates must now face this issue in the form of concrete dilemmas. What to do about the flood of disabled and diseased Pobla refugees at the border? And even more crucial, what to do about this potential saplap 'messiah', now in the hands of a fundie cult of ecoterrorists led by a former Insec agent and apparently holed up somewhere over that border?

"As the two candidates campaign down to the wire, they must also have in place a strategy to deal with new threats. A vengeful faction of refugees under a bloodthirsty warlord has obtained highly destructive weaponry, and is right now lurking in the region. As soon as a winner is virtual – compuconfirmation coming usually at around fifteen percent – that candidate is automatically the Commander-in-Chief Designate and may have to mobilize and strike instantly.

"On top of all this, only days ago charismatic yakshow power

Beau Winger launched a third-party 'symbolic' candidate. That candidate was Frank Drager, the father of Ronnie, a scarfaced symbol of hard-line 'extermigink' border policies. Winger has already shaken NorthAm society with his charges of a conspiracy of clandestine ecorads in the Conservative Party – a conspiracy aimed, he says, at advancing the fortunes of 'mixeds' and debasing humanity.

"Experts believe the independent punch-in vote will doom Stockwell's hopes of re-election, and press Adamson into a much tougher stance on genographic control – at home, a massive cleanup of Omalytown, with enforced geneprinting; and beyond the border, tight quarantine of all Pobla into cross-border camps, and selective breeding for productivity. Both Winger and Drager have, however, renounced extermination as economically infeasible; and in a few hours, at a mass rally in Capitol Park, the Big Fat Guy has promised to reveal a dramatic new plan, comprehensive but compassionate, for 'recovering the national soul'.

"So the stage is set for the most edge-of-your-seat election, the most hell-for-leather first day in office, the most pull-out-all-the-stops, make-or-break bold political gamble, in the nation's history. An unbelievably exciting show, and it will all be coming at you live, here on NHC . . . "

Donna Bradley's head has turned slightly on its smooth, muscular neck, so that an earring flashes against her thick, auburn hair. She reads rapidly, silently, for a second or two and then resumes speaking in a breathy, hectic voice.

"Here's a new development! A stunning revelation . . . a possible pinpointing, just in! Our investigative team believes Insec may have traced the fugitives to that same remote border research facility mentioned just a few moments ago! Insec spokespersons have admitted to 'contact' but will not specify whether the cult has outlined specific demands. We do know that transport personnel at the Omega base are now on alert."

A new montage: a black magrig rolling into a dock, where a row of cages shows monkeys, parrots, a crocodile, a bear waiting to be loaded; an aerial view of a small island in an expanse of sea; and finally, another aerial view: a huddle of buildings isolated on a vast plain, barren and ravined, where great clouds of dust are beginning to boil.

Donna's voice is now a continuous, headlong torrent. "We've

put together this scenario, following leads from several sources. A special biotransport rig like the one shown here was intercepted returning from a delivery to the exclusive island estate of trillionaire Homer ("Barrelhead") Morphopolous. This hijacking, we now suspect, was the work of Thorgie radicals assisted by the reclusive tycoon's ex-wife Eva, known as the 'Sewer Queen', and supervised by the outlaw agent Feiffer.

"Sealed biocargos, immune from inspection, regularly enter or leave stations like this one in chartered magrigs. Feiffer's gang, using his knowledge of Insec methods, may have smuggled itself into the research lab in order to negotiate a new set of demands. The lab's eccentric director is Doctor Tiffany . . . "

The voices in the room were now much louder; a hubbub and a scuffle of some sort had broken out. Tiffany could hear Fitzgibbon's hoarse, enraged bellow.

"Demands? *What* fucking demands? What the fuck is—"

The huddle of buildings in the desert seemed nearer now, as the newscopter dipped lower. There were parked vehicles, fences, a crowd of milling figures outside the main compound.

"Hey, that's *us*," someone called, with a whoop of startled delight. "Hey Vern, that's *us*!"

"General White, field commander in the region, disavows any knowledge of irregularity of procedure. But all holo and audio contact with the station has apparently been severed, except for lines to Insec negotiators . . . "

"Vern, go outside and wave something, wave your shirt!"

Tiffany was making way toward the door that led outside to the compound, glad for her bulk and the respect those in her path showed for partial nakedness. She heard several people calling her name, calling for Doctor Fanny to speak. She heard the fright and bewilderment, and also the thrill of excitement, of anticipation. She felt these things herself, and they merged with the driving beat of the music and the Pobla chanting – both louder now because doors were opening and a current of air moved into the room.

"Cut off? My God, are we cut off? Doctor Fanny, what—"

"We're giving ourselves up!" Tiffany cried, as she reached the doorway. She spread her arms to grip the jamb and pull herself up on tip toe. "Strip down, before they ask you. We're

409

going into the main compound, we're going with heads high, we have nothing to hide . . . "

She was raking the crowd with her eyes, looking for Tima and Ronnie, who would know what to do, and for Marvelous and Cynthia. She could see Fitzgibbon gripping PJ by his shirtfront, their faces barely a handsbreadth apart. As she watched, PJ, without losing his broad grin, lifted a knee smartly and the big man hunched, folded over with a low, resonant sound that reminded her of a cow. A window shattered then in a bright, musical cascade, and when she looked that way, Hen was already setting the chair back down carefully and Marvelous – bare to the chest – was helping Tima through the opening. Beside them, Cynthia was just stepping out of her dress.

A faint cry came from outside. "I'm waving! I'm waving my shirt, right next to the parking lot! See anything?"

There was a hiss and spat. A weapon had apparently been discharged into the ceiling, for a sprinkle of grains and fibers trickled down from overhead. "Nobody move!" someone shouted.

Beside her now was the agent Combe, fully dressed and holding a handweapon tight to his chest. His eyes were wide and his mouth open slightly in wonder. "This is weird," he said to Tiffany, "What are we thinking, here? Stay low, don't move, keep—"

"Take off your clothes," Tiffany said with cheery firmness, as to a child. "Quickly."

"See anything?"

"There's a delay, Vern. It ain't *live* live, you dumb – hey, there you are! Come back, man, see yourself waving!"

Combe was reaching for her wrist, and his expression had become a regretful frown. She stopped him with a look, then tipped her head to draw his attention to Cynthia, who was approaching the doorway, wearing nothing except her light half-bra. She had to yell with all her strength then, to carry above the whine of copters, the boom of music, and the grunts and cries of those milling about in the room.

"Strip down and come out *dancing*! No weapons but the boogie! Show yourselves free! You are *beasts from the stars*, so spin and shine! Come on everybody, *right now*! We got dancin' in the street and in the sky . . . "

Combe was transfixed and did not see Tiffany any more, as she stepped through the door, twisted out of her T-shirt and bra, dropped her panties and let the sound take her body. They moved naturally into a loose circle, Tima with her swollen belly in its center, and the circle moved into the open compound. There a hole had opened into the earth, and some who had spilled out of the room were now shrieking and trying to run back in, for dark figures swarmed from this hole like ants, loose dirt pouring from their backs.

Tiffany opened her throat and let the wind howl, wove her arms in the undulating veils of dust, shook her heavy breasts at the approaching raiders. They, too, spun and sprang to the pulse of Early Soul, and the chanting from the Pobla outside the fence. At first Tiffany thought they all bore weapons, but when they were only a few steps away she could see that most carried drums, which they hammered in a blur of blows. They were thin, but not like the Pobla she knew. These drummers were like braided leather, tough and pliant, and their eyes were a black that blazed.

Two, three, half a dozen of them surrounded her; one raider held a weapon like a live thing in his two hands, menaced her with it. She gathered herself and, on the balls of her feet, pumped her hips at him, a slow corkscrewing of buttocks – great, supple knots of muscle moving like snakes under a firm sheath of fat. He showed her a mouthful of white teeth, did a backflip, and when he alighted discharged the weapon. The streak of light was so close she heard the air sizzle, smelled the ozone. She wheeled and gave him an obscene, insulting waggle of her bottom. Their circle had opened to receive the rush, and she saw that Ronnie – no, Pahane – was beside Tima now, the two of them surrounded by a turbulence of gyrating, jerking bodies. More streaks of light were unleashed, crossing in the sky above. The air was growing dark and murky, though Tiffany was aware of a peculiar luminosity at the tumultuous heart of this collision, a kind of underwater glow.

They were chanting, a deep moan, though she could understand only the long o-o-o and u-u-u sounds of *wonakubi* and *mahanaku*, the whiplash of consonants in *Tagak*! *Tak tagak*! But then came a still deeper sound, a thunder, and from the hole in the earth, widened now into a kind of crater, rose a shining metal spear. It swayed drunkenly, nodded, and trundled finally out of the hole, dragged and pushed along by many hands. Someone was perched on this spear and now swung down, glints of light flashing from ornaments about his neck and arms. Immediately a long avenue opened through the mass of moving bodies, leading from this newcomer and his bright spear to Tima and Pahane.

Tiffany recognized finally the new thunder moving beneath the music. The drums and voices of the raiders, even the bright bolts crossing overhead, were concentrating on a single word, the hammer-blows of two syllables: *Sayat! Sayat! Sayat!*

CHAPTER FORTY

"In about ten minutes," Josh said with slow, deliberate emphasis, "you're going to be the Commander-in-Chief."

He watched Adamson's eyes, clear portholes into a furnace of ego. "Ten minutes," he repeated.

"Certainly." Adamson delivered his quick grin of confidence and made a gesture with a lightly closed fist. "So we'll be responding firmly, but with due caution, to this developing situation." His look went past Josh to roam swiftly from the verandah into the main room of the hotel suite. There aides and team members huddled around holo sets or at tables jammed with computers and phones, producing a babble of excited voices, both actual and electronic.

"That's right. Good. Although we can maybe kill caution at this phase. Check with the Tank. You'll leave right after the compucon is in, mainteamers and secret service only. Reporters ready to ambush on the exit, so the wave and crisis smile – you know the number – but field just the one question from Lynne Graves. She'll set up the responding firmly line. One smooth take."

"Absolutely." Adamson flexed his shoulders. "Pause and deliver. Presidential."

"Exactly. Then it's straight to ConRes. SamYam will meet you there. The team's got the Contingent Executive Orders. All you have to do is sign, then relax for an hour or so. At that point you'll be the Virtual President Elect, and the rescue op will be under way, so Tank will hone you for the first press conference. Okay, Bob?"

The Commander-in-Chief's attention was again straying, lured by a small outburst of cheers from one of the holo groups. "I'm going to take all the Basin States," Adamson said, pulling an imaginary blanket tight to his chest, "and most of the Borders. Even the employees at the Wilderness Theme Park endorsed us."

"That's super," Josh said, not bothering to hide his sarcasm, since Adamson would, and did, miss it. "But Bob, details don't matter here.

You're in. So as you say, *presidential* now, all the way. That's the keynote."

He had guessed Adamson was looking for a particular young assistant of the Tank's, a morsel who managed to blend a shy, breathy demeanor with a subtle suggestion of depravity. Adamson had simple, adolescent motives for seeking power, which made him easy to calculate, but sometimes difficult to manage. Today, for his own reasons, Josh found his candidate's appetites distasteful.

"Bob, you gotta job – to get in shape for that press conference. There will be casualties in this operation, maybe quite a few. Of course you had to act, had to wayne it, but you recognize the tragic dimension."

"Absolutely." Adamson looked grave, the smile gone as swiftly as a label peeled away. "A terrible tragedy."

"We have to stress the baby, the compassion theme. It's likely to be a preemie and a freak and born under an evil star, yet your intervention will save its life. You respect life."

"Life is sacred," Adamson said, jaw firming up as he recalled a climactic line, "when it has a *purpose*." He had memorized several such lines, in case his audio prompter failed for any reason.

"Exactly. You're homeworking, that's good."

"He's a fucking natural, the most natural at this gig I've ever seen."

For a very wide man, the Tank could move with remarkable stealth. He was into the room, almost beside Adamson and already speaking in a normal, conversational tone, before Josh even registered his presence. "Maybe the best since the Old Ray Gun, the original honcho. They say he never, ever, forgot a line, and this was fucking way, way before in-ear prompters. But our kid's got the mojo now, gonna turn the whole thing around for us, huh baby?"

The Tank dug a soft right hook into Adamson's ribs, and the Almost President responded with a gentle left jab and a renewed boyish grin. "Just figure out what's right," he said, winking, "and do it with all your might."

"You got it. On the fucking money, honey. Listen, Mister President, keep that edge. We wanna run one last, quick rehearsal for the Joint Chiefs' gig." The Tank was tracing his thick fingers along the lapel of Adamson's suit, straightening, picking off an invisible bit of lint. "Admiral Bowers is here to play Chair, got a mockup of the conference room in the Bluebird Wing, all set to go. Okay? Anything else, guys? You covered the exit scene, right?"

"Not sure about the caution tilt. Could go with appropriate or measured." Josh frowned. "Still no blow, so nothing to spin. Makes it hard."

"Kill the fucking caution. To the winds, men, at this point. It's wayne or wimp from here on. Okay?" The Tank lifted Adamson's lapel with finger and thumb, tugged lightly. "Firm response, decisive action, all options. You have made your position clear and no further comment. Okay?"

"Got it."

"Terrific. You're the guy and the whole fucking deck is yours. All you gotta do is wait 'til everybody is looking and then turn the cards. Now Josh and I need to fine-tune a little here, while you hustle on to the Bluebird. But you check with us before you ride out, okay?"

"Okay, coach." As he glided away toward the main suite, Adamson made a silent *wow*! face at them and enacted with his fists a small, comic parody of driving wheels.

The Tank exhaled and rolled his eyes back up into his head.

"My God, Rogers, what is this thing you have made?"

"A President. Count the rivets." Halley Rogers returned his eyes to their normal half-shut condition, the look of a crocodile pretending to doze. "But where's the fucking incident, Josh? Come on, we're confirmed any minute now. Lights, camera, roll it, baby. We gotta have a *crisis*."

Josh could not help himself, and looked at his chrono. "What can I say? Look, *something* is coming down, we all know that, but we're dealing with Ginks. Timing is going to be approximate."

"The Wing is already pumping them, man. Every holofeeb on the planet is tuned. House is sold out." The Tank inhaled through clenched teeth. "And our puppy knows his part *now*, Josh but we can't confuse him with some weird backspin. He'd lift his leg to piss and then forget it was up there." Rogers uttered a single, abrupt grunt of laughter. "My life's work."

"Relax. Any minute." Josh tried a wry, comradely smile, but he was himself cold and tense to the core. Halley Rogers was one of the most intuitively brilliant political handlers in the nation; Halley Rogers had been through a dozen major campaigns, all but two of which he won; and Halley Rogers was counting on him for perfect, darkside micromanagement.

And he in turn was counting on the cobras, on Dorothy's contacts with both insiders and free-lancers, and on Yamaguchi. Everything was supposed to be in place, with double coverage. Sam Yam's Omega force was poised to swoop, whenever Sayat's marauders made their assault, which would be right after the K-13 shot, a harmless poke at White's refugee camp. In any case the Ginks were pledged to take the couple alive, or at least the bitch. Until they could cut out her seed. This last wrinkle was their secret surprise script: to emerge from the smoking ruin of the research station with a small, bloody bundle – a living symbol, the sinister fruit of a perverted union, a mysterious and dangerous challenge accepted with brave compassion by a new President. Morphopolous would have to buy it; there would be no choice.

Who would not remain, Josh reflected with a certain bitter glee, a President for very long. The opportunities opened up by the alliance with Winger and the elder Drager were too rich, too compelling. His nervous system began to hum at the mere thought. When he had met the Big Fat Guy at their secret showdown and shootout, Josh knew within minutes that he had finally met a match for Dear Dorothy. Beau was inexorable, irresistible. *"Bend over, Joshua,"* were his first words. *"You gonna love it."*

And he did love it, as a matter of fact. The third-party gambit ensured Adamson's election, but also, as Winger explained with obscene glee, doomed him to a single term. The juice, the mojo, the roll was going to be with Winger-Drager. Or, the Big Guy hinted brazenly, with Winger-Drager-Somebody. Somebody with clout and ideas and guts. Somebody on the inside, with a *record*.

It didn't have to be spelled out. If he brought in the Adamson convoy with style and grace, it could be Winger-Drager-Tremain. He would be perfectly positioned. An inside Adamson mastermind, he could betray in the subtlest of ways. He could service Barrelhead and the cobras in ways they had not foreseen. *He* would script the future. *He* would dream Fate into being. Beau would be impresario, and Drager the great and tragic star.

A beautiful story. Old Scarface, a grandfather caring for a half-human, orphan bastard who represented everything he hated and reviled. The Exterminator, devoting himself to yoking a lesser race to a new economic miracle, and reclaiming the Wasteland for humanity. His campaign, and then his staff, would be run by the world's hottest mouth, ringmaster of a great yakshow revival circus, purifier of genetic stock and regenerator of civilization's upward drive – an expiation of the dark curse of an animal past. It was, as that bubblehead Tasha said, positively Ancient Greek, and would make a maxiseries that would break every ratings record ever compiled.

"Jesus, I can't stand this." The Tank was moving, rolling and wheeling here and there on the verandah, glancing irritably over the balustrade at the city muttering below them, at the media vehicles clustered at the front of the hotel. There was also a crowd of demonstrators, who had started an organized jeering. "Maybe there's a fuckup. This epidemic they're talking about, a morale problem, buggery in the ranks, all that shit—"

"It's not an epidemic, Halley. Relax. Some little fever, they'll figure it out, and anyway Omega is fresh, and they're always dependable. They're moving into position."

"We're down to a *half-hour*, max, Josh. I can't be responsible if your people don't deliver within the framework we discussed. When you wayne it, time is *everything*."

Josh felt even colder inside. "Listen, they'll fire it. It's a dumb bomb and—"

Rogers jammed his blunt forefingers into his ears and shut his eyes. "I don't hear you. Didn't hear you. This is not part of my area and I have absolutely no knowledge." He barely lifted one eyelid, to verify that Josh had stopped talking. "One half-hour, Josh. This is cut way, way too fucking close." He wheeled to roll away into the main room, and at that moment there was a salvo of yells, exclamations, and whistles from the holo-watchers.

An aide appeared in the doorway, beckoning urgently. "They got 'em! They were in the station but—" He opened his mouth wide and shook his head at the overwhelming burden of expressing everything at once. He stood aside to allow Josh and the Tank to charge into the main suite, where a space opened immediately for them at the closest holo table.

"You won't believe this," someone beside Josh said.

On the monitor was an aerial view of a cluster of buildings around a large, open compound, where people were running, tossing, sprawling . . . A crater of some sort was at the upper end of the compound, and figures were scurrying out of it. At the lower end something white winked or fluttered. Detail was difficult to see, because of a thickening haze of dust or smoke. "What's this?" Josh cried out as if struck in the face. "It hit but didn't go off?"

"What?" The Tank's voice beside him was impatient and venomous beneath its veil of politeness. "*What* hit?"

Josh could not answer; he was in a stupor of anxiety. The missile was supposed to precede the assault, was supposed to temporarily divert attention and justify calling in Omega. But now the Ginks had penetrated the station compound, and the whole thing was going down on holo. Where *was* the K-13? The loose cannon?

"They're *naked*," the Tank said in a hoarse whisper of awe. "They're fucking *naked*."

He saw it too, now, in a wobbling zoom shot. The nakedness was not obvious because the bodies were coated with the dust, and striped with branching rivulets of sweat. They were gyrating, weaving, bobbing . . . *dancing*! He saw a pattern emerging, lop-sided concentric circles, and at their center a half-dozen figures that seemed smudged by light. Other lances of light were striking into the sky, apparently from weapons being discharged. Finally, he was aware of the announcer's yammering.

" . . . diminishing visibility. Deer, sheep and goats, even rabbits are also contributing, but the word from command center is that these feral horses are at the largest concentration ever recorded, with estimates already into the tens of thousands. That would seriously hamper any assault, by air or ground. Nor is the tunnel complex showing up well on seismic probes, due to the reverberation of hoofbeats on shallow bedrock . . . "

At a desk in a corner, a group of aides sent up another chorus of whoops and whistles. They were watching a screenful of numbers scroll by. "Compucon!" someone shouted. Several, including Josh, looked away from the scene of the ongoing assault. Faces brightened, there was a scatter of applause and some foot-stomping, and someone seized Josh's hand and pumped it. He was aware of the Tank beside him, rising on tiptoe to hiss into his ear.

"What the fuck *happened*? Where's the blow?"

"We're in!" someone else shouted, and then began to sing. *For he's a jolly good fell-o-o-w, for he's a jolly good fell-o-o-w . . .*

" . . . now just in! The results are confirmed, with a bit under fourteen percent of the votes counted: Robert Stanley Adamson, at the age of forty, will be the next President of the NorthAm United Republics! It's official – and has there *ever* been a more dramatic entry into the highest office in the land? Adamson assumes command of a strikeforce *in the field*, where a mad, heavily armed Pobla warlord is at this very moment attacking a remote research facility!

"That would be enough to make this moment intense, and unique.

But this is no ordinary border station. The facility has *already* been seized by a small gang of kidnappers, members of a fanatic and violent cult, who are holding hostage the young, disturbed Drager, his *lapsis* consort, and their unborn hybrid – a messiah to some and a monster to others . . . "

"Holy shit," said the voice beside Josh. "There it is."

On the holo now a cumbersome, long-snouted thing had waddled out of the crater. Its metal hide glittered faintly through the veils and streamers of dust racing over the compound. The dancing naked forms were becoming indistinct; they resembled the shadows cast by moonlight through wind-shaken trees. It was no longer possible to tell attacker from defender, and the concentric circles had become a mazy, continuous writhing, a snarl of snakes.

"Yes, something *is* being moved into place, and it does appear – visibility is rapidly deteriorating – we can't take our copter any lower, can we Mark? – it *does* seem to be a mobile unit, a tracked weapon – incredible, absolutely incredible! Everything is converging at this site, viewers! This is the situation the new Commander-in-Chief – but let's flash to the Hotel Atlantis and see if Adamson has emerged . . . "

Josh glimpsed the entrance to their hotel, the ranks of uniformed security police holding at bay a now larger horde of demonstrators, a circling pack of reporters and holocorders; then he was distracted, for a door opened across the room and two secret service agents shouldered through. Adamson came next, and behind him two aides with heavy briefcases, then two more agents. The Commander's confident grin struck Josh as surreal, a dreadful mistake, the wrong mask held up at a holy ceremony.

He was aware of the Tank running across the room, heard the great political strategist yelping continuously as the whole group jostled out another door, and hurried down the main hallway to the express elevators. *Fucking caution*! he heard Rogers saying. *Extreme fucking deliberation* . . . His hand was being shaken and in front of him faces were popping up, like cutouts in a shooting gallery. They were sweaty, smiling, flushed, excited, bewildered . . . His subordinates were congratulating him on their victory.

Victory. One of the faces was telling him he had calls stacked, a hotline open. A young, adoring face, approaching the master. He nodded. Here was victory, here now. Always the best disguise of catastrophe. He looked again at the holo. A maelstrom now, but with a direction. A torrent of shapes, black and red and gray, with manes and tails like flags, a river of shadows rising, breaking, submerging . . .

" . . . very, very great peril to those inside. Yet at this time there is no, repeat no, confirmed casualty. Armored ground units could not risk firing on the massive herd without better target definition, and the herd is now running *right through* the area where the hostages and the renegade missile were last . . . "

The adoring young aide was back, bearing a black cryptphone with pulsing point of red light. "She absolutely *must* talk to you. Wants to congratulate you. Oh, this is . . . " The youngster's face convulsed in a small, wild laugh, and then spilled tears. "I could rip off my own clothes and dance *myself*! Oh God! I'm sorry . . . " From outside, from the street below the verandah, came a faint yell, a thunderous cheer.

Josh smiled, an odd and absent smile, and took the cellphone, but did not immediately lift it to his head. He was watching the holobox again, which now offered a closer view of the entrance to the Hotel Atlantis. The cluster of cameras and gesticulating reporters had contracted toward the great glass doors. There was movement, some shoving, an excited yell.

" . . . the new Commander-in-Chief. He's coming, he's in the lobby – it's an amazing moment, this young man on the threshold of greatness – ah!"

The glass doors had swung open, and the formation of agents and aides deployed through them briskly. At the center Adamson moved with swift ease, erect and purposeful but relaxed. The Tank had managed to switch the grin for a controlled, forthright smile, and some of the aides looked serious. The choreography was professional, a blend of efficiency and informality, as the vehicles rolled into place. Josh deflated his lungs with a small huff of relief, and lifted the phone.

"You want to congratulate me, I hear."

"That would be just a bit premature." Danielle's voice was sweet, soft, and charged with fury.

"You're watching, I suppose."

"Of course. What there is to watch. Those little cocksuckers."

"Now now. You of all—"

"Shut up, Josh. Homer was confused at first, but he's figuring it out now and he's not happy. He can't *see*, for one thing."

"Nobody can." Josh laughed without humor. "We could look at it as a new suspense device. Throw dust in their eyes. What happened to the Joes in charge, your *consultants*, and their—"

420

"They should be dead meat. I would personally – but we can't take the risk at this point. It was a mistake to go with a weapon that large and mobile, and a bigger mistake to trust a psych profile of a crazy Gink. But forget that. We're wasting time. We have to have a fucking baby. Without any question. A fucking baby of some kind. You understand?"

"The fucking baby was *your* idea, I believe? You and Dorothy. The fairy godmothers." Josh grinned into the receiver with private relish.

There was a pause, and he almost laughed aloud, knowing that Danny was, at last, speechless with frustration. But it was she who laughed, in quick, bright bubbles of hatred.

"You invent the most charming fables. We all saw the genius of it – though the two of us were there first, yes, it has to be said – but *you* . . . you came all over yourself with gratitude. Came to lick like a dog that night, if I recall, though I hardly do. But let's not be petty. Let's just get the whelp out. *Now*. Homer and the leading twat Tasha have their hearts set. We jacked them way high for this."

"Not that easy, with the bomb right there and a million crazy horses overrunning the whole place. If *we* kill it in some blunder . . . "

There was another pause. And when Danny spoke again he heard, for the first time, a twisted thread of desperation in her voice. "That can't happen. That's not a conceivable resolution. Sam will know what to do."

"But he can't *see* to do it. That's the problem. We have to go easy at this point. Our man is talking caution. He's poised, he'll move just as soon as he can."

"We're losing narrative momentum. Every *instant*."

"Forget narrative fucking momentum. *Pray*. Pray Sayat is not butchering the lot, as we speak." Josh was drifting away from the holoboxes and computers and phones in the main suite. Too many aides were looking at him, puzzled or hopeful, wondering *What now*? It was true: the situation was becoming excruciating.

"Joe says he's the type to gloat and spin out his fun. And he can't see much either, so maybe he'll wait. Just like a normal human psychopath."

Josh laughed bleakly. Just before sidling onto the verandah, he noted three boxes presenting three different images. There was a starred general emerging from a military limovan; then the dust cloud, through which rolled a dimly seen but tremendous river of running horses; then a sea of faces and waving arms before a

421

stage flanked by batteries of giant speakers – a stage where a big, fat man was having convulsions.

"Speaking of which, you catch the rally yet?" He had to raise his voice and cup the phone closer to his mouth, for the demonstration below had intensified its chanting and clapping.

"Just before you deigned to answer my call. A fascinating obscenity is Mr Beau, but that's a later agenda, let's not get distracted. We have to go in, Josh, have to at least make the motion, in a matter of minutes. The deal is *down*. What is that ghastly noise?"

He controlled a spasm of rage, spoke in a fair facsimile of weary tolerance. "The orders are signed, Sam's in position, the dog-and-pony is already up and running – we go the instant we can see the layout. A demonstration down in the street. Omaly louts and clowns."

"Sounds more like hyenas and loons. So then – what if?"

He did not answer for a moment, did not want to think about the chasm on the wrong side of that *if*.

"You know what happens, Josh."

"I know." He smiled grimly over the balustrade, at the city. "Too late, we cremate."

They had thought originally in terms of saving the supporting cast. Wiping the holy couple, developing the orphan theme, might establish too harsh a tragic note at the start. PJ of course had to be eliminated – had already eliminated himself, effectively – but they could use Tiffany Orr's trial as a fun sidebar, and the Petrasky and Higgins prosecutions would even have touches of salacious comedy.

But if things went awry, they all knew the safest fallback was to shred and burn every scrap of tape, disk, and tissue. Fortunately, the new angle of religious fanaticism gave them the chance to blame any holocaust on the cult members themselves. Sam had a plan for this contingency. All it took was a little spilled fuel and a spark. So at least there would be free fireworks. Everything would go up.

"A crude, lurid, stupid ending, Josh. A dead baby. A handful of charred bones. That's unacceptable. We've *got* to do better."

"We will." His weariness was not affected this time. "There's going to be a change. The dust will clear. We—"

This time the cries from the main room were long vowels of surprise, of awe. He was striding back to the doorway, even as Dorothy hissed in his ear, *"Oh yes, it's changing – take a look – it's gone . . . "* Crossing the threshhold, he understood. On the first holo he could see, a phosphorescent star had risen from the great clouds of dust and now skimmed just above them in a low arc. The lens followed its trajectory for a long, breathless moment and then light filled one whole side of the screen.

"They fired it! They shot off the sonofabitch!" People were on their feet, milling about, looking at Josh in covert anticipation and alarm. He kept the phone tight to his head, made a noncommittal gesture with his free hand, and maintained his absent little smile, to show them this development was not surprising or disturbing.

"Right, I saw it. That does it. We can go in now, we're going in. To win. Whew!" His whole body seemed to expand as he breathed deeply, sucking in the ether of adrenalin, of renewed hope. A gone bomb, Tom! Their man could wayne it now, tough and sure, as soon as the dust cleared. They would gas and stun that compound, find her within minutes, and then Sam's obstetric team would cut free their star! He was rocking from side to side, weaving back and forth, in his excitement.

"Pray, as you say. I've got to get back – Dorothy's minding Homer and Tash on the patio – so call me as soon as—"

"—the tune has played itself out. Oh yeah. Soon as the Blessed Event is o'er. The new plan. Oh yeah. Expect my call, Doll."

She laughed "Sometimes, Josh, I can almost love you. You're a fun toy. Good luck."

She was gone. Josh paused, imagining for a few long seconds a particular thing he would like to do to her. He caught himself swaying again, to the beat of the chanting – audible now even inside the main suite – and stopped immediately to punch into a top pri line. He overheard fragments of an urgent voice on the nearest holo: *muck . . . fire . . . poised . . . casualties . . .*

Adamson's transition security com spook came on the line. "Let's go," Josh said. "Sign the execs and get the little wart out of there. Now give me SamYam. I need to—" The spook interrupted him, talking rapidly, intently, without pause, cutting like a high-speed drill through Josh's own sentences.

"What?" Josh was motionless, expressionless. His lips barely moved around the word. Cold and bright, the drill was biting into his brain. *"What?"*

CHAPTER FORTY-ONE

Male and female, female and male, they had circled and twisted and braided and woven themselves together, moving both backward and forward in time. As heavy-footed shaggy ones, as long-armed swingers and howlers, as haunched and clawed foragers in desert and bog; as a muscled sheath over vertebrae, swimming or slithering, as a simple mouth dragging a bunghole, as a mere twist of their two checkered threads of self; and finally, as a shadow and its shadow, as two mirrors, they moved; and when they moved all things moved with them.

Their dance was the channel for this infinite geyser of being, and the ball of light in Tima's belly was its source. In this dance, without touching, their bodies made *naku* solid as bread. Without sound, they sang to make the stars ring. Eyes closed, they saw the world spin and burn to make the flashing jewel of life. They were molded, moment to moment, by the great serpents of dark and light, who devoured each other endlessly. They were male and female and living egg: they were together, in harmony, at the beginning.

In that single, blade-thin slice of time that pierces the open eye, Pahane saw the others gathering, dancing too, drawn around them in undulating circles. He saw the earth break apart and the drummers bound out, felt the new access of energy that came with them. He saw those with weapons, saw how the drums bent their wands of flame into the sky. He saw pair with pair, circle within circle, forming and dissolving and forming again. The dust was rising under their feet, swathing and then unveiling, turning the dancers into apparitions; but around them – around Tima – the air somehow contained and released more light. She was herself a denser shadow, erect and fluid, swallowing this light as she moved. She swallowed also the eyes of the marauders springing from the earth, pulled them inside out and threaded them like beads. Even the band that came all at once, weapons leveled below snarling faces, quick as spiders – they were bent into the bright air, flung into the circle, set spinning around, and hurled their bolts only into the sky.

The earth itself had begun to vibrate, when the *mudlati* rumbled from the hole in the compound. Beside it appeared another small band, gathered tightly around a figure that glittered and flashed as he moved. Pahane saw this warrior, the weapons slung over ornaments on his neck and arms, in a kind of tunnel; for at the first sight of the great, shining spear of metal, dragged by dozens of *tchatsinakun*, the concentric circles of dancers had elongated and separated, like a dividing cell, to open an avenue from the upthrust missile to the little nucleus of light where their shadows danced.

Tima held her swollen belly in her two hands, a thing he could see like a reflection on the blade of the present; but in the seething, inner vision that joined them, the erupting fountain of all that had ever lived and was living now, he was aware only of the song that lifted and impelled him in joy, the drums and hooves that now shook the earth under his feet. The vision *was* the song, and the song had a direction and motion inexorable as a mighty river, and he understood finally that he had only to give himself to this flow.

They were pawns, actors, shadows of something greater than themselves, and there was no escape but submission to that greatness. This paradox now flowered in his very limbs: he pranced and shivered toward Sayat, who stared at him through a mask of hatred as he, too, strutted nearer. When submission was complete, one *became* the limitless power, one was lifted and moved . . . one *danced*! And the dancer was the dance, inventing and altering, with a spontaneous and exhilarating freedom, the walls and mazes and vaults of a perfect, patterned prison.

Sayat was grinning, unslinging his weapon, his torso shaken by exultant cries. Pahane grinned, and screamed in return. He moved toward Sayat, imitating the motions of taking and holding an imaginary weapon.

The band of guards halted and contracted around their leader. Pahane could see their eyes flicker, back and forth, and the barrels of their weapons wavered ever so slightly. Sayat rose on the balls of his feet. His chest swelled, so that the necklaces strung there flashed and winked. But before he could raise his weapon, one of the small band stepped to his side and lifted a spear. It was a plain *tchatsi* spear, no more then a long, sharpened stick with a ceremonial rag of hide, a feather or two, tied on the haft.

The man with the spear was broad and not very tall, and wore a woven bag slung from one shoulder. Pahane recognized Ap, the Pobla who had first taken him into the Wasteland, who had taught him *tchat* and how to run and hide and find water, whose life Tima had once saved. Ap, twice a traitor! For he had turned from the remnants of Adza's clan and gone to Sayat, then run away to live with Kapu, and finally slunk back once more to Sayat's camp. He was speaking to his leader, and his hands supplicated even as they were moving, offering, intercepting, until the new weapons hung on his own shoulders and Sayat held the old spear.

Pahane had also stopped, and beside him someone appeared with a wooden rod, a broken rake-handle. He took the handle and unhinged his lower jaw, to gape back at Sayat, whose mask of hate had slipped for a moment, revealing uncertainty. Both Sayat's followers and those they had come to subdue were dancing and whirling more frantically now, all along the avenue between these two men with sticks. A chant was rising over the drums, the hooves . . .

The shadow is dancing!
Who is the Shadow-maker?
The stars are singing!
Who sings the stars?
Wonakubi! Wonakubi!
Show us ourselves!

Sayat was screaming, and Pahane mouthed the words, as if a ventriloquist. *Dako!* the jeer directed at him when he was Ronald, when he was dragged to Adza's underground Temple – the first Pobla name he had been given – runt, turd, idiot, half-formed pup! And it was Sayat who had given it to him, gleeful to have at last someone beneath him. Now the glittering, strutting warrior began to bellow the chronicle of his triumphs: the skulls he had emptied, the piksis he had tricked, the fearsome vengeance he would inflict. And he would begin now, by eviscerating this piksi *dako* demon with a simple spear, the old way.

Pahane wheeled and stalked and swung his rake handle with mirror-like precision, yet added a flourish of excess. He extended his lunges and stamped hard enough to make his head wobble; he scythed so far with the broken handle he almost fell flat. He anticipated the other's syllables and grimaces perfectly. He felt Tima's force behind his own: her power of shaping every atom of one's being into an image of a new self. He was practicing the most rudimentary form of Pobla humor – sheer mimicry.

Sayat bounded high in a paroxysm of rage, and shrieked more curses. Holding the spear cocked over his head, he began to run. The band of guards fanned out behind him, Ap in the center and the tunnel began to widen again into a loose circle. Pahane was running too, spear aloft, his teeth bared and lips moving to match the hurled epithets. As the two approached nearer and nearer, Pahane's knees lifted higher, his feet flapped harder in the dust, and the rake handle waggled more violently – yet the rate of his advance diminished.

Sayat's features were dark with fury and the effort of running and screaming at the same time. Thrown off by Pahane's invisible change of pace, he stumbled. Recovering a dozen strides from his target, he twisted in a skipping, side-wise step and bent his torso far back, preparing to put all his momentum into casting the spear. Pahane followed this same pattern, stumbling and skipping and bending, but he accelerated as he did so, taking quicker, longer strides before his adversary could react.

There was a chorus of whoops, as the circling dancers saw the two combatants collide, their spears cross and clash. They tumbled and sprawled, could not momentarily locate themselves. Sayat sat up, bewildered, and glared through the haze at the naked piksi glaring back at him. Then a flash of consternation traveled between them, before the fury returned. Sayat was on his feet and scrambling after his spear. Pahane was barely an instant behind – and lunged for the same spear.

They each seized an end, and Sayat began to roar, wrenching at the shaft and trying to kick his enemy away. Pahane did the same, so they began to spin around and around, like baboons manacled into a mad mazurka. Sayat's screams had an edge of hysteria, his curses were garbled, yet in the dust-flinging vortex of this tug-of-war these noises seemed to come from Pahane's mouth, which stretched and warped into remarkable shapes.

There was another sound now, emerging through the chant like a river surging around great boulders. It was the rapid, liquid murmur of laughter, spreading and rising so that a trickle became a rush, and the rush a wild surf. All around the struggling pair was a chain of white teeth. Even some of the warriors who stamped and spun fiercely, firing often into the sky, were grinning. Some were jumping up and down to the rhythm of the chant, pleased as children at a favorite reckless game.

Finally Sayat was aware of this sea of laughter. He saw his guards grinning, trying not to grin, avoiding his look, turning their backs to hide their twisting mouths. His shrieks were throttled into a croaking, and his expression underwent a change. The mask of hate shattered, and what replaced it was at once purer and more intense – a concentration of fear and malevolence so great it annihilated consciousness and left only purpose, motion, act . . .

Necklaces jangling, some breaking and scattering, Sayat broke away and threw himself into a staggering run. Pahane was immediately behind him, reeling along in perfect synchronization. The crowd of dancers rippled and elongated into another tunnel, leading like the first to the gleaming missile. The chant and the laughter sounded still more like surf, a boom and hiss that sent Sayat sprawling to the base of the squat vehicle and its lifted snout.

Ap was there, moaning and supplicating still, though he had shed all his leader's weapons. His gentle, swift hands only helped boost Sayat onto the carriage, and in a moment the Most High was astride the trunk of the bomb. There he turned his blank stare in a long sweep over the compound, where the dust rolled and swirled around hundreds who grinned up at him, even as they danced or drummed or clapped. His pursuer had paused at the base of the missile, as if baffled and awed at last.

Sayat gripped tightly with his legs, wrapped his arms around the cold metal, and glared triumphantly down at Pahane. Ap appeared to be weeping with terror, but he reached up with a sure hand and began to flip switches. There was a humming, a regular beep, and then a great cough of white fire from the base of the shaft, a fire which laced through the metal frame of the carriage and blew a sheet of dust and pebbles from the ground beneath. Sayat raised his head, his lips peeled back in a startled scream. Slowly, then more swiftly, with the sound of a great wind rising, the missile slid aloft, sagged, yawed, and then began to diminish into the sky, a retreating meteor. Sayat was all at once a mere speck on the silver dart, and then both were swallowed by the tail of fire.

Pahane had stepped back from the rocket blast, and found himself in Ap's embrace, lurching from side to side in a clumsy bear-dance. "*Dako teela yapat*! *Kish yano*! *Dyatsu*! *Dyatsu*!" Ap's face was slick with tears. The runt gone away! A good death! Cries, laughter, whoops of delight floated like debris on the steady thunder of drums and hooves, and Pahane could see over Ap's shoulder the flanks of horses flashing through the dust.

"I waited!" Ap went on, in Pobla. "I learned! I had to know and not know like the piksis . . . I had to . . . " He choked, and covered his face.

"*Kish.*" Pahane embraced him again. "*Kishta, tchatsi.* It was necessary. It was a great thing to do." He understood the other's agony. To hide in this way, to deceive – even to quell the odor of deceit – in order to injure one's own kind, was an almost unimaginable evil for the Pobla. Ap had done what Kapu could not, the piksi trick only Tima had mastered before: he had fashioned himself in the image of an enemy, understood and sympathized with the being he hunted, in order to betray and destroy.

The dancers were leaping even higher now, the drummers striking with all their strength. The horses had apparently overrun fences, for the whole area was a roiling mass of bodies, dancing and galloping, weaving between buildings and through equipment yards. Pahane could no longer see Tima, so he hurried through the murk in what he hoped was the right direction.

He found her surrounded by their company – Marvelous and Cynthia and Doctor Fanny and Henderson and Ruby – all of them clad only in mud made from dust and sweat. Like Ap, some were embracing or bawling with relief and joy. But Tima looked at him only once – and in that instant they were again inside their vision, a single being, organizing itself for a great bound to freedom. The serpents were ringing them now, coiling light into the darkness of the egg, and it was time.

"*Vasan, tohanaku!*" She smiled. Her eyes were again like a night sky, infinitely empty yet filled with countless constellations. In that wheeling scatter of stars he read the glee of their first flight, their run to the sea, their discovery of a destiny in each other.

He smiled back, remembering with her, and then the band of horses was on them, around and among them – a twisting, rearing company that did not trample them, yet cut them off from the circling dancers. The slender riders were swinging down, as if born out of the long, flaring manes and whipping tails. They were small, light-boned, with the tilted eyes of Pacrims, and they kept a hand always on the shoulder or flank of their horses. They were all around Tima, bowing and reaching to touch the ground at her feet. "*Tak tagak! Ya delo tak tak tagak!*" they cried, and other words too, in their own tongue.

The nearest to them, a handsome young female, touched Tima reverently on the shoulder and then herself on the collar bone. "*Klat*," she said. "Kapu *mahanaku* my fren. *Vasan!*" She beckoned and two of her company brought horses forward, one light gray but spattered with black, the other a deep, dark red. Klat ran a hand over the belly of the red horse, then looked up at Tima. "She *Tzasu*. Beby too."

Tima reached out, and the mare jerked her head and lifted her hooves, but did not move away. She smelled, snorted, and then her nose was in Tima's hair. Pahane had lifted his hand to the spotted horse, who reared slightly before sniffing at him, and then trembled at his touch. "He *Paloo. Ogan.*" Klat said. "Go! *Vasan!*" She made a swift, urgent movement of her upper body.

Pahane could see the woven grass sling now, though its braided light and dark stalks cunningly matched the speckled hide. There was a wider portion at Paloo's shoulder, where he supposed a rider hooked one leg, while securing a strap at the other end of the sling about his waist. One of the company now appeared beside him, and began to show him how to secure the sling and mount.

Around them the other horses were mincing nervously, sneezing, anxious to whirl free of this eddy in the river of their running. He looked around at the faces of his friends, and could not tell if they cried and choked over the dust or at what was in their hearts. But none of them had ceased moving, pumping to the rhythm of the chant, and he felt the tug of it himself, even as he swung up clumsily into the sling and felt Paloo bunch and sidle into him.

"Bless you!" the Doctor cried, his arms high and wide. "Bless the union of all, the twining into life! Bless the holy fever of creation!" He stopped to cough then, red-faced, and only waved his arms.

"We are stars!" Fanny chorused. "All of us . . . dancing star-dust! Beasts from the stars, full of lust to – but shoooo! Get down and go, don't be slow; take that child and go wild!" She made a marvelous contortion of her large body, a supple and graceful bending around an invisible, rearing icon. "We'll be fine, gonna be all right with General White . . . *Yeah!*"

Cynthia had interrupted her dancing long enough to hug Tima hard, but Pahane could not hear what she called. He saw her grief and happiness were mingled inextricably, that she, alone, yearned to travel with them. Klat was helping Tima then, settling her carefully in the sling on the red mare. In another moment Klat herself would mount, and they would be gone like a flock of arrows. "PJ?" he shouted down to them.

Fanny twirled toward him, a hefty dervish in the dust. "PJ say, gonna talk that talk!"

"Halleluja!" Marvelous croaked.

"'Cause he the spook, Luke! Gonna dicker for the sticker! Hostages! He the decoy, boy! Give you the time to run, son!"

And they were running, so suddenly that Pahane had to clasp Paloo's neck with all his strength to stay on. His face was buried in the rough hair, and he was conscious of being battered by rapid, explosive contractions of hard muscle, working against the whole length of his body, while a roaring wind raked his backside. A thrill of terror impaled him, nailed his limbs to the barrel of the horse's ribs. The thunder all around him would, he knew, grind him to a pulp in seconds if he slipped off. And Paloo seemed to know this, and in the first long minutes – they were years to Pahane – shrugged and pounded him into a compliant, unconscious mass, a muscled parasite welded to its host, so that when the first dry gully opened before them, they left the earth with the furious, headlong grace of a single, great beast.

CHAPTER FORTY-TWO

They were moving at last, hatches down, with clearance from the new topkick. Monitoring the toposcreen, deploying his armored units, Systems Master Dreyer had an outlet for his frustration and anger. Omega had been skirting the area, lurking and pacing, for hours, waiting for the politicos to get their shit together. He had been online with his officers, fretting and telling jokes and yawning in nervous apprehension, when the compucon had come through and they finally had a dependable chain of command.

Although he held his new President-Elect in contempt – first for being younger than Dreyer himself, secondly for advocating harebrained Gink policies, Dreyer was an Insec agent and therefore kept his feelings to himself. Yamaguchi was his model, and arctic SamYam had asked for execution, not analysis. That was Omega's specialty: whatever the job was, they did it swiftly, secretly, and perfectly. A weird job here, though. His weirdest ever, as a field commander. The nation's finest darkside mobile assault force was coiled to deliver . . . an incubator and a team of obstetricians!

"Dry?" It was his mate and gunner, Turlock, who had been checking their perimeter linkups with the reg units from White's Third Armored. Dreyer nodded impatiently, not looking away from the toposcreen.

"We're not synching too good with these guys. Some goof in their com staff keeps diddling us. Several vehicles stopped. Crews out and on the ground. They don't seem to want to keep up. Don't seem to take these horses seriously. Shall we back off?"

Turlock was driving, in order to leave the Master free to handle communications when the strike was launched. They were cruising in a slow zig-zag over hilly country to the north of the station, hooking around a couple of old toxic fills, where threads of steam still rose from the deeper cracks. Since morning they had also adjusted their pattern to avoid spooking the herds of hoofed animals that were congregating.

Why, Dreyer wondered with a wince of irritation, would anybody get out of a vehicle in such a place? Of course White's outfit had been giving off signs of goofiness for weeks before this, even before the rumors of a little epidemic of some low-level fever with behavior fallout. And of course refugee duty by itself had driven a lot of grunts into psych discharge.

"No. Tell their com staff to put their ass in gear. Tell them we're point and it's their job to *support*."

Finally he glanced at Turlock, and saw in the mate's eyes a reflection of his own anger and anxiety. There was a serious pattern of fuckups developing. The whole operation was timed by an election, not a field condition. No one had done sat comps and overlays in time to determine how many horses were on the move and where they were headed. And now the Ginks had a missile, for the first time ever, which intelligence had failed to track properly. Omega was moving well inside the usual range, but it was an old device and couldn't correct if anything put a warp or drag on it. And now their support was soft. There were nutcases covering their flank.

"I don't like this," Turlock said flatly, almost defiantly. "This is not professional."

Master Dreyer stared at his mate for a long moment. He moistened his lips with a flick of his tongue, preparing a reprimand, but he couldn't deliver it. He didn't like it either, didn't like any side of it.

"Something else they're doing, White's com people. Listen." Turlock lifted his headphones off and held them toward Dreyer. A faint skirl of music was audible over the throb of their power plant, the whisper of their tracks on the ground outside.

Dreyer frowned, stared harder at Turlock, whose wide mouth twisted sardonically.

"They got culture." Turlock laughed silently. "The old stuff. *Rockenroll*."

The Systems Master recoiled slightly in disgust, as if the dangling set of headphones were a snake. Against regulations to play *any* music over a com channel during an operation. But the vile, dangerous chants of that debased century when civilization had almost gone under – that would be open impudence, practically mutiny.

A light jumped alive on his control panel before he could respond to Turlock. He picked up his own headphones and snapped them on. It was his dark channel to ConCenter. Maybe things were happening at last. Maybe the ginks had shot their little wad. "Right. Alpha Prime here. Clear for–"

434

He stopped, looked startled, and his hands began to grope swiftly along the control panel, like small creatures released suddenly into a food maze. More lights were popping up, and a beeper went off. "They . . . they . . . but . . . " One hand fumbled its way to a button. The screen before him shuddered and became phosphorescent. He was aware that Turlock, expecting an alert, had leaned over inquisitively and would see the radar recon too.

They saw the bright line sweeping, the concentric circles indicating distance, the bright small star flowering and then decaying. The star was already almost at the center. Dreyer tried to swallow and could not. He heard Turlock say, with the last of a breath, *"Oh shit!"*

A terrible, completely unexpected urge swept over Dreyer. The urge to embrace Turlock. But before he could do so, the air all around them turned to fire.

Viewed from General White's frontline command unit, the blast made quite an impressive spectacle. There were after-explosions from the magazines of several of the tech and support vehicles. Tracers and tumbling meteors of cobalt and chromium fire over a bubble of white magma, and then a towering plume of black smoke shot with red tongues. For several seconds no one looked at the instruments, and those linked to speakers or headphones did not register the voices yammering at them.

General White was actually the first to return to an intent examination of the shadowy scenes being transmitted from his forward scouts, now inside the dust cloud and a bit less than a klick from the station perimeter. There hadn't been much to see so far: a shuttling blur of legs and necks and mottled hides, very occasionally a wraith-like biped, mostly Ginks from the ruptured holding-pens. Twice there was a glimpse of what might have been human, but so caked with mud one couldn't be sure. The scouts reported flashes from what were presumed to be handweapons, but had taken no hostile incoming fire.

He had passed beyond fury to a kind of cold, intense calm. The idiocy of the operation had become, finally, a structure of such magnitude and intricacy he found himself fascinated, even pleased, to contemplate it. The wayward stupid bomb was therefore not a great surprise. Nor was the information, forty-five seconds later, that Omega's field command and a considerable section of its tech element – the dark heart of the whole effort – had been blown to kingdom come.

435

He had been prepared, after all, by his witnessing of the disintegration of the army under his command. For weeks his junior officers had been unable to hide from him what was happening in the barracks, along the fences to the refugee compounds. Leaving his quarters or climbing into a scout vehicle, he had seen soldiers – or what had once been soldiers – swaying and shuffling to the incessant rhythmic chants that were always there, like a murmuring wind or a fast-running river. Many of them were shirtless, without boots, unwashed and unshaven. He saw them holding hands. He caught the smell of tobacco from their ranks. He could not glare down their simpering smiles.

Food spoiled on loading docks; switches were left on, valves open, filters unchanged; tools, documents, personnel vanished. The base stockade was full, most of the inmates charged with insubordination or dereliction of duty. There were auxillary holding cells, also full. A fleet of buses and ambulances hauled away daily the medical and summary discharges. General White heard their departure, because they usually sang at the top of their lungs. *Delirium*. A word long out of fashion, but he could find no better.

In the beginning he doubted his own sanity, had considered resigning his command, but then it became apparent that the mysterious malaise was widespread. It wasn't simply a matter of stress over the havoc created by the strange tide of dying refugees. Radical groups had gotten violent in the name of compassion for the Pobla. Then the Winger show had pumped the scandalous abduction of the Drager boy, linked it to the bombshell issue of genetic cleansing. Then the Omalytown connection, the supposed conspiracy to destroy NorthAm society. Overnight, so it seemed, the streets thronged with deranged demonstrators; and the atmosphere throbbed with a yakyammer of crazy notions.

Crazy and deadly notions. The affair had now become bloody, and the carnage was the sort that demanded, inexorably, a payback. The dead were now *official* dead, and worse – they had been the proudest and most secretive of the nation's armed agents. There would be vengeance ten, even a hundredfold. The humanitarian emphasis of the original foray would vanish like a snowflake in a volcano. The general had a fair idea of what was coming, and he knew he would have to stake his life on the most reckless gamble of his career. For he intended to pluck, from the seething heart of this volcano, the woman he loved.

"General?"

White turned slowly, his face expressionless, extending one hand as he did so.

Captain Slater transfered the code unit in its compact black satchel to her superior. "Insec Zero," she said, and did not conceal her excitement. "Do you want your cabin closed, sir?"

"No need." General White glanced at the young men and women behind the captain, now ostentatiously bent over their keyboards and screens. The plume of smoke still towered on one of the group monitors, but they no longer watched, rapt. They were humming now with the current of desire for action. They wanted new and even fiercer blossoms of fire. They would be trading glances and making faces behind his back. "I expect, Slater, we'll be going on combat alert. Possibly point. So run a systems model for retrieve. Personnel retrieve. And call up another ground scout squad."

"Yes, sir."

Slater wheeled and strode away. Skinny, tough, sure of herself. The kind of female officer he used to prefer on his staff. Before he knew Fanny. He opened the flap of the satchel and folded out the keyboard and audio helmet. It would take a few moments for Insec Zero and Third Army Spy to interface their codes, and during that time he would keep watching the scouts' images, would keep concentrating himself.

She had taught him that, had made him open himself to obsession, to a pure, single flame of being. He had gone to her desperate, doubting himself and what he thought he knew, and she had pulled him, just like that, into another world. She confirmed that something had changed in him, in the very fiber of his being. Yes, it was a physical thing. Yes, he was sick. So was she. Sick with joy, with love, with an ungovernable, lusty desire to play, to roll, to tickle, to sing, to *dance*!

Their codes had meshed to generate a self-destructing hybrid, so the general slipped on the helmet and in a moment heard Yamaguchi's voice. The voice was stilted and monotone, since it was generated out of a bank of voiceprints. Wherever he was, the Insec Director was talking about artichokes and zebras, or colorless green ideas that slept furiously – whatever his code screen gave him to say – but all this was translated, within the sealed membrane of White's helmet, into a coherent message.

"General White. Alert please. We have very serious situation. Omega now inoperative. Crisis ongoing. Response imperative. You must reconnoiter immediately, and cover own advance to current scout position. Can you surround and contain station personnel? Contain only. Do not penetrate. De not apprehend. Omega regrouping. Reply now."

General White smiled to himself. He would give a good deal to know whether circumstances had brought, finally, a drop of perspiration to the Director's famous porcelain features. Insec had no backup in the field; the elaborate rescue mission was in complete disarray; SamYam now had to beg a regular army unit to keep his quarry in its pen. Yamaguchi's staff had been monitoring all channels, so they had seen the great tide of racing horses, the impenetrable dust-cloud, the flashes from weapons inside the station.

Omega would try to regroup and launch the strike as soon as possible. They might still try to rescue the principles, especially the pregnant Pobla witch, but if they saw it was too late . . . Even as he speculated, General White was tapping out his own simple message on the keyboard of the code unit. The unit encrypted his words into a text displayed in the new code, which he began to read into the transmitter. As his voice moved on, this text ate itself.

"A tizzy is too busy for easy ampersand, and the quick blue gnu will not dismay the ox. Mickle blather, mumsey . . . "

Yamaguchi, of course, heard the general's reconstituted original: *Very serious. Acknowledge alert. Will advance to scouted position, attempt containment. Do our best.* The general hit his keys in a leisurely manner, lips pursed. He intended to be in the way as long as possible. What was left of Omega would be ready to scorch the station to the ground, and all its inhabitants and records, if their mission was no longer feasible. He intended to get lost in the dust, estimate wrongly the distance to the perimeter, stumble into the middle of the whole mess. Personally.

Yamaguchi was replying, the mechanical voice jerking out more quickly. "Emergency . . . max natsec top pri . . . expedite please . . . " General White did not even listen. He was rocking back and forth slightly, his mind once more on that last meeting with Fanny. The encounter in which he had flung aside his whole career, every professional principle he had lived by, every shred of what he had once imagined was his self-respect.

He had come to give a stern order of dismissal, and ended up dancing naked with a woman not his wife. A dance that became intimate and intense beyond anything in his prior experience. When they first met he had been maddened by Doctor Fanny – her clever, arch evasions, her sly pretense to submission. And he had ridiculed her bulk, been disgusted (he thought) by her profuse wriggling and swaying, the sinister union of size and coquettishness. He had been unnerved and off balance, angry at himself, and so charged directly into the field, into confrontation with this soft, fluttering behemoth, and had found himself ambushed, overwhelmed, and annihilated.

She teased him first with that same arch perversity, with a fierce, subtle, coyness. She rippled and retreated, undulated and hesitated, darted and dallied. She was there like a large, sweet, melon – full, ripe, bursting – and yet skittish, writhing with an excited apprehension, tantalizing in her changeable ardor. So he had made a certain move, got hold of her in a certain way, and they went down, hard.

He had never known anything so hot and rough. Had never felt himself so completely absorbed, reduced to muscle and bone with no mind, a dumb piston cabled to a jolting dynamo of erotic force. Yet even then, when he was nothing but a spinal cord incandescent with ecstasy, she contrived to provoke and prolong his spasms with a series of delicate, voracious contractions, calculated to wring from him everything, absolutely everything he had . . .

"General White, sir?"

He started, looked down to see the code unit screen was blank, then up into Captain Slater's expression of concern, now more than polite. He must have signed off with SamYam, stripped and stowed the audio helmet, on full automatic. He could do almost everything on automatic these days. Perhaps it was one symptom of his sickness, his fever.

"Yes, Captain. You've done the retrieve model? Got us some scout vehicles?"

"Yes, sir."

"Program the retrieve into the fastest one and bring it around here on active, ready to board. Give me three supports, rear and both flanks. I want the best crews we've got left. You and Carson will co-ordinate here, and make sure you follow us every inch of the way. We'll transmit and you pipe us to *all* channels."

Captain Slater's eyes widened, concern turning to alarm. "Give you . . . you mean, sir . . ."

"Yes, I mean what I mean. I'm going myself. On point. Now move, Captain."

He was conscious that the crewmen and aides in the Boomerang cruiser were indeed trading looks behind his back. They were expecting an order to halt, to set up some kind of precarious advance command post. He had to speak sharply a time or two, galvanize them out of stunned disbelief. No doubt the vehicle officer, Captain Millwright, was wondering secretly whether the military code would justify his refusing any more orders to advance.

The general ignored their fidgeting and fumbling, and kept his attention on the monitor, the terrain ahead of them. Slater would, he gambled, fend off ConCenter and even Yamaguchi himself for a few more minutes. He had taken over the navigator's desk and the mainline channel to his own headquarters, so he could cut the cruiser off from all incoming messages if necessary. Visibility was the real problem. The dust was so thick they ran over the downed fence before they saw it, and almost ploughed into a band of refugees. The skeletal forms drifted aside slowly and disappeared into the dense haze. A moment later they topped a knoll, and immediately were surrounded by the jostling, racing herd, as if they had driven into a river. The pounding of hooves was a steady, deep rumble through the metal shell of their Boomerang. They felt a slight shock through the frame, a glancing collision with the hurtling horses.

There were exclamations, a yelp, a whistle. General White did not turn away from the monitor. He heard Captain Millwright asking for a course correction to avoid further contact. The Captain's voice conveyed a certain grim insistence.

"Proceed on course. Reduce speed to six klicks an hour. And stop the chatter." Instruments told the general the perimeter of the station was only three hundred meters away, but he had to creep along now. The cataract of running animals parted and closed to allow their progress, but they could see nothing else but the boiling dust.

"Sir . . . you are our commanding officer but—"

"I goddamn sure am. And I ordered you to stuff the chatter and keep to course. If I want advice I'll ask for it."

He was fighting despair and an impulse to lunge ahead, blow a path through the compact rush of bodies. The elation and relief he had known when the K-13 rose away from the station had evaporated. To escape a fiery blast only to be cut to ribbons by these flashing hooves . . . His mind shied from the vision of his Fanny going down in this churning river. She had told him to expect miracles, to trust that dried-up old witch doctor, to believe in this holy fever . . .

An outline appeared through the dustcloud, then was erased. It might have been the roof of a guard tower. He could not tell for sure, over the rumble of hooves and hum of the Boomerang's power plant, whether the crew was whispering urgently. They could assume, at this point, that the Commander of the Third Army had lost his mind. Combat Stress Syndrome. An especially severe case of the new virus. The ConCenter channel light was blinking furiously. He had only minutes, perhaps seconds, before his command collapsed.

"There," he said with crisp matter-of-factness. "Right through that open lot. Reduce speed to four klicks."

They had reached the compound, luckily at a parking area between two buildings. The perimeter fence had been breached and toppled in several places, and the carcasses of horses were tangled in it here and there, but the main current of the great herd went outside the compound. The Boomerang slowed, hesitated, then eased ahead. They were all watching the monitor now, mesmerized.

The dancers whirled and rocked, ghostly in the haze, while the drummers formed a tremendous circle around them and an occasional band of horses wove across and through. Several security vehicles had been abandoned, hatches open, and here and there a dancer waved a torn rag from a uniform, but most of the moving figures were nude. A few had weapons, and shot into the sky from time to time.

General White had already spotted the group around Tima, picked out Fanny's prominent shape. The large, full body was no longer pink, but the color of earth. She had seen the intruder and begun to shake and prowl her way toward them, all her hills and valleys in motion. He was on his feet, undoing straps and buttons with both hands.

"Who the hell is *that*?" someone said in a hoarse undertone.

"My God," someone else said with an eerie detachment. "This is crazy."

General White removed his standard-issue Mansticker from its holster, set it on his desk, and then dropped his pants and shorts as a unit. There was a collective gasp, audible even over the tremendous thunder outside.

"Release main hatch," he said calmly. "Keep transmitting, and track me in." He shrugged off his shirt, then crossed his arms and stripped away his undershirt. He saw Millwright look away toward his gunner, place a hand protectively over a row of switches on the control panel.

General White picked up the Mansticker and pointed it casually at Millwright. "Release," he repeated, and walked to the three-step ladder that led to the main overhead hatch. "Or I'll shoot you for refusing an order in combat."

There was a long second when no one moved, and then Millwright flicked the switch and they heard the suction break on the hatch. When it lifted, the thunder from outside poured in, and White was not sure any of them heard his last words, before he swarmed up the ladder, keeping the weapon pointed at the Captain until the last moment. "I shall negotiate a surrender," he said. "Stand by."

Then the Commander of the Third Army was out the hatch, and in two jumps off the Boomerang and onto the ground. He threw the Mansticker to one side and strode toward Fanny, carrying nothing, wearing nothing on his rough, gray-haired body but a look of determined joy.

CHAPTER FORTY-THREE

Like a pianist performing a glissando, Josh brushed one hand swiftly along the row of switches to the monitors. The compound littered with bodies, the ring of armored vehicles, the long lines of chanting demonstrators, the police wielding stunners and sprayers, the yakking heads of commentators and spokespersons – every image imploded, leaving only dead, gray space in a box.

The boom and beat of the soundtracks did not cease, however, but continued to throb in the skull. The holojocks who rode the networks, roughing clips into summaries every fifteen minutes, had pointed out early in the day how the rhythms were synching in a really eerie way. Josh had noticed it himself. The chants of the Ginks and demonstrators matched the blasting speakers at Winger's rally, exactly as if they were listening to each other – though that was clearly impossible – and eventually one found himself whistling softly, or crossing a room with a certain slouch or dip, or simply *breathing* to this beat that seemed to have infected everything . . .

"You should have torched," he said to Yamaguchi. They were sitting side-by-side at the master console in the strategy room, apart from the few aides working at feeder units or handling calls. Most of the staff was with the Tank in the briefing room, trying to prepare Bob Adamson for his first press conference, now less than an hour away. Or rather crucifixion, as Josh now forecast it. "Horses and all. We could have—"

"We could not abort," Yamaguchi said. "Watch."

Methodically the Director tapped a few keys on an auxiliary board, waited for the darkside menu to come up, then flipped one of the monitors back to life. Field footage from a vehicle: a dust-shrouded plain, the corner of a building, phantom shapes emerging from the murk like creatures in one of the old bog horrorshows. There were six, the general and the big woman in the lead, and they were all naked except for a sheath of mud and dust. They walked directly toward the recording lens, hands held palm up. White's voice was audible; they caught the words "surrender" and "hostage."

"He's lying," Josh said, and laughed convulsively. "The sonafabitch is lying, and nuts besides. We should have burned them all."

"We could not. He is a general, much respected. And everything was logged on military channels." Yamaguchi killed the scene and then folded his hands carefully on his cocked knee. "They all tell the same story. Feiffer is holding the boy and the mother. We cannot be sure. We have phone contact with him, but . . . well, you have heard. He is not rational."

"Oh yes, I have heard." Josh laughed again, a sound of something shattering. "Have I heard." He got to his feet abruptly. "Jesus, Jesus, Jesus. What would please us. A meteor about now. One a couple miles across, right on that bastard. What are we going to do?"

He did not expect an answer, but began pacing before the row of dead, empty gray eyes. He could not stand to listen to the "negotiations" with PJ. The bad jokes, the raucous, mad laughter, his "readings" from the diary of his dead sidekick, who had been just as crazy. The agent was holed up in a tissue locker, which had its own independent power, water, and air supplies. They could not dislodge him except by force. And they could not be absolutely sure that the holy freak family – as the newsgurus were calling them – wasn't there with him.

Josh was sure enough. The fucking baby was gone, or dead. The one survivor of Fitzgibbon's team gibbered out a confused and fantastic story, swore the whole bunch had been trampled by horses and their corpses dragged off. Then PJ had given him a definitive clue. In his lunatic rambling, he sometimes quacked like a duck. Josh remembered their first interview, when the agent had used this rude form of signaling his new employment: decoy. He was alone in the locker, there were no hostages, the others were lying to buy time – Josh was sure of it. But why? Maybe they *were* some kind of screwball religious cult, worshipping viruses . . .

"You are in an unfortunate position." Yamaguchi sighed. "If he is tricking you. And also, if he is not."

"I know that," Josh said between his teeth. Their candidate would look like a fool or a brute, or both, but certainly not a shrewd and fearless leader. The orphan scenario was effectively blown, as was the opportunity for any swift, low-profile assault. Moment by moment, the intense focus they had managed was dissipating. Hostage standoffs got

444

boring fast, and once the K-13 had popped and the horses loped away there were no hot images to key on. Attention was shifting now to the chaos developing in the streets, the Omalys crawling from the sewer, the rumors of genetic contamination, the unraveling of public order in wave after wave of illicit sound.

Josh could not bear thinking any more about the loss of dramatic momentum. The script had been lean, tight, beautiful; and already he had sketched the sequels. A *dynastic* cycle – enough stuff to fuel major holos for two decades – and there would be a fortune just in the spinoff package, the dolls and shoes and restaurants, once the big images – the draculas and skywalkers – were locked in. Their freak would grow up to become the symbol of civilization's triumph, would be trained to lead new pioneers – redeemed Omalys and mixed bloods – to colonize the Wastelands, found a slave Eden. But it all had to begin with the bold rescue of a cursed orphan, and now . . . Josh groaned aloud. Idiotic! They had lost the fucking baby! How was it possible?

Yamaguchi said something very softly, and at first Josh thought he had heard wrongly. He stopped pacing and stared at the Insec Director, who gave no indication he expected a response. *Martial law*? Had Sam finally, incredibly, made a joke? Josh tried to laugh, but produced only a querulous grunt. Of course it was true. A President-Elect, as Commander-in-Chief, had the constitutional power to declare emergencies, if he made a finding that national security was . . .

It had never been done. It was an archaic holdover from an age when multinational blocs still tried to destabilize each other overtly, when a coup could cancel an election the morning after. He could not even remember clearly what *martial law* involved. The press – there was practically no press left, everything was holo – and public assembly and due process . . .

"You can't just shoot people for being naked and singing and clapping," he said, trying to make a joke himself. "You would gain a little time maybe, but that's all."

"Time is very valuable. In time we find things."

Josh was breathing a little faster, in spite of himself. You wouldn't have to shoot them. Maybe you could simply unplug them. Interdict holo to prevent disinfo and rumoroids. Without the electromagnetic webs that kept stimulating the mass, unifying and galvanizing it, the situation might subside into confusion and uncertainty, at least for a few hours. Long enough to smoke out PJ, find out if he was bluffing.

If so, then what? *We find things*.

"But there would be tests. Drager's geneprints are on file. So are hers, when she was Duskyrose." Josh swallowed, released a breath. He felt light-headed, as if he had stepped back from a precipice.

"In time we also lose things. A cycle. Bird in hand is no good now."

Josh had then the sensation of falling. He had been on a narrow ledge all along. His backward step was into a terrifying and exciting new dimension, mirror image of the old. There were still refugees at General White's base camp, thousands of them. Some pregnant, no doubt. Any would do. Remove baby. Baby barely alive. Baby witnessed, holoed, tagged. Baby rushed to clinic. Baby lost again . . . or – stolen!

"Oh," Josh breathed. "Oh, oh."

Yamaguchi's smile was swift and subtle. One of the aides across the room laughed at a joke they could not hear. They had a monitor operating, showing General White back in his uniform and the big woman in baggy fatigues. The woman was talking and gesturing – no, *reciting* something – before a panel of interrogators.

"We still have . . . whatshisname? Sandhurst? Sandstone?"

"Sandhill. Yes. He has been extensively questioned, of course." Yamaguchi's smile flashed again. "But he can be made operable with proper dosages. A protected witness, perhaps."

Josh laughed now with his whole heart, gulp after gulp of joy. He stood in a glorious, unexpected dawn. He saw that it was even better than their original script. It had a mad, brilliant simplicity, and a truly mythic dimension. He saw that it was the *promise* of a messiah that inspired or terrified. The savior who actually arrives, with moles and bent toes and scant hair, is immediately diminished, the object of intrigue and expectation, pressure and conflict. So spirit away the baby – any baby – and legend would flourish! Scarface would hunt his outlaw grandson everywhere, driven and damned. There would be rebel armies, impostors, rumors of miracle! Winger would *beg* for an alliance, would understand Josh had turned disaster into a brilliant plot twist.

The aides had fallen silent and were looking at him with uncertain smiles. He turned away to hide his glee. "Oh yes," he breathed. "Oh yes, what a beautiful mess!" Martial law. A measure of chaos. Communication breakdown. A few hours to find and cut out a Ginklet. The assault. Everything lost but the wee spark of sinister

446

life. And then another lightning, unexpected babynapping. He made a jigging step to one side, then back. "An orphan, absolutely," he said then. "A *legendary* orphan. Sam, you are a genius."

Yamaguchi shrugged. "We would continue investigation anyway. And we see, of course, one possible complication. We could have *two* orphans."

A cold hand seized Josh's heart momentarily. He had not thought everything through. What if the freak family turned up later, alive? Insec and army patrols were hunting the tunnel complex in the whole region, and combing the churned and dust-covered area where the horses had stampeded. He was assuming shreds of tissue would turn up, or if the fugitives survived, by some miracle, they would hide out indefinitely. But what if they gave themselves up or a routine patrol blundered across them?

"Pull back the search. Domestic upheaval. Need the troops on the street." He was thinking aloud, pacing again. "Then if the true messiah . . . " He stopped, giggled. "Send him straight to Paradise?"

"Yes. Good."

"Anyway, anything with a squeak and a dirty diaper will do us for now, give us time to get back on our feet. You've thought ahead already, Sam. You're a wonder, man. We – it's you and me, hey, SamYam? And nobody else? Not even . . ."

They exchanged a long look. Yamaguchi nodded once. "The situation must be controlled. We are in position to do this. Only a few trusted staff – medical officer and small security squad. But your employer, and your . . . partners . . . "

"Will get a new bedtime story." Josh smiled savagely. "But Sandhill is operable, you say?"

"I believe. With medication and a staff. He will not care which baby or why."

Josh was feeling lighter, easier, than he had been in a long time. Springing Sandhill would be relatively easy. Protected witnesses were kept in safe houses – hidden rather than heavily guarded – and could be liberated by a small force. Sam had informants and operatives in the Thorgy camp who could do the job. Eradicating PJ and emerging with a newborn preemie, then having it stolen from an incubator, before geneprints could establish identity, would be a greater challenge, even with the holo networks partly paralyzed.

"Speed and secrecy is all," he said quietly, and moved to take his seat again at the master console. "We'll postpone the press conference an hour. I'll put the staff to checking out procedures for declaring an emergency, generating the directives for the agencies." As he spoke he was running his hand across the row of switches, bringing the gray boxes back to vibrant, colorful life. "You and I and the Tank will have to retool Bob for the bit. But first . . . "

Yamaguchi smiled for the third time. "I locate our new hero. When we have him – a male, yes? – we will be prepared to call Mr Feiffer's bluff. The station must be sacrificed."

"But rising from the ashes," Josh crooned, swaying happily from side to side in his chair, "to bring us the word—"

"Ah yes." Yamaguchi's smile broadened, almost a grin. "I have heard this myth. The eternal firebird."

"Oh yeah! That's our sign, Sam. Yours and mine. No end to our story." His hands were weaving over the keyboard, and apprehensive, alerted faces were popping up on the row of monitors. An inner conference holo of all the major players. Looking at him in quiet desperation and wild, final hope. A President, only hours old, was already beginning to rot. They needed a miracle. Before he opened the channel to his own confident image, he giggled again, eyes shut in his ecstasy. "Which will be our gift to thy son and heir, Master Wavershaft! Oh blessed be the frozen fruit of thy withered old rod!"

CHAPTER FORTY-FOUR

They dressed each other carefully. Dorothy hung a single jewel around Danny's neck, an emerald in a plain silver setting, to offset the high contrast of a white Byron shirt and sootblack Turkish pants. Danielle gave Dot a pearl choker and matching earrings, over a pale blue wisp of frock that swirled like smoke when she moved. They vamped and teased and were silly, like actresses in a green room before a command performance. Indeed, this evening they would be called upon to exercise every wile, every stratagem, every resource, if they were to accomplish the brilliant maneuver they had devised during the day.

"A Streetcar Named Revulsion," Danny said, leaning down behind Dorothy at the vanity, so she could look over her shoulder at both of them in the mirror. "You're Noir and I'm Eartha. Together we make Josh Kowalski take off his pants."

Dorothy frowned, still examining her liner, but her mouth curved a little in mirth. "Not a difficult task. As we know." She glanced briefly into Danny's mirror-eyes. "But you are metaphorical, I realize. We need to think more in terms of getting Old King Dick subdued long enough to whisper these sweet new fantasies into his knob."

Danny laughed and ran a bright red fingernail along the inside rim of Dorothy's ear. "The beautiful fairy waves her wand. Presto, disaster into triumph."

"Stop." Dorothy twisted away, pettishly coy. "Have to get his attention. You saw how he was."

"Wheesh." Danny straightened, lifted her shoulders high and dropped them again. They were both silent a moment, remembering how Homer had stormed out soon after the catastrophe of the wayward missile, when the dust from the mad herds obscured everything. He had not come back for lunch, and the firing had gone on until about an hour ago, when he had returned, jaw still locked in rage, boots spattered with blood and hair, but steadier of hand.

"The Tush is still puking, which helps," she said. "We will have the royal attention span to ourselves."

"Yes." Dorothy swung her knees from beneath the vanity and spun around on the bench, making the blue dress float for a moment. "Another advantage for us godmothers. But you know, puss, I don't have quite your level of faith. I'm a little nervous about the spookum theories of Petrasky and the fat lady."

Danny was arrested, cocked her head alertly to examine her partner's expression more closely. "*You*? Nervous? An astonishing idea."

Dorothy sighed and crossed her feet, letting her knees protrude in an artless, little-girl manner. "Does happen. Especially when everything veers toward public disclosure, as it seems to be doing. I'm a creature of the dark, as you well know." She smiled modestly, prettily.

Danny smiled back, though with a slight delay. "Indeed." They gazed into each other's eyes for several moments. "An icy bitch, I used to think. Which you are – can be – and which I envy, as *you* well know. But what worries you about the doctor and Fanny Orr?"

"Well, of course, I've always been jealous of your brass – how you could flaunt your beauty and pride in front of—"

"Whoa, whoa. Stop. Don't hand us the poor-little-unfuckable-me number. You're scrumptious, once you decide to work with yourself. Let's just be thankful we have plenty of brass and ice and bitchery to go around. That we're not a ninety-kilo headcase, like Fanny Orr. Does she threaten you, or something?"

They burst into laughter, a laughter eddying toward the hysterical. They had been up for many hours, going over just how they would handle Josh's hoax, reviewing gossip from the networks they maintained to every significant organ in the body politic.

Dorothy sobered first. "It's her diaries, and that peculiar poem. This witchdoctor who had such an influence. I know the whole thing is ridiculous – a weird animal messiah, and worshipping *germs*, and rockenroll as apocalypse – it would be laughable, but for the fact that millions are agape with the thrill of it. Winger's people are positively clamoring for tales of dark and dirty sex with lower life forms."

Danielle shrugged. "Dirty sex is always good for a wobble on the graph."

"But all we will have, actually, is a fake foetus snatched out of a boneyard. Which Sam has to lose and then pretend to look for. Rather thin, I'd say. Suppose the real thing turns up?"

"The real thing." Danielle looked amused, a touch indulgent.

"Oh I know, *we* will create it. You are a genius at that. But suppose, before the orphan myth is quite launched—"

"If they survived – which is doubtful – and if the thing is born, the Ginks will keep it underground forever. They would never risk returning here – the doctors would take the baby and the teenage psychopath parents would go right back into the nutbin."

"You're very convincing." Dorothy remained pensive for a few moments. "Don't you wonder a little what it might look like? What it might . . . do?"

Danielle smiled ruefully. "Could be a dark Adonis. Or a hairball with ears. What's important is what it *represents*. And *we* will be in charge of that."

"I suppose you're right. I was just imagining our deranged doctors out on bail, hooking up with all the mad fringies and Ecorads. They'll be watching for signs from the holy family."

"Oh yes. Through bees, horses, and dolphins." Danielle rolled her eyes. "Of course, it's not impossible they would try for some sort of contact. You'll have to keep those marvelous ears to the ground, and if we *do* locate something . . . well, why not revert to the original script? Now that SamYam is with us, we've got a perfect sting; we can hang the whole mess, the changeling plot, on Josh and Sandhill. Winger and Frank will crash and burn. I'm more worried, actually, about this fever epidemic shifting the whole focus, starting a panic."

"What about the fever, *period*? Look what it did to Orr – to that whole team of researchers on the border."

"They were unbalanced to start with. The virus just gave the last push."

Danielle realized she sounded defensive. Dorothy's point couldn't be ignored. The fever was not just a matter of image and focus and spin. Nor a matter of finding the right antibiotic to control a mild rash and temperature. The somatic symptoms were slight, but the changes in behavior could be startling. And most troubling, those changes seemed exciting, *desirable*, to those infected.

"You saw the Pollstergeist probes?" Dorothy stood now, and did a half-turn in front of the mirror, making the blue smoke of her dress coil and settle. Danny shook her head in the bright glass. " 'Self-confirming mass hallucination.' A significant percentage *want* dirty genes, a chance to confess and writhe around on Winger's stage. The virus is both degenerative and narcotic."

Danielle uttered a quick, sharp laugh. "Lucky we're on an island."

They exchanged a sardonic look, remembering the quip "No RAM is an island." They were in fact the center of everything worth knowing. Dorothy's cadres of hacker apparatchiks and pirates, with their spy chips and bootleg slice decoders – a vast, phantom horde of tiny electronic parasites – brought her every tremor along the secret labyrinths of power. They had transmitted Orr's confiscated notes and diaries as soon as Insec had seized them. Dorothy knew of General White's defection the same instant Yamaguchi did. They were also aware now of the frenzy and disorder in the streets, the disturbing hunches of those medical investigators who were performing autopsies on the casualties from White's units.

"My dear Ears," Danielle said, proud and affectionate. Her partner's code nickname was known to every darkside power in the game, but only Danny and a half-dozen others knew the real woman. "Never fear. This boogie bug won't get us. It will even take up the slack on holonews until Josh has his changeling lined up, and we can have our bonfire."

"That's another thing." Dorothy stamped her foot lightly. "PJ. That was my mistake—"

"It's all right, puss." Danielle reached out to touch her partner lightly on the wrist. "He's the kind of mistake any woman can make, if she has an imagination. Anyway, it won't be long." She glanced at her chrono. "We should go prepare the ground. Introducing Jesus of the Wild Things."

Dorothy giggled wickedly and clapped her hands. "Exodus. To the Promised Wasteland."

"The Greatest Documentary Ever Dramatized. Or Drama ever Documented."

Dorothy presented her arm, and Danielle took it with a mock coo of pleasure, a flutter of eyelids. "Let us to the King!"

"Dingaling!"

And in a kind of processional, linear, exaggerated waltz, they swept out of the bedroom and down the hall. Before reaching the main lounge, however, they separated and adopted the pace of novitiates in a cloister. When they stepped before Homer, still in his shooting jacket and a glass in hand, they were pale, intent, and brave. They did not flinch before his drunken glare. "Well," he said finally, and lifted his glass with a sardonic tilt. "Are we come to celebrate our triumph, ladies? Have we new ruins to contemplate?" He laughed in disgust.

"How is Tasha?" Danielle asked quietly.

He looked at her, hesitated, and then drank before answering.

"Feeling terrible, of course." He stared sullenly into his glass. "She worked her heart out on this. She gave everything." He waited, but neither of the women spoke. "She's carrying my son. Goddamn that sonofabitch. Has he called? You told him?"

Dorothy had lowered her head, and now a single tear streaked down her cheek. Her voice was soft, uneven, rushed. "We decided not . . . to."

There was a long silence, when they could all hear Dorothy's breathing, shallow and catchy.

"You . . . *decided* . . . not to." Homer Morphopolous swayed, took a step to one side, then another toward them. "*You* decided. *What* in the *fuck* is—"

"Oh stop it!" Danielle burst out, and uttered one long sob before going on. "Don't you see she feels terrible too? Don't you know how we feel? How guilty? *We* made the mistake, we wouldn't listen when you tried to – and yes we should have known, should have guessed what Josh – and then you and Tasha—" She had covered her face with her hands, her shoulders hunching like an old woman's, and the sobs cut off her tirade.

Morphopolous grew red in the face, his mouth working, but produced no recognizable words. Then Danielle seemed to get hold of herself. She straightened, blinking rapidly, and managed a small, tremulous smile. "And Dot didn't decide by herself. I was there. We came . . . came to give you some good news. Of a sort." Her smile took a bittersweet bent. "Something you – and only you – could perhaps take and shape and breathe life . . . " She lifted a hand, then let it drop in a gesture of supplication.

Homer had taken another step nearer. He still glowered, but did so through an uncertain frown. "What are you talking about? Out with it."

The women exchanged a swift glance. Then Dorothy said in the same soft, rushed tone, "They are going to take the station, any moment."

The old man gave a tiny sneeze of contempt. "Of course. A burn. What of it? We lose everything."

"It will survive."

"What?" Morphopolous was directly in front of them now, his face still dark with emotion, but revealing also a wary attentiveness.

"We have an orphan. Josh has."

The old man's lips worked again, tried to sneer and failed. "You—" he began and shook his head as if bothered by an invisible fly. "*An* orphan. What do you mean, *an* orphan?"

"Josh," Danielle said, and swallowed carefully, "has enlisted us in a plan." She waited, meeting Homer's stare, drawing him out to the last, fine, maddening instant. "To betray you."

They saw him absorb, consider, and finally believe; saw a flicker of fierce glee deep in his eyes. So they told him everything in a tearful, headlong rush. How they had been stunned at Josh's daring and effrontery, had played along to gather more details, had seen the single virtue of the plan – to gain time. In a matter of minutes the President-Elect would go on national holo and, in an incredibly bold stroke, declare martial law. Moments later the assault would begin, and on their own darkside feeder channel they would see the station and the renegade agent Feiffer vanish in a glorious fireball. But a daring squad of special rangers would have discovered, only moments before the holocaust, a premature baby abandoned in one of the buildings.

The holy baby, the monstrous messiah! Or so it would appear – though nearly asphyxiated and with failing pulse. A dramatic rush to nearest emergency clinic at the border. By this time the national holo networks would again be on line, the whole nation again aroused, tormented with apprehension, desperate for a glimpse of hope. Insec in disarray after the Omega disaster, the Third Army confused by General White's nervous collapse, gangs of zealots and Omaly drifters in the streets, a breach of security at the clinic and – a nightmare miracle – the infant orphan freak stolen again!

Barrelhead lurched about the room, grunting occasionally, his features adopting various tentative expressions. Once he raised his hand as if to strike at the wall, then thought better of it. With her sure intuition, Dorothy saw that they had alarmed him with so outlandish a script, so many new variables. She uttered a low moan and sank to a cushion on the floor, and with a swift nod directed Danielle to sit on a footstool.

"We knew we had to tell you, but we were afraid . . . we didn't think you would ever forgive us . . . " She trailed off, and when Morphopolous wheeled he was confronted by both women at his feet, looking up at him in supplication, through glistening eyelashes.

"Forgive you?" Morphopolous's brow, tucked and smoothed so many times, could still form a faint crease. "What's it worth? Who has time for it? Forget it. It's *him* that I – that little prick! I drank with him, I took him shooting, I told him first about . . . ah, that miserable little—" He stopped, blinked, peered into the two upturned faces.

454

"We know how close you were," Dorothy said quietly, but with an effort. "Of course you wonder, did we make this up, are we trying to shift blame for our own mistakes, and where is our proof?"

"Very soon – any minute now – it will happen," Danielle continued. "Adamson will open his conference by announcing the emergency measures. Then the assault and the rumor of a survivor. Then Josh will call you. He'll be excited – ecstatic – and he'll tell you it's the Drager baby. The orphan we wanted. He'll say the parents were torched in a suicide pact, victims of their fanatic religious ideology."

"He would do that to me," Homer said in a hoarse whisper, as if to himself. "To *me*. So you say." He walked to the bar on one side of the room and set his glass down, carefully. "We'll move to the com room and watch. If what you say is true, I will . . . I will . . . " He closed one hand into a fist, then looked at them keenly. "He doesn't know I know."

Dorothy shook her head. Her eyes were bright.

"He believes he has managed a great counterplot," Danielle said.

"Oh? Both hands were fisted now on the bar, as if holding it down, and Homer's face was again dark with blood.

"Believes he has created an Iago or Edmund or Brutus." There was a silence, during which they heard Morphopolous breathing more deeply, through his nose. "The bastard," he said finally. "Worse than Brutus. Brutus used a knife, like a man."

He was about to go on but Dorothy burst out, as if suddenly struck by the idea. "Imagine, if Caesar or Othello had *known* what their dear friends were doing!"

"Oh, yes!" Danielle turned to her friend, eyes shining. "The villain o'ertopped in villainy!"

They looked at him, eager and hopeful. He lifted both fists and bounced them lightly on the polished wood surface. "Yes," he said.

"The proverb," Danielle said. "How does it go? Revenge is a dish . . . "

" . . . best served cold." Dorothy gazed at Homer, expectant and glowing. "And what is it, about screwing your courage?"

Morphopolous frowned, caressed his brow. "I murder," he intoned, "I murder and murder, and smile as I murder."

"O-o-oh! Danielle had closed her eyes in an apparent convulsion of pleasure.

Homer bounced his fists again, this time authoritatively. "All right. That's it. You play along, you pretend I don't know. Let him think

455

he's the capo, the master. Let him strut. When the time is ripe . . . "
He smiled, for the first time since they entered the room.

Dorothy clapped her hands together and nested them between her breasts. "We just *knew* you would come up with something brilliant! Something to save the play, make it *better*, even!"

"You are a genius," Danielle said simply, matter-of-factly, and got to her feet. "But I think we had better get to a holo set, if we want to see our plot develop."

Dorothy rose also, but before they turned definitively toward the adjoining com room, with its floor-to-ceiling monitors, Morphopolous hesitated and spoke with a streak of worry in his voice. "No sign of the actual boy and the little pregnant female, I gather. Are we sure they are out of the picture? Could they somehow, through those tunnels or with the horses . . . "

"It seems very unlikely," Danielle said, with a sympathetic frown. "The Pobla have never associated with horses. Armed units are of course combing the area all around the station, but nothing is turning up. If anything *does*, well . . . " She looked mischievously at her partner.

"We can expose our fine Brutus, ask him to explain the existence of *two* holy orphans. Or we can let the plotters eliminate the real baby, or even substitute it for the false pretender. Either way we can reveal their tricks any time. It really doesn't matter." Dorothy beamed.

They were at the threshold to the com room, where Homer had stopped, his expression one of doubt and wonder. "Doesn't matter," he repeated.

"Not really. *You* taught us that. Only genius matters. Genius makes an *image* of the truth. We don't need a particular baby." Dorothy looked up at him with simple, sunny confidence.

"People love your *story*," Danielle chimed in, on his other side. "The story of the savior and monster, rescue and redemption – all the things we've worked on. They love the adventure and surprise, the mystery and promise. But the actuality – maybe ugly or deformed or beautiful or just ordinary – the actuality is . . . " She shrugged, wrinkled her nose in mild disgust. "Boring. Everyday. Exactly what genius must transcend. And you, Homer Morphopolous, Willy Wavershaft, are making everyone's life into one drama. It's never been done, in all history. We don't need a particular baby. We don't need a particular savior." She took his sleeve, breathed into his ancient, rapt ear. *"You are the savior!"*

CHAPTER FORTY-FIVE

With his feet propped up on a rack of petri dishes, PJ could either throw darts at the blowup he had made from a clip of Winger, or watch the little holo box beside it. When he tired of these diversions, he read in Tickles's journal or scribbled in a notebook he had lifted from the lab tech's desk — his own first attempt at a diary.

Over the last twenty-four hours, in fact, he had written two poems. The only poems he could remember composing, as an adult. The first went:

> There was an old deity from Venus,
> Whose spirit was found in his penis.
> He preached a lot,
> But the thrust of his thought
> Was to screw us just to redeem us.

Then, as negotiations had begun to string out and become cryptic and tense, he felt the pressure of time and so moved on to more universal themes. The second poem was:

SUM HUM BONE HUM

> What I got
> is not enough.
> I want a lot
> of all this stuff.

These were light things, silly things, he was perfectly aware. But not without a grain of truth. Even if the truth was commonplace. Everyone knew, after all, that wanting stuff was what created civilization, the highest good. And everyone knew as well that the pecker always played its part, no matter how high and holy the vision.

Mainly, he needed relief from the wearisome job of fencing with the Insec psychs, some of them his old associates. They both knew the range of moves, the time frame, where everything was tending. He had maybe a half-hour, maybe less. He would watch if he could, he supposed, but all commercial channels had gone to test patterns. He laughed. Wouldn't even let me see myself. Really burned me up.

He had laughed a good deal, since diving into this locker and killing, as he calculated, three birds with one stone. (Gave the kids plenty of time to ride out, fucked up Josh Tremain's grand design, seized an opportunity to style his own departure.) No doubt he was infected with Fanny's sinister new microsquiggly, the rockenroll plague brought by Ginks. That would explain the poems, his occasional bopping along the narrow corridors of the locker, and this impulse to make fun.

Of course he was presented very differently in the bulletins delivered on holo. Religious cult leader holds hostages. Possible suicide pact. Dangerously unstable. Rambling and incoherent demands. Demands backed up by the fuel cans piled all around the locker, the little detonator keyed to a remote in the cult figure's pocket.

He learned this version of himself by listening to his own words before the channel died, words expertly pieced from his talk with the negotiators. "Going down . . . for good . . . taking everything . . . " And so on. Of course they left in a few of his duck quacks and whinnies of pretended alarm, as proof of dementia. A macabre sense of humor, one commentator observed. Make that Micawber, he had told the negotiators.

It no longer bothered him that few would appreciate his small gestures of disrespect and outright derision. His diary – only a few hours long anyway – would not survive. Nor would the unedited tapes. Dorothy would no doubt supply SamYam with a refabricated identity for Phillip James Feiffer: his career file at Insec would soon contain memos from doubtful superiors, rumors of erratic behavior, odd blanks or quirks in the record. He would be that rare, diabolical psychopath who slips through the most careful screening.

He didn't care. It was even partly true, from their point of view. He had guessed early that they were going to longjohn him, flip the ecohero into a creepster, and he might have bailed out or at least made some defensive move. He might have saved himself, maybe. In their sense. Which was to lose his shadow, as Tickles defined it. *No need to survive*, his old buddy had written. A line that gave PJ a whiff, at last, of that exhilarating freedom with which the Pobla stepped into their big dark river and were gone.

The light on the desk began to flash. He yawned, grimaced, and shifted his feet back to the floor. His finger hesitated a moment on the switch to the deskphone, while he looked over his notes and recalled where they had left off. Then he opened the line and began talking at the same time.

"Fiddle-dee-dee, fiddle-dee-dum. What I see, is big and dumb. That you, my sweeties? Quack quack. It's PJ the dangerous ducky, here. Notorious criminally insane cult leader. Same old demands, guys. Cleared of all charges, check for three trill, public apology from the President and President-Elect, contract for a major holo to be written and directed by me. And no, I will not allow my captives to make a statement, or show themselves. And no, we cannot select a rep for onsite negos, and no, I do not wish to discuss my terms in detail. I am, as you know, crazy. Now, would you like to hear some poems?"

The voice laughed in modest indulgence. "That's very interesting, PJ. So you're writing, now?"

"No, I'm talking now. Want me to write you?"

"No, no, that's fine . . . you're in good form today, PJ. Maybe we can get somewhere. A little humor is appreciated. That's all right. But you know people are very worried about you? About what may be happening there? I know you think—"

"The fuck you do," PJ interrupted cheerfully. "You don't know what I think. I don't even know what I think. Where is little Joshua? I want to chat with him."

"That's not convenient, PJ. You know that. Mr Tremain is now a presidential adviser, and he has nothing to do with this situation. He dealt with you and your agent solely to secure holo rights to your story, long before this situation developed. We want to keep your attention on what's happening here, on our problem."

"Good luck." PJ began to hum in a falsetto voice. The tune was the Federation anthem.

"We want you to know that we have some very good evidence that Ronnie Drager and Tima are not there with you. Evidence that is basically incontrovertible."

"Oh gee. So they aren't here? Oh gosh. Well, I guess you'll be going away soon, then. But nice talking to you."

"We'll all be going away soon, PJ. This situation has to be resolved. We've tried to accommodate you. We've gone more than halfway.

We can't justify tying up our resources or suspending the custody process any longer. We are very reluctant to use force, PJ, but you're not leaving us any choice."

"That's not true. I'm *dying* to co-operate. Just tell me what you want to know."

"We've been through this. Many, *many* times. We—" The voice broke off. PJ could hear fragments of background conversation. The verb *enfilade*, the noun *position*. When the voice came back, its tone was no longer so matter-of-fact. There was a faint color of something like interest, even sympathy.

"One thing we're asking you not to joke about, PJ. One thing you haven't really told us. A really simple thing. What is it, *really*, that you expect to gain by this stand? You know what will have to happen, if you persist in your current attitude. What do you get out of that, PJ? Tell us."

While these questions were being posed, the little holo flickered back to life. Earlier he had seen the tracked cruisers with their mounted missiles crawling nearer the group of buildings, and the shadows of the jetcopters sliding over the hoof-beaten earth. Now a tanker had also wheeled into position upwind, and soon, PJ guessed, it would begin to unscroll a thick mat of smoke.

But at this moment it was press conference time. Adamson, the handsome, forthright doll, was stern above his red necktie. His gestures were cudgels and blades. His advisers looked both funereal and fierce. The tune had changed yet again, obviously. Another crisis, another dire threat. But fear not. *We are in charge.* PJ opened and began to leaf through Tickle's journal.

"Just tell us, PJ. Tell us *why*."

He maintained the pause a little longer, during which more fragments of background chatter floated through to him. This chatter and these suggestive bits, he knew, had been carefully mixed and played to make the impending action credible. *Sweep. Surgical. Zero.*

"All right," he said. "No joke. Let me read to you. I'll let Tickles speak for me."

"PJ, we can't continue like this. We can't accept these delays. Just unlock the door, PJ, and come out slowly with your hands on your head. We've tried to work with you. We've been patient. We—"

"Wee-wee. Wee-wee wee-wee. I wee-wee on you, fucker, because you don't know who's in here with me, you don't know where they are, and you've got to find out before people lose interest, so you've

460

got to move soon, so I'm gonna answer your question and read my own epitaph, and I got maybe ten minutes to do it so you listen up or go fuck yourself, I don't care, but the dangerous duck will quack and the mad cult creep will cackle and this little piggie will prognosticate all the way home, so here it is, you assholes, listen to the dead man talk!"

He took a slow breath, settled himself in the chair, and began to read, tracing the words across the page with a forefinger.

"When I was a little boy I had a dream. The whole world was one bright, noisy toy, and it was mine. It had a musical spring and it ran and played and flashed. The lions and bears and dinosaurs were all fuzzy and happy and could talk, and everything was there just to make me laugh. But then the toy began to slow down, and lights went out and things stopped, went dead, fell over, and the music began to drag and drop in pitch. I was terrified. I saw that the dark was coming, and there would be no more toys and I woke up screaming . . ."

In the command and control room at the border base nearest the ruined station, Yamaguchi nodded wearily at the operator who had been watching his face during Feiffer's tirade, still coming at them through the room speakers. The operator expected the order, since they had just received word from the ranger team that a survivor had been recovered under cover of the tanker's blanket of smoke. He spoke quickly, intently, into his microphone, and therefore into the headset of the negotiator in the cruiser vehicle parked on a rise above the besieged station.

The negotiator shrugged, grimaced, and turned to the other members of the team, who had been watching him for a sign. He lifted a forefinger and drew it horizontally across his throat. They let out whistling breaths or soft exclamations; some got up to stretch, cracking knuckles. Their job was over. Feiffer's voice continued around them, coming over the cabin speakers, but they were no longer grinning and mugging to each other at this demented babble about toys and dreams. It was all over.

One is coming to awaken us. A tak tagak of both Pobla and piksi. Part snake and part bird. Both male and female. Coming soon. A great, great tagak. We sing . . .

Yamaguchi's operator had already switched to the band connecting him to the field commander and given a second order. A code phrase they had chosen for this op. The commander nodded, smiled at his systems officer, and repeated the phrase, which was relayed then to each copterjock and assault vehicle. Tracks engaged, circuitry hummed with a final check of infra and laser and sat co-ordinates, switches opened and cleared. The mechanism was huge, swift, precise. Four words, and it pounced.

Let there be light.

CHAPTER FORTY-SIX

At dawn he was sweating and moaning, his hands clamped around the sapling the Little Horse People had cut and peeled for him. The cramps were coming in a slow, dreadful rhythm that he foresaw would eventually squeeze out of him all memory, thought, and imagination. Consequently, his mind accelerated in the troughs between spasms, grappling desperately with the mystery of what he was undergoing – or rather of what was consuming him. The young fathers who were supposed to attend and guide him were waking up a few strides away, sitting up on their horsehair mats, yawning and grinning idiotically at him. One of them, scratching himself, said something and the others laughed. Pahane knew a flash of hatred. He had learned so far only the simplest words, enough to signal hunger and time and distance and gratitude. He could not tell them about this agony, this fear of dissolution, in one whose self was already an uneasy fusion of two ghosts.

They ought to have seen and understood. Supposedly something like this had happened to them, so it was their task to help him through. But they only squatted beside him from time to time, sang some incomprehensible song, kneaded his shoulder and back muscles. They remained offhand, cheerful, and even made fun sometimes of his gasping. *Yowa*! they would say. Good!

It was not good, it was terrifying. He swallowed and croaked the word for water, and one of the men got up and moved to the rear of the cave, where a stone bowl caught drops of water and accumulated a few mouthfuls overnight. It was not really a cave, but a stone shelf with an overhang located midway up an outcropping on a steep mountain flank. Like all of the Horse People's hideaways he had seen, this one was strictly temporary, and chosen because it provided food and water and cover for the herds.

The man brought him the water in his two hands, and Pahane lifted his open mouth to receive it in a measured dribble. "*Shi*," he said, and then clamped his lips tight again. The contraction had come with less warning, a little faster, and he felt the force of it swing at the base of his spine, begin to pull at him exactly as if gravity had suddenly increased, in a spot below his pelvis, four or fivefold. The pain advanced simultaneously – a broad pain, like a tide coming in or the shadow of a planet moving across the surface of a moon. So big, within a few seconds, that he could no longer conceive it or think about it or separate it from himself.

It took him, rolled him into bits, dispersed him into nothingness, leaving only itself. He became a universe of pain, which endured a cosmic age. And then, without knowing how, he emerged, was conscious again, and the first thing he knew was that he was not alone. That was the peculiar thing, and the troubling thing, because it made him understand why he was afraid of being a woman.

Down the flank of the mountain, in a gully crudely shaded by branches torn off and crosshatched into a shelter, Tima was undergoing exactly this tremendous magnetic coiling and uncoiling. They became each time a single force and motion, their bodies the poles in an instantaneous, completed cycle of energy. But she, he knew intuitively, was still aware of herself; she had met the pain and matched it, clung to it as to her red mare, ridden it and made it hers. She gripped her pole and opened her throat to scream in triumph, her mind ablaze with images, stricken like sparks from a forge.

That was because her shadow was a man's. A shadow independent, irreducible, and yearning exultantly towards freedom. Pahane could hear the joy and relief in her screams, which set the horses to whinnying restively. But he – there was no more escape from this awareness – had the ghost of a woman. This shadow opened to the pain, dissolved and flowed around and through, was transformed into a sea that channeled and lifted them all into the same racing wave of spirit, which was bearing a new and miraculous life, a gathering radiance of being, to the threshold of the world.

He was lifted and driven too, he had no choice. Ronald – a NorthAm boy-man, a mall roach and thief, a certified schiz possessed by a Gink raider – he was reduced to a sack of cells in sympathetic convulsion; while his ghost – this she-self and sea-self – had the boundless, brutal, stupid strength of the tides, a strength beyond the range of words like independence or freedom, and devoted dumbly and absolutely to a tiny curl of flesh.

The interval was lasting a bit longer, and he became conscious of the soft nickering of horses beyond the lip of the stone shelf. The sun would soon reach into this notch on the slope, and some of the fathers would go out to draw milk. Others would ride off with small herds and reconnoiter, read the signs from birds and watch for smudges of dust on the horizon or streaks of vapor in the sky.

Since the fireball that rose behind them on the day of thunder, the day of hooves, they had seen no indication of a massive search. The overflights and border probes were, if anything, sporadic and arbitrary. And scouts, relaying messages from the rear, brought the surprising news that there were new refugees coming over the border from the north. *Piksi* refugees! Some were soldiers who had commandeered assault vehicles and driven them until the fuel ran out and then wandered into the canyons. Some had apparently made their way on foot over service roads in the ag blocks near the border. They crawled into the Pobla tunnels when they found them, and did not come out again.

The scouts kept watch every day, nevertheless. Their party had ridden a meandering course for more than a moon and were now almost to the sea. But here, for these few hours, they were especially vulnerable. They could not ride until the labor was over, and the snake-bird savior wrapped in horsehair and given first suck. She who would rule a world must first find her own toes, and then grasp the mane above her other four legs. Then the prayer-cycle of birth could finish and they could begin the long migration that would, they believed, bring together all living creatures. Even, in the end, the piksis.

More than anything he wanted that migration to begin. He was sick of being a woman. He was too young to be the mother of a goddess. For this moon he and Tima had been crazy with the delight of being always in the open, always moving, the sun and ground running like a river around and under them. He didn't care about the radiation he might be absorbing, didn't care about the sores and burns from the sling, the jolting bruises Paloo gave him when he dozed off. He only wanted the wind in his hair, the light reaching over the warped and riven desert, and sweet forgetfulness of the prisons they had escaped.

At night, looking past the bellies of Paloo and Tzasu at the stars, they had whispered over the fragments of old stories that Klat managed to convey to them, comparing them with those Tima knew from the Pobla. If these were true, then there were other tiny bands of beings like themselves. Blow-fish and Ice and Seagull People, all with their own version of the oldest stories, all living in so hidden and unobtrusive a way that they escaped the notice of the *mudlatin*, or were recorded only as rare and unique cases of feral or psychotic behavior.

And all of them had the story of the child who was both wild animal and human, who spoke the language of all things living, who saw into the heart of shadows and into the heart of light. The child-cub who could climb trees into the sky, who could change into a hummingbird or a whale, who understood the language of the river and the wind. This was their child. And they would laugh up at the stars and turn to each other—

The force came back, a cold clamp over his belly; he felt the whole world pulling at his guts, as if to turn him inside out. He stretched his lips over his teeth, and the vision turned to smoke. A cry rose in his own throat, inseparable from another coming from Tima and the women downslope, a howl that began at the upper register and sank to a resonant, gutteral cough, which was followed by a rhythmic series of deep-throated grunts.

There were hands now running over his body, kneading his back and thighs, and a chanting that matched the grunts erupting in his chest. The air around him seemed to hollow into darkness, though he could see the sunlight beyond, on the shimmering mountain slope. The rhythmic waves of pain had reached a purity and strength that lifted him, annihilated him in a blaze of ecstasy. He was screaming, but he could not hear himself, was not even there to know this agony of joy, which had exploded every boundary of his being into a common flame. The tongues of that flame coiled, took shape, became. She was born.

"Beeg saster, bery big," Klat said. "Bery brafe. *Tak tagak*. Need goot four-legs."

All the women were gathered around, and all had at last mustered the courage to touch the new baby, for good luck. Some were still in the grip of their original awe. They had expected a miraculous birth, but not quite of this sort, and reverence was subverted by spells of fascination. Klat had spoken sharply to one of the youngest, to correct the glint of fear she had seen in the girl's eyes.

Tima's body was now a fertile, inhabited continent, a great bubble of aching, pulsing, transacting life. It existed beyond her, vaster and more powerful than she was, even in its lethargy and weariness. It was no longer merely herself. It was interfused with this small, silken slug at her breast, whose pulling drew up and through her a pleasure so intense she sometimes shuddered.

Her idiot smiles and cooings made the other women laugh delightedly, but Tima could not follow their swift, impulsive talk. She knew all the same they were wondering if rain would come now, what the wide-winged black birds would do, whether the insects would leave their hives by the sea, and most of all how they should select the four-legs for such an astonishing newborn. The excitement and delirious anticipation of the labor had given way to a certain wonder, not without apprehension. Miracles imposed a burden of speculation.

"Snek-birt *delo* keetee," Klat said with a flash of her white teeth. "Strong leetl keetee." She put out a finger and the baby took it, squeezed, and pulled herself into a half-crouch, almost erect. There was another chorus of humming and grunting from the group, and the horses grazing outside lifted their heads and whickered.

Klat yielded and let the infant curl again on Tima's breast. *"Na,"* Tima said, smiling. "My kitty. Very strong." She smoothed the silken, dark fur, saw the eyes – black as her own and as clear – follow the motion.

She understood Klat's concern. A horse might instinctively be wary of a creature so profoundly different. She had herself known, had felt, had *seen* even, what the baby was like before the birth, and still she was surprised and enthralled. The downy hair was black with a hint of fire in a certain light, and covered the small, perfect body everywhere. The legs were longer than usual, piksi legs except that the haunches would be more muscular. Her hands were broad and already could grip and pull, so that with both she could draw herself into a sitting position, something very rare even in a Pobla infant.

The tail, too, was longer than Tima had ever seen. Both Pobla and piksi newborns sometimes had vestigial tails, but while the piksis had such "deformities" removed at the hospital, the Pobla considered them a blessing, a sign of visionary power. Her daughter's reached to her heels, and indeed looked more feline than anything else, though some of the women immediately associated it with the snake aspect of the holy savior, the aspect of wisdom.

Hearing the women's horses neigh and stamp, Klat had gone to the edge of their branch shelter to look out. *"Yowa!* Ogan come!" she said with another, mischievous grin at Tima. "He look *ta pakish,* bery bad!"

There were more squeals and hoof-thumps from the horses, and answering neighs from the small herds strewn here and there on the mountainside. Then Tima glimpsed a company of legs – all she could see from where she lay beneath the canopy – arriving from the slope

467

above them. Pahane's were obvious: not only paler and marked by sores from the sling, but also unsteady, bracketed by those of the young fathers holding him up.

One of the men began to speak and went on for a good while. All the women were gathered so as to shield Tima from view, and Klat had taken up a braided hide whip which she carried loosely coiled over one shoulder. When the man finished speaking, Klat turned and began to translate for Tima, using their made-up pidgin of NorthAm, Polba, and Unat – the Horse People's tongue.

"Say *oganun* comesee. Comesee new *delo kubi*, comesee if *yowa* . . . "

It seemed at first merely a formality. The father came to see if the new little spirit was his, was well-born, was worth the pain they had suffered. But with various hand signals, squints, and grimaces, Klat conveyed that she was not to agree; she was to refuse to show the infant. She should tell Pahane to go away, because he had caused her a great trouble with his blunt little spear. He must, she should insist, bring fine horses to make up for his rudeness – horses for her and horses for the child.

Tima almost wept, in her dumb frustration. She did not want gifts, she wanted Pahane beside her. In Pobla birth ceremonies the father usually bit the cord to free the new *kubi* from its mother. A Pobla man saw his child before the mother did, as it emerged in grease and blood; and the Hive Beings taught the Pobla to do all things in common, to think of themselves as a single organism. Obviously, their black crow-god had instructed the Horse People very differently.

"Say," she answered finally in a choked whisper.

Klat looked relieved and grateful. From the first the young *tagak* had been judicious and careful in managing their integration into the group. She and Tima had established a bond of sympathy and intuitive trust, which allowed her now to shake out the whip and speak forcefully to the group of men.

The speeches went on, back and forth. One of the women produced a bundle – a shock of dried grass tied with tail strands and wrapped in horsehair blanket – and this dummy infant was solemnly presented to the men, who pretended to go away and then return in outrage. There was really no choice, Tima understood, maddening as this business might be. Their child would always be worshiped by strangers.

Her own kind were in no position to give sanctuary. Some of the Pobla had finally gone back into their burrows and were trying to

468

establish again their connection to the Hive Beings, to find again a communal life. But the old temples were still in ruins, the holy councils dispersed, and the horror unleashed by Sayat had altered their world for good. The Pobla had sacrificed themselves, had been corrupted by the power of the piksi *mudlatin*. Yet this sacrifice had also gained an extraordinary advantage: they had passed a holy sickness into the NorthAm masses, a fever that even now spread and burned, a fever that made them insatiable, thirsty for what they had forgotten, for the songs this child – this snake, this bird, this cat! – would bring.

Tima glimpsed more horses through the woven branches, some rearing or running back and forth in short bursts. The voices of the men had grown louder, more plaintive, and now took on the repetitions and syncopation of a chant. Around her the women had become more excited and restless; their eyes were glittering, their hair swung loose. Klat had stepped further away from the shelter, and now swung the whip about her head in a loose, heavy, undulating coil, as she cried to Tima.

"*Oganun* say yis! *Na*! Giff all huss, giff to beby snek-birt. *Kish*! *Kishta ya kish*! Bery goot, *kish*, *yowa*. All Unat yis, Huss Pipple yis! Say come!" The whip swung and then traveled out, a leisurely ripple that suddenly blurred into a shattering of the air, a sound so sudden and clean and shocking that it took away everything but silence.

At this explosion, the baby stiffened at Tima's breast and began to jerk in convulsions. Tima was rising, effortlessly, to her feet, though a moment before she had been exhausted. Everything around her now had a perfect clarity, like the surface of some desert planet with no atmosphere. For once she was not seething with visions, speculations, conjuring powers; the whip-crack had left her skull a mere shell of scoured bone ringing in the wind.

No one else moved a muscle as she walked out from beneath the shelter. She saw the men, heads bowed, and the great ring of horses, motionless but alert, their eyes fixed on the mother and child. On the rock outcropping where the fathers had camped were hundreds of dark, hunchbacked shapes. Tima had not heard the wings whisper overhead, or a single croak, but there they were, also watchful, eyes blacker than the stone.

Sunlight shimmered on the dry, golden grass that covered the slope, and a few scraps of cloud trailed across the sky in a light breeze. The baby was still jerking, gagging in air, its tiny fingers digging into Tima's neck. Tima was aware of all these things, aware that except

469

for this peculiar hush it was – from some now impossible perspective – an ordinary day. But this day, this moment, had a miracle at its center. She and Pahane were gazing into each other, drinking from each other the strength to bear that miracle.

He was tottering toward her. His face was drawn and his eyes bloodshot, yet he was transfigured in his exhaustion and amazement and bliss. She had heard his screams too, had understood that in a certain way his being was wrenched even more deeply than hers. He lifted a hand that trembled, but before he could touch them the baby completed its gathering of breath and uttered the first cry. It was a vigorous cry, in a major key: a high rough squall that had an immediate impact on the legion of hunchbacked birds. Most of them lifted and spread their dark wings, a strange clicking and rustling, and some answered the cry with a subdued croak.

The horses, too, started. Heads lifted higher, nostrils flared, a white ring appeared around the eyes of those who had ventured nearest. The baby lifted its head and cried louder, sounding a longer note, almost a howl. One foal whinnied and bolted a few steps, then halted and stood shivering. As Tima leaned into Pahane, lifting the baby, and his arms went around both of them, she heard the women burst into laughter and the men answer with guffaws of their own.

"My God," Pahane whispered, his cheek against the furry crown of his daughter's head.

"So they say." Tima laughed, or began to, but she was still too sore to carry it through.

Klat was beside them, grinning, the whip coiled again on her shoulder. There was a hubbub, a din, a confusion of gleeful sound. The baby's cry was steady now but not urgent, almost like a song, and the little head turned and tilted, the large eyes moving from thing to thing in wonder. Both men and women had mingled now with the horses, edging the dams and new foals closer.

"Git huss," Klat said happily. "Snek-birt *tak tagak* comesee huss, git four-leg." She beckoned, but Tima did not move.

"Please. We need . . . " Tima lost her breath, and an instant later tears spilled down her cheeks. She felt too weak even to step away from Pahane; it took their combined strength merely to hold themselves propped against each other. Something tremendously powerful, yet fragile, held them in its current. It was a form of *naku*, but traveled through this small, silken-haired creature folded between them.

Klat looked concerned, and gestured at the horses that had begun

470

to mill about, a few thrusting their noses over her shoulder. Some of the black birds were flapping aloft, too, and after circling briefly a few lined away toward the horizon. "Git huss, git four-leg. *Tonpah*! No goot stay. Git—"

She was shouldered abruptly to one side, and the little colt who had bolted earlier now danced up to the huddle of mother, father, and baby. It was still shivering, the tiny hooves striking up and down as if hot embers were strewn in its path, and the head lifted and swiveled as if to take in everything at once. The coat was a dull gold, almost the color of the grass, with a darker mane and tail and a single fleck of white on a rear ankle.

A long coo of surprise went up from the company, a sound of pleasure and anticipation. Several of the horses whinnied or snorted, and toward the rear a few were running and kicking heels high in the air. The colt stretched its neck and its nostrils flared, pinched, then flared even more. Tima and Pahane swayed apart, letting the baby ride on their entwined arms. The horse jerked back, its head poised like a drawn arrow, thin legs vibrating like bowstrings.

The infant focused on the soft, black nose, reached out to bat with her hand. The colt again extended its neck, the legs spread slightly and rigid with strain. The cooing died to a hushed sigh. The little hand bumped the nose, bumped it again, and the colt moved its head away, then back. A murmuring began around them, and a moment later the colt had its head on Tima's shoulder, had blown out its breath in a contented flap of nostrils, and the baby had tangled its tiny fingers in the thick mane.

Everyone laughed at once, a big, velvety sound, and the colt reared back again, but no longer trembled. Klat was motioning to the others to leave, and grinned swiftly at Tima over her shoulder. "Okay! *Kish*! Got huss for beby, go way. All finish. You slip, beby slip."

Tima could not even answer. The tears kept rolling down her face, and she stroked the little horse's jaw once, in gratitude. Sleep! It was an unimaginable luxury. She heard Pahane whispering to her, but did not understand him. She let him take her, in a half-dozen slow steps, back to the mats under the shelter, while the others dispersed, quickly now. Some of the men and women swung on their four-legs, while other horses trotted away to graze or frolic in their familiar herds.

In less than a minute they were alone. Tima had sunk down on the mats, the baby suckling again at her breast, Pahane stretched out beside her. The new colt stood with its head just inside the shelter, watching, listening, inhaling carefully. The sky overhead was filled with the wheeling black birds, but their circles were widening, and as they sailed over the ridgetops they veered away and stroked toward the horizons.

There seemed to be a brightness and calm in the day, as at a perfect solstice, the earth just completing its most balanced revolution. Tima felt herself, and Pahane and the baby, also balanced: weary to the bone and poised on the brink of a luxurious dark oblivion of sleep, yet too full of their love, of this light and promise and stillness, to topple into it. Everything from this hour forward, she knew, would be different for them – so immensely different that she could not, for the first time, bring herself to imagine it.

Pahane let out a long, gentle breath that terminated in a tiny grunt of laughter. "I hurt," he whispered, "so good."

She hummed, smiling.

"She is . . . " He was silent for so long, his chest rising and falling in slow, regular rhythm, that she thought he was asleep, but then the tiny bubble of laughter broke again. "Hunkysmack."

She made a hushing sound of reproval.

"Star. Maybe Star, for a NorthAm name . . . needs many names . . . "

"Be still. Names will come." Tima felt the little mouth relax, saw the baby's eyes close part way. "As we go."

Simultaneously they looked up and away, beyond the slope where the horses grazed, toward the horizon. When they woke again they would rise, breakfast quickly on milk and seeds, and ride with the herd eastward. The furthest ocean was there, but they would take many seasons to reach it.

"As we go." Pahane repeated.

She caught the odd combination of yearning and happiness in his voice, for it exactly mirrored her own feeling. It was something they had come to understand about life with the Nacuatli, moving almost every day, even sleeping while slung from a pacing horse. A paradox: *free flight*.

He lay back then, and nestled his head against her hip. She smiled down at both of them, and hummed softly again, deep in her chest. They had no need to ask where they would go, for they had understood that too. It was an old riddle, which they had learned in Unat.

Where shall we run? Where shall we hide?
Everywhere!